OUBLIETTE

A Forgotten Little Place

VANTA M. BLACK

Janeline —
Enjoy falling into
Oubliette!!
Vanta M. Black

Published by Black Château Publishing, a division of Black Château Enterprises.

Black Château and the portrayal of the castle turret are trademarks of Black Château Enterprises.

Inspired by historical events and characters, this is a fictional work. The names, characters, incidents, places and events are the concepts of the author, or are used to create a fictitious story, and should not be construed as real.

Black Château Enterprises — Publishing Division
www.BlackChateauEnterprises.com

Cover and jacket design © copyright 2015 by Black Château Enterprises.

ISBN: 978-0-9964488-1-9

First Edition: December 2015

10 9 8 7 6 5 4 3 2 1

For Bree and Dave.

I love you from the bottom of my oubliette.

Acknowledgements

Thank you Lynn and Tera for your feedback during the early days. I'm forever grateful. Also, Tera and Todd, your help with the *Oubliette* trailer is deeply appreciated — I couldn't have done it without your creativity and dedication.

Delta Wright, you gave me an insider's glimpse of the interior design world. Our conversation helped make this story come to life.

Chrishawn Simpson, your editing skills elevated my work and your enthusiasm motivated me. I'm extremely grateful to you.

Erica, the best copyeditor I know, thank you for your insights. Jeannette from Crazy Hair Photographer, you made me feel pretty during our tarantula shoot and that was damn awesome.

Kimberly Blagrove from Vogue Translations, I don't know where to begin! Thank you for jaunting through Paris with me, for lending me your magnificent editing and translations skills, and mostly, for being a dear friend.

Sean Ryan, the owner of Leap Castle, the famed most-haunted castle in Ireland, thank you for warmly opening your doors and allowing me to glimmer down the depths of the pit that inspired this book. Your hospitality, stories, and music infused my spirit and motivated my imagination.

Mostly, thanks mom. Somehow, despite the hard times, you raised a daughter who managed to produce this book. Miss you Dorothy.

True Events and Historic Legends

During the 1920s, the oubliette at Leap Castle — the famed "most haunted castle" in Ireland — was unearthed. Remains from over 150 bodies were rolled out in wheelbarrows. A pocket watch from the mid-1800s revealed how recent the oubliette had claimed victims.

There are many accounts of an "elemental" spirit at Leap Castle. One of the most renowned is Mildred Darby's. Her family once owned Leap, and there she dabbled in the occult. Some say her meddling provoked the entity to appear. Her description of it states:

> *The thing was about the size of a sheep, thin, gaunt and shadowy in parts. Its face was human, or to be more accurate, inhuman, in its vileness, with large holes of blackness for eyes, loose slobbery lips, and a thick saliva-dripping jaw, sloping back suddenly into its neck!*

One theory claims that before Leap Castle was erected, the elemental was summoned by Celtic Druids during a sacrificial ritual. It was brought into this dimension of reality to act as their guardian.

On Friday the 13th, 1307, King Philip IV of France ignited the Inquisition by charging the Knights Templar with heresy.

Leaders of the organization were pulled from their castles, keeps, farms, vineyards, and homes. They were accused of worshiping a Pagan god. Some speculated it to be the demon Baphomet, or a Muslim deity which the Templars encountered while in the Holy Land.

The Templars were also accused of keeping a magical "head" that helped them fight the crusades. The mysterious relic was rumored to be the offspring of the copulation between a young warrior and the corpse of his bride-to-be.

Empress Helena was the mother of Constantine, the emperor who made Christianity the official religion of Rome. Her pedigree is veiled in mystery and some scholars suspect she had a Pagan upbringing. In her later years she traveled to the Holy Land to seek out relics associated with Jesus Christ.

❧❧❖❧❧

In 1348 the Plague spread across France. An especially virulent strain, it ravaged indiscriminately — young, old, rich, poor, pious or heretic — no one was immune. Jews were blamed for the malady. Many were tortured and burned at the stake after being accused of inflicting the peste on society.

❧❧❖❧❧

Absinth was created by Dr. Pierre Ordinaire around the time of the French Revolution. Traveling on horseback, he sold the concoction as a cure-all elixir across France and Switzerland.

Absinth would go on to become the subject of much debate. Rumored to cause hallucinations and madness, laws were passed starting in 1908, banning it in many European countries and the United States.

❧❧❖❧❧

The phenomenon of "shadow people" has been documented throughout time. Legends of the Old Hag, the succubus/incubus, and other late-night visitors who cause sleep paralysis and a sense of mortal terror, are common across many cultures.

I've experienced these visitations. My skeptical mind once dismissed them as vivid dreams. They were just in my head — they *couldn't* be real. Then someone witnessed one preparing to attack me as I slept, and described it to me afterward.

How could it be in my head if someone else saw it, too?

— Vanta

Prologue

eronica didn't understand why they looked for the monsters in her head, that's *obviously* not where they were. Instead of listening, the doctors stuck pads with wires to her temples and increased the dosage of an IV that dripped into her veins.

They also told the nurses to tie her down with thick, leather belts every night.

The tethers didn't matter though, because when the monsters came, she wouldn't be able to move anyway. The only thing Veronica could ever do was scream.

The doctors called them "night terrors". The pudgy lady who talked funny – – she told Veronica it was her *accent* — said they were "spirits". Mommy used the term "shadow people". Veronica just called them "monsters", and wished they'd stop scaring her when she slept.

They wanted her. Deep inside, on a primal level, Veronica knew the monsters — or whatever they were — craved her, and if given the chance, they would do something very, very bad to her.

The little girl tried to explain this to the doctors, the nurses, the accent-talking lady, and her mother, but none of the adults really listened. Instead they argued and shouted at each other, and huffed in and out of the room — but the thing that frightened Veronica the most, is when the adults would simply shrug their shoulders, and admit that they really didn't have any idea what the monsters were at all.

It was almost ten o'clock — shift-change time. The night staff would come now. The nurse on duty was a plodding and lazy lady who would only check on Veronica at the beginning of the shift, and then abandon her in favor of the nurses' station and a VHS tape of the day's soap operas. Veronica didn't like her. Sometimes it would take "Nurse Lazy" a full five minutes before she'd respond. She never came fast enough.

Veronica tried to tell the doctors that the nurse was too slow, but the complaints of a ten-year-old weren't taken seriously against the word of the lazy nurse who smiled sweetly and said, "Poor dear and those dreadful night terrors. I always come running as fast as I can!"

Veronica cringed as the television automatically turned itself off. It always happened at ten o'clock; it was on a timer. She wasn't sure why, but she felt it protected her and wished more than anything it could stay on. The noise, the pictures, *The Tonight Show with Jay Leno*, there was something inexplicable about the TV that kept the monsters away.

Veronica's pleas to leave the television on all night were never honored by the adults. Nurse Lazy actually once told her, "Oh, we can't leave the TV on, it'll give you bad dreams."

Ha! Little did she know the TV *prevented* the bad dreams.

The door opened and in walked Nurse Lazy. Her metal nameplate actually read "Lucy". She handed Veronica a little paper cup with a green pill inside and waited with a thin, forced smile. The longer Veronica took to take her medicine, the longer Nurse Lazy would have to wait until she could watch her soaps.

Veronica plucked the pill out of the cup. "Aren't they 'sposed to be yellow?"

Lucy flared her nostrils ever so slightly as she replied, "No, your new doctor prescribed the green ones. Hurry up and take it."

Veronica studied the pill closely, holding it inches from her nose. She looked at it slightly cross-eyed. "I don't think I like the green ones though. Yellows are better."

Lucy's trembling hand clutched a Dixie cup of water. "That's for the doctors to decide. Now eat it up! Time for sleep."

Veronica painstakingly laid the pill on her tongue and grunted for the nurse to hand her the water.

Lucy thrust it forward. "Here, drink!"

Veronica pouted, though she knew the cute face wouldn't work on ol' Lazy.

"Thanks," she muttered as the nurse buckled down Veronica's arms and legs and pulled the covers up to her chest.

"Goodnight," Lucy grumbled. She snatched the mermaid doll that sat by Veronica's side, and tossed it on the nightstand before careening out the door.

Random acts of meanness like that weren't uncommon for Lucy. Veronica sniffed as the silence left in the nurse's wake permeated the room.

Then familiar, tinny tunes from a transistor radio wafted through the air. It hung from the janitor's cleaning cart. He always blared it while mopping the halls. There was *that* song again. Some stupid radio station played it almost every night right around this time. Veronica stared at her doll on the nightstand, just out of reach, as the lyrics began:

Dream the dream that only you can dream
Sing the song that only you can sing
Dance with me, we'll start slow
Clasp my hand, now lose control
Bite the monster only you can see
And dream the dream you only dream for me

Veronica tried to squish her head into the stiff pillow so her ears were covered, but it didn't work. The heavy metal song's pounding chorus kicked in.

Spirits in the maze
Burning brighter
Like a dream within the haze
Dancing fire
Deep inside malaise
Hungry spider
Force your screams to blaze
Spinning spiral

The song frightened her. It seemed to always precede a particularly bad episode. She really wished she had the yellow pills. She felt defenseless as sleep consumed her. The green pills would be no help if one of the bad ones came…the *real* Bad Ones, that is.

She twisted her head and glared into the large mirror on the wall across the room. People watched her from inside there. Veronica wasn't sure if they were the doctors, the accent lady, or maybe even her mother, but every now and then someone would move, the light would catch just right, and she would see a figure behind the glass. Dimly, she watched them watch her. They studied her and talked about her and wrote notes about her on clipboards. Knowing they were there gave Veronica little comfort because they weren't there to help; they were only there to watch.

Her sleepy eyes narrowed at the watchers and she whispered with dopey lips, "What, no popcorn? You gonna stare at me all night and you got no stinking popcorn? You're all a bunch of stupid heads, ya' know that? Stooopid heads…"

Sleep quietly took over while Veronica cursed the stupid heads behind the glass. She jerked her droopy neck to force herself awake, but the green pill was powerful. It pushed her into the darkness where the shadow people waited.

Veronica, here we are!

Veronica, time to steal your dreams.

Time to let us steal your dreams and break your bones and slip your soul right out of your slimy sack of skin…Veronica!

She fought to wake up. With all her might she tried to scream, but the green pill seized her motor functions and paralyzed her. She was like a petrified slab of meat laid out on a table — unable to move, unable to cry out, unable to defend herself.

Do you know the evil that you dream, Veronica?

Do you know the song that only you can sing?

Veronica!

In the limbo between sleep and lucidity Veronica sensed their heinous presence with crystal-clarity. She was hyper-alert and instinctively knew these were the real Bad Ones. Without looking she *saw* one crouching in the far corner of the room. It glared at her intently and oozed animosity. It waited patiently, almost casually, for Veronica to succumb.

With a sudden surge of intense willpower she cried out — just a little — it was a tiny whimper that was barely audible. It wasn't loud enough to scare the shadow people away though, and it definitely wasn't loud enough for anyone living to hear.

Another Bad One pulled itself onto the foot of her bed. This one was small and hairy like an animal. Scrooching under the blanket, it crept slowly along the side of her bare leg. It felt for a nook to burrow — a soft place like her stomach or side so it could squirm and writhe itself into her flesh — where it could rip her apart from the inside out.

"Help," Veronica whispered one last time before falling into the dark depths of sleep — deep, down, spinning 'round, until the darkness took a hold…

Chapter 1

Veronica's Story

Something woke her with start. The alarm clock? No. It was too early for the clock to sound. The television? Couldn't be. It broke last week and she couldn't afford a new one. The phone? Must be the phone! She grabbed it from the nightstand, swallowed, and made an earnest effort to answer in the most awake voice she could muster.

"Hello?" she said with the "o" cracking slightly.

The voice on the other end was delicate and had an accent. "Oh, dear, did I wake you?"

"No, I'm up," she grunted. "Can I help you?"

The voice was soothing — the accent French. "*Oui*, my name is Marie-Claire. I should call later?"

"No." Veronica sat up. "What can I do for you?"

"We have a lovely château we wish you to decorate."

"A château…" Veronica tried to focus. She grabbed a glass of water from the nightstand and asked, "You mean a castle?" A lock of curly, brown hair caught on the side of her mouth as she took a quick drink.

The voice lilted. "Oui, un castle! It is called Le Château du Feu Ardent. Dr. Jacobs recommended you specifically for this job."

Dr. Jacobs. The name swam in Veronica's head, but she couldn't place it. "Ah, Dr. Jacobs. Yes…continue," she said, trying to stall and recall the name.

"The château is in the Loire Valley. We imagine your work to take three months, and we will pay handsomely."

Veronica enjoyed the way the voice sounded and she smiled dreamily. "Three months, you say? Tell me more about this castle."

"It is *magnifique*. We began to renovate it twenty years ago and wanted to make it an inn, but were unable to finish. It has been vacant all this time. Help us, *sil vous plait*?"

"I think I'm available. Where did you say the castle was again?" Veronica laid her head back on the pillow.

"In zee Loire Valley of France, near le Loire River. It is a place of many castles and kings. Beautiful and green. It is like coming back in time."

Veronica smiled sweetly, briefly. "France? Did you say it was in France?" She sat up. "You want me to come to *France*?"

"Oui…"

"No, I'm sorry," Veronica interrupted politely, "that is just too long for me to be gone from my other clients."

"We understand it is so much to ask; however, as I said, we will pay well. To start, you get one million francs."

That sounded like a lot to Veronica…francs…. *How much was that in US dollars,* she wondered as the voice continued, "When the project is complete, you will receive one million more."

Veronica sat silent for a moment. "And when would you like me to start?" She let each word roll around slowly in her mouth as she tried to calculate the dollar amount in her head.

"June. We will be away on holiday. You will have three months to do the job and can hire whomever you like to help. We have a budget set aside for general labor, contractors, and assistants."

"Uh, can I get back to you? I need to think about this and see if I can, you know, clear my calendar."

"Of course. I will call you in two days. *Au revoir!*"

"Au revoir," Veronica's voice parroted.

She glanced at the alarm clock as she hung up the phone. It was 5:27 AM. Work was two hours away, but Veronica could not fall asleep as she lay imagining the fairy tale castle.

Chapter 2

Dorothée's Story

L e Château du Feu Ardent — I picked the name because of you, Dorothée. It is your wedding gift," said André-Benoit. The jarring carriage ride made his voice tremble.

He had a broad smile with a slight gap between his front teeth. Short, grey-brown bangs spread across his wide forehead like delicate fringe and deep lines framed the mouth of the man who was over twice his bride's age.

Dorothée peeked from behind the curtain. "Can we get off by the stables? I want to see the grounds before dusk!"

The carriage turned from the main road, and through the trees she glimpsed the pointed peaks of the castle. The horses' hooves pattered to a halt, and André-Benoit took her hand as she stepped down from the carriage. Her crimson hair spilled onto her shoulders. She reached up to control it.

"It came loose during the ride," she said.

"No, keep it down. Your beautiful red hair inspired the name of the Château..." He bent close to whisper, "And so did our fiery passion."

Dorothée flushed and glanced at Patricia, her lady-in-waiting, and the driver who were busy gathering her things. "André-Benoit, you should not say such things in front of the servants!"

They walked to the main road. She caught a sweet fragrance and looked to her right to see a grove of budding trees. "Apple blossoms?" she asked.

"Yes." He pointed. "There's our orchard and beyond it, the vineyard. We have a barn with livestock and horses, and a garden that is just waiting for you to plant flowers. The clergy who once lived here made the Château entirely self-sufficient. Everything you could possibly want is right here, my dear."

As they strolled under the canopy of trees, Dorothée saw the splendor of Le Château du Feu Ardent. Sublime towers reached for the clouds, two of which were a full three stories in height. A third, somewhat thicker one, reminded her of a fat, little friar with a pointed hood. Ivy climbed the walls, which were grey and green and seemed alive. Far back, behind the other towers, was a thin, solitary turret, black and anomalous. Even from a distance, she could see that it was constructed in a long-gone era — primitive — with crude bricks that didn't match the rest of the architecture.

"It is breathtaking! And it once belonged to the Church?"

"They abandoned it after the pestilence. It sat vacant for a long time. The Diocese and the King granted it to me with my lordship."

"Does that mean you *owe* them?"

He levelly contended, "No. I owe no debt. The castle is a reward for my service and loyalty."

"How queer for them to grant such valuable property so liberally. The Church is known for *hoarding* wealth. They give up nothing unless they have an agenda," she said with a huff of contempt.

He stopped and spun his bride to face him. "Dorothée, you speak like a Huguenot!"

She assumed the demeanor of a proper wife. Smiling cordially, she nodded into a quick, cute curtsy. "I tease, dear husband! The Church is most gracious, and the King generous to reward you so handsomely." She playfully tugged his arm and added, "Don't fret over my guile. After all, it is a bad omen for a husband to be cross with his bride during honeymoon."

He relaxed and wrestled her gently into his arms. She beamed up at the castle while he stood behind her. "André-Benoit, it looks magnificent against the setting sun! Perhaps the name Château du Feu Ardent has dual meaning?"

He followed her gaze. The solitary, crude turret behind the three towers gleamed, causing its ancient stones to glow fiery red.

"You mean the keep's turret?" he asked.

"Yes, it is positively perfervid."

"It does look red in the waning sunlight. See, Le Château du Feu Ardent *is* the perfect name."

Chapter 3

The Children's Story

I sabelle held Louis' hand as they sprinted across the rain-drenched courtyard. The boy whimpered, stopped short, and glowered at her with soggy, brown eyes.

"I can't run that fast!" His chubby white fists protectively clutched a leather satchel to his chest as his bottom lip juddered.

Isabelle cupped her hand under his chin, just like mama used to do when she needed the children to listen, and said, "Little Louis, don't start crying. Trust me, we have to get out of here. We have to do it fast and we have to do it tonight." She draped an arm around his shoulder and pulled him lower to the ground. "There is a crevice under the castle wall only twenty feet away. It's small, like an animal dug its way through. Come, let's go. I'll count the steps and we'll be there before you know it."

Louis nodded and followed obediently. As she counted each step, a song crept forward in her mind. It was the voice of mama singing: *A basket of apples, how many inside? Let's look and see and then make a pie! One apple, two apples, three, and then four. Five apples, six apples, soon seven more. Now eight apples, and nine, the last one makes ten. Let's put them back and count them again.*

Isabelle felt peaceful for a moment with the song and the memory swimming in her head. She and her mother both had the same wavy, light brown hair, like the color of wheat grass at harvest. Mama was tall and wispy thin. Isabelle recently noticed that her own body was beginning to take the shape of her mother's — lean and spry, with a long torso, and just the suggestion of a bosom.

She held an image of her mother in her mind's eye. The tall woman picked apples from the high branches of the tree while Isabelle held the basket. They were making pastries for her father and his men. The song started again: *A basket of apples, how many inside? Let's look and see and then make a pie...*

Louis slipped and she lost her grip on his hand. He let out a shrill cry.

"Shh!" she warned. "The guard will hear!"

Louis blubbered, "But I tripped."

She put her hand by his foot and felt a puddle washed out by rain. "Come on. We're almost there."

He started to stand but lost his balance and fell on his rump. "Dumb puddle!" he hissed with the defiance of a six year old. Louis clumsily tried again but his ankle gave way, and he fell a second time. "I'm hurt! Izzy, my foot hur-ssst! We have to tell Uncle Pierre."

Prickly cold embraced the back of her neck. "No, your foot is fine. Just a bit farther and we'll be on the other side of the wall."

She knew they couldn't go back. If Uncle Pierre discovered they were outside at this time of the night, he would become suspicious...and that would not be good.

She squatted and picked up her little brother. He buried his face in her mane of hair and sobbed while she clumsily carried him.

Isabelle was strong for a skinny girl. Her father told her so. She would cling to his broad back as he jumped around and brayed like a donkey. "My how strong you are, Izzy! You never let go!" She would howl with sheer joy and hold on tighter.

Isabelle would not let go now.

Thunder rumbled over the mountains as she navigated the muddy courtyard with her brother in her arms. She wore her riding dress because it allowed her the most freedom of movement, but the rain moistened the material, causing it to cling to her legs. She squinted warily at the tower. Her bonnet slid down her forehead and she had to tilt her head back to see.

She knew the guard wasn't watching this way. His job was to make sure no one was breaking *into* the castle, but when they got on the other side of the wall...

Louis wiggled restlessly in her arms.

"We're almost there," she wheezed. Her eyes widened in the darkness, but she couldn't see the crevice in the wall. "I have to put you down now."

Louis made a soft sound as he plopped onto the moist earth.

Isabelle searched up and down the craggy, moss-covered wall and at one point, her hand brushed across a stone's sharp edge, slicing the meaty part of her palm. She didn't feel the pain though, because it didn't really matter. Nothing mattered except their escape.

Chapter 4

Veronica's Story

eronica twirled her straw around the lemon floating in her iced tea. The restaurant patio flurried with collagen-injected ladies who carried tiny dogs in their purses. Her sister was running late and the lunch hour was quickly slipping away. Veronica drove all the way to Burbank to accommodate Nikki, and she wasn't there yet. She looked at the time on her cell phone. Twenty more minutes and she'd have to leave…Nikki came scurrying around the corner, doing a funny little hop between each step. She wore a rather short, tight, black skirt and strappy shoes with three-inch heels. Her paisley pink blouse was unbuttoned just one-too-many. *Oh lá. lá. Check out the French teacher!* Her long, blond hair was pulled back in a loose bun and wisps of hair swung across her forehead. Large dark sunglasses hung on the end of her up-turned freckled nose.

"Sorry I'm late!"

Veronica tilted her head to one side and looked at her sister with a disapproving, upward glance. People often commented on how much she and her sister looked alike, but Veronica only saw their differences.

Nikki always wore pinks and purples and sparkly things. It looked like My Little Pony threw up in her closet. In a word, she was *perky* — and super-fast with a witty comeback or snarky joke. Everyone loved Nikki; she was captivatingly playful. She made people feel just a tiny bit off-guard. Not so much as to make them uncomfortable, but just enough so they felt a sense of surprise and anticipation while in her presence.

Veronica was anything but perky. Smart in her own brooding way, her internal dialogue was too sarcastic to utter aloud and she often held her tongue. Not comfortable in most social situations, Veronica struggled with small talk about reality TV shows and celebrity gossip to the point where it was almost painful to endure. She wore frumpy, hipster attire and was concerned less with her own look than with the magnificent interior designs she created. All her energy went into her work. There was little left for her to divert to herself — and that was okay with Veronica.

"Vern, I had a crisis! That football coach I dated came into my room just as I was leaving. He was like, 'Blah-blah-blah, you never return my texts, blah-blah-blah, I miss you, blah-blah-blah.' I couldn't get away. I'm sorry. But the good news is, I got him to cover my next class, so we can have an extra-long lunch!"

"Well, that's great Nikki, but I have an appointment in Santa Monica in an hour. I gotta go soon."

Nikki flashed a super-white smile as she jabbed. "You and your appointments! Why don't 'cha pull that stick outta your ass and show up late for once? This is LA. You're always allowed to be fifteen minutes late for any appointment because of traffic. *Everyone* knows that."

"I own my own business; I have to be responsible…"

"Big deal if you're late. They'll just think you're super busy and respect you a little more. You really let your clients walk all over you, Vern."

"I do things in a consistent, professional manner," Veronica stated. "It's what works for me."

"It wouldn't hurt you to take a leap of faith and do things that aren't by the book, ya' know." She peeked at the clock on her cellphone. "You got time to at least grab a salad, right? Damn, I'm thirsty. How's the tea? Is it raspberry?"

"Passion fruit. Try it." Veronica pushed her glass across the table and her sister quickly scooped it up.

Veronica took a big breath, which was barely noticeable under her baggy T-shirt. The Flying Spaghetti Monster that decorated the front wiggled two meatball-shaped eyes as she grabbed the table with both hands and began, "Speaking of taking a leap of faith...I got the most incredible phone call this morning."

"Can I take your order?" The waiter interrupted.

"I didn't even look at the menu yet," Nikki said.

"I can give you a moment." The waiter turned to go.

"Wait," Veronica said. "We're kinda in a hurry."

"Lemme see the menu quick," said Nikki coyly as she plucked one from the waiter's apron pocket.

"I'll have a Chinese chicken salad," ordered Veronica. "Easy on the sesame dressing."

"Would you like it on the side?" the waiter asked.

"Sure," Veronica said quickly.

"I'll have...I will have...hmmm...I will have...do you have any specials?" Nikki asked.

"I thought you were just getting a salad?" Veronica glimpsed at the time on her phone again.

"*You* can get a salad because you're in a hurry. Me, I'm hungry and wanna eat, and I got plenty of time!"

"The specials today include salmon prepared with dill in a white wine sauce..." the waiter's voice trailed off.

Veronica reached into her oversized messenger bag and pulled out her "inspiration pad". It was black leather-bound book she carried everywhere. She jotted reminders, drawings, and ideas in it. Now she scanned it for the notes she took while talking to Marie-Claire.

The waiter and Nikki grew silent. Veronica looked up, prepared to discuss the notations, when her sister said, "What kind of soup does that come with?"

"The soup du jour is chicken. We also have cream of tomato or broccoli cheese."

Veronica took a drink of tea and found herself sucking air through the straw. She pushed the glass toward the waiter. He absently grabbed it while smiling broadly at Nikki.

Nikki returned the grin. "I'm not a fan of broccoli or tomatoes."

"Just take the chicken soup," Veronica snapped.

Nikki barely noticed her sister's tone. "But I don't like it if it has carrots."

"No carrots in the chicken soup, ma'am," the waiter chimed.

11

"Are you sure? Usually there's carrots in it…" Nikki looked at Veronica's cold glare and stopped. "Fine. Chicken soup."

The waiter walked away.

Nikki smiled brightly at Veronica.

Veronica's shoulders relaxed and her thick lips opened to speak just as Nikki said, "Oh, wait! Iced tea, sir, I'd like an iced tea." Nikki turned to her sister and continued. "You want more tea, too, don't you?"

Veronica's shoulders became tense again. "He's already getting it."

"Hey, sir, excuse me," Nikki called. The waiter was halfway across the restaurant. Nikki bounced to her feet. "Can you get some iced tea for my sister, too?"

The waiter held up Veronica's empty glass and nodded politely.

Veronica sat stock-still and waited, but Nikki didn't give her a chance to speak. She instantly spewed, "Oh, I almost forgot to tell you. Guess who called the other day — I think it was Sunday — Doug! Did I tell you about Doug…?" Nikki's voice trailed off.

Veronica listened anxiously. She waited for her turn to speak…and waited while Nikki told her more.

"…I met Doug two weeks ago. I thought he'd never call, but he did! We've got a date Friday, but I don't know if I should flake 'cause he's like fifteen years older than me, but he's got a great bod *and* he's a lawyer. What do ya' think, Vern?"

Veronica seized her moment to finally talk and quickly blurted, "I got a call from France this morning!"

Nikki looked confused. "France?" She nodded at the waiter who had just brought the iced teas then yelled, "Wait!"

Veronica thought for sure that she lost her again as Nikki protested, "The teas are missing wedges."

Veronica slumped in her chair.

The waiter produced a small plate with sliced lemons and oranges. "Take your pick."

Nikki squealed. "Thank you!" Plucking a piece of fruit, she said to Veronica, "Who in France called you?"

"Her name is Marie-Claire and she has a castle she wants me to decorate."

Nikki's eyes grew wide. "You're going to decorate a castle in France? No-way-are-you-yanking-my-chain?"

Veronica had an audience now. "Yes, and get this: She said they will pay me *one million* francs just to start!"

"Francs?" Nikki inquired. "What kind of francs?"

"I dunno." Veronica shrugged. "French francs I guess…"

"She didn't say euro?"

"No, she said francs," Veronica answered. "What difference does it make?"

"They don't use francs in France anymore. They're obsolete. Unless she meant *Swiss* francs," Nikki replied as she skewered the orange wedge floating on the top of her tea with a straw. Waving it around, she explained, "Swiss francs are still in use because of the Swiss banking system." She swiped a finger across her phone and tapped rapidly. "According to my currency converter app, they're worth a little more than a dollar."

The waiter came with bread, the soup, and Veronica's salad. Nikki's attention shifted once again. Dropping her straw, she said exaggeratedly, "Thank you. You're the best!"

Veronica politely smiled and opened her mouth to speak. Before she could, Nikki yipped, "Waiter! Come back! I see a carrot!"

"Miss, I don't think so. The chef assured me that there were no carrots in the —"

"But there's something orange in my soup. If it ain't a carrot, what is it? What else could be *orange* in chicken soup?" she asked as she attempted to scoop the offending vegetable out of the bowl.

"I'll bring another..." the waiter started.

"But if this one has carrots, then that one will, too. Can I just have a salad — a side salad?" Nikki pouted.

The waiter obliged, grabbed the soup, and left.

"Christ, Nikki, that was your *orange wedge* in the soup! You dropped it in there while you were flinging your stupid straw around," Veronica scolded.

Nikki looked at Veronica's salad. "They put dressing on your salad!"

Veronica glanced down. "Yeah, it's okay..." But it was too late; Nikki was already calling the waiter back.

"No, Nikki, I don't care if I have dressing on the salad. I gotta go soon. The salad is fine, okay? I'm fine...I'm fine with my *fucking salad!* Okay?"

"Okay, I gotcha. Chill out. I was just trying to help." Nikki looked slightly hurt but let Veronica continue.

"So! I'm gonna go to France to decorate a castle!"

"You *are* going? Just like that?"

Veronica nodded proudly.

"But with your cash flow problems, don't ya' think you should find out exactly what it pays first — just to be safe?" Nikki asked.

"I will. She said she's gonna call back in a few days, so I'll ask then."

"Why... I mean *how*...why...why do they want *you* to do this?" Nikki stumbled, not liking the tone in her own voice. "I mean, sweetie, I love your work; you're brilliant. But why the hell did someone with a castle in *France* decide to call *you*? Is this one of Robert's clients?"

Veronica's stomach turned at the mention of her ex-partner's name. "Robert had nothing to do with this. I got this job because of *me*. Someone referred *me* to Marie-Claire because of *my* talents." Veronica pulled out her calendar and forced the tone of her voice up an octave. "So, it looks like I will be gone all summer."

"You are going to do it *this* summer? You're going to *France*?" Nikki asked.

"Yes, that's why I wanted to tell you right away. She said I could hire people — assistants and stuff. I kinda figure I need someone to translate the language, and since you're the only person I know who speaks French..." Veronica let her voice trail off as she smiled slyly. Her green eyes blinked once, causing one of her brown curls to waggle as it caught on an eyelash.

Nikki giggled. "You want *me* to come to France with you?"

"You're off for summer vacation anyway," the older sister urged.

"Yeah! And it would be more fun than the last time I went. Hanging out in a château is much better than chaperoning a school trip. Where is it? Where in France?"

"She said it's in the Loire Valley and has been empty for, like, twenty years. Oh, and she called it — get this: Le Château du Feu Ardent," Veronica said radiantly.

Nikki's expression of glee and surprise was frozen for a moment. Then a coy look came over her. "Oh my! When translated that means: 'The Castle of Blazing Fire'."

Chapter 5
The Children's Story
1307 AD – A Time of Inquisition

Isabelle's fingers waggled through the hole in the wall. "Louis, you first."

The little boy crawled on hands and knees toward her. His ankle throbbed. "It hur-ssst, Izzy."

"I know it hurts, but we're almost there. Once on the other side, it'll be easy. Don't worry. I'm right behind you."

The hole was an eroded space under the wall, partially filled with rainwater. Louis felt with both hands, took a deep breath, and pushed his head through. He writhed in the mud, trying to dig his elbows into the wet earth and gain enough leverage to pull his body along. Isabelle pushed his backside.

Louis squinted. It was brighter on this side of the wall as it was illuminated by the torchlight of the watchtower. There was an open area of grass before him, interrupted occasionally by a large rock or knoll. In the distance, perhaps forty feet away, was a thicket of trees. Small ones at first, but they became quite dense as they climbed up the slope of the hillside. This was the back of the castle. On the front side, there was a huge gatehouse that stood before the road that led into town.

Louis knew that Izzy wanted to stay away from the road and away from town because *they* would look for them there. He peered into the trees. That is where she wanted them to go. Into the forest until they came to the river. They would then follow it upstream through the mountain pass. On the other side, they would come to a valley with several little villages. That was where they would seek refuge.

His legs slid through the opening, and as he pulled himself up on all fours, something darted among the sapling trees in front of him. Louis froze like a startled rabbit. Unable to blink, rain dripped into his eyes. Again, it jumped from behind one tree to another. It was a shadow, undefined and quick, and it was coming closer.

In the muggy nighttime air the boy thought he smelled something rotten. The odor reminded him of the dead owl in the fireplace that Papa had to flush out with a broomstick. Something smelled like a burnt, dead carcass.

He instinctively switched gears, flopped back onto his belly, and started to slide backward through the crevice. His legs kicked feverishly and he barely missed knocking Isabelle in the jaw.

"Louis, what are you doing!" she seethed. "Like it or not, you're going through!" She squeezed his buttocks with both hands and pushed with all her might.

Under different circumstances, the scene would have looked comical — a pudgy, little boy wiggling in a muddy hole while his sister pressed on his rump. Each fought for leverage, but the girl proved to be stronger. As she pushed her terrified brother, the thing in the forest crept closer.

The boy caught a clear view of the creature as it leapt from behind a tree stump. It was black — about the size of a small dog. However he could have sworn that as it bounded through the air, it grew larger, and when it landed, it was as big as a horse. It had a long, narrow snout, spindly legs, and claws that glinted like embers in a fire. It now encroached slowly, like a predator about to pounce.

"Izzy, no, no..."

She gave one last, mighty shove and Louis popped completely through. Once on the other side, he scuttled like a crab until his back hit the wall. His feet kicked at the mushy ground as if he might just be able to summon up enough traction to push the thick stone façade backward.

Isabelle slithered through next. She went slowly at first, but then faster when she heard Louis struggling. Once her upper body was on the other side, she turned to her brother. He was crouched against the wall, writhing like a worm. His face was eerily white and his eyes, huge and black, stared into the forest.

She followed his gaze and caught a glimpse of something retreating through the sapling trees. Quickly, she forced her way through. Her belly burned as it rubbed against pebbles on the bottom. Once completely on the other side, Isabelle crawled to her brother.

"Little Louis, I'm here. It's okay."

"Did you see that *devil* in the woods?"

Isabelle summoned up the calmest, most adult-like voice she could. "It was just an animal, not a devil; nothing to be afraid of. We probably scared it more than it scared us."

She tried to smile, but Isabelle knew about the creature that stalked the castle grounds. She had never seen it, didn't know where it came from or why it was there, but she did know that her father and his men considered it sacred...and dangerous.

Papa once told her not to think about the creature. It would never harm her or anyone in the castle since he was the Grand Master of the Temple Order. That meant he could command it and keep it at bay. Unfortunately, several nights ago, her father and mother, along with the rest of the Temple Knights, were arrested by the Inquisitors and taken away. *What would happen now that there was no one around to control it?*

With a flash, the light from the tower shifted in their direction, and Isabelle was pulled from her thoughts. She protectively pushed Louis back and huddled beside him, hoping that they would blend with the shadows.

A voice simply stated, "Who is there?"

Isabelle and Louis made no sound, not even to exhale the breath trapped in their tight, little throats.

They heard the voice again. "In the name of Lord Pierre Dubois, who trespasses?"

The children sat stock-still. Then they heard — no *felt* — footfalls. The guard was walking along the top of the wall, coming toward them. They could feel each step he took as the stones vibrated against their backs.

Isabelle took Louis' face in her hands. Her pinky flicked a tear off his cheek. "The guard is coming. We have to run now, as fast as we can, to the woods."

Louis shot a quick look to the trees in the direction that he saw the *devil*. He didn't have to speak for Isabelle to know what was on his mind.

She continued, "It was just an animal and it ran away." Her smile was thin and she prayed it was truly gone.

Louis huffed. "But what about Uncle Pierre? He's supposed to take care of us. He'll be so mad if we run away!"

"Louis, I told you, Uncle Pierre was there the night the Inquisitors came and took Mama and Papa away. I woke up and heard everything. We can't trust him. *He* is why we have to escape — otherwise, we may never see them again."

Louis didn't speak as he wobbled to his feet. The pressure on his ankle shot a streak of hot pain up his leg. Now he would have to run. His sister suddenly seemed far away. Her disembodied voice chimed in his ear. "We'll run together; on the count of three..."

Isabelle didn't get a chance to say the first number as her brave little brother took off like he was launched by a trebuchet. She stood for a moment — stunned — as she had fully expected to be dragging him across the grass. He ran quickly and silently. She looked up at the guard. His attention was focused on the wall, and he didn't even notice the small boy sprinting across the meadow right in front of him.

Isabelle's heart leapt. *They could do this after all!* Louis was halfway to the trees when she started to run. She hunkered down at first, trying to crouch low so as not to be seen. She pulled up her dress with both hands and galloped across the grass like a hunchback. Ahead she could see Louis disappear into the trees. Joy warmed inside of her. Now she just had to make it a little bit farther...

"You!" a shrill voice bellowed. "Stop, you, in the name of Lord Pierre Dubois!"

Only a few more feet and she'd be in the woods. She heard a sudden, odd noise in her right ear...*thwish*. It was followed by a sharp snap up ahead of her, in the woods.

A chill grabbed hold of her spine for a split second as she thought of the creature prowling among the trees. Before she had a chance to be scared, she heard the *thwish* sound again. Instantly, it made sense.

Isabelle was being shot at. The guard was launching arrows.

Chapter 6

Veronica's Story

Veronica grabbed the phone on the second ring. "Hello?"

"Bonjour, Veronica. It is Marie-Claire!"

Veronica smiled. *What an incredible voice to wake up to*, she thought. "Bonjour to you, too," she said while trying to reach her inspiration pad and pencil on the nightstand. "Listen, your offer sounds tempting. I just need to know more..."

"Of course," Marie-Claire said.

"The pay you mentioned, is that about a million American dollars or euro or Swiss francs?"

Marie-Claire hesitated for a moment, "Oui, my conversions aren't very quick."

Veronica laughed. "Mine either!" She attempted to write on the pad in the dark while propping the phone to her ear with her shoulder.

"Shit. Hold on..." Veronica muttered as she the phone began to slip. "I'm sorry. The phone slid off my shoulder."

"Oh, how delightful," Marie-Claire answered.

Veronica realized that Marie-Claire didn't quite grasp what she just said and chuckled under her breath. "I need to get some ideas from you. Tell me what you want me to do. What rooms will I be decorating? How many are there?"

"You are an artist, no? That is what *you* should decide. Look at each room and imagine how it should be. Many rooms have old furnishings still, and you may be able to restore them. There are seven bedrooms on the upper floors. Perhaps each bedroom could have an individual influence?

"There is a parlor, a library, the dining room, and kitchen. There are gardens, which were truly magnifique in another time. There is even a chapel! And, of course, the tower rooms...I cannot forget to tell you; they are in the keep, which is the oldest part of the castle. We believe you will find much inspiration there," Marie-Claire said.

"Do you have photos you can email me?" an enchanted Veronica asked.

Marie-Claire kept talking though. "There are, of course, stables and a barn, a vineyard, the orchard..."

Veronica scribbled in her inspiration pad. Marie-Claire continued describing the Château. In Veronica's mind's eye, she envisioned a fairytale palace.

Marie-Claire fell silent, and Veronica realized that she had almost fallen back to sleep while listening to the melodic French voice. She shook her head slightly to regain lucidity. The French woman continued to speak, and Veronica took notes as fast as she could until sleep finally did take over.

Chapter 7

Dorothée's Story

A man on horseback rode up to the front doors of the castle. Dorothée watched from the parlor window and thought it odd that he didn't take the horse straight to the stable. She smacked her lips as he dismounted, watching as several servants, including the stable manager, rushed to him. They appeared to speak excitedly. The horse was led off, and the servants escorted the visitor toward the castle.

She heard a commotion in the foyer. Her short, plump, lady-in-waiting waddled past the doorway, argued with the stranger, and then stepped into the parlor to face Dorothée.

This was Dorothée's favorite room. The parlor was splendid with pastoral murals, each gilded with gold framing. In a massive stone fireplace, to the left of the entryway, a blaze ravished chunks of an old apple tree. Dorothée sat on an opulent, velvet chaise strewn with imported Chinese silk pillows. She closed her book and asked, "What distress does this visitor bring, Patricia?"

Patricia's round face scrunched up; her eyes, nose, and mouth became lost in the middle of her cherub-like head. "My lady, he has an urgent message from the Cardinal. We told him that Lord André-Benoit is not here and that he can leave the scroll, but he insists upon giving it to him in person."

"He can leave the message with me. Surely he cannot deny the lady of the house," Dorothée answered. "Bring him before me."

Patricia curtsied quickly and scuttled out of the room.

Dorothée had been the lady of the house for three full weeks. She marveled at the luxury and respect bestowed upon her at all times. Her own family — though wealthy nobility — was not nearly so revered.

Patricia returned a moment later with the messenger in tow. He was bowing low and Dorothée could see the top of his greasy, hair-tangled head. "Stand up straight," she ordered.

"My lady, I have urgent news for your husband. Please forgive the intrusion, but I must speak with him as soon as possible." His voice was slightly breathless.

"He is in Paris discussing the Protestant uprising with the *King*," she answered grandly. "Can you not leave the message with me? I am the lady of the house."

"Forgive me, but no. I must present this to Lord André-Benoit and only to him." His eyes were cast downward, not meeting hers.

As she stood, her fine, red, velvet gown cascaded to the floor. She took several steps forward, and the man appeared to shrink within his own skin. "Well, as I said, he is not here and will not return until the morrow. Until then, what should we do with *you*?"

The messenger clutched the scroll tightly. "May I stay then, just for the night, and give it to him in the morning?"

"You would like to stay *here* tonight?" she boomed.

"Oh no, my lady, in the stable. Let me sleep with my horse!"

"By the scent of you, you have bedded down with that filthy animal many times." She held a perfume-soaked handkerchief to her delicate nose and walked in a circle around him. "Perhaps more comfortable accommodations can be made for a messenger from the Cardinal. That's where the note is from, correct?"

"Yes," he said, lifting his gaze to meet hers for the first time. "Thank you for your kindness."

"Yes, I am kind," she said sharply. "So, surely you can tell me the nature of the message."

"I am sure that I cannot. I don't even know. Look, you can see for yourself; the parchment is sealed." His white knuckles unraveled to reveal a ragged piece of paper, sealed with wax in the Cardinal's symbol.

"Hmm, well perhaps even bedding down with your horse is too good for you. Arrangements could be made for you, however, in the barn with the hogs." She flung her head around dramatically and allowed her lips to curl into a smile that he could not see.

His eyes fell down again. "That would be fine, my lady."

She stopped walking and stood just behind him. He remained facing forward, his knees twitching uncontrollably. She let out a huff, and her mock bravado dissipated. "Oh, there is plenty of room in the castle. You may sleep here tonight." She gestured for Patricia who was hovering in the foyer. "Please, take him to the kitchen, Patricia, and make sure he is fed."

"Thank you for your graciousness," he stammered as he was led out.

Ignoring him, Dorothée turned and walked in the opposite direction, through the parlor's French doors and into the front garden. The clergy who once tended it used it as a potager garden, planting mostly vegetables, and it had become overgrown with unsightly vines. She had recently begun to dig up the offending vegetation and was pleased with her efforts to create a luxurious flower garden.

Another set of French doors led back inside and to her quarters. Opulent and frilly, she wryly referred to it as the "Queen's Chamber". André-Benoit slept in the "King's Chamber" on the second floor. Or at least that was where etiquette dictated that he should sleep. She bent and picked up his shirt that lay crumpled at the foot of the enormous canopied bed. "Why didn't Patricia pick up that tunic this morning?" she muttered as she hastily tossed it to the floor.

From the Queen's Chamber she walked into a hallway. Two lanterns illuminated the corridor; one hung just an arm's length from her bedroom door. If she walked straight, she would enter the parlor again, and next to that doorway was the entrance to the library. If she walked down the hall and turned several corners, she would come to the keep.

André-Benoit took her into the keep only once. He explained to her that it was the oldest part of the Château, built by Pagans before France was even a sovereign country. Its walls were thick, and it served as a fortress if the Château should ever come under attack. It contained guard's quarters, prison cells, and the tower rooms. Now, it sat empty. She wondered if the keep would have acceptable accommodations for the messenger.

She passed Patricia's quarters, which were next to her own. Here, the second lantern hung to irradiate the intersection of the passageway. Next to Patricia's room, there were also quarters for the ministry, though none lived here now. She rescued the lantern from the wall and continued her private exploration.

She felt quite at home at Le Château du Feu Ardent. It fed her power like she never felt before. She was the youngest of four daughters and throughout her life had shared everything. This huge, magnificent Château, was hers though. She dreamed of her sisters coming to visit. She would order the servants to wait on them and furnish their rooms extravagantly. They would feast nightly, and everyone would marvel at her grace.

She stood in front of the door to the keep and let the lantern light reveal its wooden facade, warped with time, with metal hinges that were rusted and brittle. It made a loud, rebellious noise as she pushed it open. At once, she noticed a pungent odor and wondered if perhaps a small animal had died in a corner somewhere.

She stepped inside. The stone walls here were different from the rest of the castle. They were older and had more of an irregular shape. They fit together snuggly, as if over time, they had melded to become one. It was dirty; no one ever came here to clean. The smell was stronger now, and Dorothée felt certain that a bird or a rat must lay dead close by.

There were several small cells. Each had a massive metal door with only a slit for a window. *Food must have been passed through there*, she thought. She considered peeking into one and then stopped. She wasn't eager to see a dead animal rotting on the floor. She hung the lantern on a hook on the wall.

André-Benoit had been reluctant to show her such a hideous place as the keep, but she insisted. Chunky black chains hinged to shackles were bolted to the walls. In one corner was a monstrous device known as "the rack". She imagined showing her sisters this place and how frightened they would be. She would be the strong one, however, the brave one, in total control of her domain.

Across from the cells was a door on a convex wall. This was the door to the ground-level tower room. She had learned that there were three levels to the tower. To her right, a stairway snaked up to the other rooms. These dwellings were somewhat more "civilized" than the cells and were meant to hold prisoners of some reputation. *Perhaps my sisters would enjoy their stay in these rooms*, she thought wickedly.

She grabbed the rusty, metal handle on the door of the ground-level tower room. It felt unnaturally warm, and she automatically drew her hand back. She breathed out and noticed that she could see the vapors; the air was quite cold.

André-Benoit had opened this door and let her peep inside but had taken her no further. She had looked at him expectantly, and he said, "My dear, such a place is not suitable for a lady."

Her hand was covered with grime from the door handle. She reached into her pocket, pulled out a handkerchief, placed it back over the crumbling metal, and pushed the door open wide to let in all the light possible. It was still dim inside. There were no windows. She squinted and allowed herself some time so that she could see. She thought she saw movement against the far wall. She stood motionless and noticed that same pungent odor, only now it was more intense. She held her perfumed kerchief to her nose.

Slowly, the shadows in the room took shape. On the far wall, where she saw something move, was a short wooden door. "What on earth could that be?" she whispered. At the same time, she startled herself, as she did not mean to speak out loud. She then realized that the sound of her own voice comforted her, and she spoke again. "How long has it been since a lady stood here...two, maybe three hundred years?" She took a step forward.

The light from the doorway made her shadow huge on the rounded walls. She looked at the small door again. "Why such a diminutive door? Maybe the guards who used to dwell here were gnomes." She snickered and took another step.

Something snapped under her foot. She looked down, but her dress covered it. She could feel it, long and cylindrical, wedged against her heel. She knelt, searching with her hands for the object, while she kept her eyes focused on her own shadow which wavered in front of her. "Under my shoe, what could be hiding under my shoe?"

As she spoke her last word, her ears caught a sound. She became dead silent. *Breathing...did she hear something breathing?* Her fingers wrapped around the tiny object. She thought it felt like a piece of wood that had been worn smooth from the ocean. She stood slowly. *Was there an animal in here after all? If there was a dead animal causing that horrible stench, then maybe I have stumbled across a nest of some kind?*

She didn't want to disturb a mother and a litter of tiny critters, so she turned to leave. The bottom of her dress rustled across debris on the floor as she twirled. While stepping lightly, carefully, something scampered past her feet.

She felt instantly hot, as if consumed by a raging fever. Dorothée shrieked. Frantically, she made her way for the door, but whatever it was that had brushed past her feet did it again. She tripped, falling hard on her knees. Shearing pain struck as several small, sharp objects drove themselves into her kneecaps.

Any ladylike composure Dorothée had maintained vanished instantly. Her legs tangled in the many layers of her petticoats, making it impossible to stand. Madly, clumsily, she scrambled on her hands and knees to the door. Fragments cut into her palms, and slick blood oozed through her fingers.

With her dress bunched between her legs, crawling proved to be impossible. She dropped to her elbows and slithered the few remaining feet like a soldier in a trench. As she approached doorway, she grabbed the handle to pull herself up. However, she lost her balance and fell forward, pushing the door shut as she plunged to the floor. It slammed with a reverberating thud.

She landed on her face with her feet kicking wildly within her elegant, red velvet gown. The stench of death suddenly hung so thickly in the air that she thought she would vomit. The fumes made her freeze. She lay still and stunned for a brief moment as she fought the urge to retch.

The blackness was absolute, and though she couldn't see, Dorothée became keenly aware that something was shuffling amid the rubbish behind her. She rolled over, hiked up her dress and petticoats which exposed her defenseless legs, and sprang to her feet. The noble woman lunged into the door and tried with all her might to pull it open.

It wouldn't budge. Terror clenched her soul. Like a crazy woman, she screamed, and screamed, and screamed.

Chapter 8

Veronica's Story

The 101 was jammed on a Saturday afternoon. She was running late for her appointment with Mrs. Stevenson. Mrs. Stevenson needed to pick out different fabric for her window treatments. Veronica's suggestion was simply too "gaudy with color and patterns!"

Veronica sucked air into her cheeks, and then blew out defiantly. "Well, Mrs. Stevenson, perhaps we should find some fabric for the windows with *no* design at all. *Beige* fabric. That way it will match your beige carpet and your beige walls. If we are feeling frisky, we might just find some beige artwork to put over your beige fireplace. We can call your whole house 'Rhapsody in Beige'. Won't all of your beige bourgeois friends be impressed?"

Veronica was pleased with her use of the word "bourgeois". She had been paging through history books and felt satisfied that she was becoming quite educated in the terms of the French.

Her cell phone rang, and she fumbled for it in the depths of her denim messenger bag. Her black-framed, Elvis Costello-styled sunglasses slid down the curve of her nose.

She loved Elvis Costello. She was just a little girl when he released the song *Veronica*, and she used to think it was about her. As she grew up, Veronica realized the peppy tune had a solemn theme. She still liked it anyway; it made her feel happy and sad at the same time.

A car horn blared. She shot a quick glance in her rearview mirror to see an angry bald man in a BMW. In front of her, there was precisely twelve feet of open road. "Yes, of course, you bourgeois pig. I will certainly drive forward eight more feet so that you can get where you are going *that* much faster." Her fingers grazed her cellphone and she snatched it up.

It rang again. "Shit, shit, shit…" She quickly dug out her Bluetooth, fumbled to insert the earpiece, and then quickly pushed "talk".

"Hello, this is Veronica."

"Yo, it's Nikki. Where are ya'?"

"On my way to see Mrs. Stevenson about her beige carpet and beige window treatments." Veronica sighed.

"Well, at least you can say that her carpet matches her drapes." Nikki snickered.

"Don't you think that joke was a little *off-colored?*" Veronica snorted. They both giggled like naughty, little girls.

"Hey, I was thinking about our trip," Nikki said, trying to sound casual.

Veronica recognized her tone. "What *about* our trip…?"

"Since you have a budget for hired help, I was thinking maybe Doug could come along. He could be our bodyguard and chase away all those virile French hotties who will be breaking down the castle doors for our favors."

"Doug? Who is *Doug?*"

"Doug, my new boyfriend," she replied matter-of-factly. "I told you about him two weeks ago when we had lunch."

"Oh, Doug, the old guy with the great body." Veronica clicked her turn signal.

"He's not that *old*, and he'd be a lot of fun," Nikki persisted.

"A lot of fun for you, Nik. What would I be, the chaperone?"

"No, of course not. The three of us would have a great time."

"Oh, Nik, please don't do this to me. This *is* a job, and we only have three months to decorate an entire castle," Veronica moaned as she pulled her car into the next lane. Just then a horn blared again. She looked over her right shoulder just in time to see the Bald Beamer come up alongside her and overtake her lane. "You asshole!"

"What?" Nikki asked.

"Not you, the guy who just cut me off and is making me miss my exit. I'm late. Can we talk about this later?"

"I gotta make my plans for this trip, too, ya' know. Have you talked to Marie-Claire yet?"

Veronica made a quick move and managed to steer onto the exit ramp just in time, cutting off the BMW and sending the driver into a horn-honking fit. "Yeah, she's really great Nik. I hope you get to meet her. "

"You mean she might not *be* there?" Nikki had a sudden excited tone in her voice.

"No, they are going to be gone on holiday; that's why they want us there for the summer. It'll just be us and whoever we hire."

"Just us and Doug, you say?" Nikki asked coyly.

Veronica became impatient. "Nik, I haven't even met the guy."

"Oh Vern, Vern, Vern, come on!"

"But you know my name is *Veronica*," answered Veronica in the way she often did when her little sister used her nickname.

"Fine, forget Doug. How about if I bring Troy instead?" Nikki exclaimed.

"Troy!" Veronica boomed.

"Just yanking your chain, Vern. Relax. We won't bring any men with us. Besides, there'll be plenty there for the picking, right? Hey, where in the Loire Valley is this castle, anyway?"

"She said it was near a river."

"Well, there are a lot of rivers there, Vern. You don't know what town it's near?"

"Amboise, I think. I wrote down the address, but that's all I remember; I was half-asleep when she called," Veronica said sheepishly.

"She called in the middle of the night?"

"It was like five in the morning. That's when she usually calls; must be because of the time difference."

"Five in the morning is like two o'clock in the afternoon in France. How rude. She could easily call you later in the day."

Veronica turned her car onto Mrs. Stevenson's street. "Yeah, whatever, maybe she doesn't know that. Listen, Nik, I gotta go...."

"Cool. Oh, hey, did she say who recommended you?"

Veronica parked in the driveway and pulled her notepad out of her bag. "Yeah, I wrote it down." She looked at the illegible writing. "I think it says Dr. Jab-co Andrew."

"Huh? Dr. Jab-co-who?" Nikki asked.

"It was dark and I can't read my notes now." Veronica noticed Mrs. Stevenson walking to her car from the house. "Hey, I gotta go."

"K, I'll talk to you later. Oh! Any idea on how much you're gonna pay me?"

Mrs. Stevenson tapped on the car window as Veronica answered, "I'll pay you as much as Mrs. Stevenson pays me in a *whole* year."

"What? Christ, Vern, I didn't realize you were gonna be *that* cheap!" She chortled.

"Just kidding, I'll pay you a living wage. How does fifteen percent sound?"

"Perfect," declared the younger sister. "I feel like your agent."

"Maybe you should be," Veronica sighed as she smiled widely at Mrs. Stevenson, who now stood with her fists on her hips. "Later, Nik," she said as she clicked off the phone and went to talk color swatches with the most vanilla person she knew.

Chapter 9
Dorothée's Story
Circa 1520 AD – the Dawn of the Reformation

Patricia carried Lord André-Benoit's shirt out of the Queen's Chamber. She'd give it to the maids to be laundered. She was about to enter the library when she heard a faint cry. *Were the stable boys playing in the garden again? Lady Dorothée would be angry if they were.*

Patricia turned and walked back into her lady's bedroom and opened the garden doors. She saw that the overgrown plants and vines were quite serene.

She shrugged and walked back to the hallway. She heard the cry again. The castle echoed so much; it was often challenging to determine where a sound came from. The noise seemed to favor her right ear. She turned and gawped down the dimly lit passageway.

The solitary lantern on the wall provided just enough radiance for Patricia to notice the side corridor, about ten paces down, which branched off to the keep. *Was the sound coming from there?*

The woman wobbled on the tips of her toes and shakily removed the lantern from its perch. Then she noticed the second lantern was missing. She heard the cry again. Patricia made the sign of the cross over her chest and chased the sound through the winding hallways.

The door to the keep was slightly ajar. Illumination came from within. No one ever went in *there*.

"Hello...hello?" Her eyes searched the shadowy stone walls for a clue as she crept inside. "Is somebody there?"

Inside the tower room, Dorothée thought she heard a voice. *Was it Patricia?* She began to pound on the wooden obstruction with all her might. "Patricia, get me out!"

"My lady, what in heaven are you doing in there?" Patricia rushed to the door.

"It matters not. Please just release me." Blood coursed inside Dorothée's head. It distorted the maid's voice.

Patricia's round thumbs pressed the latch until she thought her bones would snap. "I can't open it. I'm not strong enough. Let go of the handle on your side," she said, forcing her voice to sound calm.

Dorothée released her grip.

"Now pull on the door while I push," Patricia said.

"I'm pulling." Dorothée sobbed.

"Pull!" Patricia ordered.

"I *am*!" The humidity enveloped her like a blanket.

"I can't get it open; I'm not strong enough. I have to go get help."

"No, don't leave me! I'm not alone, Patricia...there is something *else* in here!"

"Oh my...I can't open it myself. I have to find someone stronger. I'll be quick."

"Patricia, wait! Pull out the shelf and set the lantern on it."

Patricia took half a step back and saw a plate-sized wooden panel two-thirds of the way down. She fumbled with the latch for a moment; rust flaked off and stained her child-like fingers red and orange. With a screech she pulled it open, revealing a crevice in the door.

Patricia caught a glimpse of Dorothée. Her heavy velvet dress was drenched with sweat and clung to her like a wet bath towel. "Don't worry, my lady. I will find Claude or the smithy."

Dorothée crouched by the portal and savored the lantern light. On the ground, the small object that she had found under her foot was now illuminated. It was a small bone, broken on one end.

She turned her head toward the interior of the round room. Precisely in the center sat another creature, also crouching.

She vaguely made out the shape of a head, long and horse-like. The thing crawled toward her methodically on four legs, animal-like in their shape, but with humanoid hands. Each was composed of four digits and one hideously long thumb that started on the forearm; its end curled like a sickle-shaped claw.

Dorothée did not move, she did not breathe, she did not blink. Her eyes fixed on the ungodly beast before her. It took another lumbering step.

It was only a few feet away from her now. Under its matted black hair, she could see patches of red festering skin crawling with worms. Its nose got wide then thin, over and over again in a slow rhythm. Wisps of smoke escaped from its nostrils — it was sniffing her.

Prayers ran through her head, though she rarely felt sincerity while saying them in mass. Now she meant them, with all her might, she meant them. "Please, God, help me!"

Chapter 10

Veronica's Story

hy is it so difficult for you to be happy? The question randomly popped into Veronica's head. It often did. It was Robert's distinct voice, slightly condescending with a faux European accent. Robert was born and raised in Simi Valley, California. He spoke with an accent to, in his words, "add an air of sophistication to his business."

She remembered the day he asked her the question. They were in the hallway of their Beverly Hills office, and he was preparing to see an important new client from one of the cable networks. Robert was excited and had jittered around all morning picking lint off the carpet like an old fashioned lady preparing for a gentleman caller.

"I am happy," Veronica replied, wondering why she suddenly felt defensive.

"No, things around you should make you happy, but you are not. You never just 'be' happy. You never 'be' anything; so serious all the time. Can you live in the moment? Can you just stop and enjoy things as they are at this very instant? And your hair, you always pull it back like that. Why can't you wear it down?"

"What are you talking about? My hair? It gets in my eyes when I work. Why are you suddenly so concerned about my *hair*?"

Robert didn't answer. He waved his hand and shut his office door.

Veronica pulled herself back into the present. I am happy now, she thought. Right now, I am happy! I have my own business. I don't need Robert. And I have a new, huge client from France. Robert can kiss my ass because right now I am so incredibly fucking happy!

Veronica punched angrily at the keyboard on her desk. She never fit into Robert's world. Veronica was born and raised in a suburb of Bakersfield, California called Oildale. It was the kind of town that one isn't proud to be from and as opposite from Beverly Hills as it gets. She and her sister were lucky. Both bright and talented, they managed to get small college scholarships and escaped from a life of trailer parks and pickup trucks.

Hillbilly Hipster — that's what they called her in college. Unable to completely shake her upbringing, her personal style consisted of bibbed overalls and hemp tunics mixed with thick-framed glasses and vintage scarves. Her image suited her fine among the other artists in design school. It was comfortable and easy, and she resisted having to grow out of it. Even when Robert opened the office in Beverly Hills, Veronica had to make a concerted effort to dress "the part".

Veronica opened her Outlook calendar. It was May twentieth, and she hadn't heard from Marie-Claire in almost two weeks. She looked at the notes jotted in her inspiration pad. Names and numbers were scattered among random drawings. Written in the dark while she was half asleep, they were indecipherable.

Way to go, Vern!

She couldn't read Marie-Claire's phone number and didn't even know her last name. Luckily, she could decipher the address for Château du Feu Ardent and the peculiar instructions for receiving her pay.

She searched online for airplane tickets. They weren't cheap. Plus they'd have to fly into Paris, take a train to Tours, and then rent a car to get to the castle. There was a bargain fare, just $1,158.00 US per person, leaving June second and returning August thirtieth. *Should she take a leap of faith and buy it now?*

She shut her eyes as she clicked the button to "book now". Hopefully, Marie-Claire would call soon to confirm everything, the travel website only had a twenty-four hour cancellation policy.

She sat back in her chair and looked into the small, empty front office adjacent to hers. She rented it, too. When she first began *Veronica's Room* she had an assistant who sat there. That only lasted a few months before Veronica realized she couldn't afford to pay her salary and had to let the poor woman go.

The mailman poked his head in the door of the front office and looked around. He caught sight of Veronica in the back and nodded as he let a waterfall of envelopes drop onto the empty desk. Veronica thanked him even though the last thing she wanted to see was another bill.

She spun her chair around and faced sketches and swatches of fabric hanging on the wall behind her. In front of her were large French doors that revealed a picturesque courtyard. It separated her office from the whirring cars on Cahuenga Boulevard. To her left was a shelf overflowing with decorating books and magazines, including several that she recently bought from Amazon for inspiration. One was called *French Castles and Churches*, another *Medieval Design* and a third was a about medieval castle tapestries.

Veronica specialized in eclectic designs; she never once fully created a room true to any specific genre. She preferred pulling from aspects of different cultures, fashions, and time periods for inspiration. A castle in France, though, surely needed to be as authentic as possible. She felt a flutter of anxiety in her gut.

I'm out of my league. Haven't got a clue why this French woman picked me to decorate her castle — maybe she saw Robert's website and found out that I did most of his designs? Maybe somehow, someway, I *do* have a reputation?

She spun the chair again, playfully, since there was no one around to see her. She caught herself in mid-spin by grabbing the desk. She clicked on Google and searched for "Château du Feu Ardent". Nothing. She searched "castles" and "Loire Valley". Lots of hits. She clicked on the first one which had listing after listing of breathtaking châteaux, abbeys, villas, and gardens.

I guess I have to fake it until I make it. After all, this might be my last chance. Doesn't matter why Marie-Claire called me; the only thing that matters is making it work.

Veronica picked up a pencil and absently began drawing in her inspiration pad. She imagined herself standing in front of the Château. Huge tree branches canopied over her, a breeze swirled apple blossoms, and the clopping of horse hooves echoed in the distance. A beautiful structure rose before her with medieval fashioned windows, majestic steeples that arched gracefully, and tendrils of ivy, which hugged almost one entire side of a short, round belfry. A slender, red tower loomed in the distance. It seemed to glow, as if lit from within.

Chapter 11

The Children's Story
1307 AD – A Time of Inquisition

Isabelle lunged once she reached the edge of the clearing. Behind her, arrows swished and snapped as they flew into the thicket of saplings. She burrowed through the brush even though the spindly branches scratched at her face like hands hell-bent on holding her back.

Once she felt she was deep enough in the foliage, she paused to look behind her. The castle was completely out of sight — and if she couldn't see the tower that meant the archer couldn't see her.

She crawled toward the darkest, thickest section of vegetation. Coming to an upturned tree, which provided the perfect cover, Isabelle stopped to hide. The ground was covered in moist, decaying leaves that sucked around her as she sat.

Resting felt good. Her panicked mind began to focus. She needed to find her brother. "Louis, where are you? Louis?" she whispered.

Something rustled in front of her. Her bonnet covered most of her forehead. Long hair hung in her face, spilled over her shoulders, and onto the dead ground. Squinting, she could barely make out a dark form that crept closer. A twig snapped and leaves crunched.

"Louis, is that you?" She remembered the dark creature darting through the trees and a bolt of dread seared her heart.

A small beam of moonlight revealed a round, white face with a broad, goofy smile. It was Louis. He crawled to his sister's side. "Izzy! You made it!" the boy mouthed with exaggerated facial expressions.

She grinned and answered softly, "Of course, silly poppet, I'd never leave you."

Louis clutched his sister in a tight embrace. He caught a sweet whiff of blood. Pulling back his chubby fist, he held it up in the moonlight to see it was smeared with red.

"You're bleeding!"

"I am?" She craned her neck to get a good look at her shoulder. A dark patch of crimson soaked into the sleeve of her dress. "Do you have anything to wrap it; something to stop the flow?"

Louis shrugged. "Lemme look!" He reached into his satchel.

Before they fled the castle, Isabelle had told him to pack things that they would need for the trip. He wasn't entirely sure what she meant, but then recalled the things Papa would pack for hunting trips. So like his father, Louis brought a knife — it wasn't very sharp, though. He couldn't find a hunting knife, so he took a rather dull one from the kitchen — one of his mother's handmade scarves, some dried fruit and jerk beef in case they got hungry, and a flask of brandywine. Papa always said that you couldn't go hunting without a flask of brandywine...even though Louis didn't know exactly why.

Louis also brought something special; relics his father gave to him the night before the Inquisitors came.

You can keep this a secret, right, Louis?

I sure can, Papa!

It has been passed down through the generations of knights.

Is it a big secret?

Yes, Little Louis.

Louis wasn't old enough to understand the significance of the relics, yet he was smart enough to know his father wanted him to keep them safe no matter what — and that's what Louis intended to do.

As the boy rummaged through his satchel, inspiration struck. He needed the brandywine after all!

He remembered the time when a healer was called to the castle. A spooked horse had stepped on a squire's foot. Part of the flesh of the young man's ankle was torn off the bone. Louis watched with wonder as the healer pulled a draught from a flask and then handed it to his patient saying it would "chase away the demons".

He clutched the flask. "Izzy, I'm going to fix you up like I seed the healer do." The boy took a quick gulp of the sweet smelling liquid. His lips pinched together, and he coughed hard, sputtering the brandywine out in a spray. The alcohol splattered over Isabelle's open wound. She yipped with surprise. The abrasion, merely a scratch, now throbbed.

Louis thought he could hear barking dogs. He covered her mouth and got close to her face. "I think I hear them. You have to be quiet, okay?"

Isabelle writhed and obediently bit her bottom lip to make the pain go away.

"Your turn, Izzy. Take a drink; it will chase away the demons!"

The young girl shook her head. "No, Louis, it isn't that bad. The arrow barely grazed me. I don't need —" As she objected, Louis clasped her jaw and poured some of the fermented juice in her mouth. She reluctantly swallowed. The alcohol warmed her insides and steadied her uncertain stomach.

While Isabelle savored the brandywine, Louis cut his mother's scarf into strips with the kitchen knife. It took all his might to slice the fabric with the dull blade. He then wrapped the finely embroidered silk bandages around Isabelle's arm and tied them as tight as he could.

"Does it hurt, Izzy?"

"Not so much anymore. Just don't spit on me again."

"Drink some more." He held the brandywine to her lips. Isabelle made a face, but she managed to take a good swallow.

"We have to go now," Louis said as he helped her to her feet.

While gaining her balance, Isabelle caught sight of something emerging from behind the shadowy trees along the crest of the hill. Like a mangy hound, it loomed before them, about twenty feet ahead, blocking their path.

Isabelle pulled her brother's sleeve and whispered, "Wait! It's one of the hunting dogs."

Louis turned and froze. Carefully, slowly as not to provoke it, he answered, "That's not a dog, Izzy. It's that *devil.*"

His sister shook her head. "It's just a..." Before she could finish, the creature leapt forward and, in one massive stride, landed a mere ten feet away.

"That's no dog, Izzy!"

Shaded by the dense foliage, the creature didn't fully reveal itself. Animal-like for certain, it had attributes of many beasts. The long face reminded Isabelle of a rodent, the arching legs were like a spider's, the hunching posture was similar to how a rabbit sat, and the front claws — spindly and shiny as they caught glints of the moist moonlight — were like a an eagle's talons.

"Quick! Back to the castle!" the boy urged.

Isabelle firmly resisted. "No, we have to run *around* it. It can't leave the grounds and we're right on the border."

"How do you know?"

"I just do. Trust me. We can each flank it. You run to the right, and I'll go left. It can't chase us both!"

As it prepared to spring forward, the children split, each fleeing in a different direction.

The creature picked one to pursue and chased its target into the depths of the forest.

Chapter 12

Sebastian's Story

The local people whispered stories about Sebastian. Since he always wore a heavy cape with his head hidden under its hood, they called him the Cloaked Man, and everyone avoided the foothills where he lived. If encountered on the road, even the bravest of men would steer a wide path around him. He was a soothsayer, a magician, a necromancer, or — some claimed — the son of the devil himself.

Legend depicted that thirty years ago he was conjured by an evil sorcerer who lived as a hermit in the ancient caves in the hills. Sebastian simply appeared one day and could be seen traveling the country roads with the old man. Even as a lad, his eyes were steady, never blinking, and wise beyond his years. He didn't speak and never made any facial expression. Some said they could not see the boy even breathe.

He grew into a strikingly tall man and remained in the hills even after the old sorcerer died. He had long, pitch-colored hair and always wore it drawn up in a tail when he went to town to patronize The Dragon's Breath Inn. He paid for his drinks and food with chunks of raw gold, never coins. Some say he had perfected the art of alchemy and made his own precious metals.

Women were drawn to him. Even the most chaste would let their eyes linger on Sebastian and find their faces flush with an unexplainable excitement when he passed by. The whores of the town encircled him like flies, and he never had to pay for their favors.

Now, five Roman soldiers stood outside the wall that encircled his dwelling in the foothills. A centurion pushed on the fence door. His name was Cicero, and he was ordered by Governor Avitar Fabius to apprehend Sebastian. Normally, such a duty would fall onto the shoulders of one of the commanders; it was far below the esteem of a centurion. However, a commander who was previously sent to retrieve Sebastian never returned. A week had passed, and Fabius impatiently ordered Cicero to "bring Sebastian to me and make amends for your faults in basic judgment."

Cicero's foible was in not keeping the governor informed of what Cicero thought to be the "inconsequential ramblings of a mad peasant". Over the past few months, since the Romans had overtaken the Temple Fortress and claimed it as their own, Sebastian had sent several messages to Governor Fabius. They would arrive via messenger late at night, and the guard on watch would deliver them to Cicero. Cicero would glance at the notes with disdain and discard them. He never considered actually showing them to Fabius; the governor was far too consumed with important matters.

One evening however, Fabius found a message under his *door*. No one could tell how it got there, as if by magic it had suddenly appeared. The letter warned of a surprise barbarian attack.

Not only did the prophecy prove to be accurate, but the note inquired why Fabius had ignored the prior warnings. Fabius reprimanded Cicero for failing to keep him informed of any details that might put his command at risk and demanded that the Cloaked Man be apprehended for questioning.

A figure approached the centurion and his men from behind. Cicero spun around with his weapon drawn. "Who treads there?"

It was a diminutive man in dusty, brown rags. "I am Dereth. My humble home is just around the bend. I heard you marching on the road. I was hoping that you came with word about my son. He's been missing almost four days."

"He was probably rounded up as a slave," Cicero answered.

"No, not him, he was young, too young. The soldiers...your men...came several months ago and spared our family as I am too small and my children too young."

"We are here for Sebastian. What do you know of him?" one of the soldiers asked.

"He's a devil; that's what I know. He consorts with demons and necromancers. One came to visit him several weeks ago. She rode in a carriage at night with an entourage of black ghosts! I hid in the shadows and watched as..." Dereth leaned close to the soldiers and lowered his voice, "she rode right up to the gate and went inside! None dare to go in there. She must have been a witch! That was all I saw. I was afraid her magic would enchant me, and I ran back home."

"And you should run away now," Cicero warned. "We're on official Roman business, and you're an unwelcome intrusion." The muscular centurion pressed his shoulder against the gate to assess its strength. He removed his helmet and revealed a round, bald head and a thick, scrunched brow. Nodding once at his men, they simultaneously thrust their bodies forward, crashing through the fragile wooden frame.

Behind the fence was an opening to a cave, illuminated by torches. A shadow loomed before the entrance. As their eyes adjusted, they could see a figure suspended in the air; a body, impaled on a wooden stake, jutted upward from the ground. Crows picked at the decaying flesh and darted to and fro.

"It's the commander Fabius sent here," declared one of the guards as he coughed.

With an uneasy step, the centurion led his men around the corpse and toward the cave.

Dereth ventured. "I'll stand watch out here."

One of the Romans pushed the fragile man. "Just get out of here, you piece of filth." Dereth crumbled to the ground and then scurried away.

The men circled the entrance to the cave. A faint light from deep inside flickered shadows on the toadstool-covered walls.

Cicero led his troop inside. They were greeted by the aroma of cooking meat. The centurion motioned with a nod and ordered, "Follow me."

They cautiously crept behind their leader down the corridor until two tunnels branched off. One was black and stark while the other glowed with the telltale signs of a burning fire deep within.

The centurion waved his sword toward the irradiated passageway. One man stepped forward and called out, "We're here for you, Sebastian. Show yourself!"

There was no reply.

The centurion made eye contact with each of his men, grunted and nodded, and then they all careened down the corridor at once. The man in front tripped on a wire, though. He toppled and rolled head over feet through the tunnel. Everyone stopped short and watched with horror as a wooden spear sliced through the air from the ceiling. It impaled the man into the ground. He lay there, skewered, writhing, and crying. Like a child, he whimpered his last breath as blood seeped out his gaping mouth.

No one dared advance for fear of meeting the same fate. Cicero studied the floor and ceiling for signs of other booby traps. He saw none and ordered his men, "Go retrieve him."

With trepidation, one brave soldier inched his way into the corridor, flipped over the body, and slipped it off the spear with a blood-gurgling slurp.

Intestines were hopelessly entangled on the lance. As the living men pulled on their dead friend, the mangled entrails left a goopy trail across the dusty floor. While they hastily cleaned up the mess, the dead man twitched, and his eyes popped open. He gasped for breath and reached a trembling hand toward Cicero.

The centurion mercifully wielded his sword and sliced into his subordinate's chest. "Now he can rest."

After regaining their composure, the men cautiously eased their way down the corridor. Tunnels branched off in various directions, and they soon realized they were in a complex labyrinth. Up ahead, firelight flickered, and they followed it like a beacon until they entered a cavernous room. In the center was a fire pit with a bubbling pot poised above it. The massive room was an archaic burial chamber. Within the walls were tomb-sized grottos; each held decayed remains.

On the far wall sat Sebastian on what appeared to be a throne made of human bones. Skeletal remains seemed to be crawling out of their crypts to form it. They melded together to shape the chair; femurs, skulls, and pelvic bones tangled in a macabre design. Above Sebastian's head, on the backrest, was a skull encircled by rib bones. The halo-like medallion crested him like a crown.

He sat smiling. He wore a black robe, tied loosely at the waist. His bare chest was visible and glistening with an oily sheen. "Welcome, guests!"

Cicero felt a warm rush as he grasped the notion that the Cloaked Man was smiling pleasantly and holding out his arms in a friendly gesture. Bewildered by the amicable reaction, he recited his orders. "Avitar Fabius, the Governor of Touraine, commands your presence before him."

The Cloaked Man did not react; he sat rock still and absorbed every word the centurion uttered. He allowed the room to fall silent. The guards that flanked their leader began to gaze at each other uneasily. One of the soldiers pushed out his chest with mock bravado, but didn't muster the courage to speak.

Sebastian waited until the uneasy quiet made them all jittery and uncertain, and then he nonchalantly spoke. "Thank you for the invitation. I'll gladly come with you. Give me a moment to gather my things."

"Make it fast," growled Cicero. "We have orders to take you to the Temple

Fortress immediately."

Sebastian gathered up a copper bowl and several candles from a nearby table as one of the soldiers asked, "Did you make that?"

"My throne? Yes, I did. Do you like it?"

The soldier grimaced and another shook his head with disdain.

Sebastian snarled, "You may find it gruesome for me to construct a chair out of those bones, but for me, I am just making due with the things that are around me. That is how I live my life. Everything that I have, I made with my own hands. I fashion my own weapons to kill the game I eat, spin my own wool to make my clothes...all by myself."

The aroma of the simmering stew was intoxicating. Cicero absently retrieved a bowl and scooped himself a generous serving; all the while, he suspiciously kept an eye on the Cloaked Man.

"You shouldn't eat that," began Sebastian. "That is a special brew I made for myself..."

Cicero snapped, "I'll take what I want. No murdering malefactor tells me what to do."

"Murder? Who could I have *murdered?* Surely, you don't mean the carcass that I have strung up in the courtyard? It was a trap he walked into — same as your other man. You see, a local farmer and his annoying children have taken the notion of spying on me as of late. Unfortunately, one of your men walked into the trap I laid for them. And now he remains out there, as a warning to any other would-be thieves.

"I must say that his presence has kept away intruders for several days now...until your arrival that is. I am curious...does he not terrify you, even the slightest? Indeed, Rome does employ very valiant soldiers. Please, my brave men, sit, join me, and let us talk about this accusation of murder; for I surely have a right to know the details of my charge!"

One of the guards aside of the centurion snarled, "You have no rights and talking is not what we are here to do!"

"As you command. First, I must imbibe just a bit of the stew. Would you fetch me some?"

Cicero walked over to the pot that sat simmering in the pit and began to scoop out another serving. He fully intended to whip the bowl at Sebastian and scald him with the boiling liquid, but the spoon hit something big and thick. He poked in the pot. In the dim light, he caught a glimpse of something large and round just under the surface.

"My fine centurion, you don't want to scoop too deeply; just a ladle of the broth will be enough for me," Sebastian purred.

Cicero ignored Sebastian and retrieved a candle from the table for a better look in the pot. Submerged in the stew was a human skull. The flesh was partially boiled off, so that only the faint resemblance of a young boy's face remained. He recoiled in shock, and the candle plunged to the floor.

Sebastian let out a hearty whoop.

The centurion erupted, "Murderous fiend!"

Sebastian appeared genuinely offended by the accusation. "Murderous? No I tell you! The boy was a pest, always creeping around here like a scavenging dog. I tried to put him to good use and had him deliver messages to the governor. But he kept failing at getting Fabius' attention. I decided he would serve me better dead. You see, flesh and blood hold miraculous properties —"

The guards didn't give Sebastian the chance to finish. They overtook him. He didn't struggle as they carried him off to face his charges before Avitar Fabius, the Governor of Touraine.

Chapter 13

Father Michel's Story

Father Michel stood in line with the other priests. Like him, they were all recently summoned to Cardinal Jonaton Thibaut's castle to hear an official decree. Unlike the others, Father Michel had not come willingly. Guards seized him from his humble, rural church before he could even respond to the messenger. Their only explanation: "It is an extremely urgent matter".

The priests waited outside the entryway to the opulent receiving room. Deep within blazed two roaring fires, and the scalding heat was felt all the way across the enormous chamber.

Twin-robed valets motioned for the dozen men to step forward. They passed by a small audience of lords and ladies, wealthy landowners, high-ranking government officials and their families, who also had gathered for the announcement.

At the end of the receiving room sat the Cardinal between the dual infernos. Each burst from a large cauldron with a recently refashioned chimney above to ventilate the smoke. One of the robed men cautioned the group not to come too close.

The priests knelt in a line before the Cardinal, whose ivory robes and miter were stained with ash and soot. Sweat streamed down the sides of his face as his thunderous voice erupted. "This is an official decree to the diocese!" Several young scribes hastily took notes as their spiritual leader continued. "Through the manipulations of heavenly bodies, pestilence has been sent down upon mankind for our correction by the just wrath of God. The planets of Saturn and Mars and Jupiter aligned themselves three years ago to give us a portent of what has become. No one knows with certainty whose sins have summoned this retribution. Be it good men, the heathens, or the lot of us all.

"The cities are rampant with death. Word has come. Ninety-six hundred have died in Florence alone. Eight hundred perish each day in Paris, six hundred daily in Vienna. Even our dear Pope's fair city of Avignon releases four hundred souls a day upon the average.

"Neither counsel of physician nor virtue of medicine appears to avail it. Not only do few recover thereof, but well-nigh most die within the third day after the appearance of egg-sized swellings — plague-boils — on the groin or armpits or necks. The malady appears to spread by a simple touch or a sideways glance from the infected. Crowded cities are the most vulnerable."

He gestured to the caldrons on either side and continued. "We must protect ourselves and the sanctity of this diocese. Pope Clement uses fire to purify the air, and thus, we do, too. Other governments have passed regulations prohibiting funerals and the right to travel freely, thus we do. Many have sealed themselves within sanctuaries to avoid all others, and thus, we do. Until the Great Pestilence subsides, this castle will remain isolated. This is my order!"

Father Michel lifted his bowing head. Underneath the thick mop of black locks was a long face, olive in tone with crisp, blue eyes. Shocked, he shuddered as the Cardinal finished his speech.

"We will no longer travel outside these walls to tend to the sick and then return. No more will we share Sunday worship with the masses. No more will we have contact of any fashion with anyone from the outside until the peste subsides. All gathered here are welcome to stay and seek sanctuary within these fortified walls. Any who leave, though, nary will be allowed to reenter."

The ramification of the Cardinal's words soaked into the huddled crowd. There was an oppressive silence at first, and then a twitter of whispers and gasps. One brave priest asked, "Your Eminence, surely you don't mean we're not offering last rites?"

"That is exactly what I mean," said the Cardinal; his voice was flat.

"Sire, how can we abandon so many? In this dark hour, it is more imperative than ever for us to minister to the dead and the dying," another priest protested as he clutched his rosary beads.

"The dead and the dying will be absolved of their sins. Word has been passed down from Avignon — all who die of infection are saved. These are Pope Clement the Sixth's wishes," Cardinal Thibaut said. "He also instructs us to take measures to protect ourselves and the inner workings of the church. Jews, gypsies, witches, evil cults such as the flagellants roam the countryside infecting all they come into contact with. We're safe here, and our solitude will ensure that the infrastructure of the Church and government remains secure. You all should consider yourselves blessed for being among the chosen few to have this fortified castle as sanctuary."

Someone from the back of the room called out, "Pope Clement issued a Papal Bull declaring there is no proof the Jews spread the malady; their numbers are perishing like ours!"

The Cardinal answered, "In the castle of Chillon on Lake Geneva, Jews confessed to poisoning the wells in Venice to spread the peste. In St. Etienne, they are accused of the same. Even among our own diocese, we have proof that Jews are responsible for infecting our towns with the malady. Right here, in this room, is a culprit who allowed a diseased band of heathens to infect his congregation. The Pope must speak in political terms. But *we* know the truth, don't we *Father Michel*?"

A jolt shot through the simple parish priest as the Cardinal addressed him. Father Michel meekly asked, "Your Eminence?"

"Tell them, Father Michel. Stand and tell everyone how you were deceived by the Jews who came to your church. Tell them how you took them in and let them poison your congregation."

Father Michel tentatively rose to his feet. He thought about his parish — a small rural church that was mostly ignored by the rest of the diocese until it was time to collect tithes. Farmers and peasants mostly filled his congregation. It was nestled on a hillside with a handful of country houses surrounding it. They were a faithful bunch, many traveling over five miles to worship each Sunday. He opened his doors and his heart to all who needed him.

"Cardinal Thibaut, surely no one blames *me* for the misfortune that befell my congregation…" began Father Michel, shaking his head slowly.

"Blame you? Of course they do. Your congregation sent word to us asking that you be removed from the parish! They begged us to absolve you of your duties." Cardinal Thibaut rose from his chair while flames leapt at him from either side.

Father Michel glanced sideways at his peers. "Perhaps this should be discussed at a later time."

"Time is not ours to relinquish! Men have been known to go to bed healthy only to be dead by morning during this time of pestilence. Besides, everyone here knows the story, Father Michel. None chose to speak it out loud, but in the hallways, late at night, murmurs can be heard describing your exploits. Indeed, the Pope himself has heard the tale of how you took in a family of gypsies...little more than vermin wandering the countryside in a covered wagon. Witches, some say they were."

"No, they weren't witches; they were a simple family. They were hungry and sick. I ministered to them as I would my own congregation," Father Michel interrupted.

"But, unlike your congregation, what were they, Father Michel? You knew!" Cardinal's voice was loud, and it echoed off the high ceiling. Several of the other priests flinched under his words.

"They were Jews, nothing more. They weren't criminals or witches," Father Michel cried.

"That's right! They were worse than witches. They were *Jews*. And they infected your congregation and spread the peste. That's what Jews do, Father Michel — they spread disease. They are evil heathens whose only goal is to destroy the faithful. Did they cast a spell on you, Father, to deceive you? Did they taint your soul with their lies? Did they bribe you with their filthy money?" he whispered the last sentence, letting it hang in the air.

Father Michel violently shook his head from side to side. A vein throbbed in his temple. "How can you make such charges against *me*?"

The Cardinal levelly stated, "If these were charges, Father Michel, you would have been tried, convicted, and hung already. This is a warning. Make your penance and pray that God's vengeance spares your polluted soul."

Father Michel spun to face the audience. "They were a family, a mother and father...three young children and an old man. They just needed food and some place warm to sleep for a couple nights." His words echoed in the massive hall and his pleading, imploring eyes were met with expressions of disgust and downcast stares. "It wasn't like that! How could I turn them away? Isaiah 58:7 says that we are to 'bring into our house the needy and the wanderers. When you seest the naked, thou shall cover him, and thou shall not hide from him for fear of seeing his flesh!' We should not neglect to show hospitality to strangers for they may be angels in disguise!"

"Angels they were not! Satan in disguise is more apt, and you allowed yourself to be taken with his trickery!" the Cardinal erupted from behind Father Michel. "Retreat to your chamber. Go now and beg our Lord for mercy for what you have done."

Father Michel did not look back at the Cardinal. "Yes, Your Eminence," he stammered, hung his head, and walked dutifully past the rows of onlookers. Their judgment pierced him like steely daggers as he passed by. Quickening his pace, he fled through the archway, into the library, and down the hallway that led to his tiny chamber.

Once inside his own private sanctuary, he allowed tears of shame and rage to burst. While shaking, he knelt by his cot and cried, "Lord why have you brought this burden upon me? Why have you cast doubt upon my faith again and again? Do you test me?"

He reached under his collar and pulled out a gold chain. Attached to it was medallion inlaid with precious stones and an unusual, archaic cross. Gazing at it, he asked, "Or is this not a test at all but proof of a truth that I must bring into the light? I can't stay here. I must go back to my church. I just have to figure out *how*."

Chapter 14
Veronica's Story
Present Day Los Angeles

The sisters sprinted down the concourse at LAX. Nikki wore clogs adorned with yellow daisies that echoed on the floor like galloping horse hooves. Pink sunglasses rested on top of her head, pushing her blonde hair back like a flowing mane. She was hunched over, pulling a small carry-on suitcase with a sticky wheel. It caught at times, almost causing the suitcase to do a wheelie and topple over. She stopped frequently to right it.

Veronica was in the lead. A messenger bag draped over her shoulder pounded rhythmically on her right hip. Her Birkenstocks scuttled across the floor without difficulty. She wore a comfortable pair of khakis and a faded plaid shirt over a T-shirt that simply read: "The Smiths". Her curls were gathered up under a knit cap to keep them from falling in her face.

Nikki picked up her suitcase and carried it the old-fashioned way, then trotted up alongside her sister. "Do ya' think they started boarding yet?"

"Our plane takes off in less than a half hour, so I'm sure they have," Veronica said vacantly. All her focus was forward, helping her to navigate among the slow-moving travelers.

"I hate being the last one on the plane. You can't find any storage space, and everyone looks at you like you're late or something," Nikki whined.

"You *are* late, Nikki. *We* are late." Veronica shrugged her shoulder hard so the strap of her bag jumped up and rested more comfortably.

"You act like it's my fault. Freaking security didn't have to treat us like we were terrorists. Do I look like a terrorist?" she challenged.

"What were you thinking packing a..." she shouted, then whispered, "a *vibrator* in your carry-on bag? That thing looks like a freaking pink pipe bomb!"

"You expect me to spend three months in France without my Jack Rabbit? Something has to keep my va-jay-jay happy when Doug's not around," Nikki quipped as she fell behind and made two exaggerated hops to keep up with her sister's long legs.

Veronica turned back to her and yelled, "You know, there are some things that are more important than your *vagina!*" At that exact moment they walked past an elderly man with a hearing aid cord dangling from his ear. He flinched at both her volume and vulgarity, and cast Veronica a sharp look. Nikki giggled insanely.

They rounded the corner and saw their gate. A couple hundred people were milling about. The flashing red letters on the board over the check-in counter read: "Flight Delayed".

"All that running for nothing," Nikki sighed. She spied two open seats and sat down quickly. "Now I'm sweaty. I hate being sweaty on airplanes. I feel like everyone can smell me." She started rummaging through her suitcase. Veronica sat down next to her. A few moments later, Nikki emerged with her prize: a travel-sized Lady Speed Stick.

"At least you came prepared," Veronica observed.

Nikki stealthily lifted the bottom of her Hello Kitty T-shirt and quickly swiped each armpit. Just then, the same old man with the hearing aid walked by, catching her in the act. He glared at the dippy girls with an air of contempt. Veronica slumped down in her seat and wiped her hand over her face. "At least *he's* getting some entertainment today," she said while a sardonic smile spread across her chubby lips.

The girls waited patiently. Nikki got up occasionally to walk around and then quickly came back to her seat. She didn't feel like sitting, but yet, she didn't want anyone else to claim her prized chair.

"So," Nikki began, "who do we have to thank for our French adventure anyway? Did you ever find out who recommended you for this job?"

"You know, I can't seem to figure it out. Marie-Claire said he was a doctor, and I had scribbled down something like Doctor Jacob Andrews or Andrew Jacobs. I don't know any doctor by that name," Veronica said.

"No clients who are doctors?" Nikki asked.

"Nope."

"Did you ever see any doctor by that name?" Nikki persisted.

"No, that's what I was trying to remember. The doctor I see now is a woman; my dentist is Dr. Whang. Our family doctor growing up was Dr. Curtis. Hell, I even remember my orthodontist was Dr. Duffy." Veronica looked at her watch. They were behind schedule, and they hadn't even left LA yet.

"What about your gynecologist? Maybe he saw something that impressed him." Nikki smirked.

"Very funny. And no, that's Dr. Gonzales, *Amelia* Gonzales." Veronica sighed.

"Hey, what about the doctor you saw as a kid — you know, the psycho doctor," Nikki offered brightly.

"Psycho doctor? I never saw a doctor who was psycho," Veronica answered abruptly.

Nikki kept pushing. "The doctor wasn't psycho; *you* were psycho."

"Stop being ridiculous."

Nikki quit playing and said seriously, "No, I know you weren't really psycho. I'm talking about the psychologist you saw for your sleep problem."

"What are you talking about?"

Nikki persisted. "When you were nine or ten years old. I was only...like, six, but I remember Mom took you to a specialist because you couldn't sleep."

"That never happened," Veronica insisted. "If I saw a doctor when I was ten, I'd remember it."

"*I* remember it! You'd wake up in the middle of the night screaming like crazy. Mom couldn't stand it anymore, and she took you to some clinic. You were gone for a long time." Nikki was quite sincere; she huddled close to her sister.

"If that happened, why haven't you ever said anything... or Mom either?" Veronica asked, triumphant that she found a snag in her sister's fabricated story.

"*No one* said anything. Ever! I asked Mom about it once, and she jumped down my throat and told me never to bring it up again. Damn, it was so long ago. All I really remember clearly is that when you came back you wouldn't talk. You were out of it all the time. I think maybe you were taking medicine, some kind of tranquilizer. Mom was really upset, too. Then I went away to summer camp, and when I came back, you seemed fine again."

Veronica sat quiet. She felt a flash of memory, very dim, like déjà vu. In her mind's eye, she saw herself as a little girl in a cotton nightgown, running frantically down the hall to her mother's room during the middle of the night.

The two women sat quietly. Then Nikki spoke, "Now that I think about it, the name Dr. Jacobs sounds vaguely familiar." Veronica shot her a suspicious glance. "Seriously, Vern. It's like I can hear Mom saying his name; it sounds familiar to me now."

"Even if that's true, why would someone from over twenty years ago be recommending me to decorate a castle in France?" Veronica asked.

"That's true," Nikki agreed.

Silence grew between them. Nikki tried hard to remember. A distant memory danced in her head. She recalled her sister arriving with their mother in the car. Nikki ran to her with jubilation after not seeing her for so long. It was spring, and the moist grass squished underneath her bare toes. Nikki reached the car carrying a crayon drawing for Veronica. It depicted a big orange sun with two shakily drawn figures; one was she, and one was her sister.

Veronica sat motionless in the front seat, the door was open, and Mom was trying to coax her out. Veronica had dark rings under her eyes. Nikki remembered thinking that she must have been playing with their mother's make-up again. *Boy was she in trouble!* But Mom talked to Veronica very carefully, her tone soft and somewhat frightened. Nikki became scared. She was just a little girl, but she knew something bad had happened — something very bad.

An amplified voice suddenly sounded overhead. Nikki twitched and snapped out of her memories. "Flight eleven-ten to Charles De Gaulle is now boarding. Have your ticket ready and..." rambled the monotone loudspeaker voice.

"That's us," Nikki said as she stood up.

Veronica searched her phone for her boarding pass. "Maybe Mom knows."

"Huh?" Nikki murmured.

"Who the doctor is; maybe Mom knows. I mean, it could be that this Doctor Jacobs talked to Mom recently, and she gave him my number," Veronica explained as she and her heavy messenger bag lumbered into the boarding line.

"Yeah, maybe."

The old man with the hearing aid stood directly in front of them.

"I think I'll give Mom a call once we get to France," Veronica continued.

Nikki was poised like a voyeur, spying over the man's shoulder. He held out his boarding pass, and Nikki peeked at the seat number. While tilting her head toward the guy, she said, "Hey, Vern, guess who *we* get to sit next to all the way to France!"

Chapter 15

Sebastian's Story

he thick cell door slammed shut and reverberated against the stone walls. Sebastian studied his new abode. The room was square, approximately seven feet long by seven feet wide. The height of the ceiling was also seven feet, making the stockade a perfect cube. A single hanging oil lamp illuminated the slime-covered bricks. They were marred with hatch marks, which probably counted down the last days of some long-gone condemned soul's.

On the floor of the far left corner was a solitary blanket; a grey rag stained with urine and vomit. Two figures sat on the cell's only comfort. A naked man with an infested mane of white hair that grew into his gnarly beard glowered at Sebastian with contempt. The other form was a younger man. He still had a significant amount of meat on his bones and only a slight growth of black fuzz on his chin. He wore a simple grey robe — like those donned by the Temple Priests — tied at the waist by a knotty cord of twine.

There was no window. Besides the oil lamp, the only other light filtered in from the rectangular crevice in the door. A face peered through it from the outside. "Enjoy your stay, Sebastian! The governor will soon decide your fate. It will either be death by execution or death by torture." The guard chuckled at his own perceived cleverness.

Sebastian gazed at the cowering figures in the corner. "Oh, there will be death...but it won't be my own."

The guard grunted and slammed the portal shut. Sebastian studied his companions in the dimness. The hairy man dug at the stone floor with a scrap of wood, which was whittled to a nub. His labors so far had produced a shallow indentation less than an inch deep. The chubby man rose to his feet and extended his hand. "I am Baldebert, son of Amlaric."

Sebastian leered at the outstretched appendage until Baldebert retracted it. Not deterred, the outgoing Pagan continued. "I am a Temple Priest and was captured after all my comrades were slain. They keep me alive as they think I will tell them secrets about the barbarian tribes they are attempting to conquer."

"Will you?" Sebastian asked matter-of-factly.

Baldebert hung his head. "No."

"Then it seems that you are merely prolonging the inevitable. What of him?" Sebastian nodded at the dismal figure digging in the dirt.

"He doesn't talk much. And he has no teeth, so even when he does, it's arduous to understand. I think his name is 'Wassas'."

The old man perked up and reiterated, "Wassas!"

Baldebert repeated, "Wassas. That's what I said."

"Wassas!" the old man insisted.

"*Vassus?*" Sebastian inquired.

The old man nodded his entire upper body in elated agreement. "Wassas! Yes,

Wassas!"

"Well, Vassus," Sebastian continued, "why are you here?"

"Slasse got away. I shell sleep, and they got away," he stammered.

Baldebert explained. "The best I can determine, he was in charge of the governor's slaves until several of them escaped when he fell asleep."

Vassus grunted in agreement and continued digging.

"Perhaps the two of you can help me with my situation," Sebastian stated. "You no doubt wonder why I am here. It is because I have an extraordinary gift. I can see things...I know things...I have the power to enchant a snail out of its shell. But there is a price for this gift —certain sacrifices need to be made. I must say that I never do away with anything of importance or consequence. On the contrary, as I usually use those who are considered burdens and pestilence in our society — wayward orphans, occasionally a prostitute, a serf from the country who was about to die a miserable death anyway."

The Cloaked Man stood, twirled and continued to speak with his back to his audience. "What I do is for a greater good. You both understand, right? Now with you two, I seem to have equals. You are both equally undesirable; therefore, it doesn't matter which of you I choose. The matter is though; one of you shall live, while the other will be sacrificed — gutted like a hog so I can use his entrails for divination."

Sebastian looked over his shoulder and momentarily enjoyed the horrified looks on the prisoners' faces. Then he continued. "I will spare the other. The one who lives must pledge their devotion to me. Vassus, you are inane and bothersome to listen to. What a loathsome companion you would make. However, you likely have knowledge as a Roman guard that would be beneficial. Baldebert, you look like a dimwitted child. I could only hope you have information about the Temple Priests that is useful. Each of you needs to think about what you can *do* for me. The one who lives must prove his worth. Each of you should tell me *why* you should be spared to help me decide."

Vassus' scratching stick was now silent. Baldebert's lipless mouth gaped.

"Fortunately for both of you, I will wait until tomorrow. Sleep well, my friends."

With that said, Sebastian sprawled on his back and closed his eyes.

Chapter 16

The Children's Story

Louis dashed and the creature lunged after him. A thick, strong paw snatched the boy's injured foot, wrapping around it with a vice-like grip. It pulled him down. The lad's belly splatted on a damp bed of moss and the precious contents of his satchel sprayed out around him.

It reared up with a ferocious maw open wide. Despite the darkness, Louis saw into its eyes. Bright against its black matted fur, they had glistening whites — like a person's. The eyes looked *human*, and that terrified Louis more than if they had looked like a raging, wild animal's.

As the beast swooped down to attack, Louis twisted to one side and rolled over something round and hard. He grabbed what he thought was a rock and brought it down on the thing's skull with a smack. It howled in pain, swung its head around to attack again, and then froze.

Louis braced for its strike with hands shielding his head. When nothing happened, he tentatively pulled his arm back to see the creature sulk back. The boy took advantage of the inexplicable reaction and kicked his foot free. It recoiled, and Louis saw that its menacing gaze was locked on the object in his hand. It wasn't a rock after all, but one of the special relics his father had given him.

Louis scooted back. The thing hovered in front of him but did not move forward. It swayed slightly, like a dog tethered on a leash. Perhaps Isabelle was right! It couldn't go beyond the castle grounds.

He gathered up his satchel and the rest of the contents, then slowly, cautiously, walked backward, keeping his eyes on it the whole time. Once he felt there was a safe distance between him and the devil, he spun and ran toward the river.

He was small and fast and darted easily through the dense foliage. It only took moments for him to arrive. Isabelle was there on the bank, waiting for him. She hugged him and cried, "Are you all right? Did it chase after you?"

Louis nodded and tears welled up in his big, brave eyes. "But it didn't get me. It tried, but I scared it off!"

Isabelle chortled. "*You* scared it, my little poppet?"

"No, it was scared of *this*." He held up the object.

Isabelle looked confused and squinted at the gleaming globe-like relic in the moonlight, "What is it?" Before the boy could answer, she interrupted him. "Shh, listen. Barking...I hear dogs."

"I hear them, too. I think the castle hounds are loose," Louis answered.

Isabelle grabbed his shoulders and pointed him toward the water. "Go into the river. The dogs can't follow our scent if we walk in the water."

"It'll be cold," Louis said matter-of-factly.

"I know, but we can walk in the shallow part. It only comes up to our ankles, so just our feet will get wet." Isabelle took Louis' hand and cautiously navigated the craggy stones.

In the distance, one of the dogs howled. There was also another sound: heavy, rapid thumping — the sound of galloping horse hooves.

They must be on the road, Isabelle thought.

"They aren't coming from the direction we came. They're looking for us along the high-path," she said and smiled. "See, I knew this would be the best way to go."

"Then we can get out of the water?" Louis asked.

"No. They'll probably come around the back of the castle where the guard saw us. If we're lucky, the dogs won't be able smell us, though, if we stay in the water."

They navigated the stones on the river's shallow edge. The cold actually made Louis' sore ankle feel better, cooling the hot pain deep in his muscles.

Isabelle's riding boots were thin and offered little protection. She could feel each tiny stone and pebble under foot. The water traveled briskly as they made their way upstream and walking seemed more difficult than Isabelle had imagined.

The children traveled almost a mile that way. The moon poked through the clouds and reflected its ghostly image against the black water. Isabelle didn't like the moonlight; it made them more visible. In the distance, the howls of the hounds grew loud and excited; they had found a scent.

"I think they're coming this way," Louis said. His feet were numb. He lifted them high out of the water as he stepped, splashing like a soldier on the march.

"Don't make so much noise!" She could now hear an occasional horse's neigh.

Through the dense trees, she thought she saw flames flash. They had torches and were closing in.

"Louis, be still!" she hissed. Her brother froze. He now saw the torches bobbing behind the trees about two hundred yards downstream. Isabelle continued. "We have to get as far from shore as possible so they can't see us."

"We can't, the river is too deep and too cold," Louis complained.

She started wading toward the center. "Come on; there's no place else to hide. Hold onto me, okay?"

Louis grabbed her waist and they waded into the deeper water. The river was wide here and the current not as swift. He secured the satchel, twisting the opening tightly to keep its contents as dry as possible.

The dogs' barking grew louder.

"I can't go much deeper," Louis whimpered.

Isabelle turned and saw that the water was high on his chest. She reached around and grabbed him from behind. Her arms folded on his stomach, and he cinched her fingers with one hand while the other balanced the satchel on his head. His legs lifted, and he allowed himself to float with the aid of his sister.

Her feet no longer seemed to be walking on stones and pebbles; the surface below was smooth. Carefully, she walked backwards. The water reached her chest, then shoulders, and eventually she felt it lapping at her neck.

She suddenly remembered the bonnet on her head was white. *They would surely see it illuminated in the moonlight!*

She took one hand away from Louis' torso and fumbled with the tie under her chin. Louis drifted to and fro in the flowing water. Without the extra hand to steady him, he wafted uncontrollably. He let out an uneasy groan.

"Shh," she cautioned while untying the bonnet with the one hand and snatching it off the top of her head. Her dress was billowing in the icy water, and she stabbed at it several times struggling to find her pocket.

Louis' face momentarily submerged. He shook his head and struggled to keep it as high as possible.

She finally found the pocket and stuffed the bonnet inside. Her hand then immediately returned to lock itself around her brother's midriff.

"Izzy, please don't let go of me again."

"Don't worry, I got you, Little Louis."

The men on the shore were now only about one hundred yards away. There were three of them, and they each held a torch. Dogs scampered around the horses' feet. Sniffing and yapping at the air, they darted excitedly, trying to catch a scent.

Isabelle fought the consternation welling inside her gut. Slowly, she continued walking backward; the water now up to her chin. She lifted her nose up high and stood on the tips of her toes. Her boots slid across the glassy bottom.

Isabelle brought her left toe down and found no footing. She hovered there a second, standing on her right tiptoe while the current tugged her and Louis. She pulled him up, making sure he was able to get air. Carefully, her foot searched for the bottom of the stream, but there was none. A realization came over her. The smooth surface she was walking on was actually a ledge — a rocky ridge, covered with moss and slime. It was as slick as ice, and she had walked to its edge. Now she hovered there, fearful to take one more step in any direction, as that direction could be a drop-off.

The men, the horses, and the dogs were now almost directly across from them. The children had waded out ten, maybe fifteen, yards. She could hear the words they spoke. One man, he sounded like Uncle Pierre, insisted they follow the river a little longer. The other two men favored circling back around through the woods.

The current played with the children hovering in the river. Splashing onto their faces, it made watery snot trail down the sides of Louis' cheeks, and blinded his sister with thick droplets that clung to her long eyelashes.

Isabelle tapped at the slick ledge with the toes of her boots. She searched for any crack or crevice that might help anchor her down. She thought she felt a notch and tried to dig her foot into it. Instead, she slipped and found no bottom. The current gushed, and in an instant, both feet were flailing helplessly. She and Louis both sunk under the black water. Instinctively, his arms reached out, and he made a single splash. Isabelle held her brother up as high as she could, even though she was sinking under the surface.

On the shore, the men froze. "What was that?" one of them asked.

Louis's head was still above the water. His eyes were locked on the horsemen, and he was keenly aware of his sister struggling in the murky water below him. He watched one of the men dismount and swipe a torch over the shore, toward Isabelle and him, searching for the source of the splash.

Underwater, her dress wafted like a sail, making it difficult for Isabelle to control her balance. She fought the current by willing her body in the direction of the ledge. Her feet flutter-kicked, searching for a footing, and desperately she tried to keep the dress from tangling her legs. Then her right toe tapped the ridge, but it only made contact a moment before the current twisted her petticoats and pulled her away.

The remaining air in the girl's lungs escaped and bubbled up around Louis. Through gritting teeth water seeped down her throat.

Isabelle was drowning.

Water infiltrated her sinuses and the strong girl kicked like mad until her thrashing feet skimmed the ledge again. Elated, she leaned backward and toward it, searching with her toes until she tapped the slick surface. She wavered there, trying to pull herself up straight without losing her footing.

Louis suddenly twitched; she had let him slip under water again. Both her arms ached, but she forced him up toward the surface. The pain in her injured shoulder was searing, and she felt her strength ebbing. Suddenly the current shifted and pushed her *in* the direction of the ridge. Both feet found their footing and she easily stood again!

Air seared into her deflated lungs as her head broke the surface. She coughed and Louis hushed her, but she couldn't help it. Her body needed oxygen.

Dripping hair hung in her eyes. She blinked repeatedly to make out the figures on the riverbank. One was standing on the shore, facing their direction, scanning the water with an outstretched torch. Her ears popped, letting the sound back in. Just then, one of the hounds let out a loud yelp. It gnarled and barked in rapid fire.

Louis and Isabelle made no movement. The water lapped rapidly against their chilly flesh and kept rhythm with their beating hearts as the hunting dog barked and barked and barked.

Chapter 17

Dorothée's Story

℗atricia hastened down the passageway. "Help! Help! Claude, anyone, help us!" she cried as she bolted into the library.

"Mademoiselle? What is it?" a faint voice called from the kitchen.

Patricia rushed in and saw three figures sitting on stools in front of the fireplace. There was a young chambermaid and two stable boys. Each held a small bowl of stew.

"Lady Dorothée needs help. You, boy," Patricia said, pointing to one of the young lads, "go find the smithy. Tell him to bring his tools to the keep. Go, hurry!"

Patricia knew the smithy was strong. He was a large man. Strong and strapping, he would have tools if they needed to pry the door open.

The young boy hesitated and looked at Patricia with a flat, dumb stare.

"Go now, find the smithy!" she ordered.

"The *keep*?" the boy asked.

"Yes, that's what I said. She's trapped there. Hurry."

The boy dropped his bowl and rushed out of the kitchen. Patricia turned to the other two. "Where's Claude? Have you seen him?"

The young maid quickly swallowed and stood up. She was a tiny waif with braided, dark hair and milky skin. "He's off butchering a chicken," she offered meekly. The boy sitting next to her, also frail and young, nodded in agreement.

"Neither of you are strong enough to help," said Patricia dismissively.

Just then, she heard the front doors open and a voice boomed, "Why did that stable boy go running out of here like a chicken with its head cut off?"

Patricia ran into the foyer. Claude the chef stood there with a sheepish grin. He held a bloodied hand ax and the carcass of a headless chicken, still twitching.

"Claude, come quick. Lady Dorothée is in a dreadful situation."

"Oh, I am sure she is having a horrible crisis..." Claude began as he casually sauntered toward the kitchen. "Perhaps like last week when she stumbled across a dead *mole* in the garden. Thank heaven I came running to expunge the decaying rodent!" Claude chuckled.

"No, this is serious!" Patricia insisted.

"Yes, it is always serious when Lady Dorothée is involved. Does she need an urgent *cup of tea*? Surely, I can abandon this chicken and tonight's meal and prepare her one right away." Claude rolled his eyes and strode past Patricia.

"She's trapped in the keep, in the bottom tower room, and the door is stuck."

"What is she doing in *there*?"

"Surely I don't know, but she's in a panic."

"Oh, I imagine she is in quite a panic. She'll have everyone in the castle spinning in a tizzy soon, too," Claude said as he continued into the kitchen.

"For heaven's sake, help me get her out of there, Claude!"

Chef Claude looked down at Patricia's round, child-like face. His own pudgy cheeks expelled a gust of air and his bushy mustache wafted in the breeze. "Yes, I will help you, my dear." His tone was tender, but then he burst with a chuckle. "But first, I must tend to my bird!" He flopped the spastic fowl on the wooden table.

"Claude, think of how much madder she'll get the longer she sits in there!"

"I doubt she can get much madder," Claude grumbled.

Patricia clutched his arm. She was relentless, and he knew he would not get anything done until he conceded. Claude set the hand ax next to the chicken. Patricia reached behind him and grabbed the bloodied weapon. "We may need this!" she said and led him off to the keep.

Chapter 18

Veronica's Story

eronica peered into a twisted, winding pit. Hairy tendrils grew out of the mysterious opening. Nestled just inside was a black box attached to a fray of mechanical wires. Something sticky, yellow and waxy covered the mess. It reminded her of an H. R. Giger-inspired hybrid between organic material and machine — whatever it was.

She blinked. It took a moment, but she remembered being on the plane.

A gust of wind suddenly blew into her face. The "tunnel" next to her rumbled. Groggily she realized it was actually the ear of the old man sitting next to her. She had fallen asleep slumped on his shoulder and was only inches away from his hearing aid-equipped ear.

There was thundering laughter. It was Nikki.

Veronica jumped in her seat, and at the same moment, the man grunted awake with surprise. Nikki had adjusted the vent overhead, aiming the stream of air right at them.

"What the hell?" Veronica gasped.

Her sister chortled and sunk into her seat with both hands covering her guilty giggles.

"Why'd you blow air in our faces like that?" Veronica demanded.

"I'm bored," Nikki pouted while still snickering. "I was just having fun. You should 'a seen the way you fell asleep — right on his shoulder like you were gonna tongue his ear!"

The old man cast an irritated stare at the two girls and then positioned himself as far over in his seat as possible.

Veronica mumbled sorry to him and glared at her younger sister. Then reached into her bag to retrieve her inspiration pad. She pulled out her tray and proceeded to go over her drawings.

"Now what are you doing? Are you gonna work? I'm bored; talk to me for a while," Nikki implored.

"I got stuff to do. Why don't you help me?" Veronica dug deeper into her bag. "Here's a book on tapestries. Look through it and lemme know if you find any good ones."

"Fine," Nikki said unenthusiastically. She began to page quickly through the book. "These seats are so cramped, and the stewardess hasn't even offered us a drink yet."

"They're serving first class. Don't worry; they'll get to us."

"I hate flying coach. I got no room for my bitchin' gams." Nikki stretched her legs as far as she could under the seat in front of her and frowned when they only went so far.

"Get up and walk around then," Veronica offered.

"I don't wanna walk; I wanna relax in comfort. You'd think Marie-Claire, would 'a flown you first class for a job like this. Or even business class. We are on *business*, right?"

"Coach was all I could afford," Veronica snapped.

Nikki was silent for a moment. "*You* could afford? What do you mean, *you* could afford? Didn't *she* buy the airplane tickets?"

Veronica's face flushed. "No, she didn't, but I'll be reimbursed."

"She *told* you to pay for transportation?"

"Not specifically. The agreement is that I'll get the money when we get there. It's no big deal. Business is done like this all the time."

"Yeah, with business people who can afford a trip for two to France. How did you pay for it; I thought you were broke?"

"I begged the bank to increase my credit card limit. Granted, there isn't room for anything else on my card, but it'll be fine. Once we get there I'll be reimbursed, you'll see."

"This just doesn't sound right. You got a contract, right, everything is in writing so you don't get screwed?"

"It will all work out. Don't worry," Veronica answered.

"Oh shit, you don't have a contract! Vern, what the hell? You don't know these people."

"Marie-Claire wouldn't do anything like that. Why would she? This is the opportunity of a lifetime for me. Being the head designer and redecorating an entire French château is going to make my career take off. I could even be profiled in magazines. People will see my work. My *real* work not something that's got Robert's name attached to it."

"So this is about one-upping Robert?"

"No. This is about me doing something fabulous on my own for once. I have complete creative control so this is my chance to really shine and to do everything I always wanted to. No one is going to tell me to make things more *beige*. No one will suddenly step into the spotlight and take credit for my work. It is all *me* for a change! You always say that 'Sometimes you gotta take a leap of faith.' Well, I have faith in Marie-Claire. She's a little eccentric and old-fashioned. Big deal if she doesn't deal with contracts or computers or fax machines. That's okay; I have a good feeling about her, like I was *meant* to do this. Besides, you have nothing to worry about; *I'm* the one paying for the trip."

"Yeah, but if you don't get paid, I don't get paid. I just hope we aren't being taken for a ride."

"We aren't. I promise. How could someone as sweet as Marie-Claire screw anyone over?"

Nikki didn't answer.

"I am really tired. I'm going to sleep now," Veronica said. "Keep looking through those books. Remember, you're working for *me* now."

Chapter 19

Sebastian's Story

The Cloaked Man's eyes popped open. He rolled over on the slimy cell floor. In the opposite corner sat Baldebert. Vassus lay next to him hunched over and oblivious to the dawning day.

Sebastian's nostrils twitched. He perceived a familiar sweet fragrance, and allowed it to infiltrate his sinuses.

Baldebert fondled Vassus' dull piece of wood and poked absently at the floor. He gazed back at the Cloaked Man and managed a weary smile. "Morning, Sire."

Sebastian grunted and waited for more conversation.

"It seems that our friend here succumbed in the night. He lays dead."

"He does?" Sebastian rose to his feet, sniffing the slight scent of blood that hung in the air. "What happened?"

"I am not sure. He was old, and you certainly shot a bolt of terror into him yesterday. He may verily have died of fright. That being the case, if you are still in need of entrails for divination, well, there they are!"

"How fortunate he died just in time for you to be spared. It seems the gods are on your side."

"So they are!"

Sebastian continued. "I wonder if it's truly the work of the gods who sealed this man's fate."

Baldebert contemplated Sebastian's tone. Years studying as a Temple priest made him talented at the art of rhetoric. "Who but the gods has control over life and death?"

Sebastian grinned and confirmed. "Yes, who but the gods. It seems with his passing the matter is settled, yet I am curious to know the circumstances of his death."

Baldebert crouched. "I could certainly inspect the body."

"Yes, please do. It could be a bad omen if the subject in question died of disease. His blood would be tainted, you understand."

"Yes, that would be bad..."

"Not suitable at all."

"Look here," Baldebert exclaimed, in tune with the Cloaked Man's innuendo. "There is blood! He must have fallen and hit his head in the middle of the night."

"So a fall did him in. Really? Or did you kill him, Baldebert?"

The question hung in the air like a challenge. Baldebert sensed that his life rested upon the answer.

"Well, I do believe you are a man who seeks truth. Therefore, I must confess. I waited until he drifted off and used his stick to bludgeon." He gulped as the words fell off his lips, hoping his honesty would be his saving grace.

"Ah! Then he is a fresh kill!" Sebastian seemed pleased.

Baldebert relaxed and smiled broadly. "Oh yes, very fresh."

"Apparently, you are not as dim as you look. Very clever of you to do away with Vassus to save your own life. I like that. You are very cunning for one who is so young and dull in appearance. You may be of use to me after all."

Baldebert's smile faded, and he once again felt trapped by Sebastian's words. He pondered and then replied. "I may be young, but trust me, I am wise beyond my years. I was educated by the elders."

Sebastian smirked, raising a single eyebrow. "Okay, *O' Wise Temple Priest Baldebert*, then tell me; there is one priest, the Head Commander, do you know his fate? Did he escape?"

"How do *you* know about the Head Commander?"

"I *know* things about this temple. I know that the Head Commander is your leader and would have been instructed to escape if the Temple ever came under attack. He would seek refuge with the local tribes and rally them to strike back. He has a special gift and wields great power. And I must find him."

"Why?"

Sebastian answered flatly, "So I can poison him."

Baldebert wasn't able to contain his shock. "But why do you want *him* dead?" he gasped.

"You don't need to know the details of my plan. I need you to answer *my* questions. Do you know where the Head Commander is?"

Baldebert slowly nodded and confirmed. "You're right. He escaped and is among the Northern Tribe. He is convincing them to attack the Romans and regain the Temple." His eyes glanced upward as he spoke, and he prayed Sebastian would not detect his subterfuge.

"As I thought. Now I just need to gain the governor's trust and everything else will easily fall into place."

"What will fall into place?"

"I just told you; I am the one who asks the questions! You take orders from me now, and I don't want to hear your voice unless I speak first. Now hand me that stick, so I can gut this old carcass. The fresher the blood is, the stronger my visions."

Baldebert cringed as he held out Vassus' digging stick. He retreated to the other side of the small cell while Sebastian moved in on the body of the old man.

Chapter 20

Veronica's Story

𝒜 TGV terminal was conveniently located at Charles de Gaulle Airport. Veronica and Nikki bought tickets for the high-speed train from a kiosk and were soon traversing the French countryside at nearly one hundred and eighty miles per hour. Veronica watched rolling hills, provincial farmland, and adorable villages whiz by as Nikki played on her phone, updating her status to: "Watch out Frenchies, here comes Nikki!"

They arrived at Saint Pierre des Corps Gare just before ten in the morning. Veronica led the way to the rental car stand just outside the train station entrance. She burst through the door with an enthusiastic, "Hey!"

The scraggly-haired man behind the counter studied her for several seconds. "*Bonjour*," he said finally, as if correcting her.

"Oui, bonjour. Here is my, ah, reserve-ay-she-un," she stammered and meekly unraveled her rental document.

He huffed as he studied it, pushed a form across the counter for her to sign, and then handed over the keys. "Au revoir," he bid her abruptly.

Nikki quietly watched the rental car company employee *not* "try harder".

"Oh, and I reserved a GPS," Veronica said as she gathered up the paperwork.

"We are out," he said haltingly.

Nikki stepped up. "But she reserved one; how can you be out? *Nous avons déjà fait une reservation!*"

His eyes widened, surprised for a moment that she spoke French, then flatly said, "*C'est populaire*; what can I do?" He handed Veronica a map of the Loire Valley and pointed toward the parking ramp. "*Votre voiture est par là.*"

"But we *reserved* a GPS!" Nikki insisted. She wanted to argue more with the man, but Veronica gently tugged her sister's arm and led her back into the train station.

They navigated through the parking ramp until they found a short row of rental cars. Veronica held the keys in the air and clicked the remote. The car that flashed to life was theirs. It was a bitty thing with bright orange paint called a *Twingo*.

Nikki wrinkled her nose. "Christ, think you could 'a rented something smaller than this fart-box?" she quipped as they squeezed their baggage into the tiny hatch.

Veronica drove while Nikki pulled up the maps application on her iPhone. "We'd have a *decent* GPS right now if you would 'a let me at that guy," she grumbled a few times, attempting to aggravate her sister.

It didn't work. Veronica dreamily soaked in her surroundings; nothing could disrupt her elation.

Nikki managed to navigate them out of Tours, despite two unfortunate roundabout incidents that involved driving in several complete circles. Villas and cottages with delightful farms dotted the landscape. They flanked a troop of sightseeing bicyclists that traversed between them and the Loire River. Veronica slowed to their pace as a magnificent structure came into view.

Nikki sighed. "It's amazing."

"That's Amboise Castle," Veronica responded. "I looked up some of the famous Loire châteaux on the Internet. Leonardo da Vinci is buried there."

They entered the quaint village of Amboise. The narrow cobblestone streets were filled with merchants setting out their wares.

"There's a café. Oh, and a Bigot chocolate shop and a bakery!" Nikki observed with the enthusiasm of a child. She sulked as her sister drove out of Amboise and toward Montrichard.

"We'll come back for lunch. I wanna get to our Château as soon as possible," the older sister explained like a mature adult.

Nikki stuck out her bottom lip for a moment then leaned toward her sister. "Only if you promise to buy me ice-skweam," she cooed.

Many small bed and breakfast inns graced the countryside as they meandered along the rural roads. Some were old, medieval looking structures, while others seemed to favor renaissance architecture. Several had been restored into museums and hotels and had signs that read: ENTRANCE CAVE inviting tourists to come visit their cellars for wine tasting.

After several turns, they came to a T-intersection. Left was a paved road and right was a dirt trail.

"Right," Nikki said.

"Really?" Veronica asked.

Nikki raised her eyebrows yet said nothing. They followed the path for about half a mile when they saw a rickety red tractor driven by a farmer. Surprised, he stopped his vehicle to watch the two young women in the little orange car drive by.

The road twisted into a forest and led to a wooden bridge with a small river flowing under it.

"Are you *sure* this is the right way?" Veronica asked with a tint of doubt in her voice.

"That's what the map says," Nikki answered, holding out her phone so Veronica could see it.

Two signs graced the bridge: DÉFENSE D'ENTRER and PROPRIÉTÉ PRIVÉE. Veronica glanced at her sister.

"They say 'no trespassing' and 'private property'."

Veronica rode the clutch as the Twingo puttered across the rickety bridge. She grumbled under her breath. "I sure hope we're going the right way."

"If not, I'm sure some crazy troglodyte with a shotgun will be along in no time to let us know," Nikki answered. She hummed the twangy banjo theme from the movie *Deliverance* as they crossed the bridge.

Once on the other side, they pulled up to a massive gated wall covered in more NO TRESPASSING and PRIVATE PROPERTY signs.

"Wow!" Veronica had her seat belt unfastened and the door open before she shifted the car into park.

"It doesn't look like anyone's been here for years," Nikki said as she walked up to the massive gate. "How're we 'sposed to get in?"

A large metal chain wove in and out of two massive door handles and met in the middle with a huge padlock. Veronica grabbed the lock and pulled. The chain was taut and screeched defiantly as it rubbed across the ancient door.

"Help me with this."

"Are you yanking my chain?" Nikki giggled.

Veronica shot her a stern look while she clenched her fists around the padlock. The doors of the gate bowed out slightly from the effort, yet the chain held fast.

"Hang on a sec," Nikki said. She dashed to the car, opened the hatch, and emerged with a tire iron. "Stand back," she warned as she lifted the weapon high in the air. "This baby's gonna do some damage!"

"Be careful, slugger," Veronica said, stepping back.

Nikki poised herself like a baseball player. The blow rang out like a shot, and several birds flew out of neighboring trees in a fluster. The lock rattled but did not let go. She struck again. This time there were no birds to raise a commotion, and the only sound was a ringing in Veronica's head. The padlock held, but the rusty, old chain crumbled and easily broke into pieces, releasing the doors. Each woman grabbed one of the metal handles and pushed it open.

On the other side, thick foliage dripping with moss guarded the ancient Château du Feu Ardent. The trees flanked a path that led up to the magnificent structure. Like a shy child it peeked at them from behind the greenery.

"This place is huge," Nikki gasped. "A lot bigger than I thought!"

"Over fifteen acres surrounded by a ten-foot wall. The grounds actually span out slightly farther than that, about a half mile from the wall," Veronica explained. "Marie-Claire said the castle is over twenty thousand square feet."

To their right were several small buildings. They were crumbling and decrepit.

Nikki looked up at the underbelly of the gatehouse entrance. There were black metal spouts aimed right above her head. "What are those?"

Veronica gazed up. "Defense from invaders. If someone broke through the gatehouse, like we are doing right now, they poured hot oil on 'em."

"How pleasant."

They got back in the car and followed the driveway until it turned into a circle in front of the castle's façade. In the center of the roundabout sat the remains of a fountain covered in overgrowth. Inside it, three marble cherubs looked like dirty babies playing in the mud.

Veronica parked the car, got out, and walked up the massive stone steps, which were overrun with tall grass growing through the cracks. Grasshoppers darted back and forth. She felt one ram into her leg like a tiny bullet. She knelt and lifted a stone. Underneath bustled several rollie pollie bugs that resembled miniature grey tanks, and a solitary skeleton key.

"So, they left you a key for the front door but not for the main gate," Nikki started. "That's odd."

"They haven't been here for a while. They probably forgot the front gates were even padlocked. No big deal. We made it just fine."

After Veronica unlocked the door, the sisters walked into the foyer of the Château. A huge staircase swept along the wall to the left and then leveled off into a balcony that overlooked the foyer. Underneath the balcony was an archway that led to another room.

Veronica pulled open the tall shutters. Light filtered in revealing a thick layer of dust everywhere. She kicked away a patch of dirt and debris on the floor. "Look, the floor is marble. I told you this place would be incredible. The staircase — that wood is mahogany." She pulled out a flashlight. "Come on. Let's see about getting our money!"

Veronica marched forward, under the staircase, and into the library. Since the room had no windows, the women relied mostly on the flashlight to see. The ceilings were high and covered with tall bookshelves. In the middle was a table surrounded by several Louis XVI chairs.

On the wall behind them, a fireplace yawned with an enormous, charred hole. To their left was a massive set of double doors with three statues, inset in the wall, perched above them. Decades of dust muted their details, but one could still see that they portrayed soldiers of a long-ago era.

"Isn't there a light switch somewhere? This place does have electricity, right?" Nikki asked.

"Yes, it does, the electrician just has to hook it up. He's coming tomorrow, along with the plumber."

"You mean there's no running water? I can't take a shower! I've traveled half way across the world, Vern, I stink."

"I know you stink. I do too. Maybe we should get a room in town tonight. I didn't realize this place would be..."

"Such a dump," Nikki finished.

"It's not a dump. It just needs work, and that's what we're here to do."

"Thought we were here to decorate it, not renovate it," Nikki retorted.

Veronica ignored her sister and plopped her bag on the table. She pulled her inspiration pad out and opened it to a marked page. "Hold the instructions while I aim the flashlight."

There was a crude drawing on it, a map, outlining the library.

"What the hell is this?" Nikki asked while scrunching up her nose at the pad.

"Instructions from Marie-Claire. She has some money stashed away here for safekeeping. Since they can't be here to pay us in person we're supposed to get it."

"You are kidding, right? She gave you *map*? That is freaking weird. Can't this woman just use PayPal?"

"So, she's a little eccentric. They're away on holiday. This was just easier for them I guess."

"This is unreal. Who would do business this way?" Nikki practically shouted.

"Keep your voice down!" Veronica scolded.

"Why? We're twenty miles from the nearest living person. Who's gonna hear us? Christ, Vern, this is crazy. How could you go along with this?"

Veronica exploded. "Because if I don't make some big money real fast I'm gonna lose everything! My business, my apartment, everything I've worked for *gone* because I'm freaking *broke*."

Nikki bit her lower lip and stood silently beside her sister.

Veronica was shaking. "This *has* to work, Nik. This is all I got."

Nikki nodded. "Okay, then let's do this."

Veronica wiped a tear, took a deep breath, and aimed the flashlight at the statues. They looked like Roman soldiers decked out in battle gear. One held a shield, one a mace, and the one in the center brandished a sword. "The middle statue is pointing to a spot on the wall," Veronica said. She walked closer to the figure and traced a line with the beam of the flashlight. She did it over and over, creating a straight line from the sword to the wall. "Does that look like the spot he's pointing to?"

Nikki studied the movement of the light. "Close, maybe you're a little low."

Veronica adjusted the beam.

"Yeah, that's better," Nikki confirmed. "It goes straight to those books."

Veronica stepped up to the shelf. "This must be it." She pulled out an ancient tome then stood back in anticipation. Nothing happened so she set the book on the table.

"You gotta be yanking-my-chain! Are you looking for a secret passage?"

"Yep, that's exactly what I am doing. One of these books is a lever that opens a vault," Veronica said as she pulled on another volume.

"I can't believe this — no one back home is going to believe this." She took out her phone and started to click the keyboard.

"What are you doing?" Veronica asked as her sister buried her nose in her iPhone.

"Updating my status. How's this sound: I'm looking for buried treasure in a creepy castle in France — how's your morning?"

Veronica scowled at her sister and pulled on another book and then another. Nothing happened.

Nikki typed some more on her tiny keypad. "And having no luck. Guess I'll be back in LA soon!"

A loud thud made both women jump. It came from behind the bookcase. The last book Veronica pulled triggered a mechanism. Slowly an entire shelf began to slide, revealing an entrance two feet wide.

"Oh-my-God! What the hell?" Nikki stood frozen, staring at the entrance.

"What'd I tell you?" Veronica exclaimed triumphantly. "There it is; a genuine secret chamber. How far-out is that?"

"That's pretty far-out," Nikki agreed. "Now what?"

"Now we go inside."

"*We're* going inside? Dude, you're crazy. There's prolly spiders and rats in there."

"And according to Marie-Claire, there's a whole lot of money." Veronica peeked into the narrow chamber. "I didn't know it would be such a tight squeeze," she said. "I hate small spaces; I get claustrophobic."

"Well, I won't fit. You gotta walk sideways to squeeze through there, and my boobs are way too big. But you, on the other hand, will have no trouble!" Nikki said as she stepped aside.

Veronica studied the room with her flashlight. Wooden crates were stacked on the far wall and several clay amphoras nestled together in a corner. Taking a deep breath, she eased her way inside the long and narrow passage.

Nikki twitched by the entrance impatiently. "What's in there?"

"Some old, clay jars and storage boxes," Veronica answered, tucking the flashlight under her chin. She pressed several bricks on the far wall until one receded. Taking a step back, she allowed the vault to open. The stone that covered it swiveled on a rod. She stood there awkwardly with the flashlight under her chin and her chest pushed up as high as she could to see inside.

"Found it!" she informed her sister.

"Found what?"

Veronica didn't answer as she pulled out a grey metal box. It was heavier than it looked. While pulling it, the box unexpectedly slid out fast. As she caught it, the flashlight crashed to the floor and shattered one of the clay jars.

Veronica felt a wave of dread. The thought of crouching to the floor to retrieve the light terrified her. Irrationally she imagined that if she knelt down, the walls would collapse around her.

"You okay? What was that?" Nikki asked from the entrance.

Her sister's voice calmed Veronica and gave her the strength to carefully bend over. She felt on the floor for the flashlight. It lay in the rubble of the destroyed pottery. Along with it, Veronica noticed a paper scroll.

"I dropped the flashlight and broke one of those jars," Veronica answered. "And found some old scroll."

Grabbing the flashlight, she inspected the scroll more carefully. Its edges were frayed by time, and it was tied with two aged-stained ribbons. As she stood, something hairy with many legs scurried down the wall in front of her. She squealed at the spider and quickly scurried out of the tiny chamber.

"Nik, I got it!" she exclaimed, once the threatening spider-infested walls were behind her.

"Got what?"

Veronica set the box on the table and tried to open it. "Oh shit, it's locked. The key must still be inside!"

"Well, go back and get it," Nikki instructed.

"Uh-uh, I ain't going in there again. You go get it!"

Nikki shook her head. "Fuck the key. We broke through a padlock the size of a softball; we'll be able to get that little thing open. Let's get the tire iron again!"

"No need for that. We can pick it. We just need a knife or something."

"You're right. Let's go back to town, get a room, and we can open it after we eat," Nikki offered.

"You want to leave *now*? We just got here. We have the whole château to explore!"

"Let's just go. I'm hungry. You said we'd be able to have lunch back in town. We can explore tomorrow — with electricity and running water. Ya' know what I mean, Vern?"

"Fine. Grab my bag and stuff on the table," she instructed while lugging the lockbox toward the foyer. Smugly, she added, "But you know my name is Veronica..."

Chapter 21

Father Michel's Story

Father Michel mumbled, "I'll take my dinner to my room again tonight."
The cook didn't look at the priest. He motioned to some bread and
steamed turnips laid out on serving trays. Father Michel helped himself
and quickly retreated to his tiny chamber. He was a pariah since the episode with
Cardinal Thibaut earlier that week. No one spoke to him; no one looked at him.
He ate his food alone and flittered about the castle like a soulless specter.

He could hear the others in the dining room when he returned to the kitchen
with his empty plate. Someone spoke his name. "How long do you think Father
Michel will be punished?"

There was an uneasy silence followed by an eruption of hushed conversation
that Father Michel couldn't decipher. Someone snickered. Yet another
commented, "For eternity if God is truly just."

Shame engulfed the priest like a blanket and before anyone saw, he crept out
the kitchen's side door. He hoped he still had one friend — Gaston-Elise.

Father Michel recalled how they met. It was his second day at the Château —
the day just before the Cardinal's announcement — and he had decided to take a
stroll across the grounds. Gaston-Elise was sitting behind the well in the vineyard
feasting from a bucket of freshly picked grapes. This was highly inappropriate as
the grapes were designated for the Cardinal's wine.

The two men caught each other's gaze at exactly the same moment. Gaston-
Elise sheepishly swallowed a whole grape and attempted to hide the bucket
behind his back. Father Michel smiled. "I doubt one pail of grapes would make a
full flask of wine for the Cardinal!"

"In that case," the one-armed soldier answered, "join me so we may finish off
a flask's worth together!"

Father Michel laughed. He instantly liked the man's brazen spirit. They struck
up a conversation, and within a few minutes, Gaston-Elise and Father Michel
were enjoying the sweet delicacy together. The two men became friends easily.

Father Michel discovered the man once was a knight, but lost his left arm in
battle and was demoted to tower guard. The story of Gaston-Elise was biting and
tragic. The priest recalled the pain-infused tremble in his voice as he recounted.
"The Lord found disfavor with me — surely punishment for the lives that ended
at my sword. Not only did I lose my left arm, but I was unfairly stripped of my
knighthood after it happened. Then, since I was no longer a knight, I was required
to pay *taxes* on my land!

"I didn't have the money. Desperate, I went to the Church for help. They
offered me work as a sentry in Avignon to pay the debt. I didn't want to be so far
away from my family, but I had no choice. While there, word came that the peste
hit my village."

The holy man listened quietly while holding the confessing man's hand.

Gaston-Elise continued. "Father, I fiercely wanted to return home, but was denied a leave of absence. I had to go to them. You understand, don't you? So, I abandoned my post and went to my family.

"When I arrived, the children were already dead. My wife was in the deep throes of fever. I stayed by her side until she succumbed. She never even knew I was there, Father. Mad with malaise she didn't recognize me. The next day, I buried all three of them by myself.

"I had no place else to go so I returned to Avignon. I begged for forgiveness. I was granted mercy for my treason and told that I could serve as a guard for Cardinal Thibaut. Then my property was seized to pay my tax debt. My only solace; knowing that one day I may be able to earn enough money to buy it back."

Father Michel counseled the troubled man that day. He assured the soldier that the Lord didn't burden anyone with more pain than they could endure. He encouraged Gaston-Elise to be tough and hold his convictions. His faith needed to be firmer than ever, as God was surely testing him, as He had done to Job.

Now, a week later, it was Father Michel who needed to call upon that strength. He prayed the pious man would aide him in his quest.

ᘒᘖ❖ᘒᘖ

Gaston-Elise answered the door wearing only his britches. His stump of an arm dangled at his side like a folded chicken wing. The tip of it was scarred and mangled. He was a hairy man. His dark beard tangled into the curly swirls on his chest like ivy overtaking a tree. The black hair on his head was flowing now — usually it was tied back — and he looked wild and untamed. His eyes were kind, though, and they grew wide with delight upon recognizing his visitor.

"What a pleasant sight on my doorstep. Come in, Father."

Father Michel entered the cottage. In the left corner was a straw mattress. On the opposite wall was a small table and stool. A fireplace, which had no flame because wood was rationed, was centered on the wall opposite the door. Three candles illuminated the room from atop the mantle. In a dark corner hung a few articles of clothing, his sword, and finely crafted chain mail that he once wore as a soldier.

The shack's only decoration hung above the mantle. It was a painting created by an artist of questionable talent. It showed Gaston-Elise, standing proud and dressed for battle; next to him stood a middle-sized woman holding hands with two angelic children. Father Michel gazed at the painting and smiled with bittersweet compassion. Gaston-Elise motioned for the priest to sit.

Father Michel rested on the rickety stool. He scanned the table and noticed a tattered Bible; its pages fanned from frequent use.

"Can I pour you some wine, Father? I have a flask here that I have been saving for a special occasion."

Father Michel laughed. "Then why would you want to serve it *now*?"

Gaston-Elise looked surprised and chuckled. "Because I have *you* as a guest, and I must say that you are the *only* guest that I have had for quite some time." He retrieved the flask and two wood goblets. "May I ask what I owe this surprise visit to?"

Father Michel's smile dropped from his face. "I have fallen on disfavor with Cardinal Thibaut."

Gaston-Elise briefly paused. "I heard he said some cross words to you. That is his nature. It will pass in a few days. He is cross with everyone at one time or another, and no one thinks much of it after a while."

"True," Father Michel answered. "Not only am I distraught by his judgment of me, but also by his recent decree. Why is the Church abandoning so many when they need us more than ever?"

"They've been coming to the gate, you know," Gaston-Elise began. "Today villagers came to speak with the Cardinal. We tried to turn them away, but they wouldn't go. They threw stones at the towers, and one woman held up the body of an infant. She cried for us to help her; the child had died without being baptized. We said there was nothing we could do.

"One man stepped forward — a big man — and he took the dead child from her arms and wielded it at the gate. It almost flew over the top, but hit the wall instead. I can still hear the sound it made as it struck the side and slid down to the ground. The woman went mad, cursing us and the Cardinal. She clung to the dead baby and rolled herself up around it like a ball.

"The crowd went livid. They cursed us and tried to rush the gate. The guards in the tower — oh I wish they hadn't done it — they reacted hastily and opened up the hot oil spouts. Some were burned so badly that we could *smell* their burnt flesh.

"It took hours before the villagers finally left. They tried to make the woman go with them, but she refused. Eventually, they had to pull her away as she bawled and shrieked…she didn't sound human. One of the other guards eventually sent word to the Cardinal…I dread to think of the cross words *that* messenger got."

Father Michel's dark face grew visibly pale. "That is why I *need* to leave here, Gaston-Elise. I abandoned my congregation. I must go there and see if there's anything I can do to help."

"What are you saying, Father? You're leaving? He won't let you back inside once you go." Gaston-Elise's smiling eyes glazed with sadness.

"I *do* intend to come back. That is why I need your help. You can let me back in when I return. If I go now, no one will notice for days. They all regard me with disdain. I eat my meals alone, in my chambers. If I left now, I would not be missed until Sunday mass."

"Five days, that's a long time to go completely unnoticed. Even if you do return, and I help you get back inside…what if the peste…if you…" Gaston-Elise's voice trailed off.

"It won't infect me. You've heard the saying, 'once it touches someone it won't touch them again'. I had it and I recovered. The Lord saw fit for me to live then, he surely won't take me now."

Gaston-Elise's lips parted, but no sound came out. He thoughtfully ran his hand through his mane of hair and looked carefully at Father Michel. "I can't pretend to understand your desire to leave and minister people who banished you."

"Cardinal Thibaut *says* they banished me. I don't believe him, and that's why

I must find out. They were my congregation. They were my family, my children. They were to me like your family was to you. I have to go back to them like you had to go back to your family. If for no other reason, than just to find out the truth." Father Michel's voice cracked.

"Your congregation is *not* like my family," Gaston-Elise snarled. "I loved my wife and children and they wanted — *needed* — me to be with them. Your congregation cast you out. You cannot compare the two."

"There is more to it, Gaston. Our situations are more alike than they seem. I have to go and see if..." his voice faded. He sipped some wine, closed his eyes, and continued. "Her name is Claudeen. She is a farmer's daughter, a member of the congregation, and she *loves* me."

Gaston-Elise furrowed his brow. "Father...?"

"I could never return that love, though. I pushed her away. I kept my vows. But my thoughts, Gaston, were not pure. I dreamt about her every night. I dreamt about her long auburn hair that always flowed long and was interwoven with sprigs of fresh lavender. I imagined being with her in ways that no priest should ever act upon."

"*You*, Father?"

The priest nodded and muttered, "I am but a man. A weak slave to temptation; I couldn't suppress my desires."

"But you did not act upon them. All men face temptation..." Gaston-Elise lectured earnestly.

The priest interrupted him. "I *thought* about acting upon them, Gaston. I imagined us fleeing together, running away and starting a new life far away from everyone. I never dared to ask her, though. Then it was too late. Her father, Paul, brought her to see me. I was nervous, scared — did he find out? Was he going to confront me about our forbidden love? Though we never acted upon it, it was challenging to hide. She would physically flush when we were near one another, and I would lose control of my manhood.

"But the reason they came to see me was worse than our secret being discovered. Paul was happy! He grinned from ear to ear, and sweet Claudeen was sullen and quiet. Paul had come to tell me about her *engagement*. She and a local boy were arranged to be married...and they wanted me to prepare for the ceremony."

Father Michel swigged the wine and gingerly pushed his goblet forward for a refill. Gaston-Elise complied.

"I did it, Gaston. In my church before God and all the witnesses, I praised their love and blessed their future lives together in the holy union of marriage. I lied. I felt the burning fire of rage and jealously roaring in my loins as I pronounced them man and wife.

"That was only two short months ago, but it now seems like a lifetime has passed. Each day thereafter was an eternity of sorrow for me. I begged God to take the pain away. But I suffered. I am tormented for my sin of lust.

"And now I am here. Far removed from the church I served and the woman I would die to save. That is why I must go back. I have to be certain she is alright. Even though she lies with another man as his bride, I love her and have to see that she is still..." the priest's story ended in tears.

Gaston-Elise raised his goblet to his lips and looked at the narrow-faced man. "You should go now."

Father Michel slowly rose to his feet. "I understand, Gaston, sorry to burden you." He hung his head and turned to leave.

"Go pack what you need for your journey," Gaston-Elise said. "Meet me in the vineyard in an hour. And dress warm; it's cold tonight."

Chapter 22

Veronica's Story

Nikki boomed, "You get the box open yet?"

Veronica woke to see her sister coming out of the bathroom, wrapped in a towel.

"No, I must 'a fell asleep."

"Lemme take a crack at it," Nikki interjected. "Go take a shower and please hurry. I'm sooo *hungry*."

Veronica handed over the cuticle scissors she had been using on the lockbox. A thick blanket snuggled around its edges like a nest around a giant cube-shaped egg. Nikki plopped on the bed and began to investigate the lock.

Several minutes later, Veronica emerged from the bathroom with a placid face. She had showered in a claw-foot bathtub with an old-fashioned shower attachment that snaked up the wall. The bathroom was illuminated by a small stained-glass window, which cast pretty designs on the terracotta tile floor. A wood shelf with peeling purple paint held rolled up towels, soaps, and a small vase of lilacs that fragranced the room. She thoroughly enjoyed every aspect of the quaint Amboise bed and breakfast.

The bedroom was covered in creamy wallpaper with a bright red pattern of roses. Wood beams, stained black, crawled up the corners of the room and across the ceiling where they met in the middle. From that spot hung an ornate chandelier, painted white and beaded with red crystals. There was one window which was covered by rose-printed curtains.

The room had twin beds, each covered with a handmade fleur-de-lis quilt. Nikki sat on one with piles of French money stacked up around her and the opened box.

Veronica beamed. "Look at all that money! Did you count it? Is it all there?"

Nikki thumbed a stack of bills. Her eyes narrowed. "Yep, I counted it. About twenty thousand francs."

Veronica's smile quivered. She pulled her lips back and said, "Well, that's not as much as it should be. Marie-Claire said we'd have more than enough for the contractors, the carpenters, and my first payment. I wonder what happened. Maybe she'll send the rest. Twenty thousand is a start. At least it'll pay for our trip so far and lodging..."

"You don't understand. These are *francs* — Pascal, Delacroix, and Montesquieu notes. They don't use these anymore; everything has been converted to euro." Nikki tossed a pile of bills up in the air to amplify her point.

"Do you know that for sure?"

"I've been to France before, remember? People had already gone through the franc-euro conversions back then. The older money, like these five hundred franc notes, were the first to go. This money is ancient."

"But some of them might not be expired, right? Maybe we should take them to the bank. I mean, why would she leave us worthless money?" Veronica challenged.

"Because she is a wack-job trying to con you," Nikki answered bluntly.

"No, she isn't. There must be a reason..." Veronica's voice trailed off as she noticed a white envelope peeking out from under a pile of bills. "What's this?" She sat on the bed and retrieved the envelope.

"I don't know." Nikki jumped off the bed, pulled back the curtains, opened the window, and lit up a cigarette.

"Would you please *not* do that in here?"

"We're in France. Everyone smokes in France. Besides, I don't think I could stain these curtains any more than they already are. Christ, this place is a dump."

"No, it's not. I love this little inn. It's *charming!*"

Nikki grunted. "*Charming* is a word people use to describe places that are dumps."

"Well, who do you think you are? The Queen of Oildale? Last I checked you couldn't become a millionaire on a teacher's salary."

"Vern, that's just the thing. You aren't *supposed* to be poor right now. We're here to make a bunch of money, remember? But this whole thing is a wild goose chase. I told you Marie-Claire was a wack-job," Nikki spat.

"Stop calling her that," Veronica growled. "Look at this." She pulled two pieces of paper from the envelope. One had the word 'dreams' scrawled in a fancy, yet deliberate, handwritten script. The word was underlined to emphasize its importance. The other piece of paper was an official looking, yet old, document issued by a Swiss bank. It contained a series of numbers.

"It looks like a bank account," Veronica said.

"Great. She left a bank account number. How are we supposed to get money out of an account that isn't in our name?"

"It may not be in *anyone's* name. Come on; there's a bank down the street. Get dressed. We'll take all of this there," Veronica ordered as she jumped to her feet and retrieved clean clothes from her suitcase. "I have a feeling that everything will make sense soon."

❧ ❧ ❖ ❧ ❧

The two women walked into the Banque de France. The three-hundred-year-old building had been modernized. Ancient marble floors were adorned with colorful area rugs, and the row of tellers was planted behind a stainless steel counter topped with frosted glass dividers.

Veronica and Nikki stood in line and waited for the next available teller. When their turn came, Nikki greeted a stony-eyed woman. Veronica stood quietly as the two bantered back and forth. The woman glimpsed at Veronica occasionally, and then at the wad of francs that she grasped in her hands. Finally, the teller gestured to examine the bills, which Veronica then set on the counter, along with the mysterious piece of paper.

The woman examined both carefully. "Veuillez patienter. Le gérant de banque vous aidera dans un instant."

Nikki whispered to Veronica, "She said she's going to get the bank manager."

69

Within a few moments, Veronica and Nikki were escorted past the row of tellers and to a large, opulent office. There sat a man in a brown suit with large brown eyes to match. He had shocking black, wavy hair that flowed across his forehead like an ocean wave. His nose was slightly too large for his face. It stood out defiantly and hooked slightly like an eagle's beak. It was not unattractive and actually complimented the soft eyes above it.

Nikki and Veronica were ushered into his presence. He smiled broadly with thick lips that curled back and caused a ripple of dimples to appear around his mouth and chin. "So, ladies," he began in almost perfect English, "you are the women with the francs and the Swiss bank account? You created a little tizzy with Miss Desandé. She thought you were crazy Americans for a moment."

The comment hung in the air.

Nikki leaned forward in her chair and grinned. "She's right. We *are* crazy Americans!"

This caused Brown Eyes to laugh with a deep sincere chuckle. It took Veronica a split second, but she too joined in the guffaw.

"I'm Christophe Sinclair. And you are..." He reached over his desk so he could carefully shake each woman's hand while looking directly into her eyes.

They each whispered an answer, "Veronica — Nikki."

"May I offer you a beverage, coffee, tea?"

Each shook their head no. He chuckled again at their demeanor. Miss Desandé, who had been hovering just beyond the glass wall, took her cue and retreated.

"Then how can I help you today?"

Veronica paused a thoughtful moment before speaking. "We have some money — francs — that we want to cash in."

Christophe Sinclair cocked his head to the side. "The notes, I'm afraid, have no value. I collect old coins myself, but I don't know too much about old paper money. Perhaps an antique dealer would offer you a few euro for them. But the bank, we cannot honor them as it is far past the deadline for that year. The account number, though, I can access for you if you'd like."

Veronica suddenly felt foolish grasping the bundle of francs in her hand. It was as if she were coveting a stack of Monopoly money. She knew the *I Told You So* song was currently beating inside Nikki's head and would erupt the second they stepped out of the bank manager's office. She looked at the piece of paper with the account number. Everything now depended on these digits — everything — her job, her hopes, her pride. She held the piece of paper out to Christophe.

He studied it for a minute then tapped on his keyboard. His attention shifted from the screen to the paper several times. Veronica watched his fingers dance – – bare, no ring. She caught herself and quickly chased away the thought. This was not the time to be thinking about *that*. On his desk, she noticed a series of framed photos. One was of a smiling boy, perhaps ten or twelve. She assumed he was Christophe's son. Like his father, he had a chiseled nose that severely dominated his small round face.

Then she noticed the next photo. It was a family of three with the same boy.

The man in the photo, though he resembled Christophe, certainly was not him. *Brothers*, she thought. *And the boy must be Christophe's nephew.*

Another picture was of an older couple. The man was a mature version of Christophe, and the woman had a rich olive complexion with a magnificent nose — surely they were his parents.

The final photo was of Christophe. He was dressed in hunting clothes with a shotgun resting on his shoulder. At his feet sat a yellow dog and the lifeless bodies of three pheasants.

There was silence. Christophe was no longer typing. "I need the password."

Veronica looked up and blinked herself back into reality. "Pass — word," she repeated.

"Yes, to access the funds," Christophe said.

Veronica sat upright. "Yes, to access the funds!" she said as if that clue had suddenly jarred her memory. She fumbled in her messenger bag and retrieved the piece of paper with the fancy, handwritten script. "Dreams?"

He nodded his head once and typed the single word. Gazing at the computer screen, he waited. One of his heavy eyebrows lifted slightly over its sparkling brown eye.

"Did it work?" Nikki scooched to the edge of her chair.

"The account contains: two million, one-hundred, twenty-five thousand, six hundred and twenty-two point one-six Swiss francs." He sat quietly for a second. "Would you like to access your money?"

Nikki furiously thumbed her cell phone. She stopped, looked up as though she was about to spring from her chair and attack the banker like a hungry lioness, and blurted. "That's over two million, four-hundred thousand bucks!"

"You just need to set up an account here at our bank and then we can transfer the funds." He tapped with his fingers a few times to open the appropriate screen.

"Transfer the funds?" Veronica parroted.

"Yep, just need your identification."

"It's that easy?" Veronica asked incredulously.

"The account was set up in Switzerland many years ago with minimal security requirements. This money is legally yours." Christophe sat back in his chair and a huge smile overtook his face. "It is *legally* yours, right?"

Veronica felt guilty for no reason. "Of course. We're decorating a castle, and this is how the owner is paying us. Happens all the time, right?"

Christophe grinned. "Of course, mademoiselle."

Veronica couldn't believe how sweet his voice sounded as he called her "mademoiselle". She was shaking as she pulled her passport from her bag. "We'll need checks, a checking account, please."

Over the next hour, the details were set up, and the money was transferred into Veronica and Nikki's new joint account.

❧ ❧ ❖ ❧ ❧

It was mid-afternoon when the sisters left the bank. They made their way past the open-air shops where customers grazed and collected ingredients for their evening meal.

Periodically, Nikki broke into song. "I thought you were wrong, but I'm glad you're right!" she cooed to the tune of Billy Joel's *You May be Right*. She hugged her sister, making a spectacle of herself to all the passersby.

For once, Veronica was not the slightest bit embarrassed by her sister's silliness and even allowed Nikki to twirl her in the street. The girls splurged on an expensive meal at an upscale bistro and purchased a pricey bottle of wine to take back to their room.

Tired, jet lagged, but elated, they lounged on their respective beds. After finishing a glass of wine, Veronica proclaimed that she would buy herself a new car.

"Good idea," Nikki answered as she poured her sister more Crémant de Bourgogne. "And get a new wardrobe, hairstyle, boob job and a mani-pedi while you're at it."

Veronica ignored the jab and emptied her purse to rid herself of all the francs that were stuffed inside of it. As she organized the clutter, she picked up a weathered book. "What's this?" she asked, holding up a tattered leather-bound volume.

Nikki looked up from the wine she was pouring into her own glass, spilling a few droplets on the floor.

Veronica frowned then held the book out for her sister to see more closely.

"Isn't that your address book or something? I put it in your bag when we were in the castle library. Remember? You had all your stuff on the table, and you asked me to grab it because you were carrying the lockbox."

"But it's not mine." She looked at the inscription on the cover. "Oh! It's the first book I pulled off the shelf when we were looking for the vault. I put it on the table, and you must have grabbed it by accident. What does 'Journal Intime' mean?"

"That means that you have someone's diary."

"A diary? Whose diary? How old is it?" Veronica chirped. She scooted up next to her sister and opened the first brittle page.

Nikki scanned it. "It is dated June 10th, 1789."

"Wow, over two hundred years old!" Veronica wrapped a down quilt around her shoulders and cradled her wine glass with both hands while eagerly waiting for more details.

Nikki traced the handwritten words with her index finger. "The author is a woman. She's pregnant and writing this journal for her baby."

"Seriously cool. What does it say?" Veronica sipped her wine and stared at the fancy script with child-like eyes.

"Well, it starts out with a preface: 'This journal dedicated to my unborn child. This is for you, my beloved one. I want you to understand every emotion, every thought, every blessed moment that leads up to the day of your birth. You will come into the world in a few, short months...'" Nikki stopped and read a little more quietly, taking her time to translate each word correctly. "'Oh how round – – perfectly round — my belly is. The midwife says this means mine will be born a perfect child and of even temperament. And because the babe rests high in my abdomen, she says he will be a boy!'" Nikki looked up and added her own commentary. "Great prenatal care, huh?"

Veronica nodded. "Did she live in the Château?"

"I don't know," Nikki answered. "It doesn't say where she lived. She could have been from anywhere."

"Keep reading. I want to find out."

"Oh, I'm tired Vern. This wine is catching up to me. I can read more tomorrow."

Veronica pouted. "But I want to hear more!"

"Here, translate it yourself. Just use your guide." Nikki grabbed Veronica's English-French translation booklet that had spilled out of her purse with the rest of her stuff.

Veronica reluctantly took the guide, set it beside the diary, crawled into her own bed, and slowly deciphered the archaic, cursive French writing.

Nikki stood up, bent over, and gave her sister a kiss on top of the head. "You did it, Vern. Two and a half million bucks, a castle to decorate, three months in France, and by the time you get done translating that journal, you'll know how to speak the language, too."

Veronica looked up from her reading. "*We* did it."

Nikki smacked her lips and rolled her eyes slightly. She plopped onto her own bed and let herself snuggle into the warmth of the fleur-de-lis quilt.

Veronica spun the red wine around in her glass and immersed herself in the antiquated journal as her sister softly snored.

Chapter 23

Journal Intime

July 12th, 1789

Today Aunt Agathe came to visit. I have not seen Henri's sister in a year! She came by carriage and can only visit a few days, as she is afraid to be away from Paris for long. There is much unrest and rumors of revolution. She brought a slew of troubling news, but my dear Henri says that we won't be affected by the uprisings, as we are safe in the Loire Valley. Even if the strife comes to the countryside, we are secure behind the well-fortified castle walls. I am still dreadfully worried, though.

Henri told me to, "Only fancy pleasant thoughts. To think anything ill could cause you to have another nervous fit, dear."

But I do have ill thoughts. I feel dreadfully unhappy and often cry for days.

Agathe says she was prone to such fits when she carried her first child. Apparently, they are entirely normal. Still, Henri wants me to remain peaceful and stresses that Agathe's first child was sickly and grew into a wicked little imp who fights his dear mother with petulant rages at the drop of a hat. Henri says that I should be peaceful so as not to have a spiteful child like she.

Agathe brought a lovely Christening gown for the baby. It is handmade with fine lace and silk. My dear child, I can imagine you wearing it, and I simply cannot wait. I wish you would be born today!

I sit writing this in the garden, and the servants bring me a tonic as I watch Agathe and Henri play jeux de boules on the grass. The boules sparkle when tossed in the air and come falling down like shooting stars.

Agathe is leaving in a couple days. I wish she could stay longer. She says she will come back and stay with me after I give birth. I imagine us all here together, playing in the grass, tossing boules, and picking garden flowers together on that beautiful summer's day in the future.

Josette-Camille

July 16th, 1789

Terrible news has come our way! A messenger brought word that just two days ago the Bastille outside of Paris was attacked by the revolutionaries. Hundreds assaulted the prison and demanded criminals to be released. The Bastille was well protected by many soldiers and was even aided by a Swiss regiment of many men, but still it succumbed!

It began as a minor situation, a mere trifle of protesters who should have easily been thwarted. However, the Marquis de Launay, the man who governed the Bastille, didn't anticipate the mob's determination — nor their treachery. Plus, in the midst of the negotiations, hundreds of French soldiers defected. They took up arms with the vicious crowd!

The messenger says the crux of the turmoil centered on a canon, which was aimed at the street. The revolutionaries demanded it be removed. It seems odd that something as simple as a canon could cause such strife. Why the Marquis didn't oblige, I am unsure. Since my lot in life is to be a noble woman, and I do not possess a political mind, I can only wonder at the implications of the ludicrous canon.

What I do know is that de Launay flatly refused to take it down. Not dissuaded, the angry crowd next demanded the bridges to be lowered. Apparently, they thought they were entitled to simply march inside. Again, the Marquis de Launay said no.

Tensions escalated, as neither side would acquiesce. Nothing happened for the longest time. They seemed to be at a stalemate when de Launay finally said he would lower the bridges if he and his men would then be allowed to leave peacefully. But that is not what the crazed horde wanted. They refused a peaceful resolution and proceeded to break down the drawbridges! They rushed inside where they murdered the Marquis de Launay! They cut off his head and paraded it around Paris like a prized pig.

Many were slaughtered and beheaded that day. Can you imagine the horror? Blood flowed in the gutters of Paris like rain during a thunderstorm.

But the violence isn't harbored in the city. Henri said he received word from other nobles and landowners who say they fear the carnage may spread to our valley. There are rumors of banditti that go about the countryside and accuse any noble person they find of false crimes. The angry brigands drag people out of their homes. They rob them, rape them, and then the doomed souls are rounded up in the streets where they face a ridiculous mock trial. They are sentencing people by the hundreds!

Their punishment is death by a wickedly cruel device called the guillotine. It is a large blade between two long, erect, wooden planks. A rope holds the blade high as the condemned soul lays his or her head on a platform at the base. An executioner releases the rope which causes the blade to come sweeping down, squarely hitting the back of the neck of the victim. Can you believe the cruelty?

Sometimes, I am told, the blade does not slice clean through, especially if it grows dull with too much use. The unfortunate soul only has half of his or her neck sliced and is still alive. Writhing in agony, the blade is slowly pulled up again so the entire process can start over.

I chose not to dwell on what the messenger told us. Imagining such horrors is not what I desire, but the thoughts creep into my dreams like little thieves, stealing my peaceful, contented nature. I grow excessively anxious and worried. It drives me to have my nervous fits. Can you blame me?

I told Henri, "It makes me tremble to think of an irate throng of plunderers coming here!"

My husband wants me to be at peace. He gave me a tonic and told me they would not likely travel all the way to our secluded part of the valley. We are far from the hostility; we should be safe. He assured me that even if they come I should not be fearful. Our walls are more impenetrable than any others in this region. Plus, we have the keep. It is in the heart of the castle and extremely well-fortified, a stronghold that is like a fortress within a fortress. It consists of several cells for prisoners, storage bins for food, as well as quarters for guards and the castle constable.

A turret in the center of the keep contains chambers that would serve as accommodations for me, Henri, and noble members of the household. The rooms are decent enough, but yet nothing like my lavish boudoir. It won't be pleasant, but if forced to, we can stay there until the threat passes.

I pray for this unrest to be done already. Why can't the common folk just accept their lot in life and leave it at that? Why cause such disruption and chaos, especially when the birth of my first child is so close? I fret over bringing forth new life while such recalcitrants dispense upheaval and unrest in our peaceful valley.

As the tonic calms my troubled mind, I dream of my baby entering a peaceful world on a bright sunny day with the flowers in bloom. I see us in the garden. We are surrounded by the fountains and the berry bushes. Henri holds his son high in the air and lets the breeze tickle his cheeks. Agathe and the maids are there, too, enjoying the beautiful pastoral scene. I close my eyes and that is my dream for my dear, sweet child.

Josette-Camille

Chapter 24

Sebastian's Story

The Cloaked Man was covered in blood. It was matted in his hair, his beard, smeared across his chest, and soaked into his robe. He sat on his haunches, hovering over the mutilated body of Vassus. The old man's intestines, still warm and steaming, spilled out of his gut and onto the blood-streaked cell floor. Sebastian clasped bits of the entrails, holding them close to his face. He squinted intently into them as if looking for clues.

Across the room, Baldebert whimpered in horror. He was careful not to draw attention his way. It had become resolutely clear to the monk that his cellmate was capable of anything, and he had no desire to become his next victim.

Cicero opened the portal. His awestruck eyes bore inside, and he spat, "You are a sick, ghastly fiend."

Sebastian ignored the centurion's insult. "Tell the governor he should reconsider sending his cavalry into the hills today," he instructed simply. "The Gauls have arranged a trap for the horses. Deep trenches have been dug and covered with brush. The horses will fall in, and the troops will be ambushed by marksmen with throwing spears."

"What are you talking about?" Cicero asked.

"The plan of attack today. It is prudent for your commander to heed my advice. Advance through the lowlands. The outlying forces are weakest there, as they don't think an attack through the swamp is possible. However, the season has been exceptionally dry. The horses will have no problem navigating the bogs and will have the element of surprise."

Cicero snarled, "You know nothing. You could not know."

"I warn you," Sebastian began. "Tell Governor Fabius to carry out the attack as I instruct, or he will lose many men and horses."

"Your feeble, Pagan trickery will not work against me. I am a son of Rome," Cicero squawked as he clanked the portal shut.

Sebastian sat in the darkness and smiled. "But my trickery is working just fine, Cicero," he whispered. "You are like a puppet on my string."

Chapter 25

The Children's Story

𝕴sabelle clung to her little brother as she balanced on the slick ledge. The current prodded her and she feared losing her footing and succumbing to the mercy of the water again.

Louis's teeth chattered. He kept his mouth shut, doing his best to muffle the sound.

On shore, the dogs yapped sporadically. Two men remained mounted while another held a torch above his head and stood on the riverbank trying to see what was in the water.

"Mere fish jumping," Lord Pierre told him while tightening the reins of his steed. The horse fidgeted.

"I can't see what it is, but surely 'twas not a fish…" the man on the riverbank began.

Just then, the dogs started to bark wildly. One held his nose in the air, sniffed, and then yelped shrilly three times while spinning in a circle.

"The dogs caught a scent!" Lord Pierre bellowed.

The barking dog broke free from its leash, and it charged toward the river. Lord Pierre's horse reacted by rearing up.

"Easy!" he said, trying to steady the beast.

The man on the bank waded into the stream to get a better look, but before he could focus, the free dog lunged into the water just behind him, knocking him down. Both flailed clumsily on the slippery rocks.

Isabelle took advantage of the commotion and swiftly made way for the opposite shore, pulling Louis as she scuttled.

"Izzy, what are you doing?" Louis gasped.

"We're going to the other side."

"What? No, Izzy, it's too far, and I can't swim."

She leaned into her brother's ear. "We can make it. I'm walking on a ledge, and I think it goes all the way across, like a bridge under the water."

Isabelle vigorously pulled her brother along. He was prone behind her and weighted her down. She struggled to keep her own head above water, often slipping under the surface in an effort to keep him held high.

Louis watched as one of the men on horseback dismounted and helped pull his friend onto dry land. Lord Pierre still struggled to control his spooked stead. The dog, however, was not deterred, and it paddled toward the children with its eager nose in the air.

"Faster Izzy," Louis whispered fearfully.

"They're swimming toward the other side," the soaked man sputtered as he coughed up water.

"Then go after them!" Pierre ordered. "Follow the dog; it'll tear them to shreds otherwise. The rest of us will cross upstream and flank them."

The underwater ridge gave way to a normal river bottom. Isabelle's feet sank into dense mud as the river grew shallower. It slurped and pulled her, making it even more difficult to walk, but at least they were nearing the shore. Once the water level met her breast, she let go of her brother. "You can manage now."

The two slogged onto the shore. The hound was now half way across and gaining.

"It's going to get us, Izzy. We can't run faster than a dog!"

"No, we can't. Quick, give me a bit of that jerk beef in your satchel."

Louis crawled clumsily over a crop of slick rocks before finally setting his feet on dry ground. Peering at the animal in the water, he protested, "You're hungry *now?*"

Isabelle climbed over the stones and spat, "Just give it to me, fast!"

The boy obliged. His sister tore the meat into three large chunks, and threw them in different parts of the water. One near the hound's muzzle so it would catch the scent, and the others further down river to lure it away. The dog's superior sense of smell pulled its nose into the air. With a wagging tail, it veered off course to find the treats.

Gaining precious time, the children climbed the steep bank, and hastened into the woods, holding hands as they scuttled through thickets. They had one option, and that was to find a place to hide.

Chapter 26

Veronica's Story

Nikki groaned. "My brain hurts." She stood over Veronica's bed with a blanket draped around her shoulders like a vampire's cape. "Ya' got any Advil?"

Veronica opened one eye; the other refused to budge. "Yeah, but you shouldn't take ibuprofen after drinking. It's bad for your kidneys."

"My kidneys will survive. Come on; I'm in pain. I thought we drank *good* wine. I haven't had a hangover like this since drinking that bottle of Mad Dog 20/20 at the Foo Fighters concert," Nikki griped.

"Fine, it's in my suitcase." Veronica sat up and picked something crusty out of the corner of her eye. She sighed. "Grab some for me, too."

Nikki retrieved the medicine, sat down in bed next to her sister, and they shared a bottle of water. "Next we need coffee — espresso!"

"Okay, but we have to hurry so we get to the castle by eight. I have the electrician, a plumber, and a cleaning crew all coming today. Come on; let's pack up and check out."

"Check out? Where we going to stay? A nicer hotel? Oh! I saw some real swank places by the river!" Nikki chirped.

"No, silly, we're staying at the Château!"

"Vern, you're kidding! That place is filthy and full of mice, and we don't even know if there's electricity!" Nikki pleaded.

"All of that will be taken care of today, and if not, it'll be like camping," she said brightly.

"We can afford *not* to go camping! Why stay there?"

"Because we have work to do, and we'll get a lot more done staying on site. Besides, it'll be fun. We'll be fairytale princesses, remember?" Veronica climbed out of bed and headed for the bathroom.

"I'd rather be a modern day princess and stay at the Hôtel de L'Univers," Nikki pouted.

❧❧ ❖ ❧❧

Each sister juggled a Styrofoam coffee cup and a Nutella-smothered crêpe as they drove through the Loire Valley to the Château du Feu Ardent. The ride seemed shorter this time, though it was just as breathtaking.

Veronica swiped on her cell phone and frowned. "Mom didn't call me back. I left a message for her this morning and asked if she knew Dr. Jacobs."

Nikki vacantly replied, "She's prolly hanging out with her bingo buddies."

"I wonder if I should try again."

Nikki wasn't paying attention to her sister. A dollop of Nutella had dripped onto her cleavage, and she groped in the glove box for a napkin. "What's this?" Her hand pulled out a rolled up piece of parchment, brown with age and tied on each end with crumbling ribbon. "Can I wipe myself with this?"

Veronica glanced over. "Oh no! Here, use a Kleenex." Veronica dug one out of her bag and continued. "I found that scroll in one of those clay jars in the passageway. When I dropped the flashlight, the jar broke. It was inside, so I grabbed it."

"What is it?" her sister asked.

Veronica shrugged her shoulders. "I have no idea. Kinda forgot about it 'til just now."

She drove through the gatehouse as Nikki carefully slid the decaying ribbon from the edges and gently rolled out the scroll. Nestled inside was a medallion on a chain.

Veronica parked the car. "What is it?"

Nikki dangled the trinket, and Veronica snagged it for a closer inspection. "It's gold, Nik!"

"Is it a coin?"

"Maybe, it's old. There's a date: 325AD," Veronica said as she flipped it over.

"I wonder how much it's worth. Hey, I bet our buddy Christophe at the bank knows. Remember, he collects coins. We should take it to him. Plus, it's a good excuse for you to *see* him again..." she let her voice trail off coyly.

Veronica snapped her head up. "What is *that* supposed to mean?"

"It means I know you're crushin' on him!" Nikki taunted.

Veronica studied the medallion intently. "No, I'm not. Christ, Nik."

"Come on; I almost hadda put a bib around your neck to catch the drool."

"Just because he's handsome, it doesn't mean I'm interested," Veronica retorted.

"Yeah, whatever."

"I couldn't get involved with anyone right now. I have so much work...*we* have so much work to do over the next few months. There's no time for something like that," Veronica justified.

"Fine, but we can still bring this to him. Unless that would take up too much of your *precious* time."

"No, I mean, yeah. We could do that." Veronica switched gears. "Look at this paper."

The parchment revealed archaic writing and a crude diagram.

"It looks like a map," Nikki said.

"Like city streets with arrows pointing out a path," Veronica expanded.

"If those are roads, why do some end in circles?"

"Maybe they are cul-de-sacs?" Veronica offered.

"Huh, funny looking cul-de-sacs. Maybe that was the way they made them hundreds of years ago."

"What does that writing on the side say?"

"I don't know. It's not French. I think it's Latin. I can make out a couple words..." her sister began.

Veronica was interested. "Like what?"

"Like 'mort'. That means death."

"What's that?" Veronica pointed to a symbol on the end of one of the cul-de-sacs.

"Looks like an 'X'. Like on a treasure map!"

"No," Veronica answered. "It has a 'P' through the middle."

"What do you think it means?"

A white work truck pulled up alongside them.

"We'll figure it out later. They're here. It's time to get to work!" Veronica said as she folded up the scroll and shoved it in her bag. She slipped the medallion in her pocket as she got out of the car.

❧❧ ❖ ☙☙

The cleaning crew arrived first. Nikki instructed them in French, and they seemed reasonably efficient as they dusted and scrubbed. Veronica chose the large bedroom that overlooked the garden as the top priority. A plaque above the doorway read: THE QUEEN'S CHAMBER. She decided this was where she and Nikki would sleep that night.

The room had obviously been remodeled in the recent past. All the walls except for the one with the fireplace had been dry walled and painted a creamy peach. A brass bed still stood erect, though the girls both agreed that the mattress and box spring — no matter how good they looked — would have to go.

"Mice live in it. You just know they do, Vern," Nikki stated. Her sister nodded with agreement.

With the help of the maids, they maneuvered the mattress and box spring out the French doors that opened to the patio, through the overgrown garden, and into a large, rented dumpster.

"We'll use our sleeping bags and camp out on the floor," Veronica stated.

Nikki wrinkled her nose but held her tongue.

Connected to the Queen's Chamber was a large bathroom that was as big as the entire room they had at the inn. It had a definite Greek style, as ivy leaves were present in the design of the stone floor tiles, as well as on the glass that surrounded the standing shower. It also had a huge whirlpool bathtub and walk-in linen closet. The sink and fixtures, though grimy from abandonment, were decent enough and would be fine with a little cleaning. The toilet, complete with bidet, was in remarkably fine condition; however, lifting the seat revealed a nasty, black bowl void of water. The bathroom was Jack and Jill-styled with a door that led into an adjoining bedroom.

"Marie-Claire said this bathroom was actually once servant's quarters. When they remodeled twenty years ago, they converted it," Veronica commented to Nikki as they inspected the lavish vanity. "Since it's hardly been used, it shouldn't be any problem."

"Old plumbing is *always* a problem," an unfamiliar, gravelly voice said.

Both girls spun around to see a figure standing in the doorway.

The man was tall and gangly. Thinning black hair swept from the right to left side of his shiny head. He wore a grey button-up work shirt with the name "Clark" embroidered on it.

"I'm your plumber." He reached out to the girls with a lanky, filth-covered

82

hand.

Veronica lightly shook it and grimaced. "Nice to meet you. I'm Veronica, and this is Nikki."

Nikki shoved her thumbs in her pockets and nodded. He withdrew his hand and smiled with large, fake, horse teeth — obviously dentures gone wrong.

"I already checked out the septic tank, and I'm afraid I have some bad news," the man who smelled like sewage said.

Veronica caught her breath. "Yes?"

"No one has emptied it or flushed it out in twenty years, and it's seeping. It made a big sinkhole in the back of the castle. You need to get it replaced." His English was good, with an accent that included something besides French. *German?* Veronica thought. He spoke slowly — as if he had pebbles rolling around in the back of his throat — and he over enunciated each word.

"Great. How much is that gonna cost?" Veronica asked.

"Well, I need to see how extensive the damage is. If the pipes are rusted, it will be five thousand, four hundred and twenty-three euro. If the pipes are good and you only have to replace the tank, then three thousand, eighty-five euro. You also might need interior pipe work. That could run anywhere between eight thousand, two hundred euro to fifteen thousand, seven hundred." His horse teeth flashed inside a boxy smile.

"How long will it take?" Nikki groaned.

"Nine days if it's just the tank. Exterior pipes means another five days. Interior pipes would be an additional two weeks."

"So, there may not be any running water for *a month*?" Nikki whined.

"I didn't say that. The good news is that I can hook you up so that you can get fresh water for your laundry, your dishes, your douche," Clark replied.

Veronica was shocked. "Douche! Well, thank you so much for your concern about our feminine hygiene."

"He means shower. Douche is French for shower," Nikki said as she leaned into her sister's ear and giggled.

Clark's face flushed slightly. "And I can set you up with an alternate mode of excrement disposal."

Veronica paused and looked confused.

He continued. "That means I can set you up with an outhouse."

She scrunched up her nose. "We're planning on staying here *tonight*."

He shrugged. "No worries, I can set it up today!"

"Well, you certainly are the 'set up' man," Nikki chimed. "You might want to get on that as soon as possible. I drank a lot of coffee this morning."

Clark smiled, nodded, and dashed out the door. The plumber lived up to his word and had a bright blue, plastic outhouse erected within the hour.

❧❧✦❧❧

The rest of the day was spent accessing repairs, hauling out debris, and general cleaning of the Château. The electrician arrived on time and inspected the wiring and fuses. He only made a few adjustments, and the castle had power. The gasman filled the tank, inspected the lines, and made sure all the fixtures were up to code. Veronica was exceptionally pleased that everything was happening according to plan.

At five o'clock the cleaning crew left, and the plumber was the only worker remaining. Apparently, he discovered a valve that needed replacing, and it took longer than he thought. He found the girls in the kitchen as they relaxed after a long day of dusting, exploring, and sweeping mouse droppings.

"I'm no expert," he began, "but the bridge on the way up here looks unstable. You might want to have someone look at it before a city inspector does."

"Always the harbinger of good news, aren't you?" Nikki muttered.

"I just thought I'd let you know," the man with pitch under his fingernails said.

Veronica spoke up. "No, I'm glad you did. I just need to figure out who to call."

He flopped his head to the side. "My brother is a general contractor. He's licensed. I could probably set you up."

Veronica smiled thinly. "Great. *Set* that up. Right now, though, I'm exhausted. We'll see you tomorrow, Clark."

"Oh, tomorrow is Friday, my day off. I'll be back on Monday." He took his cue and made his way to the door.

"Of course you are off tomorrow...see you Monday," Veronica said as she stood to see him out.

He dwelled on the threshold of the front door for just a second. "Are you ladies really going to stay here...alone?"

Veronica's neck shivered as she nodded. "Of course we are."

"You are so far away from anyone else," the plumber continued.

"We'll be fine. Have a nice night, Clark."

"I could stay a little longer, just to make sure..."

Quick thinking Nikki cut him off. "We have boyfriends coming over soon. Yeah, a couple of big, strong American men are on their way."

Veronica shot a wild glance at her sister and swiftly confirmed the story with a bright smile. "Doug and Troy. They took a late flight and should be here aaa-ny minute."

Clark cast a crooked grin. "Well, you're in good hands then. Make sure you let the faucets run before using the water. There's a lot of rust in those pipes."

Veronica began pushing the door as he finally turned to leave.

"Will do," Nikki answered. "Thanks for 'setting us up'!"

Veronica spun to face her sister the second the door was shut. "He gives me the creeps! Nice improv about the 'boyfriends'."

"Yeah, I don't think he bought it, though. Make sure you lock the door," she instructed cryptically as she made her way back into the kitchen.

"Yeah, he's weird. I wouldn't wanna be stuck alone with him, but he seems sincere. I'm sure he's harmless," Veronica answered, casually latching the handle.

"*No* man is harmless," Nikki stated as she opened a bottle of wine.

The sisters settled in for their first night at Le Château du Feu Ardent.

Chapter 27

Father Michel's Story

Gaston-Elise stood in the shadows and waited for Father Michel. He plucked a handful of grapes from the vine as he noticed a robed figure dart from tree to tree. It was the priest. He didn't see Gaston-Elise and almost walked right into him.

"Careful, Father," the burly man said quietly.

Father Michel jumped. "My friend! There you are. Thank heaven."

"If you are thanking heaven just for seeing me, then I can't wait to hear your praises when I show this..." Gaston-Elise put his hand on the priest's shoulder and led him to a small shed.

"Where are you taking me?" the Father asked. He carried a burlap sack with a few meager rations.

"Shh...wait until we're inside." Gaston-Elise opened the door and lit an oil lamp that hung on the wall.

The building contained several round, wooden barrels and stacks of clay amphora. There was a shallow pit on one side, which was used to crush the grapes. Gaston-Elise walked to the far corner of the room and rolled up a straw mat from the floor. He revealed a large wooden trapdoor. It was several feet long and almost as many feet wide. He latched the door to a metal bar with a crooked end.

Father Michel watched with wonder. Stairs led down to a chamber that was lit from within. He heard movement — heavy, clomping footfalls — and a single animalistic snort.

"You have a friend waiting," Gaston-Elise said as he descended the stairs.

Father Michel watched him go down, unsure if he should follow or flee. The tunnel seemed foreboding and evil — as if entering it was walking down the throat of the devil himself.

"Come," his friend beckoned.

The priest wavered only a moment more, then gingerly followed.

A musty aroma filled the air. The priest coughed as he entered a narrow cavern. There stood a horse, small compared to most, but a full-grown horse nonetheless. On the floor was another oil lamp. The creature stomped the ground nervously.

Gaston-Elise patted the animal's neck and cooed, "It's okay, boy."

Father Michel was amazed. "What is a horse doing here? What is this place?"

"This is Lightning. He's for your journey, for you to ride, Father. And this place is a wine cellar, storage for all that sacramental wine. Just beyond these first caverns, though, is an ancient network of tunnels — catacombs to be exact — used as a crypt when the Romans ruled this land. They were also used as an emergency escape passage if the castle came under attack. Here, you will need this." Gaston-Elise handed Father Michel a piece of parchment. "I sketched a diagram of the tunnels. I've come here many times to get away, to explore...to contemplate. You must be careful and stay on the path I laid out. It is a maze, with some tunnels extending forever into the earth, while others dead-end into massive burial chambers."

Father Michel studied the labyrinth outlined on the paper. From this point, the tunnel continued straight for some ways and then branched out in two different directions. Then, each of those branches broke off, and so on. It reminded Father Michel of a tree.

"Where will this take me?"

"You will come out almost a half mile beyond the castle walls. The tunnel will open up into a cave at the foot of the mountains. From there, you can follow the trail to the pass and then to your parish." Gaston-Elsie pulled grapes out of his pocket and fed them to Lightning.

"This is too good to be true. I can be there and back by tomorrow night! No one will miss me in that amount of time. You're right. Thank heaven for you and for Lightning!" Father Michel stroked the animal.

"Lightning is small, but as his name suggests, he is fast. Once you are beyond the mountains, he will run like the wind. Just remember what I said about the tunnels; follow the arrows I've drawn for you, that's the safest path. Some of the passageways are narrow, and the ceilings become low. Lightning won't be able to walk through a small tunnel...I can tell you he wasn't too happy about coming down those stairs."

Father Michel reached under his tunic. "I have something." Out came the gold medallion he wore on a chain on his neck. "This is for you."

"Father, no, I don't want payment. I'm doing this because you are my friend." Gaston-Elise pushed the glistening necklace back toward him.

"Please, I insist. This is a small token. Even with all your help and Lightning, I still may not make it back, and if I don't, then you should have this. And if I do return, then this trinket's value will pale in comparison to the treasure I will have in my heart after returning to my church."

Gaston-Elise dangled the medallion. "This symbol, what is it?"

"It's an early version of the cross used in antiquity. The medallion is very old and very valuable."

"I'll take good care of it for you then."

"Thank you, my friend," Father Michel answered as he embraced Gaston-Elise heartily.

"I'll be here tomorrow's evening, waiting for you to return."

Father Michel led Lightning past the wine amphora stacked against the wall and into the bleak catacombs. "I know you will."

Chapter 28

Sebastian's Story
325 AD – When Rome Spread its Empire across the Barbaric Territories

overnor Fabius sat in the middle of the courtyard and was flanked on each side by three guards. He was a sturdy-looking man with a square head and protruding jaw. His weathered face bore witness to fifty years of life, though there were no traces of grey in his short, dark hair. It was molded around his head and tiny curls scalloped his forehead.

Next to the governor sat his wife, Esindra. She was a regal woman. Fine lines graced the corners of her eyes and framed the edges of crimson lips. She wore a creamy-white toga that clung to her curvaceous body. Beads of gold were woven into her hair, which was a salt and pepper mixture of brown, white, and grey, and piled up on the top of her head in a braided mass.

Sebastian stood before them. A guard was poised with a sword to his back. One quick move would result in instant death.

Cicero stepped forward and recited a list of offenses. "The man who stands here is Sebastian, the Cloaked Man. He is a magician and a murderer who took the life of a Roman commander. So evil and vile is he that just last night while in his cell, he committed an act of necromancy by killing a fellow prisoner to cast wicked spells and conjurations!"

Governor Fabius swiped his hand over his face and let his palm cradle his box-like chin. "Your conduct is intolerable. Culprits have spun to their death on the wheel for less. What do you say for yourself?"

Cicero chuckled and cocked his head to the side to get a better view of the Cloaked Man's reaction. The wheel was a brutal device. It looked harmless enough. A large, wooden, spoked wagon wheel suspended from an axel, mounted on a pedestal. The victim in question was tied to it, spread eagle. The wheel was spun repeatedly, first one way, then the other. The criminal was given his last chance to divulge his sins while he gagged on his own vomit. If he did try to speak, his words were often lost in the whirl of the wheel, the roar of the inevitable jeering crowd, and the gargling of his own stomach bile.

With no confession given, his legs and arms would be beaten with iron rods. His appendages were consequentially mutilated into a bloody mesh of broken bones and human meat. Once mangled, what remained of his arms and legs were interwoven into the spokes, twisted in and out to display the most unnatural position imaginable for a human body.

After being beaten beyond repair, the still living criminal would be mounted in an open space and left unattended for days. Slowly, he would die of thirst, sweltering in the hot sun and freezing in the night while birds and animals feasted on his exposed flesh.

Sebastian's shoulders hunched forward and his head hung, allowing stringy black hair to conceal his face. He spoke. "Governor, my fate is of little consequence compared to the providence of your rule. You have battle strategies to plan and a vast area of the Roman Empire to protect. Let me ask, how did yesterday's invasion unfold? I trust you heeded my warning and brought the cavalry through the swamp to avoid the ambush?"

The Governor shifted his chin to the left and let his hand drop to the armrest of the chair. "How did *you* know of the ambush yesterday?"

Before Sebastian had a chance to reply, the centurion took a hasty step forward. "He is raving mad, sir, his words are trickery, and the guards and I have learned to ignore his insane babbling."

Sebastian quickly seized his opportunity and addressed Cicero. "So, you ignored the information I gave you? You didn't even *warn* Governor Fabius of the impending danger? You put the governor's entire legion in jeopardy with your ignorance?"

Fire leapt from Cicero's eyes. "Hold your tongue, you lying villain!"

Sebastian's head lifted proudly, and his posture straightened. "Governor Fabius, I gave this man a warning of the battle in the wee hours of the morning yesterday. I told him that trenches were dug by the enemy and covered with brush so that the horses would fall through. The best strategy was to travel through the lowlands. The dry season has made the bogs easy to navigate. I implored him to warn you. He apparently did not and look at what his ignorance cost you. Your attack failed."

Cicero motioned to the guard at Sebastian's back. He obeyed the order and wedged the sword squarely under the Cloaked Man's shoulder blade.

"Make one more accusation on me, and I'll have you skewered like a hog!" Cicero bellowed.

Governor Fabius raised his fist in the air. "Enough, Cicero, I decide the fate of this man."

"I've witnessed this culprit's conniving ways firsthand, sir. His words are like spells, and he'll only enchant you with falsehoods."

Fabius lowered his arm and pointed a finger at Cicero. "I am wholly capable of deciphering his conniving ways, Cicero. Be silent now."

Cicero visibly flushed in anger and held back his words.

Divide and conquer, Sebastian thought as he continued. "Tragic as your recent loss was, you face an even graver catastrophe. An invasion is being planned with an army more numerous than you could ever imagine."

"How could you know these things?" Fabius asked.

"I have visions. You would be prudent to heed my advice. Not only for the sake of this land, but for the benefit of your lovely wife," Sebastian couched every word masterfully.

The woman sitting next to Fabius drew in a quick breath and cast a startled glare at Fabius. "He speaks of *me*?"

Fabius snagged her trembling hand. "Hush, Esindra..." he began but was cut short.

"Visions! Ha!" Cicero couldn't contain himself as he scoffed. "He is celled up with that Druid captive. That's where he got his *visions*. After murdering the old man, the Druid was probably so terrorized that he told Sebastian whatever he wanted to know."

"If the Druid finally broke down and gave up useful information, then Sebastian managed to do in one day what *you* haven't been able to accomplish in months," Fabius declared.

The centurion fell silent.

Sebastian beamed. "I can tell you more! However, I won't be able to help you if I'm dead..."

Fabius growled, "Don't attempt bargaining with me. I decide your fate. A stay of execution is all I guarantee. You'll live as long as you provide me with useful counsel. If you fail, your fate on the wheel is sealed."

The Cloaked Man nodded his head obediently. "I swear to provide you with insightful advice. I do need my copper bowl, fresh water, candles, a wooden spoon, a steely knife — all for divination."

Cicero scoffed. "No such luxuries will be given to you..."

"Then I hope you have more men whose entrails I can read," the Cloaked Man snapped.

"Make do with no bowls or spoons or entrails or consider yourself dead," the centurion retorted.

Governor Fabius interrupted, "He can have one item for his divination. Name it now. What be your choice, Sebastian?"

"The copper bowl. Filled with water. Yes, that will do."

The governor nodded. "Take him out of my sight," he ordered. "I want him brought to my chambers tomorrow at noon. If he tells me nothing of consequence, then his execution will take place immediately thereafter."

Sebastian was led out of the courtyard. Cicero followed with his dagger drawn, eager for the Cloaked Man to make one wrong move.

"Husband, why did he speak of *me*?" Esindra asked.

"It's nothing. Just words to intrigue us. The culprit is trying to bargain for his life and will say anything to save himself."

Esindra smiled meekly. "May I be there tomorrow when you meet with him?"

Fabius looked sideways at his wife. "If you must. Heed my warning, though, and believe nothing he says. Understood?"

Esindra conceded with a quick nod. The next criminal for trial was ushered before them, and they passively listened as a list of crimes was read.

Chapter 29

Veronica's Story

A mosquito disturbed her sleep. She heard a feathery buzz, which drew her closer to lucidity. It took a moment before Veronica remembered where she was. The Queen's Chamber was dark and only a thin beam of moonlight peeked through the patio doors. The hostile insect buzzed again. No, it wasn't a bug. It was her phone — buried deep in her messenger bag and set on vibrate. Sleepy fingers fumbled for it. She clicked it on and pulled it slowly to her ear as it buzzed again.

"Hello?" she squeaked.

"Bonjour, Veronica! You are at the Château. How do you like it?" chimed a familiar French-accented voice.

"Marie-Claire, it's fantastic; just like you described! We started working today. We got a lot done, mostly cleaning. The plumber found a problem with the septic system, but he's going to fix it. We got a porta potty to use in the meantime," Veronica answered.

"Port-a-prêt...what?"

"Porta potty...an outhouse," Veronica said with a chuckle.

"Goodness, you are not unconvinced, I hope," Marie-Claire replied.

Veronica stifled a giggle. "No, I'm not *inconvenienced* at all."

"The money from the account will be enough?"

"Plenty! How much should I spend on...?" Veronica started.

Marie-Claire interrupted, "Use the money as you see fit, for anything that you need. You can keep the receipts, yes? I will see everything when we meet."

"When we meet," Veronica repeated. "So, I'll see you soon?"

"Oui. Soon. Everything seems to be going just as planned."

"I'm so glad you're happy!"

"Of course, my dear, you are the answer to our dreams," Marie-Claire gushed as the phone began to crackle.

"My cell phone is bugging out on me," Veronica said.

"Pardon?"

"My cell phone..." Veronica began as Marie-Claire's voice faded in and out. "I can't hear you very well."

"Oui, I am very well," Marie-Claire said.

"My phone...yes, I am very well, too, but the phone..." Veronica's voice trailed off as she realized the connection was lost.

She looked at the display and scowled at the solitary bar. As she slid the phone back into her bag, she saw the diary. She retrieved the ancient book, cuddled next to her sister, and read as morning broke.

Chapter 30

Journal Intime

 great fear has spread across the countryside. It is terrifying! Revolutionaries are attacking entire families as they lay sleeping, pulling them from their beds, never to be seen again. Peasants have burned down the houses of their Lords, and it is rumored that many of the nobles of Paris have fled France all together. We have not heard from Agathe in days, and I pray every hour for her and her family's safety.

Henri says The National Assembly is trying to make reforms to appease the revolutionaries, and though I hope for an agreeable outcome, I have little faith one will come.

I have not been feeling well. The midwife tends to me several times a day. She says I keep her much busier than any other pregnant woman she has had the pleasure of tending. To help calm my nerves, at the request of my husband, she gives me a cloudy green tonic. Henri says it is a special medicine he bought from a traveling physician, talented in the art of apothecary, named Dr. Ordinaire. He rides on horseback across the French countryside distributing the all-purpose elixir, and calls it absinth.

The absinth humors me with gentle warmth that escalates into joy and rhapsody. Indeed, I have felt such delight that I can sit totally blissful for hours without bothering anyone! The pain in my back disappears, I become neither hungry nor thirsty, and Henri says I am easier to manage, as no one must constantly tend to my needs. All able-bodied servants can focus on preparing for the potential onslaught rather than attending to me.

At times the absinth fills my eyes with divine visions. I see dancing lights that whirl and twirl around me like angels waltzing around and around. As they circle me, I am overfilled with glee and often burst aloud with roaring jollity.

Henri says, "I am having 'fits of fancy'." He is entirely satisfied when I drink the absinth and assures me that, "It is better to be filled with mirth than fear."

The absinth is truly a wonder tonic designed to abate all ills. I look forward to its bitter taste, muddled with a hint of water, and a dab of precious sugar, which is brought to me every night. It erases all my worries and makes my fears seem like trivialities. As I drift off into the enchanted land of absinth, I feel secure and coddled, as if enveloped in a warm, green blanket.

Josette-Camille

July 22nd, 1789

A small amount of water expelled from my body yesterday. The midwife is very concerned and instructed me to stay in bed. I must remain lying down and cannot get up at all. Since the threat of attack looms at any moment, Henri decided I should take a room in the keep. If marauders do lay siege, then I am safe in the most fortified part of the castle.

The room chosen for me is the lowest of the tower chambers. It is small, cylindrical, and has no windows. With no natural light, I am forced to always have a candle or lantern burning. The smoke grows thick in the stifling room and makes my eyes water.

I have only a bed, a small stool I use as a table, my journal, and inkwell. Since I am confined to bed, I have my nightgown and bonnet, but no other clothing. All my gowns, wigs, and jewelry are left in the wardrobe next to my boudoir, which I have been told has been transformed into a temporary armory, so we have a place to store weapons in case we're attacked.

Henri was here with me earlier. He held my hand and rubbed my legs and promised everything would be okay. He noticed my inkwell and journal and said that I should write poetry to pass the time. He says it will bring peace to my nervous mind.

Indeed, one of the only things I can do is write. I sit here now with the stark light of one candle glowing over the page.

I find myself a-wondering about one thing that's mine
I will always have tomorrow
I will always have the time
The sun is waiting outside these walls
It will forever shine

There is an odor in this room. It was faint at first, and I thought perhaps it was my own body as the water that passed through my loins was foul-smelling. I was cleaned thoroughly earlier though, yet I can still detect the pong — pungent, sweet, like decaying vegetables in the garden, but muskier, like a wild animal. It makes my head ache, and I try to cover my nose with the blanket, but it seeps through anyway.

Flowers! Oh how wonderful fresh flowers at my bedside would be! They would mute the stench and brighten this dreary hole. Upon drinking my nightly tonic, I close my eyes and imagine the garden. Sitting under a canopy of apple blossoms, we toss sparkling boules across the grass to pass the time on a lazy spring day. Yes, flowers would remind me of the garden and make this dingy place more bearable.

Someone stirs near the foot of my bed, and I whisper, "May I have flowers brought to my bedside? Something fresh and fragrant from the garden?" There is no answer though. I contemplate turning my head to see which maid ignores my request, but a sudden whiff of decay overwhelms me. I can't write anymore. I need to bury my head under the covers and wait for the accosting odor to pass.

Josette-Camille

Chapter 31

The Pagans' Story
182 CE – the Ancient Ritual that Unleashed It

It was dusk on the evening of the Spring Solstice. The procession plodded across the rolling hillside as it did every year for the ceremony. The western sky was a fading array of pink, orange, and blue. Occasionally, a mourning dove emitted a velvety coo.

On the other horizon, cobalt already dominated the sky, and a few early stars flickered on. Several small dwellings, shacks made of straw, sticks, mud and bones, dotted the shadowy hills.

The procession was led by a brawny, naked man adorned with a buck's head perched on top of his own. He represented *strength* for the ceremony and had killed the stag earlier with just his hands. The animal's rack of horns was smeared with rusty blood, drying as it dripped in the cool, spring night. Meaty remnants of the deer's flesh draped down the man's back. Insects that had not yet succumbed to the chill of the night buzzed in circles around it.

Behind him walked three young men who represented *virility*. They each carried woven baskets filled with flour, mistletoe, roses, and apple blossoms. They wore swags of thinly-knit fabric around their hips, knotted on one side like a sarong.

Several older women followed, walking single file. These were the priestesses, and they portrayed *wisdom*. The first one was garbed in a black robe. A wreath of mangled twigs rested on top of her white head. It matted down her hair, making it look like a dome. The rest of her hair was wiry and sprayed around her face like a mane. She was known as the "Hag" and was the highest priestess, the oldest and the wisest. The rest of the women wore similar robes, but theirs were grey with heavy hoods that covered their heads. They chanted softly, almost whispering. The words were undecipherable. Though they kept a constant rhythm, each seemed to be reciting her own verse, like a glossolalia-ish version of *Row, Row, Row Your Boat*.

Two lines of young adults, a dozen in all, were at the end of the procession. These were the lesser priests. Several held torches, a few carried bundles, and a couple clutched chipped basalt knives. A goat, pulled on a leash, trailed behind them all.

The procession approached a dwelling made of dry, muddy grass, woven through a stick frame. In front of its doorway, an animal skin was stretched across wooden stakes, and a fire pit smoldered with wispy, swirling sparks.

A woman hunched over the smoky remains. She poked a stick into the glimmering embers, then seared the hide with the white-hot end. Upturned eyes, outlined with soot, wearily watched the procession approach. One side of her brow twitched in unison with the chanting. She cowered low, focusing on the stag-headed man. The woman's lower lip quivered as if she was about to speak, but only two faint sighs came out.

The chanting stopped. From behind the stag-headed man emerged the Hag.

She glowered at the crouching woman and then pulled back layers of animal skin hanging over the dwelling's doorway.

Inside, a man and his son cowered. The boy's tear-streaked face burrowed into his father's chest. The man crooked his neck to whisper in his son's ear. The lad grunted fiercely, as if trying to block out his father's words.

The Hag entered, followed by a priest with a torch, and two priestesses with a bucket of water and a bundle of linen. The three women sat in a circle, and the father nudged his son to stand in the middle.

He was a wild-looking boy, with matted blond curls and wise, darting eyes. His age was hard to determine because his face had the features of a lad who was at least eighteen summers old, but his physique was that of adolescent.

The women pulled off his tattered tunic and cast it aside. They untied a leather strap from the boy's waist and his britches easily slid to the dirt floor. He stood naked while the priestesses washed him. After he was clean, they swathed gauzy linen around their pledge, and led him outside.

The priestesses showed the newcomer his place in line, right behind the stag-headed man. The boy shivered, nodded, and acquiesced. As the procession moved, he despondently followed.

The father and mother stood by the smoldering fire pit and watched them march away. "Bevin is smart and resourceful. He'll be among those who come back," he said to her.

The woman stopped trembling long enough to let out a long, woeful wail, causing the cooing mourning doves to fall silent in respectful homage to her cry.

Chapter 32

Father Michel's Story

Lightning allowed Father Michel to lead him through the tunnels, though the horse protested occasionally by standing still and stomping one foot. The animal's eyes darted nervously. Father Michel patted his neck while feeding him the grapes that Gaston-Elise shoved in his pocket.

The walls were carved out of limestone. In certain areas, Father Michel could see crumbling sections. As he passed one particularly decrepit passageway, his nose was impressed with the foul odor of decay. Lightning reacted as well by hurrying past the entrance of the offending corridor.

Father Michel followed the arrows on the map precisely, stopping at every twist and turn to make sure he was on course. He came to another fork and abruptly halted. Something stirred in the corridor behind them. It was a rustling — a scurrying. *Bats?* Lightning's nostrils flared and snorted.

Father Michel walked faster, and Lightning eagerly kept stride with him. At one point, the steed stopped short and neighed uneasily at nothing in particular. Father Michel cooed softly and offered him more grapes. Even these juicy morsels did not calm the spooked beast.

A disquieting thought occurred to the priest. Perhaps someone saw them sneak into the grape shack. Were Cardinal Thibaut's guards following him?

Then he relaxed. Maybe it was Gaston-Elise...trailing behind just to make sure we are safe. Father Michel eased his pace. Surely, it was Gaston-Elise. What a magnificent friend!

He once again caught a whiff of the disturbing fragrance. He pondered the situation. *Why would Gaston-Elise risk following behind?* The stench consumed the dank air. Lightning neighed, and Father Michel felt a sheet of terror wrap around him. He started to run.

Something pursued.

He heard a grumbling...growling...yes, something growled behind him. He did not turn around. *A dog perhaps...was it Cardinal Thibaut's hunting dog?* It got louder, a cross between grunting and labored breathing, ten, maybe fifteen, feet away.

The lantern cast shadows on the walls aside him. Father Michel saw its form come up behind him. It was low to the ground, with no definite shape, just twisted, scrawny legs that arched over the top of it unnaturally as it ran. It reminded Father Michel of a cross between an elongated jackrabbit and a giant daddy long-legged spider.

Lightning was ahead of the priest and showed no sign of slowing. The animal unwittingly kicked up debris in its wake. Another turn in the corridor was just ahead. Lightning veered right. Father Michel held the map in front of him as he ran. He tried to keep it steady, but it bobbed up and down vigorously. He came to the next corridor. Unable to read the map, he blindly followed the steed through the twisting tunnels.

Chapter 33

Dorothée's Story

Dorothée screamed. The cry came out flimsy at first, merely a raspy groan, and became louder as she struggled to call out. The creature recoiled at the sound of her voice. She screamed again and did indeed perceive it to back away slightly. She cried out over and over in rapid, shrill bursts. The beast inched back with each cry until it almost completely blended in with the shadows.

She felt something cold on the back of her neck. She spun her head around. Plump fingers extended toward her through the crevice in the door. Dorothée shrieked. It was Patricia. Her lady-in-waiting peered at her with pitying eyes that urged her to be still.

Dorothée kept howling.

"We're here. Calm down. We're going to get you out of there," Patricia said soothingly.

Dorothée screeched again.

"My lady, it's okay. Claude is trying to unjam the lock. And the smithy is on the way with tools," Patricia said while Dorothée continued to scream.

"She *has* gone mad!" Claude grumbled as he fumbled with the latch.

From behind him, the dark haired boy and girl from the kitchen rushed in. On their heels was the stable boy. Breathlessly, he spat, "The smithy has tools, and he's coming. André-Benoit just arrived. They are both on their way!"

Claude held his tongue. No more acerbic comments would be heard from him in Lord André-Benoit's presence. He pulled the latch to no avail. Dorothée kept screaming.

Patricia attempted to comfort Dorothée. She reached inside to hold her hand. The air was hot and sticky.

Dorothée latched onto Patricia's arm. Her lady-in-waiting almost recoiled at the touch. Dorothée's flesh was hot, almost scalding, like tender meat that had just been removed from boiling water.

The smithy and André-Benoit entered the chamber. "What is going on here?" the lord of the manor demanded.

Patricia looked up at André-Benoit's flushed face. He still wore his riding cape. "Lady Dorothée is trapped," she answered. "The door is jammed, and we can't get it open."

Dorothée kept screaming.

"Stand back," the smithy commanded. He was indeed a strapping fellow with muscular arms that held a large hammer. His upper lip lifted into a snarl as he rammed it against the latch. Claude moved to the side, and Patricia sat back as far as she could while still holding Dorothée's hand.

The hammer delivered a mighty blow. It rattled against the wooden door, but it did not budge. He swung again with even more force, and Patricia had to duck and let loose of Dorothée's hand to avoid being struck. She shrieked again and again; sharp, short stabbing caterwauls, like a crazed seabird guarding a nest. The bolt on the latch remained intact.

"Check to see if it's loose," André-Benoit ordered.

Dorothée screeched.

"What?" the smithy asked.

Dorothée squealed.

"See if it's loose," André-Benoit repeated.

Claude reached out for the bolt just as the smithy drew the hammer back for another stroke. "Careful, man!" he warned as he stopped his swing in midair.

Dorothée wailed.

Andre-Benoit lunged next to Patricia and squinted to see inside the crevice. "Dorothée, calm down...I'm here. Everything is going to be all right, but you must stop that yowling. We can't hear with you carrying on so."

Dorothée glared at her husband through the thin hole in the door. Her red, wet hair hung in curly, matted tendrils across her forehead. Her eyes were frozen wide; she did not blink. Her bottom lip quivered each time she hesitated in between screams. For a moment, her face softened and became coherent. Her mouth began to form a word rather than a cry, but then she stopped, turned her head abruptly, and let out yet another shriek.

The smithy swung again and the latch was forced open. "I think I got it!" he cried and tried to pull the door open. It still would not budge.

Dorothée screamed.

André-Benoit jiggled the bolt. It was indeed back far enough, and the door should have opened with ease. He grabbed the handle and pulled with all his strength. It didn't move. Claude slammed his shoulder into the door in an attempt to jar it open. The smithy burrowed his fingers between the edge of the door and the jamb, pulling along with André-Benoit.

Dorothée shrieked.

André-Benoit suddenly turned to the stable boy who was standing back, taking in the horrific scene. "Run to the barn, under the floorboards in the feed chamber, you'll find a key that opens this door. Hurry!"

Dumbfounded, the boy nodded and then sprinted off.

Dorothée bellowed a low, mournful sob.

The men continued to batter on the door, but it proved impenetrable.

On the other side, Dorothée rasped, "Hurry! You have to hurry!"

"Be patient, just a little bit longer, the boy is getting the key," Patricia said in a voice so sweet and calm it seemed surreal.

"It's coming closer! Oh my Mother Mary and Lord Jesus!" the lady cried.

"What is she talking about?" André-Benoit asked. "What's in there?"

The smithy chuckled between swings. "Spiders and mice 'tis all. Nothing else been in there for years."

The boy bounded through the door with the key. "Here!" he exclaimed.

The smithy grabbed it and thrust it into the hole. It clicked.

Dorothée squawked.

The door unlocked.

Dorothée bawled.

Claude and the smithy pushed the massive door wide open. A gust of heat, as if from an oven, rushed out.

Dorothée cowered on the floor. Her red hair practically melted into her crimson dress. She reached out to André-Benoit while still in the throes of screaming.

He lunged at her, grabbing her outstretched hand, and wrapped his arm around her in one swift movement. He scooped her up in his arms and carried her out of the tower room. She clung to him like a child.

He sat her on the floor and crouched down. Patricia was also by her side in an instant. Dorothée became silent. She stared into André-Benoit's eyes like an infant. Finally, she spoke. "There is something...inside there...an animal. It wanted to ravage me."

André-Benoit looked up at Claude and the smithy. Claude grabbed a lantern and swung it inside the room. He took a few steps forward and the smithy followed him.

Shards of broken furniture, glass, and fragments of animal bones littered the floor. There was a wooden hatch on the wall directly across from them. It looked like half a stable door but had no handle. Two decrepit cots sat against the concave wall and several moth-eaten blankets lay crumpled on the floor.

Claude walked deeper into the room and kicked one of the blankets. A puff of dust momentarily clouded the room. He bent over with the lantern. Folded within the creases of the linen was a ball of white fur. It was a nest. It wriggled with life as naked, pink babies squeaked and twitched at the intrusion.

"Rats," he said to the smithy who was hovering in the doorway.

The smithy passed the message onto André-Benoit. "She must 'a seen a rat."

"No, it wasn't a rat. It was too big to be a rat," she insisted.

"Rats get big," Claude said as he emerged from the tower room. "There is a nest in there, and by the size of it, I'd say it was made by a big fat mama rat. She probably didn't appreciate company...lucky she didn't take a bite out of you."

Dorothée shuddered. "No, it was not a rat. It was black, and it had a long face with sharp claws. But the claws were almost like... hands... with long nails. It had matted fur, and it was festering...and it stank. It kept crawling closer..." her voice trailed off. She began to sob. Patricia stroked her hair. André-Benoit held her tighter.

"Yes," Claude began quietly. "That's a rat."

André-Benoit carefully wiped the tears from Dorothée's face; color was beginning to return to her cheeks. "What were you doing in there? Why are you even *in* this part of the castle?"

Dorothée methodically shook her head and her shoulders from side-to-side. "There's a messenger, and he needs a place to sleep tonight...and I thought...I thought I'd find a room for him in here."

"Some parts of this castle were not meant for a lady to see. Come now; let me carry you to bed. Girl, go fetch some tea to calm her. Patricia, make sure her gown doesn't drag under my feet." André-Benoit lifted his bride. He turned to the smithy before stepping out of the room. "Smithy, make sure that latch doesn't stick again...we actually *do* have a guest who will be staying here soon."

Chapter 34

Veronica's Story

Veronica's fuzzy dog-faced slippers shuffled into the kitchen. She found Nikki there, swiveling her hips back and forth while French pop music blared from a twenty-year-old transistor radio. Fruit, left over from the day before, was on a plate in the center of the table along with a few pieces of bread that had been toasted over the gas stove's flame.

"What is all this?" Veronica asked.

Nikki turned quickly. "Good morning. I made breakfast."

Veronica beamed. "I see that. It looks wonderful."

"I thought you deserved a little extra time in bed. Plus this way, we can eat and head straight into town and go *shopping*!" She sang the last word like an opera singer.

"I have to wait for the cleaning crew and..." Veronica began.

"Already done! They arrived about twenty minutes ago. I sent them to work on the library. That massive room should take *all* day to clean. So, you and I can enjoy our breakfast, get dressed, and *go shopping*!" Nikki exclaimed.

Veronica cupped her hands around the warmth of a cup filled with tea. It was old, porcelain, and chipped, a relic found in the cupboards. She grinned affectionately at her little sister. "Okay, we can go shopping. But remember, we have to get things for the Château. That means we are going to furniture stores, appliance stores, hardware stores..."

"I know, I know. At least we'll go to the downtown shops, right?"

"I guess..."

"Plus, I was thinking, maybe we could swing by the bank..." Nikki suggested.

"Why? We have checks and a bank card; we don't need cash."

"We need to see Christophe the hottie banker."

"Would you stop already with Christophe!" Veronica blushed.

"But you said you wanted to show him that coin we found," Nikki explained.

"Oh, the *coin*!"

"Why? Do you wanna see him for some *other* reason?" Nikki chided.

"I forgot about the coin. Yeah, we can stop by the bank," she nonchalantly rolled her shoulder. Slinging her bag strap over it, she continued, "Grab your shoes and let's go!"

❧ ❖ ☙

The sisters spent the rest of the morning shopping. They found an appliance store and were fortunate enough to have a new refrigerator and stove delivered later in the afternoon. A washer and dryer would come early next week, along with a microwave, a television, and various small appliances.

They had an early lunch at a quaint café and then searched the various shops on the quiet streets of Amboise. While Veronica studied armoires in an antique shop, Nikki slinked into a different store, an upscale boutique, and purchased several pairs of two-inch heeled mink slippers, a silk bathrobe, and an expensive bottle of French perfume.

After an hour of meandering through the town, they walked up the steps of the bank just as Christophe was walking out.

"Christophe!" Nikki exclaimed as he passed by.

His head was hung low, and he looked up in surprise. "Ah! Mademoiselle Nikki and Veronica!" He took Veronica by the hand and held her gaze a moment. "How wonderful to see you again so soon. I am just on my way out for a late lunch. Is there something I could help you with first?"

"Oh, if you are on your way to lunch, don't let us interrupt you," Veronica stated.

"You could never be an interruption to me. I'm always at your service. Hungry? Please, join me ladies!"

"Naw, we just ate," Veronica answered.

Nikki cast her sister a disapproving glance and then prompted her. "We have something to show you."

Veronica obediently reached into her pocket. She dug deep but her hand came out empty. She then opened her cavernous purse and rooted through its depths. Nikki smiled patiently. Christophe cocked his head curiously.

"I can't seem to find it now," Veronica said as she yanked out a hairbrush, cell phone, and a tube of lipstick in an effort to reveal its contents.

"Find what?" Christophe asked.

"An old coin on a chain. You said you collected coins, so we figured we'd show it to you," Nikki answered.

Veronica's hand discovered the scroll. She clutched it, unsure if she wanted to reveal that part of the mystery to him yet. Nikki snatched the ancient parchment.

"This paper was wrapped around the coin when we found it," Nikki offered as she held the paper for Christophe to inspect.

A concentration line furrowed between his eyebrows.

"I think I left the coin at the Château," Veronica finally said.

"So, you found the coin and a map together? How interesting! I'd love to look at it. Since you ladies turned me down for lunch today, how about joining me another time?"

"I dunno. We're just so busy working..." Veronica mumbled.

Christophe wasn't easily deterred. "Americans really do work far too much! What do you say to lunch on Sunday? Surely, you aren't working on Sunday?"

"Even though none of the workers are there Sunday I gotta organize..."

Her sister cut her off. "Sunday sounds like a great day to get together. We'd love to! When and where do you want to meet?" the adventurous sister proclaimed.

"I could entertain you with a Sunday tradition. Do you like al fresco?" he asked.

Veronica looked confused. "Drinking soda?"

Nikki gripped her sister's shoulder, leaned in and explained, "No, eating outside." Then to Christophe, "Yes, that would be great."

Christophe chuckled as Veronica blushed. "Wonderful. Ladies, meet me at one o'clock by the little white chapel on the outskirts of town by Rue Eglise. Wear some comfortable clothes, and I'll have a surprise for you."

"Sounds exciting," Nikki mussed.

"Great! See you then and don't forget the coin!" Christophe instructed as he fought to catch Veronica's gaze. She held her eyes down and reluctantly looked up at him. He smiled broadly. His large crooked nose flared, and she couldn't help but smile in return.

Christophe walked off leaving the two Americans standing on the bank steps.

Nikki spoke first. "Why do you get all weird like that?"

"Weird like what?"

"He was being nice, and you act like such a bitch."

"I did not! I just have a job to do and don't have time for extracurricular activities."

"Extracurricular activities...you sound like my principal. You know, making friends won't kill you. Plus, I'm dying to do something fun while we're here. Maybe one of these nights we could go out for a while. Hit a nightclub or see a show?"

"We'll see how much work we get done in the next few weeks."

Nikki rolled her eyes behind her sister's back as they made their way down the cobblestone street. Veronica's phone rang. She still clutched it in her hand and answered it immediately.

"Hi Mom!" she enthused into the receiver. "It's Mom," she reiterated to Nikki.

Nikki nodded.

"Yes, we're in France *right* now. Walking down the street in Amboise." She paused and continued. "Yes, I am decorating a castle. A real castle that dates back to the dark ages...Oh yes, she's a big help...yes...yes...no, not at all...yeah, I was wondering about Dr. Jacob Andrews. Do you know him...yeah, nightmares. I had nightmares?" She waited a long while and finally said, "I hardly remember anything...he did? No, I'm not having them again...really...okay, hang on, let me get something to write with."

"Can I talk to her?" Nikki asked while Veronica fumbled in her bag. Veronica handed her the phone, and the other daughter chatted with their mother for a few moments. Veronica found a pen and paper. "Ask Mom for the name and number."

Nikki recited, "Dr. Steven Sandbourne, 310-555-1064." She looked at her sister inquisitively. Veronica shakily wrote it down.

"Mom wants to know if you are *sure* you're not having nightmares again," Nikki asked as she pulled the phone slightly away from her cheek.

Veronica shook her head and concentrated on the busy city street.

"Okay, Mom, gotta go. We'll send you something French and fabulous in the mail. Love you, too. Bye!" Nikki clicked off the phone. "What's that about? Who's that Doctor?"

"She said Dr. Sandbourne worked with Dr. Andrews while I was going through my therapy for night terrors. She said Sandbourne said to call him if I *ever* have bad dreams again...ever. Mom didn't go into all the details, just something about an argument between the two doctors because they couldn't agree on how to treat me. She had to pick one, and Dr. Sandbourne was the winner. She said she hasn't heard from Dr. Andrews in years."

"Sounds like a plot line from *The Real Desperate Housewives*. Are you sure Mom isn't getting too wrapped up in her trash TV again?"

"No, she was serious and really worried I was having nightmares. You know, I don't even have dreams...or if I do, I don't remember 'em. Once in a while, on very rare occasions, I have the vaguest images when I wake up. I struggle so hard to hold on to them, but they always escape me. I never remember."

"You don't dream at *all*? Not even that you are flying or standing naked in front of a hundred people?" Nikki inquired.

Veronica grunted. "Nope. Never dreamed of flying or being naked. Who the hell dreams they're naked anyway?"

"I do — all the time. It's the strangest thing. I'm in a crowd of people, like at a concert, or a busy street, or even in my classroom, and then whoosh! I'm suddenly stark naked, and I can't find my clothes! I run around like crazy looking for them. Then I try to find a blanket, someone's jacket, anything to cover up with, but there's nothing around. And no one will help me. They all just stand and stare."

"Sounds awful!" Veronica sympathized.

"Not really, because then they all start clapping and cheering," Nikki quipped.

"You are so fucking vain," Veronica said flatly as her sister chortled.

"Why don't you call this Sandbourne dude?"

"No point in that. I don't dream, so I have nothing to say to him," Veronica stated as she opened the door to the little orange car.

"You know, I have these dreams about trains a lot, too. They go chugging into these long, dark tunnels..."

Veronica ignored her sister and started he car. Nikki giggled as they drove back to the castle.

Chapter 35

Father Michel's Story

Lightning's hooves kicked up a spray of dust and pebbles in the preacher's eyes. Between the dirt and the darkness, Father Michel was unable to see. Something behind him gnarled, and the heat of its breath radiated against the back of the priest's cassock. He leapt forward, tripped, and then fell.

It snagged the priest's heel with its claw and pulled him back, dragging the holy man across the ground. At the same time, Father Michel ducked under Lightning's hooves and barely dodged being trampled.

He lay on the ground with his arms over his head. He peeked out and looked back to see it lashing out with a slobbering, putrid maw. A split second before the creature's teeth could sink into the man's ankle the horse kicked up its back legs and sent the foul beast flying into the depths of the cavern.

Lightning lunged ahead at full speed. At the same time, the priest made a desperate jump forward and managed to clutch the saddle blanket. Pulled like a rag doll, Father Michel had no choice but to hold on for his life as the horse raced through the tunnel.

He looked back to see it pursuing. Gangly legs with two knee joints rather than one arched over its body and thrust it forward in one long leap. It landed inches from the priest's flailing feet and made a grab for one. However, the horse was faster and dragged Father Michel swiftly out of its way.

As the creature prepared to jump again, Father Michel threw the lantern. It splattered oil between them and erupted in vicious flames. The thing paused on the other side of the small inferno. It was clearly exposed in the fiery light, and the priest beheld the visage of its grotesque, ungodly form for a split second before Lightning skirted around a bend.

Horse and man suddenly emerged into the freshness of the nighttime air. Father Michel jumped to his feet, and Lightning paused just long enough for him to mount.

The priest whispered into the ear of the steed. "I don't know what that was, friend, but I am sure glad you were able to run faster than it!"

Despite Gaston-Elise's warning to not ride Lightning through the jagged mountain rocks, Father Michel quickly maneuvered the steed in an effort to get as far away as possible from the unholy creature in the cavern.

Chapter 36

The Children's Story

Isabelle woke to a flash of sunlight. It was morning, and someone had opened the barn door. She and her brother were lying in a far corner of the stable they had crept into the night before, under a large pile of straw. Buried, only their little faces were exposed.

A few goats, several chickens, and a small horse lived in pens near the front. The stable wall separated the children from them. Though Isabelle couldn't see the animals from her perspective, she could hear them chewing and grunting as someone poured slop into a trough. Looking over, she saw Louis still sleeping. She carefully covered his face with straw and then wriggled low to bury herself as completely as possible.

The "someone" was humming; it sounded like a woman. Isabelle waited patiently. Eventually, she heard the barn door creek again, the light diminished, and the humming stopped. They were safe. She nudged her brother. He awoke coughing with his eyes red and swollen. He sneezed several times, and Isabelle tried to hush him.

"Quiet. Someone was just in here. She might come back."

Louis stifled his next sneeze by burying his nose in his shirt. Isabelle rubbed her hand across his back until the fit subsided. Then, while the animals feasted, she got up, grabbed a bucket, and scooped some water from the horses' drinking trough. They each took a long draught and washed their faces.

"What are we going to do now?" Louis asked.

"As soon as I'm sure that lady is gone, we'll sneak out and make our way back to the river and follow it through the mountain pass. I'm so hungry...do you have anything more to eat?"

He pulled two pieces of jerk beef out of his satchel and handed her one. They each chewed the tough meat for breakfast. Once finished, they quietly crept to the door. Isabelle was about to push it open when they heard voices.

The children scrambled back to the pile of straw and quickly covered themselves again. The door opened. Isabelle frantically made sure that her brother was completely hidden before lying back and pulling handfuls of straw onto her torso. Footfalls echoed in the small barn.

The chickens clucked nervously as she heard a man's deep voice. "We have to look everywhere, in every building."

"Well, you won't find anyone in here but animals. I just fed them," a woman's voice answered.

Another man with a thin voice said, "Who are you looking for? Are they criminals...thieves...murderers?"

Isabelle shimmied her body to bury herself as deep as possible.

"Children, actually," the deep male voice answered. "We're looking for a little boy and a young lady."

"Children!" the woman exclaimed. "Why are *inquisitors* looking for children?"

There was a moment of silence. Isabelle sat perfectly still, satisfied that she and her brother were completely hidden from view.

The inquisitor finally spoke. "The children are relatives of Lord Pierre. He wants to find his beloved niece and nephew and offers a reward to he who finds them."

"A reward...how much is the reward?" the man with the thin voice inquired, his tone eager.

"What's back there?" the inquisitor asked.

"Just straw bedding for the animals," the woman answered.

Louis squeezed his eyes shut and tried not to breathe. Dust irritated his nose and throat. The voices now seemed to only be a few feet away.

"So, how much did you say the reward was?" the thin-voiced man asked again.

There was another pause, then the answer. "Three gold coins."

"A goodly amount," the man with the thin voice responded.

Louis' nose burned. He struggled to keep from sneezing by taking shallow breaths.

"What is that?" the inquisitor asked.

There was silence. Isabelle held her breath while her brother struggled for air.

"I don't know," the thin-voice replied.

"It's a satchel buried in the straw," the inquisitor observed.

Louis' chest tightened up. Isabelle felt a warm gush of terror.

"That...is...my bag I use to pick fruit," the woman's voice said. "I wondered where I left it. I picked the horse some apples the other day. Must have forgotten it."

"*You* picked apples for the horse?"

"Yes. I picked some from the wild trees near the foothills."

Isabelle and Louis could feel the straw shuffle; someone stepped right next to them.

"I'll bring it in the house," the woman said. She was practically standing on Louis. He shifted slightly and took a quick, raspy gasp of air as she swooped down and grabbed the satchel.

The inquisitor began to leave. "If you see them, let us know at once. Lord Pierre is gravely concerned for their safety."

"Of course," the woman answered as she followed him.

Louis drew in a quick, deep breath. He held it for a moment, and then it exploded in an uncontrollable sneeze.

The entire barn fell silent.

"Excuse me!" the woman announced. "Tad of a cold."

Louis struggled to keep a second sneeze under control.

"Be well," the inquisitor said as he dwelled a moment in the doorway, finally nodded, and allowed the couple to lead him out.

Chapter 37

Veronica's Story

Saturday morning. The Château was quiet except for the noise Veronica made as she unpacked the contents of various bags and boxes from the shopping expedition the day before. Pots, pans, dishware, silverware, and glasses clicked, clanked, and echoed against the stone walls. She felt energized. Her apartment back home had a tiny kitchenette. *So, this is what it feels like to have a gourmet kitchen!*

The new refrigerator was in place — a huge, stainless steel monolith with high-tech buttons on the door. The stove, also stainless, matched perfectly, and both appliances offered a startling contrast against the organic wood table and curved stone walls.

Veronica heard a noise over the din of the cutlery she unpacked.

She froze and listened.

Tick-swish, tick-swish.

What was that?

Tick-swish, tick-swish. It became louder.

She spun and faced the foyer.

Tick-swish, tick-swish.

Nikki came through the doorway. Her feet scampered across the marble floor in a pair of furry slippers with two-inch heels.

"What the hell are those things on your feet?" Veronica asked her sleepy-eyed sister.

Nikki let her heavy head drop and studied her toes. Purple nail polish gleamed through the fur of her crème-colored slippers.

"Do you like 'em? They're mink," she slurred as she continued her trek into the kitchen.

Tick-swish, tick-swish.

"You're going to scratch the marble," Veronica warned.

Nikki lazily swung her neck around and gazed at the polished stone floor. "Nope, marble is fine. Aren't these great? I feel like Cinderella!"

"They're fabulous," Veronica stated flatly.

"I'm so glad you like them!" Nikki exclaimed, too tired to sense the sarcasm in her sister's voice. "Hold on."

She kicked each foot once and let the furry heels slide off. Barefooted, she scuttled out of sight. A few moments later, she appeared again with a different pair of the opulent footwear.

"I got you some, too!" Nikki purred as she presented Veronica with a blush-colored version of the shoes.

"They're pink!" she gasped.

"Put them on," Nikki urged.

Veronica obliged. She kicked off her raggedy, dog-faced slippers and slid on the foreign footwear, exposing unpainted toenails and calloused feet.

"Eew! You need a pedi, Vern."

Veronica ignored the comment and stood on the stilts. She hardly ever wore heels, and these proved especially tricky as she navigated the slick kitchen floor.

"Thanks, Nik, these are great." Veronica did her best to sound genuine.

Nikki winked. "No problem. I'll make a princess out of you yet."

❦ ❧ ❖ ❦ ❧

Veronica teetered down the passageway to the keep wearing the mink slippers. She decided to break them in while exploring the deeper parts of the Château.

She vaguely recalled from her conversations with Marie-Claire that the keep was erected centuries ago over the site of a Pagan holy spot. Ancient priests built it and resided in it until Rome conquered it in the fourth century. The disintegrating Roman Empire couldn't keep hold of it though. During a Gaulic invasion, it was once again captured by barbarians who reinforced the walls and built the structure into an impenetrable fortress.

In the middle ages, the castle was ruled by a clandestine sect of knights — warriors who helped fight the crusades but eventually met their doom during the inquisition when they were accused of heresy.

The Catholic Church took hold until it was passed into private ownership. From the fourteenth to the eighteenth century, it was the property of French nobility. It was abandoned after the French Revolution and sat in a state of disrepair until Marie-Claire purchased it at public auction in the 1980s.

Indeed, the Château was never conceived in its entirety. It was created and expanded upon over many lifetimes. And now, Veronica had the distinguished opportunity to transform it once again. She was becoming a piece of history.

The door was locked.

Veronica ritualistically fumbled in her bag and pulled out the skeleton key. It didn't work.

That's funny, she thought. This key is supposed to open every door.

She twisted it stubbornly, but it wouldn't budge. She sighed, made plans to get some WD-40, and then ventured down the hallway toward the chapel.

The chapel — a church — someplace Veronica never went. Her family wasn't the church-going kind. Mom had been raised Catholic but didn't practice. Few Las Vegas show girls did. Veronica wasn't sure if her father was any specific religion. He left before she was old enough to question such things. She and Nikki attended church on rare occasions with friends or extended family, but Veronica never felt comfortable, even at weddings and funerals. People knelt, sang songs, shouted "Amen", and recited the Lord's Prayer while Veronica tried to copy them. She would struggle to follow along, afraid that people would notice the "heathen" in their presence. Ultimately, she decided God was just wishful thinking. If there really were a God, He wouldn't have need for idolatry, praise, and blind faith.

Now she stood inside the doorway of the castle chapel. She wasn't even sure if this was a chapel or a church, or if there was a difference. The dirty stained glass windows allowed a scant amount of sunlight to filter through. She flicked

107

on the flashlight that she carried faithfully in her bag.

The pews on either side of her, though thick with dust and grime, remained dignified. Like sentinels, they sat ready, not deterred by time or the elements, waiting for worshipers to return.

Columns, similar to those in the ballroom, flanked both sides of the room and separated the pews from the church walls. To Veronica's right, she could see faint Bible heroes painted on a dusty mural. The wall to her left, however, was covered in shadow.

She cast her light and noticed several recessed grottos. They were boxlike and spanned the entire length of the left wall from the altar to the last pew. Above them, magnificent stained glass windows cast luminosity on the opposite side, leaving the grottos below shadowy and murky. She didn't need to be religious to notice the gothic nature of the windows. They were topped with flying buttresses and exquisitely ornate with flamboyant tracery that pointed up to the sky like flames trying to lick heaven.

Veronica walked down the aisle. *Here comes the bride....* She tittered at the thought and for just a moment allowed herself to imagine yards of white lace cascading onto the floor behind her.

The altar appeared like a specter in the shadows. Behind it, something glinted. A huge bas-relief hung behind the pulpit. Though it was muted by decades of dust and patina, Veronica discerned a vague image of Christ on the cross.

She mounted the pulpit to get a closer look. Curiously, she brushed her hand across the surface of the relief. Globs of grey dust stuck to her moist fingertips. Using her sleeve, she wiped away a patch of filth to discover the immense work of art was covered in gold leaf.

"Damn," she whispered. "This must be worth a small fortune."

She turned and faced the chapel from the point of view of a sermonizing priest.

"Everyone on your knees and pray!" she pontificated in jest.

Her voice thundered off the ceiling, startling a kit of pigeons nesting in the buttresses. They fluttered and banged into the stained glass windows. Veronica squealed in surprise. She covered her head as white, fluffy feathers sprinkled down on her like snowflakes.

The birds quickly got their bearings and escaped through broken sections of the windows. She laughed and pulled feathers out of her curls. "Guess I had an audience after all."

Her remark was answered with indifferent silence. It was as if the chamber refused to acknowledge her presence. She swooped the flashlight along the grottos. They were bathed in an impenetrable darkness. She hopped off the pulpit for a closer look.

Inside the first was a rectangular, granite box with a sculpture of a reclining man atop. She studied the statue in the dim light. He lay with arms crossed over his chest. Two years were written on the side: 1284-1348. Realization spread over her like sickness. She was standing in front of a sarcophagus.

Veronica stepped back but froze when she heard a noise from the other side of the church. It was a ticking sound, like pecking.

Was there a pigeon left behind?

She spun around with the flashlight.

No birds flapped or cooed. There was nothing but silence smothering the abandoned chapel.

Then the thin beam of light caught a hint of movement. In the center of the pews stood a robed figure.

Veronica felt like she was melting. Hot terror engulfed her while her legs turned into twigs which were about to snap. The beam hovered on a black, crusted face. Wild hair stuck up in all directions around it like snakes on a medusa.

Veronica shrieked. She dropped the flashlight. It bounced with echoing clanks into the blackness of the alcove. Frenziedly, she bent to retrieve it.

A hysterical guffaw bounced off the church walls.

Veronica's head popped up like a gopher. She found the flashlight and twirled it around so that it shined on the mysterious figure.

"Nikki!" she exclaimed with both anger and relief.

Nikki was clad in a terrycloth bathrobe. A mud beauty mask covered her face and locks of her hair were twisted in silver foils that jutted out randomly. Nikki was "highlighting".

"Vern, what the hell are you doing?" she asked as her laughter subsided.

Veronica crept out of the grotto. "You scared the crap out of me! I was just looking around, checking out the church, and I found this tomb."

Nikki approached. The mud mask that distorted her face still gave Veronica the creeps. She flinched as her sister came closer and bent to inspect the grave. Under the dates, Nikki read, "Cardinal Jonaton Thibaut — The Great Pestilence."

"What is the 'Great Pestilence'?" Veronica asked.

"I think it refers to the plague," Nikki answered solemnly. "Look, this whole side is filled with graves." Nikki gestured with her hand to indicate the entire span of the wall.

Veronica studied the other coffins with the flashlight. "Oh, that is so gross! To think... just inside those boxes are dead bodies!"

"Prolly more like old, dusty bones. These things look pretty ancient. I doubt if there's too much of 'em left."

"Bones, skeletons, decaying flesh, whatever. It's disgusting." Veronica wrinkled her stubby nose.

Nikki changed the subject. "I've been looking all over for you. We had company before."

Veronica raised her eyebrows.

"A messenger to be exact...with an invitation." Nikki produced a fancy looking piece of parchment. "It's from one of our neighbors, the Fontaines — Alfred and Bridget."

Veronica admired the art of the calligraphy while Nikki read out loud. "Dear friends, welcome to the Loire Valley. We would like to make your acquaintance. Please join us for a dinner party next Saturday evening. Dress is cocktail attire. Drinks served at seven, dinner at eight. The address is..." Nikki's voice trailed off.

"They must live in one of the estates down the main road. What a nice invitation. I guess they know we're decorating the Château," Veronica chimed.

"They included a bottle of wine. Looks like it came from their own vineyard."

"This is a great way to meet prospective clients! I wonder if Marie-Claire told them we were here." Veronica gushed.

"So, we can go? Bitchin', I get to buy a new cocktail dress!" Nikki enthused.

The sisters retreated from the church, all the while talking excitedly about the invitation.

Chapter 38

Journal Intime

From this vantage there is a massive door to my left. It is the entry to my room. To the right is a smaller door boarded up with old, rotting wood. I guess it is not so much a doorway as it is an alcove. Inside is a trap door which opens to an oubliette — a vile little dungeon where enemies were thrown and left to die horrible deaths.

I endeavor not to look at the decaying wood that covers it for fear I may catch a glimpse of something through the crevices. Eaten away by time and termites, I fancy that the cracks in the wood whisper to me about something that dwells on the other side. I imagine if I stare at them too long I will see an eye gawp out at me or perhaps a spindly finger waggle through — the specter of a long-gone malcontent trying to break free. My imagination can be cruel; this I know. Such a visage would frighten the life out of me, and I dare not let my eyes dwell too long on that little door, just in case...

Henri says that once we stop rationing wood, he will have the doorway to the oubliette boarded up with fresh planks and make it more formidable. Until then, I will simply refrain from allowing my gaze to settle on that side of the room.

I turn to the other door — the massive one. It leads to the keep where there is a large hallway connected to several small cells. There are also a few chambers atop mine, up the narrow stairs of the turret.

There is a slit in the big door, designed for prisoners to be fed through. Captives who were confined here had no contact with the outside except for a guard who reached his hand inside once a day and passed moldy food and rancid water through the slit. How dreadful it must have been to be to be a prisoner in this dreary place!

Since I am confined to my bed and cannot leave, I guess I am not much different than a prisoner, am I? I imagine them lying here much like I am right now. We share the same small space, the same vantage point, the same stale air.

Oh, but there are differences. I have committed no crime, nor any sin against God. My condemnation is for a pure and noble reason — to protect my unborn child and deliver a healthy son to my dear, sweet Henri. One day in the near future, I will be able to leave this cell of my own free will. Those long-ago prisoners, they were never so fortunate. Still, there in the oubliette, they lie, condemned for eternity.

Josette-Camille

July 28th, 1789

There is not much to do to pass the time. I make the effort to write the poems that Henri enjoys so much, but the words don't come easily. I pray, but there is only so much glory I can bestow upon a God who allows such bloodshed to befall our land. So to pass the time, I sit quietly and listen to the sounds of the castle. Don't think me odd. It is absolutely interesting what you notice when you sit perfectly still for hours and listen!

I have discovered that this room conducts sound quite well. Perhaps it is because of the cylindrical shape, its central location, or maybe the constitution of the old stones. Whatever the reason, I notice that I can hear the soft dripping of condensation on my mildew-streaked walls. It is a sound that is barely perceptible unless you remain perfectly still and quiet for at least an hour.

As well, I can hear the spiders on the ceiling spinning their webs. It is almost a melodic sound, like gentle music played on a cello or bass. Oh my, I love the sound of spiders making their webs. How could I have never noticed it before? It is amazing what one can hear if they take the time to listen.

Most interesting of all the things I hear, are the voices. They sounded far away at first, but the longer I listened, and the more still I sat, the clearer the voices became.

Now I know there are a lot of voices in this castle; people are everywhere, but what makes me take notice is the fact that these voices are the serving maids. At this time of day, I know all the maids are in or around the kitchen tending to the evening meals. How could I possibly hear them when they are so very far away?

I can hear the girls whisper venomous gossip about each other. One leaves the room, and the others start in about her. Then she comes back, and they all act entirely natural until another leaves the room. How odd it is that I can hear them way over here in the keep, and they can't hear when they merely step into a nearby room!

Now the servant girls are gathered in the buttery next to the kitchen, and my how they are carrying on like a murder of magpies! Then, lo, I hear one speak *my* name.

Oh, for the love of our sweet Lord, do they dare speak ill of their mistress? I crane my neck and cock my head to listen better. Yes, there it is again; one invokes *my* name. She has a nasty, nasally tone in her voice. I hear her say that she would like to sneak a piece of bread off my breakfast plate in the morning. She sniggers after she speaks, obviously making a joke.

Another girl, with a challenging timbre in her voice, says, "Josette-Camille drinks so much of that tonic; she is only half awake most the time anyway. Go ahead; snatch an extra piece of bread for yourself. The harpy will never notice it is gone!"

They all twitter and cackle at the bravado. How dare my maids poke fun of me and plot to steal my food? I cannot endure this insubordination!

But what do you think I should do? Should I confront the maids and tell them I heard their treachery? They would certainly deny it. Lie to me; that is what they would do.

Or should I inform Henri? My husband will surely defend me and handle the situation sternly. Oh, but dear Henri is so busy with matters of securing the castle. Do I dare annoy him with such incidentals?

Alas, I could do nothing. My third option would be to simply dismiss the conversation all together. Indeed, as some time now has passed since I heard them, I've become uncertain if it was real or just my imagination. Maybe it was just a fancy brought to life by the tonic?

I'll rest now. Perhaps the answer will come tonight in my dream. Rest will do me good and give me clarity of mind for tomorrow. Then I will be able to make a lucid, level decision when the time is right.

Josette-Camille

July 29th, 1789

The evil, tricky maids, indeed, served me no bread for the morning meal! Only a small bowl of porridge was delivered to my chamber. I was right about what I heard last night!

When the servant brought the food to my chamber, I smiled sweetly and thanked the weasel-faced girl. She replied, "Of course, mistress," and I instantly recognized her nasally voice from the night before.

She curtsied, but before she left, I said, "No, dear, please wait. There is a matter we must attend to first."

Her narrow eyes grew wide for a moment. She nodded and replied, "Yes?"

I lifted my plate from the stool and, with a flourish, flung it to the floor. Her face grew pale as I commanded, "Kneel and eat it, you greedy gonoph! Steal from my plate, will you? Then all of it you shall have! Bend now like a toffer and lick it from the slimy floor."

Aghast she was and hesitated. Her thick lips worked in a circle as she fought to find words. Finally, she begged, "My lady, I stole nothing from you. I ask that you please not force me to lick food from the dirty floor. Hungry as I am, such a meal is not appropriate..."

I threw the goblet of goat's milk at her, preventing her from finishing her speech, and ordered, "Kneel and eat your slop!"

Oh, that nasty waif eyed me viciously as she crouched. The porridge was thin and traveled easily through the crusty crevices of the stone floor. Eating it required a considerable amount of licking and lapping off the filthy ground — which is exactly what she deserved.

"It would be much easier to eat with a piece of bread to lap it up, wouldn't it? But, alas, I have no bread! Wonder what could have happened to it?" I taunted her.

She cocked her head just enough to glare at me with an insipid, grey eye. I sat up straight in my bed and cast my gaze back at her. "I heard you and your cohorts talking in the buttery last night, plotting to steal food from me. I know you took my bread. I am the Lady of this household, and I am with child, and you would steal from me? This punishment is mild compared to the one that should befall you!"

Henri came in just then. The sight caught him off guard, and he stood agape in the doorway before asking, "What goes on here?"

The thieving maid was on all fours, lapping the porridge off the filthy ground. She gazed up at him hopefully. I was sitting with the inkwell cocked in my grasp above my head, ready to throw it at her.

Henri gave me pause, and I answered, "She steals bread from my plate. I heard her speak of it last night with the other maids in the buttery. Plotting to deprive me of nourishment, they were! I heard them though, and am now punishing the insolent thief!"

"Josette-Camille!" he cried. "Certainly, you could not hear such a conversation from the buttery all the way here in your chamber. Surely a dream, or one of your fits of fancy, is all it was."

"It was not a fit nor a dream, husband. I heard them call me names and plan the thievery with mine own ears," I answered.

He shook his head as he continued. "The servants would not steal from *you*. Indeed, I have given strict orders that your meals, and your meals alone, should never be sparse, despite the rationings. If you want some bread served, you need merely ask!"

He put a hand out to the girl and lifted her from the floor.

I have never been so cross with Henri as I was then. How could he not believe *me*, his wife?

He ordered the servant girl to clean the mess and fix me another plate of food. Before leaving, he said, "Please, dear, drink some tonic and try not to let your wild notions plant such fantasies in your head. Do it for the sake of the baby. We want him to be born with an even temper, don't we?"

How could Henri be so condescending? And to speak to me as such in front of a servant insults me to the core. Though he tells me not to be cross, I find myself growing more agitated. The fury burns under my skin, like a rumbling, roiling cauldron just before the boil.

Josette-Camille

Chapter 39

The Pagans' Story

Inside a cavern-like dwelling, illuminated by a small fire that crackled in a clay hearth, a family cowered and listened to the chanting priests draw closer.

"They won't stop this time," the woman murmured. She repeated the phrase over and over while two small children cuddled in her arms.

No one knew why some were selected and others spared. A secret lottery of sorts was held by the priests to determine who among the young would participate every year. All anyone knew with certainty was that the mysterious ceremony appeased the gods of nature and ensured prosperity for the coming year, even if that meant some of the children never came back.

The father poked at the fire and watched the red flames rise and fall. He coughed and shuddered. An illness ravaged his body despite all their efforts to cast out the spirits that sickened him.

On an animal skin, in the center of the room, lay the two oldest children. Karik was prone on his stomach and propped his upper body with folded arms in front of him. Trinna was curled up next to him.

Languorously, Trinna recalled last year when she had been among the chosen. The experience was blurry and disjointed. She faintly remembered being immersed in water and dancing by a fire. Then she was home, lying on an animal skin, while her mother dabbed at her face with a wet cloth. It was wrung out in a small bowl, and she watched as swirls of crimson spiraled in the shallow container — but the blood was not her own.

Trinna knew that she would not be chosen again. It could only happen once. The girl wondered though, if it would have been better if she had *not* returned last year. No one, not even Bevin, the fair-haired boy who she saw every year at the festival, had yet selected her as a wife, and her presence was a burden on her family.

Trinna gazed at Karik. If they came this time, it would be for Karik, as her other brothers were far too young. Karik did most of the heavy work since their father's illness. He fed the animals and tended the fields. Trinna knew that if they took her brother and he never came back, the family would go hungry.

Her mother began sobbing. At first, Trinna didn't grasp what was happening. Her mother had gone from whispering quietly to herself to huffing labored breaths of air while plump tears cascaded down her face. Then Trinna heard the chanting along with footfalls. They were coming up the path to the house.

They were coming for Karik.

Karik grabbed his mother's hand; at the same time, Trinna clasped her brother's wrist. Father also reached out for his family, and they sat for a moment like a human wreath, each one reaching out and holding another.

Trinna suddenly sprang to her feet. The movement surprised her father who had been grasping her hand, and he lost his grip. When he realized what was happening, he reached out for her clumsily and fell forward. In a flash, Trinna was outside, standing in front of the stag-headed man.

She quickly bent her head to show compliance and to avoid the Hag. The Hag might recognize her, and that would be bad.

Trinna's mother and father rushed through the doorway.

The Hag saw them. She had been approaching Trinna, but now she scowled at the intrusion. "Stop where you stand!"

Her father knew defiance would be met with the harshest of punishments. Whole families had been known to disappear for interfering with the sacred ceremony. He froze and clutched his wife's arm as she began to lunge forward, pulling her to his side.

Inside, Karik wondered why Trinna had sprinted out of the room when surely they were coming for *him*. Father and mother had chased after her. It took a moment, but then he realized that Trinna intended to take *his* place.

Karik tried to step past the animal skins that hung over the doorway. His father stood there, blocking him. Karik pressed his father's back, but he moved to shield his son from view. Karik realized that there was nothing he could do. Even if he managed to push past his father, his presence would do more harm than good. If the priests thought for one moment that the family was attempting to trick them, they all would be executed. Karik waited quietly. He knew that each year most of the chosen *did* return. He prayed that his sister was one of them.

Outside, Trinna was stripped, bathed, and redressed. Silent tears slithered down her mother's face. Her father stared at his brave daughter in disbelief as she stepped into line with the other children and marched away into the night.

Chapter 40

Father Michel's Story

Father Michel stopped by a small brook and let Lightning drink. Then he knelt on the downy moss by the edge, splashed cold water into his face, and then hooked his fingers together. "Was that vile creature a demon? Was it sent by you as retribution? Or perhaps it was a test. Like the family of Jews you sent to me. Are you sending things to test my faith, Lord? Am I failing?"

He recalled the family of Jews who arrived just before Sunday Mass while he was in his room preparing the sermon. One of the altar boys came running in, excited and out of breath. He said there were Jews outside and they asked to speak with the priest of the church. Father Michel did not understand what they could possibly want with him, but on that regretful day, he went out to greet them nonetheless.

An old man with a blanket shrouded around his shoulders hobbled over to Father Michel the instant he stepped out of the church. He was frantically speaking in a language the priest could not understand. Then another, younger man emerged from behind the curtain of a carriage. He, too, approached the priest.

"Please, we need help. We traveled many days, and we are weak and hungry. My children are sick. Please, help us. We have money!"

"I can't help you. I'm preparing for Sunday Mass. There's an inn just down the bend. Perhaps you can find a place to rest and get a warm meal."

"We went to the inn. They turned us away. Just like they did in the last town, and the hamlet before that," the man said. He was slight of build with dark brown hair. The older man shared his distinctive features. Each had the same crooked nose and the same quivering bottom lip.

"We are a poor parish; we have nothing to spare..." Father Michel began.

The old man grabbed the priest by the wrist, squeezed tightly, and pulled him close. Father Michel could smell the age in his breath. He mumbled something in Yiddish then held out a medallion suspended from a chain, and dropped it into the priest's palm.

The other man spoke. "See, we can pay you. Please, just for a couple days. There are women and children with us for God's sake!"

Father Michel looked at the outdated religious symbol on the gold medallion. He recognized the ancient Christian cross. He nodded his head, and the decision was made. He took the Jewish family into the church. For the next week, he tended to them one by one as they died of peste.

Father Michel was pulled out of his memory by the sound of clopping hooves. He spied a small wagon pulled by a mule slowly approaching. Two figures sat at the reins. Behind them were three more people. One coughed heavily. As the cart drew closer, he saw that the two front figures were men. One appeared mid-aged, and the other a lad of about fifteen or sixteen.

They reminded him of the outcast Jewish family. His stomach lurched as he realized that yet another test of faith was before him.

The family, who presently crowded together on the tiny wagon, obviously was not Jewish. The older man's features were now clear. Father Michel could see that he had a dirty, ratted beard and a hat with a limp plume sticking out of it. The younger lad had deep circles under his eyes. The blond hair on his head was cut round, like a bowl. He was gaunt, and his mouth hung open. He turned his head slowly as the cart pulled up, keeping his gaze leveled on Father Michel.

The older man spoke. "God must have sent you to us, Father! Indeed, the good Lord placed you here for us to find. My son, my youngest, is dead! We are taking him to be buried near the mountains. And now you can give him last rites."

Father Michel stepped back. The cart was only twenty feet away. Lightning stood patiently beside him. "In the mountains, did you say? Why don't you take him to your church, to your cemetery? He needs to be buried in consecrated ground."

"All graves full!" the young man blurted.

The older man confirmed. "Even the mass graves are filling up. And the cost just to bury the dead, it is too much for us to pay. The bodies are piling up in the street, as there is no one willing to bury the dead anymore...not without paying dearly. We are taking my son, my five-year-old..." His words broke, and he sobbed heavily for several seconds. "Someone said there is an old cemetery there. One that isn't full. And we are going to stay in the mountains; gonna try to live there. Live off the land. There is only death in the city. Almost everyone has left, except the dead and the dying."

"Go with God," Father Michel said. "You have my blessing."

"Father, can you please give our son his last rites?" the man asked as he turned to the woman in the back of the wagon. She was bent over protectively. Two children sat on either side of her, covered by blankets. She rose slightly, revealing the tiny body she had been cradling on her lap.

"All the dead are automatically absolved of their sins...word came down from Avignon..." Father Michel began.

The man took the swaddled body and held it out toward Father Michel. "Your blessing, *please*, Father."

The woman on the wagon coughed suddenly.

Father Michel recoiled.

The man dismounted the wagon with his dead child in his outstretched arms. "Father, it will only take a moment. I beg of you. We need you. My son — his soul — needs you."

Father Michel could see the dead child was swathed in torn strips from a grain sack. They were stained with dried blood and bile. The handmade bandages encircled his body like a mummy. A dirty blanket, little more than the tattered remains of a sheep's hide, loosely covered the carcass.

The man took two steps toward Father Michel. The movement jarred one of the body's tiny arms, and it flopped out. Black spots covered the bloated limb. Near the armpit were two shiny purple buboes. They were caked with blood and pus. Several flies clung to them hungrily, ignoring the commotion that normally would have shooed them away. Father Michel saw their red tongues lapping at

118

the rotting infection. His eyes glazed as the tiny offering came closer.

"Here, Father," the man said.

Father Michel said nothing. His left hand clenched the reins of Lightning's bridle. He looked steadily into the eyes of the desperate man and mouthed the words, "I'm sorry."

Chapter 41

Dorothée's Story
Circa 1520 AD – the Dawn of the Reformation

orothée lay in her bed while André-Benoit sat by her side, with a kerchief to her brow. Patricia stood at the end of the bed as the young chambermaid entered with tea.

"Dear, this will calm you," André-Benoit said.

Dorothée wiggled into an upright position. Patricia rushed forward and adjusted the puffy down pillows behind her.

"Is it mint tea?" Dorothée inquired meekly.

André-Benoit looked at the maid. She nodded once as he lifted the dainty porcelain cup from the silver tray. "Yes...mint tea. Here...drink; you'll feel better."

Dorothée accepted with both hands. The warmth soothed her trembling palms. She slowly brought the cup to her lips where it hovered a moment before she gently sipped.

"Better?" André-Benoit asked.

Dorothée smiled weakly. "Yes."

"Good. I can't have you feeling distressed right before I leave."

"Leave?"

"Yes, I have to go away again."

"But you only just returned!"

André-Benoit caressed her arm with the back of his knuckles. "The Protestants are taking hold in Freiburg im Breisgau."

"Germany?"

"Yes. The church needs a formidable force to abate them. It could last weeks, maybe months."

"Does that mean there will be fighting? Are you in danger?"

"I'll be fine. Don't fret."

"I knew it! I knew that they did not give you the Château without a cost. They give an order, and you jump like a marionette pulled by strings." Dorothée sat forward, strength returned to her frail body.

"What say you?" he asked incredulously.

"The church gave you the Château; therefore, they will call on you constantly because they think you owe them."

"I gladly offer whatever service I can, not because of the Château, but because it is my sworn duty as a French man, as a noble, and above all, as a Catholic." André-Benoit gripped her hand.

"We are only just married, and you are going to leave me again so soon. Don't you feel any duty to *me*, your wife?" Her hand twitched in his enormous palm.

"Dear, of course I do. As your husband, it is also my duty to protect you, to protect our home and our beliefs. Right now the best way to do that is to stave off any threat that the Protestants present."

Dorothée glared suddenly at Patricia, who stood dutifully by her side. Patricia reacted quickly and led herself and the girl out of the room.

She softened her tone. "Let me come with you."

"Absolutely not!"

"Then I will plan a trip to visit my parents so I'm not here alone with the insipid servants."

"You'll stay here. I don't need to worry about you traveling across the country in such turbulent times."

"So, this is the news the messenger brought. The note was about the uprising in Freiburg..." Dorothée studied his face. André-Benoit nodded his head. "And the clandestine meeting in town, what was *that* about?"

"We had to determine where to detain a prisoner."

"What prisoner?"

"No one can know his identity. It would be too dangerous if the wrong people find out..." André-Benoit's booming voice trailed off as a breeze rustled the apple trees outside.

Dorothée was completely intrigued. "Surely, you can tell me — your wife."

"It could be dangerous if the Protestants find out," André-Benoit snapped.

"Yes, danger, peril, I understand. Please, tell me!" Dorothée ordered.

"He is a leader of the Protestants. He was captured in battle a week ago, and his followers believe him dead. He is going to be held in the keep here until a trial is set. That's all I can say," André-Benoit explained.

Dorothée considered his words. "In the keep? No one can be kept in that wretched place. Not even a Protestant."

"He won't be in a cell. We'll keep him in the tower."

"The tower...especially not the tower! Something dreadful is in there. Didn't you see what happened to me? Don't you believe me?" Dorothée began to tremble.

"Dear Dorothée, yes I believe you. I am sure you saw a horrible rat, and I have no doubt you were terrified. I saw you; I know how awful it was. I also know that you had no business being in there. Now you know better! Besides, where would you like us to keep a dangerous prisoner...the Queen's Chamber?"

Dorothée ceased her protests. "Don't tease me. Very well. You are the lord of the manor. Hold the prisoner wherever you like. I, for one, won't have anything to do with him."

"As well you shouldn't. No one should, other than the sentries watching over him."

"I just don't like the thought of him being here while you are gone. I don't want you to be away. When will you leave?" Dorothée rested her head on André-Benoit's lap.

He ran his coarse fingers through her velvety, red locks. "I leave tomorrow. The prisoner arrives tonight."

"Then, husband, we should consider this time to be very precious." She slid her hand across his chest and around his neck. She tugged slightly and pulled him down to her. He fumbled momentarily with his bulky boots then sunk into bed beside his bride.

Chapter 42

The Children's Story

Isabelle bravely ventured toward the door and peeped through a knothole in the decaying wood. Outside, she could see the source of the voices. One of their uncle's men was walking with his back to the children and away from the barn. A skinny man wearing a shabby tunic and burlap britches scuttled behind him, following like a faithful servant vying for favor. Behind both men a woman respectfully followed. She carried Louis' satchel on her hip.

Two more men stood near the road with three horses. Once their companion reached them, they all mounted their steeds and rode off toward town. Isabelle breathed a little easier. *At least they were heading in the opposite direction.*

She turned toward her brother. His round cheeks were puffy and red. Moisture bleared his big, brown eyes. They were swollen and caked with mucus. Isabelle dabbed at his face with trough water and tried to clean him up as best as possible.

"We'll be out of here soon, and you'll feel much better."

Louis nodded and sniveled. "The lady took my sack!"

"We don't need it. We had jerk beef to eat this morning, and we can surely find some berries in the woods as we're walking. I have some money, so once we make it to the mountain village, we can buy food."

"But the secret things that Papa gave to me were in there. He told me to keep them safe, and now she has it! She said it was hers!" Louis pouted.

"What are these *secret things* that Papa gave you?"

Louis sniffed then sneezed. "Sorry Izzy, I can't tell anyone, not even you. Papa made me promise. But now that lady stole it!" he cried.

"She didn't *steal* it. She took it, but I think she helped us. I don't know why, but she kept them from finding us."

Louis accepted this explanation with a nod. "Izzy, maybe we should let them find us. My ankle hur-ssst, and I'm hungry for real food, not jerk beef and berries. You heard what they said...Uncle Pierre is worried and wants us back. He is even going to pay money to find us!"

Isabelle knelt by her brother. "Little Louis, they were lying. They want to find us, and they'll pay a reward, but it's not because Uncle Pierre wants us to be safe. You believe me, right?"

"Yeah," the boy murmured.

The door of the barn creaked open. The brightness of the day obscured the figure standing in front of them in a halo of stark light. Isabelle grabbed her brother's arm and pulled him toward her. He was startled and blinded and didn't react with her. As she clasped his arm, he spun in a clumsy circle and spiraled to the ground. Isabelle was also pulled off balance, and she staggered.

"My ankle!" Louis cried.

The barn door closed, and they were thrust into a dusty darkness illuminated only by the cracks in the wooden walls. Before them stood the vague figure of the woman, she was backed against the door, with one hand holding the latch. Her other held Louis' satchel.

"Children!" she gasped in surprise.

Isabelle stepped forward and guarded her little brother. Louis sobbed and clung to the folds of his sister's dress.

The woman took a steady breath and then continued. "Don't be scared. I'm not going to hurt you."

Isabelle eyed her suspiciously. "Please, just let us go. We only stayed in your barn for a little while. We didn't take anything."

"I know; it's okay. Here is your satchel."

Isabelle slowly leaned forward and snatched the bag out of the woman's hand. "You'll let us go?"

"Yes. But you can stay for a spell, if you want. The Inquisitors won't be back anytime soon. I can make you a warm meal and give you hot baths." The tone of her voice was light and soothing. She gazed at Louis for a moment. "And I can help the boy. I'll tend to his ankle."

"Why would you help us? How do we know that you won't turn us in to the in-quis-torters?" Louis said the new word slowly, absorbing its menacing sound.

"Maybe you want to collect the reward?" Isabelle challenged.

"Three gold coins...everyone knows beautiful children usually cost *twice* that!" The woman winked to let them know her guile.

Isabelle smiled thinly, then knelt by Louis. He gagged on the phlegm that continued to clog his lungs. The more he cried, the more congested he became. His eyes were swollen almost completely shut. He clutched his wounded ankle. Isabelle knew that traveling with him now would be next to impossible.

She studied the woman in front of her. The lady wore a traditional Jewish dress with a brown housecoat over the top of it. Her dark hair was bundled up in twisted braids that formed a bun on the top of her head. Her lips had no color, and they blended into her knobby chin. The only brightness came from the woman's eyes. They were sharp and blue. Isabelle didn't see any deception, and after thoughtful consideration, she acquiesced by sighing and nodding.

The woman grinned and revealed black spaces where several teeth once lived. The few remaining teeth were brown and had only a pale tongue to keep them company. "I'll take you into the house in a bit. I want to make sure the guards are far down the road first. While we wait, why don't you tell me exactly why you would want to run away from such an enchanting place as the castle?"

Isabelle wasn't in the mood to talk, but she felt she owed the woman their side of the story. While cradling her brother in her arms, she spoke. "Four days ago, our parents were taken away in the middle of the night by the men who called themselves *The Inquisitors*. I heard them call my father a heretic, and my father called them liars. My mother cried and begged them to leave, but it didn't matter. Our parents were arrested along with the knights who served in my father's order. Uncle Pierre was there, too. I heard him say he would take care of us..."

"See there," the woman said, "your uncle wants to *care* for you while your parents are gone."

"There's more," Isabelle said calmly. "I heard one of the Inquisitors tell Uncle

Pierre to kill us because of a 'legacy'."

"What kind of a legacy could be worth *killing* children over!" the woman exclaimed.

Isabelle shook her head. "I don't know. Our parents never told us!"

"Sounds like your devious uncle is interested in your inheritance?"

"We don't care about money or land; we just want to be safe and have our parents back. Do you think our parents will be okay?"

The woman smiled without showing her teeth, but didn't answer.

Louis was silent as he absorbed the words his sister spoke. "Izzy, why didn't you tell me?"

Isabelle pulled strands of straw out of her brother's hair. "I didn't want to scare you any more than you already were."

The woman spoke. "Well, you will be safe here for a while before you're off to...where are you going?" She now crouched by the children and carefully looked at Louis' ankle.

"The village on the other side of the mountains. Then we'll travel to the next town and try to get as far away as possible. We'll go back home after our parents are found innocent."

The woman caressed Isabelle's cheek. "My name is Agnes, and my husband is Aaron. You can call me Nana though."

"I'm Isabelle, and this is Louis. You can call me Izzy."

The three sat huddled in the dirty barn and waited for the coast to clear.

Chapter 43

Sebastian's Story

Avitar Fabius sauntered over the creaky wooden floorboards in the massive chamber he called "the war room". His footfalls rattled little replica soldiers poised on a topographical map. It was laid atop a large table in the center of the room. Esindra sat patiently as her husband paced. She stared vacantly at the wobbling wooden men. Some were blue, they represented the Gauls, and the white ones were the Romans.

Large windows overlooked the courtyard. Fabius watched as Sebastian was led up the path and escorted into the room. The Cloaked Man's hands and feet were tightly bound with chains that dug into his flesh. Fresh blood was visible around his wrists.

"Sit," Fabius said simply.

Sebastian was pushed down by one of the guards into the chair at the head of the table. Esindra sat directly across from him. She studied the criminal with repulsive fascination.

Fabius walked slowly toward the prisoner. "What have you to say? Oh, *soothsayer*, what are your visions?"

Sebastian took a labored breath. Esindra recoiled as he exhaled. Though several feet away, she could smell the putrid air from his lungs.

"I'm sorry if my visage offends, good woman." He turned to Fabius and continued. "Governor, thank you for providing me with my divining bowl; it served me well, and last night I was blessed with a vision. The Gauls are growing in numbers even as we speak. They're recruiting other tribes. As their numbers increase so do their chances of defeating your army."

Fabius spat, "Those barbarians could never conquer my army! You think I'm a fool? You bring me lies to save your own pitiful life."

Sebastian spoke slowly, calmly. "What I see is only an impression of what *may* come. This is preventable, and I can help you."

Fabius nodded his head in mock agreement. "Yes, you can help me. *You* can help *me*. More to the point, I can help you. Only *I* can spare your life. I am smarter than you, Sebastian. I know what tricks you play."

Sebastian continued. "Last night, the west-end outpost was attacked. Four barbarians were slaughtered, and then the rest retreated. They struck and left."

"Yes, that happened." Fabius digested the information and continued. "They strike like that often. Stupid, feeble attempts then the cowards turn and flee. That proves nothing."

"You think they retreat because your mighty forces frighten them off. This is where you underestimate them. They're testing your defenses, looking for areas of weakness. They'll make three more attacks in the coming nights. Each time, they'll strike quickly and make a hasty retreat."

"Is that all you have to say?" Fabius asked.

"I'll find out more. Fate is a choice, not a fact. What you decide today will affect the events of the future. You have a great responsibility, and I can help guide you. You *need* me. Your centurions feed you useless information. See that troop on the map to the east of the town? They moved from that spot three days ago. Your scouts have not been vigilant."

Fabius scrutinized the tiny wooden men lined up at the base of the hills. "Where did they go?"

Sebastian nodded as if he could push the tiny toys with his head. "To the south; closer to the river."

Fabius moved the wooden soldiers. "Here?"

"Yes, and they will continue south where they will join up with the Franks."

Fabius studied the layout. Strategies played out in his head as he deliberated over different moves like a chess player. "I've heard enough. Take him back to his cell. I will grant him three more nights to live. If in that time his prophecies don't come to pass, then his fate is sealed on the wheel."

Sebastian was pulled to his feet, yet he continued to speak. "Your wife is not barren as you have believed all these years."

Esindra gasped.

"She will bear a child — a son," Sebastian stated.

"How do you know this?" Esindra prodded.

Fabius turned on his wife. "Don't encourage him."

Sebastian was relentless. "I've seen his birth, a healthy boy, a gift from the gods."

"That is enough, Sebastian. How dare you speak such lies! Get him out of here!" Fabius ordered.

The guards yanked on the Cloaked Man's chains and pulled him from the room like a dog.

Esindra rose to her feet and called after him. "When? When will my son be born?"

Fabius shot her a gaze that ordered her to be silent.

As the door of the chamber closed, she could hear Sebastian's answer. "Within the year..."

The room fell quiet as the thick latch clanked shut. Esindra looked at her husband with hope-filled eyes. "What if he speaks the truth? We have tried for so long to have children..."

"Ignore his words."

"But a *child*, a son...how can you dismiss him so quickly? This is what you've always wanted," Esindra implored.

"If we were meant to have children, then we would have been blessed with one by now. We are old, Esindra, too old to think about having children anymore."

"I'm not too old. It is still possible."

Fabius shook his head. He knew it was impossible, but he could never tell Esindra *how* he knew. "Do not ponder his words. He only means to trick us, to give us false hope."

Esindra nodded and carefully urged, "Perhaps tonight, just for fun, we could at least *try?*" She smiled coyly.

Fabius grunted. "Not tonight. I have strategies to plan."

Esindra's smile faded. Her gaze returned to the wooden warriors. She watched her husband position them on the map. Before he had a chance to dismiss her, she excused herself and went to her chamber alone.

Chapter 44

Veronica's Story

eronica's belly fluttered as she and Nikki drove to the country chapel to meet Christophe. She wondered if he was taking them to a nearby hamlet with an out-of-the-way café, or a rural inn with a winery, or maybe to a castle with a gourmet restaurant!

A lone car sat in the driveway of the little white church. It was a black Mercedes and glistened in stark contrast to the pristine building. A casual looking Christophe leaned against the impressive car. He wore a faded pair of jeans and a black button-down shirt. Gucci shoes that Veronica spied at the bank were replaced with a comfortable pair of Nikes. His grin was broad, and his dark hair flowed wildly in the breeze, no longer tamed by hair gel.

Veronica rolled down the window of the little orange car and noticed the obvious contrast between the two vehicles. Nikki leaned forward for a better view. Her enormous sunglasses slid down, and she ogled Christophe with large doe-eyes over the top of the frames. Her newly highlighted blond hair was swept to one side.

Christophe spoke first. "Hi, ladies! Wow, Nikole, you lightened your hair! Now I can tell you two apart."

"That ain't the only way to tell us apart," Nikki said as she shimmied her torso and gave her sister's bosom a snarky eye-roll.

Veronica slapped Nikki's arm playfully.

Christophe shook his head with bemusement. "You two ready?"

"Yes, where we off to?" Veronica inquired.

"Get out of the car and you'll find out!"

Veronica and Nikki were both perplexed. The only building in the vicinity was the chapel. Christophe reached into the back seat of his car and pulled out the answer: a huge wicker basket with a golden baguette poking out the top.

"We're gonna have a picnic?" Nikki squealed.

"Not just any old picnic!" Christophe proclaimed as he opened Veronica's car door with an exaggerated flourish. "An outdoor dining adventure filled with freshly made culinary delights that I crafted with my own hands. You ladies are so lucky."

The women groaned at his mock conceit as they allowed him to lead them down a cobblestone path. It trailed along the side of the chapel where weeping trees roofed their heads and blades of wild grass licked their ankles. A break in the foliage revealed bounding lavender-covered hills that leapt over one another in the distance. Veronica stood still for a moment and gasped at the beauty before her.

"Lovely, isn't it?" Christophe inquired. "This is my favorite place. My parents used to bring my brother and me here when were kids. Every Sunday, after mass, we brought a picnic brunch. It's been awhile. Hopefully, I can still find our favorite spot."

Veronica fleetingly recalled a French impressionist painting that depicted two men sprawled on a blanket underneath a canopy of trees with a naked woman dining between them. Manet, if she remembered correctly. She felt like she was stepping into that famous painting.

The trail was overgrown, and Christophe apologized for their trek into nature. "Sorry, the path is a bit thick. It's not much farther."

"No problem," Nikki answered as she bounced up alongside him. "It's like hiking. I go to Griffith Park *all* the time. This is a piece of cake!"

Veronica trailed behind. Despite her better judgment, she had allowed her sister to convince her to wear a white sundress and two-inch heeled sandals. She thought for sure that Christophe must think she looked ridiculous compared to Nikki, who at the last minute decided to "dress down" and wore a simple pair of jean shorts and a tank top.

Just as Veronica considered retreating to the car so she could rummage for a pair of tennis shoes, the trees parted. A perfect picnic area sprawled before the travelers. A small pond of water was surrounded by mature oaks and willows. Clingy ivy hugged the tree trunks and a splattering of wildflowers provided pops of color like thickened paint on an oil canvass.

Christophe put the basket down and spread out a huge blanket. He leaned against one of the stones while watching Veronica sit next to him. Her creamy legs angled out like delicate scissors under the milky white dress. Christophe imagined what it might be like to be a piece of paper as he set out their picnic lunch.

"So, you grew up around here?" Nikki asked.

Christophe shrugged before answering. "Yes, here, and in Greece, Spain, England."

"What'd your parents do?" Veronica inquired.

"My father was an international investment banker, just like his father and his father before. He met my mother while she was working at the embassy in Greece." He produced several photographs from his wallet. Veronica instantly recognized the same faces that graced the pictures on his desk at the bank. The man had Christophe's chiseled features and full lips. The woman had Christophe's dominant nose and rich, dark complexion.

"We traveled a lot for my mother's work. When she became a consulate to the embassy in England, I attended university at Oxford. After graduation, I returned to France, following in my father's footsteps as a banker and a wine maker." He uncorked a bottle and declared, "My best red from 2010."

He poured, they toasted, and Veronica eyed the other photos that spilled out of his billfold. "Who's that?" She pointed to a picture of a teenaged boy dressed in a school uniform.

"My nephew, Dennis. And his parents, my brother, Tristen, and his wife, Rebecca."

"Oh! And what's this?" Nikki snagged his passport playfully from the open wallet. It was several years old. In the photo, Christophe's hairstyle was large and bushy. "Nice hair, Chris..." she cut herself off and stared quizzically at the ID before asking, "*Tervagan?*"

Christophe sighed. "Yes, my first name is actually Tervagan. Christophe is my middle name."

The girls giggled.

"Don't laugh!" Christophe mocked defensiveness as he explained. "It was my father's name, and his father's, and down the line. One day when I have a son, I will pass the name onto him. My father made me promise that I would carry on the family legacy. You shouldn't make fun of a legacy!"

"Can we call you *Tervy* for short?" Nikki asked before snorting.

Christophe chuckled. "Not if you know what's good for you." He paged through his photos until he came to the last one. He pulled it to his chest. "And now I will show you the love of my life," he proclaimed dramatically. "Beautiful Babette is my companion; she's my best friend."

Veronica's teeth clenched as she prepared herself to see a photo of his girlfriend. Slowly, Christophe let his hand drop and revealed the image. "Doesn't Babette have the most lovely, auburn hair?" he asked.

Veronica and Nikki looked down at the picture of a golden retriever.

"She's the best hunting dog a man could ask for."

Veronica and Nikki giggled as Christophe broke the bread and arranged an assortment of cheeses on paper plates. Individually prepared quiches, still warm in their foil wrappings, were also presented, along with grapes, a box of chocolates, and a container of Greek caviar.

The sisters feasted and shared stories with their handsome host. After the meal, Christophe puffed on a thick cigar. Nikki was curious and took a drag of the smelly Dutch tobacco. She coughed as Christophe warned her not to inhale.

Veronica groped in her messenger bag and retrieved the map and gold medallion. "This is what we want to show you," she proudly proclaimed.

Christophe palmed the coin on the chain. Veronica anxiously twisted a lock of curly brown hair. "Is it an ancient French franc?"

Christophe forced himself to study the coin and not Veronica. "No, this isn't a franc; the franc wasn't minted until 1360, and this is much older. Actually, this isn't a coin at all. At first glance, it *looks* like a coin made into a necklace, but it's not."

Nikki was curious. "How do you know?"

Christophe dug into his wallet and pulled out a gold coin. "This is my good luck charm. It's a Venetian ducat."

"Is it from your coin collection?" Veronica asked.

"Yes, I have several ducats — and a lot of Roman coins, too."

Nikki piped up, "You're a banker who collects money. Pretty original, Chris."

"Don't tease him!" Veronica reprimanded. "Everyone collects something."

"Is that so? What do you collect, Veronica?" Christophe asked.

Nikki answered for her sister. "She collects Little Mermaid stuff!"

"Little Mermaid...what is this?"

Veronica blushed. "You know the fairytale and Disney movie? I liked it as a kid. I had an Ariel doll once — I can barely remember it — someone took it from me. But anyway, now I collect mermaids. I have mermaid art, mermaid blankets, mermaid pajamas, mermaid mugs, mermaid soap dishes, you name it, and I have one shaped like a mermaid."

"She's a mermaid geek!" Nikki declared.

"Least I don't collect porn like you," Veronica taunted.

"It isn't porn! It's vintage erotica. It's historical," Nikki answered while swirling her wine.

"Ladies, let's not fight. I'm sure you *both* have fine collections," Christophe cajoled.

"The finest," Nikki flirted and plucked the ducat from his palm. "So, how much is this worth to you?"

"That is worth a few hundred euro. It's in good condition. Look, you can see the depiction of Christ on the back surrounded by little stars. The lettering is still clear, as well. It's Latin and reads, 'May this royal ducat be dedicated to thee O' Christ'. But even though it's in good condition', it is still irregular. That's because of the way it was minted. It was pressed with a stamp. Your necklace, however, was made in a mold. That's how I can tell it isn't a coin." He held up Veronica's medallion. Nikki held up the ducat. They raised them side by side to compare.

"How old do you think mine is?" Veronica asked.

"That symbol is called a labarum. I've seen it on Roman coins from the time of Constantine. It's an early version of the Christian cross. This medallion very well could have been made in Constantinople right around that same time — in the fourth century."

"Constantinople...modern day Istanbul," Veronica stated, proud of her small display of knowledge.

"Right!" Christophe exclaimed. "You know your history!"

Veronica shrugged. She never comprehended history well at all; she was just really good at remembering lyrics. *Istanbul (Not Constantinople)* was a song from the 1950s. A band called They Might Be Giants did a cover of it that she used to sing when she was a kid, and now the chorus echoed in her head.

Nikki squirmed with anticipation. "So how much is it worth?"

Christophe grinned. "That's hard to say. The value of the gold would have to be determined. It looks very pure. The gems appear to be semi-precious. The real value lies in its historical context."

Nikki sat up straight. "And that means it is worth how much?"

Christophe snatched the ducat from her and flipped it in the air. "I'm not an expert, but if you are pressing me to make an educated guess..."

"If I have to press you any harder, I'll leave a black and blue mark," Nikki warned playfully.

"Probably between five and eight thousand American dollars."

"Wow," Veronica stated. "All that money for one little medallion on a chain. What then do you make of this?" She held out the map.

Christophe studied the winding twists and turns drawn on the parchment. "I'm certainly not an expert, but if this map indicates where more items like this can be found, you may have a small fortune on your hands."

"Do you recognize the streets? Does this town look familiar?" Nikki asked.

"This is a map of a town?" Christophe wondered.

"That's what we figure," Veronica stated. "These dead ends are cul de sacs."

Christophe inspected the bush-like sketch and chuckled under his breath. "Cul de sac literally means 'bottom of the bag' in French. I wonder what you'd find in the bottom of *this* bag. I wish I could be of more help. This doesn't look like a map of any city or town I know of. If it's as old as that coin, it's hard to say how accurate it'd be anyway. City streets change. If you like, I have a friend who deals in antiquities. He may be able to shed some light on your little mystery."

Veronica grew cautious. "I dunno. Probably not worth the trouble."

"It can't hurt to find out," Christophe offered. "I'll give my friend a call, and we can all get together and discuss over dinner some night?"

Veronica's heart momentarily leapt at the invitation. Unfortunately, her brain got in the way. "I'm just so busy with the Château. I don't know if I have time to chase pie in the sky."

Christophe reconsidered his approach. "Well, what about next Saturday night... surely, you don't work on Saturday nights?"

"We've got a dinner party Saturday night." As the words passed Veronica's lips, she realized it sounded like she was pushing Christophe away.

They all sat awkwardly silent a moment.

Nikki spoke up. "Our neighbors invited us over to get acquainted; perhaps the following week, though. Vern, we don't have plans *then*, do we?"

Veronica shook her head quickly. "No, the following Saturday would be great!"

Christophe wasn't ready to jump at the offer quite yet. "Only if you're sure. I don't want to keep you from your work."

Veronica fought to find the right thing to say. "Today was so much fun. You did such a great job with the food, the wine, and it was so relaxing to just sit and talk. You can interrupt my work anytime!" She proudly found the perfect words.

Christophe beamed. "Very well. In two weeks, we have a date."

A date, thought Veronica. *Was this a date-date? What did he mean by date?* This question would burn in Veronica's mind for the next two weeks.

Chapter 45

The Pagans' Story
182 CE – the Ancient Ritual that Unleashed It

They navigated a narrow, jagged mountain ridge. Only several feet wide, it flanked a deep ravine. Trinna kept her head down as she followed the procession; she was fearful the old Hag would recognize her, so she did her best to stay in the back of the line.

Someone tapped Trinna's shoulder and the skittish girl spun around. She beheld familiar, smiling eyes. They belonged to Bevin, the wiry boy she saw every year at the harvest festival. They played together as children, teased each other as adolescents, and flirted once in their teens.

He bent and whispered, "How did you come to be chosen again?"

Trinna shushed him with a swift index finger to his lips. "I came instead of my brother, but they don't know that. The Hag might recognize me, but otherwise no one will know the difference."

Bevin understood immediately and stealthily shifted in front of her to help shield her from the Hag's venomous gaze. Sculpted muscles covered his chest and arms. Trinna noticed how he had evolved from a goofy playmate into a handsome young man.

The Hag began chanting and her priests whispered esoteric prayers in a monotone chorus behind her. Dimly, Trinna caught a flash of memory; bits and pieces of last year's ritual came back to her. Though she didn't know exactly what would happen next, she knew it would be bad.

A menagerie of animal bones and polished pebbles rattled in the Hag's gnarly hands. She bent and cast them onto the ground. All stepped back and gave her room to perform her divination. Crouched like a heinous cat preparing to pounce, she eyed the runes intently, then gazed down the line of potential sacrifices. She snatched up a handful of the tiny bones and threw them to the ground again, then again. Her eyes darted back and forth between the runes and the children, between the runes and the children, between the runes and the children...

A sudden gust of wind wafted by and fluttered one girl's loincloth.

The Hag moaned, "The wind has chosen."

Before Trinna understood the implication of what just happened, the man wearing the stag's head grabbed the innocent child and lifted her high in the air. Trinna watched in horror as the girl kicked and flailed while the brutish man carried her toward the edge of the cliff. Several priests raised their voices in unison, crying out to the spirits in the wind, as the girl was hurled over the ledge.

An unnatural silence penetrated the procession. For a moment, it seemed like Trinna imagined the whole scene, like a hallucination, it never happened.

Then she heard the sacrifice scream and the splattering of her body against the craggy rocks below.

Satisfied, the Hag turned to go, and the rest followed her down the mountain.

֍ ֍ ❖ ֍ ֍

Trinna found herself walking in unison to the chanting like a soldier marching in time. Without being aware of it, she rambled under her breath, singing along with the strange words that she did not understand.

They came to the river and walked along its bank until the Hag stopped. She stepped up to the river's edge and calculated the exact location of the crossing.

"Built by the priests many years before, there is an underwater bridge here," The old woman explained. "It is made of massive stones we must use to cross."

Once the precise location was determined, in single file, the procession waded across the river. The children were ordered to stop halfway, however, while the priests continued to the other side. Only the man with the stag's head remained with them.

Trinna watched the Hag on the shore. The woman rolled her bones while her subjects crooned around her.

Trinna closed her eyes tight. The only sounds she heard for the longest time were the gentle wafting of the waves keeping time with the incessant chanting.

Then the Hag cried out, "The water has chosen!"

There was a sudden violent splash, and Trinna felt water splatter against her face. She didn't want to witness what was happening, so she squeezed her palms against her sockets as the stag-headed man drowned someone mere feet from where she stood.

❧ ❧ ❖ ❧ ❧

Next, they walked through the forest and eventually came to a cave. With torches lit, the procession was led inside. A flurry of bats erupted as soon as their dwelling was invaded. They screeched and fluttered. One grazed the side of Trinna's face and she shrilled. One of the other children began crying.

The Hag shouted, "Quiet! You don't want to anger the earth!"

The excitement settled, and they marched through a series of twists and turns. Trinna focused on her feet. The smoke from the torches hung in the damp air and she coughed repeatedly. Bevin walked just in front of her. He hesitated while she cleared her lungs then put his arm around her, allowing her to lean on him.

The group once again came to a halt. The Hag began to intone and her minions joined in. The old woman threw the runes onto the earth with a snap of her creaky wrist. She pushed her nose close to the ground and studied them. Snatching several bones, she tossed them again, until finally she was satisfied.

"The earth has chosen an offering!" she stated.

Trinna stood with the others lined up against the cavern wall. Still leery of being recognized, she hung her head allowing her loose hair to cover her face. She felt the old woman's eyes on her — they carved into her flesh as if they were hot, whetted obsidian.

Trinna knew she was being scrutinized as the next sacrifice.

134

Chapter 46

Father Michel's Story

T he pauper carried his dead son toward the priest. "Thank you, Father." The morning sunlight illuminated the thin bandages over the corpse's face, causing pallor eyes to glare at Father Michel.

The stench reached the holy man's nose. Even Lightning reacted with an explosive snort. Father Michel swayed slightly and steadied himself by grasping the reins. The horse shook its mane, causing the priest to cock his head and regain lucidity. He gasped for air, stepped back, and said, "Forgive me. I can't."

With incredible agility the priest pulled himself up and mounted Lightning with a twirl of his cassock. He spurred the animal violently and rode across the plain in a matter of seconds. He turned his head only once as he sped away. The man of God watched with regret as the peasant clutched his dead child and walked dejectedly back to the wagon.

Man and beast hastened across the countryside. Hills that were once alive and abundant with crops were now gnarly and overgrown by weeds. Plows sat abandoned in the middle of fields. Occasionally, Father Michel would see a stray cow or mule meandering uninhibited through the grass. Farmhouses stood vacant. Some bore a hastily painted cross on the door — the warning of infection.

The duo crested a hill and oversaw the village cradled in the shallow valley below. It was a modest town comprised of a smattering of tiny houses that encircled a town square. A church steeple towered from the center.

Mountains flanked either side of the village. To the west, they rose swiftly and would prove very rocky and treacherous to navigate. A river ran along the east side of the town. The only bridge he could see was accessible by maneuvering through a tangle of twisting streets and narrow roads. The fastest and straightest route would be to go right through the center of town.

Father Michel rode down the hillside. The air was quiet. No birds sang, no dogs barked, no children shouted, no church bells rang. The small homes on the outside of town were boarded up.

Down one of the side streets, he caught sight of a lumbering horse-drawn cart. He observed as a man led the animal by the reins while another figure with an unnaturally large head trailed behind.

The door of a modest house sprung open, and a voice urged the men to come hither. Now in profile, Father Michel could see that the man with the large head had a pig-like snout. It was a mask of sorts — hideous and repugnant — made out of a large, twisted gourd. Father Michel could hear the street echo with their brief conversation, though he couldn't fully make out the exact words. A small bag, presumably filled with coins, exchanged between the person at the door and the pig-headed man. He entered the home and emerged a few moments later with a body encased in a shroud. Unceremoniously, he chucked it on the back of the cart next to others.

Father Michel spurred Lightning, and the horse continued at a brisk pace. As they neared the center of town, to his left, a figure appeared in the window of a boarded building. The window was low to the ground, apparently to a basement apartment, and barred shut.

The figure was a young girl — a child of nine or ten — and she called out to the priest. "Father! Father! Have you seen my mama and papa? Did they send you, Father?"

Father Michel locked eyes with the doleful imp. She was dirty and sweaty with auburn hair pulled back in a stringy braid. A festering bubo was clearly visible under her jaw.

She coughed and continued. "They've been gone three days now. They said they would fetch help. Father..." She started hacking. Her arms stretched out through the bars toward the street, and her tiny fists clenched the air as her chest heaved with convulsions. Even while gasping for air, she continued her pleas. "Father...if you see my mama and papa can you...tell them..." her voice grew weak and finally faded into a sputtering, choking fit.

Father Michel felt an urge stir deep inside. It was like a string pulling on his soul. Several weeks ago, he would have gone to the girl and prayed with her. He would have had faith in the Savior to heal her. That seemed like an eternity ago. Father Michel knew that all the prayers in the world couldn't help that girl now. As he passed, he noticed the door to her apartment. It was chained and locked from the outside.

He rode until he was in the exact center of the town square. It was an open area that he imagined once bustled with merchants selling their wares. Now it was empty except for a fountain that festered with green water. An emaciated dog limped up to the dank pool and lapped at the putrid liquid. Father Michel kept riding.

A church loomed ahead. It was majestic in scale compared to the other buildings. The steeples rose into the air, pushed up by high, sweeping arches. The windows were ornately decorated with vibrant colors and the massive doors were adorned with stone carvings of angels guarding the entryway.

He was almost completely past the church when he heard, "Father! Over here, Father!"

He prepared to spur his horse, but before he could kick, a shadow of duty loomed over his will. Instead, he forced himself to turn around. A figure limped from the doorway. He was dressed in a long, brown robe tied with a knotted rope. He lumbered forward; one hand waved at Father Michel.

"This way, Father, follow me," the man uttered.

Father Michel had no interest in what the monk had to say, but he hesitated. Being confronted with another man of the cloth compelled Father Michel to at least acknowledge him. He looked at the sight before him with pity. The monk was aged with desperate, sallow eyes that squinted in the brightness of the morning. He walked with a pronounced limp, dragging one foot behind. His left hand was coiled up on an arm that looked crippled and useless. His other hand shook as he bade Father Michel to come toward him.

"You have me confused with someone else. I'm just passing through," Father Michel answered.

The monk's eyes gazed at something in the distance. "Please, it is imperative that you come with me *right* now," he urged. "Quickly, the church will provide you with sanctuary."

Father Michel shook his head and muttered, "No, I must be off." He lifted his feet to spur Lightning. Then he heard it — a rhythmical tapping — like distant music, which made the horse shudder uneasily with a blubbering snort.

He turned and saw the visage the monk was fixated upon. Down the road marched a group of men scantily dressed in gauzy white linens. Their garments were tattered and soaked with blood. In each hand, they held a whip and flogged themselves as they softly sang a hymn. The steady "tap-tap-tap" of their whips sliced across their bare backs and kept the beat of their song.

The monk spoke again. "There are the Flagellants Brahren. I don't think they've seen you yet..."

"Haven't seen me yet? What do you mean?"

The monk continued. "They arrived in the village several days ago and have developed an impressive following as they parade through the streets performing their penance. Openly, they condemn the church for being corrupt and immoral."

The quiet town began to stir as the living and the barely living gathered around the approaching procession. Father Michel could see that one of the Flagellants carried a large wooden cross. A woman rushed forward and wiped the blood off his back. She took the bloodied cloth and smeared it over her eyes, all the while praising, "Thank you for your sacrifice. Truly your blood is miraculous, like the blood of a martyr! It is the blood of Christ!"

The monk whispered to Father Michel, "The one who carries the cross like our Lord Savior is their master. They call him the Layman. He gives sermons in the town square and charges that the sins of the church have brought the pestilence as a punishment from God."

Father Michel nodded vacantly and grunted, "Everyone is blaming everyone else for this malady. Christians blame the Jews, Flagellants blame the Church..."

"Come. Follow me," the monk urged.

"No, I have to go that way, to get to the next town. Is there a road that goes around them?"

The monk shook his head no.

"Then I must ride through them." Father Michel counted nearly thirty Flagellants.

As they drew near the center of the town square, he saw that the scourges they pummeled their flesh with were studded with iron barbs. Blood splattered through the air as they flogged their raw shoulders, oblivious to the pain.

A naked man stormed toward the procession. His skin was covered in buboes and sweat glistened off his tumor-ridden body. His insect-like eyes bulged and darted. There was a huge crimson gash on his brow, and he pushed the bloody-eyed woman down to the ground in his effort to reach the Flagellants.

A farmer holding a pitchfork hollered at the naked man. "Get back to the barn! You were ordered not to leave!"

The naked man lashed out wildly, pushing down anyone in his path, as he rushed toward the procession.

The man with the pitchfork thrust his weapon forward and reiterated, "You were not to leave the barn!" The pitchfork sliced against the naked man's chest with steely claws, but still he pushed forward, injured and staggering.

The Flagellant who carried the cross spoke. "Let him come forward if he so chooses. His death is nigh, and his sins must be atoned for."

The man with the pitchfork remonstrated. "He is employed by me and works my farm. He and his family are to all remain in the barn. I could lose a lot of money because of that ingrate."

"That man is as your brother, and you are his keeper," The Layman boomed. "Atone for your selfish ways, or you will summon the chariot the pestilence rides upon!" He wielded his whip and sliced the farmer's back. "Repent now for your sins!"

The farmer turned to the crowd as if they would support him. "I risk losing everything if he doesn't rake the field and tend the animals!"

The whip cut through his wool tunic, and the farmer collapsed as a crimson stream began to flow between his shoulder blades. The Layman ordered, "Repent!"

The farmer cried, "Forgive me!"

"Call out your sins, and be quick!"

"My sin is greed!"

The Layman spun around with his weapon and gashed the naked man. "No man is without sin. Confess! Confess now or prepare to burn in the pits of eternal damnation!"

The naked man fell to the ground. His eyes rolled. As vomit spewed from his lips, he gurgled, "Please, Lord...forgive me."

The Layman struck the farmer again. The man dropped his pitchfork and cried, "I have the sin of deceit and wealth. I am a wealthy man, and I have cheated the merchants by adding sand to the sacks of flour that I sell at the market!"

"And you!" the Layman cried as he flogged the naked man again.

"I have worked on the Sabbath," he sputtered.

The Layman's scourge lashed back and forth between the two sinners. Soon, others in the crowd chimed in with shouts of their own confessions. Some threw themselves at the feet of the Flagellants and prayed while others clamored for a bit of the Layman's blood and eagerly wiped it over their eyes, lips and tongues.

"We must not fight among ourselves," the Layman called out. "The true enemy lies within the church." He looked up for the first time and locked eyes with Father Michel.

"You should not linger," the monk warned as he scuttled away.

The Layman stood silent as the cacophony continued around him. He had long, dark hair and a full beard, just like Christ. His bare chest heaved and he slowly set the wooden cross on the ground. He took several careful steps forward. The crowd moved with him and encroached upon the priest.

"There on the horse!" the Layman called out. "He is one who brought this curse upon us!"

Father Michel shook his head. "I am just traveling through this town. I have no quarrel with you."

"No, your quarrel is with God. We are his faithful, here to do his bidding."

The townspeople fanned out and began to encircle the priest. Lightning shuddered and snorted. Father Michel tightened his grip on the reins and loudly proclaimed, "I bear no ill will to anyone in this town. I simply want to pass through."

"Your will is that of the Church. And the Church's will is tainted with heresy, corruption, and sin."

"Let me pass!"

The Layman bellowed, "Behold the demon who hath delivered the pestilence! Smite him down!"

The Flagellants rushed forward with their scourges swinging. Father Michel spurred Lightning, and the horse lunged forward as the tiny metal barbs sliced into the steed's flesh. One caught on the priest's arm, ripping his garment and scratching his skin.

Hands reached out and grabbed for Father Michel. They caught hold of his leg and pulled. He struggled to remain atop the horse as his foot was yanked out of the stirrup. For a moment, the horse turned to that side and began to gallop in a circle.

The priest lost his balance. He muttered profanities under his breath and kicked vigorously at the culprits clinging to his leg. He began to fall sideways. Urgently, Father Michel smacked Lightning's rump with his whip. The shocked horse took off like an arrow. Father Michel teetered in the saddle. He clutched the reins, pulled himself up, and barely regained his balance.

Voices jeered as he fled. Some cursed him, some damned him, and one particularly loud man just laughed wildly and cackled, "I told you he would run! The Church *has* abandoned us!"

A number of the Flagellants and townspeople refused to give up, and they chased the priest and the horse on foot. Figures darted in front of the animal to try to slow it down. One grabbed at his reins and almost caught hold. Lightning was too quick for him though, and the intelligent beast flung his head back with a quick snap. After that, he shook his snout back and forth to thwart any future attempts to restrain him.

One stubborn person grabbed Lightning's saddle blanket and was dragged alongside the horse. Father Michel pinched the persistent fingers that dug into the blanket. He could not budge them. He raised his whip, smacking the hand and Lightning at the same time. Lightning sped off even faster, and the poor soul was forced to release his grip.

As the man let go, he fell under the frantic animal and caught a hoof in the side of the head. Blood gushed from the fatal blow. Father Michel watched the flailing body twitch and writhe in the middle of the road behind him as he sped off. The gathering mob trampled their fallen neighbor and gave chase.

Once free from the confusion of the riot, Lightning reared up. He snorted defiantly before dashing off. The crowd grew smaller and smaller in the distance as Lightning and Father Michel hastened out of town and toward his small country church.

Chapter 47

The Children's Story

The peasant lady who called herself Nana served Isabelle and Louis a warm meal of roasted chicken, green beans, and sweet potatoes all baked into a butter-crusted pie. It was the most delicious food Louis ever tasted, and he took three full helpings. When they were done, Nana boiled a warm bath and washed the grimy children. She tended to Louis' swollen ankle and spread a pasty medicinal substance over Isabelle's wounded arm.

Her husband, Aaron, anxiously paced the length of the tiny house. Nana covered Isabelle and Louis with a thick wool blanket, and they cuddled together in front of the fire. Louis' sniffles subsided, and his swollen eyes shrunk back to normal.

"My sister lives in the village on the other side of the mountains. She could take you in and watch over you until your parents are freed," Nana told them.

Isabelle felt an immense responsibility slip from her shoulders. She was still a child, and felt reassured to have an adult take over the situation. "Really?" Isabelle began. "We would be so grateful!"

Aaron paused his pacing mid-stride. His scrunched face had the permanent look of someone who just ate a sour apple. He chomped his bottom jaw repeatedly and reminded Isabelle of a cow chewing cud. "What if your sister gets caught? They could trace the children back to us. They will find out that we lied to the Inquisitors!"

Nana steadied her posture. "Aaron, you dizzy donkey, my sister would never betray me."

Isabelle chimed in. "We won't get caught. We made it this far. The hard part was escaping from the castle. Now we just need to make it through the mountain pass."

The man ignored Isabelle and spoke to his wife. "We may not even get them to your sister. What if *they* come back? What if *they* find them? They'll think they were here all along."

"They *were* here all along," Nana explained.

"Precisely! If they find the children here, then we are doomed."

"We are not *doomed*. You always rant about doom and gloom. Every day of the last twenty years you have preached about one misfortune or another. Why can't you be brave for once? Sometimes I wish the soldiers would come and take *you* away, you dizzy donkey!" Then to the children she cooed, "They won't be back anytime soon. Don't worry."

The prune-faced man grumbled and plopped down in a rickety chair.

Isabelle starred into the depths of the fire and swayed ever so slightly with her arm around her brother. Louis drifted off into a peaceful slumber.

Nana knelt next to the children. "I'll leave now for my sister's village. I shall return by morning with her. If all goes well, you'll be off with her tomorrow, and she'll take you to safety."

The woman stroked Isabelle's mane of hair. The girl thought of the gold coins that she had smuggled out of the castle. Now she considered handing the kind woman one of them as payment for her generosity. *No,* she reconsidered. *I'll wait until tomorrow. I'll give her three gold coins, just like the soldiers offered, after the deal is done.*

Aaron snored in his chair. Nana bid the children goodbye and slipped out the door. Isabelle listened as Nana rode away on the horse.

Aaron jumped up with a start when he heard the galloping hooves. "Where is that bat off to!" he demanded.

Isabelle felt uncomfortable with the man. "To fetch her sister. She said she will return tomorrow."

"Crazy woman. Just gets up and takes off without thinking!" he roared. In an instant, his grey, bulging eyes suddenly softened, and he spoke his next words almost to himself. "That's what I used to like about her. When we were first married, she would do the craziest, most unpredictable things. Kept me on my toes, she did..." his voice trailed off then boomed to life again. "Now she just irritates the hell out of me! Is she out of her mind? You, girl, come with me."

He grabbed Isabelle by the arm. She yelped and struggled, but Aaron was surprisingly able-bodied, and he easily pulled her down a dark hallway to the back of the house.

Chapter 48

Sebastian's Story
325 AD – When Rome Spread its Empire across the Barbaric Territories

IFabius entered the prisoners' cell. "Remove the Druid and take him to the second level tower room. That's his cell now," he ordered.

A guard stepped forward and prodded Baldebert with the flat end of his gladius. The plump, holy man hopped to his feet and took hurried steps out the door.

Fabius turned to the two guards who crowded into the small cell with him. "Leave now, both of you."

"But, sir, he is dangerous," one of the guards protested as he pointed to Sebastian.

The Cloaked Man lay on a grass mat on the stone floor.

"I will speak to him in private. Now leave as ordered!" Fabius shrieked.

His men retreated.

Sebastian sat up.

"Stay where you are, or this conversation is over," Fabius said flatly.

Sebastian froze, then slowly eased back into a prone position.

"I have good news for you, Sebastian. Your vision was accurate. I prevented the Gaul's attack and discovered indolent scouts who were ignoring their duties."

Sebastian smiled broadly, showing teeth that few living souls had ever seen. "Now you see how my visions benefit you!"

"Don't congratulate yourself too much yet." Fabius paced back and forth in the tiny room, barely taking two steps to span each length of the cell. "I plan on sparing your life, but there is one thing you and I need to discuss."

Sebastian followed the motion of the governor's boots as they swished back and forth. "Yes?"

"You are to never discuss pregnancy with Esindra again. Never, under any circumstances, do you understand me? I don't need her head filled with crazy hope; she will never let me hear the end of it."

"Sir, she very much wants a child, and I *do* see one in her future. I was giving her good news — news that you *both* would rejoice in. I thought that..."

Fabius stopped pacing and towered over the figure on the floor. "Don't *think*, Sebastian. Don't think one more thought on the subject. I tried for many years to have a child with Esindra. She has a fine lineage, and I need an heir, but we're unable to have children. *I* am unable, Sebastian. Over the years, I sought out many other women as replacement wives, all in an attempt to carry on my family name. There were twenty, thirty, maybe more. Some of them were little more than whores. Not one of them became pregnant."

"I see," Sebastian calmly responded.

"Esindra cannot bear children."

"Well, *she* could; *you* apparently just can't father the child."

"What difference does that make? If *she* can't birth *my* heir, then she is worthless as a wife. After all, that's what a wife is for," Fabius snapped.

After several silent seconds, Sebastian asked, "Governor, if Esindra gave birth to a child, then you would have an heir, regardless of whom the father really is, correct?"

"Are you suggesting she bed another man? She'd never do that. And if everyone knows the child isn't legitimate, the state will still seize everything I own after my death."

"But what if no one knew but the two of you? And what if she was tricked into believing that *you* didn't know the child was not yours? She would never speak the truth. She would carry the secret to her grave, and you would have an heir!"

Fabius knelt by the Cloaked Man with sudden intrigue. "How could I trick her to take another man? She is far too fearful of being caught."

Sebastian cleverly responded, "The plan is already set. You just need to follow my instructions."

Fabius sat in the cell with the Cloaked Man and listened. When they were done, the governor ordered the guards to take Sebastian to the tower room. There, he would have a warm bed, three full meals a day, the service of the Druid, plus anything else he desired.

Chapter 49

Dorothée's Story
Circa 1520 AD – the Dawn of the Reformation

The prisoner arrived long after Dorothée should have been asleep. Curiosity kept her awake and she peeked out her bedroom door as he was led down the hall to the keep. A black sack covered his head, and he shuffled his shackled feet as he walked. His body was lean, thin and muscular, he wore simple clothes: brown britches, tan tights, and a white tunic with a leather vest. He certainly didn't look like the dangerous criminal André-Benoit had described.

The next day, André-Benoit said his good-byes. He promised Dorothée that he would return to her as soon as possible. She cut a lock of hair from the back of her head. The single curl formed a perfect circle, and she presented it to him in a locket. He kissed the gold charm and stashed it in his breast pocket.

"I'll keep it close to my heart," he promised.

Dorothée spent the next few days reading in the library and gardening to pass the time. On the fourth day, she strolled across the castle grounds while Patricia dutifully followed behind.

"Patricia, this isn't at all how I imagined my new life," she said while lifting her spectacularly embroidered dress. "When I lived at home, I couldn't wait to be free of Mother and Father. They hovered over me like misers. I could never venture outside without an escort. I couldn't entertain friends. I daresay that Father would have kept André-Benoit and me apart during our courtship if I had not protested so much. My sisters, you remember them, Patricia?"

Patricia barely had a chance to reply with an affirmative "Humph," before Dorothée continued. "They all wanted to rule me just because they were older. Do you know what I think, Patricia? I think that they were jealous — especially Diane. Father wanted André-Benoit to marry her and not me because she is the oldest. Poor thing; to have her little sister off and married while she still waits at home! André-Benoit originally came calling on her. Did you know that?"

"I certainly did *not* know, Lady Dorothée. Who told you?" Patricia asked.

"No one. I found out for myself. I overheard Father talking the night before André-Benoit was to arrive. He and Mother were speaking of the 'wealthy vassal who was coming to meet his daughters.' Indeed, Diane was first in line to be married, as she was the oldest, then Helen. If not her, then surely Edith, who is still over a year older than I.

"Father said that perhaps he and mother should keep *me* from meeting him. Father even knew that I was prettier than my sisters! Can you believe it, Patricia! No, he would never admit such a thing in front of them, but that night, when he thought he was speaking privately with Mother, he said that André-Benoit would find *me* prettier than my sisters!"

"How fun for you to overhear such a compliment," Patricia replied.

"That is why I instructed you to put up my hair extra special the night André-Benoit came calling. Do you remember? I scolded you three times for messing up the braids!" Dorothée exclaimed while tittering whimsically.

"Yes, I recall," Patricia answered flatly.

"Oh! Don't be put out! I knew that I had to look absolutely stunning that night to entice André-Benoit. And think of how my good fortune has benefited you! Now you are here with *me*! You are my lady-in-waiting instead of a chambermaid to four girls."

"You are positively right, my lady, it is so much better here at the Château with you. I am quite happy indeed!"

Dorothée studied Patricia with unusual interest. "I know that you enjoy being at the Château for reasons *other* than serving me. I happen to notice things, Patricia..."

Patricia's round cheeks blushed as red as Dorothée's flowing hair.

"I've noticed how the cook looks at you and how you look at him."

"Yes," Patricia uttered with a coy smile. "Perhaps I have some romantic inclinations of my own. Claude is becoming...a very dear friend..."

Dorothée interrupted her. "I know he is more than a friend. Just make sure you remember where your duties lie. I don't need to have a distracted lady-in-waiting who does not provide me with her full attention."

Patricia's smile slipped from her chunky lips. "You always have my full attention. Don't fret, my lady."

"Now back to my story...yes, my sisters looked pathetic when André-Benoit came to call, didn't they? I'm so glad to be done with them. Yet, I don't understand why I am not happier. I feel...abandoned. I know I have you and the other servants to keep me diverted, but I do feel so hollow. Without André-Benoit, and he has only been gone three days, I just don't know what to do with myself! I am lonely, Patricia. For the first time in my life, I have all the privacy and space I've ever wanted and now I am truly alone." Dorothée shuddered and let a solitary tear slip down her cheek.

Patricia looked upon her Lady with newly developing compassion. She lifted a crumpled handkerchief and carefully wiped Dorothée's face.

"Thank you, Patricia. In many ways, you are like a mother to me now." She reached out and clasped Patricia's hand. "Now, please be a dear and prepare my afternoon tea. And for heaven's sake, do make it hot this time; let the water bubble in the fire for several minutes. Be gone with you now."

Patricia hurried off while Dorothée continued to meander over the castle grounds. Apple blossoms fluttered in the air and wove a pink quilt across the grass. She eventually walked back up the path and entered her domain. To her left, in the kitchen, Claude and the maids prepared the evening meal. They eyed her cautiously as she sauntered by.

Dorothée went to the library and absently chose a book — the author, Jacques de Baisieux. She sat in front of the fireplace and sighed loudly, as if she wanted someone to inquire as to what was wrong. No one did though.

Pouting dramatically, she thought about the prisoner. She caressed the leather binding of the book and wondered what his crime might be. *Was he violent? Was he evil?* Dorothée didn't even know what he looked like.

A flash of inspiration dawned on her. She could bring the prisoner a book to read! After all, he must be terribly bored with nothing to do in that little cell. *Almost as bored as I am*, Dorothée thought fleetingly. She marched forward with newfound motivation and pounded on the keep door.

"Who knocks?" a squeaking voice asked. It was one of the stable boys. In lieu of any available men-at-arms — they were all riding with André-Benoit — the steward was in charge of guarding the prisoner. He, in turn, assigned watch duties to the stable boys. One of them now grappled with the unwieldy door.

"It is me, Lady Dorothée. I have something for the prisoner."

With a rebellious groan, the door opened wide. The stable boy, brown with dirt, stood there.

She pranced past him without a second look, and stopped in front of the door to the tower room. Memories of being trapped inside it made her pause. A warm gush spread down her back. For a moment, she thought she would turn and flee, but then a shadow caught her attention. Through the open crevice in the door, she saw movement. Tentatively, she stepped forward and knelt in front of the portal.

Candles illuminated the round room. She saw that it was entirely different than before. Scraps and debris that once littered the floor were gone. A fair-sized bed with a tall headboard stood next to the strange wooden "door" on the opposite side of the room. The prisoner was standing near her, and all she could see were his waist and upper thighs. Beyond him, to the right, there was a writing desk and candelabra. It appeared that André-Benoit had supplied him with ink and paper.

Suddenly, a face leered at her through the hole. The prisoner had swooped down, and in an instant, he was bent with his eyes in front of the portal. Dorothée gave a short, shrill cry. The stable boy took a few valiant steps forward and then came to a halt. He hesitated a moment with a perplexed glower in his young eyes.

The prisoner let out a hearty laugh. "Sorry, my dear Lady, I didn't mean to startle you. I thought my supper was being served."

Dorothée caught her breath. "No. I don't have your supper. I am sure the maid will bring it shortly. I thought you may be bored, so I brought this for you." She slid the book through the crevice in the door.

The prisoner carefully studied it a moment. From her vantage, Dorothée observed a man in his late twenties with shoulder length, golden hair. He was much younger than Dorothée had anticipated, and she caught herself starring unintentionally.

The prisoner caught her gaze. "Thank you. I will enjoy it."

Dorothée allowed a faint smile to appear on her lips. "When you are done, I can bring you another. We have hundreds of books in the library."

"How kind of you, but how will you know when I am done?"

Dorothée began to speak, caught herself, and glanced at the stable boy who stood idly by. "I will...return tomorrow to see how far you've read."

"Only if it is no trouble."

Dorothée shook her head. "No trouble at all. I often find myself with nothing to do...so picking out your next selection will at least be something of a challenge for me."

"How much we have in common then! I also have nothing to do," the

146

sequestered man answered.

Dorothée giggled and glared at the stable boy once more. "You, go see where his meal is."

"I have orders not to leave my post until my replacement arrives," the young lad stammered.

With forced patience, Dorothée answered, "I am right here to watch the prisoner. Now, go do as you are told."

The boy bravely spoke again. "The steward told me not to leave. It is my duty and..."

"Who gives the steward orders?" Dorothée asked sharply.

"Ah, Lord André-Benoit," the miniature soldier answered.

"When Lord André-Benoit is gone, *who* gives the orders?" she insisted.

"*You* do? Oh yes, you do! Yes, my lady, I'll go check on his supper," the boy whispered as he scurried out of the keep.

She turned her attention back to the prisoner. "So, I will return tomorrow. If you are done with that book, I will pick a new one."

The prisoner pondered her words. "Very well, but how is it that you will select a book to my liking? This selection, though an excellent choice, was little more than a lucky guess."

Dorothée ruminated over the dilemma and smirked. "I can't be sure I will retrieve a book you fancy. But as you are a prisoner in my castle, you don't have much assertion over the matter."

"That I am, and I am much appreciative of your kindness. If the circumstances were different and you and I were mingling in the free air, I might take offense to such harsh words. But as this situation differs, I am grateful that so fair a lady, the master of the house, would even take time to acknowledge me."

Dorothée cocked her head. "If we did mingle in the free air, then I would be quite flattered by your charming remarks. But as you are a prisoner in my castle, I take such words with caution, as I doubt you would dare speak ill of me even if you thought it."

"No matter what your deed, I could never speak ill of someone so radiant. But the subject escapes us. I am here. You are there. I humbly thank you for your generosity." The prisoner closed his mouth with a smack and beamed at her with a crooked, closed smile.

The door to the keep burst open, and the stable boy stood there with a wooden bowl brimming with meat and bread.

"Enjoy your meal, prisoner. It looks to be quite hearty," the lady quipped as she made for the door.

"I will indeed...and you may call me Julien-Luc. Julien-Luc Tervagan Roterodamus."

She absorbed the name and gently shut the door to the keep behind her.

Chapter 50

Veronica's Story

On Wednesday, Veronica's cell phone rang. A jolt shot through her when she saw the name on the screen. It was Christophe.

"Hello, Lady Veronica!"

She was exhausted from several days of non-stop negotiations with the artists and experts who were now finally mending the tattered tapestries in the library, touching up the frescoes in the ballroom, and restoring the antique table in the dining hall. His voice infused her with new energy though, and she excitedly gushed, "Hello yourself!" She sought a quiet place in the Château, away from the bustle, where she could talk.

As she retreated into the parlor, Christophe said, "I called Ralph, my friend who deals in antiquities, and he said getting together next Saturday evening would be fine. He lives in Paris. You don't mind the trip, do you?"

"That's a long drive."

"We'll take my car. I just need to know where to pick you up."

"Oh!" Veronica exclaimed, as she realized Christophe didn't know where they were staying. "We're a ways down Rue Crevier at a Château."

"A Château on Rue Crevier?"

"Uh-huh. It's called Le Château du Feu Ardent."

"Ah, I know of it! My father tried to purchase it many years ago. I didn't think anyone lived there; hasn't it been abandoned for years?"

"Yeah, at least twenty. We're remodeling it for a woman named Marie-Claire. Do you know her?"

"I was just a boy when my father bid on it. I remember he was rather upset about some American who was able to pay more than he. The only reason the American was even able to buy it was because his wife was French. Maybe she is this Marie-Claire, huh?"

"Maybe. She's my employer, but I haven't even met her in person yet."

"So, this is the work that keeps you busy all the time! But, do you know that you are decorating a *haunted* castle?" Christophe said mischievously.

Veronica laughed uneasily. "Haunted? I doubt that."

"That's what they say."

"Well, I don't believe in ghosts."

"Interesting. I wonder if the ghosts believe in *you*," Christophe teased.

"Well, you can ask them yourself when you come over to pick us up."

"I'll be sure to do that. I'll be there, say five o'clock?"

"Sure."

"Great! Oh, I told Ralph about your necklace, and he said that similar items from that era can go for thousands of American dollars. He can find a buyer if you are interested."

"I kinda consider it my good luck charm," Veronica said as she fondled the coin dangling from her neck.

"Very well. So, I will see you next week. If you need anything, or if you want to, well...please feel free to give me a call anytime," stammered the man, who seldom seemed to be at a loss for words.

Veronica grinned. "Okay. Bye now." She clicked off her phone.

Nikki had crept up behind Veronica. "Who was *that*?" she inquired loudly.

Veronica jumped and twirled around. She was sitting on an old, velvet chaise. "Christ, Nik, don't do that! You scared the crap out of me."

Nikki chuckled. "Was that *Christophe*?"

"Yes, it was. He's picking us up next Saturday at five. We're going to meet his friend in Paris."

"Paris! We are going to Paris! Kick ass! So, is this friend cute?"

"I have no idea..."

"Is he at least rich?"

"I dunno, Nik. Does it matter?"

"It *always* matters."

Veronica stated matter-of-factly, "All I know is his name is Ralph."

"Eew, that's an awful name to have to scream during sex. Can you imagine? *I'm coming. I'm coming. Oh, RALPH, I'm coming!*"

"Well, damn, Nik, don't have sex with him then."

"So, what else did pretty boy say?" the younger sister chided.

"He said the necklace could be worth several thousand bucks."

"Wow. Score! And what *else* did he say?"

"Christ, would you grow up," Veronica scolded.

"Okay! I got it. I'm growing."

"Oh," Veronica lowered her tone, "he did say that the Château is rumored to be haunted."

Nikki became incredibly serious. "You don't say...a haunted castle..." She crouched down and whispered, "I have to tell you something, Vern..."

Veronica glared into her sister's intense eyes.

Nikki continued in a booming voice. "*All* castles are haunted!" She then snorted and chuckled to herself.

Veronica pushed her sister playfully and managed to conceal most of her laughter.

A man's voice suddenly spoke. "She's right, you know."

Veronica and Nikki both jumped. Clark stood in the doorway. Sweat soaked under the arms of his shirt.

"Christ!" Veronica yelled. "How long have you been standing there?"

"Only a moment. I wanted to see if you had the key to the door down the hallway off the library. The big door with the iron latches?"

"No, I don't," Veronica snapped. She realized her demeanor and readjusted her tone. "That's the door to the keep. I tried it with the skeleton key, but it didn't work. I'm going to get some WD-40 to loosen it up."

"Okay. Just let me know when you do. I need to see if there are any clogged sewer lines in there." He hesitated.

The girls said nothing. They knew that encouraging him to speak would lead to a long conversation that neither one of them enjoyed.

He wasn't deterred and finally continued. "You *do* know the stories about this place, don't you?"

Veronica didn't want to give the man one reason to stand there and talk, so she didn't answer. Nikki couldn't maintain her discipline, and she piped up. "What stories?"

"The ghost stories. You were talking about this place being haunted. I thought you knew. After all, you were supposed to have boyfriends join you — you said they were coming to help protect you...."

"We don't need anyone to *protect* us," Veronica answered flatly. She knew the plumber had just caught them in a lie about their "American boyfriends", but she didn't care. The insinuation that they needed men to watch over them irritated her. Everything about the plumber irritated her, though she couldn't explain exactly why.

"Nothing wrong with people watching out for one another," he gently answered. "Especially in a place as haunted as this castle."

"I don't believe in ghosts or hauntings or supernatural woo-woo," Veronica stated dryly.

"Well, okay then," Clark said sheepishly. "I'll be leaving. Be back on Friday."

Nikki wanted to hear more, but as she was about to speak up, her sister cast a disapproving glance. Nikki obediently fell silent.

"See you," Veronica replied cordially.

He lingered in the doorway as he spoke. "Yep, Friday, see you then." Eventually, he turned and saw himself out.

"The creepiest thing about this place isn't any ghost — it's *him!*" Veronica exclaimed.

"I wanted to hear the ghostie stories!" Nikki whined.

"Don't be childish."

Nikki pouted.

Veronica conceded. "If you want to hear the ghost story, we'll ask Christophe. I just didn't want to hear it from Clark. He'd be here all night talking and talking, on and on."

"Yeah, you're right. Hey, I'm going into town tomorrow to buy a new dress for the Fontaine's dinner party. Wanna come?"

"No, I'll just wear my black skirt and white blouse."

"Vern, that skirt is ten years old. Come on. Let's go buy something nice. Plus, you need something to wear in Paris, too."

"I can wear my black pants and grey blouse in Paris."

"Vern! You always wear black pants or that stupid black skirt. You really gotta increase your wardrobe."

"I'll think about it."

Nikki knew that meant 'no', but she nodded her head as she made her way to the door. "Ok, well, I'm going to take a shower and get ready for bed. Good Night, Vern."

"Good night," her sister answered as she pulled the diary off of the end table. "I'm going to read for a little bit."

Veronica curled up with the Journal Intime.

Chapter 51

Journal Intime

T here has been an attack on the castle! Last night a mob came to the gate and demanded that Henri come forth to answer for his gluttony. They hurled rocks at the wall with trebuchets and created quite a bit of damage on the east side. They have laid siege and still sit out there now. No one can leave the castle, nor return.

Fortunately, Henri was prepared for this, and we are well-stocked on food and supplies. A small garrison patrols the castle walls and guards the gatehouse while the rest of the inhabitants have retreated to the keep.

I am not alone in this dismal place any longer. The sudden influx of people and activity is altogether shocking. I was growing quite used to being able to sit and listen to the sounds of the castle, but now there is commotion all the time which distracts me severely.

In the tower room atop mine, Henri has his lodgings. Above him are the head guards. I can hear them at all hours of the day marching up and down the spiral staircase that encircles my chamber. The maids and other servants have taken residence in the small cells just across the hall from me with as many as six people to a room.

My body is dreadfully sore from lying prone for such a long period of time. How I wish I could rise and stretch and walk around! The midwife came to check on me a short while ago, and I asked if I may stand and walk around for just a bit.

She denied me; said that I have to remain on my back. If I were to stand up, even for just a moment, the baby could slide into the birthing position and come out early.

She has kindness in her eyes, but I sometimes notice them avert from me. I imagine I must look affright, with no powder on my face or properly tended hair. Still, there is something unspoken in her darting glances. What does she hide from me?

As she massaged my legs, I asked her, "Dear midwife, tell me, what troubles your gaze so that you cannot bear to meet mine?"

She smiled and tersely replied, "Nothing, my lady."

"Prey, tell me then why you look away when we speak?" I insisted.

"Is not proper to look one's lady in the eye, is all. I am showing respect," she said with an awkward glance.

I nodded, and she curtsied. Annoyed with her obvious lie, I dismissed her and now sit here writing the account.

Do you know she sleeps just outside my chamber door now? Her bed is on several straw pillows nestled in the corner. I am not sure I like her being so close. Does she sit and listen to me? Does she gawk through that slit in the door at night like a spy? Why does she have to be so close? Knowing those deceitful, darting eyes are just on the other side of the door is unsettling.

I adjust myself in the bed, and it squeaks in retaliation. I lift myself on my elbows just a bit to relieve the pressure off my back. As I do, I see a shadow through the slit in the door. I stop and stare. Is that her? Is that the midwife watching my every move, making sure that I don't get out of bed?

I'm going to stop writing now. I'm going to blow out the candle so spying eyes can't watch me. And then, when I am alone in the dark, I am going to stretch and stretch and stretch!

Josette-Camille

August 6th, 1789

We just received word that the National Constituent Assembly has formally abolished feudalism. I asked Henri what such a policy could possibly mean. Our very way of life is threatened!

He answered, "You should worry not of such matters. It only applies to the clergy and their tithes and affects just a few privileges of nobility. In the end, everything will be right in the world. The policy is merely intended to pacify the revolutionaries. It is good news, my dear. It means the Great Fear will end soon as the protestors have what they want."

Though this was supposed to be good news, supplies are still being rationed nonetheless. Henri assures everyone it is just a precaution. "We have plenty to last us several months, but just to be safe, it is best to be frugal."

I can only have one candle lit at a time so that we can conserve them. It is dreadfully dark in here with no natural light. The single flame casts eerie shadows on the wall.

After enjoying my nightly cup of absinth, I held my hands o'er my head and cast long, animal-like shadows on the curved walls to entertain myself. One hand became a slender-eared rabbit, and the other hand was a crooked-eared rabbit.

I created a little puppet show with one shadow conversing brilliantly with the other. My rabbit friends spoke of the beauty in art and the darkness in war. They bounced around like players on a stage, reciting poetry and delivering dramatic soliloquies.

I laughed as they told jokes and whispered arcane little secrets to one another.

"I can hear you!" I warned the rabbit puppets.

They both stopped quickly as if caught by a constable, and we all giggled feverishly.

At last, a third rabbit shadow appeared on the scene. He was somewhat larger than the others, with a high arch to his back. He pawed at the air with claws that almost looked like human hands.

The three rabbit shadows chased each other around the circular walls. My hands hurt as I had held them up for so long, but I was so completely amused by the game we played I couldn't bring myself to stop. Until, that is, the candle flame flickered out. It had melted completely. I had been so enthralled by the puppet show I didn't even notice it was near the end.

I lay still and stared into the darkness. No longer humored, I felt the chill of the air and smelled the dankness of the room. That decaying odor was back, and I held my breath in the hopes it would soon pass. I heard it then — a low, guttural sound. Breathing, I could hear something in the room with me breathing.

Sobriety took over for the briefest moment, and I realized that I could not have made three rabbit shadow puppets on the wall — I only had two hands! Something else had joined me, and it was in the dark room with me!

I considered crying out, but realized Henri would only think it was one of my "fits of fancy". Besides, I had the feeling that if I did try and alert others, I would make it angry, and intuitively I knew that was not a good idea.

What do you think it could be? I wondered that for quite some time, considering the shape of its shadow on the wall. It had a long snout and high-arching haunches. Was it really a rabbit? But that was absurd; how could a rabbit get in here? How could anything get in here? A mouse perhaps? A small mouse could cast an enormous shadow in the right light — yes, that was the logical answer.

Whatever it was, it didn't make any threatening moves and in truth seemed rather docile. I sat quietly in the darkness with it for some time. Together we enjoyed the stillness. Eventually, I relaxed and inhaled deeply, breathing in the disturbing scent that still lingered. The fragrance wasn't so bad after all. After taking a few more deep breaths, I became somewhat used to it and accepted it freely.

The fear I felt gradually slinked away. I decided it was actually nice to have company with me! Eventually, I drifted off to sleep, but not before whispering a pleasant g' night to my rabbit-shadow confidant.

Josette-Camille

August 10th, 1789

My life has developed a regular routine. Upon awakening, the maids serve my breakfast, after which I am visited by the midwife. She checks my stomach and feels to see if the baby has changed position. We speak briefly, her eyes always downcast, and once she decides all is well, I am left alone until midday. Then, I am served my second meal and my first glass of tonic. Again, I am left alone until the evening when the third meal is served with my second glass of tonic. The evening candle is also lit then. Once it burns halfway, my evening tonic — my third glass — is delivered. I drink it until sleep takes over, and I awake the next day for the ritual to start again.

To pass time, I sit and listen to the sounds of the castle or play shadow puppets on the walls. There is not much to do when sequestered to a bed; wouldn't you agree?

Every so often, Henri will visit. I never know exactly when he is coming, so it is always a surprise. I miss him so much, and it brings me great joy to see him! He is always so busy tending to the safety of our castle that he nary can spend more than a few minutes with me.

He likes for me to pass the time writing poetry. I struggle with it, though. The poetry I used to write was inspired by the pastoral scenes of the landscape and our beautiful gardens. Here, there is no beauty to derive inspiration. My only muse is the rabbit shadow that comes to visit in the deep hours of the night when the candlelight has almost flickered out.

I find myself a-dreaming about this vile place
The creature that dwells here hides
And I cannot see its face
It threatens as it protects me
Becoming my one true saving grace

Josette-Camille

Chapter 52

The Pagans' Story

Trinna resisted the urge to lift her head and meet the gaze of the Hag. Time stood still in the silent tunnels while the old woman determined who would be the next sacrifice.

Bevin stood to Trinna's left. She risked a quick glance at him. He gave her the slightest reassuring nod, and she returned a fraction of a smile.

Someone gasped.

Trinna turned to see the girl standing to her right snatched by the stag-headed man. The Hag triumphantly cried, "Yes! The Earth has chosen!"

"No, please, no…" the victim pleaded.

The stag-headed man grabbed her shoulder and led her down a narrow corridor. He took no torch.

There was a long silence. The Hag quietly resumed her place in line.

The only sound was from one of the children who sniffled over and over again. After several minutes, the stag-headed man returned — without the girl.

જી૭ ❖ ૭૨

The procession eventually emerged outside the caverns to a chorus of chirping crickets keeping rhythm with the night. The fresh air cleansed Trinna's spirit and her lungs. She felt a shot of energy and lifted her face. In front of the group loomed towering stones, like enormous fists emerging from the ground. The moon cast long dark shadows from the ominous monoliths. They were erected in a giant circle, and the group solemnly entered. In the circle's center was a stone slab held up by several smaller stones, like a primitive table fit for a giant. The children were seated in front of the slab. As Trinna took her place, she caught a glimpse of a pit on the other side.

Everyone became busy at once. The priests emptied the woven baskets and prepared for the ceremony. Flowers, herbs, and incense were set on the slab and a fire was started beneath it.

Several of the old women priests brewed a concoction in a pot over the fire. With much revere, they prepared the elixir and poured servings into wooden soup-cups. Each child was handed one and ordered to drink. Trinna observed the other children as they obediently sipped. She took a tentative lap and, in a flash of inspiration like déjà vu, remembered the musky flavor. She quickly nudged Bevin. He looked at her sideways. She shook her head slightly while gesturing with her soup-cup and mouthed three words: "Don't drink it!" She made sure no one was watching and poured her serving onto the moist grass.

"Why not?" he whispered back.

"It will stupefy you. That is why none of the children ever remember the ceremony. It is enchanted to make us forget."

Bevin swirled his cup. "Maybe forgetting is a good thing…"

"No, look at the effect it has on them. Already they are falling under its spell."

The others had glazed eyes and drunken grins. One girl, who was crying earlier, now howled with glee. Some began to quietly sing, while others swayed in time with the chanting Hag.

Bevin sniffed the brew in his cup and took a tentative taste. "It's good! It'll help us join the celebration and end this awful ceremony. I don't think it will hurt to drink just a little…"

"Don't," Trinna begged. "I need you to keep your wits with me!"

He obliged the pretty girl sitting next to him. Anything to please *her*. Swiftly, he dumped his cup with a regretful sigh.

A few of the priests cooked flatbread over the fire. The scent reminded Trinna of home. She let her eyes fall shut. Even though Trinna had consumed barely more than a sip of the mysterious brew, she felt dizzy. Dreamily, she thought she heard a crying baby. In an instant, the sound stopped short, and the people gave out a joyous cheer. When Trinna's eyes popped open, she saw one of the male priests jumping around wildly. Red stains speckled his bare chest. In his hand was a fistful of tangled white hair. Several people were in Trinna's line of sight, so it took her a moment to realize he was holding the goat's decapitated head. The priests began to dance around the animal's carcass.

Other children joined in the dancing and drunkenly whirled in un-choreographed circles around the fire as the goat was prepared to be cooked. Bevin suddenly grabbed Trinna's hands and pulled her to her feet. He, too, began to dance chaotically and urged her to join him.

"We can't just sit here," he said. "We have to do what everyone else is doing." His kind smile was replaced with a dopey grin.

The small taste of the elixir obviously had an effect on him, too. Trinna studied his face as he fought to retain his composure. Glazed eyes focused in and out of lucidity with pupils that grew and shrunk in the glinting bonfire light.

Reluctantly, she danced with Bevin.

The festivities continued into the night. The smell of cooking meat now mingled in the air with the fragrance of the bread. They feasted and danced, drank and sang. Each time Bevin and Trinna were served more of the concoction, they cheered like revelers, pretended to greedily drink it like the others, but always dumped their servings.

At last, the Hag ordered silence. The merrymakers were deeply engrossed in the festivities and several seconds passed before she could summon everyone's attention. She waved her staff, and a quiet blanket enveloped the crowd before her. She began chanting; her words were low and baritone. The foreign syllables were spat forth from the old woman's tongue with vigor.

Trinna's shoulders suddenly felt hot and the back of her neck became sensitive, as if a single touch would cause excruciating pain. Warm bile bubbled in her gut. She felt nauseated as the woman chanted her evil spell. Trinna fell to the ground and crouched on her hands and knees while vomit spewed past her lips. She shook violently as the heaving contorted her body.

Chapter 53

Dorothée's Story
Circa 1520 AD – the Dawn of the Reformation

Dorothée returned to the keep the next day as promised. She pulled up a small stool, sat, and levelly glared through the portal into the tower room that held Julien-Luc Tervagan Roterodamus.

"Are you enjoying the book by Jacques de Baisieux?" she inquired coolly.

He rose from the small table with book in hand. "I enjoyed it greatly. I finished just now." He passed it to her.

"Already? Finished?" She wasn't sure if she believed him. "Then perhaps I should bring another?"

"Only if it is no trouble."

"I don't have much else to do."

"A lady such as yourself with no parties to plan, no games to play, no courts to attend? I find that hard to believe."

Dorothée huffed. "André-Benoit says I must stay put here until he returns. He would never allow me to venture to someone's court or attend a game without him. No parties either; though, I do hope to invite my sisters to visit soon. I am idly waiting here, trapped behind the castle's fortified walls, like a prisoner."

Julien-Luc's eyes grew wide. "Well, not *exactly* like a prisoner."

She swept a tuft of her red curls behind her ear as she laughed. "Indeed, not exactly. At least I have free range and am not sequestered to that foul tower room."

"It's not so bad in here."

"Are you sure? I ventured in there once. The door locked behind me and there was a…creature…or something locked in there with me. It was horrible, like a demon."

"A demon, say you? What kind?"

"How should I know what *kind*? It was black with festering, matted fur. It was positively evil!"

"Did you notice anything else about it?"

"Why do you ask? Have you seen it, too?"

He shook his head and said, "No, but if I do I want to know what to expect."

"It smelt rancid and burnt, like someone cooked meat that had gone bad. André-Benoit said it was just a rat though. It likely ran away when they cleaned your room before you came."

"Do you really think it was just a rat?"

She considered for a moment and silently shook her head.

"I believe you, Lady Dorothée. Thank you for warning me."

"You *really* believe me? Even the smithy and the cook said it was a rat, and they were there!"

"I can tell by your eyes; you truly saw something."

Dorothée puffed up by siting forward on the stool. "Then you are wiser than my husband or any other man in this castle," she smugly claimed.

At that, the prisoner chuckled and lightly changed the topic. "Are you sure you don't want some hint as to what book I would *like* to read?"

She considered for a moment. "No. I shall pick. Half the fun is trying to guess!" She gave him a quick bow as she rose and left in search of the perfect literary text.

Chapter 54

Veronica's Story

It was Saturday evening, and Veronica and Nikki were poised in front of the bathroom mirror applying makeup and fixing their hair. Nikki held a curling iron on the top of her head with her left hand while the other smeared liquid foundation over blemishes on her chin.

Veronica was wrapped in an oversized bath towel and carefully spread gloss on her thick bottom lip. "Are you almost ready, Nik? We gotta go in ten minutes."

"Almost, but you're the one who isn't even dressed yet." Nikki wore a new dress; it was fire engine red with spaghetti straps. Gold and ivory beads were woven into the bodice. It frayed out in layers of satin that reached to her calves.

"I just have to slip on my skirt and blouse, and I'll be ready." Veronica smacked her lips and smiled at herself in the mirror.

"No, Vern, you aren't going to wear that old lady skirt! I got another dress when I went shopping. Here, try this on." Nikki grabbed a garment bag that was hanging behind the bathroom door. The dress inside was covered in silver sequins, short, and sexy.

"I wouldn't feel comfortable in that."

"Try it on please. I bought it just for *you!*" Nikki pouted and held the dress out to her sister like an offering.

"Ah...you bought that for yourself. You told me that you couldn't decide between the two."

"Well, I decided on the red one which means you can wear the black one! Don't worry; it's stretchy so it should fit."

Veronica frowned. "I have my skirt and blouse that I *know* will fit."

"Yeah, but you'll look like shit."

"I'll look just fine!"

"You can't wear clothes you bought at Goodwill to this dinner party, Vern. Come on. It's a basic, little, black dress. You can't go wrong."

"Fine. I'll try it on, but we have to hurry. Are you ready?"

Nikki pulled the curling iron out of her hair and flipped her head from side to side. Her waves naturally fell into place. "Now I'm ready."

Veronica let her towel slip to the floor and pulled the slinky cocktail dress over her torso. She turned so Nikki could zip the back.

"You get those underwear at Goodwill, too, Vern?"

"Enough about my clothes. I'm wearing the black dress, aren't I?"

Nikki yanked the zipper and gasped as her sister spun around. "You look incredible, Vern. You *gotta* wear this dress."

"It's so short and low cut!" The front of the gown scooped down, revealing a considerable amount of flesh. Veronica tugged at the top of the dress to conceal her cleavage and caused the hemline to creep up. She then tugged at the border to cover her thighs, and the neckline plunged.

"It's perfect. Wear this wrap with it." Nikki produced a matching black scarf and twisted it around her sister's neck so it hung loosely over her chest.

"I guess it isn't so bad," Veronica conceded as she adjusted her bra.

"Not so bad...you look *smoking*, Vern!"

Veronica frowned. "Fine, I'll wear the dress. Now get your shoes and let's go."

❧❦❖❧❦

They arrived at the dinner party twenty minutes late. *Fashionably late*, Veronica hoped as they pulled up to their neighbors' château. It was Greek revival classic in style. Two staircases swooped around a flowing fountain, met in the middle, and led up to the front door. Three columns on each side held up the cornice, which was adorned with a leafy designed frieze, reminiscent of the Parthenon.

The sisters chugged up to the valet in the orange boxy car. Several sporty European models that Veronica didn't even recognize were parked in front. She reluctantly relinquished the keys while wishing she had cleaned the McDonald's bags out of the backseat.

The sisters were escorted into a huge foyer. Massive fluted columns reached up to support the twenty-foot ceiling. Neoclassical paintings hung on the walls. Veronica thought she recognized an Antonio Canova piece and a work by Jacques-Louis David.

They followed the butler, and he offered to take Veronica's wrap, but she declined. They entered an enormous, bleached-out room, with pristine white Italian marble floors, pillars, ceilings and walls. It was generously accented with gold-leaf filigrees and finials, and filled with unfamiliar people with alabaster faces.

"Ms. Veronica and Nikole Dixon," the butler announced.

The twenty-or-so people turned with vapid stares and all nodded politely at the women standing in the entry. They mingled around an elongated dinner table which was adorned with bone china, fragrant orchids, and sparkly crystal. A harpist, violinist, and cellist plucked delicately in the far corner, near huge patio doors that led to a veranda drenched in buttery moonlight.

A forty-something woman in a crème-colored skirt and blouse stepped forward. "Hello, we are so happy that you should come! We are the Fontaines. I'm Bridget and over there is my husband Alfred." She pointed to a gentleman in a maroon smoking jacket and a vibrant red scarf — the only bright spec of color in the room — who was excitedly speaking with an older woman who was smothered in diamonds.

"Nice to meet you, Mrs. Fontaine," Veronica said as she offered her hand.

The woman smirked, ignored Veronica's hand, and leaned in to plant a kiss on each side of Veronica's face. Veronica awkwardly returned the greeting. Mrs. Fontaine greeted Nikki in the same manner. Nikki was prepared and graciously received the introduction.

"Please, call me Bridget. Let me introduce you to the others." The woman with the monotone clothing took Veronica's hand and led her to the first small group of people.

160

"This is Mr. Jonathon Lebec and his wife Candice. They live at Le Château Monmouth. Oh, and this lovely dear is their daughter, Sefferine."

The girls introduced themselves to the trio. Mr. and Mrs. Lebec were in their early fifties; Sefferine looked no more than twenty-one. She wore an olive-green blouse that exposed her bare shoulders and had a neckline that plummeted to her navel. Her dark hair was pulled back in a tight bun and gold hoop earrings dangled from the sides of her tanned face. She was gorgeous with crisp green eyes and a tiny, cherub-like mouth. She barely nodded at Veronica and Nikki.

"We were just enjoying our aperitif before dinner, here," Bridget stated as she plucked two dainty glasses of rosé from a waiter's tray and handed one to each sister. "Now come, you must meet Alfred." She led them to her husband. He was speaking in French and throwing his arms wildly in the air when they approached.

"*Les voilà, les nouvelles voisines, c'est ça?*" Alfred Fontaine started excitedly as the girls were ushered into his presence.

Nikki beamed brightly. "Oui, vous pourriez dire cela. Je m'appelle Nikki et je vous présente Veronica, ma sœur."

Veronica smiled awkwardly. She was able to decipher her name and nothing else.

Nikki continued. "Ma sœur ne parle qu'anglais."

Mr. Fontaine grinned at Veronica as if he felt sorry for her. "How sad that you cannot speak the most beautiful language in the world. I speak English just so-so. It is very, ah, stupid?"

Veronica was slightly taken back by the man's straightforwardness. "Stupid?" she asked, lilting her voice to mimic his dense French accent.

Mr. Fontaine grinned. "Oui. You say 'phantom' with an 'f' and you say 'fish' with an 'f' but then you say 'pocket' with a 'p', and it is so ridiculous."

Everyone, including Nikki, twittered at his observation.

Veronica wasn't sure if she was the butt of the joke or not, and she awkwardly laughed along with them.

The butler rang a bell, and everyone took his or her seat.

Mr. and Mrs. Fontaine sat at either end of the long table. Veronica and Nikki sat across from each other and next to Mrs. Fontaine. On the other side of Nikki was a handsome man in an ivory suit jacket. He had a square jaw and finely manicured, dark hair. On the other side of Veronica was the older woman decorated in diamonds who Mr. Fontaine was speaking with earlier.

"L'entrée, mademoiselle," said the server as he placed a petite plate in front of Veronica. On it was a cucumber round with a dollop of salmon mousse on top of it. A sprig of dill made it pretty.

"The French sure do eat light," Veronica said while popping the entrée into her mouth. "In America our main courses are huge!"

The woman in diamonds leaned into Veronica and stated with a snicker, "In France, the entrée is what Americans call an appetizer. The main course is yet to come, dear."

"Oh," answered Veronica as the waiter snatched her aperitif out of her hand and replaced it with a glass of red.

At the other end of the table Mr. Fontaine proclaimed a toast in French. Nikki listened intently while Veronica pretended to understand his words. After clinking their glasses together, Veronica sipped the smoky merlot.

Bridget began the conversation. "The red is our newest batch, harvested only six years ago. A little young but we couldn't wait to try it. What do you think?"

"Delicious," Nikki chirped as she swirled the garnet colored liquid in her glass. "I can see it has a thick body." She took another sip. "Delightfully complex. I detect hints of berries and oak. Very flavorful, with a lot of textures. You should be incredibly proud."

Bridget turned to Veronica.

"I like its textures, too," Veronica stated simply.

The diamond woman spoke in a thundering voice. Her words came out slowly; she was concentrating on her English pronunciation. "It is a lovely wine. We will place an order for our châteaux."

"Thank you, Lady Florence," Bridget replied. "I'm not sure if you've been introduced to Veronica and Nikole yet."

Lady Florence tilted her head, and the girls mumbled gracious hellos.

Bridget continued. "And her nephew, Lord Richard Rennes."

The good-looking gentleman next to Nikki nodded at the sisters.

"Lady Florence owns the Rennes Châteaux. You are familiar with them?" Bridget asked.

Veronica felt that she should be, so she nodded her head.

Nikki spoke up honestly. "No, I don't believe that I am."

Richard gazed at Nikki and explained. "Our family owns several châteaux that have been converted into hotels all over Southern Europe. The first one, of course, was Le Château Rennes, just on the other side of the river Cher. We've branched out over the years. I live at Le Château Rennes here locally. You really should come by sometime. I could give you a tour."

Nikki exposed a beaming smile. "*Ça serait merveilleux!*"

Richard answered her in French, and before Veronica could interject, they were communicating quite rapidly to only each other.

Lady Florence sighed. "Tell us about you, dear," she said to Veronica.

Veronica quivered and blurted, "I *decorate* châteaux."

"*Comment?*" Lady Florence asked.

"Umm, I de-cor-ate castles. I am an interior designer. That's what I'm doing now — decorating Le Château du Feu Ardent," Veronica stated proudly as she finally found something to talk about.

"You are *decorating* your Château?" Bridget asked.

"Yes. The owners are turning it into an inn, like Lady Florence's."

There was an awkward silence.

Veronica felt many eyes set upon her, all except for Nikki and Richard. They were huddled close and clinking glasses in a private toast.

Veronica decided to showcase herself in front of her potential clients. "I have my own studio in Los Angeles, *Veronica's Room*. I once designed the interior of a Kardashian's dog's house! For the Château, I am using an eclectic mix of the old and new to create a fairytale castle for my boss. If anyone here needs any work done, I give free consultations." She shuffled in her purse for business cards.

No one spoke for a moment. Then Bridget erupted in a nervous giggle. "Oh! I didn't realize that you were *hired*...we thought you were the new *owner* of Le Château du Feu Ardent!"

Veronica felt a tremble in her gut and tucked her business cards back in her purse. "No, I don't *own* it. I was just...yeah...*hired* to decorate it."

Lady Florence spoke. "Have you decorated any *American* castles?"

Bridget chuckled.

"No, there really aren't many American castles. This is my first one." Veronica reached for her wine and gulped a hefty swig.

Lady Florence continued. "Abert-Du Clare designed our motifs. Are you familiar with his work?"

Veronica didn't recognize the name, but she nodded meekly while gazing at her sister. Nikki was twisting a lock of hair in Richard's direction.

Bridget leaned back while the main course was served in front of her — rack of lamb in a jelly sauce over a bed of baby carrots. "What do you think of our estate?" she asked. "Does the décor suit your taste?"

Veronica gazed around the opulent room. "Oh, yes, it is lovely. I especially enjoyed the Antonio Canova and Jacques-Louis David paintings in the entry way." Veronica felt a moment of pride as she was able to throw out a few notable artist names.

Bridget cast a dubious glance. "We don't have any Canova or David in the foyer. Do you mean the Mengs and the Ingres? They are neoclassical; perhaps that's why you had them confused?"

"Yes, maybe...they are very nice." Veronica reached for her knife and cut her lamb chop. It was incredibly tender and slid off the bone. She unnecessarily cut it into pieces, desperate to avoid the conversation.

Lady Florence praised the meal in a French-English combination. "This lamb is tender. *Très facile à découper.*"

"Oui, ce nouveau chef est magnifique. On a fait un bon choix," Bridget answered.

Veronica tried to translate their words. She once again sent a desperate plea with her eyes to her sister across the table. Nikki finally did look up and responded to Bridget. "Magnifique!" She grinned quickly at Veronica and then, once again, turned all her attention to Richard.

Lady Florence and Bridget continued their dialogue in French. Veronica was purposely being left out of the conversation between her hostess and the diamond woman, and her sister was all but ignoring her in favor of the French stud sitting next to her. She stabbed at her lamb and continued to cut it for no apparent reason.

An eternity passed before the main course was cleared and a lemon sorbet was served. As the waiter passed by, Veronica asked, "More merlot please?"

He gazed at her for a second as if he wanted to say something but then retreated to the buffet table. He returned a moment later and poured her second glass of wine. Eager to make small talk, she politely told him, "Merci beaucoup." Her pronunciation was tainted with nervousness though, and "beaucoup" sounded like "boy-cup". She lifted her glass and gingerly took a sip. The waiter raised his eyebrows and walked away without saying a word.

Veronica scooped up a thick helping of the sorbet and shoveled it into her mouth. It tasted bitter against the flavor of the merlot that lingered on her palate. She glanced around and noticed that everyone but she had a new glass filled with bubbling gold-colored wine.

Bridget addressed her dilemma. "The sorbet is a pallet cleanser. You should really drink the sparkling wine with it."

Veronica pushed the merlot away and hoped the waiter would return soon with her dessert wine.

Nikki finally turned to her sister. "Did you hear that, Vern?"

Veronica looked up from her mostly eaten sorbet. "Hear what?"

"Richard will be renovating three of his suites this fall. Maybe you could design them!" Nikki gleefully patted Richard's arm.

"Tell me about your work," Richard stated.

Veronica wanted to crawl into a hole. *Not this conversation again.*

Lady Florence spoke. Her words, once again, came out slow. "Veronica is the hired designer at Le Château du Feu Ardent. It is only her first castle, but she did decorate a dog house once."

Richard didn't catch his aunt's condescending tone. "Oh! Le Château du Feu Ardent has such a rich history. What are you doing to honor its past?"

"Well, I am combining old and new styles...bringing it up-to-date while, you know, *honoring the past.*" Veronica grabbed the sparkling wine that was finally placed in front of her. She saw that everyone else was now being served coffee with little trays of macarons, but she drank it anyway.

"Abert-Du Clare," Lady Florence began, "our decorator, is known throughout France as being a true master when it comes to capturing the ancient splendor of a castle. He pours over the history of each place he decorates. He diligently strives to be authentic. He did just that when he worked on Château Rennes. How have you researched your castle?"

Veronica shrugged a shoulder and in a squeaky voice said, "I Googled it." She shoved a raspberry macaron in her mouth.

"Google?" Lady Florence asked.

"You know, on the internet."

"So, you didn't go to the library, research documents, books, study the lineage of the former owners?" Bridget inquired.

Veronica froze then quickly nodded. "Sure, after I Googled it, I did all that."

"I wish I could see it when it is done. I think I might find it...extraordinary," Bridget said while Lady Florence tittered.

Nikki finally picked up on the challenge in their tones and accepted. "Oh, you will be able to see it when it is done. We are having a huge party to celebrate. We'll invite you all!"

Veronica felt her soul snap. "A *party*?" she whispered in disbelief.

"Yeah, a masquerade ball. Complete with fancy gowns and masks." Nikki sat back in her chair, proud of her quick thinking. "A Hollywood-style premiere of Veronica's work. It will be so much fun!"

"How can you hold a masquerade ball in a castle that you don't even *own*?"

Bridget quipped. "Wouldn't your employer be displeased?"

Nikki realized that she must have missed part of the earlier conversation, but she quickly retorted. "Oh, Veronica's boss simply adores her and is so proud of the work she's doing. It was *her* idea for Veronica to hold the masquerade ball!"

Veronica gaped as her sister mounted one lie on top of another.

"Sounds splendid. Who else will be invited?" Bridget asked.

Veronica could only think of one single name to drop. "Christophe Sinclair is a friend of ours. He's a bank manager in Amboise."

Sefferine, the beautiful young woman in green, spoke for the first time. "Christophe?"

"Do you know him?" Veronica asked, eager to not list more names.

"Well, of course, every woman in Amboise knows Christophe. I know him *quite* well." She knowingly flashed a glance at another woman sitting across from her.

The second woman rolled her thick head of red hair back on her shoulders. She was about the same age as Sefferine. "Yes, I also know Christophe," she replied devilishly.

Veronica wanted to learn how they *knew* her precious Christophe, but then the conversation took another quick turn.

Mr. Fontaine interjected. "A masquerade ball in a haunted castle — a magnificent idea!"

Sefferine was curious. "Oh, your castle is haunted?"

Veronica nodded. "That's what they say."

"It's one of the most haunted castles in the Loire Valley. You researched its history. Tell us about it," Mr. Fontaine urged.

Veronica suddenly wished that she had listened to Clark's ghost stories. "Well, I must admit, I don't *believe* in ghosts, so I can't really say too much." Veronica could tell by the expressions on the other guests' faces that her answer was not sufficient. "Why don't *you* tell the story, Mr. Fontaine? You're our host, after all."

The boisterous man at the end of the table gladly took over the spotlight. "Ah! If you insist, it would be my pleasure. As you probably know, Le Château du Feu Ardent is one of the oldest in the valley. No one is certain how far it dates back. Some say it was built over the site of ancient holy grounds, used by Druid prêtres, ah, how do you say? Priests. Druid priests. They practiced Pagan magic and ritual human sacrifices. They conjured primitive, evil things. To this day, something still dwells there, along with all the condemned souls who perished in Château du Feu Ardent over the centuries..."

Veronica took a moment to close her eyes now that everyone's attention was diverted from her. Her skin, however, bubbled with unnatural perspiration, and she dabbed her brow with a napkin.

Mr. Fontaine noticed her discomfort, paused, and asked, "Are you alright, dear?"

It took a moment before Veronica realized he was addressing her. She blinked with surprise and nodded.

With a somber tone, he confided, "I was a teenage boy when the castle was last inhabited. Curious, I went there one night with some friends." He stopped and quickly surveyed his guests' response before revealing his long-ago juvenile delinquency. Satisfied, he grinned sheepishly. "We were drinking wine — Renold, my best friend, and I, and two girls," he confessed. "We were maybe eighteen..." he considered the exact number and changed his mind. "No, seventeen, oui, seventeen! The people who lived there weren't around often. I think it was a vacation home they visited only on holiday. So, we didn't think anyone was even there when we climbed over the wall. Drunk and puerile, we stumbled up to the Château. We wanted to attempt to find a window to break into, but to our surprise the front door was left unlocked! Renold walked right up to it and pushed it open. Oui, we should have known better and run right then, but what can I say, we were drinking wine!"

Several of the guests raised their glasses to toast as he shouted, "Wine!" — except Veronica, who trembled as her stomach gurgled uneasily. She glared at Mr. Fontaine. He was smiling broadly, completely enjoying the attention, but then a subtle flash of apprehension flickered behind his crescent-shaped eyes, and he continued. "We went inside. Noir. Oui, it was noir, and we could not see anything. Renold led the way, and I stayed near the doorway with the girls. He went into the next room — it was large — and straight across from the front doors." He glanced at Veronica for acknowledgment.

"That's the library," She stated lethargically.

"It was the library!" Mr. Fontaine squealed as if the identity of that room had been a throbbing mystery to him all these years. "Well, Renold saw something in the library. It shocked him so that he screamed and turned and ran right past us as he fled out the front doors. The girls started screaming along with him and followed him blindly. I did not know what else to do, so I ran, too." Taking a sip of wine, he quietly looked up at his attentive guests.

Sefferine would not let him pause the story. "So, what was it? What did he see?"

Mr. Fontaine ignored her direct question. He stared ahead without seeing any of his guests, obviously recalling the episode exactly as it happened. "Renold had the car started and was shifting it in reverse right as I jumped in...had I took a second longer, he would not have waited for me; I am certain of that. The girls were crying, with the tears coming down their faces, and still he would not talk. 'Renold,' I said. 'What was it? What was it?' but he would not say."

"He would not say?" Sefferine mimicked.

"Not then," he confirmed. "But after we took the girls home, I asked him again."

Veronica felt queasy. *The wine must be getting to me*, she thought — though she barely finished two glasses. A wave of nausea rolled over her, and just as Mr. Fontaine opened his mouth to continue, Veronica interrupted, "Please, excuse me...I need to douche...I mean use the toilet...I mean your bathroom!"

The butler pointed vaguely to the hallway and politely pulled out Veronica's seat. She didn't anticipate him moving the chair and began to stumble. To compensate for her clumsy motion, she tried to adjust herself so that it looked like she was attempting to stand and turn at the same time. However, the long scarf that encircled her neck was tangled on the back of her ornate chair. Caught,

Veronica came crashing back into the chair. Her bottom wavered on the edge of the seat for just a moment before she once again lost her balance and tumbled to the floor.

The rest of the dinner party rose to their feet as Veronica flailed on the oriental carpet. The scarf was tight around her neck, choking her. Her short skirt hiked up past her hips, and her lime-green girdle-like panties were on display for all to see. Nikki rushed to her side.

Sefferine and her friend twittered. Lady Florence stood back to give everyone a good view. Mr. Fontaine rushed to the aid of his guest.

Veronica gasped for air while Mr. Fontaine pulled on the knotted scarf. Nikki managed to yank her sister's dress down to a respectable level. After an extremely awkward scene, which included Mr. Fontaine and Nikki hoisting her up by clutching her armpits, she was back on her feet.

"Vern, you okay?"

Veronica coughed, and someone handed her a glass of water. She slurped it down and eyed the onlookers through the bottom. Her only thought was how incredibly foolish she must look. She nodded her head at her sister while tears welled in her eyes.

"Let's go home, okay, Vern? I'm getting kind of tired."

Veronica continued to nod while holding the glass of water over her face, concealing the smeared mascara that was now trickling down the sides of her nose.

"Can someone pull our car up?" Nikki asked as she steadied her sister with an arm around her waist.

Together they walked toward the foyer.

"Yes, bring up their car," Mr. Fontaine ordered.

The butler loudly asked, "Are they driving the Twingo?"

"Yeah, that's us," Nikki replied as Veronica cowered next to her.

The girls dashed out of the Fontaine's dining room while a ripple of snickers echoed behind them.

"Thank you for your hospitality," Veronica spluttered.

No one returned her good-bye. As soon as the sisters crossed the threshold of the foyer, the dinner party whispered like frantically purring cats.

Mr. Fontaine loudly addressed his guests. "Where was I?"

They respectfully fell silent.

"Tell us what he saw!" It was Sefferine's voice echoing down the corridor.

Nikki hesitated by the doors, eager to hear the end of the story. Veronica moaned as the orange car pulled up.

As the girls descended the stairs, they could hear his voice in the distance. "Renold wouldn't tell me until after we took the girls home. I don't know if he didn't want to scare them, or if he feared they wouldn't believe him. I saw his face though, and I believed him. He saw something..."

His voice grew distant as the sisters got in the car, but Veronica and Nikki heard three distinct words: "That wasn't human..."

Chapter 55

Father Michel's Story
1348 AD – The Great Peste

Father Michel's cherished country church was dark and boarded up. A large scarlet cross was painted on the front doors. Not a religious symbol, it was a warning to keep out or risk infection.

He dismounted Lightning. "Wait here, boy."

Father Michel pulled a key from his pocket and walked past the main entrance to a small door on the side. It opened to an aisle that extended down the length of the church. Father Michel crept softly as dust particles twinkled in the stale air around him.

Ahead was the pulpit where he once proudly preached. Jesus Christ was there; peering back at him from the enormous crucifix suspended behind the altar. Sunlight seeped in through the blue and red stained glass windows, illuminating the Savior with a purplish hue. Outside an oak tree's branches swayed like massive arms. The twiggy ends scraped across the glass like desperate fingers.

Father Michel rushed past Christ. Bobbing shadows from the branches cast dark patches, like buboes, on the body of the Lord and Savior. The priest came to his old chamber and turned his back on the statue as he fumbled with the door.

It was locked. Perspiration bleared his eyes and Father Michel's breathing became shallow as he slid the key in the hole. Heat from the dusty sun enveloped him like a fever. The door finally opened, he stepped inside, and was greeted with the tang of rotting meat.

He didn't have time to finish his food the day the Cardinal's guards came for him. A chunk of venison, dry pudding, and a moldy black piece of bread sat on his desk as a reminder of his last meal as a parish priest. The rest of the chamber was sparsely decorated with only a cot, a small stool, and a diminutive cross suspended over the doorway.

Also on the desk was a Bible, spread open to the book of Job. Under the Bible was the parchment with the note he had written to Claudeen. It was still there!

Dear Claudeen,

Our lives face peril like no other. Chaos consumes our world and arduous decisions must be made. If it were not for the peste and the devastation it has wrought, my request would seem bold and incomprehensible. But as our community spins into insanity, we must make choices that also seem insane.

They summoned me to Cardinal Thibaut's Castle. I refuse to go. Instead, I implore you, Sweet Claudeen, to run away with me. Let's escape this dying place and leave behind all the forces that keep us apart. If indeed our days are few because of the plague, then I want to spend every last one of them with you. If God has forsaken us, then I feel no guilt in forsaking Him in return.

I need you to come with me, Claudeen. I have the money we will need. A small fortune is in my possession, and it will buy us a new life. I will wait for you tonight behind the Church. Tell your husband I summoned you for a prayer session. Or tell him nothing and simply slip off into the night. I will be there, Claudeen, waiting for...

The letter was unfinished. Before he could sign it and summon a messenger to deliver it, they came for him. The guards burst in and ordered him to come with them immediately. They had stood watch as he gathered a few personal items, making it impossible for him to grab his most valuable belongings.

Now, several days later, he was back to finish his mission. Father Michel snatched the letter and crumpled it into his pocket. Then he pulled out the desk's bottom drawer.

It was empty.

He reached in and pushed down. With just a little effort, he was able to release the false bottom of the drawer, revealing a secret chamber.

The jeweled box was still there. It had not been found either. Father Michel feared that looters could have easily uncovered it. "Is this yet another test, Lord? Is *all* this just a damn test?"

He opened the tiny latch on the box. It clicked, and Father Michel was able to set his eyes on the object of his passion.

Chapter 56

Dorothée's Story
Circa 1520 AD – the Dawn of the Reformation

Dorothée spent much of her time pouring over books in the library in an effort to provide Julien-Luc with satisfying reading material. Chaucer, Dante, Shakespeare seemed to please the prisoner. She made daily visits, usually dismissing the stable boy who guarded the room, thus giving Julien-Luc and she the liberty of talking privately...and her the opportunity to flirt freely. She loved the game, and on occasion, she caught him flirting back.

On his fourteenth day of captivity, Julien-Luc confided in Dorothée. "The books you bring are certainly a pleasure to read, but I wonder if you could find me something different?"

Dorothée taunted playfully. "Do you prefer reading material from Martin Luther and John Wycliffe?"

"Of course not. You know those are blasphemous titles. Wycliffe's writings were banned by order of a Papal bull over a century ago. Even possessing such literature is punishable with death. Surely, you don't want to see me burned at the stake like Jan Hus."

"Hmm," she pondered before she pressed him. "I must say I don't know what a Protestant likes to read other than blasphemy."

"Dear Dorothée, I am not a Protestant like those men. You must believe me when I tell you that I am not here for that reason!"

She loved his reaction. It was a splendid mix of passion and desperation. She wanted more, so she challenged him. "My husband *told* me you are a Huguenot, a Protestant leader championing the movement against the Catholic Church."

Julien-Luc chuckled as he saw through her game. He decided to play. "Obviously, your husband doesn't know *everything*. How smart can he be if he abandoned you here with me?"

She cast her eyes down demurely. She loved it when he dallied.

Julien-Luc continued. "He and the other Catholic leaders *believe* that I am on the side of the Protestants. But there is another side, one that is neither Catholic nor Protestant."

"Another side? What other side? There are but two; one is right, and one wrong."

He eyed her suspiciously. "Please, tell me I can trust you, dear Dorothée, for I suspect my fate could rest in your hands."

She gasped at his sudden candor. No longer playful, no longer harmless flirting, the prisoner's pleading eyes told her that his impending doom was real. She saw him for the first time not as an idle diversion for her amusement, but a condemned man who would surely soon perish for his crimes.

"I simply love secrets. I absolutely die for them," she said.

"Do you?" he asked seriously.

She let her thick lips part slightly and nodded.

He studied her like a priest evaluating a sinner. "I am a member of the

Brethren of the Common Life."

This revelation did not impress her. "And Martin Luther studied under the Brethren of the Common Life at Magdeburg," Dorothée flatly stated.

"And my brother, Desiderius Erasmus, did, too. Indeed, he and Luther were once great friends, bonded together by similar beliefs and their shared desire for truth. But that ended years ago. Luther called my brother a liar and heretic. They split. Erasmus even fled from Basel, Switzerland only last year when the city officially reformed to Protestant. He lives now in Freiburg im Breisgau."

"Freiburg is currently in turmoil over becoming Protestant. That is where my husband is right now."

"My brother is there, too. And it is where I am from, Dorothée. The Brethren of the Common Life has many members living there. We are caught between two factions — the Catholics and the Protestants."

Dorothée's eyes flashed. "How could you be caught between the two? Pick the righteous side and be done with it!"

"That's the problem. We *are* on the righteous side! And we're forced to watch both the Catholic and the Protestant dogmatists fight about who is favored the most by their timid father-god in the clouds who never bothers to lift one of His almighty fingers and just settle the argument once and for all! Dear, Miss Dorothée, religion is a fantasy; a dirty veil that covers people's eyes so they can't see the truth. Religion feeds off our fears and anxieties, becoming stronger and stronger the more we fight among ourselves. Our hatred makes it grow. Both sides claim to have impeccable morality, yet it is *immorality* that finds a friend in religion. Each side reduced to blind barbarism as they quarrel like babes fighting about garden fairies!" His voice crescendoed before becoming deafeningly silent.

Dorothée gazed at him, mesmerized. "I think I may stand and applaud."

He quickly fell humble. "I'm sorry. I shouldn't speak so passionately to a tender woman."

She shook her head. "No, I enjoy your candor. More, please, speak more."

"I fear I tell you too much. Possessing arcane knowledge can bring deadly consequences."

She flashed a reckless sneer and proclaimed with a pout, "You, sir, are much closer to death than *I*. If you are wise, you will confess the arcane knowledge to me. If you don't, you risk it dying with you — unless it is not really so precious after all."

At this, he cracked up. "You're certainly a talented beguiler, dear Dorothée!"

"It is but *one* of my many talents, dear Julien-Luc!" Her own words caught her with surprise, and she blushed feverishly red. It was one thing for a man to casually toss around terms of endearment like "dear" when addressing a lady, but for a woman — and a married woman at that — it was highly unacceptable, especially within the context of a statement so obviously laden with sexual innuendo. "I should go now..."

Julien-Luc objected. "Leave now? No, please stay!"

She looked at her delicate hands and suddenly clasped them like a proper lady. "I have duties to attend to." She stood, slightly curtsied, and fled the keep.

Chapter 57

Sebastian's Story

Cicero entered the courtyard where an opulent dinner had been prepared. Long tables, low to the ground and surrounded by pillows, were laid out with a feast of roast boar, wild turkey, and venison. Bread, wholly cooked vegetables, and fruit were abundant. Minstrels plucked at their instruments as Cicero took his regular seat next to Fabius.

"Not there, Cicero, move down," Fabius stated matter-of-factly.

The words confused the proud centurion. "What do you mean, sir?"

"Make room as we will be joined by a special guest tonight."

Cicero felt his neck grow hot. Several nearby soldiers cast their eyes down and avoided his disconcerted look. He rose slowly, took two side steps, and sat down on a pillow that was several feet away from Fabius.

A hush fell over the party. Cicero gaped over the heads of the other soldiers that obstructed his view. He felt a pit grow in his abdomen — walking across the courtyard was Sebastian. He wore a Roman robe. His frayed hair was still shockingly long and unkempt, though his face was clean, and he had trimmed the unsightly facial hair that the Roman's found so barbaric.

The Cloaked Man walked slowly, enjoying the moment of his entrance. He gazed at the stoic faces. One large smile greeted him; it was that of Fabius.

"Sit, Sebastian! The man of honor — it is a pleasure to have you dine with us tonight!"

Cicero stiffened. Over the past several weeks, he had observed Sebastian's transformation from prisoner to informant as he fed the governor tactical information. Once Cicero even heard them laughing from within the war room, like two old generals exchanging battle stories. Cicero fought back his anger and simply grunted as the Cloaked Man took a seat between him and the governor.

"Thank you, sir," Sebastian said with a nod.

"Ah-ha! Thank *you*, Sebastian. Because of your visions, our forces were able to conquer the Visigoth and Gaul tribes. They were forced to pledge their allegiance to the Roman State. Prime slaves were chosen from their ranks, and a new trek of land was added to Rome's vast rule."

Cicero flinched at the musings and reached for a slab of meat.

"Wait, let Sebastian be served first!" Fabius barely glanced at Cicero. He clapped Sebastian on the back and snapped his fingers so the music would play louder. Cicero sat still while the Cloaked Man reached over him and helped himself to a flank of roast boar.

The celebration bristled with excitement as everyone began to eat, drink, and discuss the magnificent battle.

"Constantine will be pleased!" erupted a voice, and the Romans clanked their goblets together.

Young servants in flowing, silken loincloths poured wine and danced among the revelers.

"What do your visions portent now?" a soldier asked Sebastian.

The crowd quieted as the Cloaked Man spoke. Even the servants paused in their duties to listen to the mystic's words.

"All the signs indicate an extended period of good fortune. You are in favor with the ancient gods. However, I do see a barbarian leader who has the ability to threaten your rule. He is known as the Head Commander. He has the power to destroy you."

Cicero scoffed. "*One* man is no threat to our legion!"

Fabius ignored his centurion. "What can we do?"

"The Head Commander is not yet capable of his destiny. And destiny is a fragile thing; it is flexible and pliable. You must act soon and eliminate him. Like a farmer who kills a wolf pup so that it will not grow to attack his herd, you must destroy the Head Commander before he grows fangs."

Fabius was transfixed. "But how? Where is he? I will send assassins. I will wage war on his tribe!"

"May I suggest something more subtle? He resides with the tribe that lies to the north. Offer to make an alliance with them to defeat their enemies to the west. The northerners will be intrigued by your offer because of the potential power...the Head Commander is still young and easy to trick. Invite them here and prepare a feast like this..."

"Ah! Then we attack him. Once inside these walls, he will be defenseless!" Fabius spoke as the epiphany struck.

Sebastian cocked his head and spoke in a quiet voice. "Such an overt attack would only exact revenge from his tribe...that would not be prudent. The Head Commander should come here, be taken in as a friend, and let to leave as a friend. After he leaves, death will befall him."

"And how will that happen?" Cicero snapped.

"With a potion that he will imbibe. I can make the concoction. The poison, when given in small doses, can take hours before claiming its victim."

"Let us make it done. We will send word to this Head Commander of the Northern Tribe. We will invite him and his men here to discuss peace. They will no doubt be suspicious of us, but we will gain their trust. We will be gracious and offer them women, food, and wine. Only the Head Commander's glass of wine will be fixed with your concoction."

"That is a marvelous plan, sir," Sebastian cajoled. "There is just one thing that I need."

"Name it. What do you want?"

"I must blend the ingredients under the moonlight and without interruption. Grant me private access to the courtyard tonight."

Cicero could hold his tongue no longer. "This is madness! He is trying to trick you, sir. He means to escape. You cannot let him go into the courtyard in the middle of the night unattended. You'll never see him again."

Sebastian shot back, "Speak not of my intentions because you don't know them!"

Fabius rose out of his chair. "Cicero, hold your tongue! Sebastian can have what he needs...the fortress walls are heavily guarded. He won't escape. Besides, why would he want to? Look at him...he's hardly a prisoner anymore."

"Though he should be! He committed horrid crimes. He should be put to death on the wheel, not given dinners and honored like a hero!"

"Cicero, this man has done more for my army in two months than you have done in two years! His crimes are irrelevant when compared to all the good he's done for us. You would be wise to learn from him, or you may find yourself sitting much, much further away the next time we dine."

Cicero clenched his teeth. Sebastian eyed him sideways, with a crooked smirk visible only on one side of his face.

After a moment of silence, Fabius twirled his hand in the air, signaling for the servants to pour more wine. Instantly, voices erupted, and Cicero quietly left his seat and sulked away.

Sebastian leaned over while pointing to one of the servants. "I have one more favor to ask. Could I have some company tonight?"

"One of the slave girls?" Fabius sniggered knowingly.

"In truth, *they* would be of more use to me." Fabius followed Sebastian's gaze to a throng of unsuspecting adolescent boys.

Sebastian continued, "I would find them to be more to my liking."

Fabius grunted. "Consider it done. They'll be delivered to your room tonight after the feast."

Sebastian rolled his eyes with anticipation.

Chapter 58

The Pagans' Story

Bevin knelt by Trinna. She was on all fours, hacking, but no longer vomiting. Bile soaked the ground, and a string of saliva dripped from the side of her mouth. He pulled strands of hair away from her face and whispered, "You're okay. I'm here."

She leaned back, wiped her mouth, and let her eyes fixate on the growing inferno that now blazed under the stone platform. An image seemed to dance deep within the flames — something sinister with spindly legs and a long snout

"Feeling better?" Bevin asked.

She nodded. "Uh-huh. I'm glad you're here."

Beside the fire, the Hag rolled her bones, over and over again until she was satisfied. Neither Bevin nor Trinna noticed her stand and lock her steely gaze on them. The man with the stag's head did though, and he advanced.

Frenzy erupted among the priests. They began to chant. "Fire has chosen, fire has chosen!" Several of them danced in a ritualized style, screeching and grunting. The Hag stood like an overseer. She shouted ancient prayers and appeared to grow taller in the illumination of the dancing flames.

The stag-headed man loomed over the young couple. He clutched Trinna under her arms and pulled her up. Her feet dangled in the air as he raised her high above the dancing crowd. A cheer erupted among the worshippers.

Several hands clenched Bevin's body and held him back. He watched in horror as Trinna was carried toward the ominous blaze. His beloved shrieked and flailed her arms. The stag-headed man fought to contain her. Trinna shimmied from his grasp and slid to the ground with a flat thud. The Hag sprang forward with unnatural agility to see the unexpected commotion.

Trinna lay on her back as the worshippers jumped and twirled around her. Hysterically, she kicked her legs and raised her body up by her elbows. Like a crab, she crawled backwards and into the thick of the crowd.

The stag-headed man lost sight of her amidst the dancing worshipers. He crouched low to see her feeble attempts to retreat. He clasped one of her ankles and pulled her toward him. She kicked violently and struck him firmly in the jaw. Blood splattered from his mouth. He roared with pain. One hand held her foot firmly, and the other rose in the air like a shield. Just as she geared up for another kick, he snatched the offending leg. Up he stood, lifting her upside down by her ankles.

A few of the priests noticed his struggle and stood clear to allow him to pass. Others danced on, oblivious to the drama. The Hag closed in and was able to witness the situation thoroughly.

The stag-headed man swung Trinna by the ankles, through the flames, and onto the altar.

"Bevin!" she cried.

Her hero snapped at the sound of his name. In a fit of courage, he twisted free from the hands that held his wrists and punched two of his captors in the face. They lunged at him, trying to re-apprehend the spry boy, but he dodged them easily.

"Trinna!" he called in response.

The stag-headed man loomed by the fire with his back to Bevin. With a cry of anger and resolve, the love-struck boy rushed into him at full speed. The stag-headed man was unprepared for the impact and lost his balance. Flailing his arms as if he were a bird that could catch the wind and stand straight, he fell face-first into the fire.

Flames roiled all around the altar. The stone slab was like a giant frying pan, and in its center, Trinna cooked like a piece of mutton. Through the wall of flame, she caught glimpses of the dancing figures on the other side. Mingled with the crackling wood and the rushing plumes, she could hear them chanting. The stag-headed man peered at her passively from the other side and then suddenly was rushing toward her, spinning his arms like a windmill. He crashed through the fire, and for a moment, she locked eyes with the dead beast upon the man's head. It was mere inches away, and immediately, its hair burst into flames before her eyes.

As the stag-headed man flailed in the pyre, sparks and embers sprayed several nearby worshippers, catching their hair and clothing on fire. They bustled around in a frenzy; desperate to extinguish one another.

The Hag barked out orders as the situation quickly escalated to hysteria. People started to run; some toward the fire to help, others away to avoid the spray of sparks that cascaded through the air.

The old woman made a sudden, sick realization. She caught a clear view of Trinna's face through the flames and finally recognized the girl. The sacrifice was one of the chosen children from last year's ritual...*Trinna was not supposed to be here. The entire ceremony was tainted!*

Bevin was momentarily surprised by his own force as he easily knocked the behemoth into the inferno. His mouth gaped as the stag head burst into flames.

The man-beast stumbled in the pyre, tripped once, then secured his footing and sprang back out. He rushed into the crowd like an animated torch, knocking into people and spreading dollops of fire wherever he ran.

As Bevin dodged around the burning man he saw his beloved wearily collapse on the slab. Flames lapped at her like hungry tongues. Before he could jump in to save her, one of the priests seized Bevin by the throat. Bevin writhed to escape, but the aggressor's grip was secure. Together they tumbled to the ground.

The frail priest was no match for the vigorous, young boy, but he sucked precious time away from saving Trinna. Bevin didn't want to kill the man, but had no choice; there was no time for a melee. In a fit of fury, he thrust his elbow into the gut of his attacker.

The priest released Bevin's throat and collapsed to one knee. Seizing the opportunity, the boy spun around and gained enough momentum to push his assailant into the blaze. Like a bale of dried autumn hay, the man burst ablaze.

One of the other children, a sweet-faced girl of only nine summers who lived around the bend from Bevin, tried to help the priest. She reached for the man through the flames. Their hands clasped, but instead of her pulling him out, he pulled her in.

Bevin didn't care; Trinna was the only one who mattered to him now. As the little girl cried out for help, Bevin rushed forward and jumped as high as he could. He leapt with the grace of a gazelle, flew through the fire — over the burning priest and child — and landed on the altar beside Trinna.

Her hair was smoldering, and her flesh was charred. Almost all of Trinna's clothing had burned off. Her near-naked body glistened with perspiration against the immense heat.

Picking her up, Bevin staggered awkwardly, not knowing what to do next. Jumping out the way he came would land them in the middle of the chaos and surely they'd be apprehended again. Without a second of hesitation, he lunged in the opposite direction.

Together, the lovers fell and missed the ground.

They spiraled into the hole on the other side of the slab. Trinna's frail body hit the bottom of the pit first; Bevin landed squarely on top of her. He heard bones snap as his flesh pounded against hers.

❧❦❖❧❦

It was oddly peaceful at the bottom. The commotion above was muted and seemed miles away. Bevin rolled off Trinna and lay beside her for a moment. He stared up at the pit's opening. The inferno raged just to the left. Beyond that, the night sky bore back at him with serene twinkling stars and a passive grey moon.

Bevin could have closed his eyes and fallen asleep, but instead he slowly asked, "Trinna, are you okay?"

She sucked in two labored gasps of air but didn't answer.

He cupped both hands around her delicate face. Her cheeks were scorched black. She smelled like fried meat. Her charred lungs heaved, and she coughed. "Bevin..."

"I'm right here. Don't worry; you're safe now."

"What happened? Where are we?" She stared up at the opening of the pit.

"We landed in a hole where they throw the..." Bevin stopped talking as he noticed the charred bones of their predecessors scattered all around them. "They must throw the ashes in here," he said quickly. "But we're safe. It was such chaos up there; I don't think anyone even saw us fall in here!"

Trinna gasped. "My throat feels like it's on fire."

"I'll climb out and get you some water."

"No, it's too dangerous. Just stay with me."

"Okay, I will. I promise."

Trinna coughed, and Bevin held her as a spasm rippled her trembling body. She found her voice again. "I always dreamed we would be together. I thought you would have chosen me as a bride..."

"Yes, I *will* take you as my bride. I am going to ask your father at the harvest festival. It has been my plan all along."

Trinna's vision bleared with ashen tears. "I won't be at the harvest festival."

177

"Yes, you will. We'll both be there. Don't worry; I'll get you out of here. The stag-man ran off when he caught on fire, and the others are in a panic up there. We'll climb out unnoticed and escape into the woods..."

"I can't move, Bevin. I can't even feel my body." She coughed out crimson spittle.

"Then we'll wait here until they all leave. And if they come for us, I will fight them off! I'll kill that Hag with my bare hands! I'll kill them all, Trinna. They can't have you."

"I love you, Bevin. Ever since that day at the festival when we first met as little children, Bevin, I do love you."

"I love you, too," he whispered as her body fell limp in his arms. "Trinna, stay with me! We will get married. We will be together!" He clutched her wrists and willed a pulse to throb against his grip.

Trinna's blood refused to flow, however, and Bevin opened his mouth to cry out. The agony was so intense that no sound came out. Instead, a thin, crisp string of bile streamed from his open jaw.

The old woman's shadow appeared at the rim of the pit. Without looking up, Bevin knew it was her. He covered his beloved's body protectively with stiff, shuddering hands. "Go away..." he managed to whisper.

The Hag seethed. "You've ruined everything! Do you even know what you have done?"

Bevin fearlessly shot back, "You killed her! You witch."

"She wasn't supposed to be here. She killed herself."

The boy looked up at the Hag. "Every year you snag us from our homes and pick random sacrifices and for what? For what?" he defiantly challenged. "I saw no demons, no gods, no spirits. It was all you and your stupid bag of bones. You have no real power. It is all a ruse because you are an evil woman. You aren't a priest of our people. You are a witch! *You* are the demon — not the wind or the water or earth or fire!"

"Insipid child! It was the spirit of fire that chose her. You doubt its power? Then just wait because it will show itself to you soon! You released it."

She waved her staff at Bevin. He glared at her until she turned and sauntered away, mumbling curses as she went. She trudged through the pandemonium and into the forest. None of her priests followed her.

In the Hag's wake, more confusion and fear gripped the crowd. Several of the worshippers continued chanting while others lay dead or dying from their burns. Children were scattered here and there. Some were mere lumps on the ground, trampled by the reckless feet of the adults. Others were spared and remained sleeping like ignorant babies. Still a few others wandered aimlessly, bewildered, and unable to process anything through the haze of the hallucinogen that still flowed in their blood.

From deep within the woods, the Hag bellowed an ancient prayer. Her chanting could be heard into the wee hours of the morning.

Chapter 59

Veronica's Story

That crazy song, *Istanbul (Not Constantinople)*, echoed in Veronica's head again; thinking of it the other day during the picnic with Christophe had resurrected it from her memory. It was a swing song, and it jumped and jived annoyingly against the throbs of a headache.

As she slowly trudged through the Château's library, she rubbed her temples to make it go away. It wouldn't.

The words were mixed up. Veronica flopped on one of the leather chairs in front of the fireplace as the verses haunted her.

> Istanbul not Constantinople
> A long time ago it became Constantinople
> Constantine named Constantinople
> Why Sebastian was a jerk
> Is nobody's business but Baldebert's

That certainly wasn't the way the song went! She couldn't get the words out of her mind. They kept looping like a dog chasing its tail. Her sister's transistor radio sat next to her on the end table. She turned it on...anything was better than that old song beating in her brain.

Something dark and heavy with a foreboding melody moaned from the tiny speakers as she pulled a throw blanket over herself.

> Dream the dream that only you can dream
> Sing the song that only you can sing
> Dance with me, we'll start slow
> Clasp my hand, now lose control
> Bite the monster only you can see
> And dream the dream you only dream for me

"Vern! Where are you?" Nikki's voice broke the cryptic spell of the song.

"In the library," she yelled back as she turned the dial in search of another station.

Nikki sauntered in through the entryway from the dining room. "This place is too huge." She sat in the leather chair beside her sister. "Only one station comes in on that stupid thing." She swiftly pushed her sister's hand out of the way and spun the dial back to its solitary channel, where that song continued.

> Spirits in the maze
> Burning brighter
> Like a dream within the haze
> Dancing fire...

Veronica punched the radio's "off" button.

"Why'd you do that? I thought you liked that song?" Nikki pouted.

"*That* song?"

Nikki nodded. "You used to sing it all the time when we were little."

"I never sang that song. I don't even know the band."

"Krimzen. It's classic 80s hair metal," Nikki answered.

"It's annoying. I wanna listen to something soothing. I have a headache..."

"Hung-over, huh?"

"Just a headache. What happened last night at the party anyway? I made an ass out of myself, didn't I, Nik?"

"Naw ya' didn't. You just had a little too much to drink; that's all."

"But, I didn't! I had one glass of merlot and a few sips of the rosé and the sparkling. I wasn't drunk," Veronica insisted.

"Well, maybe if you're lucky, they'll just *think* you were drunk," Nikki said lightly.

"Oh! I was that bad that it'd be *better* if they thought I was drunk? Oh God! I don't even know what happened. That story Mr. Fontaine told made me woozy, just creeped me out I guess. I feel like such a jackass." Veronica slid down in her chair.

"Who cares what those snobs think. Fuck 'em, right, Vern?"

Veronica grunted. "They think I'm a joke. There goes any chance I had at more business in France."

"That's not true. You'll show them when we unveil this castle during the masquerade party."

Veronica groaned and began to protest. "No, Nik..."

Nikki popped up before her sister started whining. "Shush! You just relax. Get nice and cozy by the fire, and I'll get some good music going and then make ya' some hot chocolate." She pulled her phone from her pocket.

"What am I? A five year old?" Veronica glowered.

"No, it's just a good day to kick back and relax. What do ya' want — marshmallows or whipped cream?" Nikki asked.

"We have marshmallows?" Veronica inquired coyly.

Nikki lit up. "Of course we have marshmallows!" She plugged her phone into the speakers atop the fireplace mantle and hit 'shuffle' before scampering off into the kitchen. The moment she left the room it solemnly began:

When the absinth finally takes its toll
Let the whispers guide you down the hole
Cheshire Cat, whispers near
Smiling wide, have no fear
Fight the monster only you can see
And dream the dream you only dream for me

"That's not funny, Nik!" Veronica shouted. She lobbed a pillow at her sister's phone, but it harmlessly fell short. "Stupid *throw* pillows — don't even work," she lamented sarcastically to herself.

"What are you bellyaching about now?" Nikki called.

"You played that stupid song on your phone!"

"What?" she asked, while carrying two cups of hot chocolate across the library threshold.

Veronica cast her sister a stern look and then glared at the phone.

Nikki looked genuinely perplexed. "What a freaky coincidence, huh?" She handed her sister the mug of cocoa. Veronica warily snatched it.

"Don't act innocent," Veronica scolded.

"What? I didn't play that on purpose. Hell, I didn't even know I *had* that song."

Veronica cradled her cup and sipped her cocoa. "Just turn it off, please," she said shortly. She opened the diary and began to read as Nikki shuffled to The White Stripes to make her sister happy.

Chapter 60

Journal Intime

Agathe has arrived! Dear, sweet Agathe and her family traveled all the way from Paris. She said it was a treacherous journey, and they had to ride in a modest looking carriage and dress in rags so as to not be recognized as nobles.

Agathe was dreadfully appalled at the condition of this bleak room that I am confined to. I assured her I am entirely comfortable and am used to the dreariness now. She brought flowers, picked from the garden, just for me. I thanked her, of course, for such a kind gesture. I have wanted flowers to brighten up my chamber since they moved me here!

The colorful blossoms were absolutely delightful at first, but after a few minutes I noticed they emitted a peculiar odor. It was a biting, unnatural scent, almost like the pong of smoldering metal melting in a kiln. I found it overpowering and nauseating. It cut through the room like a steely weapon and invaded my senses.

As soon as she left, I pulled the flowers from the vase. A thorn sliced my hand, and the pungent smell grew even more intense. I flung the abominable weeds across the room, desperate to get them as far away as possible.

A short while later, she came back to check on me. The flowers were scattered across the floor. I surely must have looked guilty, sitting there with the evidence all around me, yet I made no mention of the mess and warmly welcomed her back with a jovial, "Hello again, dear Agathe!"

"What could have happened here?" she asked, looking around the room as if it would betray other clues. When it did not, she let her eyes fall on me.

I told her, "The flowers are surely stinkweeds or some kind of poisonous plant as they reeked like burning metal. Plus, they are ridden with thorns and one even cut into my tender skin. I had to be rid of them and so there they flew."

She pursed her already-thin lips and slowly explained, as if I were a child, "The flowers are lilies and lilacs — your favorites. They don't smell *like metal*. Their fragrance is divine, and they have no thorns. They revivified this dismal hole so much! But if you prefer, then I shall bring no more to your chamber."

I told her, "Yes, I prefer."

She stood silently for a time, staring at the floor. She was not able to meet my gaze.

"What!" I demanded of her. "Why don't you look at me?"

"Dear Josette-Camille, you look...you have changed..." she started to say, fumbling o'er her words like prater, then paused and finished with, "Motherhood changes us, my dear. You simply seem a bit agitated. And the dear Lord knows you shouldn't be! Such a state is not at all good for the baby. We'll get you more tonic, say some prayers, and ease your troubles. Yes, that should help."

She stayed with me for several hours. While holding my hands, she whispered prayers until it was time for my evening tonic. She kissed my forehead and wished me sweet dreams before retreating to her quarters. While savoring the absinth, I wrote another poem:

I find myself a-tripping over a placid desert of sand
There are no obstacles in my way
And I don't understand
What makes me fall until I look
To see the devil's hand

Josette-Camille

August 14th, 1789

I have sores on my back, and when I sit up, my legs throb like there are sharp daggers stabbing them. Agathe, Henri, and the midwife all took turns rubbing them today, but the pain persists. I wish I could walk; I believe that would help. Lying here on this hard bed just makes it worse.

I asked the midwife again if I could get up — just for a minute — to walk around the room.

She said breathlessly, "You know that isn't a good idea, my lady."

I nodded and said nothing more. It feels heavy when she is nearby. As if a thick, invisible, impenetrable fog follows wherever she goes.

After she left, the room seemed lighter, and I was able to return to my "listening". Lying perfectly still, concentrating on the sounds of the castle, is the only remedy I've found for the pain in my legs. It keeps my mind busy and passes the time.

So, I sat, listening — and then from somewhere deep in the castle, I heard the midwife speak my name.

I cocked my head. She was in the library, me thinks, and talking with Agathe. They whispered, and though they were very far away, I heard them nonetheless.

The wily woman told my sister-in-law, "Josette-Camille is not well. I fear for the welfare of the child. We have to do something before she..."

As the midwife's voice trailed off, Agathe picked up her thought. "Harms the baby. Do you really think she would hurt her own child? Is she that bad off?"

What a vile thing to say, don't you think? They believe I would do something to cause harm to my child? My dear, sweet, innocent little one who has yet to be born? As I lay here confined to my bed, writhing in constant agony, all for the sake of my child, she would betray me with such venomous words?

The midwife next says, "We just need to make sure she stays well until the baby is born. Once the child is out of the womb, we can decide what to do."

What does she mean by "decide what to do"? What is she plotting?

It was then that I realized Henri was also there! He had been quiet while the two women gossiped, but then his authoritative voice added, "We should not overreact. She will be just fine after the birth. It is just a hard pregnancy; it will pass."

Agathe replied, "My pregnancy was demanding, too, but it didn't cause me to turn into a..." she let her own words trail off.

Into a *what*, I wondered? What did she intend to call me?

The midwife continued, "I have seen the birth of many babies, and have never seen a mother in such a state as she!"

Henri said, "The siege, the revolution, being confined to her bed in that dank, foul room — these are all things neither of you women dealt with during your pregnancies."

"Then, we will wait to see what happens after the child is born," Agathe stated. "We can decide what to do then."

They all grumbled agreements and gradually fell silent. I strained to hear more, but the conversation was over.

Now I sit here contemplating. Do they really believe I would hurt my unborn child? How could Henri, my own husband, listen to those conniving women? How dare they make such accusations!

I tremble, despite the fact I am covered with several down blankets. Hot tears streak down my clammy cheeks. I'm tired. Not sleepy-tired, but exhausted-tired. I have done everything in my power to please them — all of them. I listened obediently when the midwife advised that I remain in bed. I drank the tonic Henri prescribed without question. I welcomed Agathe into my home and took all of her sisterly advice. I allowed my body to endure torturous pain for the sake of the baby, but that is of no relevance to them! What more could they possibly expect from me?

Each of them has betrayed me, but none more than Henri, my husband. My body shudders as the pain of deception ravages me; alternating waves of hot and cold slice through me. I feel dizzy, as though I may pass out, and realize the best thing I can do now is rest. Indeed, it is the only thing I can do. Sleep will dull my anguish and allow me to escape. I shall put down the ink and paper and allow myself to drift off.

Josette-Camille

August 17th, 1789

I got out of bed yesterday. I know the midwife told me not to, but her advice has become irrelevant to me. I was determined not to let her, Agathe, or Henri imprison me with their ridiculous rules any longer. Their druthers would have me remain in that bed *forever,* and I decided not to acquiesce to their wishes. I would decide what was best for me and my baby. *Me.* It was my choice and mine alone.

The pain shooting down my legs was excruciating. I decided that standing and walking, just for a few minutes, was the only way to bring relief.

I carefully swiveled my legs so they dangled off the bed. You cannot imagine how good it felt to move them freely without the hard, hot, sticky mattress below! The movement even helped the lower part of my back feel better. It was a glorious relief that you simply cannot imagine.

I stayed there for several minutes, enjoying the way the new position felt. I waggled my toes and stretched my aching calves. Then, I rested my bare heels on the hard, stone floor. The shock of the cold was exhilarating compared to the thick, hot, sticky blankets infested with ankle-nipping bed bugs.

Then, I sat up. I waited as the baby shifted in my stomach. Lower now, yes, but I felt no extra pressure. No pain, no discomfort. Indeed, it felt perfectly natural to sit. As a mother, I knew my child was not at risk. The movement actually stimulated the baby to move. I felt him kick. He *wanted* me to get up and walk around. He was sick of being in the same position, too.

I stood. Oh, the vertigo I felt at first! The room spun 'round, and I imagined what a sailor must feel like on his sea legs. I steadied myself by holding my hand against the curvaceous wall. As I took a tentative step, I slid my fingers along the stones. My bare hands and feet felt free and light and lively. I wanted to dance!

I had made one complete lap around the room when the door burst open. In walked Agathe. I was standing across from her, just in front of the oubliette. Though the alcove was boarded up, I could feel a slight, cool breeze whisper through the crevices.

She asked, "What are you doing out of bed?"

I answered, "I'm walking 'round the room, Agathe. It feels good to move and be out of that abysmal bed."

She looked appalled and said, "But the baby is at risk. You must lie down, dear..."

"The baby is fine. I *need* to walk and stretch my legs."

She persisted. "You are not thinking about the best interest of the child. Let us get you back in bed." She came toward me with outstretched arms.

I pushed her away and said, "No, it is my decision, and I say it is *better* for the baby."

She looked stunned as she urged, "You are going to *lose* the baby, darling Josette. Even now, on the front of your gown, blood seeps out!"

I saw my visage reflected back at me from the depths of her wide eyes. I was a pale, moon-faced creature with tangled tresses that sprayed out wildly from under my deflated bonnet. My eyes bulged out of hollow, dark sockets. I looked affright — an appalling muddle of the woman I used to be.

Then I looked down. There, by my pelvis, was a splotch of garnet-colored liquid growing outward. I was stunned. I felt no pain at all. I didn't even realize I was bleeding!

She called out for Henri as I sank to the floor. With my back to the wall, I slid until I landed on my rump. The baby roiled in my womb. I held my gut as a thin, biting pain tore me in half.

My husband arrived within minutes, followed by the midwife, two guards, and several servants. They filed into the room one after another, and as they did, each stopped fast and gaped at me.

Henri grabbed his knees while catching his breath, obviously having run some distance to get to me. He stared at me with wide, sad eyes.

"Henri!" I said and reached my hand out to him.

He shook his head and tendrils of his sweaty, curly, brown hair bounced back and forth. He only said, "Get her back into bed."

In an instant, everyone surrounded me. Trepidity took hold of me, and I cried out, "Henri!"

Hands were suddenly all over me. I shielded myself by covering my head with my arms. "Don't touch me," I implored, but instead they grabbed my wrists and ankles. I squirmed in their grasp. "No," I insisted. "I can walk to the bed."

They wouldn't let me though. I was brutally carried back to that wretched piece of furniture. As they held me down, the midwife unbuttoned my nightgown and Agathe pulled it up. Before I knew it, they had it over my hips.

I lashed out and knocked Agathe in the jaw. She shrilled and slapped me back. Before I could hit her again, a servant grabbed my wrist and twisted it back. One of the guards produced a dagger, and he cut my nightgown, shredding the fine linen until my body was completely exposed. I lay writhing in turmoil as everyone hovered over my naked, pregnant form, examining me like farmers inspecting a birthing mare.

"Is the baby alright?" Henri asked. He stood on the other side of the room, averting his eyes from me.

I wriggled in agony. The sticky, hot blankets clung to my bare body. I could feel the wetness of blood seeping between my legs.

The midwife wedged her fingers between my thighs and tried to pull them apart. I fought her though and squeezed my legs tight together.

"Unhand me, all of you!" I ordered, but none of the servants would abide my wishes.

Agathe instructed the guards to help the midwife. The three of them tore at my lower body, pulling my legs apart. I cried out for my husband, "Henri, please stop them!" But Henri remained on the far side of the room and whispered an order for them to: "Do whatever it takes to make her comply."

My wrists were held by servants, and one of the little wenches hopped onto my chest to keep me from rolling over. It was the narrow-eyed girl with the nasally voice — the one who stole my bread. She smirked as her eyes glowered into mine. I flailed my head back and forth, but the struggling did not break her gaze.

On each side of the bed, a guard pried back one of my legs, as if I were a chicken wishbone. I caught a glimpse of the midwife peering into my depths. Then, I felt her searching inside me with sharp, spindly fingers.

"Dear Henri, make it stop!" I begged. There was no answer from my beloved as her hands invaded me.

I twisted with all my might.

The servant on top of me seethed. "Stop fighting, foolish woman. You are just making it worse for yourself!"

Rage overtook me, and I rocked my torso in an attempt to throw her off. As I flailed, the guards dug deeper into the fleshy part of my thighs. Their coarse, callused fingers scratched my delicate skin with dirty, jagged nails.

"Unhand me!" I spat at them. Every inch of my body was writhing in resistance. Just as I was about to bite the hand of the waif atop me, Henri appeared beside me.

"Henri," I began. Tears of relief streaked down my red face. He had finally come to my rescue...or so I thought.

Instead, without emotion, he said, "Drink this." In his hand was a cup of tonic.

I stopped struggling then.

Henri pushed the chalice to my lips. He nodded and repeated, "Drink."

Despite the fact that I was no longer fighting they continued to accost me.

I bent my head back to take a stout swig. The room tilted to and fro as the absinth streamed down my throat. It momentarily buffered me from the horror of my assault. It was like being swaddled in a gauzy, green, protective layer of cotton.

I could hear the midwife and Agathe talking, but they seemed far away now. It was as if I was listening to them from deep inside a long tunnel. I heard Agathe ask, "Is the child in the birthing position?"

The midwife groped my stomach while her hand slid back inside me. "The head is *not* in position. Praise God for keeping the baby in place!"

"Is she stable then?" Agathe asked.

"She is open just a bit, but the diameter doesn't seem to be growing. I'll have to keep checking just to make sure she doesn't get any wider," the midwife answered.

Henri's face came into my view again. He nodded at the absinth before pouring another draught into my mouth. I coughed as I gulped it down and closed my eyes. When I opened them again, Henri's face was gone. In his place was one of the guards. Henri had left me.

The guard held the absinth chalice absently, but wasn't looking at me; his gaze was cast down. I followed it and realized he was ogling my lady parts!

As the midwife inspected me, he grinned with a goofy, crooked smile that sent me whirling into another struggling fit. I cried out in anguish, but it only caused them to hold me tighter. The small servant girl that had sat on my chest bounced off as the guard threw his elbow against my throat.

"Told you that struggling would only make it worse," she snarked as she landed.

The guard pushed my head back into the smothering pillows, so I could no longer see what was happening.

"Hold still you crazy toffer," he snarled into my ear with a rumbly, low voice that only I could hear. "Or I'll snap your skinny neck like a turkey's. No one cares what happens to *you* anyway. They only want the baby. If I accidentally press down too hard and you happen to suffocate, it will make this a lot easier. We'd just slice you open, like a gutting a hog, and lift the babe out."

I could not believe a mere guard would have the audacity to threaten me so! Surely, Henri would...he would...what *would* Henri do? My husband's betrayal soaked into my frantic mind with resolute finality. My power, my stature as Lady of the castle, as a noble woman, it was all gone, wasn't it? I held no authority any longer — no respect, no status whatsoever. I was reduced to nothing more than a vessel, which carried Henri's child. That was all.

I stopped squirming and simply sobbed. Every inch of my body was being held, pressed, or fondled by strangers' hands as my husband stood and watched.

The chalice was held to my lips again.

"Here, Lord Henri wants you to finish this swill. Now, drink it up, wench!" the guard instructed.

It poured down my throat. I tried to swallow quickly, so I wouldn't choke; however, it spilt down the sides of my cheeks and trickled into my hair. My whole face was wet with the sticky substance. I turned my head all the way to one side to prevent the absinth from draining into my ear. As I did, I saw the oubliette across the room.

I lay there with the green juice dripping into my eyes and allowed that faraway doorway to become my focal point. It was a refuge from this violent attack; a place that would become my saving grace.

As I stared at it, I thought I saw movement from behind the decrepit boards. Was it my shadowy rabbit friend? Yes, I believe I saw him there, gawping back at me! His presence was comforting. He was like a helpless comrade, an ally, sharing in my pain and outrage. He could do nothing to help me now, but I knew he would be there to exact revenge when the time was right.

I went completely limp and acquiesced to their attack. They jabbed and prodded every inch of my naked body while I lay there like a corpse. Cold hands cupped my breasts, squeezing until I felt warm milk squirt from my nipples.

"She's milking," the midwife stated as if I were a goat.

I felt a clumsy hand wipe the liquid across my bare chest. My breasts were tender, and the rough motion was painful. I bit my lip but did not retaliate.

"That's a good sign. The body doesn't produce milk until the baby is ready for birth. Perhaps, even if it is born now, it will be nearly of term," I heard Agathe say.

I scanned the room one last time for my husband, but Henri was long gone. He had completely abandoned me.

I was grateful I still had the absinth though. It comforted and lulled me. As they finished their inspection, I let the soothing, green intoxicant guide me to a tranquil dream-like place. I was in the garden playing boules. The odd thing, my baby wasn't there like he usually was in my dreams. This time, I played the game with a scrawny, shadowy rabbit. We whispered fabulous secrets to one another and crowed at each other's clever jokes. As a green haze settled over the pastoral scene, the bunny and I huddled close to one another and plotted our revenge.

Josette-Camille

Chapter 61

Dorothée's Story

orothée had not set eyes on the prisoner for almost five days. She intentionally kept her distance. Teasing and taunting him like she did with other men felt somehow "wrong" to her. For the first time in her life, Dorothée felt ashamed of her behavior.

He also didn't speak to her like other men. He treated her not as a lessor, but as an equal — and that scared her.

Something was deliciously different about Julien-Luc.

She sat fretting in the library, wondering if she dare visit him again. Fearful of what might become if she went and terrified of what might happen if she didn't, Dorothée pondered her quandary. Harmless flirtation was one thing, but playing games with a condemned man...that just wasn't right. And doing it while her husband was away, surely Dorothée was not a strumpet!

She took a deep breath as if the air in her lungs confirmed her stature as a noble, respectable Lady. Besides his alluring demeanor, she also wondered what arcane knowledge he held so close to his vest. What philosophies did the Brethren of the Common Life keep that were neither Catholic nor Protestant? And what did her new husband have to do with it all? The intrigue of it gnawed at her until the young, curious bride could stand it no more. She snatched a book from the wall and marched down the corridor to the keep.

Dorothée was determined to tease him no more. This was about uncovering the truth, not about playing a petty, coquettish sport. With a cool stare, she dismissed the stable boy and sat down on her stool in front of the door. She unlatched the pass-through. He lay sleeping, and she not-so-subtly cleared her throat.

Julien-Luc jumped spryly to his feet and rushed to the portal. "I feared you would never come back!"

"I was in the library and thought you might need a new book." She set it on the tiny shelf.

He eagerly grabbed it and read the name of the author aloud. "Saint Thomas Aquinas'. Surely, you have a sense of humor!"

Her stoic face relaxed as she realized the irony of the book she had so hastily grabbed. Regarded highly by the Catholic Church, Aquinas' philosophies dictated truth was obtained solely through God. She couldn't suppress her smile as she asked, "Do you like it?"

Julien-Luc chortled loudly, and she realized it was the first time she had heard pure joy erupt from this man. She joined him, and they laughed until he asked, "Do you understand who I am, Dorothée?"

Through the crevice she gazed into the eyes of the criminal. "I do. You are a Huguenot and a Protestant leader pretending to be a Brethren of the Common Life. You are trying hard to trick me, I suspect."

He shook his head solemnly. "No, Dorothée, I have no intention to trick you.

I speak the truth." Julien-Luc sat thoughtfully for a moment and then continued. "There is so much more I want to tell you, but I can't. I have sworn to carry a secret to my death."

"A secret?" Dorothée inquired. "What kind of a secret would you risk your life for?"

"One that would reveal an ancient truth. I fight for that truth as fiercely as your husband fights to suppress it."

"My husband is a marionette pulled by the strings of the King and the Pope. I wish he *would* fight for something he truly believes in like you...maybe then I wouldn't find him so utterly boorish!" She stopped abruptly.

Julien-Luc sat quietly a moment before saying, "He neglects you?"

Dorothée's face flushed. "We are newlyweds, and we have spent more time apart than together because of his fatuous obligations to the Church," she confessed. "I am so lonely. You are the only person who I can even talk to...and you're a prisoner!"

Julien-Luc quickly changed the subject. "Dear Lady, on your next venture into the library, could you look for any Bibles that you might have?"

"Bibles?" she said, bewildered.

"Yes, old Bibles, even if they are written in another language."

Dorothée considered the request. "I can look. I will do that for you," she said graciously.

The door to the keep swung open. In bounded the stable boy, panting and heaving. "A messenger has arrived with news from André-Benoit!"

Dorothée rose to her feet. She held her head low so that the boy would not see the flush in her cheeks. "I'm on my way. Make sure the prisoner is given fresh water...and perhaps some wine. Yes. We are civilized, aren't we? Give him a bottle of wine tonight with his meal."

The stable boy blinked at the absurd notion of giving an inmate a luxury such as wine, then nodded his head obediently.

Dorothée strutted out of the room, down the hallway, and into the library. "Patricia! Where is this messenger?"

Patricia scampered into the library from the foyer. "I think he's at the stable. I will go see!"

"Hurry, and when you come back bring me some tea...and a pastry. Did Claude make fresh pastries this morning? If not, have him do so at once. I'm peckish!"

Patricia nodded and bowed as she backed out of the room.

Dorothée surveyed the volumes on the tall shelves. *A Bible...he wants a Bible,* she mulled over the odd request. Dorothée studied book after book. Her fingers trailed across their spines. A small, dirty tome was hidden deep between two larger volumes, and she almost overlooked it. "What is this?" she asked the bookshelf. As if to answer, the small book's title became clear as she pulled it into the light. "A Bible! A grimy, little Bible. I wonder..." she whispered as she opened it. A yellow piece of parchment slid from between the pages along with a gold medallion on a chain.

Dorothée gasped and quickly spun around to see if anyone else was around.

The library was empty, and the Château eerily quiet. *Patricia will return any moment with the messenger*, she thought.

Dorothée studied the beautiful jeweled object for a moment. It was clearly Roman, old, and obviously valuable.

She turned her attention to the paper. The squiggly lines outlined what appeared to be a map. Titled in Latin was "Cave of the Dead".

She hastily set the medallion, parchment, and Bible on the library table. From her hair, she pulled two lacey ribbons. She rolled the paper around the medallion and used the ribbons to tie each end, thus securing it like a scroll. *Did I just uncover Julien-Luc's secret?* She jumped up as if hit by a bolt of energy. *I must hide it someplace safe!*

Hurriedly, Dorothée scanned the three statues poised in their grottos on the west wall. She knew that the center statue revealed a lever that opened a hidden chamber. She pulled the correct book on the shelf, causing the wall to groan and a small passageway to open. She scuttered inside. There she found several ancient amphorae — left behind from the Romans that once inhabited the Château — and she popped open the crumbling cork top of one of them. It was long dried out, and she stuffed the scroll inside.

From outside, she heard the front doors push open. She backed out and hastily pulled the book-lever to close up the hidden place. As it shut behind her, a frazzled messenger entered the library.

"Finally, there you are!" Dorothée scolded.

"Sorry to keep you waiting."

"Out with it; what is the message?"

The boy spoke carefully. "André-Benoit sent me just yesterday. I rode all night straight through to get here."

"You are exceptionally dedicated; now out with the message!" she ordered.

The boy concentrated as if recalling each word from memory. "Lord André-Benoit said, 'I am returning soon. I have one more piece of business to attend to and then will ride without stopping. My return will be tomorrow night. The hour of my arrival will be late, but I won't stop until I am home.' He said, 'he misses you and is counting the minutes until he will see you again.'"

"Tomorrow! So soon!"

"Yes, that was his exact message."

"He picked a fine time to miss me," Dorothée muttered to herself and then dismissed the messenger with an angry wave of her hand. She didn't have much time.

Chapter 62

The Children's Story

*A*aron dragged Isabelle down the narrow hallway. He pushed her into a small room in the back of the house and pulled a knife from his belt strap. Isabelle gasped.

Louis had awakened during the commotion and, though bewildered, followed behind. The little boy froze in the doorway and helplessly watched his sister struggle.

"Just let us go; we'll leave right now and never come back!" she pleaded.

"It's too late for that," Aaron grumbled. He pulled Isabelle's long hair and caused her head to snap back.

"No!" Louis cried, and he sprang forward.

But it was too late. The old man drew the knife back and slashed with one quick motion. Isabelle shrieked. Louis bounded into her as Aaron stepped out of the way of the charging child.

Isabelle kept screaming. Louis wrapped his arms around his sister. "Izzy! Are you okay?"

Isabelle stopped. She wasn't hurt. Aaron stood to the side holding the bloodless knife in one hand and a fist full of Isabelle's long brown hair in the other.

"If you two are going to be traveling across the countryside with those henchmen looking for you, we're going to have to disguise you."

Isabelle touched the back of her head. It felt foreign without her ample mane.

"Here," the peasant continued. "Put these clothes on; they'll make you look like a boy. And you, young man, I have the perfect dress for you from when our daughter was a wee girl."

He reached into a battered, old trunk and produced tattered britches for Isabelle and a grimy peasant dress for Louis.

"You want me to dress like a *girl?*" the little man took exception.

"Yes, I want you to dress like a girl!" Aaron mimicked. "Your uncle's men are on the lookout for a little boy and a young girl, not a little *girl* and a young *boy.* Now, both of you put your new clothes on. And here, wear this bonnet on your head, too, son."

Louis winced but did as he was told. Isabelle constantly stroked the stubble of her severed hair and twisted her head from side to side. Aaron retreated to the living quarters of the house.

A few moments later, a different pair of children emerged. Louis wore a brown dress, stained with old dirt and grease. A lacey bonnet was tied around his head. He had it pulled forward too far and had to hold his head up so that his dark eyes could see through the tangle of black hair.

Isabelle sported a tan pair of britches. Never in her life had she worn anything but a dress. The fabric between her legs felt awkward and uncomfortable. Her tunic was made out of an old grain sack, and it scratched her skin. A rotting piece of rope was tied around her waist, and she wiggled her hips as she walked to adjust the unusual belt.

Aaron rose to his feet from his rickety chair as the children entered the room. Louis bumped into a stool and stumbled clumsily as his dress caught between his legs. Aaron scanned from Isabelle to Louis. "If you two aren't the most pathetic looking ragamuffins I've ever seen, then I'll eat a jar of tar!" He broke into a fit of uncontrollable laughter.

Louis couldn't contain himself. Without really understanding that he was the object of the humor, he joined in the peasant's merriment with gleeful giggling. Isabelle scoffed at first, but then found herself consumed by the ridiculousness of the situation, as well. The three stood together, chuckling wildly, when suddenly loud footfalls were heard outside the door.

Isabelle and the old man immediately fell silent. Louis continued to chuckle. Isabelle clutched at his arm.

Aaron walked to the door and listened. "Who is there?" he ordered.

There was no answer. He motioned to the children and shooed them to the back room. They ran toward the rear of the house as the door burst open.

Chapter 63

Veronica's Story
Present Day France

M agazines lay scattered over the dining room table. Veronica paged through them in search of the perfect chandelier. Flipping the pages, she stopped abruptly when a familiar face beamed at her.

It was *Robert*.

Veronica felt her heart leap...then nosedive into a vacuum.

He was featured in *Modern Motifs* as "Designer of the Year". She scanned the article, wishing she had the strength to set it aside, knowing she didn't.

She read about his recent success with the television show, *International Interiors*, his thriving Beverly Hills design studio, and his recent engagement to Sarah.

Something heavy churned in Veronica's stomach.

On the final page of the exposé, Robert described his humble beginnings. He praised Sarah as his inspiration, his protégé, and the love of his life. Veronica violently crinkled the magazine and threw it across the room.

Veronica was the one who was there for Robert's "humble beginnings." She began her career as an intern in his design studio in the Valley. It wasn't glamorous, just she, Robert, and a few other struggling interior decorators at first. She fetched coffee, answered the phones, and allowed herself to be swept up in an affair with her boss.

As the romance grew so did the business. Veronica was as bright-eyed as they came. She knew that now. If only she had known it then.

Nikki kept warning Veronica about Robert. "He's a cad! Honestly, Vern, I don't know what you see in him."

Veronica felt a small victory over her sister when Robert finally asked her to be his senior designer. Despite everything, Robert really did love her and respect her.

He moved his business to an ultra-modern office in Beverly Hills. Before long, his client list included names like one would see gracing the cover of *Variety* magazine.

For five years, Veronica worked hard to make Robert successful. She was the worker bee; the one who followed up with the orders, the vendors, and the one who paid the bills. Above all else, she was the one who came up with the ideas that the clients loved; the ones that made Robert a mini-celebrity in the world of interior design.

Veronica approached the crumpled magazine as if it might grow teeth and bite her. She knelt, calmly smoothed out the pages, and turned again to Robert's beaming face.

It had been almost a year since she left Robert — or to describe it more accurately — since she was *forced* to leave Robert. She certainly didn't feel like she had a choice. Nikki made sure of that. Her sister meant well enough, but Veronica still wondered what would have happened if her sister hadn't been there that day...

Robert seemed jittery and distracted as he prepared for a meeting with executives from the Traveler's Channel.

"Do you want me to help with anything?" Veronica offered.

Robert studied her and simply said, "Not this time."

After making sure that every piece of lint was picked from the carpet, he locked himself in his office until they arrived.

Veronica quietly worked and watched the traffic flow in and out of Robert's office through the glass wall in front of her desk. She was grateful when her sister poked her head around the corner and asked, "Ready for lunch?"

Veronica stroked her head. "Does my hair look okay today?"

Nikki scrunched up her nose. "No, it looks like shit, just like it always does. Why do you always pull it back like that?"

Veronica slapped her pen down on her desk. "Well, I guess that settles it. Robert said almost the exact same thing to me earlier today. I think I should make a hair appointment next week."

"You should make a hair appointment *this* week," Nikki retorted. Veronica responded with silence, and Nikki continued. "Where is the cad anyway? Usually, he's lurking around."

"*Robert* is in a meeting right now with some executives from the Traveler's Channel. He said he was handling them himself. See, Nik, he is taking some of the work load off of me and accepting more responsibility."

"What's the project? What could he be doing for the Traveler's Channel?"

"I dunno. Maybe their executive offices? He didn't tell me."

"Did you ask him?"

"Not exactly. He seemed nervous this morning before they came. He probably wants to surprise me."

Veronica and Nikki watched as one of the junior designers walked into Robert's office. Her skirt was short and her heels high.

"Who's *that*?" Nikki asked.

"I think her name is Sarah? She's new. Robert is mentoring her." Veronica blew hair off her forehead. It was coming loose from her ponytail.

"She dresses like a *hooker* for work?"

"Don't be so catty, Nik."

"Wait a second. Some new girl is in a meeting that Robert won't even tell you about? That's jacked up. You're the senior designer here. Why don't 'cha go in there and see what he's up to?"

"He isn't *up to* anything. Christ, you're so paranoid. He had a few of the interns and junior designers in there already. He's probably just...I don't know, giving them a feel for the business."

"Well, if they were all dressed like that, then *she's* the one who's prolly giving him a *feel*."

"Robert and I are a team. He's good with people. He can work a room like you wouldn't believe. I do better behind the scenes. And he knows how hard I work; that's all that matters."

"He knows he can walk all over you like faux Oriental rug!" Nikki taunted.

"Come on, let's go to lunch," Veronica said as she grabbed her bag and keys.

Robert's office door opened wide as the sisters turned to leave. Robert held it as Sarah and three men walked out. "Thank you very much!" he enthused.

Nikki stepped forward. "Hi, Robert, who are your friends?"

Veronica hung back and shuffled papers on her desk.

Robert briefly hesitated before replying. "New, ah, business associates."

"I'm Nikki; nice to meet you." She thrust her hand forward.

One of the men gave her a business card, and accepted her shake. He had shoulder length hair and a goatee. "I'm Alex, the project's casting director. Are you a designer here?"

"No, I'm Nikki, Veronica's sister; *she's* the *senior* designer here." Nikki stepped back to expose her sister.

Veronica smiled meekly.

Alex eyed Nikki. "Too bad, you have a great look."

"Look for what?" Nikki asked.

"Just a new project," Robert spoke. "Thanks again, gentlemen. The elevator to the parking ramp is just this way..."

"Yes, thanks..." Alex began. Then he turned to Sarah. "I'm looking forward to working with you. Congratulations again..."

Nikki piped up. "This project sounds interesting. What is it?"

Robert looked directly at Veronica. "We'll talk about it later."

Veronica nodded obediently.

"Oh, you can tell them. The contract is signed!" Alex said.

Sarah couldn't seem to contain herself. "I'm going to be the senior designer on the new television show, *International Interiors*! We're going to travel all over the world designing exotic homes. I'm so excited! Thank you, Robert, for making this happen!"

"*You* are going to be the senior designer...on a television show?" Veronica gasped.

"Yeah, along with Robert. And the other girls will be, like, our decorating helpers!"

"What about *Veronica*?" Nikki blurted.

Robert stepped forward. "Someone has to run the office while we're on location..."

Nikki exploded. "And that someone should be *you*, Robert! Veronica is the best designer here! Why isn't she on the show?"

Veronica stood frozen and tersely said, "Let it go, Nik..."

"No, you do all the work around here, design all the projects, and now when something huge comes along, you aren't even considered? They didn't even have you go in for an interview or audition or to suck their cocks or whatever the hell it was they were doing in there? Why is that? Why can't you give her a chance?"

Alex looked Veronica up and down one time. "Because we need women who have the right *look* for the show..."

Nikki gasped.

Sarah giggled.

Robert sighed.

Veronica fled the office...

Now, Veronica pulled herself back to the Château. She set the magazine down and caught her reflection in a gold-framed mirror. She pulled at the loose strands of hair that hung around her face and whispered, "Maybe I could highlight it and get rid of this mousy brown color; get a cut and style."

A loud crash suddenly thundered through the castle walls. The entire Château shook as if hit by a freight train.

"What was that?" she called as she frantically ran into the foyer.

At the bottom of the stairs was the antique claw-foot tub she had ordered for the upstairs bathroom. It lay in two pieces among shards of the broken mahogany staircase. Clark stood there sheepishly.

Veronica still clenched the magazine. She held up Robert's photo and said, "Fuck you, Robert. Fuuuck you!"

Chapter 64

The Pagans' Story

The pyre burned down to cherry-red embers as the thin light of day crept over the stone monoliths. The few remaining children eventually came to their senses and scampered off into the forest in search of their way home.

In the pit, six feet below the surface of the earth, Bevin stroked the flesh of his beautiful Trinna. Regret clamped his soul with a cold fist. "I never had the chance to love you like I dreamt I would."

She appeared to be sleeping as he wiped the soot from her tranquil face. He prayed beyond hope that she would open her eyes.

Her body was still warm. He unraveled the remnants of the singed robe that was wrapped around her torso and felt her chest. Bevin searched for a beating heart, hoping it would miraculously spring to life. He prayed to the gods he hated, begging them to show mercy and bring her back.

"Please," he anguished with a blubbering voice. "Gods of air, earth, water, and fire, please, bring her back. It isn't fair! She wasn't supposed to even be here! You *must* bring her back!"

His trembling fingertips lightly caressed her skin. He imagined it reacting to his touch with goose bumps. He leaned closer and trailed a solitary index finger, watching it intently as it traveled across her sternum, down her belly, around the convex contour of Trinna's hip, and back up again. The tiny hairs on her cooling flesh quivered faintly.

"We were supposed to get married," he said as he eyed his roaming hand. "I was going to ask your father at the next festival," he sobbed into her ear. "You were supposed to be mine."

Bevin rested his head on Trinna's chest and closed his eyes. He imagined their wedding taking place in a small glen near the river; the trees decorated with garlands of flowers and a small feast spread out along the bank. Their families would be gathered to celebrate the union, with song and mirth filling the day.

As the evening stars appeared, they'd bid farewell and mount a steed — a wedding gift from his father — and ride off together. Bevin and Trinna would come to a remote meadow sprinkled with wild flowers. That's where they'd consummate their union.

Bevin dreamt of this scene often. He wondered what it felt like to touch a woman, to feel her body inside and out. He wasn't entirely sure how to make love though.

He knew from watching the goats that the male forced his long, pink knob-pole into the female, mounting her from behind. The female goat would bray, but she didn't appear to be in pain. It seemed to suit her just fine as the male bounced on top of her.

The young man's eager libido caused him to swell as he thought of being inside Trinna. He wondered how she'd react to him. *Would he feel good to her? Would he be enough of a man to make her happy? Could he make her bray like a goat?*

Bevin removed his hand from Trinna and slid it down his trousers. As he had done many times before, usually right before falling asleep, the boy cupped his manhood. He squeezed. His hand was course, covered in blisters from the fire. *What did it feel like inside of a woman — inside of Trinna?*

He imagined it cushy and warm. It would surely surround him completely, snuggling him tightly as he slowly moved back and forth. *That would feel unbelievable, wouldn't it?*

Fresh tears sprang from his puffy eyes. He would never know what it felt like inside Trinna.

Urges surged deep inside. He slid the robe completely off her body and beheld her exquisite form. The morning sun cast a brash, red glow into the bottom of the hole. A bolt of lucidity made him pull his hand from his crotch with a rush of willpower. Shaking his head, Bevin slowly regained his composure. Once he felt himself go limp, he relaxed and leaned back against the wall.

Trinna's naked body was before him, and it was beautiful.

He couldn't resist touching her again; this time his index finger rested on her bottom lip. It was soft, and he pressed it gently, causing her to pout. Without his consent, his manhood swelled again.

Bevin let his hand roam freely. It trailed its middle finger down her jawline, across her neck, and swirled back and forth over her well-defined collarbone. Her perfectly round breast beckoned him. He had never felt a breast before. The shape always attracted him. He loved to catch glimpses of them through low-hanging robes when the women of the village worked the fields.

Now, he let his exploratory finger encircle the circumference of Trinna's breast. It went around and around, growing smaller and smaller as he neared the dark edge of her areola. He paused, hesitated for an excruciating moment, and then tapped the tip.

It was "squishy" and moved in a way Bevin didn't expect. The breast bounced. The sight excited him, and he felt hot longing cut through his loins with potency unlike any he'd ever experienced.

Next, Bevin cupped her breast with his palm. He held it, tenderly at first, then squeezed. He imagined that she responded to his touch by arching her back ever so slightly.

In his mind, he could hear her whisper her last words over and over again:

"Bevin, I do love you."

"Bevin, I do love you."

"Bevin, I do love you."

"I love you, too," he whispered back.

In the loneliness of the pit, he mounted Trinna, and consummated his undying love.

❧❧ ❖ ❧❧

When Bevin finished, an explosion echoed deep in his groin. Cold pain seared through his genitalia. Instantly, he loathed himself more than anything in the

199

world, more than the stag-headed man, more than the old Hag. He collapsed next to the corpse. His manhood shriveled up as if it were attempting to hide inside the body of its master. He cried out in agony.

Outlined over him, in the blearing light of morning, the Hag was back. She stood at the top of the pit and observed the disgusting scene, scowling. "Stupid boy!"

Bevin looked up. "What have I done?" He asked the question rhetorically, but he was given an answer nonetheless.

"You can't imagine what you have done. Not only is your deed repulsive, but the consequences are dire beyond your knowing," she seethed.

For the first time, Bevin saw fear behind her piercing grey eyes.

"I'm sorry," he began, but the Hag wouldn't give him the luxury of pity.

She interrupted. "You've planted an unnatural seed. You've unleashed something that I and the priests have struggled to contain for many years." She raised her head to the sky and continued, no longer speaking directly to Bevin. "How could these two cause so much turmoil? They've destroyed everything, and now their actions threaten our lives, our entire existence!"

"What do you mean?" he asked.

"Now you must do what's right."

"Do what?"

"You must build a Fortress Temple around this spot. Use the stones from this site and clay from the river. And you must complete the building before the winter ritual."

He was confused. "You're not making sense. Build a fortress, me? Alone? How..."

"You have no choice," the old woman seethed. "You did this. It is your fault, and you are going to make it right. It's now your destiny; there's nothing more for you. Your will is gone. You will do what I say, without question, do you understand?"

Bevin shrieked hysterically and began to sob. The life he had in the village was ruined. He could never return. They would likely stone him for his sins. Though he didn't want to believe her, he knew the Hag was right. He nodded reluctantly, agreeing to whatever she said.

"We must contain it here. Trap it like an animal in a cage, so it can't go far. That much we can do. I can help you." The old woman held out a long stick, and Bevin grabbed hold while streams of tears streaked his sullen, soot-covered face. He let her pull him out of the pit.

"You'll start by building a tower around Trinna's grave. Don't seal her tomb; keep the hole open. Then, around the tower, you'll build a structure to house not only you, but also others who will come and help you keep it contained after you've died. You'll spend all your days here, stupid boy. This is your fate. You can't escape it. Go now. You need to start at once." The Hag slowly turned and hobbled off, leaving Bevin alone and grieving next to Trinna's grave.

Sebastian's Story

Ⓔsindra entered the lowest tower room where the Cloaked Man now resided. It was not locked, or guarded, as everyone was still enjoying the feast. As a woman, she was forbidden to eat meals with the men. She decided to take advantage of her time by exploring Sebastian's quarters for clues.

She wanted a child. The Cloaked Man had said she would have one. *How did he know? What magic did he use to see such things?* She intended to find out.

Inside was a table, littered with an array of mysterious objects. Esindra set her candle down and inspected the spread. A shallow copper bowl caught her attention. She recalled when Sebastian had asked for it. *He uses this for divining*, she thought as she peered into it. A black pool reflected her image back to her. She searched it expectantly, hoping to see a trace of the magic that Sebastian spoke of. Only her own questioning eyes bore back at her, though.

She inspected several pieces of parchment. Did he take notes perhaps? Did he write down his predictions? She read:

I evoke and conjure thee, O spirits of plenty and fertility, those who grant life and who bring bounty. I command thee to appear before me in this copper vessel, in all your glory. To do my bidding, as I am your master, and you shall serve me or face the wrath of the darkness.

What kind of spirit did he summon? She read the spell again. The words made Esindra queasy, and she set the paper down like it was hot.

Something stirred down the corridor. The door that led into the keep banged open. Esindra's head jerked up; she thought she had more time! She wildly spun and faced a tapestry on the other side of the room. It hung there like a curtain, but low to the ground, obviously not covering a window. She ran to it. It covered a recessed area, a tiny grotto. She slipped behind it just as someone entered the chamber.

The grotto was boxy. She carefully concealed herself just on the other side of the fabric. As she took a tentative step back, her foot released a mechanism. The floor fell from beneath her with a gentle "swish", and she teetered there, balancing just on the edge of…what, she wasn't sure. Frenetically, her fingers dug into the stone wall, and she steadied herself. A noxious odor accosted her sinuses. She ventured a peek down and saw that she was hovering on the edge of a hole.

Sebastian entered his chamber with his lackey, Baldebert, on his heels.

Esindra froze, not wanting to make a single, perceivable movement from behind the curtain. She forced her breath to be shallow and her exhalations to be slow and steady. All she could do was wait and listen.

"What a fine meal that was! The roast boar, oh, that was tender…" the Druid chattered.

"I have a task for you tonight," the Cloaked Man announced.

Baldebert cringed. His master's tasks were never pleasant.

Sebastian continued. "A gift from the governor will be delivered soon. I will need your help with the...preparation. Go find a large bucket."

Baldebert grunted an affirmation and left.

Esindra squatted quietly in the little room. The curtain covered her from view, and she balanced just on the edge of the hole in the floor. She didn't dare move; one, because she didn't want to be heard, and two, she didn't want to lose her balance and plummet into the depths.

She heard metallic noises, like chains clanking together. She peeked into the room. A dividing screen now sectioned off the far half of the room. She also saw more candles had been lit. Then she noticed with dread that *her* candle still remained on the table. It was burning along with several others. *Had he not noticed it among the rest?*

She could see Sebastian's shadow behind the divider screen. She heard more sounds of metal against metal, weighty, clunking noises. She saw for the first time that a thick chain hung from the ceiling. Whatever was on the end of the chain was obscured by the screen. Metallic noises coincided with his movements as Sebastian's shadow laboriously pulled on a rope.

Baldebert returned, and she promptly heard the Cloaked Man inform him, "That is not big enough!"

Her calves began to tingle as she crouched on her haunches. There were more sounds of clanking metal, and she adjusted her position quickly, hoping that she would not be heard over the din.

People entered, and several voices chirped together. They were servant boys. Sebastian offered them some wine, and they tittered with anticipation.

Before long, there was wild mirth and laughter. She could hear Sebastian roar like an animal then whisper strange little songs, like verses, and the boys giggled. She heard Baldebert return. This time he pleased his master.

"Good, put it under the pulley," Sebastian instructed.

Esindra watched him place a bucket behind the screen. She saw the shadow of the metal device. It was laden with chains, ropes, and hooks.

The merrymaking continued well into the night. Esindra squeezed her eyes shut and listened to the stories Sebastian told his captive ensemble. Tales of magical legends echoed against the stone walls in her boxy little hollow.

Eventually, there was absolute silence. The absence of noise startled her. With a jolt she became keenly aware. *Had she really dosed off?* She remained huddled, afraid to move, afraid to even close her eyes, and wondered if it was finally safe to escape.

Chapter 66

The Children's Story
1307 AD – A Time of Inquisition

$\mathfrak{I}$sabelle and Louis hurried down the hall and ducked through the first door they came to. It was a small room filled with skinned animals hanging from the ceiling. There was another door across from where they entered. Isabelle quietly pushed it open. It led outside. She was about to lead her little brother through when she heard a familiar voice. It was Nana asking, "Where are the children?"

Aaron answered defiantly, "What children? What are you talking about, you crazy bat?"

Aaron is playing games with Nana, thought Isabelle. She clutched her brother's hand and said, "Come on, Louis, we don't have to hide."

The children burst out of the pantry. "Here we are!"

Nana stood by the front door. The children ran toward her with lopsided grins.

"Nana, you're back..." Isabelle began as she and her brother bounded into her flaccid arms, then the girl stopped short.

Standing next to Nana were the three Inquisitors who were hunting them earlier.

"Look," Aaron began weakly, "those aren't the same children. That's a little girl and an older boy. You're looking for a *little boy* and an *older girl.*"

His wife studied the children quickly. "Those are the *same* children. See how he tried to disguise them? I told you he was a tricky donkey!"

One of the Inquisitors approached Isabelle and Louis. "Come now, the game is done."

"Nana!" Isabelle cried.

The woman sweetly cooed. "Time to go home, little ones. And it's time for Nana to fill her pockets with three, glistening gold coins."

Isabelle had too much spirit to give up that easily. She dashed back to the smokehouse pantry. Louis followed, though the flappy dress made it hard for him to keep up.

One of the men pursued and the chase was on.

Through the pantry and out the small door that led outside they went. Isabelle was in the lead, her brother stumbled behind her, and then came the thick-chested inquisitor who had a difficult time pushing his way through the small pantry door.

Once outside, Isabelle saw the woman's saddled horse standing idly near the barn. She raced for the animal. Louis faltered on his bum ankle, falling behind his sister, as he struggled to lift his hem off the ground as he ran.

Isabelle sprang forward and grabbed the reins. Her foot slid easily into the stirrups, and she mounted the animal with more ease than she ever felt before. The pants provided her with freedom of movement reserved only for males. Fleetingly, she thought, *so, this is what it's like to really ride a horse!*

She bent to lift Louis onto the saddle, but he wasn't there. She looked up.

Only twenty feet from the house was her little brother, lying face down in the dirt. He had tripped.

"Get up, Louis!" Isabelle shouted. She began to turn the horse in the direction of her brother when the inquisitor came crashing through the pantry door. Louis staggered to his feet and limped to his sister. "Hurry, Louis!" Isabelle cried as she steered the horse toward her brother. Unsure of its new rider, the animal resisted and stomped an angry hoof.

The man overtook Louis and scooped him up like a real poppet. The boy kicked and scratched and cried out for Isabelle.

Isabelle contemplated the situation. Her brother was captured. She couldn't save him; however, she could flee on the horse. *She* could escape.

"Louis!" she cried as tears tracked down her face. She turned to the forest. It was thick and overgrown with dead trees and gnarly vines. She noticed a long, thick, dead branch just ahead of her. She nudged the horse. It stiffened for a moment, then responded with a slow gallop to edge of the wood.

She reached down and wrapped both hands around the tree branch. Only slightly warped, it was long — almost six feet — and it had a sharp, jagged end where it had been torn from its tree trunk. She snagged it with ease and held it to her side like a lance.

Behind her, Louis' struggles were confounding the man. He sat on his knees with Louis writhing on the ground before him, while fighting to obtain a better hold on the rambunctious child.

"Let him go!" Isabelle ordered with such authority that her uncle's henchman ceased his apprehension and looked up quizzically at the girl on the horse.

Isabelle steadied her weapon and spurred the steed hard.

The man snorted as if amused.

The horse rushed forward and Isabelle took careful aim. She knew she had one just one shot.

Isabelle had seen jousts many times during festivals. Her father even rode in them occasionally. It was a sport usually played by knights and nobles. Some people wagered money or land, but most just watched for fun. As a little girl, she dreamed of being able to play such a game. However, her mother made it clear, that as a young lady, it would never be possible for Isabelle to compete in such a tournament. So, Isabelle did the second best thing. She learned to ride, and she could do it well.

The inquisitor waved his hand in an obscene gesture.

Isabelle saw his expression. She assessed his cockiness. She lowered her lance and spurred her steed.

The inquisitor ducked just as Isabelle approached. She intuitively anticipated his movement, and at the last possible moment, adjusted her aim. The jagged end of the stick impacted the side of the man's head. He howled in agony as the flesh from his face was scraped off the bone. He fell to the side, and Louis hastened to his feet.

Nana and the other Inquisitors emerged from the front door of the house just in time to witness the joust. The three stood frozen, unable to comprehend the bizarre sight in front of them.

Isabelle spun the horse and trotted back to her brother. She reached down and pulled the boy into the saddle. He sobbed and giggled at the same time.

"Izzy, you saved me! I think you killed him. I think he's dead, Izzy, but you saved me!" Flecks of the inquisitor's flesh hung in the little boy's thick eyelashes.

One of the other men ran toward them, whistling to Isabelle's horse in an effort to make it heed.

The girl lowered her lance yet again and aimed at the advancing man. The horse charged forward, and Louis clung to his sister and braced himself for impact.

The man stood frozen a moment. His furrowed brow told Isabelle he didn't understand what was obvious…that *he* was next. Like a turncoat he snapped on his heels and ran back toward the house. The steed quickly overtook him, and Isabelle planted the end of the lance square in the middle of his back. It burrowed under the man's shoulder blade. Though his chainmail kept the weapon from piercing his flesh, he was pushed to the ground with a mighty thud. Landing face-first, dirt and pebbles burrowed into eyes, mouth and nose.

Isabelle spun the horse one last time to confront the third man, but he had already mounted his horse and was fleeing along the road. Nana was the only one remaining. She stood defiantly by the door. Her knobby fingers still clutched her purse of gold coins.

"Hope you're happy with your prize!" Isabelle spat at her.

She threw her lance at the old woman's feet as the horse galloped by. Louis held on tight as his sister spurred the animal through the woods.

⟡⟡✧⟡⟡

Inside Aaron remained. "Evil ol' bat of a woman," he groused as he sat down in his chair by the fire. On the floor, near his feet, was the blanket the children had cuddled within; peeking out from under it, was the boy's leather satchel.

Aaron spun and assessed the front door. They were all outside. He scrambled to the window just in time to see the children toss the bloody branch at his wife's feet and take off for their freedom.

"Good for them!" he huffed.

Turning back, he snatched the bag, and opened it. A curious old book, a ripped scarf, shards of stringy jerk beef, a useless knife, and an ornate, jeweled box were revealed as he riffled through it.

He jolted his head toward the door again. His wife would come back inside at any moment. Aaron shuffled quickly to the back room of the house and opened the opulent box in private. Coins, jewels, and a magnificent crystal skull beamed back at him.

Aaron knew the tales of the knights in the castle, and like most, had heard the rumors of the magic they possessed. The artifacts surely held great significance. A curious man, a disciple of Kabbalah, a seeker of arcane knowledge, he would enjoy studying them.

In Yiddish he whispered a prayer for the children, and carefully stowed their treasure in a steamer chest for safekeeping.

Chapter 67

Father Michel's Story

The ornate gold box was inlaid with ribbon-like decorations; intersecting designs accented with rubies and sapphires encircled an ancient Celtic cross. Father Michel opened it and caressed the artifact inside.

It was a crystal skull, perfect in dimension and design. Light danced inside of it. Red, orange, and yellow flickered like a trapped flame eager to escape. Father Michel recalled the first time he laid eyes on the magnificent skull...

He had just recovered from the pestilence. After taking in the family of Jews, and watching them succumb one after another, he fell ill, only to return to health in three days' time. By the grace of God he was spared. It happened sometimes. The disease did not take everyone it infected.

Only Aaron and he were left in the church. The old man was not on the path to recovery, though. As he lay dying, Father Michel prepared to offer salvation through last rites.

"Father, I have something important to tell you."

"You can tell me anything," Father Michel urged as he anticipated a deathbed confession. The old Jew lay on a flea-infested cot in a back room of the church.

"I must entrust you with something. It possesses great power and only one who is righteous should possess it."

Father Michel hung his head in prayer and noticed a leather satchel resting on the man's chest. His trembling hand cradled it protectively.

"I acquired this over forty years ago," the old Jew gurgled. Urine-colored foam seeped from the sides of his mouth. The priest held his rosary beads over the man's heaving chest while he stammered on with his story. "Many years ago there was an Order of Templar Knights who lived in the castle where the Cardinal now resides. Something horrible happened there when the Inquisitors came. The knights were accused of crimes against the church and taken away. However, there were two children who escaped. They ran away in the middle of the night. As fate would guide them, they found their way to my barn where they sought refuge.

"I tried to help, I really did! Inquisitors came and uncovered them though. Luckily, the children did escape, but they left this behind." The old man pulled a dusty tome out of the satchel and handed it to Father Michel.

"I am a man of Christ; your Kabbalah has no significance to me," Father Michel said.

"You fool! You think this is a Kabbalah? This is *your* book, *your* Bible."

Father Michel paged through the tome. Indeed it was a Bible, and it appeared old.

"You can read it later. And when you do, make sure you read the *whole* thing; it contains something significant."

Father Michel was curious. "What?"

"An inscription that commands a powerful secret."

"A secret…that Jesus is Lord?" Father Michel asked wryly.

The dying man spat, "There is a mystery to this Bible…and to the treasure in this box. It contains the *Head*."

The priest carefully answered. "You're not making sense. Rest for a while and save your strength."

"I don't have *a while*. Hear me out. The children were trying to keep this safe. They were hiding it from the Inquisitors."

"Then this Bible should be brought to the Cardinal. It needs to be seen by Church leaders," Father Michel answered smugly.

"No! That is who the Bible must be kept *from*! Your church exiled the Templars and took the castle from them for a reason."

"I am familiar with the Templar Knights. They led the crusades. But they turned on the Word of God and became heretics who worshiped false deities."

The old man coughed. Globules that looked like black cherry jam oozed down his chin. "The Knights Templar did not worship something that was false…they revered something that was very real and very powerful. The Church feared that power. That is why Pope Clement the Fifth, along with the support of King Phillip the Fair, issued a clandestine Papal bull to extinguish all orders of the Knighthood on Friday, October 13th, 1307. I remember the date well because it was only a few nights later that the children came to us."

"Why should I believe any of this? You may be trying to trick me. Everyone says Jews are not to be trusted," the priest challenged.

"Believe whatever you want. This is your religion, your doctrine, your dogma. Ignore everything that I have told you. I did my best, and God will know that when I am judged. Here, take it. A king's ransom worth of treasure I give to you because I am a *deceitful Jew*. How clever I must be, right? What a sinister a trick. I lived on the verge of poverty all those years just so I could deceive a parish priest while I lay on my deathbed!" The old man coughed as he uttered, "Do whatever your heart tells you to do. My conscious is clear as I prepare for the end."

Aaron reached into the satchel and revealed the jeweled box. It dazzled Father Michel. The old man opened the latch. Inside, the enigmatic skull glistened. It was the first time Father Michel saw the Head. Now, several weeks later, he beheld the priceless artifact once again.

Something stirred from within the church.

Father Michel pulled himself from the memory and listened. He heard the familiar sound of the church's front doors opening. He shoved the treasure box in the satchel along with the Bible and cautiously peeked around the corner. Two men were making their way through the pews. He gathered up his courage and made a dash for the side door. As he burst outside, he heard someone shout, "You! Stop!"

Father Michel raced around the side of the church back toward Lightning. The horse was not where he left him. Anxiously, he scanned the area and saw two more men near the road. One held the reins of his steed. Father Michel pushed his body against the wall. He could hear the excited cries of the men from inside.

"He was here! We saw him!"

Father Michel skimmed the hillside. A thicket of bushes appeared to be his only option. He threw his body down the bank and tumbled into the brush. He prayed that the shrubbery would provide enough cover. In the distance, he could hear the men's voices. He coiled up, making himself as small as possible. Twigs jabbed his hands and feet and thorns scratched the crown of his head. He sucked in a deep breath and waited.

"He came this way. Did you see him?" one of the men asked.

"No, we were up by the horse," another answered.

"He couldn't have gone far on foot. Did he go that way?"

"Maybe he doubled back into the church?"

"Go back inside and check. You two, go down the road and see if he made a break for it. I'm going down the hillside."

Father Michel's mind raced. One of them was coming his way. Twigs snapped and brush was trampled. He ventured to lift his head and watched as two of the men ran down the road. It was then that he saw Lightning. The horse was now standing unattended.

Father Michel sprang from his hiding spot. He ran to Lightning as fast as he could. The horse, eyeing his approach, readied himself to be mounted. Suddenly, as if he encountered an invisible force, Father Michel stopped dead in his tracks. A hand had clenched his flowing cloak and pulled Father Michel backward.

The priest struggled to retain his momentum but was pulled off balance. Both the priest and his assailant tumbled to the ground and rolled down the hillside. The satchel with its heavy, bulky contents, bore into Father Michel's side as he rolled.

Gravity released its grip as they merged with the thicket. The attacker found his bearings first and jumped on top of the disoriented priest. He straddled Father Michel and brought his elbow down on the holy man's throat.

"What are you doing back here!" the attacker demanded.

Father Michel recognized the man. It was Paul — Claudeen's father.

"Claudeen!" he blurted as the pressure on his throat cut off his words. "I came to help..." he gurgled.

"Help? You brought death to our congregation. Is that why you came back? To see the destruction you left behind?" Paul cried as he pulled his arm back slightly.

"Surely, you don't believe that I caused anyone harm on purpose!"

"I was there, Father. When the Cardinal's guards came to town looking for you I brought them to the Church. Together, we found the Jews in the back room. Their infested bodies were already beginning to rot. You allowed the peste to take hold here!" He plunged his elbow into the priest's throat harder than before.

Father Michel struggled to fill his lungs with air so he could speak. "I didn't mean..."

Paul's face contorted from absolute fury into uninhibited grief. He released the pressure on the priest's throat and began to sob. "I told the Cardinal's men to take you away! You let those infected, deceitful heathens into our Church. You caused the deaths of so many — my wife, my son, and my daughter. They are dead now because of you!"

Father Michel's body went limp. "Claudeen? She is..."

"She's dead! They're all dead! And buried. With no funeral. No absolution of their sins. No last rites. You prayed over the dying Jews and then let your congregation perish without as much as a sacrament. There will be a reckoning for what you've done, priest." Paul clenched the holy man's collar, stood, and pulled Father Michel to his feet.

One of the other men appeared on the hilltop. Paul's attention was momentarily distracted as he called to his companion.

Father Michel took advantage of the opportunity.

The satchel was hidden from view under his cloak, and slung over his shoulder. He let the strap slip down his arm. Then he hurled it like a sling just as Paul turned back around, smacking the man along the jaw. Blood splattered and showered the priest's face.

Paul released his grip, his hands went to his broken mouth, and he screeched with agony.

Free, Father Michel ran toward Lightning. The horse intuitively galloped to his master.

Paul fell backward into the thicket. He cried out to the others to "get the miscreant..." but his words were choked on his own blood.

The priest did not look back. He mounted Lightning just as the other men closed in. Trusting fate, Father Michel steered the horse down the hillside. Lightning's footing was precise. The animal maneuvered the slope and burst into a full gallop once on level ground.

The men feebly gave chase, but were quickly left in Lightning's dust, shouting and cursing the priest as he escaped into the forest. Hot tears salted the tiny abrasions on his cheeks. Father Michel cried uncontrollably as he fled the church and the people he once loved.

Chapter 68

Dorothée's Story

omorrow night! The immediacy of the words struck her with the force of a physical blow. She thought she had more time! Less than a month ago, she had been trudging around the castle grounds grumbling about how bored she was without André-Benoit. Now, she received news that he would be home tomorrow night.

She knew she needed to act quickly if she was to save Julien-Luc's life.

Dorothée crossed the lawn toward the stables. There was something inside the barn that she needed for her plan.

A buzz of flies dashed in and out of the dusty building's open door. Dorothée could see the haziness of the dank barn air seep into the freshness of the early evening breeze. She took a deep breath and stepped inside.

A surprised roost of sleepy chickens cackled to life when she entered and threw up their dirty wings in protest. Feathers flew into Dorothée's face, and she coughed as her lungs filled with the stench of poultry guano.

She hurried past the fowl and neared the horses. They also reacted with startled neighs when they saw the strange visitor.

"Shh!" Dorothée hushed as she crept past their stalls.

She came to a small room where grain was stored, near the back of the barn. From Dorothée's horrific experience while locked in the tower, she recalled that André-Benoit had ordered the stable boy to retrieve a key from a hidden space in the floor of this little room in the barn.

Dorothée needed that key.

She entered the back room. The walls were covered with harnesses and farm tools. Tentatively, she made her way past sacks of grain while studying the floor.

The square outline of the hatch was covered with cobwebs and mouse droppings. She dug her fingers into the filthy seams and lifted. With an audible creek, it pulled free, and she peeked into the dingy depths. There, among rusty chains and barbaric shackles, was a steely, black key.

She snatched it, hurried out of the barn, and ran up the pathway to the Château.

Tonight is the night, she thought to herself. *I only have one chance. I have to do this before André-Benoit returns.* As the rest of her plan began to unfold in her mind, she eagerly anticipated the looming midnight hour.

Chapter 69

Veronica's Story

Veronica walked past the workers restoring the wood on the foyer staircase, through the parlor, and past her sister's bedroom. "Do you have everything?" she called out. "Come on, let's do this."

Nikki clicked along with her fuzzy heels while holding a can of WD-40, a cloth, and a skinny screwdriver. "Yeah, I'm coming. So, tell me what the 'keep' is again?"

"According to Marie-Claire, it was the first part of the Château to be built. It dates back to around the first century. It was originally some type of temple. Then as the castle grew around it, the keep became the dungeon."

"How lovely," Nikki quipped as they arrived at the door.

"Just think, Nik..." Veronica began as she reached out and caressed the cool stone. "These walls are two thousand years old!"

"Yeah, I wonder what kind of stories they could tell us, you know, if walls could talk and all."

As if to answer Nikki's comment, something scurried in the creases of the stones by Veronica's hand. She drew back her appendage with a start as something furry whisked past her.

Nikki yelped as the mouse maneuvered over the tiny stone ledges. "Christ! That scared the crap out of me!"

"Just a mouse. This place has lots of them. All the people and the noise have frightened them out of their hiding places. Poor things are probably wondering why we've invaded their home."

"Poor things my ass. We need a cat, or twenty, that'll show those *meeces*!" Nikki exclaimed like a cartoon feline.

Veronica took the can of WD-40 and squirted it into the keyhole. After wiping her hands with the cloth, she inserted the skeleton key.

It slipped easily into the crevice, and she twisted it back and forth. It felt loose. Nothing happened, nothing clicked. Next, she twisted the screwdriver inside and tried to force the mechanism to no avail.

Nikki watched her sister struggle for a few moments. "Lemme try," she offered.

Veronica stepped back and watched as Nikki went through the same procedure. "Vern, maybe we need to let it set for a while, you know, let it soak and give it a go again tomorrow."

Veronica gazed at the locked door with a hazy expression. "Maybe I should use the *other* key."

"What *other* key?"

Veronica turned and made her way back down the hallway. Nikki stared after her, puzzled by the sudden revelation of the "other key", and followed.

Veronica strolled into the library, continued into the foyer, and out the front door.

"Where're you going?" Nikki asked.

"To the barn," Veronica stated simply.

Nikki bustled to keep pace with Veronica, uncertain what that decrepit old building had to do with anything.

The barn's door hung by one hinge, lapping open sideways. The base of the wall was made out of stone, and it stood impeccably against the elements of time. However, the wooden portion of the walls were crumbling and the roof was completely collapsed in one spot like a sagging, wet cloth. A flurry of sparrows flew up.

Nikki waved feathers out of her face. "What are we doing out here anyway?"

"The keep's skeleton key is in there. It opens the door to the keep."

"Oh," Nikki said shortly. "How do you know, and why didn't you get it before?"

"Maybe Marie-Claire told me. I guess I just remembered now."

Veronica dreamily entered the old stable. Nikki twitched her nose and reluctantly followed.

The floor was covered in dried mud that had washed in through the fissures in the structure. Decrepit beams hung from the ceiling, rotting and covered in green moss.

Veronica slid her feet across the old wood and felt it sag with resignation. The planks buckled under the weight with a sudden, rebellious creak.

"Careful, Vern, this floor sounds like it's about to give!"

Veronica chose each footfall deliberately, inched her way to the far corner, and knelt. Nikki hung back and watched, afraid that her additional weight would cause the floor to collapse.

"Vern, this isn't worth it. We'll call a locksmith."

Veronica didn't acknowledge her sister. Instead, she brushed away broken glass and debris to reveal a warped door in the floorboards.

Nikki gasped, surprised at the find.

Veronica dug her fingers into the corners of the small hatch and once again felt a rush of familiarity wash over her. She lifted the door, and it crumbled to pieces. She discarded the broken shards and reached into the darkness. She felt decaying chains and locks. She ignored these items until she brushed her hands across a single rusty key.

Nikki asked, "Did you find it?"

Veronica triumphantly held the key in the air. "Got it!"

Just then, the floor gave way under Veronica's feet. For a split second, she felt suspended in mid-air. She tumbled down as the ceiling caved in and piled on top of her.

"Vern!" Nikki yelled amidst the cacophony of the implosion.

Veronica did not answer. The air was thick with dust and Nikki strained her eyes to locate her sister through the haze. Veronica's crumpled body was covered with debris. Her legs were lost in the hole in the floor, and she was twisted amidst the wood like a broken doll. Blood seeped from a gash on her head.

"Vern! Are you okay? Vern?" Nikki pleaded, but her sister didn't answer. She lay ten feet away and wasn't moving.

Chapter 70

Father Michel's Story

Twilight was falling. Fearfully, Father Michel rode toward the village infested with the Flagellants. Lightning trudged wearily. He had ridden the horse hard, and the animal needed a rest.

From up ahead, Father Michel thought he heard singing. The holy man cringed as he recalled the melancholy songs that the Flagellants bemoaned. But this music was different. These weren't religious hymns; the music was bouncy, even jovial.

A single illuminated structure revealed itself in the dim evening. A large two-story building stood about fifty feet from the road. Several horses surrounded it, hitched at posts, under a hanging sign that Father Michel couldn't read in the fading light.

Lightning spied the other animals and neighed. They were drinking from a trough, and the tired horse could smell the liquid. Lightning swung his head and urged Father Michel in the direction of the country inn.

The priest pulled the reins to keep the horse on course. The animal was stubborn and resisted the command. Lightning needed to drink.

Hesitantly, the holy man dismounted the beast and led him to the trough. The voices grew louder, and Father Michel now understood the words: *Though the end is near, we will have no fear, grab a wench to quell the stench and pour another beer!"*

Lightning made a low "blubbering" noise, and the other horses replied with soft neighs. After the animals introduced themselves, Lightning approached the trough and drank gratefully.

The sign that hung over the door of the inn was now legible. Father Michel read: THE VELVET LION. A crude drawing of a naked female warrior riding on top of a lion graced it.

Through a small window, the priest could see figures inside, drinking around a table. A woman poured ale and urged, "Let's sing another!" She had a bursting bosom, streaked with milky blue veins, which pushed out of her corset. Her blond hair was drawn up into a mountain on top of her head. Loose strands framed her gaunt face and hung across sunken eyes.

A patron clumsily grabbed for her. The wench was too fast. She swerved her hips out of the way just in time, and he tumbled harmlessly to the floor.

Ruckus laughter erupted. A bearded, burly man pounded his goblet on the table and boomed, "Good dodge, Astrid, you get to pick the next song!"

Astrid looked up and caught Father Michel's gaze. Instead of singing, the barmaid shouted, "There's a *priest* outside spying on us!"

Several men spun just in time to see Father Michel duck out of sight. He rushed to Lightning. The animal was still drinking and defiantly shook his unwieldy head at the priest.

The door of the inn burst open. Five stout men poured out; a few of them still clutched their mugs of ale.

"There he is," one said while another cried, "He *is* a priest!"

"I am leaving," Father Michel began. "My horse needed a quick drink of water. Now we are off." He put his foot in the stirrup and was about to pull himself up when two hands grabbed his waist.

"What's the hurry, Father? Let the animal drink. Can't you see he's thirsty?" the bearded, burly man who had led the singing said. A blue beret sat on his head and a matching vest reached his knees.

"I don't mean any trouble. Just let me go," Father Michel pleaded.

The hairy man snorted with three guttural chuckles. "I didn't think for a moment *you* meant any *trouble*. I just thought you might like to join us for a drink and some supper...you look as famished as your horse." He let go of Father Michel's waist.

The priest turned and studied the hairy man. His grey eyes glinted with red flecks, and his bulbous nose was pitted like a giant, pink orange. He swayed slightly as he stood there.

Another man approached Lighting. "Your horse needs to eat, Father. He nearly took off my fingers just now! Would you like me to board him for the night? Feed and water him; make him good to ride by morning. Only charge a ha' penny."

"No, I can't stay the night. I have to go," the priest answered.

"Not sure how far you'll get. Looks like you ran him pretty hard. Keep it up, and you'll drive him straight into the ground." The man said and nuzzled Lightning.

"Come in and rest for a spell, Father. Let your horse eat and drink then you can leave in a few hours," the hairy man said.

"Thank you for the offer, but I must hurry."

The man who stroked Lightning shrugged his shoulders and walked toward the door. A few of the onlookers also lost interest and went back inside.

"Travel well then, Father," the hairy man grunted.

Through the open door wafted the aroma of cooking meat. Lightning nudged his master with his velvety nose. "Wait, maybe a quick bite. The horse *does* need a rest," Father Michel said.

The hairy man stumbled slightly as he turned back to the priest. "Yeah!" he enthused as he draped a burly arm around Father Michel. "My name is Jean-Arthur Lemoux. Let me buy you a drink!"

The stable boy returned to Lightning and nodded at Father Michel as he was ushered inside.

The inn was warmed by a roaring fire. A long bar spanned the far side of the room where a bartender and serving wenches poured goblets of ale for a thirsty crowd. On the right side, an open staircase climbed up to a closed door.

A cluster of men dined near the front fireplace. They raised their cups in unison as one man stood to proclaim a toast. He gestured at a solitary, empty stool. "To our dear friend, Bernard, who reveled with us last night but woke up dead this morning. May we not meet again anytime soon!" The men clanked their silver steins and whooped with laughter.

The other tables were littered with various people eating, drinking, and gambling. A card game near the bar had gathered a tall stack of gold and silver coins, and a few onlookers gawked at the poque players.

Jean-Arthur pulled out a chair for Father Michel at the bar and then clumsily claimed his own seat. "My friend here needs a cup of ale. And some soup!"

Father Michel flinched while his newfound friend shouted at the bartender who stood a mere four feet away.

A goblet of foamy liquid was set in front of the priest, followed by a shallow plate of stewed meat and vegetables.

"Thank you," the holy man whispered as he crossed himself and mouthed a silent prayer.

Jean-Arthur erupted with a snort. "You may not want to say grace over *that* meal until you taste it." To the bartender, he inquired, "Did you cook up another dog today, or maybe a cat this time?"

"I cook no cats and dogs!" the man behind the bar retaliated.

"Sure tasted like it yesterday," the hairy man cracked.

The bartender leaned in. "It was Bernard's horse," he said sardonically. "Cooked up nice and tender, I thought."

Tears trickled down Jean-Arthur's ruddy cheeks as he bellowed. Father Michel politely chortled with them as he drank down the sweet ale in one long draught. He shoveled several spoonfuls of stew into his mouth. He didn't care if it was horsemeat or dog or cat; it tasted delicious to the hungry man.

"Why are you in a hurry, Father?" Jean-Arthur asked as he pulled back on his goblet.

"I want to get through town before nightfall. I came this way yesterday and was attacked by some of the villagers."

"Ah, you must mean the Flagellants. Half of the people left in that town are their crazy followers. The other half are dead. Turning into a lawless place, that town is."

"Is it?" the priest asked as the bartender poured him another goblet of ale.

"Yes, I should know. I'm the sheriff." Jean-Arthur flashed Father Michel a mischievous smile. "Once they arrived, everything changed. The townspeople *worshipped* them. They wouldn't listen to me, to the clergy, not to anyone except those flogging fools. I couldn't stop them. I spend most of my days here now. Figured sooner or later everyone in the town will be dead, or I'll be dead, so what does it matter anyway?"

"Don't you have an obligation to protect the people?"

"I can't protect people who don't *want* to be protected. So, here I am. Have another beer, Father?"

Father Michel nodded his head. The bartender leaned in and continued where Jean-Arthur left off. "That's why they're *all* here. They figure if they're going to die anyway, they may as well go out having fun. See that table over there? Those men are some of the wealthiest merchants around. One or two of them even have noble blood. They come here every night, eat and drink like common folk until their stomachs are ready to explode, buy a whore for the night, and then they are on their way. Only tonight, they are one man short. Bernard was with them yesterday...as healthy as any of them. He even danced with Astrid over there for a while." The bartender nodded his head toward the blond-haired woman who had caught Father Michel peeking in the window.

Astrid was across the room carrying a tray full of cups. She noticed the bartender's nod and cocked her head to the side.

"So, eat, drink, and be merry, Father, for tomorrow, ye may die!" Jean-Arthur raised his goblet high in the air as he shouted the words. Several others around the bar imitated him and joined in the toast.

A thought occurred to the priest. "Jean-Arthur, do you think you could grant me safe passage through your town? I can pay you."

"Grant you safe passage?" The hairy man's fuzzy eyebrows scrunched together. He grabbed the holy man by the shoulders and nodded his head forward. "I hereby *grant* you safe passage...now pay me!" He crowed with laughter.

The bartender chuckled and poured the priest another glass of ale.

"I mean," Father Michel began, "can you accompany me through town? Guard me just until I get on the other side?"

Jean-Arthur's broad shoulders slumped, and he stared forward. "Will guarding a priest mean that God will forgive my iniquitous soul?"

The holy man considered his words carefully. "I cannot answer that."

Jean-Arthur leaned into the priest. "Well, as long as you pay me, why the hell not!"

"Thank you," Father Michel said. "We will leave within the hour."

"You see those men?" Jean-Arthur indicated the group gathered near the window. "Those are my deputies. Pay them, too, and you have a deal."

Father Michel nodded and raised his goblet with the hairy man. They toasted to their agreement, and the priest revealed two gold coins. "These I pay you now, and I will give you two more once on the other side of town."

Jean-Arthur snatched the gold and sauntered over to his men to inform them of the deal.

Father Michel threw back the goblet and closed his eyes as the remaining liquid flowed down his parched throat. Someone touched the side of his face, and his eyes sprang open.

There sat the bar wench, Astrid, in Jean-Arthur's chair. Her bony fingers caressed the priest's cheek, and she grinned with brown teeth. "I don't think I've ever seen a *priest* in this place. My how the times *have* changed."

Father Michel smiled shyly and pushed his empty goblet forward for the bartender. "Yes, they have."

"Tell me, are *all* priests really celibate? You never even *think* about being with a woman?" She let her hand trail around the back of his neck.

"Even thinking about it brings God's retribution."

"Oh no," Astrid cooed. "What would happen if you indeed did *it*?"

Father Michel felt warmth bubble inside of him. It was a mixture of alcohol and something else; something he only felt once before. His heavy lashes fluttered at Astrid. For a moment, her narrow eyes grew wide and bright. Her blond hair turned auburn, and she smelled of lavender. He saw beautiful Claudeen.

Astrid began to massage the priest's neck. "You need to relax. Let me rub you for a while. It will feel good. I promise." She pushed her body against the priest's back and used both hands to knead his shoulders. She struggled to get a firm grip and finally unsnapped the white collar that restricted her access. It fell from Father Michel's neck and landed on the counter in front of him. It retained some of its circular shape and formed a disappointed frown on the bar.

Father Michel looked at the collar. Next to it was a full cup of beer. He clumsily grabbed the goblet and took a long draught.

"Must feel good to have that thing off. It was practically choking you, like a dog's collar. You aren't a dog, are you?"

Father Michel allowed himself to enjoy Astrid's fingers as they pushed into his tight, sore muscles. His loins began to pulsate and dreamily he was drawn back to another time...

A young woman entered the confessional after the Sunday service. She had a soft voice, and Father Michel gently asked her to speak up.

"Forgive me, Father, for I've had impure thoughts."

"There is nothing wrong with *thoughts*. We all have them; it is very natural. It is how we *act* on our thoughts that matters to God."

"I shall never be able to act on these," she murmured. "There is a man who I love, but we cannot be together."

"Why? Would your father not approve?"

"No, he would not. But that's not the reason. There's more. The man I love doesn't know how I feel."

Father Michel probed further. "Do you know if *he* loves you?"

"No."

"Perhaps you should tell him."

"Oh, but I could not do that! It would not be appropriate!"

"Such a shy girl...will you wait for him to come to you?"

"Father, he would never come to me."

Father Michel breathed deeply. The faint scent of lavender hung in the air. "Then you must go to him. Tell him. A girl as charming as you should not be afraid as any man would be honored to have your love."

"I should tell him that I love him? I should tell him that I imagine his touch and crave his kisses!"

Father Michel beamed. "Our Lord rejoices in young love. Go, tell him..."

She sat quietly and said, "Father, I just did."

Father Michel sat stunned. She hastily sprinted out of the chamber. He pulled back the curtain, but only the subtle fragrance of lavender remained as the church doors swung shut in her wake...

Astrid stank like stale beer. Her hands slithered under the priest's cassock and felt their way down his chest. She flicked playfully at his nipples and let her breath exhale into his ear.

"You know, Father," she began. "We could go upstairs for a while. And whatever we do up there would be free of charge. I would gladly do it to see what it is like to be with a man of the cloth. To be with a *good* man for a change. Tell me, are you good, Father?"

Alcohol throbbed in the priest's head. Lust welled up from deep inside his body. He uttered a single word, "Claudeen..."

Chapter 71

The Pagans' Story

ay after day, from sunrise to sunset, Bevin hauled cumbersome stones from the mountain to Trinna's grave. He reinforced the dirt walls of the pit with rocks and mortar. Using the pre-erected obelisks, he framed a tower as a shrine to his beloved. It was well fortified. It was impenetrable. That is what the Hag had instructed.

Over the months, Bevin's young face grew gaunt while his arms grew robust. His abdomen became shallow as his chest ripped with muscle. His manhood never seemed to recover, and it remained tiny and shriveled, like the fleshy stub of a severed umbilical cord.

He thought of Trinna all the time. Like a phantom, she haunted his dreams as well as his waking mind. He remembered the day he first met her. There had been a gathering of the neighboring villages — a clan meeting — and Trinna was there with her family.

She was a shy girl who smiled modestly at the young warrior. They sat across from each other while the families feasted and danced. He plucked several daisies from a nearby hillside and wove them into a garland. Then, while she was looking the other way, he crept up behind her and gently placed it on her head. She yipped with surprise at the unexpected offering. Coyly, when he wasn't looking, she in turn tried to place the garland on top of *his* head, but he was too quick, and he playfully ran away. She chased him around the hillside until he finally let her catch him. Then it was his turn, and he chased her back.

Now Trinna appeared before him, smiling and giggling, with daisies in her hair just like on that summer's day. He laughed, too, though he knew she wasn't real. Then her outburst of joy turned to tears. She began to wail so loudly that Bevin covered his ears. The screams transformed into a cry, like the sound an infant makes, and then she faded away.

Bevin kept chiseling. He pounded harder and harder while tiny shards of splintered stone pelted his flesh. Into the night he worked, until he finally collapsed into a restless slumber.

Chapter 72

Veronica's Story

aturday morning. Veronica stirred to life from within a nest of blankets. She slowly opened her eyes to the familiar sight of the Queen's Chamber; the room that she had been confined to since the accident.

She didn't remember falling through the floor and being pinned under debris. Nikki had told her what happened. After the accident, Nikki ran into the castle screaming for help. She had tried to dial 9-1-1 on her cell phone, but then realized the emergency number didn't work in France. Clark was there, and he dialed the number for an ambulance. An emergency crew came and pulled the "silly American girl" from the rubble.

A quick trip to the hospital revealed that there were no broken bones, only a bruised Achilles tendon. The gash on her head, though bloody, was little more than a scratch. The doctor explained to them in broken English that head wounds were often very bloody, even when they were minor. He sent Veronica home that same day with a bottle of Extra Strength Tylenol and orders to stay off her ankle for at least a week.

Since then, Veronica had remained in bed. A pair of crutches allowed her to limp around the room occasionally, but they dug into her armpits and seemed more awkward than helpful.

She cradled her cell phone in her hand and tried to bring herself to call Christophe. Their "date" was tonight. They were supposed to go to Paris to meet his friend — the antiquities expert — to have a fancy dinner, and he had even mentioned dancing. Dancing! *That was certainly impossible now*, Veronica thought.

She considered her explanation to Christophe.

"You see, Christophe, I decided to go poking around in the abandoned stable to find a stupid key. The place was falling down, and the floor was rotting. No surprise that I broke through the decrepit thing! I got a cut on my head and tore up my ankle pretty bad. Doc says I gotta stay off it, and boy I will 'cause it hurts like a mother!

"Oh, and by the way, last Saturday this amazingly long scarf that I wore caught on the back of my chair at this sophisticated dinner party. When I tried to stand up, it yanked me back down, and I fell on my ass. The impossibly short dress that my pesky sister made me wear hiked up over my butt cheeks, and everyone got a view of a full moon that night!

"So, Christophe, since I have the grace and style of a fucking heifer, I can't keep our date tonight!"

Veronica groaned as the self-loathing dialogue played in her head. She pecked his number on the keypad, took a deep breath, and hit "send". Christophe answered on the first ring.

"Veronica! I was just about to call *you*! We must be on the same wavelength."

"Oh, I doubt that..." Veronica began.

"Good news. I made reservations for us at Jamin Robuchon. You will love it!

The chef, Benoit Buichard, will prepare a special dinner for us. It was a little tricky to make such a reservation on short notice, but I simply could not bring you to Paris without taking you to my favorite restaurant."

"Christophe, that is so sweet! I hate to —"

"Oh, and Ralph is excited to meet you and look at your map. Maps, ancient languages — that's his thing — must run in the family. And I should warn you; he's a little ostentatious. His family is very affluent and...it is a long story. I can tell you in the car. Oh! He wants to get a later start, so can I pick you and Nikki up at six?"

"No, I'm afraid not..."

Christophe didn't miss a beat. "Then, we'll stick with five. We can drive the scenic way and stop for a café along the way."

"That's not what I mean. We can't go at *all*, Christophe."

"Oh! I see. Okay then..." he let his voice trail off.

Veronica hesitated. She knew he was waiting for a reason, but she just sat there, silent. Finally, she blurted, "I had an accident."

"An accident? What happened?"

"It was. Christ, it was so stupid. I fell through some rotting floorboards, and I bruised my Achilles tendon. Got a bump on the head, too, from the stuff that fell on top of me."

"The castle has rotting floors? I had no idea it was in such condition!"

"No, it didn't happen in the castle..." Veronica took a deep breath. "I was in the stable...listen, that's not important..." Veronica said, trying to avoid the details of her escapade. "I feel awful canceling at the last minute."

"It's okay," Christophe said simply.

"We can make it another night, okay?"

"Sure."

"Okay! I'll call you when I'm feeling up to it," Veronica stated.

"Great. Goodbye then."

"Yeah, okay, goodbye. I'll..." The phone went silent.

Veronica clicked it off and dropped her head back into her pillow as Nikki entered the room.

"Hey, how are you doing?" Nikki bounced as she set a tray with tea and cookies on the night table.

"Why are you always so fucking happy?"

Nikki threw herself onto the bed beside her sister. "I don't know. I guess it's my fucking nature."

"Well, I called Christophe and canceled our plans for tonight."

"You *canceled*? Why'd you do that?"

"Because of my leg! I can't go anywhere like this."

"Why not? You have crutches."

Veronica shook her head. "I can barely get around on those things. I would be so uncomfortable, and I'd look like a gimp trying to hobble around. It would be embarrassing."

"Aw, Vern, I was looking forward to tonight. We were going out in *Paris*! How often do we get to go out in Paris? Try...*never*! We have *never* been out in *Paris*."

"We can go another time — maybe next weekend," Veronica offered.

"But I wanted to go *tonight*. I am sure Christophe did, too. But no, Vern gets a bug up her ass, and no one gets to have any fun."

"I don't have a bug up my ass! I just can't go anywhere like this. If you want to go out, then here, take the car, drive into Amboise," Veronica offered.

"Really? You don't mind?"

"Go ahead, if you have to go out that badly. Have fun." Veronica's tone was flat.

"You won't be mad if I leave you here?" Nikki probed.

"No, why would I be mad. Just because I can't go doesn't mean you shouldn't. I am sure you can find something to do. Have fun. I'll be fine. I can work on the designs for the upstairs bedrooms."

"Okay, as long as you're sure. I wonder if Christophe still wants to go to Paris..."

Veronica's heartbeat quickened. "You want to call *Christophe* and go to *Paris*?"

"Well, yeah, why not?"

"I just don't know if he would want to go...without me there, I mean, we had plans and...that doesn't matter, so sure, give him a call."

"I just want to hang out, have some fun. Don't worry. It's not like I'm interested in him or anything."

"I know, and I don't care...that's not the problem."

"So, there *is* a problem? You don't want me to go?"

"No, that's not what I meant. Just go. Have fun. Really, don't let me hold you back."

"Okay, as long as you're sure..." Nikki hesitated.

"Yes, go! Don't worry about me. I'll just chill here in this big old castle by myself. I'll have fun with the ghosties." Veronica smiled slyly.

"Cool, you and the ghosties have a good time; I'm going to go party with the living! Give me your phone. I'm gonna call Christophe."

Veronica begrudgingly handed over her cell phone. Nikki plucked the device out of her sister's hand and happily sashayed out of the room.

Veronica felt a pang of dread build up in the pit of her stomach. She reached for the journal and began to read.

Chapter 73

Journal Intime

I awoke to find my body tied down and bound to the bed. Only my arms are free, so I can feed myself, write, and drink the tonic. I cannot lift my legs or roll onto my side. My ankles are tied together and bound to the bedposts with thick, scratchy twine. It is coarse and scratches my bare skin.

Around my thighs are thick leather straps like the ones used to hold a saddle in place. Another belt wraps around my torso, between my stomach and breasts. The buckles are clasped under the bed, and I cannot twist far enough to reach them.

The worst part is my neck. To keep me from squirming or attempting to sit up, they secured a strap across it. I can only lift my head a few inches, enough to pull it off the pillow so I can swallow. In order to write, I must hold the pen and journal up above me at an odd, uncomfortable angle.

Henri refuses to see me. Only the midwife and Agathe have been in here since the incident yesterday. They stare at me with disdain and lecture me on how my carelessness almost lost the baby.

"Hate" does not describe how I feel about them. I dream of being free from my bindings, walking — no wait, not walking — dancing! Yes, I would *dance* up behind Agathe and the midwife as if I were gliding across the ballroom floor. Then, I would grab each woman by the hair, digging my nails in just at the nape of the neck. I would yank their heads down, jerking as hard as I could to rattle their brains, just before smashing their noggins together.

Such notions eat at my soul constantly. I attempt to break the spell. Poetry, yes, I should calm myself with pleasant rhymes and flowery verse. Henri says the poetry will bring comfort to my somnolent soul, and so I try:

I find myself a-stumbling over bodies of the dead
They are my predecessors
I'll soon lie in their bed
I'll join their rank as memories after the beast is fed
Oh, but how I'd rather try to seek refuge instead

Josette-Camille

August 20th, 1789

I lie stock-still while each day decays. Listening to the shadows brings me some comfort. There, listen! I can hear two guards sneaking a bucket of ale through the kitchen. They are drunk and not as quiet as they think they are. One of them drops the end of the barrel on his toe while the other laughs. The buffoons carry on this way for some time, and they quickly become droll to listen to.

I twist my head. Thankfully, I can hear another room in the castle. It is Henri's chamber. He resides just above my quarters. Though the floors and walls are extremely thick, I still hear him as he whispers his nightly prayer. He asks God for the birth of a healthy baby boy, a son to inherit his estate and carry on the family name. He prays for guidance during the siege and for a victorious outcome. He asks God to deliver France from this bloody revolution. He prays for Agathe and her family and asks Jesus to bless the servants and guards in the castle. I listen, hopefully, waiting for him to make mention of me — his wife — but as he mutters the last of his Hail Mary's there is none. I do not get even one prayer from my own dear husband.

Josette-Camille

Chapter 74

Father Michel's Story

Astrid took the priest by the hand and gently coaxed him to follow. "You are going to feel things tonight that are truly *heavenly*."

Father Michel staggered to his feet. The chair slipped from underneath him and almost crashed to the floor. Astrid caught it and steadied the stool. She pulled on the priest's arm with her other hand. "Come, let's take a walk."

Father Michel studied Astrid's face with sudden drunken determination. Her features overlapped; her nose danced on top of her eyes, her smile doubled, and her crooked teeth straightened. "Claudeen?"

"I'll be anyone you want me to be," Astrid smirked.

Father Michel allowed the wench to escort him through the crowd.

"Watch out for that bench..." she instructed as they made their way toward the stairs.

A booming voice called from across the room. "Father! Where are you going?" It was Jean-Arthur.

The priest opened his mouth to speak and a slur of nonsense came out.

Astrid pushed him from behind. "Hurry, we're almost there, lover."

"Astrid! Leave him alone!" Jean-Arthur ordered.

"I'm just taking him for a little stroll. He *wants* to come with me!"

"You really want to go with *her*, Father?"

The priest looked at the woman holding his hand. "Claudeen, I will follow you anywhere!"

"He doesn't even know who you are, Astrid. Let him go!"

"Most of them don't want to know who I am!" Astrid retorted.

Jean-Arthur stepped forward as Astrid pushed the priest toward the staircase. Stumbling, Father Michel used the railing to pull himself along, and he slowly mounted the stairs.

"Astrid, I have the authority to arrest you!"

Astrid spun to face the burly man. "Your *authority*? What are you going to do? Take me into custody? Put me in *jail*? Oh wait, the Flagellants run the jail now, don't they?" she taunted.

"Wretched whore, bite back your tongue! I am still the sheriff..."

"You stopped being the sheriff weeks ago. Now, you're just a depraved drunkard trying to hold onto your pathetic past. You are nothing. A joke. A craven sheep like all the rest of us just waiting in fear." Astrid puffed out her ample breast like a cock preparing for a fight. She was half the size of the robust man and her display caused the crowded tavern to twitter.

Jean-Arthur lowered his voice. "This isn't a game. The priest is drunk. Leave him alone." He took three long, stomping strides across the flimsy wood floor. Nearby patrons rushed out of his way while several onlookers from the back of the room moved in for a closer look. He stopped inches from Astrid and glared into her rodent-like eyes.

"This isn't your business," she spat. "You leave *us* alone. Go to your buddies and drink another round. We'll be back before you take down another pint."

"Filthy trollop, I said leave him alone!" the burly man shouted as drops of spittle sprayed across Astrid's sickly white face.

She drew up her right arm and slapped him with the back of her hand. Jean-Arthur grabbed for her, but she was too quick and easily ducked around him. Several men jeered the action, and the bartender jumped on top of a table. "There is no fighting in my tavern!"

Within seconds, Jean-Arthur's deputies were behind him, grabbing his arms. Astrid spit at the sheriff's face but missed, hitting one of his men in the forehead. He pushed her back with his free hand and shouted, "Keep your dirty juices off me, whore!"

Astrid's voice was shrill. "Look at the big sheriff now! What are you going to do? Huh? Come on, come and get me!"

The bartender came up behind Astrid and grabbed her shoulders. He pulled her away from the men and warned, "Don't tease them, Astrid. A fucking priest isn't worth all this. Now get back to work."

Astrid pretended to struggle in his arms while Jean-Arthur was dragged away.

Father Michel sat perched halfway up the stairs. He observed the commotion with his eyebrows raised high. Every once in a while, he attempted to speak but his words were lost in the uproar below.

"Father!" Jean-Arthur bellowed from across the room. "You didn't want that unclean strumpet, did you?"

Father Michel rose precariously to his feet at the mention of his name and yelled back, "I want *Claudeen!*"

The voices in the room fell silent. Even Astrid, who was preaching her side of the story to anyone within earshot, paused to listen.

"Claudeen...was Paul's daughter. She always wore sprays of lavender in her hair, and she was young and beautiful and shy. I wanted to be with her, but how could I? I made a promise to God! But at night she always crept into my dreams. I fought so hard to push the impure thoughts from my mind...and I succeeded. I was *not* tempted!" Father Michel stumbled on his perch, but clumsily caught himself on the railing.

"Then the Jew came, and he made me regret *ever* taking my vows. He showed me the truth. An ancient truth that devastated everything I believed in. He brought me my salvation. A Jew saved me! Or so I thought. I was going to take her away...I had the Jew's money. And I could take her away from that wretched life as a farmer's daughter, in that wretched little town infested with this vile disease."

The priest's eyes welled. "The peste is God's punishment. Don't you see? We are all being punished! Rich, poor, humble, proud, good, evil, sinners, saints, young and old, no one is safe from a vengeful God."

He raised his face to the heavens. For a moment, one could imagine him standing on a pulpit, lecturing before a congregation. "The Jew opened my eyes. Oh, did he ever show me! If you knew, then you would understand that our Lord has been deceitful! I can show you. I can show you all!" His arms waved in the air, and he stumbled again. This time he slid down two steps before catching himself.

"You are not well right now," Jean-Arthur spoke. "You aren't even making sense, Father. Be careful before you fall!"

"What was my first sin? Was it the lust I felt for Claudeen? I resisted! I tried so hard to resist. Then the Jews came and I took them in. I told myself I would have taken anyone in because that is what the Bible teaches us to do. Or did I give them refuge because of the money? I don't even know why I did it, but I did."

Two men went to the aide of the priest and steadied him as he sobbed. "Testing me...always testing *me*! Why must you always test me and watch me fail? Do I amuse you, Lord? Is smiting us with pestilence and fear not enough for you? I am done with your tests. Peasant families begging for last rites, little dying girls reaching out to me from a barred-up apartment, I reject them all! I refuse to take your stinking tests anymore. Stop giving them to me because I won't take them you wicked, vengeful, spiteful God!"

Jean-Arthur slammed several coins onto the top of the bar and spoke to the innkeeper. "Give him a room for the night. Let him sleep off the drink. I'll be back tomorrow. And no matter what, keep Astrid the hell away from him!"

"You don't have to worry about her anymore," the bartender stated as he nodded toward the doorway.

There stood Astrid with her arm around a bewildered looking man who just entered the inn. She talked excitedly in his ear while reaching over to stroke the beard of another man.

Two men assisted Father Michel while the innkeeper barked instructions to them. "Take him upstairs to the room at the end of the hall."

Father Michel resisted feebly while he was led away. "I can't sleep now. Gaston is waiting. I have to get to Lightning...where is my horse?"

One of the priest's escorts said, "Your horse is waiting for you upstairs."

Father Michel nodded as he willingly followed them. They gently tossed him into a room and locked the door. He was left to sleep until morning.

Chapter 75

Sebastian's Story

Esindra pulled back the tapestry and poked her head out of the grotto. The bacchanal that transpired earlier had ended. There was a noise. It was tinny and quick — a *ping*. She cocked her head. There it was again. It had a rhythm.

Ping...ping...ping...

Carefully, she stepped out of the chasm and straightened her back. She had been crouched over for hours and a hot pain shot down her spine. She took another tentative step when she heard the voice behind her.

"Esindra!" It was Sebastian, hovering by the tapestry like a cat waiting for a mouse to emerge from a hole. "You finally decided to come out."

Esindra whirled and faced the Cloaked Man. "You knew I was here?"

He held the candle she had left on the table. "I've been waiting for you to come out on your own. Didn't want to frighten you and have you take an unfortunate fall."

He took a step toward her.

"Stand back or I'll scream," Esindra warned.

He was calm, almost amused. "Please do. The guards will come, along with Fabius, who will want to know why you are hiding in *my* chamber. I would verily like to find out, too, so do scream. Go ahead..."

Esindra carefully considered the situation. "Fabius cannot know." Consternation clutched her throat and made it crack. "You said I would have a baby. I thought I might find something here; a clue or a hint that would tell me if it was true. Fabius forbade me to even speak of it, so I had to find out on my own."

She took a slow, calculated step toward the door. From behind the dividing screen, she could hear the noise.

Ping...ping...ping...it echoed off the stone walls.

"I've seen a child in your future. But remember, the things I see are not absolute. They are merely specters of what *may* happen. If it is truly a child you seek, I can help you. But it is you and only *you* who'll ultimately make it happen."

"I want a son more than anything in the world. So does Fabius. I fear, though, that he's given up hope."

"I can help you, but only if you trust me completely."

The word *trust* made Esindra shudder. She took another hesitant step toward the door.

Ping...ping...ping...the sound grew louder.

"What would you have me do?"

"Follow me."

"Where?"

Baldebert lumbered in, carrying a bucket. He nodded at Esindra, hid himself behind the screen, and trudged back out.

"Baldebert has everything ready. Come, before the night grows cold."

ᦂ᥊ ❖ ᥊ᦂ

Esindra followed Sebastian into the courtyard. Baldebert was the only soul in sight. He stood by the garden bath with a bucket. Fabius designed it like those in the bathhouses of Rome. It was a square slab of white marble surrounded by warrior statues covered in ivy. The moonlight illuminated the tub, and its contents gleamed like a pool of liquid obsidian.

"What is this?" Esindra's voice quivered.

"A special bath to make you feel young. Young women bear children easier than old."

Baldebert poured the last bucket into the pool. "It's ready."

Sebastian took Esindra's hand and led her to the tub. "Hurry, while it's still warm."

Esindra gazed into the foamy liquid. It was dark with a red hue in the moonlight. "I don't think Fabius would want me to do this...the bath is only for men; women aren't allowed."

"Fabius isn't here."

"I should have female slaves tend to me, not Baldebert."

"Baldebert is a Druid priest; he may as well be a eunuch."

"What if someone comes?"

"I told Fabius I needed privacy to prepare poison for the Head Commander. A little lie. That way no one will disturb us as we perform the ritual for you."

"You knew I would come?"

"I see many things, Esindra. I always knew you would come to me."

"I don't know if I *should* be here."

"You want to have a child, yes, Esindra?"

"Yes, more than anything."

"You understand I can help you, yes?"

"Yes, however..."

"Esindra, do you want to have a child?"

"Yes."

"Then you understand that I can help you, yes?"

"Yes."

"Then you must do exactly as I say, yes?"

"Yes."

"Then let's prepare you for your bath." The Cloaked Man removed the broach that held her robe in place. He held her gaze for a moment and then averted his eyes.

Her robe slid down the curves of her body. Baldebert removed the adornments decorating her hair. He pulled out her delicate braids and combed his fingers through her twisty locks, causing her hair to fall long and free. While cupping her elbow, he guided her into the bath. Esindra felt herself melt into the liquid. It was warm, indulgent, and had a perfumed redolence. She sat in the tub

228

and wallowed in the experience. Her entire body began to tingle, and she eased herself lower and lower, enjoying the sensation as she submerged deeper and deeper.

Baldebert tended to her like a servant. After he used a cloth to wipe her face and arms, he wrung it out over her hair, and saturated every strand. No one spoke a word. The only sound was the tranquil movement of the liquid, splashing lightly against the sides of the tub. When Baldebert lifted his cloth, it dripped with a tiny *ping...ping...ping* back into the tub.

Esindra recalled the familiar sound. In front of her face was the Cloaked Man. "You want to have a child, don't you, Esindra? Esindra, tell me you want this. Tell me 'yes', Esindra."

She lifted her arms. They gleamed ruby red. Droplets of blood, freshly drained from the young boys, dripped down her forearm with a *ping...ping...ping.* She answered in a steady rhythm, "Yes...yes...yes."

Chapter 76

Veronica's Story

It clicked. The lock had never done that before. The latch gave way, and Veronica cautiously pushed the door to the keep open. She was greeted with a warm gush of stale air. It had the tang of rotting leaves and mildew. She drew up the neck of her t-shirt and pulled it over her mouth and nose to filter the rank aroma.

Clicking on her flashlight, she swiped the beam around the dismal corridor. This place was like no other in the Château. The scene before her materialized like a medieval nightmare. Large iron sconces dangled overhead. One wall curved outward, and from Veronica's vantage, she could just make out the impression of a door inlayed on its convex surface. *That must be the tower,* she thought as she swung the light to the right side of the narrow room to see three enormous wood doors fitted with black metal hinges. They each had a small slat near the bottom.

Veronica pushed the door all the way open. It rebelled with an antagonizing screech. She let the shirt slip off her nose and took a shallow, timid breath. She almost gagged. It was the sweet, musky, gaseous fumes of rot and decay. Coughing twice, she pulled the shirt quickly over her face again like a bandit. She held her breath until her lungs could bear no more then slowly sucked in a small amount of air through her mouth. The tip of her tongue sprung to life, as she now tasted the stench.

"Gross!" she sputtered while building up a supply of saliva in her mouth. She spit on the floor and awkwardly backed into the hallway. Here, she took several labored breaths before re-entering the keep.

Her ankle was still tender from the fall, but she moved as quickly as she could. She noticed the stairs that hugged the round wall and spiraled up into darkness. That climb would be for another day.

The door to the tower room was covered with a thin layer of white mildew that melted onto her fingertips as she nimbly felt for the handle. Aiming the flashlight, she peered through its narrow slot. The room was perfectly round and littered with debris. A hollowed out square on the opposite wall looked like a massive fireplace without a mantle.

Then, the designer inside of her took command.

This will be so cool to decorate. I've never had the challenge of designing a perfectly round room. We can get that fireplace working; add a circular area rug...

She hurried into the room, momentarily oblivious to the smell, the dirt, and the darkness. She flashed the light back and forth, and instantly determined that a canopied bed should be on the far wall. Veronica imagined the colors — bright, flowery — to compensate for the lack of natural lighting. She considered painting the stone walls...would she need to hang drywall? She felt the surface and found that it was relatively smooth and, therefore, paintable. As her hand brushed across the stones, something sliced her thumb.

"Ouch!" she squealed, more in surprise than pain. She drew her hand back and then gingerly reached out again, curious as to what nipped her. The stone was smooth — almost soothing to touch — except for one odd protrusion. Like a sliver poking from a wound, a sharp object jutted from the wall.

Veronica breathed shallowly, desperately craving fresh air. With more effort than she was prepared for, she plucked the dime-sized object and curiously inspected it. It was slightly curved and jagged on the end. Veronica tried to determine if it was a rusty nail — it would be just her luck to need a tetanus shot!

From across the room, she heard something stir. She steadied the beam and let it fall squarely on the decrepit remains of a cot. There was something under it. Air escaped from her lungs, but she didn't want to inhale again. Two tiny reflections caught in the beam of light. It was quick, and before she could focus, they disappeared.

"Were those eyes?" Veronica whispered as she scrambled to the door and let it fall shut behind her.

She drew in a deep breath and wobbled down the hall. As she went through the library, she held up the sharp object. It had ridges, like a tiny potato chip. Her sister called to her from the kitchen.

"Hey, Vern! In here."

Veronica entered while Nikki continued. "Where were you? And what stinks? Is that *you*?"

Veronica sniffed the air. It smelled fresh to her compared to what she had just experienced. "I don't know, maybe. I was in the keep, and it smells bad in there."

"So, you finally got inside the freaking keep, huh?"

"I wanted to make sure the key worked, so Clark can check the sewer lines."

"By the smell of it, I think he may have his work cut out for him. Is there a leak?"

Veronica went to the sink and scrubbed her hands with hot, soapy water. "Maybe, I didn't see anything. I was only in there for a minute. I couldn't stand the stench. I did find this though — it sliced my hand when I touched the wall. What do you think it is? Do you think I need a tetanus shot?" Veronica held up the miniature potato chip.

Nikki squinted at it before declaring, "It looks like a fingernail. See the cuticle?"

Veronica screeched at the revelation and flung the object into the air. It landed on the counter.

Nikki leaned in for a closer look. "Vern, where did you get it? One end is torn like it was ripped off someone's finger!"

"It was stuck in the keep's wall in the tower room."

"That's so gross! What the hell happened in that room?"

"I dunno. Maybe it's from a prisoner who tried to claw their way out?" Veronica stammered.

"That is just freaking morbid."

"I saw some kind of animal, too. Maybe it was a skunk?"

"Is *that* what a skunk smells like?" Nikki asked.

"I guess. The only skunk I ever saw before was Pepe Le Pew. He was French, ya' know? That would explain a lot," Veronica quipped nervously.

"Speaking of amorous French men; Christophe and I had a blast last night. We had drinks at Place Plumereau in Tours. I'll have to take you there sometime...if you're not too *busy*," Nikki began carefully.

Veronica's gut tightened as she swept the fingernail into the garbage with a paper napkin.

Nikki continued. "He seemed concerned about your ankle. I told him what happened in the stable and how you went to the hospital. I know that you say you're not interested in him, but I kinda think he likes you."

Veronica felt a gush. "Really?" she prompted.

"Yeah, he kept talking about you most of the night. Don't worry, I set him straight though."

"Set him *straight*? What do you mean by that?" Veronica felt her stomach roil as it always did when her sister interfered.

"I told him you wouldn't be interested in dating him — too busy decorating the castle. That's what you said, right?"

"You *told* him that?"

"Yeah," Nikki answered. "Like I said, he kept asking about you, and I didn't want him to get his hopes up."

"I can't believe you just came out and said that to him!"

"It was no big deal. We had a few glasses of wine, and we talked about a lot of things."

"Like what? What did you tell him about *me*?" Veronica fought to keep her tone steady.

"You know, the basics, like how you lost your fancy-shmancy job in Beverly Hills and started your own business, and how it's kinda sucking ass."

"Why would you tell him that?"

"Well, I wanted him to know why *this* job was so important to you, so he would understand why you work so much, and why you're kinda bitchy sometimes."

"Nikki, just don't get involved, okay?"

"Involved with what?"

"With me, with my life."

"What the hell did I do?"

"It's just like with Robert. You always have to go poking your nose into things."

"So, this is about Robert?"

"No, it is not about Robert. It's not about anything. Just don't...don't talk about me, okay? And don't talk *for* me, okay?"

"Uh, okay...can I still talk *to* you?"

Veronica clenched her teeth together. "Can we just drop it?"

"Considering the fact that I'm not even sure what it is that we're fighting about..." Nikki let her voice taper into a whisper.

"We're not fighting. I'm fine," Veronica said brightly. "I wonder when we should reschedule our trip to Paris."

"Oh, we talked about going next weekend. I'll give Chris a buzz and confirm. It's okay if I talk to *him*, right?" Nikki fished her phone out of her pocket.

"Yeah, of course you can talk to him. I need to take a bath anyway."

Nikki smirked. "Good because you really reek."

"Okay, I'll be in the tub." She hesitated before asking, "Let me know what he says, okay?"

Nikki eagerly began dialing and nodded her head.

Veronica limped back to her room and prepared a bath. A stream of rust colored liquid escaped from the faucet, and she cursed Clark under her breath.

Chapter 77

The Children's Story
1307 AD – A Time of Inquisition

Isabelle and Louis sped across the forest road. It was little more than a dirt trail, overgrown with weeds. Branches hung down from the canopy, so the children had to duck several times.

"Slow down, Izzy, we're going too fast," Louis warned as he clung to his sister like a frightened monkey.

"They might be chasing us!"

Louis watched over his sister's shoulder. He bounced violently on her lap, and his jaw clanked against her collarbone.

"Ouch," Isabelle scolded. "Sit still, or you'll fall off."

"No one is behind us, Izzy!"

Isabelle relaxed her legs, and the horse slowed to a comfortable gallop. "They still may be coming," she cautioned.

"Where are we going? Aren't the mountains in the other direction?"

"We can't ride to the mountain village anymore because that's the direction the Inquisitor on the horse went. Plus Nana knows our plan, and that's where she will tell them to look. We have to go someplace else."

"Where?"

"I think this road leads to town. No one will recognize us because of our disguises. Plus, we have the horse. We'll ride through and just keep going and get as far away from Uncle Pierre as possible."

"The satchel! I don't have it," Louis exclaimed.

"Don't worry about..." Isabelle began.

"But it is still back there. We need it!"

"No, we don't. I have money to buy food," the older sister assured him.

"It had Papa's secrets in it."

"Secrets from Papa?" she asked.

Louis dropped his voice low even though no one was around. "Papa gave me something to keep safe for always, and now I lost it..." The child's words trailed off and subtle sobs took over.

"Papa will understand that escaping with your *life* was more important than whatever it was in that satchel. What was it anyway?"

Louis sniffed. "I can't tell anyone about the secret." His face suddenly brightened. "But I still have part of it! I thought I would forget what Papa told me, so I wrote it down just inside the cover of the book. But I didn't need to write it down after all because I remember!"

"Remember what?"

"The secret name..." he whispered. "I am the only one who knows it."

"Well, good, Little Louis, just don't ever forget it," Isabelle cajoled. "Now hold on tight; the road is getting rocky!"

❧❧ ❖ ❧❧

Around mid-afternoon they came upon a village. She drew up Louis' bonnet to cover his face. Though she did her best to keep to the outskirts, several wagons, steered by farmers and pulled by donkeys, passed them by. Isabelle prayed they would not be recognized.

The evening shadows began to grow long in the setting sun as they rode away from the town. Isabelle directed the horse off of the road and tied him to a tree in a small glen. He nibbled happily at the foliage.

"What are we doing here?" Louis asked.

"Resting for the night where no one can see us."

"What about wild animals?" Louis griped.

Isabelle patted his head. "I'm here to protect you."

She inspected his ankle, which was swollen and purple. He yipped like a puppy when she pressed on it. Though the sprain looked severe, she didn't feel any broken bones.

"It'll be fine, Little Louis. It'll hurt for a few days and then be all better."

The children snuggled in each other's arms and listened to the whir of insects buzz around the horse.

"I'm going to call him Stinker," Louis proclaimed just as Isabelle began to nod off.

"Who are you going to call Stinker?" she asked sleepily.

"The horse. He needs a name, and I think it should be Stinker."

"Why Stinker?" Isabelle mused.

"You have to ask?" Little Louis questioned as he deeply breathed in the musty fragrance of the animal and let out an exaggerated cough.

Isabelle chuckled as they drifted off to sleep.

Chapter 78

Father Michel's Story

father Michel's breath was hot and dry. There was no moisture in his mouth. He swallowed several times in an effort to summon up bile. His eyes opened slowly, painfully, as he sat upright in a dusty bed. It was draped with billowy red blankets that were stained and smelled like vomit. He touched a damp spot on the pillow where his head had been. An image of Claudeen lingered as he surveyed the room and tried to determine where he was.

Fragmented memories came back. He remembered stopping at the inn so that Lightning could get water. He recalled Jean-Arthur, the merriment of the bar, eating, drinking...

He brushed crusty remnants from the corners of his mouth and rose to look out a small window. The blue sky was streaked with pink and orange, and for a moment, the priest thought that night must just be falling. With dread, he remembered that he had arrived at the inn near dusk. The colors in the clouds were not from the setting sun; it was the hazy light of morning.

Father Michel rushed for the door, clasped the handle, pulled, but it held fast. The door was locked from the outside. He pounded with his fists and yelled, "Hello? Is anyone there?"

His pleas were answered by stillness. From outside, he heard the coo of mourning doves, taunting him with their freedom. He pounded and pounded, but no one came.

"Someone please help me!"

A far-off voice yelled, "Shut up and go back to sleep!"

"Just open the door. I'm locked in!"

No one responded. Frustrated, he rested his forehead against the door. Then there was a noise, just on the other side, a soft click, and it pushed in.

"Thank you..." the priest began, but he stopped short when he saw the figure that entered the room. Covered in blood was a woman dressed only in her under garments.

He pulled her inside, laid her on the rank bed, and wiped blood-soaked hair out of her eyes. Her face was swollen and lacerated. One eye was open while the other was almost completely caked shut by dried blood.

"Look who saved me," she spoke. "Never thought I'd see you again."

The voice stirred his memory. She was the woman who had been serving drinks, the bar wench...what was her name? Father Michel felt embarrassment flood his gut as he recalled her touch on his flesh — massaging him. The memory was hazy but began to clarify as he dabbed at the open wound above her eye with the corner of the bed sheet.

She coughed with tired lungs and a small glob of bile, red with blood, squirted from her thin lips. The priest now remembered watching those lips flap, beckoning him to follow her.

"Astrid..." he recalled her name. He made the sign of the cross over his chest and continued slowly. "What happened to you? *Who* did this?"

Only one of her eyes focused on the priest. The other appeared to be glued in place by the dried blood, as if it were already dead. "Two men, they came in at the end of the night; one had a beard..." She gagged as fluid filled her lungs.

"Where are they?" the priest asked as he propped up her head with a pillow. More scarlet phlegm spattered from her mouth.

"I think they're gone now. They heard you pounding and ran out. We were in the bedroom next door."

"They attacked you?"

"It happens; a hazard of my profession. I screamed and screamed, but no one came to help. No one wanted to get involved. I couldn't fight both of them by myself, so eventually, I just let them do whatever they wanted...and they did — again and again — all night."

Hot guilt pierced his abdomen. He slept in the room right next door and never woke up.

Astrid continued. "I usually don't take more than one at a time — it's risky — but they had a lot of money, and *we* need money so bad."

"I'll get Jean-Arthur. He's the sheriff and can catch them before they go too far." He began to stand, but she tugged his robe.

"Jean-Arthur won't do anything to them, especially not on *my* behalf."

Father Michel recalled the confrontation between her and the sheriff. "I didn't know you needed money," the priest whispered, more to himself than to her.

Astrid grunted. "Everyone needs money. I just need it a little bit more than most. I have a son, and once we have enough, we'll be able to leave this town before it kills us. Go off into the city where it's safe..."

The priest thought of the treasure that he carried under his robes and felt his face flush. He saw that she was shivering and pulled a blanket over her pasty-white legs. They were ridden with deep, thin lacerations, like marks that a barbed whip makes — a flagellant's whip. Father Michel also noticed a pool of blood under her thighs, pouring out her loins.

"You have a son," the priest began brightly, but his voice was hoarse. He struggled to find more words but was at a loss. His head began to throb, and he suddenly became intensely thirsty.

"He's seven years of age. I know what you must think, but I *am* a good mother! There is no other way for someone like me to make money. No one will take care of us; no man would want a whore as a wife. What else can I do?"

Father Michel nodded as she spoke. He realized that she was confessing to him, and he quietly listened.

"Mary Magdalene, she was a prostitute, wasn't she, Father? And Jesus forgave *her*?"

Father Michel instantly thought of the Bible that the old Jew had given him. "That's what the Good Book says." Father Michel winced as the thumping in his skull intensified. He desperately needed water.

"Maybe, then, Jesus will forgive me, too, right, Father?"

Father Michel smiled at the broken face. "He forgives, yes. You need rest now. I should get someone, a doctor or maybe..."

"No! I don't want you to go. Please, don't leave me." Tears trickled down the sides of her bumpy cheeks, and her thin mouth trembled. "I just wanted to be with someone *good* for once!"

"What?" Father Michel scrunched his eyebrows.

Astrid sobbed. "When I tried to lead you upstairs, that's what I wanted, Father. I wanted to know what it felt like to be in the arms of a man who was *good*. Someone who didn't curse at me or spit on me or beat me."

The priest's dry throat tightened. "I'm here now."

"I didn't want to hurt you or *tempt* you. I just wanted to be held by you." Astrid's one eye wearily closed. Her chest heaved and then froze.

Father Michel cradled her blood-soaked body before administering last rites and then quietly slunk out of the room.

Chapter 79

Sebastian's Story

Esindra's body was speckled with chilly bumps. The early morning breeze lapped at her naked skin through the veranda doors. Memories from the previous night snapped her awake, and she hastily grabbed her regal purple robe, swathed it around herself, and left her quarters.

She mounted the stairs and crept up to Fabius' room. With a sly smile, she pushed the door open.

Fabius lay on a sea of billowing pillows. Two young slave girls hovered over him. She caught them in the middle of a candid giggle as they kneaded his massive, bare back. Fabius lifted his head to see who the intruder was. "What are you doing here?" he asked flatly.

The girls froze and turned their shy faces away from the Governess. Fabius didn't wait for Esindra to answer. "Don't stop!" he barked. "My neck, rub my neck."

"What's going on, Fabius; why are these girls here?"

"They are obviously giving me a massage. I awoke with a kink in my neck. Now answer my question; what are *you* doing here?"

"I thought we could be together. I thought you might like some company this morning, but I see you already have..."

Fabius grunted, "Yes, I do."

"Fabius, my love, surely you can make yourself exclusive to your wife right now. If it is a massage you want, then let me do it."

The girls once again lifted their hands off their master's back. Fabius whined like a disappointed child, sat up, and dismissed them with a reluctant flick of his hand. They briefly glowered at the Governess as they romped out of the room.

Esindra approached her husband. Though a blanket thinly covered his loins, she could see he was swollen. "You should come to *me* when you want to be massaged."

"You were sleeping. There was no reason to wake you."

Esindra sat next to Fabius and pulled his hand to her face. "You may wake me. I won't mind. You come to see me so seldom. I miss you sometimes. I miss your touch." She led his hand down her neck, across her breasts, and used it to open the front of her robe.

Fabius pulled his hand back. "I dismissed the servant girls because you said you'd rub my neck."

"But it appears something else needs to be rubbed first." She pushed her fist between his legs and cooed, "Shall I rub this instead?"

Fabius grabbed her hand. "No, Esindra, not now."

Coyly, she asked, "Why not now? Fabius, it has been so long." Her fingers felt him grow limp, and he hastily pushed her probing hand away.

"I said not now! I have a lot of work to do today. I must go."

"Go? I just got here? Fabius, you aren't serious?"

He stood. "Just leave, Esindra, you're distracting me."

"But I *want* to distract you; just for a little while, come lay down."

He began to dress. "Not today. Go now."

Esindra muttered, "If that's what you wish," then fled from the room.

As she made her way down the corridor, she noticed the two slave girls huddled in an alcove. They twittered as she passed by. Esindra bolted down the stairs. Once in the foyer, she continued to run. Through the courtyard, into the narrow passageways, and to the keep she went.

Two guards called out to her at one point, "Is something amiss?" but she ignored them and kept running.

She burst into Sebastian's room. "It didn't work!"

The Cloaked Man sat at his writing desk as he studied Esindra. "What happened?"

"You consulted the stars and said the timing was right, but it wasn't."

"The timing *is* right. The moon indicates your cycle is peaking now. It will work. Go to Fabius if you want to have a child because *now* is your chance!"

"You don't understand. Fabius didn't want me. He sent me away."

"Why would he do that?" Sebastian asked incredulously.

"I went to his room early this morning, just like you told me to. I wasn't the first woman to join him in bed though; two slaves were there, rubbing his back. After they left, he had no interest in me. He told me to leave; dismissed me like a servant!"

"He was with two other women; what an awful thing for you to find."

Esindra sat on the edge of the bed and stared at her trembling hands. "They were there to massage his stiff neck."

Sebastian approached her carefully. "Those women were surely there to do more than massage his neck."

"Do you think I'm stupid? I know that. I just thought — I hoped — that when given a choice, he'd pick his wife over those whores."

"As he should — as any good husband should!"

Esindra's usually steady voice cracked. "He's been with them before...and others, too. I try not to think about it because if I ignore it, then it isn't real."

"You can't ignore what Fabius has done. He betrayed you."

"We always wanted to have children. Fabius needs an heir to his estate, a son to carry on the name. If we had a child, then Fabius would have everything he wants, and he wouldn't need those other women."

"It isn't too late, Esindra. You can still have a child. And I can help."

"That's what you said before, and it didn't work!"

The Cloaked Man sat next to her on the bed. "It will still work...with me instead of Fabius. You can have a child, *my* child, and Fabius will never know. He'll think the baby is his own. You and he will be the parents, Fabius will have an heir, and he will cease his wanderings."

Esindra recoiled and pushed Sebastian away from her. "How could you suggest such an abhorrent thing?"

Sebastian lowered his voice. "If you want a child, then you must conceive right now. The ceremony we performed last night makes you fertile at this precise moment, but it won't last much longer. We don't have time to argue, Esindra. *Right now* I can do this for you. Consider it a service, nothing more."

"But Fabius would know the child is not his."

"Tomorrow I will convince him to have relations with you. I'll tell him I had a vision, and he *must* make love to you. He'll listen to me. He listens to everything I say. He will never know I fathered your child. It's a perfect plan."

"I can't betray him. He's my husband."

"He betrays *you*, Esindra. Every time he fucks another woman, he does so with the intent of impregnating her. He told me so. He'd banish you if another woman conceived his child. He'd take her as a wife so he'd have an heir. What if he succeeds? What if one of his courtesans eventually becomes pregnant? What then would become of you, Esindra?"

Hot tears burst out of her eyes. "I don't know!"

"If you bear a child, he will never leave you. That's what he wants, and it's what *you* want." The Cloaked Man pulled her to him.

She sobbed and melted into his dark form.

"It is a service that I do for you *and* for Fabius *and* for the benefit of our Roman state. It'll make everything right, and most importantly, you'll be a mother. And what a magnificent mother you will be. I can see you with the child in my visions, Esindra. Relax and allow me to perform my duty."

"Will you hurt me?"

"Hurt you? No, no, of course not," he answered. "Just close your beautiful brown eyes, lie down, and imagine a time in the future with your child."

She obliged and curled up on the Cloaked Man's bed.

He slid off his robe and nuzzled behind her. Caressing her bare neck, while cooing in her ear, he said, "I am at your service, Esindra. Like a slave to a master, I am doing a humble duty."

She nodded and answered, "Okay, but do it quick."

"If that's what you will," he said as he pulled up her robe so it bunched around her midriff. Instead of immediately pulling her thighs apart as Fabius would have, he simply lie there and delicately trailed a single finger in circles around her belly.

Esindra bristled, "Why are you doing that? Just make the deed done."

"Imagine the child in your womb. A son I declare! A strapping, smart lad who will be a leader of men," he whispered.

"I beg you not to torment me. I want the child, but I also want this moment to end."

The finger made one last circle before taking a downward trajectory. Slowly it went, tickling across the fine hairs of her underbelly, causing goose bumples to prickle as it passed. Just before it came to her tender spot it diverted its path and trailed down her inner thigh.

She huffed at the unexpected change in direction.

Then his finger ran back up, toward the target, but again he steered it off course just before contact.

Esindra squirmed slightly, unconsciously moving her pelvis in the direction of his roaming index finger.

He swept it back and forth several more times, stopping only when Esindra caught her fervent breath and let out a solitary sigh. "What *are* you doing?" she asked.

"Making sure you're ready," was the answer. "Making you want me. If you *want* me, then I won't hurt you. I don't want to hurt you, Esindra. I don't want you to loath me as I do this simple, beautiful, precious duty for you. I *need* you to want me."

"Sebastian, I won't 'want' you no matter how long you tease me with your silly finger. Please, just be quick and stop playing your pointless game."

He slipped his finger inside and answered, "As you will." His lips spoke against the hot skin on the back of her neck and twists of her wild, peppery hair slid across his tongue.

As he drew his finger back out, he let it linger lightly in just the right place.

She gasped. "Why are you doing that with your hand?"

"You mean this?" he answered and waggled his finger.

Esindra arched her back and pushed her posterior against his groin. "Fabius has never done such a thing!"

"Do you want me to stop?" he asked as he ceased all movement.

Esindra spoke haltingly. "I'm. Not. Sure..."

He pushed himself inside with a deliberate, measured pace. "Would you still like me to hurry?"

"You should..." Esindra started as he slowly pulled out and hovered just at her entrance. "...hurry and be fast..." But she was unable to continue to speak as the finger began jiggling again.

Her hips refused to stay still. They writhed, searching for him. Her hand reached around and clasped his thigh. Pulling him close she pressed against him, forcing him re-enter her. The Cloaked Man hesitated, letting her wiggle around and position herself perfectly before pushing back. Gently they rocked back and forth.

She turned, shoved her face into his shoulder, and stifled tears. A strange combination of passion, fear, and disgust overtook the regal woman of Rome.

"Sebastian, I think you should take your time."

"As you will, Esindra. Remember, I'm here to do my duty for you."

Chapter 80

Journal Intime
August 24th, 1789

The siege has lifted! We are no longer under attack. Henri negotiated an agreement with the revolutionaries, the details of which I do not know. What I do know, however, is they have retreated, and that is really all that matters. The savages no longer surround our castle, which means we are no longer sequestered to this God-forsaken keep!

This wonderful news was just delivered by one of the servants. Henri was too busy dismantling the stronghold with his garrison to tell me himself. Hurt, of course I am, but I also rejoice because with the siege behind us, it means Henri will have more time for our baby and me! Surely, my husband will now see how awful he treated me the last few weeks. Perhaps he will even come to understand how Agathe and the midwife manipulated the situation.

Yes, of course, with his mind free to return to matters of his family, Henri will easily realize the mistakes he made. And I will forgive him. As a good wife, it is my duty to abide him, and I will not hold a grudge like a mulish woman would. I understand that Henri simply had too many other things on his mind; that's why he did what he did.

I can hear everyone outside my door, bustling and moving their belongings out of the keep. People are cheering, laughing, and singing. It is a joyous time!

As I wait patiently for someone to come and escort me out, I imagine being back in my own bed. How marvelous it will feel to sleep on my on downy pillows again. I wonder if they will undo my bindings when they move me. They most certainly will, I determine, which means I will soon be free! Perhaps they will even allow me to go outside — dare I dream of it? Yes, I dare! How could they refuse me now? There is no longer any danger. I will breathe fresh air again soon!

More time passes as I sit here writing and waiting for them to come for me. What could be taking so long? I call out, but there is no answer. They all go about their business, moving their own belongings, and ignoring me.

Growing impatient I call out several more times. Finally, the servant returns. With a halting voice, he says thinly, "My lady, everyone is...is moving back to the main part of the castle. Everyone, that is, except you. Lord Henri says you are to...you must...remain in the keep because moving you may...cause harm to the baby. You are so close to delivery; he doesn't want to ta-take any chances."

I don't know how to respond. *Henri is making me, and me alone, stay in the keep?* The servant's words come as such a shock that I just sit and stare agape at him. Before I know it, the boy is gone, and I am left completely alone.

The keep becomes instantly silent. Everyone is gone to the main castle, and I am left absolutely abandoned.

I find myself a-falling into an endless hole
Down deep, deep down, spinning round
The darkness takes a hold

There's emptiness within me, a sickness in my soul
Everyone has gone away and left me all alone

Josette-Camille

August 28th, 1789

Solitude feels like death. Cold, lonely, and grey, it is like falling into a void of nothingness. Or, more aptly defined, it is like descending into a hole, one with no bottom. Down, down, spinning round, I feel a constant sinking sensation in my stomach. The darkness clutches my heart like an icy hand, and I can't make it let go.

My only saving grace is the child in my womb. He grows heartier every day. I know once he is born, I will also be reborn.

I will be free to move and stand and walk. I will once again live in the civil part of the castle, taking my rightful place as the Lady of the house. It won't be long now, this I know. These thoughts of freedom give me the determination to survive from one day to the next!

The baby kicks now as I write these words. Do you think he knows my thoughts? Are his kicks a signal he also wants his freedom? Is he ready to come into the world? He is growing inside of me. My blood is his blood. We are two souls in one body after all; therefore, our thoughts must surely intermingle.

I place my hands on my stomach. His little foot presses against them in response.

"All will be right in the world soon," I whisper to him. "Must wait a little longer."

Josette-Camille

August 30th, 1789

The midwife just came for her evening visit. Twice a day she inspects my body for signs of labor. She enters the room quickly as if eager to get in and out as fast as possible. It is amusing to watch her. Because of my acute state of awareness, I notice subtle signs of agitation all over her. The tiny blonde hair on her forearms stands erect on goose pimples. A thin sheen of perspiration appears suddenly across her upper lip. And her breathing — I can hear it quicken along with her rapidly beating heart. She is like a scared little rabbit in the presence of a predatory fox.

I stared blankly at her without saying a word. She looked not at my face, only under my nightgown. Her hands moved quickly and for that I am grateful. She makes her inspection fast, and before I can exhale, she turns to leave.

I intentionally sigh heavily as she walks out the door, allowing my voice to level off into a low, guttural growl at the end. The sound makes her quicken her pace, and in an instant, she is gone like a skittish little mouse.

I smile now as I recall the frightened look in her tiny, darting eyes. Knowing I make her nervous gives me divine satisfaction.

Josette-Camille

September 2nd, 1789

I awoke to rumbling pain in my gut. Worse than any cramp from my menses, the contraction shuddered through my loins. It was the little hours of the morning — what time I did not know — but my candle still burnt low, so I knew it was before sunrise.

The pain subsided, and I waited for several minutes. I almost decided it was only an uneasy stomach, then it hit again, stronger than before. I writhed on the hard bed, the sores on my buttocks and legs stung as they slid across the soaked mattress — my water had broken. The baby was about to be born. But was it too soon? I did not know and could only pray that he would be born a big, healthy baby boy — or girl — if God so chose.

Again, the pain came, this time quicker than the last. I cried out. It was intense, and I knew I needed the midwife's help. Being tied up meant that I couldn't even open my legs to allow the baby to pass. I arched my back as high off the bed as possible. It was only a few inches and would barely allow enough room for the child.

Desperate, I tore at the strap around my neck. If I could free it, then I could sit up and reach the other tethers. As I pulled, the leather cut into my palms, causing them to bleed. With all my might, I yanked but to no avail. Another contraction gripped my stomach as I fought with the straps. It shot down my left leg like a bolt of lightning.

"For the love of God," I cried out. "Please, help me!"

No one came, and I cursed them for their insolence. How could they not have a guard stationed to watch over me? How could Henri allow himself to be so far away from his pregnant wife? And the midwife should surely be close by! But not a soul heard my cries, and not a one came to my aid.

Unable to remove the strap from around my neck, I then tried to rip the one from my chest. This tether was twice as thick as the first and gave up no inches. Hot, frustrated tears burst from my eyes, and I pleaded, "God, please help me. Someone please come..."

Something stirred from within the oubliette. I could hear the rustling behind the boards. Whatever foul specter might dwell there mattered not, I was desperate for any companionship, and I begged of it, "Help me, please. Free me from these binds."

I felt a pain in my gut so sharp that it made my vision blur and go black. I arched my back as high as I could. The baby's head was pushing its way out. I felt the swelling between my thighs. With all my might, I tried to spread my legs, but the constraints held firm.

I reached out with desperate, waving hands, trying to find something — anything — that could help me. I grabbed the small stool beside my bed and pushed it over, hoping the noise would alert someone. Nobody came. Flailing wildly, my fingertips finally came into contact with the stone wall. I slid them down the crevices of the mortar; the cool, slick, grainy texture brought relief to my burning, hot skin.

Another contraction ravaged my stomach. This time it reverberated not only through my leg but also up into my back. I dug my desperate fingers into the mortar of the wall. As the contraction gripped me with a pain beyond compare, the world twirled to a stop. Digging and burrowing, my fingernails kneaded the rock, quickly becoming raw against the hard, jagged surface. The pain in my fingers was sharp and stinging, and insanely, it felt better than the tormenting aches of labor — it actually provided a distracting *relief* from the contractions!

I dug my fingers into the mortar of the wall again, scratching and tearing in an attempt to divert my attention from the agony of giving birth. The nail on my forefinger became lodged in a hairline crack in the mortar. As a contraction sliced through me, I pulled back my hand, and the nail stayed fixed. It tore straight off my fingertip!

In agony, I beat my fist against the wall. Warm blood gushed from the wounded finger. It hurt, but not nearly as bad as the labor pains.

The baby's head once again pushed into my thighs, this time harder than before. I forced my legs to spread, my fleshy thighs bearing against the leather belt until they bled.

Beside me, I sensed movement. Something stirred alongside the bed. I allowed my bloody hand to pause from scratching the mortar and dropped it slightly to let it connect with the creature. It was small and hairy; it was the shadow rabbit — my imaginary friend come to reality as I lay struggling in misery!

I stroked the rabbit's fur as the baby's head once again pressed into my thighs. I forced my legs as wide open as I could. The belt burrowed into the meaty sides of my legs as I spread them. Arching my back gave the child just enough room to force its head through. It was almost born!

The baby let out a tentative whimper; as if unsure of the outside world he was being forced into. Then, he sucked in a deep breath and let out a bold, forceful cry.

Happiness overtook me, and I cried tears of joy along with my child. All the while, I remained posed with my back arched and my legs spread as wide as possible — lying down or closing my legs would smother the child. It hurt tremendously to remain in that position, but I had no choice. Another battering of labor pains accosted me. Coughing and crying, I bore down hard, pushing with all my might so that the baby's shoulders would pass through. However, they did not.

I needed hands to pull the baby free. I frantically tried to reach down with mine. The belt around my neck choked me, but I fought for every inch, trying to grip the baby. It was to no avail. Though I was mere inches from pulling him free, I simply could not reach.

My back ached as waves of labor pulsated through it. I felt weak beyond compare, and my body trembled with frailty. I was losing strength. If I lay down now, I would crush my child's skull.

I pushed again, battling to force the baby from my loins with every muscle in my body. Then, he moved slightly. I felt him wiggling and heard a gasp for air. He gurgled a moment and then stopped making any sounds. He couldn't breathe!

I squirmed, attempting to adjust my body so he might reposition and find air. Still, he did not cry out. As another contraction sliced though me, I pushed with all my might, willing the baby to be expelled. He stayed in place, though, where I knew surely he would die.

"Please, someone help me!" I begged hoarsely. I stretched my arms as far as I could. The belt around my neck gripped my throat. I couldn't breathe, but I didn't care. The only thing that mattered was freeing my child. The room swirled like a vortex, like I was falling into a hole, as I began to lose consciousness.

Then, with a snap that was as liberating as having the noose cut for a hanging man, the belt around my neck gave way. My head was free! I could now reach my baby.

Quickly, my hysterical hands clinched my child's head. His skin was cool to the touch. In anguish, I cried out, "No! God, please no!"

I gently cupped the back of his head and the top of one shoulder and pulled. There was resistance. I slid my hands down and felt the cord that was coiled around his neck. I untangled it with numb fingers. Again, I pulled my child with my hands and pushed with my internal muscles. At first, there was only the slightest movement, and then in a rush, a quick release as he easily slid out. I held onto him as he squirmed between my legs. I heard him breathe in — the most beautiful sound a mother could hear — and then let out a long, loud, trembling cry.

My back was still arched, and I feared I would lose the strength to hold the position. If I came down now, I would lay right on top of my child. I twisted to the side and pulled on his little arm, moving him out of the way. Gradually, I pulled him up along my body, across my chest, and into my arms.

Exhausted, I collapsed into the wet, slimy bed. It didn't matter though; nothing mattered but holding my — I checked to make sure — my son. I had given Henri his boy.

Through bleary eyes, I looked around the room to see if that creature was truly there with me. I saw nothing. My imagination playing tricks with me during the throes of labor, I decided. But what of the tether around my neck? It had been cut. How could that have happened?

My baby cooed. His cherubic lips nuzzled for a breast. Sobbing silently, I fed my child and waited until morning for the maid to find us.

Josette-Camille

Chapter 81

Veronica's Story

Veronica set the book down and gazed through the parlor window. The rain had been falling for three days, and the driveway, the grass, the entire earth, was sloppy and moist.

Headlights, yes, she saw their glow through the greyness. It was only five o'clock in the afternoon, but the day was obscured by thick clouds that smothered it like a jealous lover.

"He's here! Are you ready?"

Her sister's voice answered. "Almost. Five more minutes!"

Veronica knew that meant Nikki would be ready in *twenty* minutes. She opened the massive doors, holding them wide as Christophe came running. His parka was pulled up high to his cheeks and partially covered his broad smile.

"Hi..." she began as he simultaneously greeted her with, "Look at *you!*" Veronica smirked and became quiet so that he could continue his thought. He did. "Look how ravishing you are!" He seemed to surprise himself with his enthusiastic compliment and chuckled sheepishly.

Veronica knew she had scored with her simple, but elegant, ensemble. Her trusty black slacks and white peasant blouse were suitable for any occasion.

"You don't look so bad yourself!"

"The rain, can you believe it! The fields are like swamps. We had to rent pumps to drain the flooding in our vineyard."

"Yeah, it's bad. The ground is saturated, and the plumber is having a terrible time installing the new septic tank. It's a mess out there with the ground half tore up."

"But tonight, you should enjoy yourself. Forget about work, agreed?"

Veronica playfully nodded. "Since Nik is still getting ready, let me give you the five cent tour."

"You would charge me five cents! I am hurt!" he teased as she led him through the castle.

They were admiring the Roman statues in the library when Nikki emerged wearing a shocking hot pink dress with tiny black polka dots. It was tight and sheer and had fringe encircling the hem and neckline.

"Let's go!" she exclaimed.

The three made their way to Christophe's car, all huddled under the protection of one umbrella.

❧✤❦

They arrived in Paris as the sun set on the rain-soaked horizon. It caused a double rainbow which arched across the River Seine. Christophe drove through the moist streets of the Sixteenth District, also known as Arrondissement de Passy. It was one of the most exclusive places to live in the City of Lights. They pulled up to a fortified gate, were waved through after Christophe showed the guard his credentials, and drove until they reached an opulent, nineteenth century villa.

The house's door swung wide before they got out of the car. There stood a smiling, stocky man. He flipped a mop of black hair back as he called out. "Come in, come in!"

Christophe led the way, opening his arms wide as they walked up the garden path. The two men shared robust kisses planted on each cheek. "Ralph, my friend, thanks for having us!"

"My pleasure, Christophe. And you brought gifts! Look at these two lovely ladies. Which one is *mine?*"

Veronica gasped at his candor.

Nikki challenged him. "I'm not sure you could handle either one of us, sweetie."

The fat man laughed with a deep baritone guffaw. "Oh they have spunk! I love the ones with *zee spunk!*"

Veronica recoiled while Christophe and Nikki both chuckled.

"Ralph, these are my two new friends, Veronica and Nikki. They're American women, so you might want to check your manners."

"American women! No wonder they are so feisty and gorgeous. I see this one has some meat on her bones. I like a woman who packs some padding. Those skinny French models are just walking bags of bones. I mean really, who wants to jump on top of a bag of bones?"

Veronica felt her face get hot as she realized that she was the one with "meat on her bones".

Christophe interjected. "You have to excuse my friend, ladies. He seldom thinks before he speaks."

"You mean he *does* think?" Veronica retorted quickly.

Ralph's face contorted into an exaggerated pout. "I am sorry if I offended you, beautiful demoiselle. I truly meant it as a compliment! Voluptuous women are by far my preference. Like a painting by Rubens, they are vibrant and curvaceous and sensuous." He growled playfully and winked at her.

Veronica smiled thinly as Christophe gently cupped her arm and led her forward. "Come, let's go look at your map before dinner."

"Oui," Ralph said. "To my study and where I can get a good look at your mystery."

They stepped into a cavernous room lit with a raging fire. Glass cases spanned the wall, each holding a variety of vases, bowls, and archaic looking pieces of art. There were several Egyptian-style statues roped off behind dusty, red velvet sanctions. In the middle of the room, piled with papers and books, was a huge, dusty, oaky desk. Ralph invited his guests to sit by the fire where a leather couch and two billowy chairs were situated around a huge trunk that looked like a treasure chest.

"Have a seat!" their host offered as he ambled his way over to a bar on the far side of the room. Above it was a gigantic painting of seraphim and angels frolicking around a blue sky. "What can I pour for you?"

"A glass of red," Nikki answered quickly.

"Perrier," Christophe said.

Veronica mimicked, "I'll have a Perrier, too."

They settled in the overstuffed furniture while Veronica admired a series of sketches and photographs on the wall aside the fireplace. She recognized a picture of a black tablet from a history book — the Rosetta Stone — if she remembered correctly. One of the drawings depicted a man leaning over the artifact with a magnifying glass. He had his head turned up, as if someone caught him by surprise.

Ralph spoke right behind her left ear. "Here is your water, ma petite chérie."

Veronica jumped as his warm breath wafted onto her neck. "Thank you."

"My great-great-great uncle was Jean-Francois Champollion," he said matter-of-factly, as if Veronica should know the name.

"Oh!" she answered, as if she did.

"Who was that?" Nikki asked.

"He deciphered the Rosetta Stone. That's him, looking over his Holy Grail."

"The Rosetta Stone, that's a religious relic, isn't it?" Veronica questioned.

"Not exactly. It is a decree written by Egyptian priests. It had three different types of writing; hieroglyphs, which is what all important Egyptian documents were written in; the common script of Egypt, which was demotic; and Greek, because Egypt was under the rule of Greece at that time, just a couple hundred years before Christ. Now, since Greek is a *known* language, he was able to use it like a key to read the hieroglyphs."

"And your uncle deciphered it! That's amazing," Nikki chirped as she sipped her Bordeaux.

"And it almost killed him, too. He was so excited after he figured out what the hieroglyphs meant that he went running through the streets of Paris like a wild man, rushing to announce his discovery. He promptly fell down in a fit of delirium and almost died of pure joy."

"No one could die of joy," Nikki purred.

Ralph grinned. "One certainly could. If you want to come into the chambre à coucher, I could show you how..."

"Quoi, tu vas me montrer ta bite? Alors, c'est sûr que je vais mourir de rire!" Nikki cracked.

Ralph and Christophe laughed, and though Veronica couldn't be sure of what was said, she was sure that her sister got the better of Ralph.

"Now, what is this treasure that Christophe speaks of?"

Veronica drew the medallion from under her blouse and lifted her chin slightly so Ralph could get a better look.

Ralph exploited the opportunity to get near Veronica and closed in on her like an eager wolf. He palmed the coin and stared past it and into the depths of her blouse. Veronica instantly regretted not taking the necklace off as he commented, "Oh, that is quite a treasure! Yes, I can see how very valuable *that* is!"

Veronica pulled back, undid the latch, removed the chain, and handed it to Ralph. He pouted again with the same irksome expression as before, and grudgingly took the necklace from her hand.

"It's a fine piece, in good condition. I've seen other labarum like it. They were made for the Roman elite in the fourth century. I like it, very nice."

"And..." Nikki prompted.

Ralph glanced over at the woman sprawled out on his sofa.

"And, I will give you six thousand euro. That's fair market price."

"I don't want to *sell* it!" Veronica declared.

"Oh, then why did you want me to look at it?"

Christophe interjected. "Show him the map as well."

Veronica reached into her messenger bag and pulled out a Zip-lock baggie, which contained the map. Ralph snagged it and pounced over to his desk. He removed the parchment from the plastic bag with dainty tweezers and held it out like a wet, developing photograph.

"Now *this* is interesting! Where did you find it?"

Veronica was hesitant. "Hidden in the castle that we're staying at."

"How enticing."

"We found it with the labarum necklace, so we think it might be a map of where we can find other valuables, you know, like a treasure map," Nikki explained.

"As long as we don't run into any damn pirates," Ralph answered absently. He studied the parchment intently, and for a moment, he looked intelligent to Veronica. She thought he resembled his great-great-great uncle pictured in the drawing on the wall.

Ralph held the map up to the light and wagged his fingers behind it. Then he brought it to his nose and took several short sniffs. *Now he looked ridiculous.* Veronica wondered if he would nibble it, too, but he didn't.

"The map postdates the coin by almost a *thousand* years. It is similar to parchment that was created in France around the first wave of the plague. It is grainy and naturally brown. You see paper was hard to make during the plague, what with everyone dying and such. We see a lot of this kind of parchment when looking back on that period. There, if you look closely you can see strands of grass in it."

Nikki was growing impatient. "What about the map; do you recognize the town?"

"Oh, this isn't a map of a town."

"Then what is it? Aren't those roads?" Veronica asked.

"No, these are laid out like tunnels. And the writing on the top, it's Latin, and it reads 'Caves of the Dead'. It reminds me of the Paris underground."

"The Paris Underground? What's that?" Nikki asked.

Ralph stared quizzically at the paper and didn't answer. Christophe jumped in. "The Paris Underground is a series of tunnels underneath the city, also known as the Catacombs. Many years ago, the cemeteries became too full to bury the dead during a cholera outbreak. So, they unearthed the old bodies to make room for the new ones. They dug tunnels under the city to dispose of the old bodies."

"Oh, how disgusting!" Nikki snarled as she bounced her slender legs over the arm of the black couch. Her black, polka dotted, pink dress matched the furniture perfectly.

A mischievous grin spread across Ralph's face. "There was no place else to go with the dead, and disease was spreading. That happened in the late 1700s, but the catacombs originated even earlier than that. Some say they date back to Roman times. Over the years, more bodies were added. Some from the riots of Place de Greve; some were enemies of the state that were slaughtered and hidden away. I can take you there if you like?"

"No, thank you," Veronica stated quickly, while Nikki's eyebrows rose in contemplation of the offer.

Ralph's voice raised an octave and he rolled his shoulder "We can go tonight. I can even get you into the areas the tourists aren't allowed. It's illegal, of course, but I know the way."

"I think we should stick with our dinner plans," Veronica stated flatly.

Ralph felt that he struck a nerve and decided to probe. "The bodies are stacked on top of one another and literally make up the walls in some places. There are specific crypts designated to different groups, such as those taken from the graveyard of Saint-Nicolas-des-Champs."

Nikki became intrigued. "How many people are buried there?"

"Thousands and thousands. There are over 300 kilometers of tunnels, stretching all over the city. A tunnel probably lies under our feet at this very moment. You can access them through the sewers, and some passages are even available if you know where to look in the subway system. I've been to parties in the underground...secret parties. Sometimes you hear of religious groups — cults — that hold clandestine ceremonies; all very illegal, of course."

"So, is our map of the Paris underground?" Veronica asked.

"No, it is too small, and it doesn't match any portion of the underground that I've ever seen." Ralph began rummaging through a stack of books and paged through them quickly. He finally held open the pages of one for all to see.

"Is that the Paris underground?" Nikki inquired.

"Yes, see, nothing like the tunnels on your map."

"Then what *is* our map?" Veronica demanded.

"That's hard to say, but if you found it in your castle, then I'd say that you should start by looking in its tunnels," Ralph replied.

"My castle...*the* castle...doesn't have tunnels," Veronica answered.

"Are you sure about that?" Ralph challenged.

"It has that funky, secret hiding spot," Nikki chimed.

"Marie-Claire would have told me if the castle had tunnels."

"All castles have secrets," Ralph said. "You might want to look for yours."

Christophe rose. "We should go if we want to make our reservation."

Ralph grunted and strode out of the room while unbuttoning his shirt.

Veronica stared quizzically after him.

"He's one of a kind," Christophe stated.

Veronica and Nikki nodded their heads.

A few moments later, Ralph returned wearing a different shirt. His pudgy digits punched a keypad on a wall intercom. In a flat voice, he said, "Bring up the car," then swiftly marched out of the room calling, "Come on!"

They trailed behind their host and filed into a black Bentley that waited for them outside.

It was a short drive to the restaurant. Veronica was surprised to see that it was in fact a charming, converted townhouse, painted in subtle shades of pink. It was much cozier than she anticipated.

Once seated, the chef personally greeted them and described the dish that he was about to prepare. Christophe translated from French into English. "For the entrée, you will begin with miniature frankfurters wrapped in a veil of dough..."

"Yum, sounds like pigs in a blanket," Nikki murmured. She and Ralph tittered as the chef coolly continued. "For the main course, I am going to prepare lobster ravioli in a champagne sauce with grilled asparagus. The fromage is goat and will be served with figs and a dandelion salad. Dessert will be a classic chocolate feuilletée with pink grapefruit sauce and citrus granité on the side."

Next, the sommelier presented a list. Christophe asked several questions, and the men conversed so rapidly that not even Nikki could keep up. Veronica felt mesmerized by the animated wine steward's conversion and gasped as she observed a small ball of snot shoot out of the man's nose as he recommended the Château de Gourgazaud from 2007.

She wasn't the only one who noticed. Nikki gasped, giggled, and then slumped in her seat as she whacked Ralph on the shoulder. He snickered along with her, having also witnessed the unfortunate flying phlegm.

As the man retreated, Christophe gave a knowing chuckle. The group burst into laughter as the regal banker pretended to check for stray boogers on his shirt.

"Oh my God, Vern! He's another 'Booger Face'!" Nikki exclaimed.

Veronica cried, "Oh no, Nik, not the 'booger moment'. Please stop bringing that up every chance you get." She felt the blood drain from her face and knew her complexion just went pale.

"But why not?" Nikki replied. "It's so Goddamn funny."

Veronica sat stoic as her sister stared her in the eye and erupted with giddy amusement.

After several moments, Ralph asked, "What in the hell is the 'booger moment'?"

Nikki piped up before Veronica could cut her off. "Only the most mortifying episode of my big sister's life! She tried to kiss her first date with a big ol' fatty hanging out the side of her nose."

Veronica slunk into her chair. The night had been going so well up to this point. Her sister always found a way, though, to make her the butt of a joke. "It wasn't that big of a deal," she stammered and then sat quietly. However, all eyes were on Veronica, and she had no choice but to elaborate further. With resignation, she breathlessly explained. "It was my first date *and* my first kiss. As we stood on the doorstep after a night at the roller rink, I prepared for the big moment. I took a deep breath and exhaled through my nose...and kinda halfway blew a booger out. It hung on the side of my nostril and then I leaned in for the kiss...let's just say he got grossed out and..."

Nikki happily continued as her sister's voice trailed off. "And he pushed you away and called you Booger Face! The name stuck all through middle school."

"I was so embarrassed," the older sister continued without mirth, "that I ran into the house and didn't date again until I was twenty."

Nikki poked her sister's arm playfully and cooed, "Aww, you just didn't know how to handle boys! Don't blame it on the booger."

Christophe was curious. "Well, what would you do if that had happened to you, Nikki? What if you blew a booger out as you were about to kiss a man?"

Without missing a beat, she replied, "I would 'a wiped it on him, of course. Maybe chased him around with it on my finger, you know, boogers make great foreplay."

The table roused again.

"You're the only woman in the world who could make a 'booger moment' sexy, you know that?" Ralph observed.

"Yeah, actually I do," Nikki admitted with mock bravado.

The entreé came. Veronica was grateful for the conversation to turn to food as everyone commented on the delicious "pigs in a blanket".

⤎⤏ ❖ ⤎⤏

The chef returned after the meal. In fragmented English, he asked, "Enjoy, did you, dinner?"

Veronica beamed at him. "Yes, everything was delicious."

"And where you...ce soir...uh, to-night?"

Christophe answered. "I think dancing is on the agenda."

Ralph snorted.

Veronica was leery of tackling a dance floor. Her tendon was still bruised, and though she could now walk on it, she wasn't eager to overdo it.

Christophe saw the reluctance in her eyes. "You'd rather do something else?"

"*I'd* rather do something else," Ralph answered.

"I thought we were going to check out the Paris underground!" Nikki interjected.

"Yes! Now that sounds like a plan!" Ralph exclaimed.

The chef gave a short hoot. "These ladies, in their pretty garments, in the tunnels! How farfelu is this?"

"That is very far-fe-lu," Veronica replied flatly.

"I know a place," Ralph began. "On the other side of the bridge. It's very exclusive. It has a little of everything and will make everyone happy."

"Does it have dancing?" Christophe asked.

"Yeah, they have dancing, even billiard tables and English darts. I think you'll enjoy it."

Veronica perked up when Ralph mentioned billiards. She could play pool! Her father had taught her the game when she was just a little girl. He would often take her to smoky pool halls and then forget to drop her off at afternoon kindergarten. While the other kids were learning their ABC's, Veronica was learning how to put English on a cue ball.

"That sounds like fun. You play billiards, Ralph?" Veronica asked.

Ralph noticed her sudden change in demeanor. "Why yes, I do. Would you like to engage in a game?"

Veronica nodded.

Christophe was pleased that they had come to an amicable decision.

The drive to the club took them on streets that flanked the Eiffel Tower. It was luminous with a sparkly display that lit up the hazy night. Veronica peeked out the window with her nose almost touching the glass. Occasionally, Christophe would lean over, whisper in her ear, and point to a landmark.

The car turned down a narrow street, not even wide enough for two vehicles to pass one another. It then veered again down an even smaller street, not much more than an alley.

The driver cracked the partition glass and said, "I must leave you here. The car cannot go further."

Ralph led them on foot through the wet, cobbled alleyways, past dumpsters of garbage and under clothing that hung from lines suspended between the narrow buildings. They finally came to a dead-end. A chain-linked fence blocked their path. Veronica expected Ralph to turn around and admit that he was lost when he walked up to a small red door and knocked.

"C'est qui?" asked a grumpy voice.

"We want to see the Paris Underground," Ralph said simply.

Veronica moaned. Nikki squealed with delight.

The door opened, and a hairless, grey man stood wedged between the door and the jamb. He sized up the party, snorted, and escorted them into a tiny room with one hanging black light bulb, which cast a purple tint on everything. The man grinned with yellow teeth.

The wall on the opposite side of the room slid back and revealed a descending staircase. Ralph led the way as they followed, spiraling down, until they came to the bottom and a narrow passageway. In the distance, Veronica could hear the dull thud of music, and she and Nikki shared a quizzical sideways glance.

Ralph gallantly pushed a door at the end of the hall open, and they were engulfed in heavy bass. The music was fast and repetitive, like the trance music Veronica's friends listened to in college.

"Welcome to *The Paris Underground*!" Ralph exclaimed as he swung his arm out like a tour guide. "The most exclusive club in all of Paris!"

"So *this* is the Paris Underground? You said it was it was an underground *maze*!" Nikki moaned, disappointed.

Ralph laughed. "It's like a maze, getting here was quite tricky, don't you agree?"

Nikki pushed on his arm playfully. "You had us going!"

Ralph gleamed. "Don't worry, ma petite chérie, you haven't seen anything yet. Come, I'll show you around."

He led them past the crowded bar. A collection of twenty-somethings decorated in an array of piercings glinted at Veronica as she passed by. A Marilyn Manson look-alike smiled, and she cringed as she caught a glimpse of several steel spikes bobbing up and down on the tip of his tongue.

Ralph led them through a tangle of sweaty bodies bumping and bouncing on a neon dance floor. A disc jockey was perched in a catbird's seat, several feet above his servants, who jigged and jagged to every scratch and beat that he pounded on the turntable. Veronica noticed several girls, thin as waifs, swaying to their own beat like enchanted snakes, standing in a circle on the dance floor. Veronica thought she recognized them but dismissed the notion quickly as a case of déjà vu.

To the right was a staircase that led to a loft. Veronica gazed up and saw several people hanging over the railing, observing the view below. She bent her head back even farther and noticed old pipes and rusty ducts that crisscrossed the ceiling.

Ralph led them to a table that was sanctioned off with a gnarly red rope. He raised his hand and waved in the direction of the bar.

The bartender nodded at Ralph and then barked something in French to a stocky man standing beside the bar as if awaiting orders. The man crossed over, parting the sea of dancers without raising a finger. He opened up the sanctioned area, and Ralph slipped him a wad of cash.

The foursome gathered in their seats while a cleavage-bearing waitress brought over a bottle of champagne. Veronica noticed the Cristal label and gaped at the opulence juxtaposed against the eclectic decor.

"This is something else," Nikki remarked as she surveyed the room.

In another corner was a similar roped off area, and several men in suits and ties were raising their glasses in a toast.

"You have all kinds of people here," Veronica added.

"This is the naughty playground of the Paris elite. What makes this place different than the stuffy tourist clubs is that people can be themselves here. There are no rules, so to speak. It is very exclusive, not just anyone can get in," Ralph explained while he gawked at the waitress pouring his drink.

"So, this is what you meant when you said that there were parties in the *Paris Underground*," Veronica observed.

Ralph answered coyly. "I can be deceptive, now can't I?"

"I want to dance!" Nikki exploded as her leg began to gyrate to the music. It was impossibly fast and fed her vivacious spirit.

"I'll dance with you!" Ralph offered.

Veronica gaped. "I thought you said you *didn't* dance!"

"Like I just said, I can be deceptive. Let's go, ma chérie!"

Veronica was sure that her sister would turn down the invitation, but instead, she gleefully snatched his hand and led her trophy to the floor.

Christophe leaned back in his chair and turned all his attention to Veronica. She felt a jolt of excitement as she realized they were alone. She thought for a second and decided that she had something clever to say.

"Christophe, I want you to know —" her sentence was cut short by a squeal of delight directly behind her. Christophe's attention was diverted and she turned around.

There stood three women, the same super-thin-model-types that she noticed when they first entered The Paris Underground. One of them cocked her head and encroached upon Christophe. He looked surprised as she pushed past the sanctions and planted an exaggerated hug and kiss on him.

The other two women followed suit.

"How long it has been?" one of them questioned. "Christophe, you should really stay in touch."

"What a surprise to see you here!" Christophe exclaimed.

The three overtook the chairs at the table without glancing at Veronica.

One of the women spoke. "Christophe, I never thought I'd see *you* here! I thought you always hung out at that bistro...oh, what is that place called...the one you used to take us to inside that old townhouse with the pink walls?" She wore a blue sequined top that hung off her shoulders, and her breasts were almost nonexistent. Her amber hair was cropped tight around her face in a boyish bob that accented her jutting cheekbones. Her neck was adorned with several silver rings that hugged her throat. The ostentatious necklace reminded Veronica of photos of African tribal women in *National Geographic*.

Christophe was fast to interject. "This is my...friend, Veronica. Veronica, this is Bianca, Naomi, and Sefferine."

Veronica smiled politely and was about to speak when the one called Naomi blurted, "Christophe, you must come see the villa again. Mama and Papa gave me the deed for my birthday last month, and we are celebrating with a soirée next week." She flapped thick eyelashes at him and flicked back a wave of her bouncy blond hair.

"That sounds lovely, but I have so little time lately —"

"Oh, but you have time to come to *this* place and hang out with all manner of unsavory sorts!" the bobbed-haired one called Bianca bubbled.

Veronica eyed Bianca savagely, but she refused to acknowledge the challenge.

Naomi piped up again. "When was the last time I saw you...was it during the fashion show in Cannes? I think so, that was in the spring. Oh, so maybe it wasn't too long ago. It just seems like ages. You know, Sefferine has a new agent now, and she's going to be in Vogue next month — on the cover."

Sefferine didn't respond. She gazed sleepily at the crowd and clicked her red nails against a champagne glass.

Veronica attempted to make eye contact with the demur Sefferine, but the black haired beauty would not even glance in her direction. She had thick, pink lips and sparkling blue eyes. Her dark hair hung in wavy tendrils. It was pulled up and twisted on the top of her head, but was still long enough to reach all the way to the middle of her back.

Dully, Veronica recognized the woman. *From a magazine...or a commercial*, she thought. Then it hit her. Sefferine was at the Fontaine's dinner party!

"Well, Seff...Sefferine," Christophe began, "how wonderful for you. I wish you much success." He raised his glass to toast.

Veronica reached for her champagne but was interrupted by Bianca, who snatched up the glass with a giggle and clinked with Christophe and Naomi. Sefferine didn't imbibe.

Nikki and Ralph returned from the dance floor. Sweat beads twinkled on the top of the portly man's brow, and he swiped at his forehead with the back of his hand. Nikki opened her eyes wide at the variety of women who had overrun their table.

"Well, Christophe, you have quite the party happening here!" Ralph exclaimed as he twirled his hand in the air, signaling for another bottle of champagne.

"Just some old friends. They probably need to get going though; no need for another bottle…"

"Oh, we'd love to join you!" Bianca perked.

"The more the merrier," Ralph noted as the waitress brought more champagne.

"We need more glasses, too," Nikki announced as she eyed her former beverage that was now nestled in Naomi's palm.

Ralph pushed his way into the mix and settled between Sefferine and Naomi. Nikki also squeezed in and nestled between Veronica and Bianca. Bianca gave her a disapproving glance, and Veronica noted a sharp stare in retaliation from her sister. She felt relieved that Nikki was there.

"So, who do we have here?" Ralph asked as he eyed each woman hungrily.

Christophe made the customary introductions and tried to lock eyes with Veronica. Veronica was busy eyeing Sefferine, who was now staring down Christophe.

"So, what do you girls do?" Nikki asked. "Do you work, are you *working…*" She let the word hang a moment, "girls?" She knew the term would be lost on the French, but Veronica emitted a knowing snicker.

Bianca whirled her head around and addressed Nikki directly. "Oh yes, we work. We work it on the runway. What kind of work do you do again? Teach kindergarten?"

Before Nikki could comeback, Ralph's voice boomed. "A trifecta of models. You hit the jackpot, Chris!"

"I think I'd like to play billiards now," Veronica announced. "Are you ready for the challenge?" She directed the last statement at Ralph.

"A challenge; I am always ready for a challenge. Let's go, lovely lady, the billiard tables are up the stairs. Who else is in? You, dear, would you like to play?" He had turned his attention to Naomi.

Naomi leaned over to catch an affirmative signal from Bianca. "Yes, let's go," she declared.

Nikki was already moving away from the table.

Christophe was about to speak when Ralph cut him off. "Can you order another bottle, good man? I think we need one upstairs."

Christophe opened his mouth to call out to Veronica, but she was already making her way through the crowded dance floor. Nikki was fast on her heels, and Ralph swiftly ushered Naomi out of her chair.

Bianca stood as Christophe turned his back to hail the waitress. She smiled secretively at the solitary model remaining at the table and scampered along with the rest.

Veronica pounded across the floor. A dancing man with his eyes closed bounced into her, and she pushed him back with a flourish. Nikki scooted up beside her. "What was *that* all about?"

"Nothing, it's about *nothing*. I just don't like those women. They are snobby and rude."

"Of course. They're models, *and* they're French," Nikki answered.

"They are annoying."

"And they are fawning all over Christophe, and one is still sitting with him. I recognize her from the dinner party —" Nikki was cut short.

"I don't care who she is. I just can't have any fun with them around."

"The other two are behind us along with Ralph," Nikki continued.

Veronica turned around and saw Ralph with a girl on each arm. The trio strolled by and stopped at the bottom of the stairs.

"You first ladies," Ralph said while ushering up Bianca and Naomi. He grinned deviously as he watched them from behind.

He offered Veronica and Nikki the opportunity to step in front of him.

"No, go ahead," Veronica said.

Ralph mounted the stairs then turned and quipped over his shoulder, "You just want me to go first so you can watch my ass."

"We won't be able to *miss* it," Nikki jabbed.

Ralph snickered and strutted. He stopped halfway up, turned back, and said, "It looks like there are already people on the billiard table!"

"That's okay; we can take them on in doubles," Veronica answered, confused by his change in demeanor.

Ralph howled heartily. "I didn't know you were into foursomes!"

Nikki peeked over the railing to catch a glimpse of the pool table on the balcony. She saw a woman with her legs lifted high in the air, lying back on the green slate while a man with his trousers around his ankles stood next to the table and pushed himself into her.

"Christ!" Nikki exclaimed.

Veronica peered over her shoulder.

The models were at the top of the stairs staring at the couple questioningly. Several other people were mulling about on the ledge, watching and veering at the sexual display.

Veronica decided to catch a glimpse of Christophe from her bird's-eye vantage. He still sat at the table with Sefferine. The model was talking; her hand gestured in the air dramatically.

Nikki leaned against Veronica's shoulder and whispered into her sister's ear. "Something's going on down there, isn't it?"

"Probably. And I don't want to go back over there and be in the middle of it. And I certainly don't want to play pool anymore with the freaking peep show going on. What the hell kind of place is this anyway?"

"Let's go to the bar. Screw these guys," Nikki announced as she grabbed her sister's hand and led her down the stairs and through the crowded dance floor.

At the bar, they nuzzled next to a thick woman dressed head to toe in black and red lace. Her face was painted white, and she wore a fake set of vampire teeth. The girls grinned at her cautiously as they ordered drinks. A man standing next to Nikki offered to purchase their beverages. He was attractive and wore skinny jeans and a faded Ramones T-shirt. Nikki accepted the offer with a sultry, "Why not, big boy?"

Veronica spent her time nodding along as her sister flirted with the rock musician. Apparently, he was in a band, moderately popular in Europe, and they were about to start their North American tour. She absently stirred her drink, shoved several books of matches into her purse, and occasionally muttered to the vampire lady that: "boys are dumb".

Every once in a while, she casually peeked over her shoulder to catch a glimpse of Christophe and what's-her-name. *Sefferine...what the hell kind of a name is that?* The two leaned into each other from across the table. Veronica heard Robert's familiar voice in her head, "Dear, you know you need to give me my space when I work with the junior designers. They're young and have so much to learn." Her trembling hand fanned cigarette smoke out of her bleary eyes.

Vampire lady leaned over and coolly whispered in Veronica's ear while nodding at Sefferine, "You want me to rupture that bitch's brittle little neck?"

Veronica teared up for a brief moment and sincerely answered, "Aw, that's so sweet of you to offer. But no, that's okay. Who needs him anyway? Not me."

Ralph eventually found the sisters sitting at the bar. The two models still followed him like puppies, and they hovered as he leaned into Veronica and Nikki and said, "I have something to show you. Come with me."

Nikki shrugged at Veronica who rolled her eyes as if to say, "Why not." Reluctantly, the girls fell in line behind the waddling man like a string of ducklings. He motioned for Christophe who quickly jumped up from his chair. Sefferine grouched and folded her arms in front of her chest until her friends chided her into joining the gang.

Ralph led them through an "employees only" door and into a storage area where boxes of wine were stacked along a wall. Silently, he began to move the boxes.

"What are you doing?" Naomi asked.

"Are you looking for your *own* box of champagne now?" Christophe asked coyly.

Sefferine huffed as he spoke. Her arms were still locked across her bra-less chest.

"I have something to show you," Ralph sang as a sheen of sweat formed on his forehead after moving only three boxes.

Christophe helped him clear the area.

"What is it?" Bianca asked.

Nikki was more demanding. "Just tell us what you're doing, or I'm going back to my rock star at the bar."

"Be patient, Nikki, you'll enjoy this more than anyone else." Ralph stepped back to reveal a door.

"What's that?" one of the models asked as Ralph pushed it open.

"Is it the wine cellar?" another one inquired, but he didn't answer.

Instead, he rummaged inside the desk and produced a lantern and two flashlights. He tossed one to Christophe then ducked his head and entered the dark cavity.

Christophe glanced at the apprehensive women and shrugged his shoulders, urging them to follow.

"It's *the* Underground!" Nikki gasped, and she eagerly tailed Christophe.

When Sefferine saw Nikki follow Christophe, she, too, went inside. The other models fell into suit behind her. Veronica stood on the outside, not at all interested in participating.

"You guys go ahead. I'll just stay here and, uh, guard the door."

Nikki's voice echoed from the depths. "Come on, Vern! It isn't even scary!"

Ralph goaded. "Nothing to fear. Everyone down here has been dead for at least a hundred years!"

Then Christophe offered, "Please come, Veronica, it really isn't so bad."

Veronica paused, scuffed her foot on the ground, and warily followed the crowd.

The tunnel was cave-like. Some areas were held in place with wooden support beams and metal fencing that held back sliding rocks. The Paris Underground seemed primitive, unkempt, and dangerous.

As they passed two small passages, Ralph briefly shined his light in each to show long corridors that seeped into the darkness. "Whatever you do, don't go off exploring, some of these small branches aren't very sturdy. We need to stay in the main tunnel where it's safe."

Christophe hung back by Veronica. "You okay?"

"Yeah, I just don't like dead things; cemeteries, even churches, just give me the creeps. And small places make me feel claustrophobic."

Christophe reached out for her hand, and she reluctantly accepted.

"Do you want to go back?" Christophe asked.

Before Veronica could answer, Nikki called, "Hey, Vern, you gotta see this!"

One of the models yipped. "Oh, disgusting!"

Christophe and Veronica caught up to the others in a large, open area. The far side of the cavern was covered in human skulls. They were stacked one on top of another, like bricks in a brownstone. Most were whole and intact, a few were fractured. It looked like some had been intentionally removed by mischievous hands.

The center of the chamber was the most disturbing. There was an altar of sorts, a pedestal with a large flat rock on top of it. Upon closer inspection, it appeared to be a natural formation, like a deformed stalagmite that reached from the floor and then was molded into some kind of wicked sacrificial platform by human hands.

A few empty bottles of wine littered the ground, and one wall was covered in brightly colored graffiti. There was a detailed drawing of a devil-like creature with its arms raised in the air. The artist in Veronica became transfixed, and she walked over to get a better look.

The devil had the body of a man, traditional ram horns and a beard, but sported feathered wings that were white, like an angel's.

Another scene contained cartoon characters like those on the cover of a Beatle's album. A rabbit smoked a joint, and a miniature soldier flashed the peace sign. The lower right hand side contained a faint signature, *Morgan Star*, and the date "1968".

Other bits of graffiti resembled the twisted letters that one would see tagged on the sides of buildings in Los Angeles. There was a myriad of names and dates. One faint and primitive drawing of a skull had the year "1786".

"Look at these," Veronica marveled at the paintings.

Ralph beamed like a proud preacher standing before his congregation. "This place has witnessed many visitors over the years. If the dead could talk, imagine what tales they might tell." He waved his hand in the air dramatically, and Nikki grunted with a skeptical snort.

"I wonder how many bodies are down here," Naomi observed.

No one answered her.

Veronica caught a glimpse of Sefferine whispering into Bianca's ear. A sly glance was shot Veronica's way from the girls. They were like cats teaming up for a pounce.

Veronica decided that she didn't want to play their game. Whatever was going on between Sefferine and Christophe, and it was obvious now that there was *something*, Veronica was not going to get caught up in the middle.

"People have become lost in here, haven't they?" Naomi asked.

Ralph acknowledged her. "Yes, many times. Usually, it's a foolhardy tourist who wanders away from the group. They do have guided tours, but people who think they're cataphiles come roaming around down here all the time. Every once in a while, one strays from the pack. It doesn't amount to much, though; they're usually found in a few hours, maybe a day or two.

"There is a marker down here to commemorate a fellow who got lost a couple hundred years ago though. Seems he decided to come down here alone and was never seen again. Twenty years after he disappeared, they found his body...only a few meters from an exit. He didn't even know how close he was to getting out."

"How ironic." Naomi sighed.

"So, what is this pedestal thing for?" Nikki asked.

"What would you like it to be for? Maybe a *virgin* sacrifice?" Ralph goaded.

Nikki rolled her eyes and pushed his arm. "I'm serious. What do they do in here?"

"You name it; they do it. I know the owner of the club very well. He doesn't allow just *anyone* to use his entrance to come creeping around in here. It's illegal to be in here, you know, and he could get fined if the cata-cops found out."

"Cata-what?" Nikki asked.

"Cata-cops," Ralph answered. "The cata-cops are a special division of the police that patrol the catacombs."

"So, how'd *you* get permission to come down here, Ralph?" Nikki pried.

"The owner and I are great friends. Plus, I greased him with a wad of cash. You can do almost anything you want in the Underground if you're willing to pay. I know a fellow who threw his birthday party down here; brought in live music and everything. And there is a club that celebrates every New Year in this very room. And I am sure there are others who come here to use it for things that we can't even imagine; things only the dead have witnessed."

Veronica partially listened to Ralph's pontification. Another part of her was engrossed in the art that spanned the walls from tunnel to tunnel. She used her flashlight to admire the variety of drawings, symbols, and messages. "How far does the graffiti date back?" she asked.

"To the late 1700s."

"Amazing, isn't it? To think of so many people over time who left their mark here. This place is like a time capsule spanning the centuries. It makes you wonder why people do it, you know..." Everyone quietly looked at Veronica as she lapsed into a mystical discourse. "Why do people feel compelled to draw and paint on the walls, to leave their mark behind? Is it a primeval instinct? Is it the same motivation that Neanderthals had when they began drawing on their cave walls? It's beautiful, all of it. Like a communal, single piece of art that so many people, maybe hundreds, have contributed to, and more than likely, they never met one another. They probably weren't even born in the same lifetime. It's like a patchwork quilt, added onto again and again, a little bit more every year."

She turned and saw Christophe with his head cocked. Nikki stood with her mouth gaping slightly.

Then Sefferine spoke loudly, and Veronica realized that it was the first time she heard the woman speak all night. "I remember you now. You are the American woman who fell off her chair at the Fontaine's dinner party."

Veronica watched Christophe's brow furrow. "You know each other?" he asked.

Sefferine quipped, "We met just once before. I doubt if she remembers me though. She was too drunk."

Veronica felt searing heat envelope her body, and she hastily spat, "I wasn't drunk!"

"You mean you are naturally *that* clumsy? Then you should really go back to finishing school. Oh, but that is right, you likely never went to begin with, being the hired help and all at Le Château du Feu Ardent."

Christophe glared at Sefferine and then carefully turned to Veronica. "The art on the walls is magnificent. You're right."

Sefferine scoffed. "It is ugly and should be removed. Scribbles on cave walls is not art." Her English wasn't good, and she spoke haltingly.

Veronica summoned up a deep breath and was about to retaliate when Ralph spoke. "Actually, this isn't even the good stuff. The entire place is covered in graffiti. One chamber is completely adorned like an Egyptian tomb. In some of the old World War Two bunkers, there are oodles of drawings and paintings. It's pretty remarkable."

Nikki spoke next. "What amazes me are the skulls, the bones, all the dead on display. How sad and eerie."

Sefferine decided to jab at Nikki's comments, as well. "It isn't sad. It is just bones. Once the body is dead and the soul is gone, it doesn't matter."

Nikki spun and faced Sefferine with determination. She was about to speak when Ralph interjected, "That's what the 'mosh pit of the dead' is all about." Ralph didn't even realize that he diffused a confrontation between the women. His random comment hung in the air for a moment. He waited dramatically for someone to probe him for an explanation.

Nikki sneered at Sefferine then obliged. 'Mosh pit of the dead'? What the hell is that, Ralph?"

"It is a pit, filled with bones — miscellaneous bits and pieces — tons of them piled up. All the scattered, broken shards from over a thousand corpses made into a giant sea. There are people who call themselves 'Death Skaters' who go there and 'dance with the dead'. They jump into the pit and slide down ramps made out of bones like skateboarders."

"That's sick," Veronica and Nikki said in unison.

"I want to dance with the dead," Sefferine said flatly.

"I wouldn't recommend it for a lady," Ralph said.

Sefferine insisted. "Take me to the pit. I want to go right now."

"Like, I'm sure you'd actually do it," Nikki taunted.

"Let's go," Sefferine demanded. "I want to see this 'mosh pit of the dead'. I want to go in it. I am not afraid. What would happen? Nothing. Dead people can do nothing to the living."

Christophe began quietly, calmly, "You could get hurt. Jumping around in a pit of broken bones, you'll cut yourself. It isn't safe."

"I won't get hurt. Take me there!"

"If you insist. It is a ways down the tunnels, but be careful in your high heel shoes," Ralph said as he gestured to the corridor.

Sefferine snatched the lantern from the stone altar and began to march down the passage. The other two models followed. Ralph giggled as he tailed them. Veronica and Nikki brought up the rear with Christophe, who vaguely tried to talk Sefferine out of her escapade as they walked.

The tunnel was deep, and Veronica felt her ankle throb. The models' long legs were striding briskly, despite their high heels. Numerous twists and turns made navigation tricky, but Ralph called out directions, and seemed confident at all times.

Within a few minutes, the models and Ralph were several meters ahead of the others. Veronica was trailing, hobbling slightly.

A shrill cry was heard up ahead. Then Sefferine exclaimed, "It is bigger than a pit. It is like a sea! Let me take off my blouse as it is Dior."

Then Ralph exploded. "Bravo! You take it off! Yeah!"

Christophe began to trot ahead. "Seff! Don't be stupid. Don't go in there without a shirt!"

Nikki followed, eager to see the display.

Veronica lagged behind as Christophe and Nikki ran ahead. Her foot was swelling. She paused a moment to slip her shoe off and instantly felt relief. Someone called for her to hurry up — two voices — it sounded like Christophe and Nikki. She couldn't thoroughly make out what each of them said as their words echoed off each other in the hollow halls.

"I'm coming!" she called as she watched Christophe and Nikki turn right. Veronica shined the flashlight on her foot; her tendon was red and the heel was bulbous. Tentatively, she made her way down the corridor as voices from her friends and enemies guided her.

In the distance, Sefferine yowled like an angry hound while several others shouted at her. Veronica followed the cries. She turned to the right; the same direction that Christophe and Nikki had gone.

Veronica stopped suddenly. Something was different, and it took her a full ten seconds to realize that she had not heard a peep from Sefferine or the others since she ventured down this tunnel. She looked at the dirty ground as if it would tell her whether someone had just walked across it. There were no footprints, no fresh scuffmarks — no breadcrumbs to lead her.

She called out. "Nikki! I can't hear you. Are you up this way?"

She waited...nothing...then a far off cry. It sounded like Sefferine again. Veronica began to walk; convinced she was on the right path. Then, she heard the quick, shrill cry again. Was that Sefferine? It was sharp, like a crow squawking from atop a telephone pole.

Veronica waited again. Was she hearing Sefferine?

What else could it be?

Veronica called out again. "Hey! Can you hear me?!"

She waited. No answer.

She looked back the way she came. *Did she turn too soon?* She saw Christophe and Nikki go to the right, but did they actually go down this tunnel, or maybe it was the next? She could hear them fine before, and now she could hear — well, she wasn't sure what she was hearing.

Something cold seized her. A single, frantic thought squeezed her throat. *Am I lost?*

Her neck felt prickly and became super sensitive. She pushed her back up to the wall. A thousand bones held her up. She looked both left then right, flashing her light for a clue. Should she continue or trek back? On the wall directly across from her, a design of skulls shaped like a cross seemed to point in both directions at once.

The path before her seemed forbidding. It seemed *wrong*. Like a girl scout who ventured too far from the campfire, she scuttled back the way she came.

She could hear the voices again. Yes, they were up ahead!

Veronica tittered with immense relief. She trotted a few feet and saw that there was indeed another tunnel to the right, and she quickly followed it, now eager to find the rest of the gang.

She began to yell. "I'm coming!"

She heard a voice cry, "Vern!"

"Nik, I'm almost there!"

The tunnel split, and she heard the voice from the left, as if it were only a few feet away. The passage widened, and she burst into a cavernous area. "Christ, Nik, I took a wrong turn and..."

But it wasn't Nikki's face that she saw right before everything went black.

Chapter 82

Sebastian's Story

Esindra lay prone with one palm cradling the teensy bulge of her belly, and she imagined a tiny, perfect baby swimming in her womb. Fabius stirred next to her. Sebastian had convinced her husband to have relations with her. It took a few days, but eventually Fabius summoned her to his chamber. It was fast, mechanical, and now as she lay watching her husband's naked, hairy, body emerge from the bed, her thoughts drifted back to Sebastian's gentle touch.

Fabius wrapped a toga around his waist and fastened it with a gold belt. "I'm going to a meeting with Cicero."

Esindra snapped to attention. "You're leaving so soon?"

Fabius huffed as he left. "It was fortunate I found time for you at all. I have matters to deal with."

For the first time, she didn't experience a nagging tug on her heart as her lover left; instead, a strange, blissful feeling of peace envelope her. She wallowed in it and stretched her body on the sea of pillows as she rolled over. There across the room hung Fabius' robe. He forgot it and would surely catch cold in the drafty castle.

She dressed, grabbed his garment, and went in search of her husband. She found him in the war room with Cicero. The two huddled around the table, pouring over strategies.

"Now isn't a good time," Fabius spoke. "We're planning our assault on the Head Commander."

"You left this behind." She held out the robe and Fabius snatched it. "How are you doing the assault?" she asked.

"Poison," Cicero answered, holding a vial.

Esindra's eyes locked on the glass container. "With the elixir Sebastian made?"

"You *know* of that?" Fabius bellowed. "Who told you about the poisoning? Sebastian?"

Esindra retracted her words. "No, it wasn't Sebastian."

"I warned you to stay away from him."

"I know. I haven't spoken to him."

"Then how could he tell you about the poison?"

"*You* must have told me."

Fabius approached her with quick, purposeful strides. "You have orders to stay away from him. I don't need him to fill your head with fantasies. You are much too susceptible to such notions."

"Don't speak to me like I'm a child! I am verily capable of thinking for myself, and Sebastian hasn't filled my head with any fantasies!"

"So, you *have* spoken with him!"

Cicero attempted to deflate the confrontation. "Sir, should I put the poison in his *food or*...?"

Fabius directed his attention to his first in command. "No, his drink."

Esindra persisted. "What if I did? Surely, I can have a simple conversation with the man."

"No, you can't. If you see him in the hall, you turn and walk the other way. If he enters a room, you leave it. If he speaks to you, ignore him. It's that simple."

"I am the *Governess,* and you've given Sebastian, a criminal, free-range of the grounds. How can I avoid him when he can go anywhere? Certainly, you don't expect me to stay…"

He cut her off. "In your room? That's a grand solution. Cicero, take her there."

Cicero gently cupped Esindra's arm and led her out. The lady held her composure; her regal features barely cracked as they walked.

Turning down a quiet hallway, Cicero whispered, "I am sorry. He's just overwrought with this plan and easily angered."

"He's always angry. I'm used to it."

Once they arrived at Esindra's room, Cicero entered with her and closed the door behind him. "I dared not say anything before, but you should know about Sebastian."

Esindra took a quick breath. "What do you mean?"

"I know why Fabius pressed you about him. I think he's jealous. Perhaps, I should hold my tongue but, earlier when I went to meet Fabius in the war room, Sebastian was there. They didn't hear me approach, and I overheard them. Sebastian *told* Fabius that you came to his chambers two nights ago. Fabius asked him what happened, but before the villain could answer, they heard me outside and fell silent." Cicero respectfully dropped his head and continued. "I can't be certain what Sebastian was going to say next, but I'm sure that's why Fabius attacked you like that. He'll likely confront Sebastian next."

She sat thoughtfully for a moment. "Sebastian won't betray me."

"Governess, please tell me you don't have a confidence with Sebastian." Cicero's concern was genuine.

Esindra thrust her palms into her eye sockets.

"You *can't* trust him! He will surely betray you to Fabius. That is his way. He will trick and manipulate you and do anything in his power to bring havoc upon us all."

"If he tells Fabius…Cicero, I'll be put to death!"

"He won't *kill* you. You'll be punished for speaking with the rogue but Fabius won't…"

"It was more than a simple conversation."

An uneasy silence lapsed between them. Cicero held her gaze just long enough for him to understand.

Esindra continued. "Now it all makes sense. Everything Sebastian told me was deception. He tricked me so that he could destroy Fabius and me."

Cicero agreed. "He's a villain. A swindler and prevaricator."

"I am ruined. I shouldn't have trusted him. It was like he cast a spell on me. He made me trust him and believe there was no other way. Maybe Fabius will grant me mercy if I tell him I was enchanted?"

"Fabius doesn't grant mercy."

"Then I'm doomed," she whimpered.

"No. We just need to take *care* of Sebastian."

"How?"

Cicero raised his fist like he was casting a vote at a Coliseum tournament. Then he thrust his thumb down and toward his chest.

She answered her own question. "You mean murder?"

"It isn't murder to kill someone guilty of treason. It's justice. We have to act fast, though, before he tells Fabius. And we have to be clever. He's smart and not easy to trick. Will you assist me, Esindra?"

She nodded.

"Good." He grabbed a quill and ink at the desk.

Together they worked out a plan.

Chapter 83

Veronica's Story

lackness. Veronica tried to open her eyes. More blackness. *Why won't my eyes open?* She blinked, but the dark was absolute. She lifted her arm — *what happened* — and put her hand to her face. She felt her eyes. They were open; she just couldn't see. *Am I blind?* Her head hurt. The left temple throbbed. She touched it. It was tender, swollen, and wet. *Blood.*

She remembered with horror: *I'm in the catacombs!*

She was lying on the ground face up. Tiny rocks poked into her back. She held both arms out and flailed wildly in the air, reaching for something, anything, but there was nothing there. She felt the ground around her. It was dusty and scattered with debris. Pushing herself up, she came to a sitting position. Her palm rested on something hard; it was a small cylinder. She picked it up. It was her tube of lipstick. She felt around and discovered more items: her compact, a brush, the map! *Couldn't lose that.* She automatically clasped her neck. It was bare. Her necklace was missing, though.

Did she trip and fall? Her mind raced. She opened her mouth to call out to Nikki and then froze as the memory came gushing back. *Someone else was there, and it wasn't Nikki.*

She remembered racing down the corridor and turning the corner, expecting to see Nikki and the others. Instead, her flashlight shined on an old man's mangled face. He had stringy tendrils of dirty hair, a long, unkempt beard, and startled, wide eyes that were filled with crazy. Then the blackness came.

Was he still here? There was no way to tell in the darkness. *How long had she been unconscious? Where were Nikki and Christophe?* And her bag...her hands brushed the ground frantically. She found the strap and pulled it toward her. She searched the inside. More familiar items: her perfume, several crumpled receipts, pocket change, her wallet. She opened it and felt the emptiness. Her cash was gone...and her credit cards. *Damn!* She began to put her items back into the bag when she felt something else — a small square-ish item — *matches!*

A faint noise caused her to freeze. It sounded like someone taking short, shallow breaths. She waited and listened and held her own breath. The breathing stopped. Everything was silent.

Veronica couldn't hold her breath forever. She finally exhaled and then slowly drew in a steady stream of air. Just a few feet away and to her left, she thought she heard another breath. She held hers, and the other stopped. *Was he mimicking her? Breathing only when she did so she wouldn't know he was there?*

With conviction that sliced into her like a knife, Veronica knew she needed to get out of there — and fast. She slung her bag over her shoulder and started to crawl. Bits of stone, bone, and debris from her purse dug into her knees and palms. She still held the matches, and she deliberated whether she should light one or not. It might reveal the way out. It also might reveal her location to the crazy man who stalked her in the dark.

She froze again. This time she heard rustling somewhere behind her. It stopped a split second after she became still. Veronica sat confused and scared. For several minutes, she didn't move.

Hopefully he would lose interest and go away. However, he didn't. After three minutes of being stock-still in the dark, Veronica heard him rustling ever so quietly. He was moving toward her.

Frustrated tears welled in her useless eyes. If she kept moving, he would hear her and catch her. If she stayed quiet and still, he would eventually find her. She had to make a run for it.

Veronica stood and struck a match. There was a spark, nothing more. The matches were wet, and she smelled something sweet. The perfume had seeped onto to them. She fondled them, maybe two or three were still dry. Gently, she plucked one of the driest and struck it. A flame flickered.

The tiny light revealed a cavernous room, and like the others, it was filled with graffiti and stacks of skulls. The edges were cloaked in darkness though, as the light wasn't bright enough to unveil the entire cavern. In the center of the chamber was a pile of rubbish. There were tattered clothes, a bicycle tire, a battered shopping cart, a rolled up sleeping bag, and an empty jar of Nutella with a rusty spoon in it. It looked like she stumbled across someone's "camp". She turned around as the flame of the match crept toward her thumb and forefinger. There were two corridors leading out, but nobody else was there.

The match burnt out. Veronica stood in the darkness. *Was she alone after all?* She wondered if he was hiding in the shadows where she couldn't see him.

Maybe he was just as afraid of her as she was of him? Perhaps he was simply a homeless man, and here she came bounding into his camp shouting and screaming like a crazy person. She probably scared the crap out of him as he sat alone in his peaceful, little hermit hole!

She heard something rustling, like feet sliding across the dusty ground. The sound came from the direction of the corridors.

He was in front of her.

She mustered up all her courage and said, "Hello?"

The noise stopped. No rustling, no breathing.

"Hello?" she repeated louder. "Bonjour?"

There was silence. Veronica waited and listened. Though the dark was absolute, she thought she detected a faint, red shadow that danced across her line of sight. She squinted, but the blackness gave her no more clues.

Vertigo crept over her. Without vision, she couldn't determine up from down. Her head throbbed, and she feared she might pass out again. To stay alert, she bit her bottom lip. As she took a calculated step forward, a gruff voice rambled.

"Que faites-vous ici? Sortez de ma caveme! Sortez d'ici maintenant!"

Veronica squealed and jumped back. "Who's there?" she cried.

"Stupide touriste américaine. Tirez-vous!"

She couldn't decipher the French. He spoke too fast. One thing she did realize, though, he was *not* friendly.

"I just want to leave. I don't know which way to go. You can keep my money. Just tell me which way to go! Ah, quelle maniére?"

She heard footfalls approaching, and he spoke again; this time his voice was closer, maybe six feet away. "Tirez-vous!"

"I'm *trying* to leave. I can't see, and I don't know where to go!"

His breathing became loud and raspy.

Veronica screamed. "Nikki! Help!" To her attacker, she said, "There are others here. Don't touch me, or they'll find you!"

"Tirez-vous!" he repeated with authority.

She understood the request. He was saying *leave now*.

"I'm trying. I don't know where to go!" Desperate tears filled her blind eyes. She struck one of the dry matches. There he stood, maybe five feet away, he held a whisky bottle in one hand, and his other arm stretched in front of him, like a blind man feeling his way.

Veronica shook the match, and under the cover of darkness, she took several quick side steps so that she was no longer standing in the same spot. Then she froze. She heard him scuttling. He was trying to find her like a child playing blind man's bluff.

Slowly, carefully, she crept toward the corridors. She felt something warm on her shoulder through her sheer blouse. Short gusts of hot air.

He was breathing on her.

Fear gripped Veronica, and she careened forward. She heard him move, too, and he made a guttural cry. There was a crash, the sound of breaking glass on stone. She realized that he flung the bottle against the wall. She took a step and shards crunched under her foot. *Did he take a swipe at her and miss? Or was he fashioning a more brutal weapon?*

"Just leave me alone!" she pleaded.

Then something "clicked" with a tinny metallic sound. A light flashed on and blinded her eyes. *The flashlight. He had her flashlight, and now he had her in his sights.* Veronica ducked low and crawled across the debris-ridden ground. The light turned off, and she sat still again in the blackness. With a flash, it was back on, then off, then on again like a strobe light. She tried to get her bearings with each burst of light, but instead found that she was becoming more and more confused. Glass sliced into her palm as she crawled. Oozing blood caked with dirt, causing her palms to feel bulky and awkward. She heard him closing in on her. The flashlight continued to click on and off, and the only thing she could do was stagger to her feet and make a run for it.

For a brief second, she saw the corridors in front of her. The man and the flashlight were to her left. The light went dark and stayed that way. She heard him encroaching.

Veronica bolted like a blind bat. Sheer terror had consumed her and all sense of reason was lost. She missed the corridor and rammed her body into the wall with a thud. Instant dull pain engulfed her as her head and shoulder connected with the bone-infested wall. She cried out in agony.

A crusty hand snatched her arm and pulled her back. Veronica twisted her body and swung blindly with her other arm. She smacked the attacker in the neck, but he held his grip.

"Let go of me!"

He sputtered something incoherent, and Veronica could smell his whiskey breath. His grip tightened, and he flicked the light on again. His face was next to hers. He held both the flashlight and the broken whisky bottle in one hand. He clumsily tried to manipulate the two while maintaining his grasp on Veronica. She let her body fall back against the wall and brought up her knee fast, forcing it into his groin. He retaliated with a cry and swung the bottle at Veronica's head. She ducked just as he thrust his fist into the wall. The bottle smashed, the flashlight shattered, and everything went black.

Veronica raced in the direction of the first corridor while shouting, "Get away from me! Leave me alone!"

She raced down the dark passageway. Her left arm grazed the wall, tearing the sleeve of her blouse. She didn't care though. Veronica felt no pain as adrenaline forced her to flee for her life. Down the bone-decorated corridor she sprinted, knocking into the wall from time to time, righting herself, only to run blindly into the stacked-up skulls on the opposite side. Like a pinball bouncing back and forth on bumpers, she made her way back to the main passage way.

Her ankle throbbed in unison with her head. After several minutes of running blindly, she slowed, leaned against the wall to steady her balance, and felt her way with shaking hands. She could light a match, but she feared there was only one good one left. Plus, she wasn't sure if she had lost her attacker. The light might give away her location. She sat a moment and stared into the darkness behind her, wondering how close he was.

Alone in the Paris Underground she felt like one of the dead, silently waiting in the dark. Her throbbing heart slowed to a normal pace. As the adrenaline subsided, the pain returned. Her ankle, her head, the sliced palm of her hand, all seared. Veronica closed her eyes and wished the nightmare would soon be over.

Chapter 84

Father Michel's Story

Father Michel spurred Lightning toward town. The image of Astrid's frightened seven year old son, holed up in a dingy apartment or flimsy shack, alone and unknowing, rattled in his brain. The boy would surely die on his own. The best hope would be that someone would find him and take him in as a servant. The worst, the flagellants would discover him...

Another test, thought Father Michel. The Lord decided to throw one more at him, like a toff playing knucklebones, hoping one of the jacks are finally caught.

I said I was done with your trials! Every one ends miserably. Why take a test when I'm doomed to fail? I refuse them, all of them. I'm not an object for You to torment.

Truly a just, loving God wouldn't subject his servants to tribulations. Such vengeance is an act of hate, of spite and evil.

God delivers the peste. The peste is evil, therefore evil comes from God...

"I can't condone evil. I know in my heart, and through my own ability to reason, that evil is not acceptable. Therefore morality does not, cannot, come from God. If morality is independent of God, then why do I need Him? Why does anyone? He is just an imaginary monster in a world filled with real demons." Father Michel grumbled as he clutched the old Jew's satchel.

His thoughts returned to the boy: an innocent soul cast into a world where God is dead and fear runs rampant.

I know morality — I can reason what is just, right, and good — without God. I don't need to appease Him. Morality comes from me. I am my own God.

In the distance, three figures approached on horseback. Uncertainty accosted the priest, and he considered steering Lightning off the road to avoid a confrontation.

One of them waved his cap in the air. It was the sheriff, Jean-Arthur.

"Good morning, Father!"

Father Michel felt relief. "Thank you for returning. I didn't think you'd come back for me."

"We made a deal. Of course I'd return."

Father Michel rode up to the sheriff and quickly spoke. "The woman from last night —Astrid..."

"She's a whore, Father."

"She came into my room this morning..."

Jean-Arthur interrupted again. "She just doesn't give up. I'll take care of her. Don't fret the strumpet. Come along now," he said as he spurred his mount and turned around. "Let's quickly ride through, before the town wakes up."

Father Michel rode astride his escort and persisted. "You don't understand. She's dead. Passed away about an hour ago."

"Dead? Of peste? Dirty trollop; it was inevitable."

"No, she was beaten in the night. I thought you should know since you are the sheriff."

"I see." Jean-Arthur's attitude shifted, and he appeared to physically shrink in his saddle.

"Did you know she was a mother? She said she had a son."

"No, didn't know. Undoubtedly, he was a bastard, no father, no future."

"Do you know where Astrid lived? Now that she's gone, the boy is alone," the priest pressed.

"She lived on the streets. Each night a different man's bed was her home."

"But the boy had to stay somewhere."

"It was probably all a lie, Father. Her kind are filled with lies. There's no child. She just wanted money or..."

Father Michel insisted. "Her *kind*? What kind is that? You and the others caroused every night with her *kind*. You allowed her to pour your drinks and suck your cock and now you denigrate her because she survived by the only means she could? It seems her kind and your kind are more kindred than you believe."

"*My* kind don't lie. She had a wicked tongue and this tale of a child was likely another ploy concocted to trick you."

"She wasn't lying! She was confessing to me on her deathbed. In my experience, no one speaks falsehoods to a priest as they prepare to meet their Lord and Savior. The boy is real, and you have to find him. He's out there somewhere, and he just lost his mother."

"Even if I found him, where would I take him? There's no place for him. He can't go to the church because the clergy there aren't...well, let's just say that wouldn't be a good option."

"Please, Jean-Arthur? Last night in the inn you asked me if it was still possible for your soul to obtain absolution for the many sins you've committed. I knew then that you were a good man, because those who are evil care not about such things."

"So you think I'm a good man, Father? Is that it, you're appealing to my 'noble' nature?" Jean-Arthur chuckled.

"I'm appealing to your reason. You know the difference between good and evil and don't need God to condemn or condone your actions."

"This truly is the end of times if a priest is telling me not to believe in God."

"Believe what you will, but know this — even though you were helpless to save so many, it doesn't mean you should be complacent when you have the opportunity to save one. The boy still has a chance, but only if you help him. Just because so many are damned, doesn't mean he has to be one of them, Jean-Arthur."

"You make me feel almost as guilty as the church used to." The gruff man's eyes gleamed as the sun broke the distant horizon. His ruddy face flushed more brightly as he chortled.

"I'll give you money to take care of him. Here, use this to buy him a place to stay, food, clothes..." The Priest handed the sheriff a pouch of gold.

The big man inspected the pouch and thumbed one of the coins. He nodded. "I'll ask the innkeeper. If anyone knows about Astrid's kid, it would be him. If he's out there, I'll find him."

After several quiet moments, the sheriff asked, "A pouch of money, the gold coins you are paying us to watch over you, you carry a lot of coinage for a simple parish priest."

Father Michel felt his neck grow hot. "Church tithings..."

"It's dangerous to have that kind of money on the road. We'll stay with you, Father, riding for as long as you need us to."

Father Michel sighed with relief. "Thank you. I can pay you more…"

"Stop, stop with the money. I'm a *good man*, after all, I don't need to be bribed." He laughed without mirth.

The stench of death permeated the damp morning air. They rode past a long, narrow trench, dug out of fresh earth. Inside, bodies lay scattered haphazardly; their arms and legs were split open like over-cooked sausages; their faces distorted with mouths hanging wide to reveal black tongues. Many were marked with the sign of the peste, displaying the telltale buboes on their necks, arms, and — as some of them were naked — their groins. Father Michel held his breath as they rode by.

Something stirred. Within the pit of bodies, there was movement. Father Michel tried to turn his head from the scene. He didn't want to look, but he couldn't help himself. A hand wagged its fingers and then suddenly shot straight up from underneath a rotting corpse. There was a raspy groan, and he watched in despair as someone from within struggled.

"One is still alive!" Father Michel shouted.

Up ahead, just off the road, sat a wagon stuffed with corpses. Two men unceremoniously heaved bodies from it into the trench. One wore a familiar, distorted gourd-mask with a long, pig-like snout and two holes carved out for eyes. The clunky head turned in the direction of the riders. The other man kept his focus down as he tugged at a ring that stubbornly held onto its owner's finger.

Father Michel repeated his words and pointed. "There! Someone is alive. He moves! Don't you see him?"

The masked man cast a slow gaze into the trench and looked directly at the wriggling form. "No. I *don't*."

"But he is there. He moves. You are burying him alive. Take that stupid thing off your head, and you will see!"

"This 'stupid thing' is protects me from the peste, and it works much better than your hollow prayers. I will not take it off to gawp at an infected corpse. Tell me what you'll do to me Father, damn my soul to hell? I'm already damned and live every day on Earth in Hell."

Father Michel waved his hand at the other man. "Then him. He can see the one that is alive. He can help."

Without turning, the other said, "We are paid to collect and bury the bodies, not to be doctors. If you want him out, then please, go in and get him."

Jean-Arthur spoke. "Let it go, Father; there's nothing anyone can do for him now."

Father Michel contemplated dismounting Lightning and reaching into the trench to pull the poor soul free. He watched the man struggling, trying to get out from under a festering body that pinned him down. Puss and bile bubbled out of the corpse causing the living man's hands to become slippery and clumsy.

Father Michel flinched. He made the sign of the cross over his chest and asked, "Jean-Arthur, is there nothing we can do?"

Black birds danced in the air, screeching with excitement. They swooped onto the bodies, landing just long enough to pull off a bit of flesh, and then ascend upward with their bounty.

The Sheriff nodded. "One thing — an act of mercy." He pulled out a bow and arrow. Taking careful aim, he easily skewered the doomed man, shooting him dead, as they rode by. "We can't save them all, Father. We just can't."

Chapter 85

Veronica's Story

Ａ distant noise echoed through the catacombs. Veronica thought it was a voice, but she wasn't sure if it belonged to the crazy man or someone in her party. She didn't dare call out in fear it was the first.

Rising to her feet caused Veronica to swoon. She wondered how much blood she had lost. "Is someone there? Nik?" she whispered.

More noises, clearly voices this time; she could hear them calling her name. They didn't sound far. "Nikki?" she howled again, louder.

Her sister answered. "Vern! Where are you?"

"Nikki! I'm over here. I'm lost! You have to find me!" She waited. At first there was no answer, then several voices seemed to call out at once. They echoed off the walls, but she couldn't understand them.

"I'm over here! I don't know where to go!" she cried.

Again, several voices mashed together seemed to answer her request. Then, one loud voice clearly demanded, "Quiet!"

Veronica sat still and listened. The voice slowly repeated, "Quiet." There was another pause. "The walls echo, and we can't hear her if everyone yells at once!" It was Ralph. He sounded angry, but authoritative. After a moment, he continued. "Veronica, can you hear me?"

"Yes!"

In an instant, another frantic voice chimed in. It was Nikki. "Follow our voices! Come to us!"

"Okay!" Veronica replied.

At the same time, Ralph answered. "*Don't* follow our voices! I repeat, don't attempt to follow our voices! These caves echo; plus, there are many levels. We could be directly above you or beside you, and you wouldn't know the difference."

Veronica considered his words. "Then what should I do?"

"Stay where you are. We'll come to you!"

"How will you find me?"

"Just keep your flashlight on. We'll find *you!*"

"I don't *have* my flashlight. I'm in the dark!"

Silence.

"You don't *have* your flashlight?" Ralph asked.

"No, it was taken from me. I was attacked."

Nikki's voice came next. "Attacked! Who attacked you?"

Ralph ordered her to be quiet.

"Are you okay?" Christophe called. "Are you hurt?"

"I'm okay, but I don't know where he is. He was right behind me, but I ran to get away. He took my money, the flashlight, and my necklace."

Christophe again. "We're coming; stay calm. We'll find you!"

Veronica let her body slide down the wall. She crouched in the darkness, and a spell of nausea fell over her. She gagged twice, but kept the bile from spilling out by swallowing it back.

"We're going to split up. We have two lights. That way we can cover more ground and find you!" It was Ralph speaking.

"We won't split up! Stupid!" It was one of the models arguing. Veronica thought it was Sefferine. She was right because Christophe scolded, "Shut up, Seff. Veronica wouldn't be lost if it wasn't for you!"

Nikki added, "This isn't an episode of Scooby-Doo. I don't think we need to split up."

Ralph said, "But we will cover more ground..."

"Just find me and fast!" Veronica pleaded.

A beam of light cut through the dark.

"Finally!" The injured American girl gasped. "Thank God you found..." but her joy was cut short when she saw the transient man standing in the shadow of the flashlight.

Veronica shrieked.

He rushed toward her. In the distance, Christophe, Nikki, and Ralph all cried out: "What is it? Are you okay? Hold on, we're coming!"

Veronica scuttled on all fours as the man converged on her. "Just leave me alone," she pleaded.

He answered. "Connasse! Vous avez révélé ma cachette secrète."

Veronica felt his breath on the back of her neck. She rolled over to see him standing over her with the flashlight angled to strike her head. She feebly covered her face and braced for impact. None came. Instead, she heard the man squeal with surprise. Flashes of light mixed with shadows danced across her field of vision.

She hoisted herself up on her elbows and saw Christophe standing there. The man was beside him, lying in a heap. The flashlight rolled across the ground, causing the shadows to rise and fall on the wall like wicked dancers.

"Are you okay?" Christophe inquired.

Veronica nodded, too stunned to speak.

Nikki was there in a second. She knelt beside her sister and dabbed at her wounds. "Where does it hurt, Vern?"

"My head, ankle, and my hand," she said holding up her injured paw.

"He got you good," Ralph commented as he nodded at the crazy man.

Veronica's attacker stood suddenly as if he knew he was the subject of conversation. He stared wildly at the group, spit at the ground, and rushed off down the corridor. As he fled, he called, "Putains de touristes. Allez-vous faire foutre!"

"Should we call the police?" Bianca asked.

"No," Ralph snapped. "Remember, it's *illegal* to be down here."

Christophe jumped up to give chase. Ralph put up a cautionary arm and warned, "He knows these tunnels better than you. Better not to risk it, my friend. Besides, we need to get Veronica out of here."

Christophe puffed out his chest as if to protest, then took over. "You're right. Let's get out of here." He knelt and said to Veronica, "I'll carry you."

With a quick, pouting nod she allowed him to pick her up in his arms. Peering over his shoulder, she caught sight of the models walking behind them. Sefferine's arms were wrapped across her chest. She sneered at Veronica, but the American girl merely closed her eyes and allowed his strong, comforting arms to make her feel safe and secure.

Ralph felt the need to comment on everything. "We didn't even notice that you weren't behind us. You have to be careful in this place. It's filled with the dredges of society: vagrants, drug addicts, criminals, gang members. You're lucky he didn't kill you."

Veronica narrowed her eyes at Ralph. "*Now* you tell me."

"There is little danger if we're in a group. There's safety in numbers. If I thought you'd be exploring by yourself, then I surely would have warned you..."

She didn't want to listen to Ralph's sermon. She buried her face in Christophe's shoulder so she could quietly sob unnoticed.

"We *have* to call the authorities and tell them she was attacked and robbed," Nikki demanded.

Ralph was quick to point out: "Don't you understand? We aren't supposed to *be* here. It's against the law to be in the catacombs. Not to mention that we would be revealing the location of my friend's entrance. No, we can't report this. Besides, the cata-cops would do nothing, could do nothing."

They entered the cavern with the altar. Ralph spoke. "See, you were very close to getting out of there. Had you traveled just a little farther you would have come out here. How did you manage in the tunnels anyway? How did you find your way in the dark?"

"Even though I kept running into walls, I just kept going," Veronica replied.

"You were very brave then. You know the best way to defeat a maze, is to pick one wall and follow it? As long as it's not an interior wall, you'll eventually find the way out."

"Again, *now* you tell me." Veronica snickered.

The group emerged in the storage room of the nightclub. The models hurried out. Ralph requested that they "call him sometime", and they grunted an affirmative reply as they split from the group.

Christophe did not put Veronica down as they made their way through the crowded bar. She opened her eyes once to see a sea of faces staring blankly at her. Among them, the Vampire Lady smiled broadly and raised a drink as if to toast Veronica as she passed by.

The remainder of the evening was a blur. Veronica faded in and out of sleep as they rode first to Ralph's and then back to the Loire Valley. She felt herself being carried once again before she was set onto her cushiony bed. She languidly opened her eyes and caught a glimpse of Christophe. He was leaning over her. She felt something soft on her forehead. *A kiss?* Veronica was unsure as she drifted off to sleep.

Chapter 86

The Pagans' Story
182 CE – the Ancient Ritual that Unleashed It

Bevin slowly drifted out of the miserable reality that was his life and into an enchanted world. Images of Trinna floated through his mind. She was dressed in wedding attire, wearing a flowing robe that immodestly contoured to every slope of her curvaceous body. A wreath of blossoms was woven into the braids piled high on her head. She stood at the side of the river, just like Bevin always dreamed she would on their wedding day. He happily went to her with outstretched arms, calling her name.

"Trinna!"

She stepped back as he approached, entering the water, and slipping out of sight, just as he got close enough to touch her. Bevin playfully splashed in the water where she went under.

"Come on now, stop teasing me!" he called.

Trinna did not come up.

Several agonizing moments went by, and Bevin's humor was replaced with alarm. He dunked his head under but couldn't see beyond a few inches in the murky water. He felt around for her, flailing his arms under the surface where she had gone under.

Desperate, he took a big breath and dove down to the bottom. Instead of being a few feet, it was inexplicably deep. He swam down, down, deep down. The water turned around him like a tempest. He did not relent, however, and continued to plunge until he felt his lungs begin to implode. A searing pain ripped through his chest. His survival reflex kicked in and forced him to gasp, causing water to enter his lungs.

The water roiled around him like soup in a spinning, bubbling cauldron. He closed his eyes, preparing for imminent death, but instead, he felt a rush, and the water was gone. He was suddenly standing in a field of incredibly tall grass. Surrounded on all sides, he had no choice but to push the long stalks aside and search for a way out.

Then she was there. Lying in a nest of wild flowers, Trinna was curled up, sleeping peacefully.

He dove to her side and snuggled beside her. "Trinna, Trinna!" he pleaded in his dream. She did not stir. He entwined his fingers around hers. They were ice cold. Bevin spoke into her ear. "Trinna, come back to me."

Her eyes popped open. Bevin relaxed. His fear ebbed, and he began to laugh, too. "Trinna, you scared me! I thought you were —"

Trinna interrupted him. "Look, Bevin, a baby. *A baby!*"

Bevin looked down the length of her body. Something dark and blurry stirred in the weeds by her pelvis. Bevin was unable to see it clearly.

He turned back to Trinna. Her beautiful, creamy white skin rotted away before his eyes. A blood-streaked skull grinned back at him.

He cried out, "Trinna!"

She didn't answer, but in response to his outburst, there was another sound –
– a primeval cry. It wailed like an insane child. Bevin spun his head just in time
to face the black thing that pounced on him like a malicious beast, clawing and
scratching. He shrieked and drove away the nightmare. He awoke in the real
world, sweating and panting as he lay on a pile of rubble at the base of the shrine
he was building for his beloved.

The Children's Story
1307 AD – A Time of Inquisition

A question bounced around in Isabelle's dreamy head. "What are you doing here?"

She murmured with her eyes still shut, "Louis, I'm sleeping."

"Wake up. Come on..."

"We need our rest for tomorrow. Go back to sleep," she said.

"But you shouldn't sleep *here*."

"We'll be fine; no wild animals will attack us. Now go back to sleep, Louis!" Isabelle scolded. She felt her shoulder being shaken and she shrugged defiantly.

"Is this your horse? It was wandering near the road."

With a shiver, Isabelle realized the voice accosting her sleep was not Louis. Her eyes popped open, and she sat with a start. The morning light revealed a figure, crouching in front of her, dressed in a long, white tunic. A gold crucifix dangled from his neck. The horse, now known as Stinker, stood behind the man and was no longer tethered to the tree where they had left him.

Isabelle fought to find words as her brother slowly stirred to life beside her. "Yes, that is our horse. He must have wandered off."

The man smiled warmly. "Young man, you should be more careful."

Isabelle didn't respond right away. She was momentarily confused by being addressed as a "young man". Then she remembered her appearance and spoke with a deepened voice. "I will be in the future. I don't want my horse to get away. My father, the farmer, would be displeased."

Louis rubbed his eyes and sat up next to his sister.

Isabelle continued quickly. "This is my *sister*..." She struggled for a name, and as none immediately came to her, she uttered, "Her name is Isabelle."

Louis looked confused. He momentarily hesitated before saying, "Hello."

"I'm Father Gabriel. You really shouldn't be out here. The highway can be a dangerous place for children. Where are your parents?"

"We live...far from here," Isabelle answered. "We are traveling to...to go to our relatives to get some things for our parents. They are sick and need...things."

"That's like quite a journey for two so young. Where do your relatives live?"

Her brain scrambled for a location. "In a village over the mountains!"

"Our party is going in that direction. It is not safe for children to be on the road by themselves. Let me talk to the Bishop. Perhaps we can escort you at least part of the way."

"Oh no, that's okay. We'll be just fine," Isabelle answered quickly.

"Goodness, I insist! We're traveling on the same road in the same direction. Come now; let's go back to the others."

Isabelle tried to think of an excuse. Louis looked up at her from under the drooping bonnet. "Izzy..." he began, then caught himself quickly as his sister glared at him with cautioning eyes. "Zzz-eee-rid," he finished. "Izzerid," he stated as if confirming the new name he had given his sister. "Our parents told us not to mingle with strangers."

Isabelle was relieved by her brother's fast thinking. "Yes, that's true. We shouldn't defy our parents."

"Well, Isabelle and Izzerid, I am reasonably sure they would be relieved if they knew you were able to travel with the Bishop's caravan. What harm could possibly come from *us*?"

He took each child by the hand and led them back to the road. A long procession stretched out before them. Men on horseback were in the front carrying flags adorned with crosses. A fancy carriage stood behind them. It was gold and paintings of angels and an official crest decorated the side. Curtains hung in the windows, hiding the rider inside.

"Who's in there?" Louis asked.

"My dear, that is Bishop Thomas Duforcquet. He's on his way to an important meeting. He ordered us to stop when we saw your wandering horse on the road. Now, I'll go request that you be allowed to join us."

"You don't have to do that. Don't disturb him..." Isabelle began, but Father Gabriel was already mounting the step to the carriage.

Isabelle considered grabbing Louis and mounting Stinker so they could make a quick getaway. Surely, the Bishop wouldn't be inclined to chase after them. Then, she considered the situation more carefully. In truth this might be good for her and Louis. After all, they would be with religious men, men of God, *good* men, who would protect them and maybe even help them find their parents. After all, Uncle Pierre couldn't harm them if they were in the company of a *Bishop*!

Gabriel returned from the carriage. "You are invited to join the Bishop. Come, he wants to meet you. You can ride with him."

The children were escorted inside the regal coach. The Bishop sat facing forward on a bench covered in velvet pillows and satiny blankets. Isabelle and Louis took a seat across from him, next to a tiny man in a valet's uniform. The valet scrunched to the side and brushed a few flecks of dust off the Bishop's creamy white robes.

Bishop Thomas Duforcquet had no beard or mustache, and the only hair Isabelle could see were his snowy white eyebrows, which haloed his kind eyes. He smiled warmly. "Welcome aboard. Sit and enjoy the ride. I am sure it is much more comfortable than traveling on horseback."

Isabelle and Louis graciously thanked the man for his hospitality.

"Careful," the valet warned as he observed the mud on their fine shoes.

Isabelle pulled her feet back, suddenly aware of how odd the expensive ladies' riding boots must look on a "peasant boy".

"Tell me about your parents. They are ill?" The Bishop leaned forward.

Isabelle swallowed hard as she repeated the lie. "Yes, very sick. They are both in bed and are hot if you touch them."

"Have you prayed for them?"

"Every day," Isabelle replied.

"Let's pray together now. Give me your hands."

They awkwardly clasped the Bishop's hands as they traveled down the road, back in the direction that they had been running from.

Chapter 88

Sebastian's Story

Esindra squealed sharply.

"Shh, Governess." It was Cicero, waiting for her outside her door. He pulled her into an empty passageway and held a tiny vial inches from her nose in the darkness. "Here's Sebastian's poison. There's enough for several doses."

The startled woman caught her breath and asked, "Okay, what do you want me to do?"

Cicero pulled her deeper into a dark, recessed corridor where he had everything set up on a small side table and explained. "One dose causes death after several hours, but two doses will do him in faster. Just to be sure, we'll give him *three*, so his death should be quick, and we'll still have plenty left over for the Head Commander." He grabbed a goblet of wine from the side table and poured the poison into it. He swirled the cup, lifted it to his nose, and smiled. "It's true; there's no odor, and no odor means no taste. Take this to Sebastian." He snatched a second goblet. "And this one's yours."

"You want me to drink *with* him?"

"Yes, of course. You have to make sure he drinks it *all*. Suggest a toast. After all, you and he are...close friends."

She huffed, snagged the goblets, and decisively walked down the hallway to the keep. Cicero followed and cased the corridors to make sure no one caught sight of them. The tower room was not guarded. He waited outside as Esindra slipped through the doorway.

"Sebastian, it's Esindra," she announced as she entered.

The Cloaked Man lay on his back, sprawled on the bed, with his hands clasped under his neck. His head remained still as he spoke. "I see that."

Esindra carefully set the goblets on the desk, noting which was hers and his. "I brought you some wine." A forced smile glimmered at the corner of her lips.

Sebastian studied her until her smile faded. "Wine?" he finally asked. She nodded, slowly approached him, and sat at the foot of the bed. "What's the occasion?"

"None," she quickly answered. "Fabius is preparing for the barbarians to arrive, everyone is busy, and I stole off with a carafe and thought you might like to share a glass."

"How enchanting, but not now. I also must prepare for tonight. Something isn't entirely right. I can sense it, but I can't see it."

"Perhaps a bit of wine will help relax you. It helps me quite often."

"No, I don't need to relax. I need to *sharpen* my senses."

"Oh, wine can do that, too. I develop the most enchanting notions when I have a taste of wine," Esindra quipped.

"You're persistent, aren't you?"

"I just poured the chalices and came *all* this way with them. But if you're busy, I'll be off..."

"No, stay. I'll have some; bring it here."

Obediently, she scampered to the desk, grabbed a goblet, and handed it to him.

"Are you going to join me?" Sebastian inquired.

Esindra looked at her solitary goblet on the desk. "Of course." She retrieved her cup and anxiously swirled the liquid.

Sebastian studied her and cajoled, "Your beautiful brown eyes betray you. I know why you're really here, Esindra."

She froze. "You do?"

The Cloaked Man rose to his feet and stood before the Governess. "I sense things, Esindra. I know you're afraid. I can smell your fear."

"You can?"

"Yes, but you need not be afraid. All is going as planned. Let's drink to us!"

"Yes, to us," Esindra whispered as she lifted the cup and let only a few drops of the wine penetrate her lips.

The Cloaked Man drew back on the chalice and quaffed a massive swallow.

"And let's drink to the defeat of our enemies," Esindra offered slyly.

The Cloaked Man nodded and took back another hefty swig. "And most importantly, Esindra, let's drink to our child and a brilliant plan."

She nodded and held her cup to quivering lips. "A brilliant plan indeed."

They toasted and drank, and Esindra even lapsed into a genuine giggle as the Cloaked Man exaggerated his final pull on the goblet by raising it dramatically in the air.

When he finished, he asked, "Is there more? You said you stole off with a carafe."

"It's stashed just down the hallway. Shall I fetch it?" Before he could answer, Esindra eagerly trotted out of the tower room.

Relieved to be done with the deed, she ran to Cicero. He waited just around the corner.

"Did he drink it?" the Centurion asked.

"Yes, now we just have to wait for him to die."

"He should be dead already. Are you sure he drank it all?"

Esindra held out the empty goblet as proof. "See?"

"Perhaps we should give him more? He has to die *now*. We can't wait, or we risk being caught."

"But you need to save some for the Head Commander," Esindra reminded him.

Cicero carefully studied the vial and assessed its contents. "There's still enough."

He mixed a small amount with another cup of wine. "Here, this will finish him off."

"You want me to go back in *there*?"

Cicero grew impatient. "Of course! You're the only one who can."

She reluctantly returned to the tower room and again found Sebastian reclining on the bed. He did not stir. Esindra crept closer and carefully held her hand above his open mouth. She waited, feeling for the slightest breath with her tender palm — nothing, no breath, no movement. She spun and skittered out of the room.

"Cicero! The deed is done. He stopped breathing."

"We have to be certain; feel his chest to see if his heart still beats."

Under her breath, Esindra muttered, "Alive or dead, I don't think he has a heart to beat."

Cicero shot the lady a stern look, and she once again tiptoed into the tower room. This time she lightly placed her hand on the center of his chest. She felt nothing. She turned to call Cicero when Sebastian sat up like a shot. Startled, Esindra shrieked and jumped back.

"What are you doing?" Sebastian asked.

"Oh! You startled me! I was checking to see if you were still ali...awake."

"How disappointing. I thought perhaps you were sneaking into bed wid' me," his speech slurred.

"That wouldn't be appropriate," she said demurely.

"You already done inappropriate things in this bed. Ha' you forgotten?" he stammered.

The poison was taking effect.

"That was for a reason. Remember, it was a *duty* that you performed — nothing more."

Sebastian sat up and leered at her with sleepy eyes. "But you enjoyed that duty, didn't you? At first, you lay stock-still like a marble statue obliv'ous to everything around you. But then you began to move with me. I felt your hips push back into mine. Your breath became quick, and I heard you stifle your sighs. Come, Esindra, come lay wid'me again."

She swallowed hard as she spoke. "If someone came, we'd be caught."

"I thought you said that everyone was preparing for tonight?" He rose and walked around the Governess with a wobbling gait.

She flashed over her shoulder to see Sebastian close the chamber door. "Yes, but there's a *chance* someone may catch us," she cautioned.

He circled the room and returned to his bed. "Join me Ezzind'a. If anyone comes, we'll hear der footsteps. You'd be surprised how these walls echo."

"Okay." She grabbed both chalices of wine from the desk. "And we can have another toast...to victory over our enemies!"

Sebastian carefully cradled the goblet in his hand. He leered at Esindra hungrily as she carefully sat on the bed next to him. He drank, but just a small sip. "You're an odd bird, Ezzind'a. The first time I laid eyes on you, you bore back at me like you were beholding a raging beast. Now, in just a short period of time, you've become drawn to me, have you not?"

Esindra felt strangely enthralled by Sebastian's words. The revulsion drained from her soul, and she began to feel a flutter in her loins. "I do find you appealing, yes. I can't explain why." Before she could prevent the words from escaping her mouth, she found herself speaking her exact thoughts. "I thought you were disgusting. Even only moments ago, I was dreading the thought of your touch.

But now, I find myself anticipating it."

"Why'd you come here den, if only a few moments ago you foun' me repulsive?"

Esindra felt woozy, and she took a long sip of wine. "I was curious to see you again after the other night..." her voice trailed off as she fought to contrive a lie.

"So, though you have since bedded your husband, you have thoughts of me?" He seemed pleased by the admission he so easily conned out of her.

She caught herself slipping into his spell and held out her goblet. "I don't think we should talk about *him* right now. Let's drink to us!"

Sebastian obliged and sipped from his cup. "There's something you should know 'bout Fabius though."

Esindra trembled. "It isn't right for me to speak of my husband while I sit here with you. Let's drink our wine."

"Ezzind'a, Fabius *can't* father children!" Sebastian blurted.

Esindra stared into her chalice. "What do you mean?"

Sebastian paused as if struggling to find a clear line of thought and finally answered. "He's fallow. And when you tell him you're pregnant, he'll know he's not truly the father."

"No, that can't be..."

"It's true. Fabius came to me several weeks ago and told me dat for many years he had affairs with od'er women. Noble women, women of modest means, slaves, and even prostitutes shared his bed. He was desp'rate to produce an heir. If any of dem had become pregnant, he would've left you. He would've replaced you with a *whore* if she gave him an heir. But not one of those women did, so he *knows* he can ne'er fad'er a child."

Esindra bore at him incredulously. "Then why did you tell me he would think our child was his own? You tricked me. Why have you done this? Fabius will have me imprisoned and charged with adultery. I may even be sentenced to death and our child sold into slavery."

"He already knows dat I'm the fad'er of your child," the Cloaked Man confessed.

"What are you talking about?"

"Fabius ordered me to trick you and seduce you. His plan was for you to get pregnant by me, yet he would fad'er the child and have an heir."

"That doesn't make sense..." Esindra began as the warmth of the wine stung her temples.

"He knew you desired a child as much as he 'id and that you'd do *anything* to have one. He also knew dat you'd be as curious as a mountain cat af'der I told you I saw a child in your future. He knew you'd come to me to find out more. He planned it all from da start."

"The first time I saw you, you said you saw a vision of me having a baby...was that a lie, too?" Esindra's wailed. "You tricked me all along!"

"I saw da vision. I never lied about dat. The moment I lain my eyes on you, I knew'd your destiny."

"What is my destiny now? To be tried as an adulterer and executed!"

"You'll have our child, but Fabius won't live to see it. You'll be free of him.

It w' all make sense tonight after da meal with da Head Commander. I'll be your protector. You *will* see!" He patted her arm, closed his eyes, and laid back down.

"You? You will *protect* me? But you..." Her words trailed off. Shooting a look in the direction of the door, unsure if the centurion was able to hear them.

He forced himself upright. "Yes, I have double-crossed Fabius, and he'll soon meet his end. Bu' fear not, for you'll be spared, and togedder we will raise our child here in dis castle. It'll soon all be ours."

"I must go." She stood abruptly and gathered up the wine goblets.

"Leave dat. I'll drink it."

A chill accosted Esindra by the spine. "No, the wine is flat."

"Id is fine." Sebastian grabbed his chalice. "Are you sure you don't want to stay? Af'er all, soon you'll be lying in bed wid'me every night."

Esindra watched with dread as the Cloaked Man held the wine to his mouth. Her tender lips parted and words caught in her throat. Sebastian pulled back and drank, slurping and lapping. At that moment, she loathed him, despised him; his trickery had reduced her to his servitude. Turmoil grasped her. *He is the father of my child!*

"Don't drink that!" Her hand shot up and knocked the cup from his mouth. It crashed to the floor, spilling on the bed sheets and across Sebastian's chest.

"Don't be angry. I saved you from a miser'ble life with a philanderin', sterile husband who treats you like a used-up whore."

Esindra stood speechless. Her mouth opened, but no words came out.

The Cloaked Man rose to stop her from leaving, but then swaggered back. "Da wine is quite potent. My head is cloudy, my body weak..." A veil of realization spread across his face. "You laced da wine! You mean to kill me..."

He reached his bony white hands out to her, she dodged his advance, and he tumbled across the room and fell to the floor. He lay there on his stomach, gasping for breath. His legs kicked back and forth. He writhed like a snake, struggling for strength as the toxin seized control.

"Cicero made you do dis, didn't he? He convinced you to serve me my own 'lixir." Esindra stood over Sebastian as he convulsed. "You betrayed me..." his voice trailed off as his body rippled with one last spasm and then lay still.

Cicero burst into the room. "The deed is done?" He spied the Cloaked Man crumpled on the ground.

Esindra's statuesque face cracked. As the tears flowed, she said, "It's done. Sebastian is..."

The Cloaked Man's hand lashed out suddenly. Esindra shrieked and stepped back, but was too slow. His clasped her ankle and yanked her to the floor. Cicero leapt forward, grabbing Esindra by the hands. He pulled the Governess toward him, but Sebastian held strong. He jerked her leg, and she was pulled in two directions like a rope in a bitter game of tug o' war.

Cicero kicked Sebastian. His chunky boot smashed into his mouth, and Esindra heard bone break. Blood gushed out of the fresh wound. His lips parted and revealed a wet, red mouth with a hanging front tooth. The blow didn't slow Sebastian down. He pulled on Esindra, grasping her thigh, as though he were climbing up her leg.

Cicero drew his foot back again and kicked, but this time Sebastian rolled out of the way. He loosened his hold on Esindra, and she took advantage by thrusting herself free. Cicero pounced on Sebastian, clenching his throat. The two men rolled back and forth while grunting and cursing.

"Guards, we need help!" Esindra called down the corridor.

Turning back, she watched as Cicero beat Sebastian in the head and stomach with his fists. Three men came rushing in and beheld the sight. They stood there a moment, unprepared for the visage before them. Cicero barked orders, and the guards converged on the fight, kicking and punching Sebastian as he struggled against the Roman soldiers.

Sebastian was a bloody, beaten, shell of a man when Fabius entered the room. "Stop!" he ordered.

The three guards drew back, but Cicero remained locked in combat. His hands were cinched around Sebastian's throat, gyrating the head back and forth.

"Cicero, enough! Stop!"

Cicero rolled off the culprit, his eyes locking with Fabius'. Fabius glared at his first command.

"What's going on here? Answer me, Cicero, or you'll face charges for treason."

Cicero stood. A bloody welt gleamed under his right eye. "I heard Esindra calling for help, and when I came in here, I saw him attacking her. I fought him off and saved your wife!"

Esindra gaped as her husband turned to her. "Is that true?"

She ruefully bore at Cicero and then consented. "Yes. Cicero saved me."

"Damn it, Esindra; what were you doing in here? I forbade you..." Fabius began, but his words fell short as the Cloaked Man twisted back to life in a spasm.

He flailed on the floor, gasped, and cried out once in pain, then lay motionless again. His eyes remained open and staring. His tongue swelled and pushed its way past the lips. Blood continued to drip from his wounds. A delicate *drip...drip...drip* echoed in the dead silent room.

There was a sudden flurry in the hallway outside the chamber door. A young foot soldier burst in. "A carriage has arrived!" he uttered excitedly. "Governor, come quick, we have a guest —" His words stopped dead when he saw the bloody body.

Fabius absently addressed the messenger. "The barbarians? Already?"

The foot soldier replied. "No, Roman. It is Helena, mother of Constantine."

"What is *she* doing here?" Fabius scanned the room and spat when he spoke.

"She said she urgently needs council with you," the boy offered.

Fabius glared from Cicero to Esindra and back again. "I'm not finished interrogating you two yet. But right now I have to tend to our unexpected visitor. Everyone make haste. Cicero, prepare your men for tonight. Esindra, go to your chamber and stay there until I send for you."

Everyone scattered. The governor remained alone and knelt before the corpse. From his waist pouch, he retrieved two copper coins and lightly placed them on the eyes of the dead. He whispered in the stillness. "I know not what will happen to a soul such as yours in the hereafter. I pray the gods show mercy."

Chapter 89

Journal Intime

I awoke to the sound of a single Charleville musket being fired. It echoed through the whispering castle walls. I would later find out it was the execution of the guard who had been assigned to watch over me last night. He had left his post to play an illegal game of poque in the courtyard.

Beside me, in the bassinette, was my son. We gave him his father's name, Henri the Second, or Henri Jr. as I prefer to call him. He is a perfect child, with wide, wondering eyes and a tuft of dark hair on his perfectly round crown.

We spent most of the day sleeping. Agathe and Henri both came to visit, but I was too exhausted to speak to them. I remember seeing them come and go but not much else.

When I awoke later, Henri Jr. and I were alone. I sat up so I could gaze down at him. It felt good to be finally free of my constraints. Tentatively, I rose from my prison of a bed. Stretching my sore legs felt divine. The dull, constant pain in my lower back was instantly relieved once I stood. I stretched and walked slowly across the room. It felt splendid, despite the soreness between my legs. I did bleed, just a little. It soaked through my nightgown. I am sure the midwife would scold me for being out of bed if she caught me, but I didn't care. I was free!

I took short, tentative steps. I couldn't move faster if I wanted to, but it was okay; the slow, methodical tempo was soothing. I stopped once in the exact center of the room. There I stretched and allowed myself to savor sweet liberty. A palliative wave of tranquility swept over me. This tower room was my home — — our home — and it made me feel safe and secure.

I heard things there in the center of the room. Whispering voices from other parts of the castle were crystal clear. From the library, I heard servants gossip as they served the afternoon meal. I turned slightly and was privy to hearing the guards in the receiving room plan a meeting with townspeople. Apparently, Henri wants to ensure no more sieges will befall the castle. I turned a little more, just a bit, and I heard workers on the other side of the castle. They spoke of preparing the wood to reseal the oubliette in my chambers. Henri is keeping his promise to have the old rotting wood replaced. He does care about my wishes after all!

As the day passes, I slowly spin, stepping lightly, making the circle a little wider each time I turn completely around. Every spot is like a direct line to a different area of the castle. By taking my time and walking the circle methodically, I capture all the voices everywhere. The practice keeps me entertained until the maids return and tend to Henri Jr. and me. The whet nurse feeds him. They clean me and change the bed linens. As soon as they leave, I start again, in the center of the room, pacing in a circle to hear all the wonderful secrets of the castle!

Josette-Camille

September 5th, 1789

Workers came today and tore away the decrepit boards covering the entrance to the oubliette. The wood was old and brittle, and they easily removed it. Henri Jr. awoke from the noise, however, and howled like a little animal. Feeling much more agile, I swiftly attended to him, lifting him from his bed. To calm him, we danced around the room. I swear a hint of a smile crossed his pouting lips as we twirled. For a brief moment, I imagined the pounding hammers were the beat to a ballroom song and my young price and I were dancing a waltz!

The workers gave me a queer look as I threw my head back with jollity. Despite the noise, I could still hear the whisperings in the castle. Curious, I asked them, "Do you hear the voices, too, when you are in here? There! Listen, do you hear the maids gossiping in the kitchen?"

The guards didn't answer.

Just then, Agathe entered. "What are you doing with that child?" she gasped.

I spun and confronted her. "What do you mean, Agathe?"

Before I could react, she snatched my boy from my arms. "Thrashing him around like that is not safe!" she scowled. "You could drop him! You need to be more vigilant with Henri Jr."

"Don't be muddle-headed," I told her. "I would never *drop* my son. How could you say such cruel..." before I could finish, she rushed out of the room with him and slammed the door.

I chased after her but the wretch locked it from the outside! I pounded angrily and cried out, "Bring him back! Agathe, bring him back!"

The two workers were still in the room with me, and one put a hand on my shoulder. He said I should calm down, but I didn't want to hear his stupid mouth. I spun and slapped him across the cheek. I was filled with wrath.

"I want my son back!" I commanded. "Bring him here!"

That's when Henri peered at me through the slit in the door. "What is this outburst?" he demanded.

Tears erupted in a warm gush of absolute ire, and I answered, "Your bitch-sister took my baby! I want him back. And I want these insolent workers out of my chamber!"

Henri scowled. "Don't distress. The baby will be returned when you calm down."

I stomped a foot and insisted. "I will calm down when Henri Jr. is returned to me!"

"Fine!" Henri shouted. His face shot red, and he glared at me with a stab of odium before unlocking the door. "Go get Agathe and tell her that I said she should return with Henri Jr.," he ordered the workers. Then under his breath, he grumbled, "Tell her to give the child back, so I don't have to listen to this incessant harping." He gestured with an abrupt wave of his hand. The men quickly scrambled out of the room.

Henri and I were completely alone. We were seldom by ourselves anymore, and the tension in the room was as heavy as a steel anvil. I stammered, not sure what to say but was eager to seize the moment.

"Henri, I don't like how your sister is so quick to steal Henri Jr. from me. I want him with me at all times. It hurts like a stabbing blade through my belly when he is away." I stepped toward him and held out my hand.

He did not take it. Instead, he stoically said, "She knows more about tending to children than you do, Josette-Camille. Agathe is here to help. *Let her.*"

"Still she should not take him off so quickly and leave me agitated," I explained.

Agathe entered the room before Henri could answer. She held Henri Jr. I stretched out my arms to take my baby, but she remained clutching him. Her narrow, black eyes cast an icy stare.

"Give me my son, Agathe," I said with a quivering voice.

"I will hand him over slowly," she scolded. "He is a newborn, a fragile babe, and you should learn to handle him more carefully."

How dare she imply such a thing? I scowled at her before turning back to Henri. "I am sorry, dear husband, but it pains me to be away from our son for even a second."

He didn't acknowledge my apology. Instead, he said, "We are having a council with the townspeople to ensure that peace has been restored to this land. Until then, it is best if you stay here where you are safe. Agreed?"

"Stay here?" I asked to confirm his words. When he didn't answer, I asserted, "I have been in this room for far too long, Henri. When will you let me out? Surely, it can't be that dangerous in the castle? If trouble rises, Henri Jr. and I can make a hasty retreat."

I couldn't help but notice that his eyes fluttered as he spoke, not locking with mine for more than half a second at a time. "It is better this way. You'll remain here until I decide it is safe."

"Can we take just a short stroll in the garden? I long to see the sunlight again. Please, Henri, let's take our son for a walk. Then we can talk about this some more."

He avoided my question. "I have matters to attend to. Rest now."

"You would leave me again? But the matter is not fully discussed!"

He simply shook his head and walked out the door. Agathe followed quickly behind him, casting me a derisive glance as she hastened out the door.

"Why are you cross with me Henri?" I cried out. "Why will you not speak with me?"

But Henri did not respond, and I sat calling to no one, with only Henri Jr. to react with a soft whimper that blossomed into a wail.

Josette-Camille

292

Chapter 90

Veronica's Story

ikki burst into the Queen's Chamber. Veronica set down the diary and watched her sister bounce onto the bed beside her. It was eight o'clock in the morning, and Nikki already had two cups of espresso in her veins.

"Vern, good morning! You a' right?"

"Yeah, I'm fine."

"What a wicked-cool night, huh? It was fun, I mean, up until you got lost. If it wasn't for that, it would've been perfect."

"You had *fun?*"

"Yeah, we were in the *freaking Paris Underground.* I just updated my status. Everyone back home in LA thinks that was so tight!" She studied her phone for a few seconds, laughed, and continued. "Oh and that restaurant was yummy-licious. And Ralph, that fat little fuck, he has some serious game, doesn't he? He cracks me up."

"I'm glad you were amused."

"Those girls were *cray-cray* though. I got the story from Christophe about them. He's sorry by the way."

"What do you mean?"

"We sat and talked over a cup of coffee last night, after we put you to bed. Dude, we must have stayed up until three, three-thirty in the morning. Anyway, that Sefferine chick, she and Christophe used to date...kinda."

"I figured that."

"He broke it off and hadn't seen her for months until they ran into each other last night."

"That makes sense."

"Her family comes from *big* money — money they keep in Christophe's bank. But she's a hot mess from what he says. She's got a full-on crazy clown circus going on in that cracked head of hers. Obsessed with weird shit like witchcraft and cutting herself and death. She seemed normal enough at first. I mean, when we first met her, she didn't act psycho, did she?"

"I guess not."

"So, anyway, he felt bad about them crashing our party."

"Well, whatever." Veronica sighed.

Nikki continued. "Dude, I think Christophe really likes you. He was worried that you thought there was still something between him and her."

Veronica considered confessing her feelings, telling Nikki right then and there she had a huge crush on the brown-eyed Adonis. This was her *sister* after all! That's the way they were *supposed* to talk.

Veronica watched Nikki nod her head forward as if that would nudge a response. She smiled devilishly and raised one eyebrow like only the mischievous Nikole Dixon could.

Veronica held back. Experience taught her that every time she let Nikki insert herself into her love life, something bad happened. So she said, "It really doesn't matter to me if there is something between them or not. Not my circus, not my monkeys."

"Vern, you should have seen that Sefferine though! When Christophe and I came around the corner, she was standing there in nothing but a leather thong. Leather! Chaffing, ouch! Anyway, there was this pit literally filled with bones...skulls and femurs and rib cages. It was gross. And she was going to do it, jump in there with all those bones and slide across them on some kind of surfboard. There was a small ramp, and apparently, people just zip right down it. The funny thing is that when Christophe and I got there, he just stood there and shook his head like she was a fool."

"She certainly acted like one."

"She started pouting and talked about 'becoming one with her ancestors.' She said that it would be good for her soul to look the dead in the face. In the middle of her little speech, we noticed that you weren't there. Christophe freaked when we looked down the corridor, and you were gone. That's when we started searching for you. He just left her standing there half-naked in front of a pile of bones. I think she was pissed."

"I know she was."

"And Christophe was sorry about your money and necklace being stolen. He said he'd put tracers out there for your credit cards to see if they can catch anyone attempting to use them, and he'll make sure your bank card is changed right away so nobody can withdraw any money."

"Cool. The cash was no big deal, maybe thirty or forty euro. The labarum necklace, though, was worth a lot! Plus, it was my good luck charm." She trailed her bandaged fingers across her bare collarbone. "What else did you and Christophe talk about?"

"Ah! See, you *are* crushin' on him!"

"No, I'm just curious. Christ, Nik, can't I just be interested in what someone has to say without wanting to jump their bones?"

"Hmm, yeah, I honestly don't know what that's like."

Veronica started to push the covers back to let her sister know she was done with the conversation. Nikki skillfully offered, "Christophe and I also talked about the rumors surrounding the Château..."

"What rumors? Are the neighbors talking about me?"

Nikki groaned. "Christ you're vain. No one is talking about *you*. But they do talk about the past owners, must have been the ones before Marie-Claire. Apparently, they just vanished one day. No one has any idea what happened to them. Poof, just like that, they were gone. Rumor says the ghosts got 'em. Christophe said he was surprised that we were here fixing it up because this place was vacant for so long. He said it looks really good though."

"Yeah, it does look *good*. It wasn't easy though. We've worked hard. This place was filthy, the animal droppings, the septic tank, restoring the old stone and woodwork. We're getting there, and when it's done, in just a few more weeks, it'll look great!"

"Yeah, and that's why Christophe is so excited about the masquerade ball that we're throwing!"

"No! Nik! Not again with the party. We can't do that; this isn't our place! We don't *own* it!"

"Come on, Vern, you know that Marie-Claire doesn't care. Besides, it will be good publicity for her new château; plus, publicity for you!"

"What do you mean *publicity*?"

"Well…" Nikki began slyly. "I made a couple phone calls. I talked to Alex from the Traveler's Channel, the guy I met at Robert's office the day that…well, you know, *that* day."

"You called that creepy producer from Robert's television show! Why would you do that?"

"We sort of kept in touch over the past year because I kinda hooked up with him for a while."

"You dated that slime ball!"

Nikki retaliated. "Dated? No! Just fucked him a couple times. I never told you because I figured you'd get pissed…and apparently, I was right."

"I'm not pissed," Veronica scowled. "I couldn't care less who you date…or fuck."

"Well good, because like I said, I called him and told him about how you've been redecorating this castle. And guess what, he's doing a new series for the Traveler's Channel about castles! They have that famous designer, Gigi Jones, hosting it. And, are you ready for this…they are filming here in Europe in a couple weeks which means they can come to the party! Cool, huh?"

"No, not cool! Why do you always have to mess things up for me?"

"I'm not messing anything up! I'm your agent, remember? I'm doing what agents do, that's why you're paying me 15-percent!" She said with a proud snicker.

"Why do you take the things I joke about seriously, but never the things I'm serious about, seriously?"

"Because I take the things that are *best* for you seriously, Vern!"

"But you know my name is Veronica…" she grumbled in an effort to change the subject.

Nikki kept pushing. "Alex told me Gigi and her crew will come and check out the place during the party. If they like it, they might feature your castle in their new series. That could be huge for you!"

"But what if they come and decide that I suck? Think of how embarrassing that will be. And what if Robert finds out?"

"So what if Robert finds out? If you get featured on their series, then dear old Robert can sit back and suck his balls."

"I'm not ready for this! This place isn't finished. It's not perfect!"

"But it will be perfect soon; you're almost done."

"Who the hell are we going to invite? We don't *know* anyone!"

"That's where Christophe comes in. He's a member of the Chamber of Commerce, or whatever they call it in France. He said he'd help us create a super-tight guest list. He knows so many people, influential people; the kind of people who could give you more work. That's what you want, isn't it? To get noticed? To become a bitchin' world-class designer?"

"The Château isn't near being finished! I have to get the hardwood floors refinished, and the marble in the ballroom is chipping..."

"Vern! Knock it off! Listen to me; you need to stop making excuses. You're just afraid. Admit it, you *are* afraid. Afraid you're going to fail, so you don't even want to try. But this is your chance. That batty Marie-Claire lady asked you to renovate this place for a reason. She gave you the opportunity to showcase your talent. You keep saying that this is what you always wanted. You told me yourself this was your chance to get noticed. Now it's here right in front of you, and you wanna wimp out? This is your opportunity to grab your dream by the balls, and damn it, I'm not going to sit here and watch you throw it away. Now I'm planning this party. We're inviting the people from Christophe's guest list, the press, the Traveler's Channel, the stuck-up neighbors, and you are going to smile and be gracious and be all froufrou-fancy just like you've always wanted to be and you are going to *like* it. Got it?"

Veronica gaped at her sister. "What if it isn't good enough? What if I am just an inexperienced American who has no right decorating a French castle like the neighbors said?"

"This place looks great! The colors, the furniture, the freaking toil accents in the bathrooms..."

"But it's *English* toil! The French are going to hate *that*, and I didn't even know the difference before I had it installed!"

"Who cares? If they don't love it, then the hell with them, at least you tried. You gotta try now, okay?"

Veronica nodded her head. "Okay."

"Besides, it's going to be a party. *I* can throw parties, and I'll take care of everything, so all you have to concentrate on is the decorating."

"That's the reason you're doing this; you just want to throw a party?"

"I do love my soirees." Nikki flashed a beaming smile. "And I also like seeing my sister get the recognition she deserves. Okay?"

"Okay," Veronica repeated. She placed the diary on the nightstand as she climbed out of bed. "I guess I better get to work then."

"Are you still reading that thing?" Nikki asked as she eyed the tattered journal.

"Yes, I am. It's fascinating, Nik. This poor woman was bedridden for months while she was pregnant. They even strapped her to the bed." Veronica stood and a wave of vertigo washed over her. She steadied herself by reaching out for Nikki.

"You okay, Vern?"

"Yeah, dizzy. And a weird déjà-vu feeling."

"Well, lay back down and relax," Nikki ordered. "I'll get started on the party planning. I'll have to order invitations, something classy, yet fun. And food, I need to find a caterer, not to mention music — a band — maybe? And I'll pick out costumes; that'll be fun..." Her voice trailed off as she scuttled out of the room.

Veronica braced herself. When her sister threw a party, it was always epic.

Dorothée's Story
Circa 1520 AD — the Dawn of the Reformation

He was ridiculous as a guard; a stable boy wearing oversized chain mail and carrying a clunky battle axe. He hobbled past Dorothée as she lurked in the shadows. When she spoke, he dropped his weapon.

"You! Go into town right now and get some things for André-Benoit's return."

The boy quivered a moment before he uttered, "I am to stand guard...have orders..."

"Haven't we been through this before?" Dorothée growled. "I give the orders — *me!* Your shift has been covered. I instructed the first boy to stay longer. Now, take this list and go."

He slowly took the scrap of parchment. "But it's late," he said quietly. "Where can I possibly get —"

"The merchant on the other side of the river. Wake him if you must, he won't deny my request. Is running a late-night errand too hard for you?"

"No, I mean yes...yes, I can do this." The boy bowed and hastened off to do her bidding.

Once he was out of sight, she clutched the tiny Bible and the key beneath the folds of her flowing nightgown. Quickly, she sprinted to the keep. The other guard was there, poised and ready for his relief to come. As Dorothée entered, she heard him say, "You're always late..."

He turned and saw her standing in the doorway and stopped short.

"You can go," she said. "Since you are so eager."

His expression was similar to the first young guard's. He blinked as he tried to comprehend her words. "I thought you were my relief. I am sorry, my lady, I did not know."

"Obviously," Dorothée said flatly. "Now go. I just saw your replacement; he'll be here any moment. Off with you." The boy nodded and fled.

Once he was gone, she peered through the door slot of Julien-Luc's room. Even now, several weeks after her first frightful experience in this place, she still felt a sense of dread as she looked inside. It was dim with only a thin beam of light filtering through the slit.

Quietly, she slid the key in the lock. It creaked then caught, clicked, and opened the prisoner's door. A rush of warmth engulfed the woman as she took one tentative step over the threshold. This moment would change everything. Once she awoke the figure on the bed, there would be no turning back. Her decision would be absolute. And if André-Benoit ever found out that it was she who freed the prisoner...

She took another careful step, silently, contemplatively. She could still turn and go back...tuck herself into bed and wait for André-Benoit's return tomorrow night. Her life would continue normally, better than normal actually. She was nobility, after all. She commanded respect in the house and among society. She was privileged. Her life was pampered — even luxurious. *Was it worth risking for a criminal?*

A subtle sound behind her made her spin like a top. A frightening image materialized in her mind's eye as she flashed back to her first dreadful experience in the tower room.

Would she see that swarthy animal-like form hunched at her feet again?

While still turning to see what was at her back, primal fear made her feet begin to run. Dorothée stumbled. She didn't have the grace to make the motion fluid and like a marionette cut from strings, she crumbled to the floor. Slightly stunned, she sat there a moment. As her eyes adjusted to the dark room, she saw a swarthy figure loom over her. It grunted softly, as though it was laughing at her.

Chapter 92
Sebastian's Story
325 AD — When Rome Spread its Empire across the Barbaric Territories

The matriarch of Rome was an elderly woman decorated in elaborate jewels, including an exquisite medallion that hung from her crinkled neck. Inlaid with precious stones, it bore the symbol of the labarum and represented her elite Roman status.

Fabius knelt before her as she rested on a throne of pillows in a hastily prepared chamber. On either side stood her entourage; exceptionally trained Roman soldiers, garbed in black, specifically selected to escort her on her journeys.

She spoke with a level, velvety voice. "I received news of your meeting tonight with the native peoples. You intend to negotiate an alliance."

Though she didn't frame her observation as a question, Fabius answered. "Yes, Mother Helena."

"I look forward to attending."

Fabius lifted his bowed head. "Mother Helena, it wouldn't be appropriate for a royal lady to dine with such barbarians. Besides, you're tired from your long journey. Rest and I'll have a fine meal brought to you."

The matriarch studied Fabius and answered flatly. "I'll dine with everyone tonight. I want to see how the negotiations are conducted."

Fabius carefully chose his words. "I can assure you that matters of the state will best be handled by my advisors and me."

"You would deny me, Fabius?" Helena challenged.

"No! Of course not. It seems like such an odd request..."

"I'm here to ensure the peace talks go smoothly. A promise was made many years ago, years before you were even born. This Temple and the worshipers from this land were never to be invaded by Roman forces."

"I've never heard of such an arrangement, and I am here under orders from Constantine, your son."

"Constantine gave you *direct* orders to conquer *this* Temple?"

Fabius slowly answered. "He said that we needed to gain rule over this region. I determined that taking the Temple was an essential tactical..."

"The conquest of this Temple resulted in the murder of fifty priests and priestesses. They were peaceful, and they provided comfort and spiritual guidance to this land. You cut them down and stole their home like they were uncivilized Philistines."

"It had to be done. We ordered them to surrender, but they refused."

"You had no right to even ask them to surrender, Fabius!"

Fabius countered. "*I* was granted governorship of this territory. Constantine knew my plans and —"

She cut him off. "Constantine's insipid tyranny is no excuse. You and he can claim ignorance; whether it be true or not is of no consequence now. The only thing that matters is justice."

"Why does this petty little temple and a few Pagans matter so much to you?"

"I hail from this land. The Temple priests and priestesses you so valiantly massacred were my brothers and sisters. This Temple was once my home," she said.

"But you are a Roman woman, the wife of a Senator, the mother of the Emperor...how could *this* place be your home?"

"I was a member of the Temple Order a long time ago. When I was young, only sixteen, a Roman General came and threatened to pillage our land. I caught his eye, though, and he asked me to leave with him. I agreed and in return made him promise that Rome would forever spare the Temple from invasion. That General was Constantius, Constantine's father. And because you broke that treaty, I'm here to ensure justice is done."

"I didn't know..."

"Obviously. You're going to form an alliance with the Head Commander? That is your plan, correct?"

Fabius nodded. "Yes, we want to join forces to fight a common enemy." The lie tasted like acid on his tongue.

"Then all should be set right," Helena stated.

"Yes, of course Mother Helena. All will be set right," Fabius echoed as he stood. "I must prepare to meet our guests."

Helena nodded, and he rushed out of the room.

Chapter 93

Journal Intime

pparently, the negotiations did not go well. An attack occurred just last night, and the ungrateful villeins launched rocks at the walls with a trebuchet. A canister of Greek fire was also hurled over the gatehouse. It exploded near a hay cart and started quite a blaze. Everyone went running around in a tizzy, and I—well I enjoyed the solitude. No one paid much attention to me and Henri Jr. for the entire night, and I rather liked it that way.

The entrance to the oubliette is still not boarded up. The guards had no time with such treachery about. They were much too busy with more important matters. They did cover it with a curtain, though. With no one around to scold me, I took a moment to inspect it just now. I crept over and pulled back the veil. The grotto around the entrance was shallow, only a few feet deep, and not very high. I had to stoop slightly, so it could not have been more than five feet tall. The actual hole was merely a few feet wide. It seemed relatively benign; considering it was a crypt for centuries' worth of condemned souls.

Looking into the depths revealed nary a secret. It was black like pitch, and I could only see about a cubit down. A subtle fragrance wafted to my nose; that familiar odor was back. A sweet, sour, and musty scent, like decaying leaves mixed with something else. The scent once annoyed my senses, but now I rather fancied it. I had become used to it and inhaled deeply. Ah, yes, that was a divine aroma now, wasn't it?

I held the candle above the hole. It was a weak, flickering flame, and only illuminated a couple more feet. I could see the pit was rather deep, and the sides seemed to widen the further down it went. I couldn't see the bottom, though. Curious, I found a small shard of discarded wood and, holding it in the center of the hole, let it drop. After it fell out of sight, I waited a full three seconds for a gentle "thump!" as it hit the bottom.

It was deeper than I thought, maybe twelve or fifteen feet! I bent over and reached into its depths with the candle. I could just barely see the bottom. Vague shapes, merely grey shadows, revealed themselves slowly, like shy players reluctantly taking a stage. I squinted, forcing my eyes to adjust to the darkness. It took a moment, but slowly I learned to see. Bones from ages gone-by unveiled themselves to me. The oubliette was strewn with a collection of crusty old skeletons — carcasses of sinners and criminals condemned to rot together for eternity.

I don't know how long I hunched there, gazing into the abysmal nadir, and nary do I know why. Such a vile scene is certainly not one I would naturally seek out, but even though I knew the visage was unsettling, I found comfort in it. I felt peaceful and calm knowing the bones below me were once alive like me. They spoke to me with their silent stares; telling me that I would one day join their ranks. We are all destined to turn to dust and decay. Everything dies eventually, and I am no better than them just because I currently breathe and have warm blood flowing in my veins. My life, like theirs, is as brief as my flickering candle flame. It will eventually end, and I, too, will become a lonely, grimy pile of forgotten bones someday.

The souls in the oubliette don't judge me. Those sinners, criminals, madmen, and heathens, they don't look at me with superior stares. Unlike the living I deal with every day, the dead in the oubliette are blasé. They are simply there — understanding, nonjudgmental, and patient. I like them. I like them. Yes.

Henri Jr. whimpered. I rose and tended dutifully to my dear child. He has a stubborn chin that scrunches up when he is fussy, much like his father's. I kissed it and calmed him.

Sadly, I know that he too will also die one day. Though only a week old, he is also on a journey that slowly takes him closer and closer to death with each passing day. The thought of my precious Henri Jr. becoming a dusty stack of bones makes me shudder, and I hugged him to my shoulder, patted his back, and hummed a joyful tune to comfort us both.

We stood in the center of the room, and I slowly moved to and fro. We were sad, lonely dancers. We made our way 'round in a methodical circle. Henri Jr. altogether enjoyed it and fell back asleep easily. It calmed me, too, and I spent hours spiraling around the room.

Josette-Camille

September 9th, 1789

As I sway, I listen. I hear all the secrets spoken in the castle. Not a single conversation is kept from me. From Agathe's quarters, I just heard the most dastardly, treasonous remarks imaginable!

She spoke to the midwife about me. That jealous sister-in-law said I was not a fit mother, and she feared for Henri Jr.'s safety. The midwife agreed with her, calling me "mad" and "dangerous".

Blast them both! Evil demons. How dare they speak of me as such? Vile wretches them both! I stood swaying in just the right spot to hear them as they devised a plan to take Henri Jr. away from me.

Agathe said they would come in the night when I was asleep, and "slip out carefully with the baby so as not to waken the mad-woman. Once Henri Jr. is safe in our hands, we'll lock the door and board it up. She can rot in that tower room until either her senses return, or she goes completely mad. Whichever happens is of no concern to me. I'll take Henri Jr. with me to Paris. He'll be schooled and raised in the most proper fashion."

The thought burns into me like a white-hot smithy's poker and ignites a fury unlike any I have known before.

As I sit here transcribing this treachery, I shake and tremble. I will not allow them to take my child. Under no circumstances will such betrayal befall me, especially not at the hands of my own sister-in-law.

I must tell Henri of their devious ways. Surely, once he sees how Machiavellian his sister is, he will come to my side. My husband will not allow such perfidy. He will throw both those abhorrent women to the revolting peasants behind the castle walls! I will demand to see him at the first light of day. Until then, I dare not fall asleep in case the wicked women chose to steal my child while I slumber.

Josette-Camille

September 10th, 1789

Last night I slept not, and as the late afternoon approaches, I grow weary. Only a servant girl has come into my chamber today, bringing food, the tonic, water, and clean linens for Henri Jr. I asked her several times to send word to my husband to see me at once. She smiled sweetly each time, nodded and curtsied in an appropriate fashion, and said, "Yes, my lady."

I know she is merely a spy for them, waiting for me to fall asleep, so she can alert Agathe. Then as I slumber, they will steal away with Henri Jr.

I am foiling their plan, though, as I refuse to sleep! I will simply stay awake, making it impossible for them to carry out their treachery.

Here comes the servant girl again; this time with the evening meal. She lights the night candle, wishes me pleasant dreams, and scuttles away before I can say nary a word. The food is cold. I notice a peculiar odor to the porridge and decide it is best not to eat. They may have laced it with chamomile or lavender or perhaps a tint of belladonna to make me fall asleep. Best to be safe!

As the night creeps in, I struggle to stay awake. Forcing myself to my feet, I spin slowly in my rhythmic circle. Inaudibly, I sing, "Down deep, deep down, spinning 'round, until the darkness takes ahold…"

Then I hear Agathe again!

I pause and listen. Her voice is muffled and far away, but I am sure it is she. She is speaking low, as though what she offers is of grave importance. I can't altogether make out her words, though. I sway slightly to the left in my circle, seeking the exact spot that will conduct her words to me. Then there is another voice; a deep one, one that is few on words. It is Henri! Their conversation becomes clearer as I pinpoint the precise spot in the room from which to listen.

Agathe tells him, "I fear for your son's wellbeing. Your wife is sick, she can't properly take care of him, and you are too consumed with the revolution. Please, Henri, I am your older sister; I know best. Let me take the child with me back to Paris. Tensions have calmed there. He'll be safe. Trust me, brother."

After a pause that seems to last an eternity, Henri replies, "Very well, Agathe, I approve. In the morning, whether Josette-Camille is asleep or not, we'll remove Henri Jr. You can leave with the boy by noon."

Josette-Camille

303

Chapter 94

Veronica's Story

The huge fans reminded Veronica of the kind that replicated hurricane winds. A disaster movie was once shot outside her office, and she remembered watching from her window as they ravaged Cahuenga Boulevard with a faux tornado.

Now similar fans roiled the castle air. Clark suggested that the keep might be the root of the plumbing problems. Apparently, medieval castles often had ancient toilets complete with septic systems, and this one could possibly be filled with sludge. He planned to air out the keep first, and then drain the archaic plumbing system.

Veronica was eager for him to finish so that she could decorate the tower rooms. She had selected the linens, the furniture was ready, the designs were laid out, and once the stench was gone, she would be able to put it all together.

While she waited for Clark, she spent her time monitoring the finishing touches on other areas of the Château, such as the gold leafing that accented the fireplace mantles and the restoration of the stained glass in the chapel. As she strolled through the library, studying her clipboard, Nikki called out, "Vern! Come here, the party planners are with me in the ballroom, and we need your opinion."

"No, you don't."

Nikki batted her eyelashes and persisted. "Yeah, we do. We can't decide on the appetizers. What do you prefer, the chutney baked Brie, escargot in a creamy garlic sauce, or tapenade-topped toast?"

"I don't care." Veronica continued to walk past the ballroom.

"Vern, I just want to know what you'd like to eat!"

Veronica let her arms drop to her sides, and she spun to face the party planners. Nikki smiled widely. The busy designer relented by stepping over the threshold of the enormous ballroom.

The decorations were lovely. Luxurious linens were draped along the walls and drawn up with huge bows. A stage had been erected on the far side, and cocktail tables were interspersed between the columns that lined either side of the hall.

One of the planners eyed Veronica as she assessed the scene. "The flowers will arrive the morning of. They will be fresh, of course, and will really make this place pop!" He splayed his fingers quickly for emphasis.

"Great," Veronica said flatly.

Nikki held out a menu. "So, what do you think? We could also have stuffed olives or eggplant caviar...you prefer?"

"I don't *prefer*...I don't care. You pick; I'm busy." Her cell phone rang, and Veronica eagerly accepted the interruption. "Hello?"

"Hi." It was Christophe. His voice was velvety.

"Hey, how's it going?" She escaped back to the library.

"I'm fine, but how are you since Saturday night?"

"The cuts on my hands are a little sore; otherwise, I'm fine. Nikki said she had a great time, though!"

"Nikki would have a great time partying on the Titanic. She can make the best of anything."

Veronica considered his insight into her sister. He was absolutely right. Nikki had a knack for making any situation an adventure.

He continued. "I leave Monday on business for two weeks...I just thought I'd call and let you know."

"Oh, well have a nice trip." Veronica immediately regretted the curt reply.

"Yes, okay, thank you. I'll be back for your masquerade ball. I'm looking forward to it..."

"Yeah, Nik is busy planning away. It should be a blast."

"And you must promise to save a dance for me."

"Oh, I don't dance...not really. I've been known to have spasms while standing on the dance floor, but that's about as close to dancing as I get." Veronica snorted at her own joke.

"Then maybe we could have a spasm together?" Christophe offered.

"Sure, you and I can spasm anytime."

Christophe chuckled. "I will see you in two weeks. Take care until then."

"Okay, you, too," Veronica clicked off her phone.

Instantly, she wished she could re-do the conversation. He was leaving; gone for two weeks...*Should she have suggested that they get together before he left?*

Veronica wailed loudly in anguish.

Nikki heard her sister's moan. "You okay out there, Vern?" she called from the ballroom.

"Yes!" Veronica yelled. "I am just freaking fine. Clueless, but fine!"

Father Michel's Story
1348 AD – The Great Peste

𝕴ather Michel's ride went swiftly with the sheriff and his men accompanying him. No one dared confront a troop of well-armed men on horseback. At one point they saw the Flagellants in the distance, gathered around a makeshift altar — a crucifix of twisted, rotting barn beams that were soaked with fresh blood — in an overgrown wheat field. The Layman and his brethren chanted, prayed and sang distorted versions of hymns as their followers strung up another sacrifice.

The riders quickened their pace. The only thing that followed them were a few menacing stares and yowling insults.

"Theirs is not the path to salvation," the sheriff said. "It's a decent into darkness. Why can I see that while others cannot?"

Father Michel didn't answer. Instead he nodded toward the deputies who rode ahead. The men gazed at the revelers in the field with wide eyes.

"They'd never forsake me, Father."

"Some men lead while others gladly follow. It doesn't take much to beguile the masses. Promises of absolution wrapped in the threat of damnation. However a true leader is not feared, but admired. You can be a true leader, Jean-Arthur. That, I have faith in."

As they approached the mountain trail the sheriff reached into his pocket and pulled out a sack of coins. "Here, take this back."

"No, that is your payment for your service…"

"I think you already paid me for that."

"It's money for the boy…"

"I'll find the child and take him in. Plenty of room in my big house without the wife and kids anymore…" His words trailed only a moment before he quipped, "Don't worry, I'm not giving it *all* back. Saved a few coins for my men. They need a little incentive to *admire* me, you know. That's what a *good man* would do, right Father?"

❧❧❖❧❧

Father Michel and Lightning approached the entrance to the catacombs alone. His entourage had left him a few miles back. With a mixture of dread and anticipation brewing in his belly, the priest led the animal inside.

The darkness was a stark contrast to the bright blue day they left behind. Father Michel used a candle to light their way, eyeing the map that Gaston-Elise had drawn for him, being careful to follow it exactly.

Would his friend still be waiting as they had planned? He was to arrive under the cover of the night. Would it be too dangerous now to emerge on the other side in the light of day? He could surely make his way out of the tunnels, to the wine cellar, through the trap door, and out the grape shack, but what about

Lightning? A horse would surely look odd if someone saw it emerge from the tiny building above the wine cellar. Once Father Michel would have prayed that Gaston-Elise was waiting to help him reemerge. Now he could only hope.

He kept his hand cupped in front of a candle, shielding the flame as he and Lightning crept through the twisting caverns. Then he heard something up ahead. Father Michel froze and listened. Lightning also held still; his ears pointed forward, catching the subtle sounds.

Glass crunched under the horses' tentative hooves. Father Michel shined the candle near the ground and saw remnants of the shattered lantern from their first episode in the catacombs.

Footfalls approached from deep in the tunnel.

He considered turning back. He had no desire to face that vile creature again. As he reached for Lightning's reins, a thin beam of light flickered down the corridor. Then a voice...it cracked at first, but then became clear.

"Are you...there, Father? Father Michel...is that you? It's me. Gaston..."

The Priest's shoulders fell as the trepidation festering in his neck dissipated. "Gaston-Elise! Yes! I'm coming, my friend. Thank you so much for waiting. I feared you would not be here upon my return."

Father Michel tugged on Lightning's reins and quickened his pace. The animal resisted slightly, preferring to take its time while navigating the twists and turns.

Gaston-Elise didn't answer, so Father Michel continued. "I didn't mean to be gone so long. Did anything happen? Did anyone notice?"

There was no reply.

Father Michel stopped.

He waited a moment and called out again, "Gaston-Elise! Where are you?"

There was a pause and then an abrupt answer as Gaston-Elise cried, "Run, Father! I'm not alone! It's a trap..."

His cry was cut short with a *thud.*

Father Michel stood frozen in the glare of his solitary candle. He could hear footsteps up ahead, rushing toward him.

The priest stepped back behind the horse, removed his satchel from the saddle, and with all his might, he whacked the buttocks of the beast. Lightning reared up, neighed ferociously, and galloped down the corridor in the direction of the ambush.

Father Michel ducked down a passageway and came to a dead end. He looked at the map...all the passages were dead ends, like branches that ended in rounded half-circles. *Could he turn and go back the way he came? Back out into the mountains?* He considered his options...maybe hiding would be best. There were so many tunnels they would never find him.

He descended down a particularly long passageway that took several zigzagging turns. When he came to the end he hunkered down and crossed himself reflexively. He looked around the alcove. Crypts spanned the walls. Each was little more than a ledge carved out of the rock, with one on top of another, all the way up to the ceiling. Ancient Roman numerals and painted faces marked the tombs.

The priest sat on the ground and thrust his hand into an alcove. He could hear commotion in the distance. Men were shouting and Lightning was braying. Father Michel had hoped the horse would buy him some time as it barreled into the guards.

His desperate fingers dug into the hole, pulling out bits of ancient bone to make room. On the side of the crypt was a faded portrait of a young woman with wide, desperate eyes. They glared at Father Michel as he shoved the satchel into her grave and placed her broken skullcap over top of it. Once again, he quickly surveyed the room, looked at the hand-drawn map, and with a bit of charcoal, hastily drew a symbol where the treasure was now stashed. He shoved the map into his pocket.

Voices echoed in a chorus of caterwauls. Then he heard the patter of footfalls. They were approaching. Father Michel drew in a quick breath and blew the candle into darkness. He sat perfectly still as she shadows enveloped him.

Eerily, with the candle out, there was no sound, no shouting or running. Father Michel suddenly felt alone, as if he were the only one in the catacombs keeping company with the dead. Though he didn't want to get caught, the thought of being alone in the dark terrified him. He contemplated lighting his candle again when he heard men running down the corridor. First they came closer, with the sound growing louder, then it became softer. They ran *past* his hiding spot!

He had outsmarted them — for now. *How long would they search for him? Hours? Days?* The Cardinal would not give up. *Would he post a guard at the entrance to the tunnels?* Father Michel felt a twinge of regret. Maybe he should have retreated to the mountains...then he'd at least be free. He could have gone back to The Velvet Lion and pulled back a pint with the sheriff and his men. Now he wasn't sure if he'd ever get out.

Distant voices called out. Faintly, he could hear someone address him directly. "Father Michel, you can't hide. We know you're here."

Then another sound, something scuffling, snorting, and growling. Father Michel stiffened. An animal approached in the darkness. Claws clicked the stone floor as it rushed forward. It snarled and leapt on top of him. The priest cried out. A wet muzzle burrowed into the priest's neck and gnashing teeth clamped down. Fortunately they chomped his collar and not the tender flesh of his throat.

He thrashed with the beast as a flurry of guards burst into the tiny chamber. One of them whistled as another pulled the Cardinal's hunting dog back by its leash.

"Stop flailing around," one man ordered. "You act like prey, he'll treat you like prey."

The priest went limp. The dog withdrew and the man who whistled rewarded the animal with a scrap of meat. Two others apprehended Father Michel by clasping his arms. The priest did not resist, even though one of them kneed him unnecessarily in the stomach as he rose to his feet.

Father Michel was led through the caverns while doubled in pain. His breath gradually came back as they dragged him through the wine cellar, up the stairs, and into the shed.

Gaston-Elise was there. His head hung low, and he avoided eye contact with his friend. One of the guards spoke. Father Michel recognized him as the commander, Gaston-Elise's superior.

"The Cardinal is seething, Father Michel. You defied him. He wants to deal with you directly."

The priest nodded compliantly. He knew that a single word could provoke another blow to his gut or jab to his face. While holding his head down he nodded at his friend and asked, "What of Gaston-Elise?"

"Your accomplice? He'll be reprimanded, too. And since Gaston reports to me, his punishment will be according to *my* wishes," the commander said.

"He only did what I asked him to do. Please, don't blame him."

"Rest your tongue. You'll need it to beg for mercy from the Cardinal."

As they began to walk Father Michel held his hand to his mouth and coughed loudly. He made a display of it, wheezing up phlegm from the back of his throat. The guards surrounding him gave him a wide girth.

"Are you okay?" Gaston-Elise asked.

"Fine," he answered. "Just giving us a little privacy. This might be our only chance to talk." He gestured at the guards who now walked a good distance from them.

"Are you sure you're not sick? The peste…"

"Once it touches you, it never touches you again, remember? I'm okay."

"You're a smart man. I knew you'd make it back. With the Lord on your side I never doubted for a moment. I always had faith in you, Father."

The priest smiled sadly. "I'm glad someone still has faith."

"When you didn't come for your dinner, the cook went to your room and noticed you gone. They asked me if I knew where you were. I tried to protect you! I said you were merely in the caves, on a sojourn, praying for guidance, and that you'd be back soon. I didn't think they'd pay you much mind, but the Cardinal was furious. He wanted to have words with you. They forced me to take them there and we searched for you. When we didn't find you they made me wait with them. I had no choice. I'm sorry, please forgive…"

"Enough, Gaston, it's okay. My punishment and yours will merely be a small tribulation for us to endure. I will likely serve a short sentence in one of the tower rooms, you'll be confined to your quarters for a spell. Once it is over, I have…"

"Stop with the whispers!" A guard grunted while poking the priest in the back with the tip of his rapier.

Both men fell silent and walked with their heads down. They were nearing the castle and Father Michel knew his time was short. He fingered the map in his pocket.

As softly as possible, he whispered, "Take this, Gaston. It leads to something *they* must never find."

The one armed man didn't take notice.

"The Cardinal will have me searched. But you can keep it safe until my sentence is over."

The big man kept pace silently. Then he turned his head, just slightly, and cast a crooked grin at the holy man. "Your secret is forever safe in my hand."

The map passed between them as they were led to face their judgments.

Chapter 96

Sebastian's Story

As Fabius marched down the corridor, Cicero fell into step beside him and spoke. "The tribesmen are here, gathered in the courtyard."

Fabius grunted. "You ready?"

Cicero thumbed the vial. "Yeah."

"You better be, Cicero. You've tested me for the last time."

Cicero stammered, "Believe me, I acted in your best interest. Sebastian was..."

Fabius snapped around and faced his second in command. Cicero stumbled to a stop as the governor bellowed, "If you want to act in my best interest, then you'll obey my orders to the letter. Do not question me; do not second-guess me. I don't want you to wipe your ass without my permission!"

"Yes, sir, of course! You have my sworn allegiance."

"You must give that poison to that damn Head Commander. And whatever you do, don't let Helena or her guards know about it."

"Why is she *here*? Isn't she usually traipsing around the Holy Land looking for cross shards and spear heads?"

"She says she *hails* from this land," Fabius answered. "This temple was once her home, and she intends to oversee our 'negotiations' to ensure all goes smoothly. I insisted she not attend, but she refuses to stay in her quarters."

"She thinks the negotiations are genuine? What if she figures out the truth?"

Fabius paused at the entryway and quietly ordered, "If she interferes with our plan, then she and her guards die."

"*Die?* She is the mother of Constantine!"

"She's a Pagan whore..." Fabius grumbled.

Cicero stood stunned.

"You questioning me?" the governor snarled.

The centurion quickly shook his head. "No, I follow your orders to the letter!"

Fabius studied his second in command a moment then stepped past him into the courtyard.

Cicero obediently followed to see thirty barbarians mulling about anxiously. They were a stark contrast to the blossoming trees, flowering ivy, and elegant statues. Their garments were raggedy, flea-infested animal skins, and their frizzy, braided hair frayed in sprays of tangles and knots. Most bore mangled battle scars, and each had a streak of indigo brushed across his forehead.

Fabius clapped his hands. "Welcome, tribe from the north! I'm Fabius, governor of this region, representative of Rome. You have no need for your weapons here; we are friends!" He gestured, and two Roman soldiers assisted the wild men by cautiously disarming them of battle-axes, spears, and knives. Fabius continued. "Sit, recline, relax; our feast is served!"

The barbarians peered at each other. Two or three of them bowed slightly to their host and then gruffly snagged pillows and sat at the dinner table. It was lavishly set with enormous plates spilling over with fruit, bread, pies, and meat. Servants poured ale and wine as one of the barbarians spoke.

"Why'd you bring us here, Fabius?"

Fabius laughed at the question. "I like your straightforwardness! You, men of the Northern Tribe, were summoned, so we can discuss a peaceful alliance. Our vast army and you share the same enemies, so it stands to reason that we can benefit from working together to destroy those who oppose us." Fabius glanced sideways and watched as Helena and her entourage entered the room.

"Who is she?" a barbarian asked.

Before Fabius could introduce Helena, she spoke. "I'm the Matron of Rome, Helena. I was part of the Temple order many years ago. This is my home. I'm here to oversee the negotiations — an ambassador, if you will — for both sides, to ensure peace."

"You're here to make sure we aren't raped and brainwashed by Rome like you were?" one of the tribesmen retorted.

The stabbing remark didn't sway her. "Yes, I am."

Fabius broke in. "That is not Rome's intention at all! We're suggesting joining forces to combat a common enemy."

Another wild man spoke; his voice a barely audible growl. "Yeah, and that means joining Roman tyranny."

Fabius shirked off the scathing defiance with, "We're not asking you to acclimate. Instead, I propose a peaceful alliance so that we may work together. Your borders are constantly being infiltrated by Germanic tribes, and we can help defend you."

Still, another barbarian asked, "And what do you want from us?"

Fabius felt confident. "Nothing more than an alliance. Together we are formidable."

From the far end of the long table a one-eyed, exceptionally hairy tribesman inquired, "You specifically asked the Head Commander to be here...why?"

Fabius didn't miss a beat. "Your leader and I must be in agreement. Who among you is he?"

The tribesmen broke into laughter.

One of them pulled back with a long slurp of ale, belched loudly, and snorted back the bile in his throat before mocking, "Which one of us is the Head Commander, you ask? Ha! We're *all* the Head Commander!"

The governor remained jovial. "Your inhibitions are understandable. Perhaps after we feast your leader will be ready to reveal himself. Until then, you *all* will be treated with the respect and honor of the Head Commander. Raise your glasses now and let us drink to the future!"

The tribesmen toasted with their host, and a few of them even chuckled. A ruckus ensued as the wild men tore into the meal. The Romans sat silent. A few of them managed to say their prayers over the feast while the northerners gnarred the food.

One of the wild men snatched an entire turkey and flopped it on his plate. As he ripped the bird's leg off, he seethed. "You've pillaged the lands to the east and the west, enslaved the able bodied, killed the weak, and raped the women. You expand over our land like a disease. Why should the Head Commander trust you?"

"Because if you don't, you will fall to the Germanic tribes, and we will watch it happen," Fabius stated flatly. "So, you can gain an ally, or an apathetic neighbor. Which do you choose?"

The barbarian slammed the turkey leg on the table and proclaimed, "Don't threaten me with your Roman rhetoric. *I* am the Head Commander!"

Fabius grinned genuinely. "Then let's discuss how we can work together."

Cicero took his cue and stealthily reached over the Head Commander's drink and pretended to grab at a plate of bread. Instead, he emptied the vial into the man's wine. Pleased with the ease of the task, he reclined and nodded at Fabius.

The Head Commander snickered. "I'm *not* the Head Commander, you fool! He will not reveal himself so easily."

Cicero cursed under his breath. All the poison was in a random boor's cup. He watched the wild man quaff down his drink.

Fabius glared at his second in command.

Cicero leapt to his feet and dashed into the kitchen. A few servants busy carving a stag eyed him warily. He grabbed one by throat. "Tell me where that monk is," he ordered, "Baldebert, where is he?"

The servant gargled. "I don't know!"

Another meekly offered, "In the keep, I think."

With determination, Cicero scrambled into the foyer, through the parlor, down the corridor, and to the keep.

It was quiet. Everyone was in the courtyard.

"Baldebert!" He broke the silence. "Where are you?"

Peeking inside the tower room, he saw the body of the Cloaked Man still lying on the floor. He studied the desk as he entered. *There must be a container of poison here; surely Sebastian did not mix up only one little batch.* He turned over bowls and flasks, looking for more elixir.

There was a sound behind him. Cicero turned to see Baldebert poised in the doorway. The plump man starred dully at his fallen master.

"You!" Cicero called out. "You were his manservant, so you know where he kept his concoctions. He made this poison." Cicero held up the empty vial. "Where can I find more?"

Baldebert turned his head to the centurion. "I don't know. He mixed it in secret during the night. What happened to him?"

Cicero causally scanned the body. "He's dead...from his own poison. But now I need more for the Head Commander. He is here now...with the Northern Tribe..."

Baldebert eyed Cicero inquisitively. "You speak of the Head Commander...you say he is *here*?"

"Yes, you stupid clodpate! The tribe from the north is gathered in the courtyard for the peace talks."

"You intend to murder the Head Commander?" Baldebert asked.

"Yes, that is the plan. Don't you know anything?"

"No. Sebastian ordered me to stay in the upper tower room. I've been sequestered for days. Tell me, please, what is going on?"

"I don't have time to explain it to a dim monk. Just do as I say."

"I'm not a monk; I am a priest of the sacred Temple Order —"

Cicero cut him off. "I don't care if you are Jesus Christ of Nazareth. I need you to help me find the poison. Can you do that?"

"Yes, that would be easy," the Druid said as he lifted a small mixing bowl from Sebastian's table. It had a grinding stick, still moist with a syrupy brown liquid.

"That's it! And there's just enough..." Cicero stirred a goblet of wine with the tainted stick.

"You are going to serve that to the Head Commander? What if he doesn't drink it?" Baldebert inquired with a smirk he was barely able to contain.

"Don't you worry about that. He'll drink it. Those barbarians feast like hogs, and he won't turn away a fine glass of wine. I just have to make sure I serve it to the right one. You know these people; you'll help me."

"Help you how?"

"The Head Commander is cowardly and will not expose himself. Do you know him?"

"I..." Baldebert began. He was cut short by a moan from the other side of the room.

Cicero and the Druid both turned to see the Cloaked Man lift himself off the floor. Coins fell from his eyes with a tinny "ping-ping". Sebastian locked his gaze on Cicero.

Chapter 97

Veronica's Story

A familiar voice greeted Veronica as she clicked on her cell phone.

"Bonjour, Mademoiselle Veronica!"

"Marie-Claire! How are you?"

"Magnifique. The castle is coming along nicely, oui?"

"Yes, everything is going great. Still having some problems with the septic system, but the plumber is working on it. Everything should be finished right on time."

"We are proud of you, Veronica."

"Thank you! Who do you mean by 'we'?"

"Oh, everyone of course!"

Veronica scrunched her nose. "Of course..." she replied slowly and then continued. "Who is —"

Marie-Claire interrupted. "I have to go now. We'll talk again soon."

"Oh wait. I have something to ask you..." Veronica cringed as she thought about the party that her sister was feverishly planning. "We were thinking of having a little soiree after the Château is done. A party, something to showcase the new Château, and we might even have it filmed for an American television show."

"Well, you should! Feel free to show off your work any way that you see fit. You deserve it."

Veronica felt a giddy bubble in her belly. "Really? Great, thank you...will you be able to attend?"

"No, I am afraid not. We'll be there in spirit, though."

A twinge of disappointment fell over Veronica. "Oh, that's too bad."

"We will meet soon enough; don't worry about that. For now, enjoy yourself and the beauty you've created."

"I have a few bills and expenses that we should probably go over..."

"No need, my dear, I am sure everything is in order. There is enough money in the account, oui?"

"Oh, plenty..."

"Then everything is fine. I must go now. Au revoir!"

"Good-bye!" Veronica said hastily as another voice called from outside her bedroom door.

"Miss Veronica? Come quick!" It was the plumber.

She poked her head out of the Queen's Chamber and called, "Clark? Where are you?"

"In the keep!" he replied. His voice echoed down the corridor and could have come from anywhere.

She followed the sound to the tower room. He stood there with a variety of tools and pipes strewn across the floor. In his arms was a dark, dusty blanket, and he held it out to her like an offering. "I found this. I thought you'd want to see."

Veronica carefully approached him. "What is it?"

He grinned sheepishly and nodded at it eagerly. "Have a look-see!"

"It looks like a ball of greasy, old blankets," Veronica spoke slowly as she backed away.

"It's a dress! I found it stashed in a box in the corner. It looks very old."

"It looks very dirty," Veronica remarked.

"Dusty, yes, but otherwise it is in remarkably good shape. I think it might be authentic."

He held the shoulders of the gown with the tips of his fingers and let it sprawl out. Veronica could see that it was made of red velvet. The bodice was exquisite with intricate lace and beads. He rustled it to shake the dust and the fullness of the magnificent dress billowed before her.

"It does look vintage. Too bad it's infested with spiders and moths."

Clark shook the dress again and looked down. "I don't see any moth holes. The box was cedar, and it kept pretty well. Here, take it."

"Naw," Veronica drawled. "I don't wanna touch it."

"It would look beautiful if it were cleaned up. I bet it would fit you!"

"That would *not* fit me," Veronica sneered. "It must be a size six, and I'm a..." she let her voice trail off.

"It doesn't have a label. Looks like it was hand-made. You can tell by the stitching...see the cross hatching; this dress is a work of art!"

"Do you have some weird *thing* for women's clothes? Maybe *you* should wear it, Clark," she said dryly.

Clark chuckled without sensing Veronica's sarcasm. "No, I don't wear ladies clothing. It would have been beautiful on you. I just thought you'd like to see it."

"Well, thanks, but it would be nice if you thought about the plumbing a little bit more."

"I'll throw it away." He tossed the dress to the floor.

"So, *how* is the plumbing coming? I have a ton of work to do in here, and I can't get anything done until you're finished."

"I am working as fast as I can. There's a leak, and I can't install the new septic tank until I find it..." Clark began.

Veronica didn't let him finish. "You had over a month to figure out where the problem is! What's taking so long?"

"I'm trying to set up a very old system of pipes. This isn't a regular house. It's much more complicated than most of the jobs I do."

"Then maybe you aren't the right man for the job. I could find someone with more experience who could get this done!"

Clark glanced at the tools that were scattered around the room. "I can do it. I'm sorry that it's taking so long. I had to get rid of that awful stink and set up the upstairs bathtub and the shower..."

Veronica huffed, "I know, I know. Just get it finished. Okay, Clark?"

He kicked at a PVC pipe on the floor and nodded his head. "You'll be incredibly pleased when I'm finished. I promise. I just have to find the old sewer lines," he waved at the grotto in the wall, "probably in this alcove here. That hole might have been a latrine a few hundred years ago."

Veronica looked at the grotto. "I thought that was a fireplace?"

"No, see, there isn't a chimney."

"Damn!" Veronica cursed. "I had a mantle and everything picked out for this room."

"You can't build a fire in there. Sorry to disappoint you."

"Well, I'm getting used to you disappointing me," Veronica spat.

She froze.

So did Clark.

Wiping his grimy palms on his overalls, he stammered, "I'm sorry..."

Veronica interrupted, "No, Clark, I'm sorry. I didn't mean that. I'm so stressed out with this stupid Traveler's Channel thing and the party and...other things. Just keep up the good work, okay?"

"Yes, Miss Veronica, I will. You'll feel better once it's all over with; just wait and see."

Veronica turned to leave and then stopped by the crumpled dress. She gingerly picked it up. "It is a pretty dress. Do you really think I could pull it off?"

Clark sheepishly grinned with half his mouth and nodded.

"Maybe I *will* take this to the cleaners and see what they can do with it," Veronica said before she left the room. "Thank you, Clark."

Chapter 98

The Children's Story

𝕿he Bishop prayed with the children as they bobbed along the pothole-infested road. The holy man lifted his hands as though he was speaking directly to God, then stroked Isabelle's short hair and said, "The Lord is watching over us."

She felt bile churn in her throat and suddenly wanted to be back on Stinker with Louis, galloping across the fields.

The Bishop sensed her apprehension. "We're almost there."

Isabelle wondered exactly where *there* was. Her sense of direction and time was distorted. *Had they ridden east or west? Were they in town or traveling away from it?*

The procession stopped abruptly, and she heard a man bellowing. "The Bishop has arrived; make his presence known to the lord of the house!"

The Bishop cupped Isabelle's face. "We have arrived! We will provide you with food and even baths! And we'll see about helping your parents."

There was a lilt in his voice as he spoke, and Isabelle felt uneasy again. She pulled back the curtain, and for a moment, didn't recognize the scene outside.

Flags decorated a stone façade and were draped down long, double doors. An archway covered the entry, and it was decorated with flowers and fauna. A flurry of movement was happening everywhere as horsemen dismounted their animals and valets rushed to and fro.

Isabelle swallowed, and it felt as though an icy rock fell into her gut. "No! We can't be *here!*"

She turned to the Bishop with terror oozing from her soul. He cocked his head almost playfully.

"Don't fret, child, everything will be okay..."

"You don't understand!" she spoke quickly. Time was precious as the carriage doors would soon be opened to reveal them. "This is *where* we are running *from.* Our Uncle Pierre has been chasing us! We had to escape because I heard him say that he was going to kill us."

She realized that her story was rambling and disjointed. She needed to make it simple so that the holy man in front of her would understand. "We have to leave now. We can't be here! He'll have us killed!"

"That is ridiculous. You are with me and everything will be okay. I'll have words with Lord Pierre to see what this is all about. Don't worry; Lord Pierre takes his orders from *me.*"

Louis was now wide awake and silent tears streamed down his round, red cheeks. Isabelle squeezed his hand reassuringly. Though she knew the Bishop indeed had power over her uncle and would be able to protect them, uneasiness still tugged at her heart. The carriage door swung open.

Her Uncle Pierre stood before her with his head slightly bowed to greet his regal guests. A large, welcoming grin turned sullen as he slowly recognized his niece and nephew, seated in the carriage, cowering alongside the Bishop.

Chapter 99

Father Michel's Story

There was a crawl space at the base of the castle wall where the Cardinal's hunting dog had dug its way through. The animal frequently took advantage of the passage to the outside world, and scurried back and forth between the confines of the walls and freedom. Gaston-Elise had noticed the animal come and go many times.

Now the sequestered man watched as the dog poked its head through the crevice. Something dangled in its mouth. Something that flapped and waved as the proud animal trotted across the expanse of grass. *Another disgusting offering*, Gaston-Elise thought. He hated that dog.

The mongrel snapped its head back and forth. The thing in its mouth, obviously dead, flopped like a rag doll.

He watched the scene from the tiny window of his quarters. His punishment for his involvement with Father Michel's escape was confinement for three weeks. Plus, he had been demoted one full rank, losing his entire pension and a good portion of his pay.

Gaston-Elise unfolded the parchment that Father Michel entrusted to him. It was merely the map that he had previously sketched for the priest, with an addition. One little mark was scratched on it with charcoal. Obviously it indicated that something was there, hidden deep in the labyrinth.

Gaston-Elise used ink and quill to draw over the smeared charcoal. He thumbed the necklace that Father Michel had given him and drew the same labarum symbol on the map. He tapped the quill in the well and near the top of the paper wrote in Latin: "Cave of the Dead".

Looking back out the window, he watched the dog drop the thing on the ground. It took two steps backward, lowered its head, and barked. *That is odd behavior*, Gaston-Elise thought. His curiosity was piqued, and he wished that he could stroll over and have a look. However, there was likely a nearby guard instructed to keep an eye on the quarters of Gaston-Elise. Not worth the risk.

Usually, the dog took its offerings to the back door of the kitchen, as if it intended to contribute food for the evening meal. It would haul in squirrels, rabbits, an occasional bird, or unfortunate cat. The cook would usually come across the carcass, jump and swear at the unexpected corpse, and then brush it into a burlap sack and bury it behind the apple trees.

On some level, the dog thought it was doing the right thing by catching small vermin, chewing off their heads, and leaving them to be added to the nightly stew. The animal suddenly seemed weary of its latest kill, though. Gaston-Elise could see the dark form lying motionless in the grass. The dog continued to bark as it lifted its front paw in a hunting stance and howled at the dead thing.

A thin voice called for the animal. Gaston-Elise shifted his attention and saw the cook at the back door, waving a ham bone. The dog bounded off, forgetting about the corpse in the grass, eager to retrieve its treat.

The cook threw the bone into the air. The dog gleefully retrieved it then jumped up on the man, gratefully licking his face as if to say, "Thank you for the treat!"

Gaston-Elise grimaced. If the cook had only seen where that dog's mouth had just been...

❧❧ ❖ ❧❧

On the third day of his confinement, Gaston-Elise heard the dinner bell ring, but he knew it wasn't calling him. He wasn't allowed meals with everyone else. He had been granted a meager, weekly supply of hard boiled eggs, dried meat, and a bag of potatoes, most of which were already sprouting eyes. Tonight, he would slice one potato, put it in a pot of water above the fire, and add just two or three small bits of meat for flavor. That would be his supper. Tomorrow, a peeled egg and one potato, cut into slivers, and fried in a black skillet would serve as both breakfast and lunch.

As he huddled near his tiny hearth, a savory, spicy aroma wafted in from outside. He followed the scent to his window where he saw the setting sun cast a fiery glow on the landscape. He noticed the dead offering the hunting dog had abandoned. It was still on the lawn, where the animal had abandoned it a few days earlier. The corpse was surrounded by frays of grass that were illuminated by the sun, making it look like it was engulfed by flames.

A few feet away stood the cook, holding the kitchen door open, and leaning out. Deep, belly-twisting coughs rippled through his body several times before he doubled over and heaved. This was odd; Gaston-Elise knew the cook well. He was young and hearty and didn't take ill easily.

Gaston-Elise hoped his comrade merely had eaten a bad egg and that his sickness would soon pass. He whispered a prayer on the man's behalf. With everyone living in such close quarters, it would be devastating if a contagion broke out. And if that contagion was the peste...Gaston-Elise dismissed the thought. That was impossible. They were immune from the infliction behind the castle walls. God's grace surely protected them. After all, the Cardinal said they would be spared. As a direct conduit of the almighty Pope, surely he was right.

❧❧ ❖ ❧❧

Under "quarantine" said the Cardinal. It was a new term used to describe a period of time that ships had to wait upon coming into the harbor if they were suspected of carrying the pestilence. The Spanish coined the term. They found that by making the ships wait a period of thirty days, they could keep the plague from spreading into the seaport cities.

Father Michel would spend his quarantine in the oubliette. The Cardinal decided that would be the safest way to contain him if indeed he did contract the deadly illness. He thought about telling his Grace that he had already been sick and recovered. Once touched by the peste, you won't be touched again — everyone knew that. But then the Cardinal would ask when and how he was

319

infected. If he told him it was from the Jewish family then he'd surely be accused of using sorcery. No, best to endure the punishment he was given. It was much milder than what could come.

Thirty days. That was his sentence. He'd be given food and water once a day, thrown down to him as if he were an animal in a cage. After his quarantine he would be brought back up and allowed to go on as normal. All would be forgiven and eventually forgotten.

They fashioned a rope harness around his chest and slowly dropped him into the depths until he reached bottom. It was strewn with the dry bones of his predecessors.

It was deep. Father Michel estimated that he must be at least fifteen feet below the surface. Though the oubliette was long and narrow, it was wide enough to foil any attempts to climb back up.

They gave him two blankets, three candles, a pot for defecation, and a Bible. He cleared an area on the floor and made a "nest" with one of the blankets. The other smelled like donkey manure, but he didn't care, he covered himself with it to keep warm in the chilly pit. The pot he shoved in a far corner along with the Bible, which he used for wiping. The candles he never lit. He preferred not to see the company he kept.

He spent much of his time those first few days lying face up and gazing at the small opening above. In a way, he felt relief. His journey was behind him, and he had accepted his punishment. This was the last test he would have to endure. He had solace knowing that the old Jew's Bible was stashed away, along with a handsome treasure. It was safe.

He would be able to return to it in thirty mere days. He decided he would take Gaston with him. They would escape the Cardinal's castle with the small fortune. Gaston could buy his estate back. Perhaps they could live there together...and he'd ask Gaston if he could plant lavender in the garden.

On the fourth day he heard muffled chanting and singing. *It must be Sunday morning. Amazing how the sound traveled all the way from the chapel!* It was as if the sermon was taking place right above him. He listened to the fluctuation in the Cardinal's voice and imagined everyone gathered there; kneeling, praying, eating, and drinking the body and blood of Christ.

Father Michel chewed on a bit of stale bread. He listened as the Cardinal preached of eternal damnation from an angry God, as the depths of the oubliette cradled him like a comforting new friend.

Chapter 100

Journal Intime

This will be my last journal entry. They will come to take Henri Jr. today. But I have decided not to let them.

I savor my last bit of tonic and revel in the warm, green waves that wash over me. I think of the glorious dreams I once had and despair that I will never see them realized. I will never hold my son outside in the bright sunlight after all. We will never lounge in the garden and toss the pretty boules across the silky grass.

Agathe the witch has stolen my dreams.

But I will not be undone. In retaliation, I will steal hers.

If I can't live the dream I wish for my sweet child, then no one can. If Henri, my own husband, would betray me, then who could fault me for exacting revenge? Indeed, my jury — my predecessors — those who dwell in the oubliette don't fault my judgment. They support me. They are my saving grace, and for them, I am most thankful.

A gentle breeze whispers up from the oubliette; my predecessors beckoning me to join their ranks.

"Soon," I murmur back to them. "It won't be long now."

I know I have made the right choice. Indeed, it is the sanest decision considering my circumstances. You would do this, too, wouldn't you?

I hear them now, coming down the hall to my chamber, lumbering footfalls, belonging to Henri, and quick, snappy steps, those of the culpable Agathe.

Behind them, the marching of two guards; likely ordered to hold me down while they steal my boy. Do the guards intend to tie me up again? Would they grope my noble body while my reprehensible husband turns the other way? Would they snicker as I am left here alone — weeping and bawling — without my beloved child?

I refuse to give them the satisfaction.

Henri is knocking at the door. He says, "Josette-Camille, darling are you awake? I come with great news!" His tone is light, almost happy, but I can tell he is forcing it so. There is an ever-so-slight tremor in his tone that he can't hide.

I decide not to answer. Let them quandary the silence.

Another tap.

This time it is Agathe. The sound of her nasally voice rattles me like a physical assault. "Dear sister, please put on your dressing gown. We are going to take you and Henri Jr. outside. The danger has passed, and you can come out of that dreadful chamber now. It is a beautiful autumn day with the leaves turning brilliant shades of red and orange!"

She lies. Like a snake in an abandoned garden, she tells a tale of utter deceit.

I can't hold my tongue any longer. I lash out, "Don't feed me your mendacities, Agathe! I know of your duplicity."

"What could you possibly mean by that?" she asks.

The door rattles. I can hear them unlock it. Henri Jr. whimpers as if sensing the tension in the room. He is bundled in his bassinet right beside me. I cup his little face and hum soothingly. Bright, curious eyes lock onto mine. With a sudden burst of inexplicable joy like only babies possess, he waves his tiny fists in short, spastic jerks as a glint of a smile hovers on his chubby lips.

The door pushes open, but it stops short, hitting the bed which now blocks it. I smartly moved it there during the night.

Henri asks, "Wife, what is this? Come now, help us move the bed, so we can get you both out of there."

Flatly, I say, "No, we're not leaving, Henri."

"What do you mean?" he asks.

I know I don't have much time now. The guards are pushing against the door, slowly sliding the weighty bed across the floor. It scrapes and screeches with a deafening sound, causing Henri Jr. to cry out again.

I soothe my son. "Fret not little one. All will be right in no time."

He purses his lips together, scrunches his chin, and blows bubbles at me.

I don't want to turn away from my adorable child, but the hammering on the door makes me look up. Henri is forcing his shoulder through, pushing with all his might. He is yelling to his men, ordering them to help. I can see their hands reaching into the room. To me he asks, "Why do you block the door, darling?"

"Because you intend to steal away with Henri Jr.," I answer. "Agathe is an evil witch, bent on taking my son. I hear your secrets at night. Don't deny what you say when you think no one can hear — because I do hear! I hear all and know all. Don't try to hide your confidences from me!"

Agathe calls out, "Nothing could be further from the truth, dear! All this time we have been doing what was best for you and the child. You have gone through so much. New mothers are often sad and given to nervous fits after giving birth. It will pass in time. Now just let us in, so we can tend to you and Henri Jr.!"

The door "thuds" as the men plow into it, trying to shove it open. I was clever when I pushed the bed in front of the door. I positioned the feet to lodge in the crevices on the cobblestone floor, making it difficult to slide it backwards.

Anger now fills Henri's voice. "You are having fits of fancy again, 'tis all. There is no way you could hear conversations from your room. You are much too far away. Dreams perhaps, or delusional notions brought on from being a new mother must be filling your head. Now, please, let us in so we can help you."

One more shove and the door is almost open. My time here is done.

To those who read this journal, I implore you, believe my story. Don't let naysayers tell you otherwise. I am guilty of no artifice. You understand, don't you, that I am protecting my child? I am *saving* both of us?

Before they break through the door, I grab Henri Jr. He giggles and swats at my forlorn face with a plump fist. I kiss his brow and then together we jump into the oubliette. Joining our predecessors to lie in their bed. We'll join their ranks as memories after the beast is fed.

Au revoir!

Josette-Camille

322

Chapter 101

Veronica's Story

Her shrill cry echoed through the castle walls. Veronica sat bolt upright on the velvet chaise in the parlor. Her bottom lip quivered, and she scanned her surroundings with wide, wild eyes.

She surprised herself with the sudden outburst. The journal was clasped in her trembling hand, and she stared at it with reproach and disdain.

"How could you kill yourself and your child like that?" she whispered to a long-dead Josette-Camille.

Veronica ran toward the foyer, calling for her sister. "Nik? Where are you?"

Nikki was upstairs painting trim on the wainscoting in the hallway when she heard her name. She could tell by the quiver in her sister's voice that something wasn't right. She scrambled down the stairs, and the two met at the bottom. "What happened? Vern, you okay?"

"She killed herself and the baby! He was just a newborn. She flung herself down some kind of hole!"

"Who? Where?" Nikki asked.

Veronica's loose ponytail allowed her hair to fall into her wild, wet eyes. "Josette-Camille, the woman who wrote the journal. She was kept prisoner in a room during her pregnancy, and she went crazy. She flung herself and her little baby into a pit!"

Veronica held out the book as if it suddenly had turned into something hot. Nikki gently took the tattered diary. "Okay, relax. It happened a long time ago. No need to get all hysterical about it *now*, right? Take it easy, and just tell me what happened from the beginning, okay?"

"I read the journal a little bit every night. It started with a siege on the castle she was living in."

"Was it *this* castle?" Nikki asked.

"I think so, but I can't be sure. I only remember bits and pieces of it. It's weird. It's like the memory is right there, but when I try to focus on it, it kinda slips away from me."

"Just tell me what you *do* remember."

"Something about her being tied down, like she was strapped to the bed...I remember being strapped to the bed...I mean *she* was strapped to the bed." Veronica squinted as if attempting to see the image dancing in her mind's eye. "She gave birth while tied down. Yeah, I remember that. It was a hard labor, and she was alone when it happened. Her husband...that's right! I remember her husband. He was the dude in charge, and he had locked her up during the pregnancy..."

"Is that it?" Nikki asked as Veronica trailed off.

"No, in the end they were coming for the baby. She wanted to protect him. She was out of her mind and paranoid of her husband and of a woman — that's right, there was a woman who was trying to steal her baby — and I think that's why she killed herself and the child. It's all right there; just read it." Veronica pointed to the book as if it were guilty of a heinous crime.

Nikki scanned the pages while nodding. "Let's see what we got here, okay? French can be tricky to translate, especially an older dialect that was handwritten like this, maybe you weren't getting the full story."

Veronica suddenly felt small, like a child. She collapsed onto one of the lower stairs, pressed her palms into her eyes, and waited for Nikki to translate the diary.

Nikki sat, too, one step above her sister, and flipped through the pages intently. After several moments, she finally said, "I can't find the part about killing herself and the baby. Where is it?" She held out the pages for Veronica to see.

"At the very end. The last page."

"But it doesn't say anything like that. As a matter of fact, it doesn't say much of anything at all. There's only a few entries and some poems — badly written poems at that. I don't see anything here about being locked in a room or giving birth alone or a woman wanting to take her baby."

Veronica looked at her sister sideways and caught a quizzical expression on her face. "Of course it's there. I read it. I translated the entire thing."

"Well, I don't see it. She just talks about wanting to play ball with her child in the garden and being visited by someone named Aunt Agathe. Is that the woman who tried to take her baby?"

"Yes!" Veronica gratefully recognized the name. "That's the one. She was her sister-in-law! It's coming back to me now."

"But it just says she came to visit. She brought a Christening gown..." Nikki trailed her finger across the ornately written script as she carefully cited the text. "It talks about the French Revolution, the midwife making her stay in bed, something about her husband giving her medicine — a tonic — to calm her down, but that's it. It ends after four entries."

"I remember the tonic, too. It's coming back to me. It was green, and they gave it to her every night and, and...damn, I can't remember. I can get flashes, but that's all. But it has to be there. I read it!" Veronica snatched the journal like a defiant child reclaiming a favorite toy. "The last entry..." She scoured the book and flipped the pages several times, from the beginning to end. "I don't see it now."

Nikki spied over Veronica's shoulder as she thumbed the pages. Together they studied it, until finally Nikki spoke. "Honey, there's nothing there."

"I saw it. I read it! I've been reading that book since we found it. There were more than just a couple pages. It was a *whole* diary."

"You said you were lying on the chaise in the parlor? You prolly fell asleep. You dreamt about her; that's all. That's why you don't really remember it. It was a dream, and now the memory is fading."

Veronica grew more defiant. "I didn't *dream* it! It was real. I mean, it was like I was there, and I could see everything happening. It was more real than any book I've ever read."

Nikki forced her voice to sound calm, but it cracked as she carefully explained. "That's a *dream*, Vern. That's how dreams are. They feel real, and you get wrapped up in the emotions, but it isn't real. Just relax. It was very bad dream — a nightmare by the sounds of it — but it didn't really happen."

"I don't *have* dreams, though. I told you that." Veronica let the journal fall onto the hard marble floor and glared straight ahead with defiance.

"Well, that proves it then. It *was* a dream. Since you don't have dreams a lot, you don't even know how to recognize one! Don't worry, this just goes to prove you're normal after all." Nikki wisecracked, trying to ease the tension, but Veronica insisted, "Gawd, you don't understand! It was real. This woman was going mad, and I was there watching her. I was in her *mind*, and I knew what she was going to do. I knew she was losing it. I couldn't stop her. All I could do was watch like a bystander."

"Yeah, and that's how dreams go. Sometimes you become the person you're dreaming about; sometimes you are watching like an observer. I'm telling you, it wasn't real, so just chill."

"Fuck, Nikki, stop treating me like a baby! I know what I experienced, and it wasn't just a dream! Why can't you get that through your head?"

"Because it couldn't be real, dumbass! Now you're the one acting crazy. Obviously, it was a dream. What else could it be?"

Veronica began to sob. "But it was sooo real, Nik!"

Nikki eased her tone and said, "Maybe this is why you saw a doctor when you were a kid. I mean, if you were having dreams like *this*, I can see why mom got help for you."

Veronica let herself sink down one step. Nikki followed and placed her arm around Veronica's shoulder. Veronica spoke thoughtfully. "Is this what my dreams are like? Vivid nightmares?"

"Yeah, I guess so. No wonder mom was worried about you dreaming again. She gave you the number of that doctor?"

Veronica didn't allow herself to blink. Her eyes grew misty as she considered her sister's words. "Mom said I should call him if I had nightmares again. She sounded worried, and I just thought she was mom being mom, ya know."

"Give him a call and see what he has to say. Maybe he can help."

Veronica suddenly snapped. "I'm not crazy, Nik!"

"I didn't say you were! I just suggested you call him. See what he has to say."

"Yeah, I know what you said, and I also know what you meant. I don't have any psychosis or anything. I just don't dream very often, and I guess I have nightmares once in a while."

"You told me that you *never* dream. And now you have a dream — one dream — and damn, look what happens! It really freaked you out, Vern. Hell, it's freaking *me* out. Just because you call this stupid doctor it doesn't mean you're crazy; it just means that you're trying to figure out if this will happen again and if there's something you can do about it."

Veronica placed her hand on her abdomen. "I think I feel sick. I can still see her face, wearing that bonnet and the blood smeared all over her nightgown. Maybe mom's right. It's too late to call that doctor tonight. I'll do it tomorrow."

Nikki helped her sister up. Together they settled in the library with cups of warm tea while Jack White's voice squeaked out songs on Nikki's iPhone.

Chapter 102

Sebastian's Story

He's *not* dead!" Baldebert howled.

Cicero scowled at the monk for stating the obvious. He began to draw his dagger as the not-dead man barreled into him with unexpected speed and agility. Together, they slammed against the desk. Paper, candles, mixing bowls, and ink flew into the air. Both men twirled to the floor, punching and kicking each other like wild beasts.

Sebastian rolled free of the centurion and scrambled to his feet first. He grabbed a nearby wooden stool and held it above his cowering enemy, preparing to smash it into his head. "Die, Roman filth!"

As the furniture came crashing down, Cicero drew back his blade and thrust it deep into Sebastian's gut, just under his rib cage.

The Cloaked Man staggered backward and cupped his hand around the offending dagger. Black blood oozed from the wound, and Sebastian reached out to Baldebert with a vague swipe of a desperate hand, lost his balance, and crumbled to his knees. The Cloaked Man wavered for a moment and then fell face first to the floor.

"The villain simply didn't want to die today," Cicero remarked; anxious laughter exploded as he spoke.

Baldebert didn't share in the centurion's moment of humor. "Why was he to die?"

"That's not something that concerns you. Come with me, I need your help."

The two men hurried out of the room. Baldebert reluctantly followed his new leader, cursing and wheezing as he plodded along. Under his robe, he clutched something nervously. The Druid knew his time was coming, and he both welcomed and dreaded the moment.

Down the hall and toward the courtyard they ran. "Hurry!" Cicero commanded, and the chubby man-boy obliged.

❧❦❖❧❦

Just around a corner, Esindra hunkered and watched Cicero and the monk pass by. She crept forward, curious yet cautious. She had heard the commotion from the tower room. It sounded like a fight and she thought, during the scuffle, she heard Sebastian's voice. *Could he still be alive?*

Hope rumbled in her heart. She'd give anything to take back her betrayal.

Afraid of what she might find, but unable to control herself, she made her way toward the tower room. She decided she must see the body of the father of her child, if for no other reason, to pray over his corpse and beg forgiveness.

Something stirred around the corner ahead. Esindra froze and listened. It lumbered slowly and grunted as it drew near.

She ducked into a dark alcove and cringed as a shadow shuffled by. Esindra held her breath and then exhaled quickly as she recognized Sebastian.

He walked crumpled with his hands clenching his abdomen. Esindra reached for him. As she clasped his arm, he shrieked and pulled away.

"Sebastian, it is I, Esindra. You *are* alive!"

"Gid away from me!" he spat. "You did dis. You would ha' me murdered!"

Esindra grabbed his arm to steady him as he hovered like a drunkard ready to tumble. "I didn't know! Cicero had me believe that you would betray me. I thought you intended to destroy Fabius and me. You should have told me the truth from the beginning!"

With blood seeping from the corners of his broken mouth, he sputtered, "How could I? How could I tell you dat your husband *wanted* me to seduce you? Dat he conspired with me to impregnate you? Even if you belie'ed that, how could I den tell you that I intended to double-cross him and would actually destroy him and would take care o' you and our child? You would ha' thought me mad, Esindra!"

"How could you *not* tell me? Even now I wonder if you are spewing more lies...nothing you say makes sense!"

"My mother and I made a great plan toge'der. It was brilliant and would 'a united dis land and our people. But we didn't take into account your treachery, Esindra."

"My treachery? Your mother? I don't understand." Esindra gently cupped his elbow and dabbed at the blood dripping from his mouth. "You're not making sense. Let's get you into a safe place where you can rest..."

The Cloaked Man spat blood onto the floor so he could speak clearly. A tooth also flew out, making Esindra cringe as he spoke. "My mother was a priestess here many years ago. She wanted to take back the Temple Fortress and rid it of the Roman occupation. As her son, I also have the blood of the Temple Priests in my veins. So, when she asked me to help her, I, of course, agreed."

"You're a Temple Priest?" she asked.

"No, not exactly. I also have Roman blood. I'm a man between worlds, and neither one accepts me. But all that was to change! That is why our plan was so brilliant."

"How..." she began, but he was already excited relating the story to her.

"The first course of action was to gain Fabius' trust. As it turned out, you were the key to gaining it. Once I could manipulate your husband, I merely had to convince him to invite the Northern Tribe here, so he could 'murder' the Head Commander. That's when the plan becomes truly brilliant..." With a wide, red smile he paused and waited for Esindra to react.

She wasn't sure what to say, so she gently urged, "How was the plan to kill the Head Commander so brilliant?"

Sebastian spit out more blood, grabbed the nape of her neck, and pulled her close to his face. His black eyes bore into hers as he explained. "The poison I made is not deadly, my flower. I told Fabius that to fool him. You see, it only immobilizes the imbiber. They fall into a deep sleep and *appear* dead. So, while Fabius thought we were murdering the Head Commander, we were really putting him into a deep, deep sleep.

"Then the plan was for me to escape from here. Indeed, Fabius hardly considered me a prisoner any longer; slipping away from the Temple in the dead of night would have been easy! I'd go to the Northern Tribe's camp and 'resurrect' their leader. Like a miracle, like Jesus raising Lazarus, I'd bring him back! They'd have no choice but to accept me then. No longer would I be an outcast among my own people. Together, the Head Commander, the Northern Tribe, and me, we'd return and lay siege on unsuspecting Fabius. I'd give them tactical information, so we could take the temple back. And I'd be a hero!"

"And me...what would become of me during this siege?"

He winced and hunched over, cradling his wounded gut. "I would have protected you. You would not have been harmed," he answered contemptuously. "Then you, me, the baby, we all would have had this temple as our own. But your betrayal changed all that, didn't it?" He wobbled back into the wall, which propped him up.

For the first time, Esindra noticed the dagger protruding from Sebastian's stomach. "You're stabbed! What happened?"

"Cicero came back to finish me off."

"So, the poison would not have killed you. You were never in danger of actually dying." As she slowly comprehended the reality, she burst out, "But now *this*! This belly wound may do you in! Come with me, quick, before someone sees us. We'll find some place to hide, and I will mend your wounds..."

"No, I must go to the courtyard. I have to see this through." Sebastian stumbled down the corridor.

Esindra tugged on his arm. "You can't! Cicero is in there and will finish you off."

Ignoring her, Sebastian kept shuffling.

Esindra followed, pleading. "We have to get out of here. I beg of you, do as I ask. Do it for our child!"

"I *am* doing this for our child," he said and rushed into the courtyard.

⧉⟡⧉

Minstrels played, dancers frolicked, and the Roman soldiers pretended to partake in the merry-making. The wild men clashed cups of ale together and proclaimed lavish toasts to their host while gobbling down fine pastries and cakes. Fabius stood tall at the head table. He held his goblet high and grunted happily as he chugged it, obviously putting on a show to mimic their rambunctious ways.

Baldebert waddled behind Cicero on the other end of the courtyard. From time to time, the centurion would turn around and seethe, "Do you see him? Do you know which one is the Head Commander?"

Baldebert just shook his head over and over again. He noticed Helena perched at a side table surrounded by her entourage. The old woman gazed at the barbaric feast. Baldebert thought he saw a smile on the old woman's colorless lips.

At that moment, Sebastian burst into the room. A few near him gasped and gawped at the wild-looking, wounded man who ran through the crowd. He

328

splayed his arms out and rushed forward until he reached the center of the courtyard. With Cicero's dagger lodged in his gut, he bellowed, and the entire room was instantly captivated by him.

"There is treachery here! The one called Cicero tried to murder me again and again. Tonight he also tries to murder the Head Commander...that is why you are called here! It is not an offering of peace..." his voice sputtered, and he coughed up jelly-like clumps of blood.

Helena rose and cried out, "Sebastian!"

The Cloaked Man turned in the direction of her voice, and they locked gazes. "Mother!" he cried.

Several Romans sprung from their seats and converged around the wounded man. Cicero advanced on Sebastian with his sword drawn. It was held high in the air, and it came down on the back of the hunched-over man. It hit him square, with the flat side of the blade, knocking him to the ground.

"No!" Helena cried, but no one heard her over the din of the surprised shouts and jeers from the barbarians.

Cicero raised his arms to draw attention to himself. "Ignore the ravings of that madman! He is a prisoner and speaks only lies!"

"What is this murder he speaks of?" one of the barbarians spoke. "I demand to know!"

"Murder? There is no plan of a murder..." Fabius answered awkwardly.

Another barbarian stepped forward; his hand rested on the handle of the dagger hidden in his belt. "We demand answers or the peace talks are over."

Baldebert stepped forward, becoming visible for all in the room to see. The burly barbarians paused as the young priest found his voice. "And I'll leave with you."

The barbarians all fell silent. One by one they bent down on one knee and saluted Baldebert.

Fabius jerked his head back and forth, dumfounded by the situation. The Roman soldiers stood poised for action.

Fabius burst out to Baldebert, "You go back to your chambers! Now!"

Baldebert's fearful eyes seared with intention. He was no longer a fluttery prisoner. "No, Fabius. Your army invaded my Temple and killed my brothers and sisters. I won't stand by and watch you destroy our people."

One of the wild men pointed to Baldebert and spoke, "Hail the Head Commander!"

Others cried out in a cacophony. "It *is* the Head Commander! He is alive! Hail the Head Commander!"

Fabius' face flared with red energy. "*You* are the Head Commander?"

Baldebert reached into his robe. "I'm the keeper of the Head. I'm the one who commands it. Yes, I *am* the Head Commander!"

The Roman soldiers snapped to attention; readied to overtake the crowd of Barbarians.

Fabius reeled, pulled his dagger from his belt sheath, and advanced on Baldebert. "Then you will be the first to die, Druid!"

Chapter 103

Father Michel's Story

It was Sunday, and since Gaston-Elise could not attend mass with all the others, he read his old, tattered Bible as he sat by the window, watching the day drift by.

Around midafternoon, two servants carried the cardinal's lifeless hunting dog across the grass. Each man held two paws and hastily flung it to the ground. They dug into the earth with picks and shovels and created a shallow grave.

Gaston-Elise was shocked. What could have befallen the animal? A hunting accident? He also wondered where the Cardinal was. Why did he not come and pay respects to his beloved pet?

A short while later, he watched as the same two men emerged from the front doors. They pushed a wheelbarrow heaping with linens.

What an odd time for wash, Gaston-Elise thought. Sunday was not a day for chores. And why were the guards tasked with such menial work?

Then he saw an arm dangling from under the pile. The men weren't washing clothes; they were disposing of a body! The lifeless appendage waved "good-bye" as they wheeled the cadaver to the vineyard behind the castle. Gaston-Elise knew where they were going...to the caverns to bury the cook.

❧ ❧ ❖ ❧ ❧

The chapel bells rang early Monday morning. It was an unusual time for them to chime, and Gaston-Elise figured that service must be underway for the cook. Everyone was likely gathered to pay respects in the chapel. They would hold mass, the Cardinal would give a eulogy, and together they'd pray for the soul of their colleague and friend. All except Gaston-Elise, who couldn't join them. Instead, he paid tribute with his own private prayer.

The bells chimed again at noon, marking the midpoint of the day with a clang that woke Gaston-Elise from a light nap. A growling stretch brought him to his feet, and he faced his little window. Groggily, he watched the front doors to the quiet castle thrust open.

The same two wheelbarrow-pushing men rushed out. This time their unholy load was heaping with bodies. Gaston-Elise now feared the worst — the peste had infiltrated the stronghold of the Château.

The men scrambled across the lawn, nearly losing balance at one point and toppling the cargo. They made their way to the back of the grounds, to the catacombs most likely again, to dispose of the dead.

Gaston-Elise watched, frozen; a veneer of dread washed over him. Not one to give way to emotion, he bit back a rush of hopelessness that griped his soul and slumped into his chair. With his face buried in his palms, he succumbed. The big man wept.

Every so often, he'd look out the window at the castle, hoping to see some clue as to what was transpiring within. Were they inside struggling to contain it? How many were sick? How many would die? What would happen if the peste ravished the castle like it did so many places across Europe, leaving everyone dead? Would the Lord Jesus truly let that happen?

The next day, several people carrying packs, as if they were prepared for a journey, walked hurriedly from the front doors of the Château. Gaston-Elise could hear yelling, and he strained to see the drama unfold from his vantage. Guards barked orders to those who apparently intended to leave the grounds. There were several altar boys, a couple women who worked as maids, and an old man who served as a valet. Gaston-Elise heard one of the boys declare: "You cannot stop us if we choose to leave!"

The guard retaliated with, "Your duty is to the Cardinal."

To this, the old man replied, "I relinquish my duties. Now let me pass!"

With that, the small mob pushed past the guards and marched toward the front gates.

Gaston-Elise struggled to see. His little house was at an odd angle, and the action was occurring far down the path, through the trees, which obstructed his view.

He heard a commotion, and a woman shouted, "He was a weaponless old man, and you skewered him just because he wanted to leave? Don't you see this place is infected? We all will die unless we go right *now*!"

More shouts. Gaston-Elise couldn't discern the words as several voices collided in argument. Then he saw the young men and women marching back toward the castle. Behind them were two guards; they each had their sword drawn and were poised to attack if provoked.

Gaston-Elise's worst fears were reality. Not only was he sequestered, but everyone who resided in the castle was also trapped. Their only escape was succumbing to the specter of the Black Death.

When the next morning came there was a knock on his door. Gaston-Elise sat silently within. The bolt was latched and locked from the inside.

He recognized his former colleagues when they called out to him. "Gaston! Are you in there? The commander wants to know if you are still...Gaston, answer me!"

The sequestered man held his tongue, unsure if he should answer or not. *If he told them he was alive, would they enlist him to help guard the servants from fleeing?* Not a deed he agreed with. If people wanted to leave, they should have free will. No, that wasn't something Gaston-Elise wanted to be a part of.

He listened to the dialogue outside. "He's probably dead."

"We need to find out. Those are our orders."

"He's dead, or he would have answered. If we break in the door and find his rotting bones, then we'll be the ones who clean him up. I don't want to touch one more dead body. Let's come back after the corpse is dried out. It'll be easier to move."

They certainly didn't seem concerned about his welfare, but that was fine with the one-armed warrior. It meant they would leave him alone.

Gaston-Elise huddled far back from the window so that no one could see him even if they happened to glance inside. He stayed there frozen for many hours, not moving even to use the excrement bucket near the door. He remained balled up in that corner for hours, begging the Lord to have mercy on their souls.

Chapter 104
Veronica's Story
Present Day France

It was late afternoon. Veronica steered the little orange car over the rickety bridge. Clark told her that his brother had reinforced it with support beams in time for the party, but it didn't feel different to Veronica.

She scanned from the road, to the "to-do" list in her hand, to the clock on her dashboard. It was finally late enough for her to make a phone call to California. She pressed the buttons on her cell phone and listened as a female voice answered on the second ring.

"Doctor Sandbourne's office..."

"Yes, is Dr. Sandbourne available?"

"Are you a patient?"

"No, but I was."

"Do you need to make an appointment?"

"No, I just need to speak to him."

"Then you need to make an appointment."

"I can't. I'm not in California right now. I was a patient of Dr. Sandbourne's a long time ago. It's a little hard to explain, but I need to..."

"Dr. Sandbourne isn't available right now. He's with a patient."

You could have told me that in the first place, Veronica thought, then nicely, she spoke, "I really just need a moment of his time."

"Ma'am, would you like to make an appointment?"

"No, I can't make an appointment. I need to *speak* with him."

"He isn't available right now."

"Can I *please* leave a message?" Veronica fought to contain her frustration.

"Who may I say is calling?"

"This is Veronica Dixon. He can reach me at..."

"And what is the nature of your call?"

"I can't really explain. I just need to speak with..."

"Ma'am, I have to let him know why you are calling."

"Fine, tell him I am a former patient, and I'm having nightmares that scare the fuck out of me. Okay?"

The woman didn't miss a beat. "Okay, can I get your number?"

Veronica rattled off her number and clicked the phone off. She leaned back on the vinyl seat and settled in for the long drive to Orleans.

❧❧❖❧❧

Later that evening, she felt a rush of anticipation as she hung the garment bag in the back of the Twingo. The red dress that Clark discovered had been repaired and dry-cleaned, and to Veronica's surprise, it looked amazing. Whimsically, she wondered if she could possibly fit into it as she spied a rustic antique shop nestled behind an ivy-guarded gatehouse.

Veronica couldn't resist. Before she knew it, she was perusing the store for last-minute odds and ends for the impending party. She found a lovely table cloth for the dining table, several throw pillows, and a crystal vase for the credenza in the foyer that she planned on filling with flowers from the garden. And a gorgeous red mask, beaded with sequins, and laced with a silky red veil that hung over the wearer's mouth and neck — it would make a beautiful decoration.

She rushed to her last stop; praying she'd make it before it closed. Nikki had ordered their costumes from a vintage store, and Veronica was in charge of picking them up. Luckily, the lights were still on.

The shop reminded Veronica of the kitschy specialty places that lined the streets of Hollywood Boulevard. Only this one had more than just naughty negligees and sparkling '70s mini-skirts. It had fairy-princess wings, wizard hats, and pirate costumes.

She walked sideways along narrowly spaced racks filled with silky, billowy dresses. Recreations of Marie-Antoinette gowns hung on vacant-eyed mannequins who passively watched her pass by.

A pale-faced girl with mascara-soaked eyes gazed lazily at a computer monitor while Veronica recited an order confirmation number. She eventually rose and pushed her way to the front of the store. A dress hung in the window. It was black and covered in orange feathers. It was part of the "Fantasy Collection", according to the sales girl, and was a vintage sorceress' dress, apparently made in the early 1970s. It had a long, sheer train accented with glitter, but the dress itself was short — five-inches-above-the-knee short. The back scooped to a wicked "V", and the sleeves were flared at the ends. The girl also produced a feathery mask. It was black, studded with cheap, orange beads, and had a fray of feathers and ribbons fanning out from each side.

Veronica tried it on. It was so unlike anything she would ever pick out for herself. *I look like some bimbo dressed-up for Halloween!* Veronica's gut cringed as she slithered out of it like a snake grateful to be rid of its dead skin.

As she emerged from the dressing room, the clerk clumsily shoved Nikki's dress into a garment bag. It was olive-green and silver with steampunk goggles and an adorable miniature top hat. Victorian in style, it had a high collar, billows of fabric, and an intricately-woven corset. It was much prettier than Veronica's — which didn't surprise her at all.

⊰ຈ❖ຈ⊱

It was late when she arrived back at the Château. Once inside, she laid each of the costumes on their beds. Then she zipped around the castle, arranging her various shopping finds throughout the rooms. Her sister was in the kitchen, and the air smelled like garlic and oregano.

"Vern? Is that you? Are you home?" Nikki called as Veronica fluffed pillows in the library.

"Yeah, it's me!"

Nikki walked through the double doors of the dining room with a ladle in her hand. "Where've you been? I made dinner over an hour ago, it's already past nine

334

o'clock."

"I went into Orleans and picked up the costumes *you* ordered. Yours is on your bed. I got some things for the Château, too. Like the pillows?"

"They're lovely. Now you wanna come eat?"

"Yeah, it smells great."

They sat at the kitchen table, and Nikki scooped bow-tie pasta onto her sister's plate and smothered it with tomato-cream sauce.

Nikki chatted over the evening meal. "So, what do ya' think of your costume; pretty funky, huh?"

"It's pretty funky alright."

"Oh! I just got a confirmation from Alex and the Traveler's Channel. They *are* coming to the party. Plus, there's a lady who reviews European Castles for a vacation guidebook. She's on the guest list and several photographers from different magazines, including *Better Homes*. Get this, a bunch of people from the US Consulate's office and some city officials from Tours and Amboise are coming. This party is going to be huge, Vern!"

"How huge? How many people?"

"Well, we sent out over four hundred invitations."

"How are you managing to get these people? Who could you possibly know at the US Consulate's office?"

"Christophe knows people there. Trust me, Christophe knows *everyone*. Ralph invited some on our behalf, too. Oh, and the rock singer that we met at *The Paris Underground*, he's coming with his band. Plus, a bunch of our neighbors, including the Fontaines, the Lebecs, Lady Florence..."

"Oh no! Not her. She'll poke fun of everything."

"Vern, this is your chance to show her what a great job you've done decorating this castle! Plus, Lady Florence's nephew is coming, too. Remember Richard? I sat next to him at the dinner party."

"Richard's going to be here, plus the rock star, plus Alex; how many men do you want at this thing?"

Nikki twisted a strand of hair around her pinky. "As many as I can get!"

Veronica rose from the table. "Well, I have a lot of work to do then." She whirled from room to room making adjustments. She decided that the library chairs needed to be closer to the fireplace, and after careful consideration, determined that the linens in the upstairs master bath were a little too pink, so she replaced them with rose-colored ones.

While straightening the paintings in the parlor, she heard the familiar breep-breep of her cell phone. She looked at the clock above the fireplace. It was twenty minutes before midnight. *Who could be calling at this hour?*

She clicked the "talk" button. "This is Veronica?"

A strange male voice spoke. "Veronica Dixon?"

"Speaking..."

"This is Dr. Sandbourne. I got your message."

"Oh! Yes, hi! Thanks for calling back."

"My secretary said you wanted to make an appointment?"

Veronica murmured expletives inaudibly and then answered brightly. "No, actually, I told her that I *couldn't* make an appointment. I just wanted to talk to you on the phone."

"I see. What can I do for you?"

"This probably sounds a little odd. My mother told me to call you if I ever had...if I ever needed to...I don't even remember you. My mom said that I saw you when I was a kid because..."

"I remember *you*, Veronica. You were special to me. When you were first brought to me, you were suffering from some awful night terrors." His voice was even, with the slight rasp of an older gentleman.

"Yeah, I guess so. I only remember bits and pieces. Mom told me to call you if I ever had a bad dream again."

"You're having dreams, Veronica?"

"Yeah, not very often, well, almost never really. But I had a bad one yesterday. It was so vivid and I was screaming and I thought it was real. It seemed so real. Anyway, Christ, this must sound so stupid..."

"Please continue. What you experienced as a child was one of the most extreme cases of night terrors we ever saw. Tell me everything." His voice was gentle. He was familiar to her now, like stumbling across a forgotten childhood toy.

"I dreamt a woman threw her newborn baby into a...pit. The thing is, I had been reading this diary, and I thought I was *reading* about this woman. For several nights, I read a little bit more. But there was nothing in the book after all. None of it ever happened; it was all just a bad dream. See, sounds crazy, doesn't it?"

"Not at all. Your dreams are anything but crazy. Dr. Jacobs and I discovered that a long time ago. It's so good to hear from you again. I always wondered how you were doing all this time. I would like you to come in. Can we make an appointment tomorrow?"

Veronica chuckled to herself. *They sure want me to make an office visit.* "I can't. I couldn't make an appointment to see you for several weeks..." Then the name Dr. Jacobs struck Veronica, and she interrupted herself. "Dr. Jacobs?"

"He and I treated you together. I actually saw you first, but then called him when things got...challenging."

"I wonder if it was he, who recommended me?" She became pleased with her sudden revelation. "You see, I got this job here in France decorating this castle. The woman I'm working for, Marie-Claire, said I was recommended to her by a Dr. Jacobs, and I don't remember..."

"Did you say Marie-Claire?"

"Yes, she owns this Château. I always wondered who..."

His calm voice shattered. "In France, you say?"

"Yep, that's where I am right now. That's why I couldn't possibly make an appointment for tomorrow, but I could probably..."

"Are you at the Château du Feu Ardent?"

"Yes! How did you know —" Veronica began, but was abruptly cut off.

"How did this happen? How did *you* get *there*?"

"Like I said, Marie-Claire called and offered me a job. She..."

"She *called* you?"

"Yeah, do you know her, too?"

"Veronica, listen, I have to see you right away. I'll come to you."

She chuckled and tried to clarify. "That is a pretty big house call. Maybe you didn't understand me. I am in France *right now*..."

"Yes, dear, I know, and you are at Château du Feu Ardent because Marie-Claire hired you. Listen, you need to do something, okay? You have to get back on your medication. It will help your dreams. I will call in a prescription to...uh...let's see." He spoke off the phone for a moment. "Nurse, find me a pharmacie in France. Something in Amboise where I can phone in a prescription..." His voice trailed off, and Veronica heard the familiar "breep" of her phone as the battery began to die.

The doctor came back on the line. "Veronica, you need to go to this pharmacie right now and fill this prescription..." he rattled off an address.

"Uh, wait, I need a pen and paper." Her phone breeped again. Veronica rummaged through her purse in search of something to write with. He repeated the address as her phone sounded a third time.

As soon as he was done speaking, she maintained, "Look, I only had one dream, and I don't really like to take medicine if I don't have to..."

The doctor became stern. His easygoing nature replaced with something more desperate. "You have to get the prescription filled. As a matter of fact, you should get it *right now*..." His voice faded into static.

"I can't go *now*. It's almost midnight."

The phone breeped.

Through the static, he said, "Sleep with a radio or television on..."

"What? My phone is going dead. I'll charge my battery and call you tomorrow..."

The doctor was still talking, and Veronica could make out a few words. "Going to take a flight..."

"What flight? You're breaking up. I can't even understand you. Let's talk in the morning, okay?"

His voice was scattered, but Veronica could hear his urgency, and it confused her. "Veronica, get the prescription filled...need to sleep deeply or...difficult to understand..."

"Yes, it is difficult to understand you right now, too. You're fading in and out." Veronica wasn't sure if he heard her.

The phone breeped urgently yet again.

The doctor spoke rapidly. "Marie-Claire Jacobs..."

"Marie-Claire *Jacobs*. Her last name is Jacobs?"

"She has," the phone crackled before she heard four final words from Dr. Sandbourne, "dead for twenty years."

The phone went silent. Veronica looked at the dark display. *I charged this stupid thing this afternoon!*

It was 12:02 A.M. The thought of going into Amboise to fill a prescription at that hour was crazy. *And what kind of prescription was it?* She looked at the notepad. "Tranquillisant" was the word he had spelled out. Veronica was pretty sure it meant "tranquilizer". She didn't want to take any tranquilizers, not with everything going on. She still had things to do for the masquerade ball, she needed to get ready, make sure the castle was presentable, and she couldn't be greeting guests while she was floating in a cloud of drugs.

Veronica slid into bed and let sleep take over. She would be fine. No need for drugs. She would have no dreams. After all, she *never* had dreams. Just because she had one nightmare after how many years, that didn't mean much.

The shadows crept around Veronica as she slipped from lucidity to someplace else. *No dreams*, she thought. *I just won't have any.* The voices started to whisper, and Veronica answered them. *No dreams tonight. Sorry, not gonna happen.* The voices swept around her and guided her. *No dreams*, she insisted, but the dreams came anyway, one right after another.

Chapter 105

The Pagans' Story

Morning crept up on Bevin. He had once again worked the stones until the early hours of the next day. It happened more times than not. Then he would fall asleep right where he had been laboring. Upon awakening at midday, he would grab his hammer and pick up precisely where he left off.

The tower he built, a tall turret, cast a long shadow in the dawning light. It was three stories high, and a staircase wound around it like a snake, leading to the top levels. The bottom level housed the pit that had become Trinna's tomb.

He was hungry. Bevin's diet was meager and consisted mostly of rabbit meat. He hunted the stupid creatures in the small mountain quarry. A warren resided among the rocks, and he stalked them by standing on a ledge over top of them. He would cast a hawk-like shadow with outstretched hands while they romped in the sun. This seemed to mesmerize the animals, and they would freeze for a split second, just long enough for him to sling a sharpened stone. This hunting tactic was known as "tervagan" — a method his father taught him to convince the prey that the attack was overhead, when it was actually coming from the side. His aim had grown precise, and he never failed to strike one of the rabbits in the head, knocking it into kicking, squealing death throes.

A shadow now loomed over Bevin. Still shaken from the attack in his dream, he cried out and thrust his arm over his face like a shield.

"You've done well," the Hag purred. Her frail frame seemed huge as he groveled among the dusty stones at the entrance of the Temple.

Bevin stammered humbly, "Thank you."

"You must stay here until your end of days. You are the guardian and have sole power over your offspring. Do you understand?"

Bevin feared that he did, but feigned ignorance in hope that the truth of the matter would differ than the one he imagined. "No, tell me."

The Hag adjusted her grasp on her staff. "You have given *fire* a new life. Your actions unleashed a power into our world; one that wasn't meant to be here. Now it is your duty, and mine, too, to keep it contained. Do you understand now?"

Bevin comprehended what the old woman was saying, but still he shook his head. He felt comfort having her there and wished to keep her crackling voice speaking as long as possible. Though he feared her more than anything, more than the dreams that accosted his sleep, he welcomed the company of another human being. He had been toiling alone for months, and even his worst enemy was an appreciated companion.

The Hag knelt to the ground and leveled her gaze at Bevin. "Every year the ritual provides offerings to the four elemental spirits. It is our obligation to make these sacrifices in return for their blessings.

"Air gives us the wind that cools the summer days and provides us with breath. Water sustains our bodies and washes away impurities. Earth gives us soil to till so that our crops may grow. And fire. Fire warms us and cooks our meat.

It also is the most destructive force of all the spirits. It burns unmercifully and erupts in violent anger when not appeased."

Bevin listened carefully to the old woman's words. Answers to numerous questions that had haunted him were being revealed.

"Each spirit must be appeased with an offering. For example, air must not be angered, or it will blow up fierce storms. Water should be placated so that ample rain falls. The earth must be pacified so that it remains rich and fertile. Fire, above all else, must be content so that it does not erupt in a blaze that destroys our homes and fields."

The old woman patted a barren patch of dirt in front of her. She smoothed it with the palm of her hand and then scratched at it with a grimy, gnarled fingernail. "The ritual is necessary for the wellbeing of our people. It has traditions that must be upheld to ensure harmony and balance. You and Trinna disturbed that balance. Each year a *new* batch of young people are chosen to make the sacrificial trek. Since Trinna had taken the journey before, her knowledge tainted the proceedings."

She outlined various symbols in the dirt. It was a writing that Bevin did not recognize. She continued. "Fire is tricky, you see. Have you ever thought the wood in a pit was burned up, only to have it spring to life again unexpectedly? Or maybe you watched as the men of your tribe burn the brush in the fields to make way for tilling, only to have the fire leap out of control and consume an entire countryside? That is fire. Of all the elemental spirits, one can never trust fire."

The Hag dug under her grey cloak and cupped something gently in her hand. "Fire was extremely cunning that night. It recognized Trinna; knew she wasn't a first-timer. It also knew that she hadn't drunk the elixir. It saw a weakness and took advantage of our mistake. That's why it *chose* Trinna."

Bevin was confused. "But Trinna had an advantage over everyone else. *We* had an advantage. We didn't drink that potion. We were *smarter* than you."

"You still don't understand. The elixir *protects* you. It would have protected Trinna as she perished. The fire elemental is drawn to those who are dying. When a person nears death they become a portal from our world to its world. They act as a conduit as they hover between two realities. For a brief moment, as fire consumes the soul that has been sacrificed to it, it can enter our world completely."

Her hand waved over the runes that were etched in the earth. She paused to mumble something that Bevin did not understand.

She spoke again. "The altar, the ritualistic circle of fire, it traps the fire elemental while it claims the sacrifice. At the precise moment it entered Trinna, you pushed her *out* of the circle. You liberated the spirit. You gave it the opportunity to manifest itself into our world. It has generated itself now. You gave it life, and you now must be its guardian. It is bound to these grounds; that much I was able to ensure. You alone command it. You control it, with *this*."

She opened her hand and revealed a crystal object. It fell with a puff onto the earth, landing in the center of the symbols in the fine dirt. It was white, pure, and shaped like a skull. Deep within its dimensions, Bevin caught a glimpse of red and orange light, as if it were burning inside.

"This Head controls the elemental." She waved her hands over the crystal. "The spirit will be born today into flesh. From Trinna's decaying loins will come the unnatural birth. It will be an atrocity against nature. It will be your offspring, your prodigy. You are its father, and you must name it. With its name and the Head, you have power over it."

"So you want me to stay here and oversee some wicked devil," Bevin whined. "Me? Alone with it for the rest of my life?"

"I told you that you sealed your own fate. Don't worry, boy, others will come in due time. I will send several priests here, and together you will continue to build this structure into a temple. You'll start an order that will control the elemental and use its power wisely."

Her last words gave Bevin comfort. He instantly looked forward to the day when others would join him. "What must I do now?"

"Give it a name," she answered.

Bevin mulled over her words dully. The tower trembled slightly. The structure was several feet behind him, and Bevin turned as a muffled cry came out of the entry.

The old woman swiftly rose to her feet with the agility of someone half her age and faced the entrance. Bevin remained squatting and uneasily glared into the empty eye sockets of the skull. It lay on the ground, grinning back at him.

The cry became louder and more pronounced. It was similar to a crying infant, but had undertones of something animalistic — like a goat being slaughtered. It sounded scared, injured, and angry.

Hot fear suddenly exploded on the back of his neck. Bevin realized the noise was coming from within Trinna's crypt and that everything the old Hag had told him was real. He was about to be a father — to something evil and unnatural. He tried to wake himself, certain that what he was experiencing must surely be another dreadful dream. However, reality and his nightmares had now merged.

"Name it!" the Hag ordered with a sense of urgency.

Bevin let fear seize his body, and he sat petrified. His mind momentarily produced no thought. He was frozen, like a young rabbit in the shadow of a hawk, unable to move because of overwhelming terror.

"Give it a name, *now!*" the old woman commanded.

For a faltering second, Bevin saw a hint of consternation in her steady eyes. He snapped out of his stupor as his brain raced for a name. Nothing came to him. From deep within the stone walls it wailed — stronger, louder, closer. It was making its way to the entrance.

Bevin was on the verge of trepidation. He fought to retain his wits and think of a name.

The Hag pleaded with him. "Name it now, you fool!"

Bevin opened his lips, but no words came out. The thing behind him crept forward. Dark, like pitch, it came into view, and the Hag recoiled at its sight.

Bevin snatched the Head from the dusty ground in front of him. In one quick motion, he whirled around and faced his offspring. It rose on its hind legs, growing taller as it prepared to pounce, while its long shadow covered him as though he was a mesmerized rabbit.

Bevin's jaw dropped and he uttered the first word that came to his mind. He shouted it, more out of fear than with authority. His voice echoed against the hillsides like a trumpet.

Bevin gave it a name.

The thing that was Bevin's prodigy skulked back to the doorway. It hovered there, out of the light, and only the vague outline of its long head and spindly haunches were visible. There was a glint, though, from its human-shaped eyes — and from its razor-like claws.

It bowed its head, as if acquiescing to its master. The thing snarled several times and retreated back into its new domain.

Chapter 106

Dorothée's Story

Julien-Luc leaned against the wall by the doorway of his cell with his arms casually wrapped over his chest. He observed the nightgown-clad woman tiptoe past him. He made a soft "psst..." sound and watched her twirl in a quick half circle, stumble, and fall into a heap on the floor by his feet.

"Who is this sneaking into my chamber?" he asked with a chuckle.

"It is I, Dorothée. You startled me!"

"I startled *you*! You are the one slinking into my room. *I* am the one who should be startled." He took her hand and helped her stand.

Dorothée trembled. She suddenly felt shameful, like a thief caught in the act. "I had to come. André-Benoit is to return tomorrow night, so now is your only chance to escape. You are free to go!" She waved her hand as if to shoo him out of the room, but he stood there and smirked. She insisted, "The guard is gone. I saw to that. You can leave undetected!"

"I can't escape..."

"Yes, you can! I left a rope near the gatehouse, so you can scale the wall easily and be gone."

"You would do that for me? I'm your *husband's* prisoner!"

"You shouldn't be here! You are not a criminal. They made a mistake."

"I am here for a reason, dear Dorothée. That is what I have been striving to tell you. Being captured and taken as a prisoner was no accident. I posed as a Protestant leader and *allowed* myself to be taken into custody. There is something important hidden in this castle, and the only way I could get close to it was to be brought here. I can't leave until I find it."

Dorothée grinned slyly. "I have what you seek! This Bible, yes? I discovered it in the library earlier today." She held it out to him.

"You found it!" he exclaimed and took the fragile little text. His excitement quickly waned though, as ruffled through it. "This isn't it."

"Maybe you are interested in what I found inside its pages then?" she masterfully teased. "It is a piece of parchment that looks to be quite old and a medallion on a chain. The parchment has a maze drawn on it, like a map, and a funny x-shaped symbol. And handwritten across the top, it reads, 'caves of the dead' in Latin. I stored them in a cubby for safe-keeping."

"It was a map then? Perhaps it leads to my Bible and the other artifacts. Yes! That must be it! Bring it to me, Dorothée. I must see for myself."

"I can easily bring it to you, but only if you tell me what all this means first."

He chose his words carefully. "You would keep it from me and sentence me to remain here?"

"Of course not. You just have to tell me what this is all about. Then I will fetch your precious map and medallion and you will be free to escape."

"Don't you see I am trying to protect you, Dorothée? These are dangerous secrets to reveal."

"Then I swear an oath to always hold your secrets!"

"You won't relent with your niggling, will you?" Before she could answer, he grabbed the lantern that hung outside the doorway. In that moment Dorothée realized if he wanted to escape, he could have easily ran, but instead he ducked back into his cell.

"Listen close to what I'm revealing. There are few in this world who know these truths."

He snagged a spoon from his empty supper bowl on the table, and while crouching to the floor, used it to draw onto a small patch of dirt. He explained, "Lifetimes ago, before Christ, a sect of ancient priests, called Temple Priests, built a fortress here to contain an unholy demon. I believe the creature you saw in here, the 'rat', was this demon. It is a long-headed beast with spindly legs that arch over its small body. They made drawings like this to symbolize it.

"Yes, that is what it looked like!" she confirmed.

"This symbol eventually turned into this one, known as the skull and crossbones, or the Jolly Roger. You no doubt recognize it as a symbol for pirates and other unsavory bandits."

"So, the priest became pirates? I'm confused."

"It's more complicated than that. Look here," he said as he scratched yet a third pictogram.

"This is a labarum. The Jolly Roger became more abstract and turned into the labarum."

"That is the symbol on the map and the medallion," she gasped.

"Which is what I suspected," Julien-Luc said with satisfied huff.

He brushed away the etchings to create a clean slate in the dirt, then once again dug in the spoon to illustrate yet another symbol. "As Constantine transformed Rome to Christianity, the labarum was taken as a Christian symbol. This happened often in the early days of Christianity. Pagan symbols, rituals, celebrations, even their mythology was usurped by the Christians and given a Christian connotation. That's what they do, you see. Steal lore from other cultures and integrate it into their own. It is an evil mind-trick really, a way to control the masses into adapting a new religion."

"I am aware of how the Church manipulates, but such talk is blasphemy," Dorothée taunted.

The prisoner shrugged and said, "Will you report me for my blasphemous speech? Will I be thrown in a prison cell for it?" They both chortled wryly and he continued, "The labarum would see many transformations over the centuries. Because of interactions with various barbaric tribes like the Celts and Gauls, the labarum influenced their symbols, specifically the Celtic Cross. Which is another symbol that Christianity eventually took over. Indeed, many of the cryptograms I'm showing you merged with others over time."

Dorothée stared vacantly at the crude sketches. The lantern light flickered against her pallid cheeks, causing deep shadows to dance manically like frenzied dancers.

"I am boring you. I see," he said.

"Bored! No! I am listening and studying intently. I may be a maiden but my mind is sharper than most men I have met. I am absorbing, sir. Continue, please!"

With a quick nod he answered, "I meant no offense. I've never met a woman who…"

She glanced upward and stopped his words.

"Let's continue," he stammered. "The Temple Priests gradually increased their influence. The Christian Church eventually revered them. As their power and authority grew, so did their need to strengthen their alignment with Christianity. Around AD 1100, they started to call themselves the Order of the Temple. They changed their symbol yet again, this time to the even-sided cross. Many scholars believe this is when the Templar Knights first formed, but as I have just shown you, their history is much deeper and murkier."

He etched the Templar cross into the dust and continued. "They wore this on their breasts and shields, painted bright red, when they guided pilgrims to the Holy Land. You are familiar with it, I am sure."

Dorothée leaned over the etching, rubbed away one spoke, and drew an extension. "And this led to the shape of the cross we have today, I'm guessing?"

"Yes, that is how it evolved, more or less, over the years. Church leaders gradually adjusted the shape to match that of the crucifix Christ died upon. Memories of where the symbol actually came from were erased from history. It was a way to control the people — an explanation simple folks, farmers, and the gullible, could easily accept."

"Christianity is rooted in an obscure order of priests who became the Order of the Temple, the Templar Knights?" she asked without making it sound like a question.

"That is the *true* history, one the Church would like never revealed. They sought to destroy the Templar Knights during the Inquisition. They killed many, but some escaped. A handful of them were bitter and angry, and they would use the early symbol of the skull and cross bones as they pirated and pillaged the seas. That is why you recognized the Jolly Roger.

"Others, like my brethren, continued our beliefs in hiding. Louis, my great, great, great grandfather, escaped from here during the Inquisition. He was just a boy, but he understood his heritage, and he passed it onto to his son, my great, great grandfather, who went on to settle in the town of Freiburg with a handful of other survivors. Indeed, the city's coat of arms is a Templar cross! Intent on keeping their legacy a secret, they joined with the Brethren of the Common Life. Each generation is taught the ancient beliefs and those beliefs we keep to ourselves for fear of persecution."

Dorothée pointed at the first drawing. "So what is this demon that started it all? Was it real? Was *that* the thing I saw? You know of it, tell me. My husband, Patricia, the cook and smithy, all thought me mad for thinking it was anything more than a rat!"

"It is actually a love story," he said with a coy grin.

"A love story? *How?* Now you tease me, I am sure. If it is a love story then tell it now, or I will never believe your lips again," she insisted.

Julien-Luc rolled back on the balls of his feet and steadied himself with the hand that held the spoon. Gazing into the smoldering eyes of a woman who tempted, teased and tested him, he prepared to tell her a tale that was a sworn secret among his Brethren.

Chapter 107

Sebastian's Story

The Barbarians brandished weapons which were stealthily hidden under layers of animal skins and furs. The battle started to simmer as everyone poised for combat. Before a single sword clanked, however, the unassuming priest captured everyone's attention by stepping forward and pulling a shimmering crystal skull from under his robe.

It glared with a blinding brightness beyond natural capability. Baldebert pressed his lips against where the ear would be and incited the ancient name.

The courtyard walls vibrated. The air grew thick and misty. No one saw it, but everyone felt a presence as the Baldebert invited something evil to the party.

"I invoked the ancient name. You should pray to your God, for even *your* God knows the power that is held within a name!" Baldebert shouted while staring directly at Fabius. "Surrender now, and I will command the elemental to show you mercy."

Fabius gaped incredulously at the druid.

The rumble slowly increased. The tribesmen and the Roman soldiers were all poised for battle, yet they stood frozen like statues, their senses keenly aware that something unnatural was brewing.

Baldebert preached, "You wanted easy answers, didn't you? You wanted Sebastian to *feed* you instructions. You never considered what his true motives were. Your ignorance is what defeated you!"

Sebastian stirred on the ground. He rolled over and locked eyes with Baldebert. "It was *you* all along? Why didn't you tell me?"

Baldebert's stern expression wavered and it almost looked like he pouted as he explained, "Because you said you wanted to poison the Head Commander! I thought you intended to kill *me*. You were the fool for not telling me who you were and your true intentions."

The air grew warm and thick. Smoke from an unseen source wafted through the air, encircling everyone in the courtyard like a sultry, smoldering blanket. The barbarians grumbled. They surveyed the atmosphere, not sure if they should fight, flee, or stay frozen.

Baldebert spoke slowly, almost with pity. "And now I give it permission...to come and take the enemy." He pointed the face of the skull at one particularly fearful Roman soldier.

The man grunted at the druid and then gazed at his comrades while shrugging his shoulders. He opened his mouth as if to speak, but then his eyes scrunched with bewilderment. He coughed twice and then let out a billowing shriek.

Another soldier took two steps toward him but then stopped when he saw smoke swirling from the top of his friend's head. For a moment, it looked as though his hair might be on fire, then his eyes, now round with dread, bulged from their sockets. They were being pushed forward by something rubescent and oozing. Not blood — something brighter — seeped from every orifice of the man's face. It was lustrous, and flaming, like molten lava. It escaped from his nose, mouth, and ears. It forced his eyes from their holes until they finally popped like heated kernels of corn. Several men near him leapt back as the victim fell forward. His body ignited in a blaze before them.

"Now to him!" Baldebert exclaimed, randomly pointing to another Roman soldier.

This victim wheezed as smoke slowly engulfed his head. It encircled him from the neck up, churning like a vortex. He ran, searching for clean air, but the cloud hung with him. Blindly, he smacked into a pillar and fell to the ground. He crawled on hands and knees, reaching out for something — someone — anything that could help him. Everyone backed away, creating a large circle for him to flail within. The dirty halo smothered him until he collapsed to the floor, screaking for breath, and then slumped over dead.

Esindra emerged from the corridor just as the second man fell. She tried to run back, but was pushed forward as several guards rushed past her with brandished swords. She fell to the ground and sat stunned.

Baldebert scanned the room for his next victim. One soldier panicked and fled for the courtyard doors. Baldebert took aim, and the soldier instantly began to slow down. It appeared that his feet were too heavy to lift. Each step became more labored and lethargic, like a man running in slow motion. He blubbered a Pagan prayer, reverting to his old gods at the moment of his demise. It then became evident that his feet weren't just moving slow; they were *melting*. Those who stood nearby jumped back as though they were avoiding a leper. The soldier's feet became sloppy globs — formless and smoldering. Torrid heat rose up his body, and the flesh fell off his skin like creamy pudding. He slowly slumped over. His body reduced to a gurgling puddle.

Fabius bellowed out, "Fight! Soldiers of Rome, raise your weapons!"

The Roman soldiers took up arms and began to attack. The wild men were prepared. Those who didn't have armaments hidden under their furs or in boots, improvised by hastily grabbing table knives.

As metal clanked and blood flowed, one of the tribesmen pulled an ivory horn that was stashed in the folds of his tunic. Blowing it fiercely, an ominous note carried to a nearby hillside where an army of a thousand men waited. Upon hearing the battle horn, they sprang to life and stormed forward, charging the Temple of their Head Commander.

The Children's Story
1307 AD – A Time of Inquisition

There was so much fanfare that the children barely recognized their home. The foyer was splendidly decorated with garlands of flowers and elaborate, billowing linens. Minstrels played instruments as a procession of immaculately dressed lords and ladies marched through the library, past the Roman sculptures, and into the long ballroom.

The Bishop walked several paces in front of the youngsters. Noblemen, women and wealthy land owners lined either side and bowed as the Holy Man's procession passed. At the end of the ballroom was a long table, with several men and women who held esteemed positions, seated along it and facing the audience. Uncle Pierre was in the center and he glared at the children as they were led in.

The music stopped and the room became silent. A man at the end of the long table stood and announced, "Good people, presenting Bishop Thomas Duforcquet — the Grand Inquisitor!"

He did not speak right away. Instead, the Bishop, now also known as the Grand Inquisitor, walked toward the center of the table. He glowered into Pierre's darting eyes before turning to face the audience. Then, with his back to the table, he motioned the children to step closer. Each went to either side of him. Clasping their hands, he pulled them close, protectively, allowing them to sink into the folds of his flowing robe.

Finally, the Grand Inquisitor said, "Lord Pierre of Loire, thank you for the gracious reception. I hope that our time here will be eventful. As you know, I take great care to see that my will is dispersed with both authority and compassion. Your servitude is, and always has been, most appreciated. Before we continue, we have the unexpected business that these two children present. You know them, yes?"

Lord Pierre's left nostril twitched and flared, but he didn't answer right away.

Isabelle was keenly aware of her uncle right behind her, and she felt his anger wrap a tentacle around her neck. She shook it off like a chill. *The Bishop was proving to be a formidable ally!*

Finally he said, "Yes, though their clothes are different, and they seemingly have changed sexes, they appear to be my niece and nephew."

A nervous ripple of laughter made the room feel smaller.

"They were found sleeping in a field on the other side of town. They told us an outlandish lie, and it seems that they intended to escape from *you*. Do you have any idea why they would do such a thing?" the Bishop asked.

"No, Grand Inquisitor Duforcquet, I do not. I became their guardian just a short time ago; after their parents were taken into custody."

"It appears they are frightened and confused. Such little angels should be sheltered and taken care of. Do you have any idea why they would not feel safe behind these walls with you?"

"I certainly do not. I have given them nothing but comfort."

"Their father was the lord of this manor, a Templar Knight and a Head Commander of the Order. Though he and his ilk are accused of worshiping a false god — a Muslim deity no less, these children are innocents."

"Yes, your Grace, innocent children indeed."

The Grand Inquisitor's voice echoed against the cavernous castle walls. "We must not let anything unfortunate happen to them. If their stay here is so distressing that they want to run away, then let's find them a home elsewhere."

"Sir, I believe the children will be fine here. I think their foray into the night was caused by the anguish of the unknown fate of their dear parents...my own sister! Perhaps, I can set aside my personal grief and tend to them more. They do belong here — with me."

"I think it may be prudent to allow the children to return with me. They can start fresh, in a new home. These poor angels have been through so much. It would give the good people of this land peace of mind to know that these innocent souls will be taken care of by me personally."

The noble crowd erupted in affirmation. A few ladies even clapped as Lord Pierre hung his shameful head.

The children nodded vigorously, and Louis actually giggled. Isabelle felt victorious over her evil uncle. She dared to take a glance over her shoulder and eyed him momentarily with a contemptuous stare.

The Bishop looked down at the imps cuddled within his robes. He smiled. "Then it's settled. They will return to Avignon with me until their parent's trial is over. Now, let's continue with more official business."

The rest of the conversation was inconsequential to Isabelle. As the Bishop discussed the loans, assets, and monetary holdings of the Templar Knights, the children were led away and given baths. After a warm, hearty meal, they were tucked in their beds and left to sleep until the morrow, when they were told they would leave for Avignon.

᪥ᖇ ❖ ᖉᥬ

In the middle of the night, Isabelle heard the chamber door creek. She opened her eyes just in time to see two swarthy figures enter their bedroom. They converged on the little angels and pulled them from their beds before either could cry for help.

Louis kicked as hard as he could, and Isabelle bit and scratched, but the men held firm. Despite their fierce efforts, the children were easily overpowered and dragged into the depths of the castle's keep.

They were brought to a dimly lit, circular chamber where each was sat on a tall, wooden stool. Isabelle knew they were in the tower room — a place her father had forbidden the children to play. Lord Pierre crouched against the concave wall across from his niece and nephew.

"What have you *done*?" he asked rhetorically.

Isabelle answered defiantly. "We've done nothing. It's what *you* have done! You are an evil, evil man! The Bishop knows about you. He'll chastise you if you hurt us."

Uncle Pierre shook his head methodically from side to side and leveled his gaze at Isabelle. "You don't understand, do you?"

"Yes I do!" Isabelle insisted. "After they took Mama and Papa, I *heard* you tell the other men that Louis and I were to be killed."

"That is only what you think you heard! It was he, the Bishop, who I spoke to that night. It was *he* who wanted you eliminated. He is the *Grand Inquisitor*!"

Isabelle scoffed. "I don't believe you! The Bishop is helping us. He wants us to be safe."

"The conversation you heard was only a ruse. I was pretending, agreeing with him so that I could gain his confidence and then save you! Don't you see? I was going to make sure that you were taken from here and protected. I didn't want to see you dead like your parents."

"Mama and Papa are dead?" Louis cried.

"No, they're not. They're being held someplace, waiting for trial. Louis, don't listen to Uncle Pierre; he's a bad man."

The door opened and in stepped Bishop Duforcquet. Louis jumped off his tall chair and ran to him, burying his face in the Holy Man's robes.

Isabelle cried out, "You've come! See, he tries to capture us again!" She spun skillfully, with fury, and challenged her uncle. "You can't lie to us anymore. Now you are caught, and the Bishop will punish you."

The Bishop pushed Louis aside and surveyed the family before him. "You failed, Pierre, on a splendid scale, didn't you? I asked for one little favor and promised you riches and power beyond your dreams. And you let them escape — children — insipid children?"

Uncle Pierre continued to eye Isabelle. Tears ran down his face. "Insolent children! Why did you run away?" he cried.

"No..." Isabelle whispered.

The Bishop grumbled at Lord Pierre. "It was lucky I came along when I did and managed to apprehend these little wretches on the highway. Our Savior, by His grace, returned them back to me. Thank you, Jesus!"

The two inquisitor guards mumbled, "Amen", in unison at the mention of their Lord.

The Bishop continued. "I am the Grand Inquisitor, I make all the decisions, and if you ever betray my orders again, you'll regret it, Pierre."

Isabelle watched Uncle Pierre nod in submission as the awful comprehension gnawed into her brain. *He was telling the truth! Uncle Pierre had been trying to protect them all along!*

The Bishop pointed at his men. "Dump the children in the oubliette."

Louis reacted quickly. He yanked the Bishop's flowing robe, causing the Holy Man to lose his balance and careen to the floor. The scuffle granted him a few precious seconds, and he took advantage by darting out the door.

"Hurry, Izzy!" he called to his sister.

Isabelle tried to follow her brother, but she wasn't fast enough. The men overtook her. Before they covered her mouth with an oversized, smothering hand, she cried out, "Run, Louis, run!"

The boy sped around a corner and stopped fast when he realized his sister wasn't behind him. "Izzy?"

From the depths of the keep, he heard her urgently command, "Don't wait for me, Louis, just goo...!" Her cry was cut short.

Louis hesitated in the lonely corridor. "Izzy, hurry," he whispered.

Hefty footfalls approached; he knew they weren't his sister's. The boy had no choice. He fled out a door and into the vineyard.

Isabelle's hands were tied behind her back. She thought the men would surely trammel her, but instead she was ushered forward, toward a section of the circular room that was veiled in shadows. One man pushed the small of her back with the butt of his blade, forcing her to walk forward, while the other steadied her shoulders.

They positioned her directly in front of the darkest part of the room. One of the men held forth a candle, revealing a cavity in the wall. It was a grotto with a trap door in the floor. He tapped it gently with the heel of his boot, and it swung open easily. A vile, ancient odor wafted up, and the girl gagged reflexively.

"Be done with it," the Bishop said from behind them flatly.

Isabelle squirmed, thrashing her head from side to side, looking around for her uncle, but he was no longer there. She was utterly alone and helpless.

To her surprise, she was hit again in the small of her back, this time hard. Caught off guard, she tumbled forward, head first, into the oubliette.

A smart girl, Isabelle had always been able to get out of challenging situations using her wit, skills, or agile body. Her greatest asset being that most people simply underestimated her. With crystal-clear vision, she now saw all those past situations dance before her. Sickening realization consumed her because this time, Isabelle knew, there was nothing she could do to save herself.

This time — the last time — Isabelle lost. Her only prayer was for a quick and painless end.

Down, down, spinning round, the darkness took a hold. She landed on top of a pile of dry bones, face first. Sharp, broken pieces sliced into her cheeks, her belly, and legs on impact.

She cried out, but the sound was drowned by blood rapidly filling her windpipe. She had been skewered like a bit of mutton over a fire pit. A jagged femur had ripped into her gut, through her lung, and out her fragile ribcage.

The pain was overwhelming. Mercifully, she quickly passed out. For how long, it was impossible to say. When she awoke, she could hear distant yelling. They were searching the castle for her brother. Isabelle was forgotten and completely alone in the oubliette.

Through the odor of death Isabelle perceived a sweet familiar aroma. It was the perfume her mother wore. With a broken, bloody hand she reached out, and felt the still face of her mamma. A few inches beyond her, was Isabelle's dead papa.

Sweet serenity consumed the broken girl as she caressed her parent's rotting cheeks. Knowing that her fight was over caused all anxiety and apprehension to wash away, leaving her with a sense of peace unlike any she had ever felt during her short life. Now, Isabelle could sleep.

Louis was the important one. After all, he held the secret that her parents had tried so fiercely to keep hidden. As long as he escaped, that was all that mattered. His big sister had done everything she could to save him. Now, as she lay dying, she could only hope that she had done enough.

Isabelle exhaled her last breath. With blood-soaked, trembling lips, she mouthed the words, "Run, little poppet, run!"

❧ ❧ ✦ ❦ ❦

Louis scuttled blindly through the vineyard in search of a hiding place. He could hear men shouting from inside the castle. They weren't outside yet, but would be soon.

Crouching low, he weaved through the rows of grape vines. Though his wounded ankle hurt, Louis remained focused and kept his head down as he followed the furrows. Every few seconds, he'd make a choking-gasp as he stifled sobs. *His sister was still back there. He left Izzy behind!*

Louis quickly concocted the best plan he could. He'd make his way through the vineyard, toward the back castle wall, then he'd follow it until he came to the crawl space he and Izzy had originally used to escape. He'd go through it, run to the woods, and follow the river to one of the small mountain villages where his sister wanted them to go in the first place. There, maybe he could find help. A constable would surely listen to his story, come back and arrest the Bishop, and free his sister...

His strategizing was interrupted by a pair of turnshoes blocking the path before him. The boy rapidly scrambled backward, but wasn't fast enough. A swift hand grabbed him by the scruff of the neck and pulled him up. Louis' mouth was covered before he could cry out.

Uncle Pierre's forlorn face appeared before him.

Louis dangled in the air, but he continued to fight. His arms and legs flailed wildly, and the muscular man almost lost his grip.

"Be quiet. They'll hear you!" Pierre said.

The boy howled as his uncle awkwardly tried to cover his mouth and hold onto him at the same time.

"Fear not, nephew," Pierre urged. "I'll help you!"

Louis continued to squirm and whimper.

Pierre clutched the boy's shoulders tightly. "Child, *I'm* the only one you can trust. If I intended to hurt you, don't you think I'd be dragging you back inside already rather than warning you to be quiet?"

Louis stopped struggling. His trepid eyes searched his uncle's for signs of deception. "What about Izzy?" he asked.

Lord Pierre shook his head. "There's nothing we can do for her now. But *you* can escape. Come, this way!"

Scurrying from shadow to shadow, the man led the boy to a small shed at the edge of the vineyard. They squatted on the dark side of it. Pierre held his pointer finger in the air, signaling Louis to wait. They both listened. In the distance, they could hear men yelling. One of them shouted orders to inspect the crawl space under the castle wall.

"Now I won't be able to escape," Louis sniveled. "They know about the hole under the fence!"

"You don't need that hole to escape. I have a better plan for you." Louis tightened up as the man once again tried to lead him. "Boy, you must trust me. I'm your blood; the only relative you have left. Come on, we have to hurry."

Louis half followed and was half dragged into the dirty little barn. He knew it was for storing wine. He had only been inside a couple times. There wasn't anything *fun* to play with in there, so he never had much interest in it.

Though dark, the shed was illuminated by beams of moonlight that filtered through holes in the roof. Uncle Pierre grappled with something unwieldy on the floor for several minutes. Dogs barked in the distance, and Louis knew he didn't have much time. He was about to bolt out the door and make a run for it, when the piercing squeal of rusty metal caused him to stop in his tracks. Pierre lifted a hatch and revealed a stairway in the floor.

The man handed the boy an oil lamp. "These stairs lead to the wine caverns, and from there to a maze of passageways. They are your only hope for escape. They end at an opening far beyond the castle walls, near the mountains. I only just traversed the path a few days ago, and therefore, left my footprints in the dirt. Follow my tracks, don't stray from the trail, and you'll come out on the other side just fine."

"It's dark. I can't go alone. I want Izzy!"

Lord Pierre gently cupped his nephew's face. "You have to be a brave man now, son. Your sister is gone. And I must hurry back before they discover I'm missing. You can do this; just follow my footprints to freedom. Once there, you must never come back. Do you understand? You're the soul surviving descendent of the Templar Knights. You must make it!"

"I don't understand what that means," the boy sobbed.

"Did your father ever reveal any of the Templar secrets to you? Did he ever show you the ancient texts or artifacts?"

"Those *secret* things?" Louis whispered. "Yes, Papa gave them to me to keep safe. I smuggled them out when Izzy and I escaped."

"You have them? They are safe..." Uncle Pierre began with a sudden burst of joy.

Louis started bawling again. "I lost them, though. The things that Papa gave me are gone! I left them in a Jewish man's house. The only thing I remember is the secret name —"

Lord Pierre slapped his hand across the child's mouth. "Don't say it! Don't tell anyone the name, not even me. If the Inquisitors tortured me...let's just say that you alone must protect the name. It's all that remains of your legacy. It has great power, and you must carry it on."

"But what about the satchel I left behind with the book and the sparkly skull..."

"Don't worry about those things. They'll return to the castle one day. They're connected to this place, and they won't stay lost forever." Lord Pierre squeezed the boy in a hearty hug. "Come on, we have to get you out of here," he said as he led Louis down the stairs.

"Where am I supposed to go once I get to the mountains?"

Pierre reached into his trousers and pulled out a small sack of coins. "Use this to buy room and board. Take it to some...people I know. There are women who live in a house — an inn — in the little town through the pass. It's called *The Velvet Lion*. Find it and ask for Elizabeth and Merrie. Tell them you're a friend of 'Pepe', and you need a place to stay for a while. Give them one coin a month, and they should take good care of you for nearly a year. Do chores for them, work, earn your keep, and you'll likely be able to stay longer. Never tell them who you are or where you came from, though, okay?"

"Okay," the boy said and then he asked, "*Pepe?*"

"Don't worry about that," Pierre said, brushing away the boy's curiosity while lightly blushing. "Just know the ladies will take good care of you. They'll help you grow into a man. And one day when you have a son — and this is imperative — give your son the secret name. When he's old enough, instruct him to do the same. Your lineage must pass the name down the line from generation to generation. It can't ever be forgotten."

Louis tightened up and seriously asked, "Does that mean I will have to get married, to a *girl?*" He scrunched his nose.

Uncle Pierre paused and then released a rumbling chuckle. "Yes, you will need to get married to a *girl,* so you can have a son. Don't worry, it won't sound so bad in a few years."

"And one day my son will come back here?"

"Perhaps. Or it might be your son's son. Or even your son's son's son! All I know is that this legacy must not ever be forgotten. Quick, let me tell you a story. Listen close and put it to memory, okay?"

The man and boy crouched together on the final step of the cavern's stairs. Pierre took a deep breath and related as quickly as he could: "Many years ago, Pagans who once lived on this land performed an ancient ritual to appease the gods. It happened right here on this spot, where the castle stands today. They had done this ceremony many times, and it always kept peace and harmony in the land. One time, however, something went horribly wrong. An ancient creature not of this world was set free. If left to its own evil devices, it brings death and devastation."

He lit the oil lamp and continued. "One Pagan sorceress was smart, though. She cast a spell that captured the creature, binding it to just a small area, roughly equal to the size of the castle grounds. It was forced to remain here, trapped and unable to cause havoc and mayhem in the world. To keep it under control, the sorceress crafted the skull, which is now known as the Templar Head. Using the Head and invoking the secret name is the only way to command it."

Louis gaped at his uncle and asked, "Is that the devil I saw in the woods? It was afraid when I held up the sparkly skull."

"Probably," Pierre answered. "It roams the outskirts hoping to find wandering souls that are too far to be protected by the 'sparkly skull'. If you held it up, it surely would have been frightened off."

"If it's so bad, why not kill it? Knights are stalwart! They could have sent it back to wherever it came from!"

Pierre chose his words carefully. "It isn't that simple. Though the creature is spiteful and bitter, it's also powerful. When controlled by the right people, it can be commanded to do great good. It's only bad if used by the wrong people. The Church is the 'wrong people'. That's who you must keep it from at all costs."

Louis digested his uncle's words as best he could. "So, Papa and Mama, they were knights, and they kept this secret?"

"Your father was a Head Commander, the one specifically ordained to control it. All the Knights who lived here were Temple Knights, or Templars as they have become known. They were descendants of the Pagans who first unleashed the creature."

"Papa said he'd share the teachings with me one day. Nos-ick, he called them."

"Gnostic," Pierre corrected. "It means knowledge. Your parents and the rest of the Templars were keepers of esoteric knowledge they kept hidden for centuries. They became friends with the Church, but it was more like 'pretending'. A strategic ploy so as not to raise suspicion. They carried out crusades and fought in the name of the Lord Jesus. Being aligned with the Church gave them the ability to grow and amass more recruits. However, as the order grew, they became more and more powerful and wealthy. And the Church didn't like that."

"Why?" the boy asked.

"The Templars threatened the Church. Their wealth, power, and their heretical ways put the Pope's tyranny in danger. That's why the Inquisitors came and laid siege to your parent's castle. Not only was *this* place attacked, but Templar leaders all over Europe were obliterated. They made false accusations — told lies — and sentenced hundreds to their deaths!"

Dogs barked nearby.

"Don't worry, Uncle Pierre, I'll pass down the legacy. I promise — pinky-cross promise." Louis made the sign of the cross with his two little fingers and nodded.

"I know you will," Pierre said. "Time to go. Use the lantern to follow my tracks. Don't leave the path for anything, just stay on course, and you'll be on the other side in no time. Travel well, dear Louis, and never forget the things you've learned here tonight."

Louis clutched the lantern with his chubby fist. "I won't." He hugged his uncle one last time, turned, and hastened into the austere depths of the caverns.

Chapter 109

Veronica's Story

Nikki sat at the mahogany dining table with a throng of RSVP slips spread before her.

Veronica pulled up a chair. "How many are there?"

"One hundred-seventy-two. We'll prolly get at least fifty more in the mail today. Can I throw a party or can I throw a party, huh?"

"Yeah, but will we have working toilets?" Veronica noted as a coverall-wearing plumber, carrying an armful of copper pipes, lumbered past the French doors. Clark had not come to work in several days. Veronica was used to his long weekends, but this was different. The man didn't answer calls, and no one else had heard from him either.

Veronica feared he may have just up and quit, leaving her hanging. He was an odd, seemingly inept man, and she cursed herself for hiring him in the first place. The thought of scrambling to find a new plumber jarred her nerves. Fortunately, her sister was working on a solution to the problem.

"The subcontractor plumbers that Clark hired are managing to get things under control," Nikki explained. "The new septic tank still needs to be installed, but they're putting in a temporary sump-pump, and promise to have the bathroom off of the ballroom working in time for the party."

"Lovely, so in the meantime, we are still using the porta potties?"

"Yep."

Veronica scrunched up her nose in disgust and then softly began. "I got a call back from that doctor last night. Dr. Sandbourne..."

"You did? Did he remember you?"

"Yeah."

"Whad' he say?"

"He said he'd been wondering about me over the years. He said he and *Dr. Jacobs* treated me when I was a kid. I figured that it must be the same Dr. Jacobs who recommended me! I was pretty happy to figure out that little mystery when he started to freak out. Told me to start taking medication for my night terrors. That's what he called them — *night terrors*. He even called in a prescription for me." Veronica held up the paper, and continued. "I think it's for a tranquillizer. But I can't take something that'll knock me out!"

"Let me see," Nikki said. She snatched the paper and nodded.

"I couldn't understand everything he said. My phone went dead."

"Are you gonna take these drugs?"

"I don't like the idea of taking medicine like that. I only had *one* nightmare. He's probably just one of those doctors who prescribe pills at the drop of a hat."

Nikki nodded. "Right now we need to be getting ready for this party, not taking naps. It's two days away."

"Agreed," Veronica said and spent the rest of the morning perfecting her castle.

Chapter 110

Father Michel's Story

Gaston-Elise awoke the next day to more chiming chapel bells. They rang for hours, and that was highly unusual.

He knew they signified something more than the deaths of ordinary men.

Shortly after the bells stopped, he watched several priests and servants scramble from the Château. They carried few belongings and hastily made their way to the gatehouse. Like rats evacuating an infected ship, they scurried wildly toward freedom.

They weren't allowed to leave, though. Several loyal guards stopped them with rehearsed commands. "By order of the Cardinal, you are bound to his service and cannot leave!"

The threats weren't enough to keep the desperate from trying. They rushed the doors, and the guards brandished weapons, cutting down the brave ones who led the revolt. Blood flowed freely as chaos erupted.

Gaston-Elise saw the commander march onto the scene.

The man's uniform was covered in crimson and his helmet missing. The hair on the left side of his exposed head was matted with dried blood.

One priest wandered the grounds with his arms raised to God. "The Lord is my Shepherd! He is *your* Shepherd as we walk through the valley of darkness!" he called out. A guard ordered him to go back inside. The priest stumbled toward him, but before he could take more than two steps, the guard cut him down with one swift stroke of his long sword.

Gaston-Elise turned his face away, and when he summoned up the courage to look again, he saw several people scaling the castle walls. A sniper from the tower fired arrows. He was a poor shot, but still managed to strike two unlucky victims. They fell wailing to the ground.

The riot continued until one of the bishops stepped onto a second story balcony of the Château. He called for everyone's attention. Surprisingly, slowly, it was granted to him. The people were desperate for leadership, for someone to give them direction, and they turned to the highest ranking Church official left alive.

The bishop grasped the railing and leaned forward, scanning the atrocious scene before him. His robe fell open, and in a flash, Gaston-Elise saw bright red welts on the man's neck and chest.

Pulling his robe shut to conceal the infection, he clumsily tied it and then called out, "Don't allow the darkness of the black death to enter your hearts. It may infect our bodies, but we must not let it infect our souls! Please, hear me as I spoke with the Cardinal as he lay on his deathbed. He wanted peace in his final hour, as we should all find peace now. Pray with me..."

The mob of people transformed into obedient sheep. The dutiful guards, the panic-stricken escapees, the infected — they all paused to listen.

The bishop steadied himself by leaning forward against the balcony rail as he asked, "Lord, forgive our sins. Walk with us for we are the faithful..."

Everyone hung their head as they listened to the prayer. They weren't looking at the bishop, but Gaston-Elise was. The preacher's upper body bent over, far over the railing. A sheen glistened on his bare, heaving chest.

"As we stand on the threshold of darkness, we will not fear evil. Lord bestow your grace upon us as we humbly beg salvation. Lift us in your loving arms as we prepare..."

He swayed.

Gaston-Elise held his breath as the bishop's eyes rolled back. Reaching out to the heavens, the preacher made a vague swipe of his arms toward his Lord just before falling head first off the balcony.

He called out to Jesus as he plummeted to the cobblestones below. His head hit first and exploded like a blood-filled melon.

The docile crowd erupted. The guards, once again, sprang into action and tried to force the hysterical mob to submission, but pandemonium was unavoidable. Without regard for rules, people fled in mass, fighting for their lives as they tried to escape the plague-infected castle. Some of the guards even turned on their commanders and joined the revolt.

Gaston-Elise slunk back into his corner and covered his ears. He closed his eyes and rocked back and forth while chanting prayers.

Someone rattled his door. He pulled a knife, prepared to defend his humble refuge if needed.

The lock held. Whoever tried to get in sobbed loudly and eventually went away.

Gaston-Elise fought to drown out the calls for help, the blubbery sobs of pain, and the mournful caterwauls of the dying. He burrowed under the small blanket on his bed, covered his head, and continued to clutch the knife. Still he heard the cries of the doomed. The pleas followed him into the night and haunted his dreams until the silence of morning broke.

Chapter 111

Dorothée's Story

Julien-Luc felt timid, like a lad reciting a story before a headmaster, as he prepared to recite the ancient Templar legend of the Head. It was a story so profound and esoteric, only the highest masters knew it. Now he was revealing it to his captor's wife.

He began, "Ages ago, when Pagan beliefs prevailed across France and most of Europe, an evil witch known as 'the Hag' sacrificed a young warrior's betrothed to an unholy demon. The maiden was a rare, brave beauty and the boy loved her fiercely. She was the light that guided his every thought, a beam of happiness and hope in a world filled with toil and death. When she died, his soul fractured into a thousand pieces. He wished more than anything to be able to hold her one last time."

Dorothée closed her eyes and soaked in the prisoner's words. She sighed, "A passion so deep is a rare thing indeed. Such tragedy to not have it fulfilled."

Julien-Luc noticed how Dorothée's thin nightgown, coated with a glint of perspiration, clung to her body as she sat on the floor beside him. She urged, "Continue, please…" and he did.

"He imagined her touch every night in his dreams. He knew he'd never feel her soft breath on his skin again or stroke her long locks of hair. And he would never, not in a million moons, be able to consummate their love. So, in the deepest, darkest of nights, he crept into her tomb, and found her there. She appeared to him as she did while alive — fresh and warm, beautiful and inviting. He could not resist…"

"Did he…?" Dorothée began.

Julien-Luc nodded. "In the small hours of the morning, as the sun began to peek over the tips of the mountains, he made love to her. They shared a moment of passion that few could understand. But their union was not a secret. The Hag found them there. She was spiteful, mean and bitter. She cursed him for his undying love and cast a spell that made the maiden's corpse give birth to that unholy demon."

"That is what I saw then, the 'unholy demon'? It was frightful. Why would the Temple Priests want it here? Why keep such an evil, vile thing?"

"The warrior boy made a pledge to his true love. He vowed to build a beautiful monument to her memory. For months he toiled all by himself, building a tower over her tomb, to forever mark her final resting place. This turret that we are in right now, is that monument."

Dorothée looked around uneasily. She nodded at the boarded up hole in the wall, "And that…?" she asked.

"That is where she rests, deep down a hole that has been since transformed into an oubliette. It is a cursed place now, a pit, where victims are thrown and left to die. The Hag came back, you see. And when she saw the magnificent monument the young warrior built, she cursed it. She condemned the demon to reside here, unable to ever go beyond the castle grounds."

"Why did the Temple Priests stay here? Why does anyone stay here then if it is cursed?"

"The Temple Priests learned how to control it. They established dominion over the demon by using its name and a sacred relic known as the Head. They used its power for good and to defeat enemies. That is what I am looking for, dear Dorothée."

"You're looking for a *Head* that controls the demon?"

"I have to find it. My brethren and I were resolutely content to keep to ourselves until we heard this castle was granted to Lord André-Benoit by the Church. As the newest vassal of this land, we knew he'd be responsible for housing Protestant criminals. And we knew it might be our only chance to infiltrate these walls and try to find our lost treasure. That's what I came to uncover. I have to find out if it is still here, somewhere...and you, dear Dorothée, may have found a map that will lead me to it!"

"Lost treasure?" she asked.

"The Bible handed down from Empress Helena herself; an original from the council of Nicaea. Plus, gold, gems, jewelry — such as the medallion you found — and of course, The Head. Those are the most valuable artifacts the Templars possessed. During the Inquisition, the Church went mad looking for them."

"They wanted to steal the Templar treasure?"

"They wanted to *destroy* it!"

"But why?"

He explained, "In the early 1300s, while they were sending the Templars to fight crusades in the Holy Land, the Church leaders learned a secret about Empress Helena."

"What secret could there be about Saint Helena? I have read about her. Not much is known, though. It is like the history books about her were lost."

"Not lost. *Erased.* Her story was eradicated by the Church. She was the mother of Constantine, the Roman Emperor who in the year AD 325 became the architect of Christianity as we know it. She was a crucial player in the early formation of the religion. Mostly known because she went on pilgrimages to Jerusalem and Bethlehem to bring back religious relics."

"Yes, this I already know," she said hurriedly. Dorothée grew excited and impatient.

"What you *don't* know, is the secret the Church discovered. She had also been a member of the Temple Priests, and had bestowed them with ancient knowledge from those pilgrimages."

"Saint Helena was part of the Temple Order — part of *your* order? Let me guess, the Church wanted to suppress that knowledge! Just as they do today."

Julien-Luc grinned at his pupil. "Yes! The Pope found out about The Head, and accused the Templars of worshipping a 'Muslim God', as they called it, because of Helena's connection to the Holy Lands. Trumped-up accusations of heresy, blasphemy and practicing witchcraft were leveled against them. This was the start of the Inquisition."

"The bloodiest time in history. And it all stemmed from Saint Helena."

"It wasn't all because of Helena. The Templars amassed great wealth while escorting pilgrims to the Holy Land. They established a powerful banking system and were the holders of much land and property. Knowledge and wealth equaled power — and the Church would not allow the Templars to usurp them. *That* is the real reason for the Inquisition." Julien-Luc finished with a wink and a nod.

"Now I understand the animosity you hold for the Church — and why it is your mission to find the Templar treasure."

"I only hope it's still here, hidden, waiting to be found."

"The map is titled 'caves of the dead'. Do you know where that is?" she asked breathless.

He frowned. "No. But it must be close. Are there any caves nearby that you know of?"

Dorothée started shaking her head, then stopped and brightened with revelation. "There are underground crypts, a network of tunnels; André-Benoit told me about them! That must be it!"

"Can you take me there?"

Her excitement deflated. "He said the entrance is in the vineyard, where the remains of a grape house once stood. But it was sealed centuries ago. We can find it though — dig our way through. Let me get the map at once!"

"I doubt we could dig through in a single night. We don't know how deep it is, nor how hard the ground."

"André-Benoit returns tomorrow! You must escape *now*."

"I can wait. No harm will come to me as long as André-Benoit thinks I have Protestant intelligence. I can stall him; feed him bits at a time so he keeps me around. You, in the meantime, can talk to him. Tell him..." he thought fast, "you want to plant a *garden* on that spot! Get his men to excavate it for you. They will loosen the ground so I can easily break through on the night I choose to escape. Use your *charms* to get him to do it. That shouldn't be too difficult for you."

Dorothée caught her breath as her deepest desires spilled out from within. "No! I don't want to charm *him*!"

"No?" he asked.

"No, of course not. And I want to come with *you*!"

He leaned closer to her. "You would *come* with me?"

Her hands clasped together. "Yes. Please take me with you! I am a prisoner, too, in this damned place. We'll escape together!"

"Darling Dorothée, you jest me in the most cruel ways."

"I make no jest. I want to come. I want to be rid of this drab, boring fortress."

"What about your husband; you would dishonor him this way? Don't you love him?"

"I do not," she said simply. "I thought I did. He gave me everything I ever wanted. An opulent life, all the gowns a girl could dream of, jewelry and perfumes, a prestigious title, my own servants. I thought that would be enough, but it isn't."

"You would be a fugitive, and it would be dangerous. Forever you would be running, always hiding, always afraid of being caught."

"We'll escape to Germany together. You have your friends there, and they'll help us. We won't get caught. Besides, I already know too much for my own good. Would your brethren feel safe with *me*, a *Catholic* noble, who knows all their secrets, pining away here for her lost love?"

Julien-Luc searched her eyes. "You would pine for me?'

"I pine for you even now, and you are merely inches away."

He visibly flushed in the flickering lantern light and quietly spoke. "You should go back to your room, Dorothée. Before someone finds you here."

"No one will find me. The boy who was to guard your room is in town and won't return for hours. Everyone else is asleep, and my husband isn't due back until tomorrow. I can stay here, at least a little longer, there's plenty of time...." Red locks of hair hung over her eyes.

"But you *shouldn't*."

"But, I *want* to..." She leaned forward, merely an inch, and swiped the hair away from her face to reveal slightly parted lips.

"You don't understand. You *can't* stay here."

Dorothée withdrew. She leaned back on one arm, contemplating his last statement. "You mean you don't *want* to be with me?"

"That's not what I said. I want...very much...I have to honor my duty though. I swore an oath. Nothing can cloud my judgment. I have but one mission to accomplish here. I have to find that treasure. Being with you, here like this, compromises my objective. My brethren would not be pleased."

Bubbles tingled in her loins. Rather than becoming dissuaded, she found herself rippling with deeper desire. She leaned back further and breathed deeply. The ties on the front of her nightgown were loose and gave way easily as her chest heaved. She relaxed her shoulders, and her nightgown began to fall open. "And I just swore an oath to you...to help you find your treasure. So, which oath would you prefer?"

"Dorothée, you are beautiful, desirable, but there is too much at stake, and I can't take foolish risks."

Dorothée plucked the ties on the front of her nightgown until her bare chest was fully exposed. Like a siren she sang. "Are you calling me foolish?"

Julien-Luc shook his head.

Dorothée perched on her knees and let her nightgown fall. It cascaded to the floor like liquid. She leaned over and gently kissed his forehead. At the same time, she let her breast brush across on his chin.

"Dorothée, we shouldn't..."

As his mouth talked, she carefully allowed her nipple to connect with his lips. He sat still, not accepting her advances, but also not avoiding them. She breathed deeply and looked down at him, dominating him with her naked body.

He did not respond.

After several long seconds, she pouted with a huff. "Very well then. I will do as you wish and leave. After all, my husband returns tomorrow night after being gone for quite long time. I shall save my charms for him. Is that what you'd like me to do? Seduce *him* so he unearths the entrance to the catacombs for my fake *garden*?"

His desire swelled.

Before she could pull away, Julien-Luc wrapped his arms around her, drew her to her feet, and buried his face in her mane of hair.

She rolled her head back, exposed her neck, and he devoured her skin, kissing, nibbling. She tugged at his shirt, pulled his arms through the sleeves, and yanked it overhead. His trousers came undone easily, and once they fell to the floor, their skin melted together, warm and fiery.

Feeling his hardness sent a thrilling bolt through Dorothée. She grinded her hips against his, but Julien-Luc pulled away. As she pushed forward, he stepped back, and together they fell onto the bed. He went down on his rump, and she quickly climbed on top of him, straddling like a rider on a horse.

Holding her buttocks, he prevented her from finding him.

"Why do you tease me so?" she moaned in his ear.

He twisted her to the side, so she twirled and lay on her back. "Because you deserve it," he challenged and climbed on top of her, pinning her down with his weight.

She squirmed underneath and giggled as he dodged her roving pelvis. "I know what I deserve..." she goaded.

His response was absolute stillness.

"What?" she asked and also froze.

"I thought I heard something..."

"This creaky castle; I *always* hear something. Relax, we have nothing to worry about," she cooed and nibbled his tilted ear.

Julien-Luc acquiesced and looked at her deeply. "Promise me this is no game, Dorothée. You will help me find what I'm looking for. And you'll come with me, leaving your husband behind. Tell me."

"I promise, my love."

He entered her, gradually, timidly, while gently nuzzling her neck. She gasped as he filled her and then chuckled at her own outburst.

Julien-Luc's confidence grew, and he pushed again, this time harder and faster. She pressed firmly against him, and they moved in unison.

His world disappeared, and he felt blind and blissful, with no past or future. Everything was contained in the moment. He absorbed it eagerly, hungrily. At that instant, nothing mattered but the way he felt inside Dorothée. His promise to his brethren, his mission, the prison cell he was in, her husband, none of that held any importance. Breathing her scent in and out consumed him totally. Just as the intensity was about to overpower him, Julien-Luc slowed his pace to extend the moment.

She groaned hungrily, clutched his backside, and pulled down, forcing his hips to press into hers. A strange lucidity engulfed her. Her entire body tingled, and she felt as though she was hovering on a ledge, but she didn't allow herself to jump in completely. Her lips, her nose and then her whole face became numb.

Dorothée drifted into a stupor. Dreamily, she imagined another presence there, as if she was being taken by two lovers.

Opening her eyes confirmed that only Julien-Luc was hovering above her. On the edge of her sight, however, just beside the bed, a shadow lurked.

She wanted to say something, but Julien-Luc felt divine inside her. The sensation of him pushing into her again and again caused her mind to go numb with a dopey kind of pleasure. Like an intoxicant, it made the real world insignificant. Closing her eyes, she ignored what was surely just the flickering lantern light and enjoyed the rhapsody of making love to Julien-Luc.

Something hot and hairy brushed against her naked shoulder.

Dorothée squeaked in surprise, but before she could fully react, Julien-Luc pulled her up into a sitting position and away from whatever it was.

My imagination is playing tricks with me, she thought as he positioned her like a doll. She was paralyzed with passion, barely able to move, as her entire body rippled with pleasure.

An instant before a surge of energy could erupt from inside her, Julien-Luc stopped. She took two deep breaths as he spun her around and laid her on her stomach.

He entered her again. This time even more slowly than before.

She steadied herself on all fours as her husband's prisoner cupped one of her breasts and tapped her nipple in a deliberate rhythm with his steady glide. His other hand moved across her stomach and pushed her into him with each exquisitely deep thrust. His fingers trailed down, down, until they found her moist warmth and began to dance.

She felt him all over her, caressing every aching part of her body at once; like smoke he engulfed her.

There it was again.

As her body grew stiff with excitement, she clearly felt something *underneath* her. Something that was not Julien-Luc crouched between her belly and the bed. It was moving, twitching with the rhythm. Waves of pleasure and terror simultaneously washed over her.

She wanted to cry out, but her throat tightened as a whiff of decay accosted her sinuses. Strands of fur lapped at her exposed underbelly. It hovered there as though it was waiting....

Julien-Luc thrust hard and pushed her down. She felt the thing buried under her gut writhe like an animal. It couldn't be the Templar Demon, could it? Preparing to burrow its way into her, clawing and scratching like a rabid rat, into her stomach!

Dorothée went stiff. Ecstasy engulfed her like a tight glove, and she couldn't move. She was completely paralyzed as roiling bouts of passion assaulted her over and over again. She forced out a sound, just a whimper, as that's all her body would allow while on the verge of rapture.

Julien-Luc's index finger suddenly dug deep and sought out her warmest, wettest, most sensitive spot. He played her like a harp.

This caused a new level of intensity to shoot through her. Dark waves of pleasure swirled in Dorothée's head. She knew she was vulnerable at that moment. Her intuition told her the creature was about to attack, but the ravishing made her powerless to do anything about it.

Julien-Luc pulled her upright, and in an instant, they were both on their knees. *She was free of it!*

While he pushed from behind, she saw the black, mangy thing on the bed in front of her. As her loins exploded, she screamed with both ecstasy and fright.

Julien-Luc released. The thing hissed. The door burst open.

Dorothée experienced several things at once.

Bolts of orgasm rippled through her body like a glorious melody.

The thing beneath her careened off the bed. It was fast, and she only caught a bleary glimpse of its human-like eyes as it disappeared into the shadows.

In the doorway, she saw André-Benoit. His mouth was a gaping hole, and his eyes round like the full moon.

Julien-Luc was still inside her, warm, throbbing, coming, and oblivious. His hands came around and each cupped a breast as he pushed tenderly inside of her, one last time, and whispered, "I love you."

Chapter 112

Sebastian's Story
325 AD – When Rome Spread its Empire across the Barbaric Territories

Esindra pressed her back into a crook, trying to swathe herself in the shadow. She knelt to become as small and insignificant as possible. As long as no one noticed her, she might be able to ride out the battle.

It didn't work. One of the wild men summoned by the horn advanced on her. He was fresh to the skirmish, fully armed with a studded battle axe, and he snarled at the governess with what she determined to be a mixture of fury and lust.

From across the room Baldebert saw his approach. "Stay away from her!" he barked. "She's not to be harmed!"

The roar of combat was too loud, though, and the invader did not hear the Head Commander's order.

Esindra cried out to Fabius. "Help me! Fabius!"

Her husband stood ten feet away. He turned and saw the brute stalking his wife. "You were ordered to stay in your room!" he bellowed to her.

"Fabius!" Esindra cried.

He scowled, turned away, and pushed a dagger into the gut of an attacker.

Baldebert charged toward Esindra as fast as his wobbly legs would go. Again he called out to his kinsman, "Stay back from her!" and still was not heard.

The boor snagged Esindra by her coiled braids. She squealed and kicked.

Baldebert quickly aimed the crystal skull in the direction of the attacker and whispered, "To him, now!"

The barbarian's hand burst into flame. He screaked and let go of Esindra. Staggering backward, his arm, then his torso, burst into flame. He fled across the courtyard like a human torch.

Esindra stood dazed.

Baldebert rushed to her side. "You're okay now," he said.

"You killed your kinsman to save me?" she asked.

"Yes, you're safe with me. Just stay close," the Head Commander answered.

Several feet away Fabius pulled his dagger out of the stomach of an enemy with a blubbering slurp. He wiped bloody tendrils on the fallen man's fur vest and looked around for his next conquest. He spied Baldebert.

The Druid had only a split second to react. He dodged out of the way as the Roman governor sliced the air with his weapon.

Baldebert spun, lifted the Head, and gave the instructions.

Fabius didn't react at first. He continued to draw back his blade, intent on skewering the barbarian leader.

Esindra yelled to her husband. "Baldebert saved me just now! Don't hurt him. Please, spare him on my behalf."

Fabius didn't look at her. Instead, he swiped his weapon again. This attempt was feeble, though, and Baldebert easily dodged out of the way. Steam wafted off his attacking arm, but the governor didn't seem to notice. Out of the corner of his mouth, he answered his wife. "This is not your concern."

She stepped in front of Baldebert, between him and her husband. "You would slay the man who saved me when *you* would not?"

He pulled back, intent upon backhanding his wife, then paused. He stared at his extended arm. Boils formed. The skin stretching into tiny pustules that were red and wet, as if his flesh was being boiled right on the bone.

Esindra saw the fire blisters spread across her husband's arm and recoiled, stepping back into Baldebert. The Druid held her close and said, "There is no hope for him now, my lady."

One of the boils erupted and sprayed yellow pus. It was like a tiny firecracker detonating just under the surface of his skin. Then another burst on his wrist. Fabius cried out and jiggled his hand violently as if he could shake them away. A large one formed on the side of his brow. Esindra and Baldebert both skulked back, preparing for the inevitable pop.

Fabius suddenly seemed frail and vulnerable to Esindra. Trembling lips pleaded, "Make them stop, my wife, please." As he spoke, the ripening furuncle on his temple splattered hot beads of blood across her white robe.

Fabius cried out and placed both palms on his face. There were several fire blisters on his hands and forearms. Esindra and Baldebert turned away as the doomed man's flesh snapped like boar fat in a skillet.

Fabius called out to his men, but none came to the aide of their leader. The barbarian army had infiltrated the outer perimeter, and the entire hoard was now storming the fortress. All the soldiers were engaged in combat — fighting for their lives — there was not one who could help him.

His body, now ridden with steaming, bubbling pockmarks, collapsed forward. The lesions frothed with bodily fluids, causing blood, sweat and bile to brew together in a puddle around him. He sloshed and squirmed on his belly while crying for mercy.

As his heart neared its final beat, the dying man lifted his head onto its chin, keeping his mouth and nose raised so he wouldn't drown in his own juices. His upward glaring eyes beheld the attacking army as it poured into the courtyard. Everywhere weapons clanked, men caterwauled, and Roman soldiers fell.

Using his good arm, Fabius rolled onto his back. The pain ripped through him like a thick, searing blade, but at least he could breathe.

As he pulled in his last few breaths, he caught a glimpse of a swarthy shape climbing near the top of the courtyard walls. Its appendages were long and gangly. Like a spider, it lurched in and out of the shadows. The creature cocked its narrow head and knowing eyes locked momentarily with Fabius'. Then Baldebert barked out another command, and the creature shifted its attention to someone else.

Suddenly, something loomed over Fabius and blocked his view. It was Esindra. Her soft features were drawn up sharply. She said nothing; just watched like one might curiously observe an insect roasting on a burning log.

He reached for her. His arm was a fuming kabob of grey, boiled meant. The governess stepped back as her husband's forearm grew several more fire blisters. She shielded her eyes when they exploded. Upon opening them, her husband lay dead and smoldering at her feet.

Chapter 113

Veronica's Story

Pain. Dull, throbbing, constant, and then a sheer jolt rumbled from within. Rising and falling like waves, subsiding for a few moments, and then another stab brought her closer to consciousness. Veronica rolled over, tangling herself up in her own bed sheets. She groaned. Her hand slipped under the covers and she cradled her abdomen. Reluctantly, she realized the gnawing cramps were unmistakable. Veronica was getting her period.

She strained to see the clock on the nightstand — three-fifteen. Why did it always come in the small hours of the morning? She flung her legs over the side of the bed, felt the floor for her slippers, and discovered the obnoxious furry footwear that her sister had given her. Not being particular while half asleep, she slid them on. She grabbed her bag from the top of the dresser, and while taking short, slippery footsteps, scuttled to the bathroom.

Veronica kept her eyes squinted. She was tired, and her sleepy mind reasoned that if she kept her eyes nearly shut, maybe her body wouldn't realize that it was awake.

She flipped on the bathroom nightlight. She made her way to the toilet and just before she sat down noticed that the water level in the bowl was almost nonexistent. One eye opened wide, validating the situation in the toilet bowl. She muttered, "Damn!" and jiggled the handle. Nothing. No flush, no rush of water — the toilet wasn't working again.

Veronica cursed Clark as she hurried out of the bathroom. She made her way through the kitchen and exited out the side door. The porta potties were just around the corner, and she needed to get to one in a hurry.

White flashed, flooding the darkness with brightness. It was a motion sensitive light. Clark had installed it to illuminate the path between the kitchen door and the porta potties.

She made a wide circle around an area that was sectioned off with yellow tape. Underneath it was the old septic tank — the cause of all their toilet troubles. To one side was a huge, orange machine. A backhoe. Its metal-toothed scooper was dripping with mud.

The ground was soggy. It had been raining for weeks almost non-stop. "Unseasonably wet," the locals declared. Veronica sunk into the grass; her insensible shoes digging in with pointed heels. She pulled her bathrobe tight around her neck as a crisp wind blew flecks of rain down her pajama top.

She reached the Porta Potty and settled inside to take care of business. It took a while. Severe cramps rippled through her gut. Veronica rummaged in her bag for a bottle of ibuprofen. She swallowed several mauve pills dry and coughed a little as she sat in agony, waiting for the medicine to quell her pain.

Once finished, she stepped back outside into pitch-blackness. The motion light had turned off. She waved her arms in the air as she trudged across the soggy lawn, attempting to signal the light to turn on again.

Something rubbed against her bare ankle.

Startled, she wavered in the blackness and tumbled forward, head first into the muck.

"Freaking Christ! What the hell was that?"

She pushed herself up; her palms slipping into the soggy goop. Up she came to her feet and took two tentative steps forward. Muck and slime seeped between her toes. Though she couldn't see it, she knew the fuzzy mink slippers were a mud-soaked mess.

She dug like mad into her bag. Her hand rubbed against her organizer, lipstick, Tic-Tacs. Finally, *thank God there it was — my trusty little flashlight!* She snapped it on and surveyed the ground around her.

Veronica was standing in the middle of the yellow taped-off area, above the seeping septic tank, where the ground had been dug up by the backhoe. It was uneven and soupy. Behind her was a length of the tape, smeared into the mud. She had tripped over it.

She tried to step forward but fell down again. Her left foot wouldn't move. Shining the flashlight she saw it submerged in the sewage. Veronica pulled hard with her right foot as leverage, but it also sank. The moist earth slurped at her flesh. Like the wet mouth of a giant, it sucked her legs like drinking straws.

She collapsed to her knees awkwardly and attempted to crawl. The terrycloth robe grew heavy as it sucked up moisture and tangled between her legs. *Well that fucking didn't work!*

Next she rose so she was standing on her knees. Her legs bent unnaturally beneath her, causing hot pain to sear her calves as she struggled.

"Shit!" she cursed while waving her arms wildly, as if she could flap hard enough to fly away.

Falling to her hands again, Veronica attempted to wiggle free. She slithered in the mud, but instead of moving forward, the American girl sank deeper. The consistency of the mud became more fluid as she churned it.

Liquefaction, she thought, *it's what happens when soil becomes saturated with water. And it's not something you want to get stuck in.* Being a California native, she knew the phenomenon, as it was associated with earthquakes and mudslides — and apparently old, French castle septic tanks, too.

"Help!" She jerked and thrashed as her thighs began to submerge.

Veronica was sinking.

Next, her hips disappeared beneath the surface. She shimmied like a hula dancer and grunted like a linebacker, as if sheer willpower would be enough to break free.

The muck reached Veronica's belly.

Her desperate hands searched for anything firm to hold on to. Finally, she wrapped her hand around something round and hard. *A rock?* Her slime-covered, wiggling fingers gripped the object. Grasping for a firm hold, her thumb and forefinger pushed into two tiny holes. It felt like...*a bowling ball?* She shined the flashlight to see she was holding a human skull. Its dead grin beamed gleefully as her thumb dug into its eye socket.

With snap, she threw it like a hot potato. Then the tears started streaming down her pitch-covered face. Veronica sobbed manically.

She called out for help, chanting her sister's name over and over again. "Nikki! Nikki! Nik-eee!" The only response was that of a nearby owl, hooting at the disruption of its peaceful morning.

Another skull popped up in front of her. This one had black skin hanging from sallow cheek bones. She pushed it away and tried to swim in the muck; however, her struggle only caused the murky liquid to splash in her face. It got in her mouth, up her nose, and she could both taste and smell the defecation and death. Veronica clamped her lips shut and held her breath intuitively. She was slipping deeper and deeper. She recalled the description of quicksand; how it pulled you under the more you struggled.

She tried to clear her mind.

Stop fighting! She ordered herself, and slowly, her legs and arms became still. In front of her bobbed two, now three, corpses. They floated in the goop with her, like a stew of flesh and bones.

Disgust seized her, and she opened her mouth and called out. Sewage seeped down her throat. She waved her arms in the air, and the bodies encroached around her. Her legs kicked deep within the murky depths, and it pulled her deeper, down, down. The filth rose up to her ears. Desperate, she grabbed hold of one the corpses and tried to use it like a life preserver, hoping beyond reason that she could stay above the surface by pulling her body on top of it. It crumbled into miscellaneous bones beneath her.

She gasped for air, but more slop filled her mouth and lungs. *I'm going to drown!* The sewage reached the bridge of her nose. As she sank, her horror-struck eyes caught the grotesque image of a raggedy beast with a horse-shaped face. It sat on its haunches just out of reach, on solid ground, on the other side of the yellow tape. Like a spectator, it watched her.

She forced her face to the surface one last time and breathed deeply before the sewage pulled her down to swim with the dead.

The thing on the sidelines pounced on top of her. *What the hell is that?* She wondered as she felt the weight push her deeper.

It dug its front paws into her scalp. She imagined it preying on her like a saber-toothed cat feasting on a mammoth in a tar pit. She wished one of its claws would wrap under her chin and pull her face up, despite the fact it would slice her throat, that way she'd at least get fresh air into her lungs. However it only scratched and clawed, then pushed her down deeper when it leapt off.

Veronica felt her lungs begin to implode as the remaining air expelled. The horror of suffocation consumed her as her head slid under the surface.

With a rush, the mud began to flow, and Veronica cascaded like a child slipping down a water slide. The dead bodies luged along with her as gravity forced them all down, down, down.

Suddenly, solid ground was beneath her. Her feet skidded on the bottom, but she couldn't gain footing. She tumbled forward. Her eyes remained closed, and she became instantly aware that her head was no longer submerged. Instinctively, she gasped and was relieved to pull air into her lungs. She coughed and gagged, but at least she was breathing!

Veronica rolled end over end. It was as if she was bobbing along rapids, but instead of foamy white water, she was being propelled by sewage, and rather than dodging jagged rocks, she was being jostled around disembodied skulls.

The current finally subsided and she jumbled to an abrupt stop. The entire ordeal only took a few minutes, but she felt battered and beaten as though she had been struggling for hours. Her eyes opened to complete blackness.

She jangled the flashlight, which thankfully she never let go of, and shook the sticky mud off its bulb. Veronica clicked it on. She was in a large cavern. A stream of sewage coursed around her like she was sitting in the middle of an underground river. Its source was the ceiling and it poured down like a waterfall.

Various waxy, rotting bodies jutted out of the sludge. *What is this? Hell? Am I in Hell and this is the freaking River Styx?*

She was like a beaver's dam blocking the surge. Veronica coughed and spit as the corpses flowed past her. She tried to stand but the current was too strong, so she began to crawl instead. Shards of bone and debris cut into her palms and knees. The pain assured her she was still alive.

One of the bodies churning around her wore decaying tatters of a cape pinned under its chin. *These bodies are old*, she thought. *I must have fallen into some kind of ancient crypt.*

The backhoe, Veronica surmised, apparently dug into it while unearthing the old septic tank. Then the rain loosened the soil making one huge, mess of sewage and corpses.

It made sense. This was probably the reason Clark was having such a hard time fixing the tank. It had rotted through and seeped into a mass grave.

Veronica studied the ceiling where the flow originated, where she fell in, and knew that was the way back out. That would mean digging through tons of sludge and bodies to get there. As she contemplated the task, a skeletal face with hollow, beetle-infested sockets popped up like a buoy. It smiled broadly at her with a full set of black, snarling teeth. Remnants of curly hair clung to bits of decomposing flesh on its skullcap.

Quickly, she turned away from the horrid sight. The thought of digging through a pile of decaying corpses was too much for the interior designer. Repulsion took hold of Veronica, and she rose to her feet, finally far enough from the deluge so she could stand. She slogged down the imposing corridor and away from the scene.

The tiny flashlight cast a thin beam, and it only illuminated a short distance in front of her. Before she knew it, there was a fork. One tunnel veered left; the other went to the right. She stayed right and continued without any forethought as to where she was going. She just needed to get away from the bodies, the many, many putrid, rotting, dead bodies.

She traveled several more feet and came to another fork. She remained constant and stayed to the right. She coughed and gagged, bits of grime still hung around her eyes and nose, and she desperately cleaned her dirty face as best she could with filthy hands. Her pace slowed as she came to still another fork. This time the tunnels branched off three different ways.

She stopped.

Veronica flashed her light from tunnel to tunnel. Each seemed equally ominous and gave no clue to its secrets. She folded her arms across her chest and vaguely realized that she was freezing cold. Hot tears squeezed out of her muddy eyes, and she wailed. Veronica crumbled to the ground. She sat on her knees and heaved from grief and nausea.

She stayed there for several minutes before reason reclaimed her agitated mind.

This place is like the catacombs, she thought; *a maze of freaking tunnels, one branching off from the last.* She could go left, straight, or right. Her little light gleamed down each one. She shivered with brattling teeth.

She remembered what Ralph said about the map. "...if you found it in your castle, then I'd say that you should start by looking in its tunnels."

"My castle...the castle...doesn't have tunnels," Veronica had answered him.

She dug into her bag. It was wet and soppy, but still held her possessions. Her fingers grazed over her now filthy brush, useless tampons reduced to clumps of paper, and half a pack of soggy gum. Then, there it was. Sealed up tight in a Zip-lock bag was the map. She carefully pulled it out; making sure her dirty fingers only touched the outer edges.

"Are you sure about that?" Ralph had challenged.

"Mother fucker, you were right, Ralph," she said aloud. Her thin voice cutting the murky silence like flint.

The drawing certainly did resemble the tunnels she now stood in. She studied it for a moment, calculating where her starting point must have been. It appeared that there were two "entrances" — one at either end. She determined that if she was near the one at the bottom of the page, took three rights, she should come out in one of those circular cul-de-sacs.

She rose and cautiously walked down the tunnel to her right. She didn't go far before it rounded off. *The cul-de-sac! Just like on the map.* She knew exactly where she was. And if she was able to come in one end, she should be able to get out through the other. As she turned to leave, the light scanned the far wall of the circular chamber. It was inlayed with several grottos, and each contained a corpse. *This whole place is one huge freaking crypt,* Veronica thought.

Slowly, with sudden respect for the dead who she now kept company with, she retreated from the room. She came back into the hall with the three forks and chose the one to the left.

Excitement filled her gut as the map matched each turn. She studied it, making sure that she didn't make one single wrong move. Every step was made only after careful scrutiny. Her fuzzy high-heeled slippers proved to be impractical for walking, and she eventually bent over and snapped the annoying heels off.

She eyed the mysterious cross-like mark on the map as she stomped her new "flats" on the dusty ground.

"All castles have secrets," Ralph had said. "You might want to look for yours."

She forced herself to concentrate on the task at hand — escape! She just needed to get the hell out of there. Though she wanted to rush, she resolved to make slow, steady progress as to make no mistakes.

Veronica grew closer to the strange mark on the map. It was just off her current path and down a few other corridors. It's right there, just a hop skip and a jump. If I go down this next tunnel, take a left and then a right...there I am!

She hesitated, contemplating her next move. *I should come back later. It's better just to get out of this place — this dead, disgusting place.* The skin on the back of her neck felt raw and exposed. Her heart continued to flutter. *Leaving would be the best thing to do. I can bring Nikki and Christophe, maybe even Ralph, later.*

She started forward, prepared to follow the path to freedom. At the last second, she veered left. Without being able to explain why, she found herself scurrying down the tunnels in search of the thing that was marked on the map. Anticipation now tingled her belly and the fear dissipated. Veronica was *almost* having fun.

She turned right and came to another cul-de-sac. She calculated, made an approximate guess as to where exactly the mark indicated, and shined her flashlight on a wall of bodies. Each was inside a crypt carved into the stone. Faded Roman symbols and a crude, wide-eyed painting of a long-dead face, marked each one.

Veronica illuminated a corpse. It was dusty. Years of dirt had settled on top of it, camouflaging its features. She observed the boney digits, looking for a ring or some kind of jewelry. A thought: *Maybe there was something here once, but someone else already found it? Maybe I'm rifling this corpse for nothing.*

Her flashlight flickered and Veronica jumped. She shook it, and instead of regaining its normal intensity, it darkened a little bit more.

"Shit!" she muttered out loud. Her own voice startled her, and she quickly apologized to the skeleton before her. "I'm sorry." As she gazed at the dusty features, she noticed something behind the head, tucked in the corner. It was box-like, also covered in the dust of time. The light flickered again. The flashlight was dying, and she knew she didn't have much longer.

The body disgusted her. To reach the boxy object, she would have to grab the skull, pull it off of the body, and move it out of the way. The light dimmed again. Veronica felt a stab of fear in her gut. Without hesitation she stuck the little flashlight in her mouth and thrust her hands into the grave. Dusty bone caressed her skin and the dirt clung to her moist skin. She winced, but snatched the item nonetheless.

To her surprise, it was a bag made out of leather. It was brittle but intact. It had molded to the shape of a big book that was inside. Along with the book was an intricately detailed box decorated in jewels. It was obviously old and valuable. Veronica didn't have time to inspect her prize, though. The light flickered again. This time it almost went completely dark. Black fear fell on top of Veronica, and she regretted veering off the path.

If the flashlight stopped working, she'd be in total darkness and unable to navigate out. Veronica had little time to figure out what to do. She shook the light, and it came back a little bit; just enough for her to read the map. She studied it, trying to quickly memorize the way out. Right, then right again, then straight, then a sharp left...

The light went off.

She was alone in the darkness with the dead.

Tears streaked down her pitch-smeared face. She thought wildly that she must surely look like hell, but it didn't matter because there was no one there to see her. Eerily, she wondered if the dead could. She wondered if they were watching. If they were enjoying this, laughing at her...waiting for her.

She held the map inches from her wide eyeballs. The way out was right there before her; she just couldn't see it. She squinted, hoping her eyes would somehow adjust to the absolute darkness, but they didn't.

Franticly, she shook the flashlight. Nothing. She flicked the switch off and on. Still nothing. Angry, she slammed it against the hard stone wall, and miraculously, it flashed, just as bright as when she first turned it on.

Veronica sung out with sheer joy. Knowing that she may not have much time, she illuminated the map. Navigating the tunnels in total darkness would be tricky. One wrong turn, one missed pathway, and she'd be lost forever.

The light began to dim, and she suddenly remembered what Ralph told her when they were in the Paris catacombs. He had said that following one wall was the best way to find your way out of a maze. As long as it wasn't an interior wall, it would eventually lead to an exit.

Veronica studied the map in the dying light. Sure enough, it would take a while. She'd follow many unnecessary tunnels, but if she stayed on this one wall, eventually she would come to the exit. The light flickered two more times and died. She clutched her bag and the newfound satchel, and pressed her back to the wall.

Without losing contact, she slithered along, following the wall from one tunnel into another, and into another crypt. She passed many grottos, layered with long-dead corpses, as she went. No matter what she touched, no matter what it felt like, she stayed on course. This was Veronica's only hope for escape. She couldn't risk becoming disoriented just because her body was rubbing against a few dead things.

Her foot kicked something solid, stubbing her naked big toe. "Damn!" she cried and pendulously swayed her arms like a blind man. She connected with the obstruction. More bones, sleek, piled up. She continued to feel them, to find a way around them, but they weren't *just* piled up. They were a distinct shape, melded together in the shape of a...could it be?

It was a chair.

She felt the arm rests, the seat, the high back — like a throne. *Who would make a throne out of bones?* She navigated past the obstacle.

She could smell herself, covered in a mixture of mud and feces. *And what else...the smell of death? The odor of dry bones?* She never thought that bones had a scent. Decaying flesh sure, but she soon realized that even the oldest bones had a distinct odor. It was earthy and dry, yet had a twinge of decay. *It was a persistent bouquet,* she decided, *as once it got in the nostrils it wouldn't leave. It was a lingering aroma that faded and returned with each passing breath.*

Then another scent came to her. It was sweet and steamy. Like the smell of a pile of rotting October leaves after an autumn rain. Not a dry smell, nor was it the smell of the mud and sewage. This was something new, yet something familiar...

I'm imaging things. I guess it makes sense. My sense of smell is all I have since I can't see anything. My nose is developing its own overactive imagination!

She tried to ignore it as long as she could. It consumed her totally, though, causing each inhalation to be an assault on her sinuses. It stank. Like an animal, a filthy stinking...skunk. It was that skunky-odor from the keep — that nasty tang Clark cleared out with the fans. It shared the darkness with her now.

Veronica coughed and unconsciously held her breath. It was like a noxious gas, and on some primitive level, she imagined that it would poison her if she inhaled too much. Her pace quickened. Even though she knew it was extremely important not to rush in case she became disoriented, she felt angst overtake her. Her primeval instincts kicked in, forcing her to hurry.

The tips of her fingers trailed across the smooth bones in the crypts as she trotted along. If she lost contact with the wall, she could miss a turn. She began to run and a fevered image of a priest manifested in her mind's eye. She saw him running, horrified just like her, as he carried an ancient lantern. On his tail was the shadow of a creature in close pursuit. Its long, spidery legs galloped behind him. It had a narrow snout, like the creature that she thought she glimpsed right before her body submerged in the muck. In the blackness, Veronica imagined that same creature stalking her now, gearing up to pounce.

She couldn't contain her fear and a scream exploded from her lungs. The release felt good, invigorating, and she cried out again and again. All the while she kept running, her hand sliding along the wall. Suddenly, there was a sharp turn, and for a brief second, she lost contact. She tripped over her own feet as she brought herself to a dead stop. She reached out again for the wall, but there was nothing there. She had lost it. The one thing that led to freedom was gone.

"I'm so fucked," the frightened interior designer said out loud. A total loss of control and helplessness enveloped her, and she sobbed heavily. "No! No! No!" The scared, primitive part of her brain took control. Despite a dim echo of logic in the back of her mind that told her to remain calm, terror shot through her like a seared poker, and she lunged blindly for the nearest wall. She knew following the wrong one could lead her off course, but she didn't care.

She couldn't remain standing there in the dark waiting for that thing to pounce on her again.

Scratching paws moved across the dusty floor. It came from behind, and she guessed that whatever it was could be no more than a few feet away. In the darkness, she began to spin. Her arms flung out wildly, and they connected. For a split second, she felt a burst of joy as she thought she found a wall! That moment quickly subsided, though, when she realized that her hand did not touch stone, but something flocculent and sticky — something that felt like moist, fur-covered skin.

It was wrinkled, leathery, hot, and clammy.

It moved.

Veronica squealed, and she felt it cringe and leap out of her way. Blindly, Veronica ran, hoping that she picked the right direction. With a thud, she collided with the wall. Stabbing pain shot through her shoulder. The thing that she touched snorted behind her. It sounded angry, and she imagined it was about to attack.

Her hand stroked the wall, and she dove forward, running as fast as she could while still feeling her way. It was on her heels, mere inches away. She hoped with all her might that she was going in the right direction. Otherwise...before she could finish the thought she felt its steamy breath on her back. It stunk so bad she felt dizzy.

Veronica struggled for a clean breath of air and then suddenly got one! A fresh, cool breeze greeted her along with the sight of a turquoise morning sky. She could see the outside; it was just ahead! With added vigor, she pulled her hand from the wall and burst forward.

She emerged from the tunnel into the early cool, misty daylight. It felt divine on her scorching skin. Throwing her arms in the air, she sprinted with absolute abandonment into the dewy morning.

From behind, she heard a growl that transformed into a distinct voice. "Veronica! Come back. Veronica, the dead want you to stay. Don't you want to play with the dead? Veronica? Don't you know the song that only you can sing? Veronica!"

She couldn't resist. Veronica turned and glared back into the tunnel. A hunkering form hovered just at the entrance. Though swarthy, she made out its gangly appendages which angled over its low-to-the-ground torso. A long snout flared slimy nostrils in the brisk morning air.

Veronica sobbed.

The thing glared at her with disturbingly human-like eyes.

She fled into the forest, and the creature lumbered back into the caverns.

Chapter 114

Dorothée's Story

ndré-Benoit stood frozen in the doorway. Dorothée saw her betrayal reflected in a single tear that shimmied down the side of his stalwart jaw. She wanted to run to him, to comfort him, to beg forgiveness...but then something dark consumed his expression.

"Demimonde!" her husband cried.

Dorothée struggled to find words, but the only excuse that came out was, "You are to return *tomorrow*...."

André-Benoit stared at her, momentarily dumbfounded. "That is *all* you have to say? Are you suggesting it is *my* fault for returning? Well! How rude of me to return to my home and interrupt your fucking."

"I didn't mean..."

"The messenger likely told you I'd return 'tomorrow'—those were my exact words to him yesterday. Yet *his* ride was near a full-day. Next time I'll make sure the stupid boy is more accurate with the news of my return. Then I won't be so rude as to disturb your liaisons. Would that make you happy, dear wife? I must clearly give you enough time to jump onto the cock of mine sworn enemy while I am away!"

His acerbity turned to tears as André-Benoit continued, "This castle, servants, your beautiful gowns, perfumes and scents imported from the far ends of the world, anything you want is but yours for the asking! All I expect in return is you to be a faithful wife..."

Dorothée watched her strapping husband's body quiver as his words trailed off. "He attacked me! I-I brought word of your return, and he overpowered me...I tried to fight but..."

André-Benoit was across the room in two massive strides. He slapped Dorothée; reducing her to a sobbing pile on the bed.

Julien-Luc jumped up and stood naked before his opponent. André-Benoit closed in on him like an ominous storm. Dorothée pulled her red face from the pillow and beheld the image of her cowering lover.

"No!" she cried out. "André-Benoit! Don't!"

The big man ignored her and continued his advance. Julien-Luc expertly assessed his situation. He spied a sconce on the wall just above his head and pulled an extinguished torch from it, holding it high like a club.

André-Benoit hesitated when he saw the naked man arm himself.

Dorothée fell silent, knowing that there was nothing she could do but watch.

Julien-Luc waved the torch in his hands majestically. André-Benoit could see his opponent was a skilled swordsman and imagined that if he were properly armed they would probably have a fair duel. He pulled a gleaming dagger from his belt and grinned. *This was not going to be a fair fight, though.*

André-Benoit swung first, a low swipe intended to test the prisoner's agility. Julien-Luc dodged the dagger like an acrobat, slipping out of the way at the last possible moment and wielding his weapon at the same time. The tip of the torch grazed the side of André-Benoit's head.

The two men danced for a moment, each sized up the other. Julien-Luc was the first to act and aimed the blunt object again at André-Benoit's head. The big man avoided the blow and swung the dagger. This time he connected with the prisoner, gashing into the flesh of his forearm. Julien-Luc cried out and blood splattered across the bed and Dorothée. She yipped and smeared the red out of her eyes with shaking fingers.

André-Benoit pulled back and aimed again, but this time his action was parried, and the dagger's blunt side fell flat against the makeshift club. Julien-Luc used the leverage to swing his body around, and his free hand formed a fist. It came down on André-Benoit's face, smacking him solidly, causing spit and sweat to squirt into the air.

The big man shook his head like a wet dog, and the naked man attacked again, pushing the torch into his gut like a battering ram. André-Benoit doubled over while coughing and swearing.

Julien-Luc thrust his knee up under André-Benoit's chin. The big man bit down on his own tongue, and blood spattered from his lips. He remained hunkered down and barreled the full weight of his body straight into the naked man, pushing him up against the wall, pinning him.

Julien-Luc brought his club down on the broad back of his attacker, clanking it against the chain mail under his tunic. The blow was forceful, though, and directly struck the kidney. André-Benoit collapsed, and his dagger fell from his hand. He crumpled to the floor and rolled onto his side, grimacing with pain.

The prisoner sprung to the dagger which had skidded across the floor during the melee. He snatched his new weapon and spun to face his attacker. André-Benoit slowly rose to his feet and winced as he straightened his back. Julien-Luc took advantage of his pain and closed in.

André-Benoit dodged out of the way and drew a rapier from the scabbard on his hip. He held the weapon high as the naked man charged again. This time there was an ear piercing screech as metal met metal and the two weapons collided. André-Benoit brought the sword down toward the prisoner's face, but it was blocked by the dagger, poised inches from his nose. Julien-Luc held the pose for a moment, balancing under the weight of the big man, holding back the slender sword. He trembled under the pressure, until finally, he leapt to the side, causing André-Benoit to fall forward.

Julien-Luc spun and lunged, but the big man twirled just in time to parry. His force was immense, and the ruby-adorned dagger flipped in the air, forced out of the naked man's hand.

Julien-Luc was unarmed now.

André-Benoit towered over him like a bear. Instead of finishing him off, the burly man stepped back and tore his fingers into the wood panel on the wall. It was bolted into the brick, and André-Benoit ripped it out with his bare, claw-like hands. Splinters sliced his fingernails, but he seemed oblivious to the pain.

André-Benoit exposed a box-like grotto. He grabbed the prisoner by the hair and heaved him across the floor like a puck on a shuffle board. The naked man careened into the hollow and struck the back wall with a thud. His weight triggered a trap door, and he plunged out of sight.

Dorothée gawked at the scene before her. André-Benoit straightened himself before spitting a clot of blood from his busted lips.

She rose from the bed and rushed into his arms, sobbing. "You saved me, husband!"

André-Benoit placed a hand on each of her bare shoulders. "Are you okay?"

Dorothée willed tears to bulge from her eyes. "Yes. Now that you're here."

He kissed her tenderly on her forehead. "You were my bride, my precious bride," he whispered tenderly.

She began to cry ferociously, and he let her sob in his arms for a few moments. He knelt down, grabbed his dagger, and walked to the door. "I'll leave you now."

Dorothée's thick lips quavered. "Leave me...you don't mean in *here?*" She rushed him as he approached the door, grabbed hold of his arm, and tugged fiercely. "André-Benoit! No!"

He shook her off, and she tripped to the floor. She snagged him again; this time wrapping her arms around his leg like a stubborn child. He bent and picked her up effortlessly. He hurled her back into the room, and she landed on her naked rump with a splat.

She continued to call out. "André-Benoit, you can't punish me like this! I am your wife, the Lady of the house! This is not proper."

"*You* are not proper!" he growled.

Dorothée would not relent. "And it is proper for a husband to abandon his new wife? This never would have happened if you weren't always gone; leaving me, time and time again."

He fired back. "As I fight for our beliefs, you bed down our enemy? It would be wise to hold your saucy tongue and accept your punishment until I decide what to do with you."

"They are *your* idiotic beliefs, not mine! At least Julien-Luc sought the truth."

"You want truth? You can have your truth — with your Huguenot lover." He grabbed her wrist and dragged her toward the oubliette.

She shrieked and kicked and cried. "No, don't! I tease. I simply tease, dear husband!" She vainly tried to giggle, but it was without guile or mirth. Hollow, it sounded like the lonely caw of a mourning dove.

With absolute ease, he flung her into the pit while calmly explaining, "There's your truth."

Dorothée landed squarely on the body of her dead lover.

He was mushy, covered in sticky blood, and still warm. She scrambled to get off, her hands and feet kicking and smacking him as she scuttled to the other side of the pit.

André-Benoit peered down, holding a lantern, which allowed Dorothée to see Julien-Luc's broken neck. His head was cocked at an extreme angle and his kind, brown eyes were half open. His gaze reminded Dorothée of the beguiling expression she had seen so many times when peeking through the opening of the tower room door.

"Julien," she whispered, half expecting him to answer. Instead, his head flopped forward. It was completely broken, and only a few tendons kept it from totally rolling off. She shrieked. "Husband, no!" she called up. "I won't be able to bare a night in this place. Let me out! Banish me to my room if you must! I will stay there a week, even two!"

"You will stay *there*," André-Benoit said quietly as he peered down at her. Desperate hands reached up to him. He could hear her whining as he finished. "And it will be for much longer than a week or two."

Dorothée became hysterical. She jumped up and down. "How long will you punish me? How long would you banish me to this vile pit?"

André-Benoit whispered three soft words as he turned to leave. "Forever, dear wife."

Chapter 115

Sebastian's Story
325 AD – When Rome Spread its Empire across the Barbaric Territories

𝒜 few remaining Romans huddled in a corner with arms extended and heads bowed in surrender. Around them, bodies of the dead and dying littered the once festive courtyard. The massive table, which had been set with plates of pies, roasts and fruit, was now flipped on its side and smeared in blood. Several craven men cowered behind it.

Hooting barbarians pulled them out and dragged them across the floor, all the while kicking and spitting on them. Rings and broaches were pulled from their fingers and breasts. Finely crafted weapons were lifted from their hips.

In the background, men and women bellowed for help. The cries came from the kitchen, where both male and female slaves were being trammeled and raped.

A man with a slice through his bottom lip pointed his spear at Baldebert. "Should we scour the rest of the fortress?" He spat blood on the floor after he spoke.

It took a moment before Baldebert realized that the tribesman was asking his permission. He scanned the carnage and calmly slipped the crystal skull back beneath his robe, dismissing the demonic force that he alone commanded. "No, that's enough."

"That is enough!" the bloody-lipped man bellowed, mimicking Baldebert's words with a much louder voice. "The Head Commander says that is *enough*!"

"And in the kitchen, make them stop."

With a scoff he growled, "Tell them to stop waxing their wicks in the kitchen, too."

A few of the men went around, repeating the orders. After a moment several boors came out of the kitchen with their britches unfastened. They sneered defiantly, but nonetheless they nodded obediently at Baldebert while buckling their pants.

Slowly the wild men settled down and gathered in a loose circle around their leader. "What about *them*?" one asked while pointing to Helena and her entourage.

During the melee, Helena's men had surrounded her in a protective circle, not allowing anyone near. Baldebert had noticed them moving with choreographed precision, like a single unit rather than twelve separate men. He knew they were special, and though they could easily have slaughtered many during the fight, they instead remained oddly neutral, only concerned with keeping the stately woman safe.

"Are they our prisoners, too?" a bald, pock-faced tribesmen asked. "They fight good! They'll make vicious warriors for us."

Helena swiftly rebuked. "My knights are not yours to conquest!"

"*Everyone* is mine to conquest," the bald barbarian answered.

Several others grunted in agreement, and a few fondled their weapons, ready to strike.

"Why should you be spared?" Baldebert asked. "Who *are* you?"

"I'm Helena, mother of Constantine and a former priestess of this Temple. I came to help with the peace talks."

A gruff, red-haired barbarian retorted. "Didn't go so well, did they?"

Baldebert ignored the sarcastic remark and studied the woman carefully before asking, "You're the matriarch of Rome *and* a Temple Priestess? How can that be?"

"Don't lie. I can smell it when a woman lies," the redhead snarled.

Helena lifted her chin regally as she directed her answer at Baldebert. "I was born here. This place is my home, Head Commander." She bowed slightly to him before continuing. "As a young Temple Priestess, I offered myself to a Roman general in exchange for peace. It happened many years before you were born."

The pudgy Druid's face lit up. "Your legend is known to me; to all of us it has been passed down. I heard the stories about you!"

The old woman looked pleased. "My memory remained! It was so long ago."

"Beautiful princess Helena sacrificed herself in the name of the scripture of the ancient tome, by wedding the rogue king from Rome..." he recited as if recalling a children's verse.

Helena picked up where Baldebert left off. "Yes, and the rogue king was named Constantius. He was a Roman general then and intended to conquer our land, our people, our Temple. I was barely into my sixteenth summer when he and his men arrived under the guise of peace. We welcomed them and invited Constantius and his centurions into the Temple...that was when he found favor with me. Once it became clear, however, that they meant to subjugate us, I went to Constantius and pleaded with him to spare the Temple and my people. He agreed to leave in peace on the condition that I go with him, as his concubine, never to return."

Esindra stepped forward. "And so you left with him?"

"I did. I saved the Temple and my people. Constantius was a good man. He treated me with all the respect and honor of a real wife. However, when he became Emperor, it was required that he put me aside to marry Theodora, as she had a royal lineage. I bore him two sons. Constan-*tine* was my first. Sebastian, my second, was born after Constantius married Theodora and therefore deemed illegitimate."

Esindra gasped. "Sebastian is *your* son!"

"He *was* my son. I saw what happened to him. That's not what we planned...no, not at all..." Her voice faltered just a moment.

The bald barbarian taunted her. "And now your boy is just another dead sack of bones we added to the funeral pyre. I lost *three* sons to the bloody Romans! I don't think we're even yet..."

Baldebert held up his hand and commanded, "Quiet. Let her speak her peace. She deserves fair judgment."

To everyone's surprise, Helena snickered heartily. "But my son was a fool! A suspicious idiot driven to fits of madness. Oh, he surely got what he deserved!"

The Gaulic warriors all gaped at her outburst. Everyone in the room quietly watched the old woman as her mirth escalated.

"He was crazed!" Helena exclaimed. "He was a bitter, conniving madman!"

"So, you're *pleased* he's dead?" Baldebert asked.

"Oh, no. He was mad, but he was my son, and I still loved him. Sebastian and I had worked out a plan, you see. We intended to liberate this region from the tyranny of Rome." She turned to her audience. "Yes, you heard me. I, a Roman matriarch, would devise a plot against my own people...indeed, against my own son, Constantine. We wanted to *liberate* you all! I guess I should start from the beginning."

She stood silent a moment. The quiet deluged the courtyard, and even the most unruly barbarian gave her his full attention.

"Twenty years ago, when Constantine took the throne, he wanted to make sure there was no way his illegitimate, younger brother, Sebastian, could ever steal it. He plotted to have his brother murdered. I intervened, though. When I discovered the plan, I bribed the assassins. Instead of killing Sebastian, they brought him here, to this Temple, to stay with my father who was still a Temple Priest."

"So, Sebastian grew up *here*?" Esindra asked.

"No. He wasn't allowed to live here after all. The Temple Priests wouldn't accept him. The creed states that no outsider may join their ranks. Despite his heritage, he was turned away. This embittered my father, and he left the Temple to raise Sebastian among the local tribes, but they too cast them out because of their distrust of the Romans. They saw Sebastian as a possible spy, an outsider, a traitor. Exiled from everyone, my father and son took refuge in the caverns in the mountain, right at the mouth of the catacombs. My father did his best with Sebastian, but his bitterness led them both down a dark path."

"We heard rumors about necromancers who lived in caves in the mountains," Baldebert mumbled. "No one went near them."

Helena's pallor face flushed and she nodded slowly. "There was little I could do for Sebastian as I had to remain in Rome. But I did teach Constantine the ways of our religion when he was young, hoping he would grow up and use the teachings to become a great, noble, just leader. But something happened to him at the Battle of Milvian Bridge. His beliefs took an ominous turn. He said he was given a sign by the Christian God; saw the symbol of the cross in the sky like an omen. He claimed that Jesus held his sword in battle that day and delivered him to victory. That was the turning point for my eldest son. He brought the religion of Israel to our land and converted the mighty Roman Empire to Christianity."

"And the Christians have been persecuting us and any religion they consider Pagan ever since," the bloody-lipped barbarian grunted.

"To make me conform to the Christian cult, Constantine sent me on quests to the Holy Land. He thought if I could find proof, actual artifacts from the time of Christ, that I would succumb to Christianity and turn my back on my Pagan upbringing."

"Your pilgrimages are legendary," Esindra spoke. "You found pieces of the cross that Christ was crucified on."

Helena confirmed. "Yes, I've uncovered many relics, like the Spear of Longinus, which sliced Christ's side at His crucifixion. I also unearthed the graves of the three wise men, the magi, who visited Christ at his birth. I discovered many artifacts in their crypt, including an amazing recipe for an elixir that makes it possible to seemingly raise the dead! I decided it would be a useful potion to have, and I brought it to Sebastian."

Esindra jumped in. "Is that the poison Sebastian made? The one he wanted to use on the Head Commander?"

Helena nodded and explained. "I came to Sebastian with it several months ago, and what I found horrified me. He was *not* my son anymore. He had become an animal! He was so filled with hate and animosity for the local tribes, the Temple Priests, and for his brother in Rome that he became a bitter, evil necromancer. I only hoped he wasn't too far gone and could still become the leader he was destined to be. Then I gave him the recipe so he could brew the elixir."

"How does this elixir work?" the redhead asked.

"It makes the imbiber appear to be dead. The heart slows its beating so much that it's barely perceivable. Breathing seems nonexistent. It lasts several hours and then one wakes up as if from a miracle!" Helena answered. "We made a plan to feed it to the Head Commander, to cause him to fall into a death-like state, so that Sebastian could raise him and become as revered as Christ who raised Lazarus from the dead. Such a miracle would secure his status as a messiah, and the Temple Priests, and you the tribesmen, would have *all* accepted him as your savior."

"So, he never intended to murder me," Baldebert affirmed.

Helena nodded her head solemnly. "Exactly. The plan was for Sebastian to gain the trust of Fabius. Once in his confidence, he would reveal a magnificent plan to 'poison' the Head Commander. After the deed was done, Sebastian would escape through the catacombs, and he'd go to the barbarians. He'd resurrect — as if by magic — the Head Commander and be touted as a hero. But the plan went hopelessly wrong because we didn't know that you, Baldebert, were actually the Head Commander! We thought you escaped and were among the barbarians.

"As a former Temple Priestess, I knew the protocol if the Temple was ever attacked. The Head Commander must escape through the catacombs and seek refuge among the local tribes. I thought you were surely among them, planning your next attack."

Baldebert nodded. "Myself and a few select others did try to escape through the tunnels with the Head. All the other priests stayed behind, sacrificing themselves so that the Romans would not know anyone had fled. But the tunnels were teeming with traps. Daggers thrust out of the walls at us, skewering my brothers. I was the only survivor and was forced to retreat back to the Temple Fortress and accept being captured."

"The snares that Sebastian set! The fool! So distrustful of everyone that he constructed elaborate traps to keep everyone at bay. He turned out to be his own worst enemy, didn't he?" Helena sighed.

"What is that...Head?" Esindra pointed to the bulge in Baldebert's robe.

Baldebert answered. "The Head commands something that's incredibly powerful — and dangerous. For nearly two centuries, we Temple Priests, have watched over it."

Helena composed herself and continued. "And it must remain here! Protected and passed down from one Head Commander to the next."

"But all the priests are dead except for Baldebert. There are none left for him to pass it to," Esindra explained.

"No, there's one more," Baldebert said. "You carry Sebastian's child."

Helena steadied her gaze at Esindra. "You're the mother of my grandchild?"

"Sebastian deceived more than just Fabius," Esindra stammered. "He tricked me, too."

"But you're the Governess; how could that happen?" Helena asked.

Esindra explained with an uncomfortable quiver in her throat. "He performed a spell to make me fertile so Fabius and I could have the child we always wanted. Fabius turned me away, though. I was distraught, and Sebastian took me into his bed. He said no one would know he was the *real* father. Fabius was to believe the child was his own, and his noble heritage would be carried on."

"Ah, that's what he told you," Helena answered. "Sebastian's *own* heritage was more likely on his agenda. He beguiled you. His methods are abhorrent; for that I apologize," Helena said with a slight nod to the Governess.

"Now my husband is dead, and I'm carrying a bastard child. I may as well go live in the mountains with the goats as I'll surely be thrown in the coliseum when I return to Rome," Esindra bemoaned.

"You should stay here, Esindra," Helena stated with authority. "You and your child, along with Baldebert, you can start over. Build this Temple back up and carry on our traditions."

"We won't be safe here. The three of us are hardly able to defend an entire fortress!" she replied.

The redheaded barbarian offered, "Our tribe will protect the Temple. They'll be safe under our watchful eyes."

"And what of *me*," Helena asked. "Have I passed your judgment?"

Several barbarians nodded while Baldebert confirmed, "You won't be harmed, nor taken prisoner, and neither will your men. You are free to leave."

"In truth, my guards will remain here with you," The matriarch countered. "Their skills as warriors will be useful, and with their help, you'll reform the order together."

"And then you'll stay here, too, Mother Helena?" Baldebert asked.

She shook her head. "I have more journeys to the Holy Land ahead of me. And as long as I do those quests for Constantine, I can keep him from sending another legion here. While I'm alive, I can protect you and the Temple Fortress."

Baldebert proudly declared, "We'll keep the traditions of the Temple Priests alive and rebuild everything as it was."

Helena shook her head. "You'll rebuild, but things are going to be different. They *must* be different, or the Temple will come under attack again. My guards are fierce fighters. They will teach you to be warriors as well as priests. So, if you are ever attacked, you'll be prepared and able to defend yourselves."

"Will I study your teachings, too, and turn away from the Christian faith?" Esindra asked.

"Yes and no," Helena answered. "Our teachings and Christianity must be *integrated*. Constantine proclaimed Christianity the official religion of Rome, and that must be respected or you'll come under suspicion." She addressed Baldebert directly. "Hold true to your heart our gnostic teachings and keep the Head sacred. But also learn the ways of Christianity. You and Esindra must teach each other."

"So, you want us to be Christian as well as Temple Priests?" Baldebert asked.

"I want you to use Christianity as a ruse to protect our beliefs," she answered flatly and waved her hand at one of her guards. He produced a large, leather-bound tome. "Here's one of the Nicaean Bibles," she continued. "Constantine had fifty of them created at the council of Nicaea, and it is the absolute Word as accepted by the Holy Roman Empire. Read it, learn it, but remember that its teachings are only an illusion compared to the esoteric, gnostic teachings that we keep as Temple Priests."

Baldebert took the book, understanding intuitively that it would become one of their most revered relics, just like the Head.

Helena let her eyes linger over Fabius' corpse for a moment and continued. "I must prepare to return to Rome. I'll bring the governor's body with me. I'll tell Constantine all his men are defeated, but not to retaliate as a friendly band of Christians reside here now. I'll make sure he leaves you alone. If Roman soldiers ever do visit, remember to behave like real Christians. Keep their suspicions at bay and gain their trust; that way this Temple will forever be safe."

Baldebert nodded.

"Not exactly what Sebastian and I had planned, but somehow things worked out, didn't they?" the matriarch of Rome said with a fluttering voice. "The Temple is safe, our ways will remain, and that's what really matters. That and keeping the elemental force contained. Most importantly, always keep that *thing* concealed. It can never escape, and that is for the good of all people, Christians and Pagans alike. Do you understand?"

Baldebert agreed. "If there's one thing I'm positive of, keeping control of *it* is paramount compared to the petty things mortal men fight for."

෴ ✣ ෴

Cicero dragged Sebastian's body down the corridor. He managed to slink out of the courtyard unnoticed with his prize, while everyone was gathered around Helena.

He wasn't sure if the Cloaked Man was dead this time or not, but *he* intended to be the one to make sure. No barbarian was going to throw his enemy's carcass on a funeral pyre and take the much-deserved satisfaction away from him. He earned that sweet moment of reckoning!

Sebastian was on his belly and a smear of blood trailed the floor behind him. Stopping, Cicero gave the carcass a kick in the side to evoke a response. There was none. Sebastian had most likely bled out and was unconscious. This saddened the Roman soldier. He wanted his nemesis to be awake, so he could watch the last moments of his wretched life being choked away.

Hurriedly, Cicero continued to the keep's tower room. Once inside he slapped

Sebastian's face. "Wake up, you wicked lurch. You're not poisoned after all."

The Cloaked Man did not respond.

The centurion pressed his fingers over Sebastian's mouth. Dried blood crusted the stubbly facial hair around it. No breath came out.

"Dead you are then," he sighed reluctantly. "The dagger likely doing you in."

He contemplated slicing his enemy's heart out or chopping off the head, just to be certain. Knowing from many years of battle that neither was an easy feat, he decided instead to give the rapscallion a slow, excruciating death — if, indeed, he happened to still be alive.

Cicero opened the curtain covering the grotto. He knelt and lifted the trapdoor, revealing the bowels of the oubliette. The stagnant release of air was warm, as if he had just opened a portal to hell.

He dragged his enemy by the ankles toward the cusp, guiding first the feet and then the legs over the edge. As the body was about to topple, Sebastian groaned softly.

"Hades damn you!" Cicero cussed. "You *are* alive!" He pushed hard on Sebastian's shoulders. "This is good. May you slowly rot in agony down there."

Just as Sebastian's lanky frame slid into the darkness, his eyes burst open. He jolted as his body started to fall, and spat, "What are you doing?"

Cicero kicked the rogue's face with the pointed tip of his boot. It connected with his right side, causing crimson to splatter across the bricks in the grotto.

Sebastian dug his fingernails into the mortar of the stone floor and caught some traction just before skidding all the way in. He hung there. His head and arms the only thing above the surface.

Cicero kicked him in the jaw again. The force knocked Sebastian's head back with a snap. Saliva, blood, and one of his teeth shot from his broken lips. He slipped three inches deeper.

Blood on the stones in front of Sebastian made them slippery. His fingers began to slide and he submerged past his elbows.

Sebastian fell into the oubliette.

As he plunged, he grunted, "I'm not going down without you, friend." He grabbed for the centurion's foot as it came down to kick one last time.

His grip held.

Cicero was pulled off balance and landed with a smack on his back. His head bounced on the stone from the impact. He skidded across the floor and into the oubliette with his enemy.

Both men descended rapidly.

As he skimmed the floor, though, Cicero reached for the corner of the wall. With a jerk he snagged it and stopped sliding. His position was incredibly awkward as he was laying on his back, and it arched painfully, with his lower body in, and the upper body, out of the oubliette.

Sebastian still clutched Cicero's boot and dangled below. He used all his remaining strength to grasp onto the centurion's calf, and then the knee. Sebastian climbed up.

Cicero kicked vigorously with his free leg. He came down on the top of Sebastian's head with the heel of his boot.

Crunch!

The pain cut through the Cloaked Man's skull like a white poker. It blinded him and made him dizzy, but it did not make him let go.

Voices called from below.

Sebastian, we're waiting for you.

Let him go and you'll be free.

Join us where the world is dark and souls ripen into rotten fruit on a moldering vine, intertwined around the loneliness of time.

Cicero's heavy boot struck Sebastian's temple, causing his ears to ring with a deafening clang. The only thing the Cloaked Man could decipher were the soft voices beckoning him.

"I'm coming," he answered them. "I'm taking *him* with me, though."

Sebastian scaled his way up to the centurion's stomach. The man's tunic was ripped and open, revealing a soft, fleshy belly.

Sebastian bore into it. With one hand wrapped around Cicero's waist, the other ripped into the man's gut. Shredding, like a raptor gutting a mole, the Cloaked Man dug into the hairy navel with pointy, jaggy fingernails. Once a tiny flap of skin was tore back enough, he pulled it further with gnashing teeth to reveal clumps of gooey, yellow fat underneath.

Cicero wailed. He wiggled his waist, trying to shake the madman off. His fingers slipped, causing his rump to slide further into the pit. If he dropped past his shoulders, he'd surely plunge all the way. Desperate, he tried to roll over while maintaining his grasp on the grotto wall. Sebastian's weight was too much, though, and he merely wobbled back and forth like broken rocking chair.

Below Sebastian burrowed into Cicero's entrails hungrily; biting, tearing, and gnawing at the thick, tough skin. Blood and belly fat slathered his face.

"Off me, wretch!" Cicero cried.

The Cloaked Man obliged and pulled himself up another notch. Now atop his enemy's chest, Sebastian reached for Cicero's face. With thumbs digging into the eye sockets, the Cloaked Man bashed the centurion's skull against the stone floor several times. Cicero heard his skull crack. Like a sharp, quick, thunderclap, it reverberated with a tremble that nearly drove him into blackness.

With his bloody fingers splayed around the centurion's bald head, Sebastian beat it up and down, over and over again.

Cicero wanted to push his assailant back, but doing so would mean releasing his hands from the wall, causing him to drop into the abyss. Instead he thrashed his neck back and forth, trying to make Sebastian let go.

The Cloaked Man held tight, and used the sudden momentum to slam his nemeses' head against the grotto's sharp, protruding corner.

Cicero's neck snapped.

Like being submerged in searing red-hot wax, the centurion lost first his sight, then his breath, and finally his consciousness.

Then Cicero finally let go.

The Roman champion only went dark for a brief moment — not more than a couple seconds — but it was long enough for him to release his grip, causing both men to tumble down.

They clutched each other's throats, fighting fiercely even as they fell to their deaths. Gravity was the only victor, however, as it pulled them down and spun them 'round.

They landed side by side with their bodies facing each other; hands, arms, and legs intertwined. Cicero was unconscious and his head bled until death came in a few, mere hours.

Sebastian was fully aware, however, but he could not move. Something happened during the fall. He was wide awake, knew exactly where he was, and felt every hot breath his enemy exhaled into his face until the final one.

The only thing he could even twitch was his left, unswollen eye, and his bruised, roaming tongue, which pushed the blood out of his mouth and throat so he could breath. He lay like that for several day. Never did he regain his ability to move or to even cry out for help.

During that time, Esindra came, and so did that stupid Druid, Baldebert. They hovered over the top and bemoaned his death. One of them threw flowers on top of him. He felt a soft bud bump his fluttering eye and could smell the sweet fragrance of lilies — they momentarily masked the smell of shit and piss and blood and decay.

Once the fallen necromancer fancied he heard his mother overhead. The woman cried, moaned, and prayed to gods who no one knew anymore. Surely *that* must have been a dream, though. His mother was with her other son, her favorite boy, the Emperor of Rome and the Bringer of Christendom — the beloved Constantine.

The watchers above didn't stay too long, though. He heard one say that the oubliette needed to *feed*, and the bodies were best left to lie where they were. They held a simple ceremony, sang ancient songs, and blew out the candles when they left.

So there he lay, for hours that turned into days, cradled in the arms of his nemesis. Fierce enemies locked in a lover's embrace in the eternal bottom of the oubliette.

Chapter 116

Father Michel's Story

This new day was the most frightening for Gaston-Elise. There were no sounds, no bells, no woeful cries of pain and misery. Dead silence — that was all.

He nibbled a rotten potato for breakfast and waited until noon before looking out the window. There hadn't been any movement all day. He unlatched his door, braced his shoulder against it, and pushed it open. The first thing he noticed were the massive gatehouse doors which were always locked and guarded. They hung open like a gaping wound.

A few bodies were scattered here and there, and Gaston-Elise avoided coming too close to them, yet he did eye each one carefully as he went. He was on the lookout for Father Michel.

Across the threshold of the castle doors lay a corpse, face down. Gaston-Elise stepped around the fallen soldier. He made the sign of the cross over his chest as he entered. The inside was rank with the scent of death. He held his one arm over his nose and mouth and breathed through the sleeve of his tunic.

In the parlor, in front of the fireplace, lay two bodies, huddled together as if the flames would somehow be their salvation. Their flesh was grey and red veins swelled through thin, rotting skin. Neither of them were Father Michel, so Gaston-Elise trudged on.

In the library were more bodies; some were dead for days. No one had been willing or able to clear them, and their faces were plump and distorted. *Even if I find Father Michel, I may not recognize him,* he thought.

Gaston-Elise considered the fate of the dead; lying exposed, rotting, stinking, discarded like trash. What if their families come looking for them? What will they find? Bodies half eaten by insects and rats? Blank staring faces with gaping mouths; the skin pulled so tight from decomposition that tongues push out and teeth jut forward like snarling animals'?

Will they come across the same visage as I did when I returned home to find my children dead in their beds?

A sense of duty weighed in the big man's noble heart. He wrapped a kerchief around his face like a bandit and slipped on a leather ridding glove. Then Gaston-Elise filled the wheelbarrow with as many bodies as he could manage to steer with one arm.

As he pushed the cumbersome load across the lawn, he noticed something hidden in the grass. It was the thing that the Cardinal's hunting dog had retrieved and then abandoned. A swarm of insects covered it. Gaston-Elise approached, but instead of finding a dead animal, he saw the corpse of an infant. He recognized the raggedy garments that still clung to it. They were the same as those worn by the dead baby that was thrown against the wall by the angry crowd many days before. The Cardinal's hunting dog — a retriever — had brought the child's corpse inside, spreading the disease.

Using a shovel, he scooped up the remains of the innocent babe and added it to his load.

He trudged over to the wine shed and pulled open the door in the floor, expecting to be able to haul the bodies down one at a time so that he could stack them in a crypt. The entrance, however, was not passable.

Apparently, those in charge of burying the dead had let their duties slack. Maybe they had followed through at first, hauling each individual body into the catacombs and placing it in an empty crypt. But then, the sheer number of corpses must have become overwhelming. There were, after all, almost two hundred people living behind the walls of the Château. How many succumbed during the first few days? How could two men successfully discard all those bodies? They couldn't, and that was why Gaston-Elise beheld the grizzly sight before him.

The stairs leading down to the caves were covered with bodies, one slumping over the next. A small amount of dirt was sprinkled on top of them, as if the living half-heartedly attempted to bury them.

There were at least thirty, maybe more. Gaston-Elise could not move them all, not by himself. He decided that the best thing to do was to carry on the tradition. He hauled several corpse-filled wheelbarrows to the entrance of the catacombs and dumped them inside, letting the bodies pour down the stairs.

He searched every room of the castle, every chamber, plucking the dead out of their beds. He looked in the church and retrieved one repentant soul who sought refuge in the confessional. In the barns were the farm hands, lying dead amidst hungry cows and chickens. He scraped the Bishop's body off the cobblestones in front of the castle, as well as the corpses of those who tried in vain to escape by scaling the walls.

The dead were all laid to rest together in the one mass grave. After the bodies were collected, he covered them with fresh earth from the garden; thereby filling the entrance to the catacombs, sealing it up like a dirty little secret.

Not one of the bodies was Father Michel. Gaston-Elise counted nearly twenty, and his friend was not among the dead. *Perhaps he was one of the first to die? If he perished first, then he may have already had a proper burial.*

Gaston-Elise pondered. Some of the survivors no doubt managed to escape. *Could Father Michel have been one of the lucky ones?* More plausible was that Father Michel was kept someplace as prisoner. But he had searched every bedroom; there was no sign...then a thought struck him — *the keep.*

The burly man ran back inside, down the narrow halls, and found the door to the keep. It was shut tight. He slammed his shoulder into it.

Far below the surface, Father Michel heard a noise. It had been quiet for so long. Now there was something — a thud — from overhead.

Gaston-Elise pushed on the door, forcing it to yield under his strength. He burst inside and ran to the tiny cell doors on the right-hand side. He peered in each one but saw no one. "Father Michel!" he called out.

The priest recognized his name. Was it a voice from beyond? Maybe it was it dear, sweet Claudeen calling out to him?

Gaston-Elise squinted through the slat in the door of the ground-level tower room. It was empty; no one was inside. He spied the spiraling stairs that slithered up the side of the ancient tower and ran up. His footfalls reverberated throughout the turret.

From deep below, Father Michel felt the vibration.

Gaston-Elise threw open the door of each room and called out repeatedly. "Father Michel! Where are you?"

From the depths of the oubliette, Father Michel heard his name. It was real; someone called out for him. It had been three, maybe four days, since anyone had brought him food or water. He felt weak, delirious, but through the haze, he became certain of one thing — one *real* thing — he was positive someone was there, calling out to him. It wasn't one of the shadow people, no; they only spoke to him in his dreams. It was his friend, his one true, faithful confidant. It was dear Gaston-Elise.

Father Michel swallowed. His throat was dry. He pushed air out of his lungs and cried, "Gaaassston..." His voice failed; barely a whisper was all he uttered.

Gaston-Elise came down the stairs and back to the main level. There were no other rooms or cells to keep a prisoner. He looked one last time into the bottom tower room. It was vacant, yet rather clean. The other tower rooms were dusty and filled with grime. Obviously, this one had been recently used.

He entered and saw a solitary plate of food and a flask on a table. He picked up a moldy loaf of bread and waved it in the air as tears leaked out of the crinkled corners of his eyes. "Father?"

Several feet below the surface the gaunt priest mustered all the strength he could. He pushed his voice forward as if it was a physical thing. It escaped from his peeling, white lips, and this time it *was* audible. Not entirely a cry, but certainly not a whisper as it had been before. With all his might, the Priest said, "Gaston!"

The burly man sobbed as he stood on the threshold of the tower room holding a rank piece of bread in his one hand. His sobs echoed in his head, and he heard nothing. With a sullen heart, he trudged out of the keep.

Father Michel drew in his breath again. "Gaston!"

Gaston-Elise paused. *Was that a voice?* It was coarse and low. He waited, listened. *Would he hear it again?* He stood in the hallway for several moments.

In the oubliette lay Father Michel. He smiled and murmured, "My friend is coming to save me now. All the rest of you can just go away. I don't need you anymore because Gaston will soon rescue me."

Gaston-Elise dismissed the sound. *Only my wishful imagination playing tricks,* he thought. The burly man shuffled down the lonely passageway and pulled the map from his pocket. He unclasped the necklace Father Michel had given him and placed both items between the pages of his humble Bible.

"Your secret will remain here, Father. It will be safe, hidden, and I pray if you are still out there somewhere that you will come back for it one day and find it here, tucked away in my Bible."

He slid the book between two others on a library shelf and ducked out of the Château forever.

Chapter 117

Veronica's Story

Veronica ran and ran and ran. Desperate to escape the thing in the cavern, she tromped blindly through the woods with her most primitive of survival instincts pushing her forward.

After an hour, her reasonable mind took over, and she wondered where she was in relation to the castle. Veronica was completely lost.

She came to a mountain stream where she paused to wash her face and hands. She could still detect the decay-like stench of the sewage that covered her like a mud mask. She heaved a little, drank some water, and then heaved again.

What was that thing in the tunnels?

No matter how logical Veronica wanted to be, she couldn't deny that something bizarre had chased her. It had actually stalked her and called out her name. Like it *knew* her.

"No," she said aloud. The sound of her voice in the quiet woods was jarring. "It was an animal. Maybe a stray dog or a coyote. Its howl just *sounded* like a voice. I mean, what the hell else could it *be*?"

That seemed to satisfy her. She nodded at no one, stood, and surveyed the sun, which was now high in the sky. She knew the river ran east and west, and quickly determined the right direction to follow. As she meandered along the bank, her personal dialogue continued...

The septic tank was buried near that crypt. The rain and Clark digging up the ground must have caused the sewage to flow into it. The entire thing turned into one sloppy mess, and I stepped right into it. The dog-thing, a fox or a badger or whatever, well, it just saw me as an easy meal! That's why it jumped on me like a saber-toothed cat pouncing on a mammoth stuck in a tar pit. When the whole thing gave way, it fell in with me and then followed me. There. Makes perfect sense!

The terrain proved tough to navigate. Her fuzzy slippers, stripped of their pointed heels, were slick and uncomfortable on the rocky ground. For a while, she walked barefooted, but her tender feet soon became gnashed with welts. Exhausted and guessing it to be early afternoon, she stopped to rest in a glen of fir trees. Soft needles were spread across the ground like a cozy blanket. She intended to only sit for a short while, but instead, woke up as the long shadows of late afternoon crept through the woods. Veronica had slept the day away.

She was desperate to get back before dark and ran along the riverbank until she reached the road to the Château. She trotted through the open gatehouse and under the branches that canopied the driveway. She couldn't wait to see her sister, to take a warm bath, to eat, to drink, and then to sleep yet again.

In her excitement, she hardly noticed the strange car in the driveway. It took her a moment to realize Nikki must have called someone, perhaps the authorities, to help find her. The car was likely that of a detective, or maybe someone from a search and rescue squad. Nikki must be worried sick!

Veronica burst in the door and waited to hear the surprised shouts of joy at her return. But there was nothing; no welcoming committee, no worried cries of "where have you been!" There were hushed whispers, though, coming from the library.

Veronica still wore the filthy, heel-less slippers, and she slid clumsily across the marble floor. She was covered in dried pitch from head to toe. Her hair was matted with crusty feces that hung like gnarly dreadlocks. The silky robe was stained to a dull grey, and the bottom was ripped to shards. She still carried her messenger bag, as well as the heavy satchel. She entered the library and saw her sister sitting with an older gentleman. They each held a coffee cup, and were in the middle of a conversation when she rambled in.

"Nikki!" Veronica exclaimed and held out her arms for the inevitable warm embrace.

"Vern! Christ, where'd you get *that* outfit?"

Veronica stuttered for a moment. "I-I'm not...this isn't an outfit! This is my, it doesn't matter. I'm back! I'm okay!"

"You don't look okay. Where'd you go?"

"I was lost in these tunnels, underground, they were...well, I fell into this...the septic tank made a sink hole, and I fell into it last night..."

Nikki cocked her head. "Last night? You've been gone since *last night*? I thought you went shopping or something."

"You mean...you didn't notice that I was even *missing*?" Veronica stammered.

"I slept late. This freaking place is so huge; thought you were decorating sumptin' upstairs. When you didn't come poking around at lunch time, I figured you must've gone to town."

"Then who's this guy? Isn't he like a detective or something?"

The man wore a tweed jacket over a faded green T-shirt that bore a faint image of planet Earth held in a pair of cupped hands. Though almost completely bald on top, the long hair on the back of his head was pulled back in a scraggy ponytail. Wiry spectacles framed sad, grey eyes that shyly studied Veronica. He reminded her of a hippy college professor. He was probably quite attractive in the 1970s, but today was a faded replica of his former self.

He spoke calmly, almost soothingly. "Veronica, nice to see you again. I'm Dr. Sandbourne."

"He got here about a half hour ago," Nikki spoke. "We were having tea, thinking you'd show up sooner or later. I just thought you'd be a little cleaner."

"Dr. Sandbourne!" Veronica exclaimed. "You really came all the way *here*?"

"Yes, and it's a good thing I did. Are you *okay*?" the doctor answered.

Veronica caught sight of herself in the mirror that hung alongside the fireplace and jumped back. "Oh Christ! I look like shit!"

"And you smell like it, too," Nikki replied.

"Listen, Dr. Sandbourne," Veronica began, ignoring her sister. "I gotta get cleaned up. I'm gonna take a shower; wash this crap out of my hair."

"By all means. Anything we can do to help?" he replied.

"I'm so hungry, starving actually..."

It took Nikki a moment to comprehend the hint. "I'll make you a sandwich."

Veronica smiled thinly and raced out of the room, anxious to have her hideous self out of sight.

❧❧ ❖ ❧❧

It was almost an hour later when Veronica returned to the library and re-greeted her guest. She felt guilty making him wait. She tried to hurry through her shower, but her hair was completely matted with filth. She didn't feel clean after the first washing and ended up taking two complete showers back-to-back.

Dr. Sandbourne once again rose and greeted her with a warm handshake. Veronica nodded, smiled politely, and wondered, *why did this man travel half way around the world to see me?* She was cautious and waited for him to start the conversation.

"Now I see the face of the child I once knew. I'm relieved you're well, after all."

Veronica chuckled. "Well? I don't know about that! I'm still pretty shaken by what happened."

Nikki came out of the dining room with a sandwich, chips, and a glass of juice. She pulled up a chair, and the three sat around the library table. "What *did* happen anyway?"

Veronica took a huge bite, washed it down with juice, and wished she could just sit and eat in peace for a moment. Both pairs of eyes eagerly awaited the details of her story. She swallowed the half-chewed food and related her tale, starting with her early morning need to use the latrine.

Her audience was captive, and she quickly explained how the saturated earth pulled her down like quicksand. She watched the expressions of disgust as she described the animal that clawed at her head and the corpses, rotting and decayed, that floated in the soupy pitch with her. She took another bite but found that her own memories disgusted her so much that she couldn't stomach food.

The fall into the entrance of the tunnels, running wildly with terror, using the map to find the way out, Veronica related the entire experience with the exception of discovering the boxy leather bag. She didn't want to mention it in the company of the strange doctor.

She described the distress she felt when the flashlight began to fade. "I was so freaked-out. I just followed the walls just like Ralph said. Remember, Nik, when I got lost in the catacombs in Paris, Ralph said that the best way to get out of a maze is to follow one wall because it will eventually lead out. Thankfully I remembered because it worked!"

"You were lost in catacombs before?" Dr. Sandbourne asked.

Veronica blushed. "Yes, in the Paris Underground. I got separated from the others and attacked by a vagrant."

"He hit her in the head, stole her wallet," Nikki added. "She's lucky to be alive."

"Must've been very traumatic," the doctor stated.

"Hell yeah, but it was nothing compared to this. I was chased by a thing — an animal — I'm not sure what it was, but I'm sure as shit, it wasn't human."

"So, you're convinced it really happened," The doctor stated.

Veronica began to nod then questioned, "What do you mean '*I'm convinced it really happened*'?"

"Veronica, doesn't it seem like a coincidence that you found yourself lost in an underground maze just like when you were lost in the Paris Underground; chased by an animal like when you were chased by that vagrant? Don't you see, you had a terrifying experience, and it manifested as a night terror. You were dreaming about the Paris catacombs."

"You saw me when I came in. I was a mess. Was that a dream?"

Dr. Sandbourne lowered his voice. "No, we saw you. However, you must understand how it all could have been *caused* by a dream. You were probably walking in your sleep. I know from experience what happens when you dream."

"It wasn't a dream. I'm positive."

Nikki spoke. "You were positive about the lady in the diary and that was a..."

Veronica didn't let her sister finish. "I know what happened to me! It wasn't the same thing. I woke in the middle of the night to use the bathroom..."

Nikki didn't back down. "You could've been *dreaming* you were looking for the bathroom. I had that happen once. I dreamt that I got up and went to the bathroom. Only I didn't really, and I peed my bed." Nikki caught herself being too candid and quickly added, "That happens to a lot of people, right, Doc?"

Dr. Sandbourne conceded by nodding his round head. "That can happen. It's called a lucid dream. You're aware of your surroundings and believe you're awake, but are actually dreaming. Veronica has lucid dreams, but hers are often accompanied by a deeper degree of 'openness', which makes her extremely vulnerable. She needs to be careful and take her medicine."

Veronica watched the doctor turn his head and address her sister, and she suddenly felt small, distant, like a child peering up at two adults while they conversed. Then, like a child, she rose quickly to her feet and stomped out of the room while shouting, "Listen, I had *one* dream. One. About Josette-Camille. And it happened because I was reading that stupid diary. This is very different. I'll prove it."

"I don't doubt it was *real* Veronica," The doctor called after her. "But that doesn't mean it wasn't a dream."

Veronica went to her bedroom, grabbed the grimy satchel, turned on her heels with a snap, and proudly marched back into the library. "You might've been my doctor when I was a kid, but a lot has changed since then. I've grown up. You don't know me anymore."

"You're right, a lot's changed, but I've seen you like this before, Veronica, I recognize your symptoms. Do you remember your first visit to my office when you were just ten years old?"

Veronica stood in the doorway. The leather sack dangled in her hands as she spoke. "No, I don't. Honestly, I don't remember you at all. The only reason I called you is because my mom gave me your number and said to talk to you if I ever had bad dreams. I'm not sure if that was such a good idea anymore. I mean,

I appreciate you coming all the way to France to see me, but it wasn't necessary. I really don't need to listen to this...and I'm not paying you! If you don't want to believe what happened to me was real, then fine. But then please explain where *this* came from. I found it in a crypt in the catacombs." Veronica took long deliberate steps forward and thumped the satchel onto the library table.

Dr. Sandbourne sat quietly and waited for the tension to calm down. Nikki opened and closed her mouth several times, not sure if she should speak or not, then decided to stay out of the fray. Instead, she poked charily at the bag and pulled out a book and a tarnished, yet ornately decorated, box.

The doctor squinted at the items on the table before calmly stating, "This isn't about those things on the table. It's about *you*. I'm not charging money for coming here. That's the farthest thing from my mind. I came here because I know you're in trouble and need my help. When we talked on the phone, I knew things weren't right. I couldn't explain it then; you probably wouldn't have believed me. I know it's hard to understand because it's been so long since you've seen me, and if you don't even remember me...well, all I can say about that is that our treatment must have worked, — at least to some degree. You see, I *made sure* you forgot everything that happened to you."

Nikki flipped through the pages of the book and frowned at the mysterious script. She caressed the box, eager to open it, but was also enthralled by the doctor's account of her sister's history. "What happened to her?" she asked.

Veronica nodded and echoed, "What happened to me?" Her anger and frustration slipped away as she studied his thick, round spectacles. His far-away eyes were wide, and he slightly bowed his dainty, oval head. He reminded Veronica of a light bulb.

"Those awful night terrors, all the treatments, the studies, the tests, the sleepless nights, the crying fits — it was almost as stressful for me as it was for you," he recounted. "When you first came to me you were this fragile little thing wearing Little Mermaid pajamas. You were shivering and clutching your mother's neck as if your life depended on holding onto her. At that point, your mother said you'd been awake for three days straight. She had taken you to the family doctor, but he couldn't help you. Then she brought you to me, and I tried my best."

"What do you mean you *tried*; I thought you made the dreams stop?"

"At first I prescribed a sleep aide, nothing stronger than what you get in over-the-counter cold medicine. You were so tiny, I was afraid of overdosing you! It seemed to work for a week or two, but it didn't last. I tried a higher dose, then higher, but your night terrors kept breaking through. You got violent, were out of control, and...well, let's just say I finally had to get outside help, and that's when I called Dr. Jacobs."

"So, he got the night terrors to go away?" Veronica asked.

"Not exactly, but he was at least able to diagnose you."

Nikki piped in with, "You mean she had a disease?"

"Oh no, Veronica's condition wasn't physiological. Dr. Jacobs was a parapsychologist, and he diagnosed you with a severe case of sleep paralysis — said it was the worst he ever seen."

The girls' perplexed stares prompted the doctor to elaborate. "Imagine sleep like a long elevator ride. As you fall asleep, you descend past numerous levels until you get to the bottom. And at the bottom is the stage of consciousness known as *deep sleep*. It's where most of us go when we slumber. Veronica, you don't take the elevator all the way down, though. You consciously fall into a light sleep while your body falls into a deep sleep. The result: you are aware of being asleep. You become lucid, but sleep paralysis takes over, and you can't move."

"So, I have bad dreams because I never really fall into a deep sleep?"

"You have bad dreams because you become prone to extraneous influences."

Veronica and Nikki simultaneously said, "Huh?"

"When sleep paralysis takes over, it's like you're standing in front of a doorway, and those from the other side can use you to come through. You're accessible by spirits, ghosts, entities. *They* cause your night terrors."

"Wait a second, you saying my night terrors are caused by *ghosts*?" Veronica stood up to create a substantial amount of distance between herself and the doctor.

"I know it sounds crazy. Even as a child, you never fully understood what was happening to you. You were so completely innocent. That's why I covered up your memories with hypnosis. Just recalling them could've spurred more episodes."

"I don't have dreams about *ghosts*! I thought you were a doctor — a serious, professional, scientific guy — not some kook."

Sandbourne persisted. "I saw what happened to you twenty years ago, Veronica. I was there! I saw your crazy fits of hysteria. I watched as you descended into madness because of what those *things* did to you."

"What, so, you're saying I'm *crazy*?"

"No, I didn't mean it like that. It was because of the spirits. They drove you to the brink of madness, and they'll do it again unless we stop them. Veronica, did you fill the prescription I gave you?" He didn't wait for an answer. "Did you at least try to block them? No, you didn't, and look what happened to you last night. Listen, you must..."

Veronica took three quick short breaths before rage blasted out of her. "No! You listen! Everything is going good for me now. Decorating this castle is my dream job. It's almost done, and tomorrow night we're having a party to celebrate. The Traveler's Channel will be here, and I'll finally get noticed! This is my big chance, and I don't need to worry about your stupid ghost stories and all this crap you *claim* happened over twenty years ago. And I certainly don't need to be taking tranquilizers! I need to be on the very top of my game. Do you understand that? I didn't ask you to come here. I don't need you here fucking with my brain right now!"

The doctor's eyes scanned the floor like an ashamed child. He nodded his light bulb head and muttered, "I didn't mean to upset you. The night terrors can get worse when you're stressed. Before I leave, please promise to do one thing. After your party tomorrow night, please start taking the medicine? Once you are 'off your game', will you take care of yourself?"

Veronica felt a guilty stab as she watched the fragile old man shuffle toward the door. "Fine. After Marie-Claire approves my work, and I'm done with this job, I'll try your pills."

"No, you mustn't listen to Marie-Claire! Whatever you do, *don't* listen to her."

"She's my boss. I have to..."

"Marie-Claire and her husband, Dr. Jacobs, vanished *twenty* years ago. The authorities in the US declared them *dead* five years later." The doctor's face brightened as he delicately explained. "I think Marie-Claire's ghost contacted you through your dreams. She wants something, and she tricked you into coming here."

"So what — a ghost called me on the phone and lured me all the way to France? Ha! A ghost freaking hired me to decorate the castle it haunts. Guess we better call *Paranormal Ghost Hunters* then; screw the Traveler's Channel's show..."

"Have you seen her, Veronica?" Sandbourne insisted. "Met Marie-Claire in person? What proof do you have that she's real?"

Nikki addressed the room. "This is getting way too weird. I always figured this Marie-Claire chick was a nut, some kooky old rich bag, but she's not a freaking ghost."

"Sometimes ghosts, or spirits, lose their path from God," Dr. Sandbourne said. "They are influenced by other forces, powerful forces..."

"Oh, I get it," Veronica sneered. "This is about *God*. Well, I have news for you, Doc. I don't believe in God. I don't know what kind of religion you're preaching, and I don't care."

"Veronica, I'm not preaching. I'm just explaining what kind of forces we're dealing with..."

"Sounds like preaching to me," Veronica gritted her teeth.

"Both of you need to chill the fuck out," Nikki proclaimed. "Fighting isn't going to help the situation." She waved a frazzled hand in the air. "Why don't we change the subject?"

"What do you suggest we discuss? Who's on this season's *Dance with the Stars*?" Veronica asked venomously.

Nikki quickly surveyed their faces, deviously glanced around the room, and then commanded, "Let's talk about what's in that box!"

All three shifted their attention to the ornate chest.

Nikki pressed a thumb to the edges of the lid. "Ready?"

Veronica and the doctor nodded. Nikki lifted it up.

"Wow," Dr. Sandbourne sighed. His stilted demeanor seemed momentarily caught off-guard.

Inside was a mound of coins; luminous and glistening. They were ducats, like the one Christophe carried as a good luck charm. Something protruded from underneath the coins. It was buried; only a slight sparkle indicated its presence.

"What's that shiny thing?" Veronica pushed the coins to the side, and unveiled a white, lustrous, crystal skull, about the size of a softball. It was beautiful and disturbing, exotic and arcane. Veronica cupped it gently. The flames that danced in the fireplace seemed to be magnified within, and it gleamed like an iridescent jewel.

It grew warm in her hands.

She turned to the doctor. "I'm not dreaming this."

Nikki seemed to snap out of a trance with a jolt. "That's it!" she exclaimed. "The ghosts. Okay, so, let's say you are right, Doc. Marie-Claire is dead, and she contacted Veronica from the other side. Maybe she did, so Veronica could find this treasure. Makes sense, right? She wanted it to be found, along with the money in the Swiss bank account!"

Dr. Sandbourne let his head sway from side to side. "Not likely. The dead don't reveal money or treasure to the living. Such things have no value to them, and they certainly have no desire to make the living wealthy."

"Then what does Marie-Claire want? A shabby-chic castle to haunt?" Nikki quipped.

Sandbourne chuckled without humor and turned to Veronica. "I don't know what she wants, but until we figure it out, you have to protect yourself. Here, I brought these." He handed Veronica a bottle of pills.

She pensively studied the prescription and nodded. "Okay, I'll take them tonight. Just tonight, if that'll make you happy."

Sandbourne grabbed Nikki's transistor radio from the fireplace mantel. "And sleep with the radio on, too."

"Why?" Veronica questioned.

"Electronic transmissions block *them*. Not sure why; something to do with how they affect electromagnetic fields."

"You're saying the radio protects me?"

"Yes, in a manner of speaking. Televisions, too."

"You always sleep with the damn TV on," Nikki noted.

Veronica vacantly agreed. "Yeah, until recently. The picture tube went out on the one I have at home a couple months ago; couldn't afford a new one. And we don't have TVs here."

Sandbourne nodded his head as if that proved his point, but he held his tongue as Veronica shrugged, swallowed a pill, and took the radio with her into the bedroom.

Chapter 118

Veronica's Story

When she woke, Veronica didn't feel groggy or tired because of the pills. She actually felt a surge of energy, like she had the most restful sleep of her life.

Nikki and Dr. Sandbourne were in the kitchen. He had spent the night at the sisters' request. Having him there made them feel safe in the suddenly frightening castle. "Besides," Nikki had said, "this place is supposed to be an inn. There are plenty of rooms, so why shouldn't you just stay here?"

Veronica poured coffee while the doctor paged through the ancient tome from the satchel. She asked, "Can you read it? Does it say what that skull is?"

Dr. Sandbourne chuckled. "You know what they say; *it's all Greek to me*...and I mean that literally. It's written in ancient Greek."

"So, you can't read it then, huh?" Veronica sighed.

"Well, truth be told, I'm managing to get some of it. I did study Greek and Latin in college, but that was some time ago. I have to take it slowly. Perhaps, if you take it to an expert, they could translate it much more effectively than I can."

"Ralph's an expert in ancient languages. He could do it!" Nikki proclaimed.

"Yeah," Veronica agreed. "He's, ah, a friend of ours...an antiquities dealer. Is he coming to the party tonight?"

"He is!" Nikki enthused. "He was one of the first to R.S.V.P."

"How do you feel this morning, Veronica?" Dr. Sandbourne asked.

"Fine. Actually *very* fine. Listen, I'm sorry about last night. I didn't mean —"

The doctor cut her short. "Don't worry about it, dear. Under the circumstances, it was perfectly understandable. I would like for us to sit and talk for a session; maybe a little later this afternoon?"

Veronica frowned. "I really can't. There's too much going on today. First, I gotta see if Clark is around to fix that septic tank, then I have to make sure every last room is presentable because we have people from magazines and television coming. Maybe tomorrow? Please feel free to stay the night again. We have plenty of room. And join us tonight at the party."

"Thank you for the invitation, and yes, I will stay."

Dr. Sandbourne inspected the mysterious volume while Veronica and Nikki prepared for the evening. The caterers arrived shortly after eleven, and then came the flower delivery, the band, and a flurry of preparations filled the rest of the day.

⇜ ❖ ⇝

At four o'clock, Nikki chased Veronica out of the ballroom. "I have everything under control, Vern!"

"But the people from the band are dragging equipment across *four* hundred year old marble floors, and someone spilled something brown on the velvet chaise, and the caterers have completely taken over the kitchen!”

“The band will be careful; *I* spilled a coke, and *I* cleaned it up; and the caterers are *supposed* to take over the kitchen. They’re professionals. Relax!”

“You don’t understand, Nik. I am responsible for this place.”

“And I’m responsible for the party, remember? You put me in charge. Trust me!”

“But everything has to be perfect with the Traveler’s Channel people here and the Fontaines and snotty old Lady Florence...”

“Vern, you’re acting cray-cray! Everything is under control. Why don’t you go take one of those Valium the Doc gave you?”

“No! I don’t need a pill. It’s just that I can’t sit around and do nothing. I have to stay busy.”

“Well, I can’t get anything done with you hovering over my shoulder.”

“What am I supposed to do?” Veronica moped. “I can’t relax. Just let me help.”

“No, Vern, this is *my* thing. Here,” Nikki flipped Veronica the car keys, “run into town and get some ice.”

“Ice! We need *ice*? The caterers should have brought ice. See, they’re going to ruin everything!”

“The caterers *did* bring ice...” Under her breath, she finished her thought, “I just need an excuse to get you the hell outta here.”

Veronica snagged her bag and hurried out the door. “You can never have too much ice! I’ll be back in a little bit. Anything else we need?”

“No! Just go!”

Veronica ran a shaking hand through her hair as she sped to town. The recent rain and humidity had really brought out her curls, and she vainly tried to keep it under control by pulling it back with bobby pins. She scanned the main street shops for a place to buy ice, spied a market with a rusty, white ice machine outside the front door, and pulled up.

Once parked, she jumped out of the car, slammed the door, took two steps, realized that she left the keys in the ignition, and stopped cold in her tracks. She spun back around and opened the car door again. “Can’t leave these behind,” she whispered to herself as her shaking hand snagged the keys with a flourish. This time she slammed the car door before making her way across the street.

When she came to the front step, she realized that her bag was also still in the car. She huffed, turned quickly, tripped forward, and nearly fell over. Veronica sheepishly cursed under her breath as she opened the car door. While leaning in to grab her purse, someone behind her said, “Veronica!”

Her frizzy head jerked up and hit the roof of the tiny car. A hand grabbed her waist as she yelled, “Ouch!” and twisted her torso to see who was behind her. As she did, her hip thrust into the steering wheel, and she fell, bottom first, into the driver’s seat. She looked up. Christophe stood there with outstretched hands.

“Are you okay? I didn’t mean to startle you! Did you hurt your head?”

Veronica rubbed her crown. “No, I’m fine. Hi!”

Christophe grinned. “Hi.”

“What are *you* doing here?”

"I was having a coffee, reading the paper and looking forward to tonight," he gestured to a quaint café on the corner, "and I saw the orange car, and I thought it might be you." Veronica followed his gaze and realized that he had a perfect view of her from the moment she parked the car. She blushed lightly, smiled, and he continued. "What are *you* doing here?"

Veronica eyed the decrepit ice machine outside the market and vaguely pointed as she tried to regain her composure. "Oh, I'm getting —"

"You're hair done!" Christophe interjected.

Veronica blinked rapidly, momentarily confused, and then she noticed the hair salon next to the market.

"My hair, why did you say that?" she asked as memories of Robert stabbed within.

Christophe beamed. "Your party tonight. All women get their hair done before a big party."

Veronica chuckled. "Yeah, you're right. Very perceptive! Gotta get some of those highlights!"

"It's a big night for you. How's everything? How are you doing?"

"Nikki has the party under control, however, last night I...well, let's just say it was a crazy night, and we got an unexpected visitor from the States. And I'm a little nervous, I mean, there's going to be TV people there judging my work; plus the neighbors, and people I don't even know..."

Christophe grinned with an easy, dimpled smile. It made her anxiety automatically wane. "Everything will be fine. It'll be a great party, and everyone will see what a magnificent designer you are!"

"Thanks for the vote of confidence."

"So, tell me what your costume looks like!"

"Oh, it's black and...wait! I'm not going to tell. You'll find out later."

Christophe smiled coyly. "And I can't wait."

"Well, I better get going and get...my hair done," she said apprehensively.

Christophe lifted her hand and helped her out of the car. She walked toward the salon, turning once to see him watching her. He smiled and waved as she reluctantly went inside.

She had no choice. Veronica was *finally* getting her hair done.

Chapter 119

Veronica's Story

$\mathcal{A}$t eight thirty that evening, Veronica peeked into the ballroom. It was decorated with enormous swags of fabric, garlands of flowers, and twinkle lights. It had the ambience of a fairytale garden; the perfect place for a masquerade ball. She wanted to praise her sister for a job well done, but Nikki was nowhere in sight. She didn't have time to search for her as guests were to arrive in a half an hour.

In her bedroom, Veronica was surprised to see that the black dress was no longer laid out on her bed, but instead, Nikki's green steampunk dress was there, along with a note. Veronica picked it up and read: "Vern, the green dress is too big for me, but it should fit you just right! I took the black one. See you at the party!"

She frowned as she held the olive-green dress up to her chest and stood in front of the mirror. It clashed fiercely with her deep *red* hair. She would look like a Christmas tree.

Red hair. "Vibrant Vixen Red" to be precise. Veronica still could not believe that she let the beautician convince her to dye it. When Veronica first entered the salon, she asked for blond highlights, like her sister Nikki.

"Do you really want the *same* hair as your sister?" the woman questioned her.

Veronica conceded. "Well, everyone says we look a lot alike. Maybe I don't?"

"It is better..." according to the smock-clad hairdresser who smoked thin, brown cigarettes, "to *not* look like your sister. Be your own person! She wants to be a dippy blond girl, aw, let her! You! You should be passionate because you are in love, right? Don't deny it. I can see in your eyes. You have passion, and therefore, your hair needs to have passion. The color will accent your fair complexion and make you glow! It will *ignite* your love. You will see."

Now Veronica pulled at the crimson locks that spiraled around her forehead. She smiled at herself...and then she considered the red velvet dress that Clark had found.

It was clean and hung in the closet.

Veronica slung the green dress aside and pulled the red one out of the drycleaner's bag. It smelled fresh. She laid it out on the bed. It was perfect — no stains, no rips. But would it fit? Veronica continued to study her figure in the mirror. She looked more slender than she used to. All the hard work and missed meals had caused her to lose at least five pounds, maybe more.

She decided to take a chance and pulled the red dress over her head. It fit perfectly. *Better than perfect,* she thought as she studied her body in the mirror. The bodice had strings that pulled tight around her torso, and she looked thinner than she ever imagined possible. Her breasts pushed up and were ample and sexy. This was the kind of dress she thought she could never get away with wearing, but she was!

"The red mask!" she exclaimed as she ran to retrieve it from a sideboard in the hall where she arranged it like a decoration. She slipped it over her face.

The mask covered her eyes, and a semi-translucent, silky veil hung from it, covering her mouth and neck like an Arabian princess. She stood in front of the mirror and didn't recognize herself. She was sexy...and Veronica had never felt sexy before. As the party awaited her, she gave her reflection a coy, snarling smile and sashayed out of the Queen's Chamber.

A line of guests were being escorted through the foyer, then through the library, and into the ballroom by hired butlers. It was quarter after nine, and there were already a good number of people in attendance. They were dressed in elaborate gowns and wore fanciful masks. Some of them were sprinkled with glitter and garnished with feathered wings like woodland fairies. Others wore renaissance clothing and looked like French nobility from long ago. One man wore furry pants like a mythological beast, complete with hoofed feet and horns.

She scanned the parade as they passed. Many of them wore Victorian attire with steampunk accessories like goggles, gears, and various gadgets. She was grateful she didn't wear her sister's dress, she would have been just another steampunker.

From the foyer came a woman garbed as a nun. Two others wore sheer fabric draped around them like togas and prosthetic, pointed ears. A man walked through dressed entirely in green armor...the Green Knight, Veronica recalled, from English literature. Another gentleman and his female companion wore elaborate turn-of-the-century Spanish attire. When they turned, Veronica saw their faces painted like Día de Muertos sugar skulls.

Delighted by the enthusiasm, Veronica joined the line and entered the ballroom like a regular guest. A blonde woman in a black gown, bordered with orange feathers, stood near the doorway and greeted people as they entered. She wore a matching mask bedazzled with orange plastic beads and feathers. Ribbons weaved in and out of her hair, which was pulled up on the top of her head in loose, fanciful curls. It took a moment for Veronica to recognize her own sister. Somehow she made that hideous dress look hot!

She leaned over to offer a compliment, but Nikki spoke first. "Hello, so glad you could come. Enjoy yourself, and remember, we unmask at midnight!"

Veronica grinned as she realized that Nikki didn't recognize her. She was about to speak, but hesitated. Finally, she said with a snicker, "Why thank you, ma'am. It looks like a wonderful party!"

Nikki smiled politely and turned to the next guest. Veronica giggled and made her way through the crowd. She'd think of a way to surprise her sister later on. It would be *her* turn to play a prank on Nikki!

The band played a waltz, and a few brave souls took to the dance floor. A mile of food was laid out on banquet tables, and there was a castle sculpted out of ice in the center of the spread. Servers also carried trays with mini quiches, coconut shrimp, and glasses of champagne. She snagged one and sipped the bubbles while admiring the party scene.

Across the room, Veronica noticed a dark figure wearing a tattered cloak. She tilted her head to get a better look. Most of the costumes were bright and striking; however, this man caught her attention, as he was swarthy and dirty. He disappeared from her line of sight.

She started to walk and then, on the other side of the room, she saw him again, facing her. He seemed oddly familiar. Someone crossed between them, and she lost her view of the cloaked man. Veronica remained in position, hoping the crowd would part again so she could get another look. She waited a moment, but the sea of people seemed to thicken, so she decided to make her way to the spot where he had been standing.

"Pardon, pardon," she whispered as she weaved through the partygoers. When she finally came to the other side of the room, he was nowhere in sight. Veronica thought she knew him from somewhere, but she couldn't place the face. It was long, dark, covered with a scraggly beard and mustache. Stringy hair hung in his eyes. His eyes — they bore into Veronica. She knew those eyes. A cold stab shot down her spine, and she felt someone tap her arm.

She spun and saw a short, plump man dressed like a leprechaun. He grinned warmly and asked, "May I have this dance, my lady?"

Veronica nodded politely, and the two began to waltz. They spun clumsily among the other dancers. Veronica felt his sweaty hand on her back and wished she had declined the offer. He struck up a conversation just as she again spied the familiar man across the room. This time she was certain that he was staring directly at her. *Who was he? Was he wearing a costume? There was no mask, but that hair, could it be a wig?* She held his gaze as her dance partner persisted.

"I said are you enjoying yourself?"

Veronica dropped her eyes upon the leprechaun. "Yes, I am. It's a great party," she answered absently and then looked up, but the strange cloaked man was gone again.

"My name is Lawrence Farrell, and yours?" he spoke with an English accent.

"Veronica. Nice to meet you. You aren't French, are you?"

"Goodness, no. From England. I work at the consulate's office. Everyone there got an invitation to this ball."

Veronica knew that the invitation was the work of Christophe, and she wondered where he was.

"One of the many perks from my job. Invitations to the best parties, large expense accounts, free hotel rooms..." he rambled, in an attempt to impress her.

The music faded, and she quickly replied, "Thanks for the dance, Lawrence," then she stealthily escaped from the sweaty leprechaun.

As she shuffled through the crowd, a young boy dashed in front of her, almost making her trip. She cursed him as he disappeared into the sea of partygoers. *Who would bring their kid to a party like this,* she wondered as she noticed drops of champagne had splashed on her dress.

She grabbed a napkin from a nearby table, whipped her bodice, and when she looked up saw a striking, broad-shouldered gentleman enter across the room. He had wavy, moussed hair and wore a dark tuxedo with a simple, black mask. It didn't disguise his angled chin or luscious lips, though. There was no doubt, Christophe had arrived!

She waved her hand eagerly, trying to get his attention, as she made her way through the crowd. The place was packed, and fleetingly, she wondered if the people from the Traveler's Channel were there yet, too.

Suddenly, Dr. Sandbourne was standing in front of her. He wore the same type of brown tweed jacket as he had the evening before. A blue mask covered his eyes, but it was small and fit awkwardly over his wiry glasses and didn't leave much to the imagination. "Hello, dear, wonderful party!"

"You recognized me! My own sister didn't even know who I was."

He pointed to the hand she held in the air. "See that scar; I'd recognize it anywhere."

"This?" Veronica asked as she turned her hand. I hardly even notice it." On her wrist was a tiny gash just under the meaty part of her palm.

"I was there when you got it. Maybe that's why I'll never forget it."

"You were there when I got this scar...?" Veronica prompted. Her interest was piqued, yet she wanted to see Christophe. She scoured the room for him, but he was lost in the crowd.

"At Dr. Jacobs' Clinic for Parapsychological Research. You were on your third week there, and your night terrors were getting worse. You were such a sad little sight, hooked up to monitors and machines with wires coming out of you everywhere. Dark circles under your eyes, and no matter how many blankets we gave you, you always trembled like you were cold."

Veronica listened, slightly distracted by the party around her. "Sounds awful. Maybe it's better that I don't remember."

"We watched you while you slept. I'm not sure if you ever knew that, but there was always someone looking over you," the doctor persisted. It became obvious to Veronica that he had a story to tell, so she politely gave him her full attention. "We had a one-way mirror and observed you from the room next door. The night you got that scar you had barely fallen asleep when you started screaming. You had done this many times before. Usually, the night nurse would go in, wake you up, and you'd tell her about an awful night terror, and then go back to sleep."

Veronica felt frozen claws grip her heart and pull it down to her bowels. The sickening, sinking feeling made her woozy and desperate to steer the conversation in another direction. She turned away from Sandbourne and locked eyes with the shadowy cloaked man again. He stood a few feet away from Veronica and the doctor. His piercing stare fixed on her as if he was penetrating her soul...and was enjoying it.

"Do you see that man there?" Veronica pointed. The doctor turned. Again, the crowd converged, and the cloaked man was hidden from view. "Huh, he's gone now. Never mind."

Dr. Sandbourne cocked his little head. "What did you see Veronica? Is something there?"

She shook her head. "No, just some guy who keeps staring at me."

He managed an awkward grin and said, "Can't blame young men for staring at you, dear. You're stunning in that dress! You've grown into a beautiful, young woman."

She gushed and bowed her head at the unexpected compliment. Veronica wasn't used to people telling her she was beautiful.

The doctor continued. "That night, whatever came to you while you were dreaming, it didn't want to let go. It grabbed onto you, Veronica. Somehow it stayed with you when you woke up. Do you understand? We couldn't see it, but when the nurse went into the room it *pushed* her. We watched her fly across the room! Then I ran in to help, and I could *feel* it. Heavy is all I can say to describe it. The room felt like it was filled with pudding!

I could barely move as I made my way to you. I unclasped your bed restraints, but you still couldn't get up. It pinned you down. I tried to pull you off the bed, but it started clawing at you like a rabid dog fighting for a bone. I saw that scratch appear on your wrist, but there was nothing there. It was like an invisible claw sliced into your flesh. It was some kind of creature, a demon, something absolutely evil."

"A demon, huh, I thought you said I was visited by *ghosts*?" She hoped her skeptical demeanor would shut him up. Instead, he eagerly continued. "Ghosts are just one type of spirit, my dear. There are many things out there, and they go by a lot of different names. They're known as demons in Judeo-Christian doctrines, succubae and incubi in mythology, and in the Middle Ages, they were known as the 'old Hag'. The difference is that a ghost was once human. The other things, well, they never were."

"So, I got this scar from one of those 'other things', from something that was *never human*?" She smirked as she displayed her right hand.

Dr. Sandbourne lifted the blue mask and let it rest on the top of his shiny head. He was serious as he said, "I think so, my dear."

"So, how did you save me? I mean, an 'old Hag' attack; that sounds pretty brutal."

"It might sound funny, but it isn't, Veronica. The old Hag is a demon bent on stealing souls while people sleep. I think your soul would have been taken that night if Marie-Claire hadn't arrived just in time and somehow *banished* it."

Veronica perked up at the name. "Marie-Claire? What do you mean by *banished*?"

"She *ordered* it to leave you alone. She had the ability to see spirits and communicate with them. She marched into your room and commanded it to go back where it came from."

Unable to quell her skepticism, Veronica scrunched up her nose and asked, "So, you're telling me she was, like, psychic?"

"Marie-Claire was *clairvoyant*. She could actually *see* the spirits and communicate with them."

"So, she helped me, right? She wasn't as bad you make her out to be, after all."

Dr. Sandbourne chose his words carefully. "She did help you and took care of you. After that episode, she sat with you every night to make sure none of the bad ones came for you again — that's what you called them — the *Bad Ones* — and 'monsters' . You hated it when I tried to tell you they were *only* night terrors. Got so mad at me when I said they were *just in your head*! I quickly found out you were right, though."

Veronica didn't want to talk about monsters and night terrors. She *did* want to learn more about Marie-Claire, though. "She sat at my bedside every night?"

He lowered his voice as he explained. "But she had ulterior motives, Veronica. Marie-Claire told me that she had 'limited' clairvoyance. She said her connection to the other side came through fuzzy, like a bad connection with a transistor radio. You, on the other hand, had a unique thing happen when you slept. You were a clear conduit. Like that elevator I told you about, you hovered right in the doorway of the spirit world. And the spirits constantly tried to use you to break through. And Marie-Claire, well she wanted to use that doorway to break through from *our* side to *theirs*. She and Andrew wanted to *experiment* with you. You were a means to an end for her, and she didn't care what the experiments might do to you."

"*Experiments?* What experiments?" Veronica didn't disguise her irritation.

"Please, don't get upset. I'm going to tell you the truth. After everything you've been through, you deserve to know."

Veronica grew solemn and listened as the doctor explained. "When your mother first brought you to me, I didn't know what to do. I'd never seen a case like yours before, nor had any of my colleagues. I got a second and third opinion, and they both diagnosed you as schizophrenic. I tried my best, but you were so violent, so out of control, that you couldn't stay in the regular hospital. Since your parents couldn't afford the special care you needed, your attending physician recommended you be institutionalized in a state-run psychiatric hospital for the clinically insane."

Veronica felt dry heat in the back of her throat. She wished the light bulb-headed, hippy-doctor would stop talking and just go away. She didn't want to hear any more of his stupid story, but he wouldn't relent. "I was desperate. That's when I brought you to Andrew and Marie-Claire, to their 'new age' parapsychology clinic. I didn't put much stock in that kind of stuff, but I knew you'd be given a safe bed in a private room, and I'd be able to continue treating you. It also meant that Andrew and his wife would be allowed to study you."

"Study me for what?"

"Andrew surmised your night terrors were caused by spirits attempting to *break through* into our world. I thought he was nuts. He wanted to give you electro-magnetic therapy. I thought it was a bunch of bunk. I still prescribed you tranquilizers and figured his therapy was just a bunch of hocus-pocus that wouldn't do anything anyway. But Andrew switched your medicine without my knowledge. Gave you sugar pills that did nothing! Then he created an electro-magnetic field around you while you slept, and all hell broke loose! It was like he opened a flood gate and couldn't close it."

Veronica stopped him. "Electro-mag-what? What the fuck did you do to me?"

"It wasn't me. It was Dr. Jacobs. He created an *electro-magnetic* field around you while you were asleep. I remember you all wired up like a lab rat. You were terrified, and there was nothing I could do. Andrew said the electro-magnetic field would 'shut down' areas of your brain that were receptive to other worldly influences. But like I said, it made everything much worse. The night terrors became increasingly violent as more and more *Bad Ones* broke through."

"Then why didn't you stop him?"

"I tried! After the incident when you got that scar, I begged Andrew and

Marie-Claire to quit, but they wouldn't listen. They got the crazy idea to bring you to France. They wanted to take you *here*, to the Château, and do the experiments. Marie-Claire had just purchased Château du Feu Ardent. It had a reputation as being haunted, and she wanted to bring you here to use you to summon up spirits, mostly victims of the oubliette."

"The oubliette?" Veronica asked.

"Yes, the oubliette...you haven't seen it then? It is a dungeon, a narrow pit. Literally, it means a *forgotten little place*. People were thrown in and just left to die."

"Like the pit Josette-Camille jumped in with her baby?" She wondered aloud.

"Who's Josette-Camille?" the doctor asked.

Veronica didn't want to start a conversation about the diary, so she shrugged and said, "Never mind, just someone I read about."

"Do you know where the oubliette is, Veronica?" he pried.

"No clue," she answered. "If it's here in the Château, then I haven't seen it."

Dr. Sandbourne continued. "There's something else, too. Something sinister haunts this castle. It's an *elemental.*"

"A what?"

"Elementals are ancient, primitive and unpredictable. Marie-Claire said the one in this castle is trapped between worlds."

"Like a ghost that can't find the white light?" she said with a smirk.

"No, this is more like one of those 'other things'. It isn't a ghost. It was never human. There are many different types, and Marie-Claire said the one in this castle is known as a *djinn*."

Veronica's eyebrows scrunched.

The doctor paused, smiled, and explained, "It's like a demon. There are all kinds of different demons. Legend has it the djinn were created at the dawn of time out of 'smokeless fire'. They are powerful and evil. You are familiar with the legends of genii?"

"You mean like, blink-blink?" Veronica asked. She crossed her arms in front her chest like Barbara Eden and nodded her head.

"Yes, genie legend sprung from the djinn."

"So, Marie-Claire wanted to get three wishes?" Veronica snickered. Dr. Sandbourne frowned, and Veronica continued seriously. "I'm sorry, but this all seems so freaking unbelievable. Do you really expect me to believe that *I* was some kind of a doorway to the spirit world?"

"I thought you deserved to hear the story...your story. Even if you don't believe me, you should at least hear me out. What I'm saying might sound crazy now, but someday, it will all make perfect sense. But you decide. Do you want me to continue?"

Veronica noted how skillfully the old man made her feel guilty and grunted, "I'm sorry. Please continue."

"Marie-Claire wanted you to be the conduit between her and this elemental-djinn thing. She didn't care how dangerous it was. I wouldn't allow it, though. We fought — Dr. Jacobs, Marie-Claire, and I. They even went to your mother and told her *I* was standing in the way of curing you. They told her there was a special research center here in France that would help you. They lied to her! They would have done anything to bring you here. I called your mother and told her the truth about the spirits and the djinn and what Andrew and Marie-Claire *really* wanted to do with you. Your mother, rightly so, became extremely upset at all of us and put an end to everything. She came early one morning and pulled you out of the clinic. She tore the wires right off your little head, yanked you out of bed, and drove off. That was the last time Andrew and Marie-Claire saw you."

"And was it the last time you saw me, too?"

"No. I went to your mother the next day, and though it took a while, I convinced her that I could help you, and she let me see you again. I managed to reverse the damage they'd done. I hypnotized you with the objective to *close* all those doors in your psyche they had opened with electro-magnetic therapy. It took several weeks, but I finally planted enough hypnotic suggestions in your mind to keep those doors shut. That's why you don't dream; your own psyche blocks your dreams to protect you. That's also why you don't remember anything. Weeks of hypnotherapy blocked everything. It's also why you are in denial now. I made it so your psyche wouldn't accept seeming irrationalities like spirit dreams. I did that to *protect* you. The less you remember, the less you accept them, the more resistant you are to them."

Veronica glanced at the huge clock on the wall; she had spent a good amount of the party talking with Dr. Light Bulb and was growing weary of him. "Okay, fine, I can believe you gave me a post hypnotic suggestion, and it helped to alleviate my bad dreams. But all that stuff about Marie-Claire and summoning evil demons and spirits from another dimension...I mean, I'm sorry, Dr. Sandbourne, I just can't buy that. You're a very kind man and —"

He cut her off. "Veronica, I'm afraid the spirits are back, and they're knocking on your door! Marie-Claire is behind this —"

She kept her cool, but interrupted him back. "Please, the Marie-Claire I know is a sweet, generous lady and my best client. She's not a *ghost!*"

Dr. Sandbourne would not relent. "You need to understand how much danger you're in. She lured you here for a reason and I'm afraid that..."

Veronica suddenly wanted to be far away from the odd, little man. She didn't want to listen anymore. He blinked at her through his delicate spectacles while the mask on his forehead also stared at her with hollow sockets.

"You know, you shouldn't take your mask off 'til midnight!" she quipped.

The complete change in her tone made Dr. Sandbourne freeze for a moment. Then he exhaled and pulled the flimsy cardboard back over his eyes. He sensed her frustration. "Maybe this isn't the time to tell you all of this. After all, we're at a party, right? We should be having fun, not reliving the shadows of the past."

"Yes, now you're getting it. Let's enjoy the evening. Maybe we can talk tomorrow," Veronica lied. She hoped she never had to speak to the creepy, old hippy again. He raised an eyebrow and opened his mouth to speak, but Veronica cut him off. "I know! Let me grab us a couple glasses of wine." She hurried off to fetch the beverages and escape from the doctor forever.

Ten minutes later, Veronica still stood at the bar. She was relieved to have fled Sandbourne's morbid story and was in no hurry to return. She chatted with the bartender about "all the extra ice in the kitchen if you run low" and other random trifles.

The server nodded along with her, then grinned widely when two men approached and interrupted the conversation. They carried cameras, a boom mic and light bounces. One leaned against the bar and asked for a couple bottles of water.

The Traveler's Channel! Veronica thought and quickly introduced herself. "Hello! My name is Veronica Dixon. I'm so glad you came."

They shook hands as a short woman with a booming voice prattled behind them. "Don't forget, we need exterior shots!" The woman wore a bright blue cocktail dress with a feathery purple mask that splayed from her head like a peacock's tail. She looked annoyed that Veronica interrupted her and strained to be polite. "Thank you for having us. I'm Gigi Jones; that's Justin and Alex."

Veronica then recognized the goateed producer and smiled sheepishly.

Alex flaccidly shook her hand. "Nice to see you again."

"This is quite a spread," Gigi noted. "If the rest of the castle looks as nice as the little bit we've seen so far, then we should be able to include it in our series. Don't you agree, Alex?"

Alex nodded.

"You mean you *are* interested in shooting here then?" Veronica inquired.

"Yes, it looks marvelous," she said without emotion. "We'll be able to come back on Monday and Tuesday to shoot. We'll need to have full access to the grounds, the castle, and so forth. You should be here. We'll do some designer interviews, ask you questions. What do you look like under there anyway?" She reached without regard and pulled Veronica's mask down so that she could catch a glimpse of her face, then continued. "You'll need at least an hour in makeup."

"She'll need a wardrobe assistant, too," Alex remarked as if she weren't even there. He then turned to Veronica. "You don't mind if we check out the rest of the castle?"

Veronica nodded compliantly and pulled her mask back up. "Let me show you around."

Gigi snapped her fingers and pointed to the hall that led to the dining room. "I want a shot of that, Justin. Get over there." Turning to Veronica, she said, "Come, come, we don't have all night!"

Veronica opened her mouth to answer, but before she could, Gigi was gone in a ruffle, chasing down Alex and squawking about the lighting. Veronica followed behind, reluctant to leave the party, yet thrilled to finally have her moment in the spotlight.

Chapter 120

Veronica's Story

Afterᵉ nearly an hour of showing Gigi the castle, Veronica politely excused herself outside the corridor to the tower rooms. "You've seen just about every room. The only part that's left is the keep, down this hall. Feel free to look. It's the oldest part, built as a fortress before the dark ages by a tribe of Pagans."

Gigi sniffed her nose down the narrow hall. "Smells, doesn't it?" she asked.

"The plumber has been trying to air it out. Something with the septic system..." Veronica began, and finally said, "Look, I have other guests to attend to. You're free to explore wherever you'd like!"

Alex cocked his head. "Did you hear that?"

"What?" Veronica asked.

They all stood and listened. Music and distant voices from the party echoed through the halls.

"I thought I heard someone cry out."

"Someone from the party," Gigi answered thinly.

"No, it was closer, yet farther," Alex said cryptically.

Veronica's impatience burst as she said, "No one's down there; everyone is in the ballroom — which is where I should be. Have a wonderful evening, and thank you again for this amazing opportunity!"

Veronica fled as Gigi nodded and feebly wished her, "Good night. Call me tomorrow!"

❧ ❖ ❧

The morose music hit Veronica like a wall of sound as she reentered the ballroom. Heavy and thundering, it filled the room like something solid. She scanned the crowd for Christophe or her sister, but didn't see either of them. As she made her way toward the veranda, she was forced back as people pushed their way to the dance floor. She stopped a moment to observe.

The music twanged and wailed. It was a mash-up of Irish folk, classical, and hard rock. The band was a strange, medieval assortment, including dulcimer and lute players alongside a keyboardist and bassist. A female singer would occasionally belt out high pitched, melodic verses, then oddly enough an electric guitar player — the guy Nikki met at the Paris Underground — would wail out a few rock chords, and the percussion would bang away with a danceable beat.

The floor was now packed. The crowd lined up like square dancers; the men on one side, the women on the other, and they began to bow and curtsey. The music flared up, and Veronica froze as the woman's voice melodically began:

Dream the dream that only you can dream
Sing the song that only you can sing

Dance with me, we'll start slow
Clasp my hand, now lose control
Bite the monster only you can see
And dream the dream you only dream for me

Not this freaking song again! she thought as she watched the dancers pace to and fro. They swelled together, joined hands with a partner from the other side, and then broke away and rotated. As they pulled apart, Veronica noticed a woman in the middle of the floor. Her head hung down, focused on her feet, which barely moved. She wasn't dancing, though she did sway slightly. Like a snake being charmed in a basket, she hypnotically wavered.

The dancers once again smothered her out of sight as they gathered in the center. She remained there, in the midst of it all, yet no one chose her as a partner. Everyone else paired up, did a little jig, then separated into a line on either side; all except for the woman who remained in the center. *Like the cheese,* Veronica thought, *the cheese stands alone...the cheese stands alone.* But the music wasn't *The Farmer in the Dell.* It was growing faster and faster as the momentum for that song, *Spirits in the Maze,* increased. The dancers sashayed back and forth, keeping pace with delighted grins on their faces.

Spirits in the maze
Burning brighter
Like a dream within the haze
Dancing fire
Deep inside malaise
Hungry spider
Force your screams to blaze
Spinning spiral

The woman in the center was turning; Veronica saw that now. Slowly, with the speed of the minute hand on a clock, she rotated in a circle with her head hanging down. Veronica strained to see her face, but it was covered by a bonnet that flopped over her brow. The front of her dress was ragged. Something dark stained it from her waist down. It was brown; no, Veronica decided, more of a rust color — like dried blood. Veronica braced herself. The image was recognizable now, familiar, but impossible for Veronica to accept.

When the absinth finally takes its toll
Let the whispers guide you down the hole
Cheshire Cat, whispers near
Smiling wide, have no fear
Fight the monster only you can see
And dream the dream you only dream for me

The dancers began moving at lightning speed. The song was nearing its fastest point. The beat was thumping, repetitive, and Veronica thought for sure everyone would leave the floor. It was nearly impossible to keep up, but they did. With delighted faces, they twisted and twirled. Veronica thought they looked like a scene in a movie that had been sped up.

It didn't look natural.

The woman in the center became exposed yet again, and Veronica saw the deep red stain from giving birth on the front of her nightgown. She watched, transfixed, as Josette-Camille slowly lifted her sullen face while the crowd of dancers whipped around her, furiously keeping time to the music.

Veronica wanted to look away; to take her eyes off of what surely could not be possible. But she stood frozen, like a rabbit mesmerized by fear.

The music came to its final and fastest verse. The vocalist hollered now.

Calling you to play
I'm your master
Don't you want to stay
Falling faster
Looking for the way
Hidden answers
Now you must obey
Stupid bastard

Josette-Camille was revealed one last time as the crowd backed away, and the music lifted to crescendo. There was no doubt in Veronica's mind that it was the woman who penned the diary. She looked just like Veronica knew she would: matted night gown stained with blood and afterbirth, hair tangled and falling out of her bonnet, wild bulging eyes that were determined, yet oddly confused, which stared directly at Veronica.

The music quelled then sharply stopped. The dancers had pulled together one last time. As the room became silent, they huddled in the center. They laughed, nodded to each other, and clapped. Not a one of them was out of breath or damp from the vigorous workout. Josette-Camille was nowhere in sight, and Veronica struggled to find her again. She greatly wanted to see that it was *not* Josette-Camille; that it was merely just another partygoer. But as everyone left the floor, there was no sign of the bloody dancer.

A hot surge of dread swept Veronica away to the veranda. Air. She needed fresh air. She pushed her way through the double doors and felt instant relief as the evening breeze neutralized the perspiration on her face. There were several people enjoying the outdoors, most of them smokers, escaping the party to puff in private.

Veronica's rational side took command in the lucid, cool night. Whatever she saw was not real. *It couldn't be.*

She peered back into the ballroom through one of the warped stained-glass window panes in the French doors. The room was a distorted smear of colorful figures, streaks of light, and shifting shadows. Obviously it was just someone in costume. It couldn't be Josette-Camille — *she's just a dream.*

Veronica breathed deeply and felt her lungs assaulted by the pungent odor of cigar. She coughed, turned back to the night air, and as she did a hefty gentleman beside her casually muttered, "Sorry, didn't mean to offend."

Veronica instantly recognized Ralph's condescending tone. "Hey!" she exclaimed, relieved to find someone, anyone, who was familiar.

He studied her, smiled, and graciously laid a balmy palm on her bare shoulder. "Well, hello there. It's a bit chilly out here tonight for no coat, sweetheart. Would you like to share mine?"

From his tone, it was apparent Ralph didn't recognize her. She gave him a gentle whack on the arm. "Ralph! It's me, Veronica, not some floozy!"

Ralph tilted his head in an effort to get a better look at her. A silky white top hat brimmed the crest of his head. It matched perfectly with his white suit. Melded to his face was a *Phantom of the Opera* mask. "Veronica? Is that *you*? You look *ravishing*! I never would have guessed!" He stood back and eyed her as he sucked the thick, Dutch cigar.

"Gee, ah, thanks." Veronica said nervously. She wasn't used to being ogled.

"That dress looks smashing. I could've sworn I saw you earlier in a *black* dress with orange feathers."

"Oh no, that's Nikki."

"You two look so much alike."

"That's what everyone says," Veronica answered and then quickly changed the topic. "Do you know where Christophe is?"

"Last I saw him, he was talking to some incredibly boring people who have an incredibly large amount of money in his bank."

"So, he's busy," she groused. "Hmm, maybe we can find him later. But while I have *you*, I have something un-freaking-believable to tell you..." she let her sentence hang like bait.

"Are *you* teasing *me*?"

"You know that map we showed you..."

"Yes...no! You figured out what it's a map of?"

"Oh, better than that..."

He paused with a cocked head and asked, "You found the booty?"

Veronica grinned devilishly. Her eyes fluttered behind the sultry mask. "Yes-oh-yes, I did! And it's a *big* booty."

He squealed, delighted by her play on words. "Well, what is it?" He clapped his chubby palms together like an excited boy.

Veronica glanced at the smokers standing on either side of them. "I think I should *show* you. Follow me?"

Ralph enjoyed the game and returned her devious grin with one of his own. "Of course. Lead the way to your booty, you gorgeous, red devil, you!"

❧ ❧ ❖ ❧ ❧

In The Queen's Chamber, the *Phantom of the Opera* mask and top hat sat on the edge of the writing desk. On the other side was the ancient tome, spread open, with Ralph leaning over it. Veronica stood beside him. She had just finished telling him about her adventure in the Château's catacombs. He thumbed the book and excitedly rattled, "This is old, oh yes, very old. And you said the catacombs are filled with crypts? Did you notice any inscriptions, drawings, symbols...?"

"They had paintings of people next to them. Faded, like they were there for centuries."

"Describe them."

"I dunno. They were multi-colored, and they had big almond-shaped eyes."

"Ah-huh," Ralph grunted. "Must be Roman. Did you see any dates?"

"Nah-uh, I was trying to get the hell out of there, so I didn't pay much attention."

He rambled inaudibly to himself and studied the text. Veronica jittered impatiently behind him. Finally, he spoke. "Rome occupied this area sporadically throughout the fourth century, so based on that, and the lexicon of the writing, this has to date back to around 325AD."

"You can read it?" she prodded.

"Well, I'm getting the gist of it. It's in Greek; looks like Christian scripture. It would take time for me to read it thoroughly though and translate it." He squinted and turned a page. A modern slip of bright yellow paper lay between the pages. He interrupted himself. "What's this?"

Veronica starred quizzically at the legal-pad style paper. "Dr. Sandbourne was looking at it earlier today," she realized. "He must've marked that page."

Ralph squinted at the doctor's writing. "Apparently, he tried to translate part of it. A name or something. But he's obviously no expert in ancient languages. Who's this Dr. Sandbourne?" Ralph smugly slid the yellow paper back between the pages.

"He's, ah, a friend visiting from America."

"You should be careful who sees this until we know exactly what it is."

"Why? Is it worth anything?"

Ralph chortled and washed down his amusement with a sip of champagne. "No. A text as old as this, in excellent condition, isn't worth *anything*...it's more than likely *priceless*."

Veronica shuddered. "No shit?"

Ralph snorted and mimicked her American accent. "No shit."

She narrowed her eyes and asked, "What should we do then, Sherlock?"

"Let me study it, carbon date the paper, translate it..."

"I'm going home in a week and a half. Is that enough time?"

"Maybe. I'll take it with me tonight and send the sample to the lab first thing in the morning."

"Or if it's that valuable, maybe we should report it to someone..." Veronica second-guessed herself.

"Don't worry, Veronica," Ralph calmly stated. "I'll take good care of the book. I am an *expert*."

"But it really isn't mine. Marie-Claire owns this castle; therefore, *she* owns the book."

"Call her. I can even talk to her; explain how significant this find is."

Veronica shrugged after contemplating for a moment. "Marie-Claire is on holiday...just take it with you tonight, and I'll explain everything the next time I talk to her. Besides, I haven't even shown you the best part yet." Veronica reached under her bed and retrieved the box. "I found it with the book." She set it on the desk. The semiprecious gems refracted specs of light, which reflected off Ralph's pristine, white suit.

Ralph brightened and began to ramble. "How exquisite, so ornate. The cross embossed on the lid looks Celtic. But why would it be in a *Roman* crypt then? It could be early Christian..."

She opened it, revealing the crystal skull nestled among the gold ducats.

"Christ in heaven is that a *crystal skull!*"

"I guess..." Veronica began, but Ralph prattled off a series of rhetorical questions.

"Is it real? You mean to tell me you found a crystal skull here in France! Do you have any idea how much that must be worth?"

She jumped in with her own question. "What's a crystal skull?"

"Shamans make them to control spirits. You find them in numerous ancient cultures: the Mayans, Druids, Egyptians, the Hopi Indians. They all made these finely crafted mysterious skulls. We've never had one turn up in *France* before, though!"

"So, this could be pretty important?"

Ralph wiped beads from his brow. "Shit yeah! And a treasure trove of ducats to boot! Here." He picked one up while giggling and flipped it to her playfully. "Now you have a better collection than Christophe!"

Veronica's tummy tingled at the mention of the banker's name, and she caught the ducat with a quick snap. "I can't wait to show him..."

Ralph exploded in epiphany. "The Celtic cross on the cover! What if it's really a *Templar* cross? The Templar Knights had treasurers, enormous wealth, and most of it was never recovered. This could be *Templar* treasure!"

Veronica earnestly tried to follow. "Templar Knights...?"

"Yes, an order of extremely righteous men. They wore tunics with red, even-sided crosses, like this Celtic cross," he tapped the top of the box, "on their chests."

Veronica formed a visual image in her mind. "Yeah, okay, I've seen them in movies..."

Ralph rose from his chair and patted her heartily on the head while chuckling. "Yeah, but the movies never got their history quite right. They show the Templars as extremely pious, faithful knights who fought bravely in the crusades in the name of the Church. Most history books date them back to around the eleventh century. But the truth is their origins go back *much* earlier."

"Marie-Claire mentioned that some knights once owned this castle. Do you think that's who she meant?"

"Quite possibly! It is all starting to make sense. According to arcane texts, the Templars actually branched off from the ancient Pagans. They were like some kinda splinter group of renegade priests. Their symbols have similarities with the Celts because, as some theorize, they integrated with various Celtic, Gaulic, Visigoth and barbarian tribes.

"The Templars only became revered when the Church hired them to cleanse the Holy Land. That's when they became known as the Templar Knights. Though they fought for Christianity, they were, in fact, Pagan masters of dark magic and controlled the elements with a mysterious *Head*."

"*Head*? Veronica asked. "What kind of Head?"

Ralph laughed as if she just told a joke. "What kind of Head. Excellent question! The thing is, no one knows. Some said it was the mummified head of John the Baptist. Some said it was the head of a slain demon. Others said it was made of pure crystal. All agreed the Templar Head wielded great power that no one dared challenge."

Veronica tapped the skull with a tentative pointer finger. "Well this is crystal. You think *this* is the Templar Head?"

Ralph flipped his pompous head. "The legends all seem to fit together. And if it is, it could be very powerful."

"Those are just silly myths. You don't really believe in crap like that, do you?"

The smirk that always hung on Ralph's pudgy lips vanished as he stated, "I'm an expert in antiquities, a researcher into the past, and if there's one thing I've learned, it's that there's always a grain of truth behind every legend. They're never pure fantasy. Distorted over the years, misunderstood and misinterpreted, it takes an open mind to figure out what is true and what is fallacy."

She huffed slightly. "So, why does this little rock have so much power?" She held it up so it could grin directly into Ralph's eyes.

Ralph snatched it and cupped it lovingly. "According to the Templar legend, there is a shocking story about that."

She bit and asked, "What story?"

Ralph peered into the hollow sockets of the skull as he spoke. "A long time ago, before there were countries or even kingdoms, when Europe was ruled by warring Pagan tribes, a young warrior fell deeply in love with a poor, provincial girl. He was going to ask her father's permission to marry her, but he didn't have the courage. Before he knew it, the girl was chosen as a sacrifice in their autumnal equinox ritual. She was slain as an offering to the fire god. The young warrior was heartbroken. He never had the chance to tell her he loved her. He mourned, and no one could console him."

Ralph paused for effect.

Veronica obliged and sighed. "Aww..."

Ralph continued. "Then, after she had been laid to rest, the grieving, young lover crept into her crypt. He lay beside her, confessed his undying love to her, and held her into the night. He felt an unnatural compulsion to consummate his devotion, and that night, he made love to her corpse. When he finished, his manhood shriveled up inside of him, never to return. Then a mysterious witch appeared and reprimanded him for the horrific deed he had done. She ordered him to wait by the grave for nine months, so he could claim his unnatural offspring. The warrior obeyed the injunction, and after nine months, he opened the crypt, and out of the earth, crawled a head mounted on the leg bones of a skeleton. It was an unnatural aberration; a demon that could change form at will. It had human-like eyes and stunk like a rancid corpse."

Veronica scrunched her nose as she recalled the animal-thing that chased her through the castle's catacombs. She held silent, though, not wanting to share her delusion with Ralph who would surely tease her mercilessly.

He continued. "The witch spoke again and ordered him to become the demon's guardian. He was instructed to use its powers for the protection of a sect of priests who eventually became the Templars."

"He raped a corpse," Veronica wryly declared.

"I'm just telling you the legend. Like I said, all legend is based on some fact. Unfortunately, it's convoluted through the ages, and often the exact details are lost. That's why people don't take them very seriously. But I study them, Veronica, and I know there is more truth in myth than most people want to believe."

"You remind me of Sandbourne. He thinks a genie is haunting the castle. Ha!"

"A what?"

Veronica snickered at her own sarcasm. "A *djinn* is actually what he called it. Says it is an *elemental* demon."

"I know what a djinn is. I wonder why he thinks one haunts this castle. Djinn are from Persian mythology."

Veronica was surprised Ralph took a serious interest in what Sandbourne had to say and regretted bringing it up. "He's just a weird, little old hippy. I don't put much stock in what he thinks."

"Well, the djinn are a lot like demons in Christian mythology. They both can be summoned to do nasty things. They're evil and manipulative and like to collect souls. That's the amazing thing about legends, Veronica. There is a magical spot where the truth surely lies. That spot is where you have two legends from completely separate cultures cross. Both Persian and European myths have the same type of creatures. They just go by different names."

"Fine, djinn — demon, tomato — toma-toe, whatever!"

"This is a clue, Veronica. Don't be so dismissive. What else did Sandbourne say?"

"He said Marie-Claire told him about the djinn, and she wanted to summon it. This all happened over twenty years ago, back when I was just a kid. He said she held séances and tried to connect to the other side. And she wanted to use me to...well, I dunno. Like I said, Sandbourne is kinda *out there*, and you really can't take him seriously."

"No, that's actually quite interesting. You see, there are a few versions of the legend about the Head being Muslim in origin. When the Pope accused the Knights of heresy it was because they were suspected of worshipping a *Muslim* Idol. Since the djinn are Islamic in nature, it's all starting to make sense. Get it?"

Veronica didn't want to get it. "I have no idea what you're talking about anymore."

Ralph breathed deeply and said simply, "When the Templars were accused of heresy, the official charges stated it was because they worshipped a *Muslim* deity. That may be why Marie-Claire calls it a djinn. If Persian in nature, then she would have referred to it as a djinn rather than a demon!"

"Okay, I guess that makes sense."

"All these clues point to this being Templar treasure. This is exciting, isn't it Veronica? We could be uncovering one of the greatest finds in history! I need to talk to this Dr. Sandbourne. Introduce me to him?"

"Ah, sure. He's here at the party somewhere..."

"Let's go find him. It's almost midnight anyway, and we don't want to miss the unmasking."

She spun to see the clock. "It's that late? We gotta find Christophe and Nikki, too."

Veronica quickly packed the treasure back into the leather satchel. She and Ralph both primped for a moment, straightening their costumes, before hurrying to the ballroom.

❧❀❖❀☙

Ralph gently guided Veronica through the crowd. The sea of people was thick, and their progress slow. As they weaved, a woman in a velvety red gown slithered up to Veronica. She was beautiful, with vibrant crimson hair loosely gathered on top of her head, enormous smoldering eyes, and thick, pouting lips. What struck Veronica was the woman's red dress. It was *identical* to Veronica's.

"We're wearing the same dress!" she exclaimed to the woman.

Rather than respond with the usual girly-shrill of "*Oh-my-God-we-are!*" the woman hissed as if insulted. Her breath hung in the air like a haze. It was putrid and made Veronica exhale fast and deep.

Undaunted, Veronica asked, "Where did you get yours? I thought mine was a vintage one-of-a-kind."

Before there was an answer, Ralph grabbed Veronica's waist and pushed her through the crowd. While pointing, he instructed, "Look, Christophe is just over there!"

The dapper banker stood next to the center banquet table, in front of the ice sculpture, holding a plate of coconut shrimp. He surveyed the crowd, as if expectantly looking for someone. Veronica wondered if it was her.

"Lead the way!" Ralph ordered.

Veronica turned back to the woman in red, but she was no longer there. Apparently gone. Lost in the crowd.

"Okay, follow me," Veronica said and she snaked through the bodies. As she moved, something scampered around the border of her dress. She recognized the boy that was running amuck earlier careening around her legs. "Hey! Careful kid. You'll make me trip..."

He was dressed like an *Oliver Twist* raga-muffin. The imp jerked his head around and stuck his tongue out menacingly. Veronica scolded, "Watch it, young man!" He weaved through the crowd and out of sight. Veronica thought she heard him call, "I'm not a young man. I'm a girl, fool!"

Veronica complained to Ralph. "Can you believe that? It's almost midnight, and someone has their snotty kid here."

Ralph was focused forward and called out to Christophe. "There you are, my good man!"

Just then, Veronica noticed Nikki come up behind Christophe and tap him on the shoulder. He jumped in an exaggerated fashion, feigning surprise. The foursome stood there, all finally converged.

Nikki spoke to Ralph and gestured toward Veronica. "She your date?"

"Oh, yes!" he joked. "The only problem is she can't seem to keep her hands off me! All night long, she's *begging* me for sex...I really wish she'd control herself in public." He playfully snagged Veronica's wrists and rubbed them up and down his chunky chest. Veronica pulled a hand back and playfully whacked Ralph while smirking.

Nikki suddenly recognized her sister's familiar smile from under the gauzy veil. She began to say, "I was wondering where the hell..."

Just then, Christophe leaned in and softly spoke in Nikki's ear, cutting her off. "I have a question for you..."

Nikki gazed up at the strapping man. "Yes, Christophe?"

"I've spent the last two months dreaming of the moment when I could finally confess my feelings to the most fascinating, exciting, beautiful woman I've ever met..."

Nikki cast a sly glance at her sister, who stood several feet away from the hushed conversation. She spoke loud enough for all of them to hear. "Really? So, you gonna do that now, Chris? Declare your undying love to someone right here, tonight, huh? Ya' *finally* gonna do it?"

He blushed under his black mask and quietly confessed, "Yes, that's my plan."

Nikki waved a flamboyant-gloved arm toward her sister. "Then maybe you should plant a big, wet, sloppy kiss on her lips just as we hit the stroke of midnight...that'd be *very Cinderella*."

Christophe looked down shyly and chuckled. "Really, is that what *you* think I should do?"

The music faded, and the singer called everyone's attention to the huge clock on the far wall of the ballroom. "Mesdames et messieurs, il est presque minuit!" Then she repeated in English, "Attention, everyone, it iz almost midnight!"

Veronica giggled and spoke to Ralph. "Standby for a *Cinderella moment!*"

The woman with the microphone drowned out most of their conversation. "We'll begin the countdown, and at exactly midnight, everyone must take off zee mask to reveal their true identities!"

Ralph answered Veronica. "Yes! And I must say it's about time!"

Veronica coyly smiled at the pudgy man in the white *Phantom of the Opera* mask. She took a careful step forward to be closer to Christophe.

The woman with the microphone began to count, and the whole room chanted with her. "Dix, neuf..."

Veronica beamed at the finely dressed man. She had resisted Christophe for so long, had been so afraid and hesitant, but through it all he pursued her, never gave up, just like a prince in a fairy tale...in Veronica's fairy tale.

The counting continued. "Huit, sept..."

Veronica saw Dr. Sandbourne approach from over Christophe's shoulder. He was heading straight toward her. "No!" she sighed out loud. Ralph wanted to meet the doctor, which would mean she'd have to introduce them, and her moment with Christophe would be ruined.

No, not now. Not right as Christophe is about to kiss me!

As her mind raced, she noticed someone dressed as a priest step in front of the doctor, effectively blocking him for a moment.

Yes! Veronica thought. I just need a few more seconds.

"Six, cinq…"

Another figure, a young girl in a toga, bumped into the frail, little doctor, yet he righted himself and continued to walk toward Veronica with a big grin plastered on his light bulb head. Veronica watched while muttering, "Please not now…."

Then the woman in Veronica's red velvet dress was walking astride him. With a large flourish, she wrapped her arms seductively around the doctor.

The counting wound down. "Quatre…"

Veronica turned to Ralph. "Hey, there's that woman in red I told you about before. I don't know why, but she's *hugging* Dr. Sandbourne."

All in one instant:

Ralph asked, "What woman in red?"

Nikki turned to see whom her sister was talking about; her chin lifting slightly in Christophe's direction.

The crowd chanted, "Trios, deux…"

The woman in red pulled at her jaw as if she was removing a mask, but instead, she tore her face off — completely *off*. Tendons, muscle, and veins ripped away and revealed a dry, rotting skull. Veronica thought she was imagining the visage and stepped forward to get a better look. She watched as maggots dripped off the woman's face like cascading pearls. She transformed into something dark and shadowy and engulfed the doctor like a smoky specter.

The entire party ripped off their masks and whooped and hollered in revelry.

Veronica strained to make sense of what she was seeing as Dr. Sandbourne seemed to disappear in a cloud of blackness. Then as the crowd shouted, 'un!' she watched in astonishment as Christophe pulled back his mask, leaned down, and gently, tentatively, with love and passion like she had never and would never experience, kissed *Nikki* squarely on the lips.

Chapter 121

Veronica's Story

Veronica felt her body spin around. Slimy, clammy hands gripped her arms and twisted her, so she suddenly faced the opposite direction. There stood Lawrence in the leprechaun suit.

"I've been waiting all night to see your lovely face! Don't be shy!"

He reached up and lifted her mask. Underneath, the true face of Veronica was waxen, with fluttering eyelids and a trembling lower lip.

"Are you okay? You look ill," the leprechaun who worked at the consulate's office, asked.

Veronica ignored Lawrence and turned to her sister and Christophe. The kiss was still taking place. He now had his arm wrapped around her, pushing her body into his. His other hand gently held her chin. His thumb grazed ever so lightly over her flushing cheek.

Nikki stood stiff and carefully pulled her mask onto the top of her head. She stood in profile to Veronica, and her visible eye was wide and staring; however, her mouth moved slowly, carefully working up and down as Christophe kissed her. Then she tried to pull back, but her effort was meek and he simply pressed closer. She relented and released her inhibitions. As her eye closed, she seemed to melt into him. Pushing her body against his, her head tilted back and she parted her lips wide, allowing him to kiss her deeply and passionately.

❧❦✤❦❧

A cry pierced the merrymaking. Over the din of the music, Veronica heard a man shout, "Help! Someone call an ambu —" the voice was sliced short by a woman yelling, "There's blood everywhere!"

Ralph trailed behind as Veronica rushed forward. As they passed Christophe and Nikki, she heard her sister say, "I had no idea you felt this way about *me!*"

Veronica felt nausea wrench her gut like a screw. Her steps were off-balance as she pushed through a circle of people.

On the freshly polished wood floor sprawled the body of Dr. Sandbourne. Blood collected in a puddle under his head. A man in a Prince Charming costume knelt beside him with his hand on the doctor's chest. Insanely, Veronica expected him to lean over and kiss the little man like Sleeping Beauty, but instead, he gasped, "There's no heartbeat."

"Did he fall? Did anyone see what happened?" Ralph inquired, but the only responses were blank stares and shaking heads.

Veronica rushed to his side. Guilt wrapped around her like a hot, sticky wool blanket as she regretted her treatment of the kind man who flew half way around the world to help her. As she knelt, her mind whirled and tried to comprehend the impossible thing she witnessed. *It was that woman — that rude woman in red who wrapped her arms around him and did this to him. She pulled the skin off her face and became black and cloudy and engulfed him like smoke. Oh-my-fucking-God!*

Ralph barked at the crowd to stand back. He put a comforting hand on her shoulder as Veronica leaned in and shakily implored, "Dr. Sandbourne, are you okay? Doctor?" She felt his boney wrist for a pulse then held her hand over his mouth to see if he was still breathing.

"We called an ambulance," a voice from the bystanders stated.

"Maybe we should start CPR..." Veronica began.

"What about the blood; where's it coming from?" Ralph asked.

Veronica lifted Sandbourne's head, attempting to clear the passageway. As she did, blood so bright it was almost neon poured from underneath. "His head," she surmised.

Ralph quickly removed his pristine white jacket and slid it under the man's neck. It soaked up the crimson.

Veronica blew through the doctor's cold lips while feeling his wrist for a pulse. She pushed on his chest carefully, knowing his fragile bones could shatter under the pressure. Over and over again, she breathed and pressed while the macabre skeletal face of the woman in red throbbed in her mind's eye like a spastic dancer.

Veronica squinted through tears of frustration and denial and watched Ralph join her. He pressed on Sandbourne's chest so she could concentrate on giving mouth-to-mouth. Together, they fought to revive the old man.

The rhythmic breathing made Veronica lightheaded. She kept her eyes shut tight and ignored the gasping crowd around her. She forced herself to concentrate, even though she felt slimy, icy-cold vomit creeping up the back of her throat.

After several minutes, Ralph grabbed her arm. "Veronica, it's not working. He's gone."

Everything stopped.

Veronica opened her eyes. Ralph's brow dripped with sweat. He sat back and huffed as he dabbed his face with a handkerchief.

She remained hunched over the body and blinked mascara-tinted tears onto Sandbourne's lifeless chest. An image of her sister locked in Christophe's arms slammed in her head amidst a background of blood red. The crimson in her mind grew deeper and darker until it became the smoky, black figure of that woman. Dizzy, she reached out to grab Ralph and steady herself. As her hand extended, it was clutched tightly. She looked down and saw the frail fist of Dr. Sandbourne holding her. She gasped. He twisted his lips — the dead man was attempting to speak.

"Dr. Sandbourne, you're alive!" she exclaimed.

"No, Veronica, he's dead," Ralph stated.

Veronica ignored Ralph and continued. "Dr. Sandbourne, don't worry, an ambulance is on the way."

The doctor pulled her closer, and at the same time, Ralph placed a reassuring hand on Veronica's shoulder. "Dear, he's gone. You did everything you could..."

Veronica leaned in as the doctor feebly whispered to her. "Read the Bible..."

"What?" Veronica asked.

The doctor's hazy grey eyes glared with intensity. With vigor, almost angrily, he spat, "Read the Bible!" Then he released Veronica's wrist, and his eyes fluttered shut as his body went limp.

For the first time, Veronica looked up at the faces that surrounded her. Lawrence the Leprechaun, Gigi Jones and Alex, Mr. and Mrs. Fontaine, Lady Florence, members of the band, hundreds of familiar and strange faces, plus Christophe and Nikki, all blankly gawked at Veronica and the corpse.

Nikki towered over her crouching sister. Her hand rested lightly in the crevice of Christophe's bent arm. "Poor guy, what a way to go," she stated.

Veronica was afraid to stand, certain vertigo would consume her if she did. She sat hunched over the body like a scavenging animal caught next to a carcass.

Christophe's brow scrunched as he spoke. "Veronica...you..." he let his words trail off, and he glanced down at Nikki nuzzling beside him.

The next thing Veronica saw where men in pale blue jumpsuits converge on the scene. They carried a stretcher and quickly surrounded the body. Urgently they spoke to one another in French. Everyone cleared out of their way.

Someone grabbed Veronica from behind and helped her stand. She didn't turn to see who it was. Her only thought was to escape. She just wanted to get out of there, away from the consternated faces, away from Dr. Sandbourne's bloody body, and away from her sister and Christophe.

She pushed through the crowd. The partygoers looked upon her with pitying eyes. They all stayed clear, giving her space as she fled to the patio.

Once again the cool, outdoor haven helped calm her. She darted to the farthest corner and allowed the tears to flow as she collapsed into a pile of red velvet. She sat on the cool terracotta tiles, drew her knees up to her chest, and alone she wept.

A voice whispered. It was deep and the language foreign. Surprised she wasn't alone, she lifted her head to see the man in the medieval priest's costume, on the opposite side. He was talking — almost to himself. Like a real priest uttering prayers, he murmured under his breath while his bony hands caressed a rosary chain.

Veronica felt violated. After all, she had come out here to grieve alone for a moment. *Why was he interrupting her?*

The man in the archaic cassock gazed back at her with stabbing eyes, physically accosting her with his stare. She felt it bore into her like a torrent of nails slicing her flesh. Veronica gasped, but didn't breathe. It was as if he had sucked up all the air and left none for her.

The priest took a few, slow, calculated steps toward her. He continued to pray, but Veronica couldn't understand the words. They were rhythmic and ancient, possibly Latin. He crouched beside her. The broken American girl wanted to run, to be as far as she could be from the peculiar priest, but her body refused to respond.

Instead, she managed to pull in one shallow breath and asked, "What do you want?"

He leaned close, only inches from her face, and tilted his long head back like a horse getting ready to neigh. Veronica caught a whiff of his pungent breath, it was putrid like the woman in red's. He simply stated, "Veronica, read the Bible."

"Wha...what?" she stammered.

"You need to find God, Veronica. Need to make peace with the Lord!"

She was appalled. The man in the priest's costume must have heard Dr. Sandbourne's dying words. *And now he stood there mocking the dead?* Veronica recoiled and covered her face with her hands. She stayed that way for several moments, shaking her head in harsh denial of everything around her.

Her fit didn't last long. Keenly aware that the people were likely watching her through the glass doors, she swallowed and summoned all the courage she had left to confront the rude man. She opened her eyes to wipe the tears from her face...but he was gone.

Veronica was alone on the patio.

The doors opened, and Ralph called, "Veronica, dear, come. Let's get you inside by the fireplace where it's warm. The authorities want to talk to us."

She scanned the deck for the priest, even looking over the balcony, but he wasn't there. Only Ralph, with an outstretched hand, was in sight.

She threw her arms out to him, and he lifted her up. The Phantom of the Opera held her snug against his side and led her back through the gawking crowd and into the library.

∻ ❦ ∻

Veronica sat in one of the large, leather library chairs. Out of the corner of her eye, she saw them point at her. Two women dressed like steampunk princesses whispered to the detectives and nodded accusingly at her. Veronica continued to stare into the fireplace flames and didn't even turn her head as the man in the red scarf tapped her shoulder.

"I'm Inspector Hertel. May I ask questions from you?" he said with a stilted accent.

She nodded. "Kay..."

"You knew the victim?"

"The victim?" Veronica parroted.

"The deceased. Dr. Sandbourne."

"Yeah."

"How you know him?"

"He, ah, knew me since I was a kid."

"He is your family?"

Veronica scrunched her nose and broke her stare from the fireplace to scan the room. Not seeing a familiar face, she looked up at the bug-eyed detective and answered. "No, he was my...doctor..."

"You are sick?" Inspector Hertel's voice lilted and sounded genuinely concerned.

"Oh no, not like that. I'm fine."

Hertel suddenly snapped. "Then like what? If you aren't sick, then how he is your doctor?"

The remaining self-pity Veronica had been wallowing in evaporated as the Inspector changed his tone, and she retorted, "He's a psychologist not a medical

429

doctor!"

"Psychologist? Vous souffrez de psychose?"

Veronica nodded slowly. "Yeah..."

From behind, Nikki jumped in. "No, she doesn't!"

Veronica spun in her seat to see Nikki, Christophe, and Ralph standing there. "Elle ne souffre d'aucune psychose. L'homme était son docteur il y a longtemps quand elle était petite. Elle avait l'habitude d'avoir des cauchemars. C'est tout!" Nikki prattled in French. Then she quickly explained to her sister, "You just told him you have a psychosis. I set him straight, though."

Inspector Hertel now addressed Nikki, even though he spoke in English. "Do you know why she argued with the deceased?"

"We weren't arguing..." Veronica answered.

He then addressed Veronica in French. "Vous êtes disputés plus tôt ce soir. Les témoins vous ont vus."

"Were you and Sandbourne fighting?" Nikki translated.

Veronica shook her head. "What do you mean *fighting?*"

Her sister quickly explained. "Some witnesses said they heard you and the Doc arguing earlier during the party."

"No, we were *talking.* I got a little annoyed 'cause he," she caught herself, "he was telling me messed up stuff about when I was a kid..."

Hertel lifted an eyebrow. "What is this 'stuff'?"

"I used to have night terrors, and Dr. Sandbourne admitted me to a clinic for parapsychological research. He did it so I wouldn't have to go to a state mental hospital. It's a long story..." Veronica let her voice lapse to a whisper, and she timidly added, "but he did it all to *help* me. He came all the way here from the States because he wanted to make sure I was okay. He was worried, and *cared* about me. Even his dying words were for me to read the Bible. Right before he passed he said, 'Veronica, read the Bible'. It was like he wanted me to find God or something."

"None of the other witnesses reported him saying any such thing. He never regained consciousness," Hertel quipped.

Veronica firmly stated, "He grabbed my wrist, told me to read the Bible, then went limp. That's what happened. I know what I heard."

"Funny, no one else saw such a thing. But several people reported seeing *you* grab *him* right before he collapsed," Hertel challenged.

Hertel nodded at one of the detectives who stepped forward and read from a notepad. "A woman in a red dress with red hair gave Dr. Sandbourne a hug. It was just before midnight. After she squeezed him, he fell to the floor, and there was blood everywhere..."

"That wasn't *me!* There *was* a woman in red. She was dressed like me, but it wasn't *me!*"

Hertel shrugged and flashed over her shoulder, surveying the crowd. "What other woman in red? Show her to me. No one has been allowed to leave the crime scene, so she must still be here..."

Veronica turned and scanned the sea of costumes for the striking woman in red, but Hertel was right — she wasn't there.

"What do you mean 'crime scene'?" Nikki asked.

"Dr. Sandbourne's ribs were shattered, his clavicle broken, and his neck snapped. That is not a heart attack."

"We tried CPR," Ralph jumped in. "His ribs could have cracked then..."

"Who gave the CPR?"

Ralph pointed gingerly to Veronica. "We did."

The detective studied the foursome then gestured to his men. "Put restraints on them. We're taking all of you to the commissariat de police for more questions."

Chapter 122

Veronica's Story

eronica let her body collapse onto the hotel bed. The mattress was stiff, and under normal circumstances, she would have complained, but at that moment, the only thing she could think about was sleep.

It was six-thirty in the morning. She had been at the police station for over five hours. They questioned each suspect separately, and since Veronica needed an interpreter, her questioning took longer than it did for Nikki, Christophe, and Ralph.

Veronica told inspector Hertel her story several times. She explained how Sandbourne was her doctor many years ago when she had a sleep disorder. He came to visit her in France because she had some bad dreams recently. That's all, just a couple of meaningless nightmares. He was a little senile and kept pestering her with crazy stories. He was annoying, but he meant well. Like the other witnesses, at midnight, Veronica also saw a woman in red give the doctor a big hug. Since everyone was hugging and celebrating the unmasking, it could have been anyone. The dance floor lights must have distorted what Veronica and the others saw. Maybe the woman was wearing orange or pink, and her dress just looked red.

That was Veronica's story.

To herself, though, she thought, *and that lady must've worn a mask under a mask. Yeah, she didn't pull off her face; she pulled off a mask to reveal another mask. A skull-like mask cocooned in a gooey mess of decaying veins and muscle. Covered in juicy maggots and rotten flesh that easily slid off the bone. It was the most realistic skull mask she had ever seen. That's all, just a real good makeup job. Yep.*

That part of the story Veronica wisely kept to herself.

The police released her shortly after six in the morning with strict instructions *not* to return to the castle. It was considered a crime scene, and no one could enter it until the investigation was over. Veronica was too tired to argue and willingly allowed them to drop her off at the nearest hotel.

As she peeled off her costume and crawled under the covers, she clicked her phone and listened to her voicemail. There was a message from Nikki. "Hey, Vern, it's five in the morning, and the police just let Christophe and me go. We can't go back to the castle, so I'm going to stay —" she cut herself off. Veronica could hear her sister mumbling to someone and then return. "Yeah, I am gonna stay with Christophe tonight. Give me a call when you get this message. We can pick you up...or...just give me a call, okay?"

Veronica clicked her phone off and imagined that, at this exact moment, her sister was with Christophe, at his home, most probably in his bed, cuddled in his arms. After popping two of Sandbourne's sleeping pills, Veronica allowed herself a moment to cry. And this she did, until sleep mercifully took over.

Chapter 123

Veronica's Story

It was seven o'clock on Sunday evening. Veronica lifted her head from the pillow as her phone buzzed. She answered to her sister's voice.

"Vern?"

"Yeah."

"Hey! How are you? Are you okay? I've been calling and calling you!"

Veronica didn't hide the annoyance in her voice. "I'm at a hotel, and I'm fine. I'm sleeping. Going to get cleaned up in a little bit and head back to the Château..."

Nikki interrupted. "The police just called and told us that it would be a couple days before they'll let anyone in."

Veronica sat up in bed. Her head pounded, and she kicked the covers off. "What?"

"I talked to that inspector, Hertel, and he said the Château is still a crime scene. He's going to escort us inside, so we can get our personal belongings, but that's it. We can't stay there. He said we might have to wait 'til Wednesday."

"But the Traveler's Channel is coming *tomorrow* to shoot the special..."

"I know, I know, but there's nothing we can do. We can't get in 'til they let us. So, anyway, Christophe has to go to his vineyard to get ready for the wine-tasting event. He said that I, well I guess *we*, could go with him, both of us, since we can't stay at the Château."

Veronica's gut churned as she listened to her sister speak his name. He sounded so familiar to her — so intimate. "No, I'll just stay here," she said flatly.

"Why? It'll be good to get away for a few days; let this all blow over..."

"I don't wanna. You go ahead. I'd just be a third wheel."

"It wouldn't be like that, Vern. We can't just leave you..."

"You and Christophe go. I have to stay near the Château. Plus, the police might wanna talk to me again, so I should stick around."

"Christophe talked to them. You don't need to worry about the police anymore," Nikki explained.

"Then why can't we go back to the Château?"

"They're just being assholes and making it hard for you."

"For me? Why? What did *I* do?" Veronica insisted, her anger welling.

"You're an American."

"That's insane!"

"Listen, Christophe knows the mayor, and he's gonna pull some strings to get them off your back. He's right here. Do you wanna talk to him?" Nikki offered.

"Christophe is *right* there?"

"Yeah, he said he wants to talk to you," Nikki forced a casual tone into her voice.

Veronica cringed. "No, thanks."

"You're not upset, are you?"

"Gee, Nik, why would I be upset? A man died while I tried to save him, the police think I had something to do with it, the Château is a crime scene, and I'm supposed to have the Traveler's Channel there filming tomorrow, and..." her voice drifted off into indulgent sobs.

Calmingly, Nikki said, "Vern, we'll come get you. What hotel are you at?"

"I wanna be alone right now."

"Are you sure? Chris and I can be there in ten minutes."

Chris...she called Christophe *Chris*. "No, Nik, you and *Chris* just do your own thing."

"You're not mad at me, right?"

Veronica wished her sister would shut up. "Why would I be mad at you?"

"I don't know, maybe 'cause of Christophe and me hooking up? I mean, even *I* didn't see that coming. I had no idea he had the hots for *me* all this time. It doesn't bother you, right?"

Veronica bit her bottom lip to keep it from trembling. Mustering all her strength, she nonchalantly asked, "Why should it bother me?"

"I don't know. You're acting like it does. I mean, you said all along that you weren't interested in him, so it's no big deal, right?"

"Right," Veronica said simply.

"Then why are you acting like this?"

Veronica exploded. "I'm not acting like anything. Go wine-tasting with Christophe. Go have fun with your new *fuck*. I don't care. I have stuff to do here. The plane leaves from Charles de Gaulle next Monday. Just make sure you're there." Veronica clicked the phone off and threw it across the room. It banged against the door.

The room suddenly seemed hollow and lifeless, like an empty masquerade mask. The only sound was the rush of blood Veronica heard in her skull as violent sobs consumed her.

She pulled her knees up to her chin and pressed her teeth into her kneecaps. Veronica remained like that until there was a knock at her door almost two hours later.

"What!" She scolded the intruder.

"It's Ralph. Can I come in?"

She tilted her salt-streaked face and groaned. Wearing only her underwear, she swaddled the blanket around her body and waddled to the door. Before opening it, she picked up her cell phone and lobbed it on the bed.

Ralph wore the same shirt and pants from the night before. He held the leather satchel and Veronica's messenger bag. "They let us back into the Château to pick up a few things. Your sister packed some stuff for you. I also managed to sneak this out without being questioned. The book and the box are in it." He handed her the tattered satchel and messenger bag.

"Thanks," Veronica said.

"Are you okay? It was a very traumatic night. Can I get you anything? Did you eat yet?"

"Veronica slowly flopped back onto the bed. "Naw, I'm fine."

"If you'd like, I can still look at the text. I can bring it back before you leave."

Veronica shrugged. "Sure, go for it."

Ralph let his pompous demeanor fall. "Listen, whatever happened to that old man, it wasn't your fault. The police aren't going to find any evidence against you, me, or anyone else. Sandbourne obviously had a stroke. I told the inspector we tried to give him CPR; that's how his bones must have broken. We were just trying to help him. I think the police know that. They're just suspicious of outsiders, especially Americans, so they're being tough on you."

Veronica closed her eyes and lied, "You know, I didn't get much sleep, Ralph. Just give me a call when you are done with the book, okay?"

Ralph took his cue and rose to his feet. He mumbled something more about the text, but Veronica barely listened. She rolled over as he closed the door.

Once he was on the other side, he called, "I'll call you about the book in a couple days to give you an update. Sleep well, my dear. Let me know if you need anything!"

435

Chapter 124

Veronica's Story

When Veronica woke on Monday morning, she reached for her cellphone. She was roaming and only had one bar. Plus, her battery was at twenty percent, and her charger was still at the Château. She hoped that her call would go through as she carefully plucked the numbers.

Gigi Jones answered on the second ring. "Jones here."

"Hi, Gigi! It's Veronica..."

"Yes, the camera crew is on their way right now. What do you need?"

"Ah, well there is going to be a slight delay. The police said no one can go into the Château yet. It's still considered a crime scene."

Oddly, Gigi did not inquire about the police investigation. Instead, she said, "There can't be any delays. We need to start shooting today."

"But you *can't*. No one can get in while they are investigating Dr. Sandbourne's death. There isn't anything that I can do."

Gigi cursed. "Damn it! We had an agreement. Alex put off our assignment in Germany just so we could fit you into our schedule..."

"I know, and I'm sorry..."

"We have to arrive very early tomorrow then. We'll have to fit a two-day shoot into one day. You can expect us at five in the morning." Gigi sounded as if she were about to hang up, and Veronica quickly spoke.

"Tomorrow won't work either. They'll open the Château back up on Wednesday, though. You can come at five in the morning *Wednesday*!"

"Wednesday!" Gigi Jones shouted, sounding nothing like the pleasant, smiling host from the Traveler's Channel. "Impossible. We're leaving for Germany Wednesday. It has to happen Tuesday, or it ain't happening at all."

"There has to be something we can do. I've always dreamed of having my work featured like this. Maybe we can..."

"Nope!" Gigi interrupted. "There's nothing we can do. Ya' had your chance. I can't put off any other projects just for this one. Sorry, sweetie, you blew it, and to top it off, you fucked up my entire shooting schedule. Hope you're happy."

Now, Gigi Jones did hang up.

Veronica sat stunned in the lonely hotel room for several minutes. She still wore her underwear from two days ago, but she didn't care. Her hair was snarled in clumps, and she struggled to pull her fingers through it. She caught a glimpse of herself in the reflection of the black television screen. "I'm pathetic."

Sitting up, she declared, "I have two choices. I can continue to lay here like a loser and feel sorry for myself, or I can get my ass out of bed and become a human being again."

She rubbed a crusty eye booger out the crease of her lid, sighed, and pushed the blankets off.

❧❧❖❧❧

It was mid-afternoon, and Veronica sat in a fluffy, white robe with an array of room service trays on the bed around her. Her phone rang. As Veronica answered, a familiar "breep" indicated that her batteries needed to be charged.

Without saying hello, Detective Hertel stated matter-of-factly, "The investigation has been closed. The coroner declared Sandbourne's cause of death to be from natural causes. The broken bones were a result of the fall and attempts at CPR."

Veronica politely began, "Thank you..."

"Don't thank me," He snidely quipped. "Thank your friend who knows the mayor."

Veronica silently let his jab hang in the air. After an awkward pause, he concluded the conversation by stating, "You may go back to the Château at any time. It is now open," and then hung up.

Veronica quickly snapped off the phone, then turned it back on and punched Gigi Jones' number. Through the fading connection, she heard Gigi answer.

"Jones here."

"Gigi! It's Veronica! The police just called, and we can..."

"Hello?" Gigi asked.

"Fuck!" Veronica exclaimed. "I'll call you back on a landline."

Veronica turned off her cell and picked up the hotel phone. It was a black and bulky antique with a huge dial that moved painfully slow.

Obviously annoyed, Gigi answered again. "Yeah?"

"Gigi, its Veronica. Sorry about that; my cell phone was dying and..."

"What is it?"

"The police just called, and they're done with their investigation. The Château is open!" Veronica waited for a reaction, and when she got none, she continued. "We can do the shoot!"

"I'm driving to the airport right now. We're on our way to Germany. We switched to an earlier flight. Sorry, you're too late."

"But I just found out! Can't you switch your flight back?"

"I'm not playing games with you anymore. This is getting obnoxious. Goodbye."

Chapter 125

Veronica's Story

Shards of orange *CRIME SCENE—DO NOT CROSS* tape littered the front steps of the Château. Veronica snagged a few of them that were illuminated in the taxi's headlights before it turned and drove back down the tree-lined pathway.

The overwhelming aroma of rancid meat greeted her upon entering. She buried her nose in her sleeve. The odor grew more pungent as she walked through the foyer and toward the library.

She clicked on the light. Half-empty champagne glasses and wilted crepe paper decorations were scattered about. Veronica gaped as she realized that the whole time the police were here, they never bothered to clean anything.

That meant all the food from the party was still in the ballroom — sitting out in the humid August heat.

Disgusted, Veronica cautiously made her way to the double doors between the library and the ballroom. She hovered at the entrance a moment, letting her eyes adjust to the darkness.

The shadows slowly took shape. Tables, chairs and the banquet table were all still set as if the partygoers would return at any moment. Suspended in time like whispers of Veronica's hopes, they taunted her like a dream that would never come to pass.

Food was left just as it had been set out. Decaying mini quiches, moldering coconut shrimp, and rancid cherry-flavored punch now attracted flies and scavenging rodents. They angrily scuttered out of Veronica's way as she slowly crept inside.

"Sorry to ruin your party," she muttered to the vermin.

In the middle of the room was more orange tape. It sectioned off the area where Dr. Sandbourne had fallen dead. She approached and saw the floor saturated with a large stain of crimson. Two mice scuttled from the spot, each with a crumb of crusty blood in their maw. Blinded by the sudden illumination from the library, they ran chaotically toward Veronica, rather than away.

She bounced back and cursed. "Damn mice!"

The heel of her shoe connected with something "mushy". Veronica cursed again and fled the ballroom. As she did, she glimpsed something scurry up the wall alongside the double doors. It was quick, and just a shadow. No doubt it was a huge rat climbing one of the tapestries.

She burst out, keeping her eyes focused forward. She didn't want to see the beady yellow eyes of the huge, mangy rodent as she passed it.

Once safely in the center of the library, she felt more at ease and a shiver of relief reverberated through her. She twirled and faced the entrance to the ballroom. It was a dark, sinister, portentous hole. No animal eyes peered back at her — at least none she could see. "Guess I better call an exterminator," she whispered to herself.

She dashed back to the ballroom entrance and pushed the double doors together with whirling outstretched arms, closing off the stench and the scavengers within it.

The air in the library rapidly cleared with the doors shut. She slid her messenger bag off her shoulder and flopped into a huge library chair in front of the somber fireplace. She breathed deeply, enjoying the scent of the leather. The chair wrapped around her in a comforting hug from behind.

Alone.

It was the first time Veronica was completely alone in the castle. Her sister was no longer by her side. There were no workers cleaning or fixing or building. The castle was completely hers.

She soaked up the quietness for a few moments as a surge of despair welled in her gut: the Traveler's Channel opportunity was blown, the party that was intended to showcase her talents ended with a tragic death and ruined her reputation, and her sister took off with Christophe.

"Way to go, Vern," she told herself.

The tears came again, and Veronica indulged in a good, long cry; one that she hoped would be the last.

Meanwhile, something slithered across the gold leafed ceiling panels in the ballroom. It crawled upside down as it maneuvered. Though it had a long snout and spindly claws like a rat, it certainly was not. Darker than death, older than humanity, it was like something straight out of Veronica's night terrors. It quietly pushed the ballroom doors open from the top. They spread mere inches. It took its time so as to be imperceptible. With the speed of a minute hand on a clock, it opened the doors, slinked through, and crept across the ceiling and into the library.

On the recliner, Veronica sidestepped from pity to anger. *Screw the Traveler's Channel*, she thought. After all, it was just *cable*. To hell with the snotty neighbors; she didn't want to work for them anyway. And who cared about Christophe, just another dumb guy for her slutty sister to fuck. What did it matter to Veronica? She was *done*. She rose from her chair and shouted, "I'm done! Ya' hear that? *Done!*"

As her voice vibrated off the cold stone walls, vertigo grasped her. She wobbled and fell back into the chair. She sat there a moment as the castle seemed to answer her: *No, Veronica, you're not done, not yet.* It was like a thought in her head, but not one of her own. Forced there by someone, or something else, it struck her with an invisible impact that left her stunned.

Veronica melted into the chair, feeling like the wind was knocked out of her. She patiently waited for the queasiness to pass. The quiet was interrupted by delicate tapping mixed with the soft undertones of something scratching. It sounded like nails scraping across stone. She sat motionless and listened.

It came from above.

Veronica stared at the crown molding where the wall and ceiling met over the fireplace. She thought she saw a dim shadow wavering there, as if something behind her and above her was casting it.

Without moving her head, she scanned the ceiling above by rolling her eyes back as much as she could. Her line of sight only went so far, though. She desperately wanted to tilt her head, just a little, to see what lingered directly above her, but she was paralyzed and unable to move. Like a frightened rabbit sensing a predatory hawk in the sky, she sat mesmerized as something stalked her from above.

She heard it again, scraping and scratching just above her head. Hot panic stabbed her spine. For a moment, she thought she would pass out from fright, but she remained lucid. Then, just on the edge of her line of sight, a distinct shadow quivered on the ceiling. Any doubt she harbored dissipated. Veronica was positive something menacing hovered directly above her. Intent on doing bad things to her, it was something that *craved* her. She didn't know how she knew its intentions; she just *did*. It wanted to tear into her flesh and shred her into a bloody mess of sinewy tendons and muscle and skin.

Should she run?

To her right was the foyer. On her left, the short hallway that led to the Queen's Chamber. She considered bolting each way. The foyer was farther, but it offered the immediate freedom of the castle's front doors. The Queen's Chamber was closer, but then she would have to go out the patio doors and have a farther run to the orange car in the driveway.

Stay still. Veronica intuitively knew she shouldn't move. So she waited, hoping it would eventually lose interest. The standoff continued for several minutes that seemed like hours. The desire to run was overwhelming. In her mind's eye, she saw herself scrambling for the foyer and the freedom of the front door. Somehow though, she knew the thing above her was quicker than she. It would easily overtake her.

The clock above the fireplace ticked away three, then five minutes. Veronica barely allowed her chest to move while breathing. Her neck grew stiff and the muscles ached. Eight minutes passed. Gradually, her primal apprehension subsided. The hot perspiration that trickled down her spine grew cold, and the urge to flee diminished as the minutes benignly ticked.

She blinked. Her eyes suddenly seemed more focused, and the shadow that once hovered above her was gone.

Logic strolled into the room like an old friend. Veronica realized she let her imagination get away from her. After all, *what* could possibly be hovering over her head?

She slowly straightened her back. Nothing happened. She splayed her fingers to stretch them. Still nothing happened. She exhaled deeply, and the tension in her muscles eased.

She scolded herself. "I'm such a pathetic loser..."

As she began to rise, something tapped the center of the top of her head. Like a solitary raindrop, a dollop of saliva, or a bit of blood, something landed directly in the middle of her part. Cautiously, Veronica swiped her hand through her hair and felt sticky wetness.

Something from above had dripped on her.

Afraid to look, she shut her eyes and shakily wiped her tainted hand across her jeans as if it was infected. It stung, whatever it was. Adrenaline shot through her body and infused her soul.

Veronica snatched her bag and lurched forward just as something plopped on the floor directly behind her. She could sense it falling, whooshing the air as it landed. It brushed the back of her bare calves — feeling like a ball of hot, sticky, wiry hair.

In a blur, she was gone. Dashing for the hallway, it followed right on her heels. A razor thin slice of skin ripped from her ankle, and she realized it took a swipe at her.

Veronica careened down the hall and barreled into the Queen's Chamber, slamming the door behind her. She staggered as something bashed into the door from the other side.

Walking backward, unsure what to do next, her buttocks hit the edge of the huge, comfy bed. For a mad moment she just wanted to crawl into it and hide under the covers. Like a child, she thought if she hid well enough, the monster couldn't get her.

It slammed into the door again. It gnarred, howled, clawed and hissed.

She allowed herself to fall backward. Veronica landed in a sea of pillows and blankets that consumed her like protective arms.

❧❧❖❧❧

Insanely, she flung her hands in the air and pushed back the downy covers and velvety pillows that smothered her. She sat up. Her crazed eyes locked on the door.

All was quiet. Nothing fought its way through from the other side. Nothing slammed into the door, clawing and scratching. It was gone.

Or was it ever there at all?

Veronica scanned the room and all seemed serene. The lamp on the nightstand cast a warm glow over her surroundings. Her messenger bag sat securely on the chair next to the bed, and the alarm clock glowed calmly with the numbers 11:10pm.

Don't tell me I just dreamt that? Did I really fall asleep and dream all that?

She scooted out of bed and into the bathroom. There she flicked on the light and glared at her bloodshot craze-filled eyes in the mirror. *A night terror? Was that a freaking night terror? Is that what Sandbourne warned me about?* Veronica flopped onto the toilet seat and rationally told herself it was just a bad dream. It wasn't real. *I'm not crazy, just had a bad dream is all.*

She clutched her hands behind her neck, rested her elbows on her knees and rocked herself quietly. She felt safe there and rationalized that nothing bad could happen to you while you sat on the toilet. Did you ever see horror movie monsters attack anyone on the can? Nope. The commode is off-limits, she surmised.

Veronica slid her pants down, peed, and savored the mundane moment. As she wiped, a small puddle of crimson pooled on the terra cotta floor by her feet. She felt her ankle with jittering fingers and found the source. It was a razor thin slice, as if something extremely sharp had grazed the cusp of her anklebone.

It wasn't a dream; something *real* had scratched her.

441

What the hell could it have been? A mouse, a rat, an animal of some kind...then it hit her. A bat! It must've been a bat. Dizzy bat swooped down from the ceiling; it did! Made sense. It was hanging from a gold-leafed finial minding its own bat-business when she came barging in, turning on lights, slamming doors, blabbering about being *done* and generally doing everything humanly possible to piss off an unsuspecting bat. Then it took a shit on her head. That's right. She got guano in her hair. She didn't know it at the time, so she went running out of the room like a spaz, causing it to freak out and swoop down and scratch her ankle. There — a rational explanation! She was dive-bombed by a bat — just a furry, little, fiendish bat with a kamikaze complex.

Veronica scrambled back into the bedroom. She'd avoid the stupid bat and leave through the French doors. She grabbed her messenger bag and hoisted it over her shoulder. She thought about the orange boxy car waiting for her in the driveway. It had sat unattended for days, and fleetingly, Veronica imagined the car not starting. Like a scene in a movie, she would try to turn it over while something sinister encroached upon the vehicle.

She laughed at herself. I'm just gonna stroll out the door, get in the car, and go back to town. I'll call an exterminator and come back tomorrow — I just won't come alone.

She slunk out of the patio door into an opaque night with no moon or stars. Thin light from the front entry sliced across the driveway several meters away. Through the pitch she trotted, until her heel came down on something hard and round. It rolled under her foot. She lost her balance and awkwardly fell back into the dark, dewy grass with a bone-jarring thud.

The fall stunned her. After a dazed moment, she scrambled to her feet and saw the silver ball that made her fall, then another ball just a few feet from the first. Then there was another, and yet another. She stepped carefully because the entire lawn was suddenly covered in silver jeux de boules.

Like a minefield navigator, Veronica tiptoed through the boules. The car was just around the corner, only about thirty feet away. She dug the keys out of her pocket, so she was ready to unlock it.

She looked up, but someone blocked her path.

Veronica staggered to a halt. "Who's that?"

Before her was a shadowy silhouette. It swayed rhythmically — methodically — like a charmer's snake. Next to it, a bassinet was nestled in the grass.

Veronica didn't wait for an answer. She darted to the left, in the direction of the orchard, intent on circling around the spectral vision. However, her escape was blocked by another swarthy phantom. It appeared from behind the fragrant apple trees like an insect. Its antique cassock flapped in the evening breeze like the wings of a June bug.

Startled, she stumbled on a boule and fell again, landing square on another metallic ball with her kneecap. It rammed into her bone with a crack, and she gasped as the pain seared up her leg. Her hand instinctively cupped her wounded knee and dropped the car keys. Ridiculously, she saw the scene from a third-person perspective. It was just like a campy movie.

She fleetingly hoped her zany sister had set her up for some outrageous reality show and the host would jump out of the trees and yell, "Relax! You're on *Fear Tactics*, Veronica!" But instead, the black June bug figure emerged from the trees. As it approached, she saw it was actually the same gangly priest from the party. His long face was grave, yet this time his searing eyes had a glint of pity.

There was no way Veronica was going to stick around to see if he was a good priest or a bad priest. Scrambling on all fours, she retreated back toward the French doors. Another figure crept out of the night to her right. This one looked like the infamous Woman in Red, but her eyes did not betray any kindness. Just behind her, another appeared. A young girl wearing a wispy toga with a sooty, singed border.

Veronica lurched into the Queen's Chamber, flung the French doors shut, latched them, and drew the curtains to obscure the hideous figures that loomed outside. They stirred a twang of recognition that resonated within her like déjà vu, as if recalling a distant dream.

Am I still fucking dreaming, she thought, and tried to force herself awake. *Scream*, she thought, *I have to scream!* Veronica threw herself on the bed, opened her mouth, and squeezed out a screech that was mellow at first, but quickly became an ear-stabbing wail with a quick crescendo.

Veronica screamed and screamed until her throat became raw and exhaustion overwhelmed her tired body.

Chapter 126

Veronica's Story
Present Day France

Morning brought clarity. The menacing images of the previous night's dream became harmless phantoms as Veronica blinked herself awake. While getting out of bed, she understood for the first time what Dr. Sandbourne had warned her about. Her night terrors did seem real — frightfully real — no wonder he believed they were caused by spirits.

She changed into clean clothes, brushed her teeth, and fumbled with her hair and makeup in the bathroom for about a half hour before realizing she was stalling.

Veronica was afraid to walk outside.

She swept back the flimsy curtains hanging from the French doors. The early morning sun casually swept across the soft, dewy garden. There were no silver boules, no bassinette. No sign of last night's specters. Despite the pristine scenery, Veronica felt trepidation. She haphazardly packed her suitcase, chucked her messenger bag over her shoulder, and approached the door. It was still locked from the night before.

She couldn't bring herself to open it.

She stood there twenty minutes.

The bathroom, she considered. *It has a door that opens to Nikki's bedroom.* Through there she could sneak down the hall that led past the keep. If she kept following it, she'd come to a side door that opened to the vineyard. Then she could walk around the back of the Château to get to the car in front.

Veronica chuckled at herself. *Seems stupid to walk all the way around the freaking castle when the car is just forty feet outside the front door.* She had walked through the Queens Chamber door hundreds of times. Now it terrified her.

Ten more minutes passed before Veronica turned on her heels and walked through the Jack-and-Jill style bathroom into Nikki's room. It was disheveled. Obviously, her sister packed in a hurry, not even bothering to make her bed.

Veronica continued swiftly out the door and into the hall. She veered right and followed the passageway as it twisted into the oldest part of the castle. Not much farther was a door on her right that would open to fresh, glorious air!

❧ ❖ ❧

Was that a voice? It was a thin sound, incredibly subtle, like a kitten crying from a way-too-high tree branch.

Veronica stubbornly refused to accept hearing it. Muscles she didn't even know she had, tightened inside her head and muffled her ear drums.

Again, something whined from inside the bowels of Le Château du Feu Ardent. There was no doubt. She distinctly heard, "Aaauuu secours!"

Probably the wind or rumbling old pipes? It couldn't be a voice. She was the only one there after all. *I'm the only one here!* she bellowed inside her head.

She heard it again. This time it was clear. "Au secours!" From her meager French vocabulary, Veronica knew "au secours" meant "help".

Veronica was poised at the junction of the corridor leading to the keep. The darkness was so complete she couldn't see the door at the end. Could someone really be down there calling for help? Or was it something else — baiting her — one of those *visions* from last night? Straight ahead was the side door that would release her to the outside world and freedom from the Château.

The voice called out to her again, "Au secours!"

It definitely came from deep inside the keep.

She remembered something Marie-Claire told her. "The tower rooms...they are in the keep, which is the oldest part of the castle. We believe you will find much inspiration there."

Instead, Veronica had found several decrepit rooms that needed fumigation. The top two weren't so bad because they had windows to help air them out. The bottom room, though, seemed to be the source of the stench. It had an odd grotto that Veronica initially mistook for a fireplace. Clark explained it was likely an ancient toilet, and the source of the pungent odor. Nonetheless, she placed a mantle around it, determined that it should *be* a fireplace that would make the room cozy and inviting. Clark was supposed to connect a gas line to it, so she could convert it...

Clark! He had been missing for days.

"Clark, is that *you*?" Veronica called out.

Dead silence.

"Hello?" she tentatively asked.

Still no answer, but Veronica didn't really want an answer. She wanted to get the hell out of there. She wanted nothing more than to plop her fat ass behind the wheel of the little orange car and race back to town. She wanted to check into a hotel and sit at the bar and pull back two or three cosmopolitans and convince herself that everything she'd experienced in the last twenty-four hours was just a bad dream.

Most of all, Veronica didn't want the voice to be Clark. He hadn't shown up for work in several days, and Veronica much preferred the thought that the annoying plumber just up and quit than to think he was trapped somewhere in the depths of the keep all that time. She hovered at the mouth of the corridor, staring down its throat, hoping the darkness would remain silent. It didn't.

"Oui! I'm here."

A fierce, primitive surge of terror clenched her reason. Instead of coming to Clark's rescue, she wanted to flee. She fought her instincts and diligently asked, "Who's there? Is that you, Clark? What's wrong?"

"Oui, yes it..."

The answer was weak and trailed off as if too frail for all her questions. Veronica abandoned her suitcase and crept down the corridor, tracing her pinky nail along the cool, slimy stones as she navigated the darkness. She remembered the mouse that startled Nikki and her and promptly pulled her hand back.

The voice beckoned her. "Aidez-moi!"

"Coming," she answered.

The door to the keep wasn't latched, and she easily pushed it open. Oddly, she didn't need to hit the light switch as the main room wasn't completely dark. The door to the bottom tower room was ajar, and light seeped from behind it. That must be where the voice came from.

She stepped into a brightly lit fairytale bedroom. The dank, disturbing room where she once found a crusty old fingernail, and Clark discovered the mysterious red dress, was hard to even recognize. It now featured a canopy bed brimming with fluffy pillows and blankets dotted with a pastel floral pattern. The hand-carved side table held an antique Tiffany lamp, which was the source of the illumination. On the far wall was the fireplace mantle surrounded by abandoned workman's tools.

"Clark?"

"Oui," came a weak reply.

"Where *are* you?" She welled with a moment of joy as she realized it really was Clark. That meant another human being was in the Château with her. She wasn't alone! Clark's presence brought a split second of comfort. She couldn't tell where his voice came from and spun around wildly searching for a clue. "Where the hell are you?" She laughed to try and force normalcy into the situation, but only managed to sound scared and uncertain. She noticed a flashlight inside the fireplace. "Did you come today to fix the gas line?" she asked, hoping Clark had arrived earlier that morning to finish his work.

"Get me out of here!" the plumber cried from within the hole in the grotto.

Like an echoing radio drama, Dr. Sandbourne's conversation from the night of the masquerade repeated in her head: *"She and her psychic friends were able to contact spirits, mostly victims of the oubliette."*

"The oubliette?" Veronica had asked.

"You haven't seen it then? It is a dungeon, a narrow pit. Literally, it means a forgotten little place. People were thrown in and just left to die."

With sick realization, Veronica realized the oubliette was real. It was the same one Josette-Camille jumped into with her baby. It had become a tomb for them both and for how many others? Veronica didn't have time to think about that, though. She shuffled to the edge of the pit. Around it were planks of wood, a saw, and a hammer. It looked as though Clark had been attempting to seal it when he fell in. Veronica peered over the edge while wondering how long he'd been there. The oubliette was black as night, and Veronica couldn't see anything.

"Clark?" she ventured.

A tired moan replied, echoing in the narrow chamber.

Veronica grabbed the flashlight and shined it into the abyss. Directly underneath, at the bottom of the oubliette, was a pair of legs wearing blue workman's pants and scuffed, brown boots. Veronica couldn't see Clark's upper body as the rest of him was out of sight because the oubliette was wider at the base. It was shaped like an elongated cone, with the opening being the narrowest. This most likely ensured that no one would be able to escape by scaling the walls. It also meant that Veronica could not get a clear view of Clark.

One of the legs twitched and a shaking hand reached for her. It was pasty with paper-thin skin bulging with turquoise-colored veins. She heard him mutter, "de l'eau, de l'eau." He was asking for water.

"Hold on, Clark. I'm gonna get help."

Veronica spun around and faced a woman standing in the middle of the room. She was petite and wore a yellow jumpsuit with a crisp, white sweater tied loosely around her neck. Chunky gold hoops dangled from dainty earlobes, stretching under the weight. Her black hair was pulled into a tight bun, and a tuft of fringe hung just over thick eyebrows. She was elegant, yet matronly; frightening, yet familiar, and a smile quivered on her bowtie lips. She spoke softly.

"Bonjour, Veronica!"

"Marie-Claire!" Veronica gasped.

"Oui!" the woman answered.

"You're here! I wasn't expecting you...yet. The Château is a mess. You see, there was a party and, oh my God, so much has happened. But right now there's a man stuck in this pit-thing, you know, the oubliette."

"Mademoiselle Veronica!" Marie-Claire brightly exclaimed.

Veronica continued to ramble. "He must have fallen. He's one of the workers — the plumber. His name is Clark, and we gotta get help."

"You aren't leaving, are you?"

Veronica stopped mumbling when realization hit her. "Oh, you must've seen my suitcase in the hallway! I was *about* to leave, but heard someone calling for help, and I found Clark. He's trapped down there."

"I know, Veronica, we all are."

"Pardon?" Veronica stammered.

Marie-Claire approached Veronica. The round room seemed to shrink as the diminutive specter closed in.

"You'll help us, oui?"

Veronica nodded carefully. "I have to go get help for *Clark*..." She stepped forward, and Marie-Claire moved swiftly in response to block the advance, cornering her at the cusp of the oubliette.

"No, Veronica, you have to help *us*. We've been down there *a long, long time*."

Veronica shook her head from side to side. "No! You're not real. I'm dreaming, just like Dr. Sandbourne said."

"Dr. Sandbourne, you say? He's down there, too, Veronica. Don't you want to help him? After all, he traveled all the way from America to help *you*. Don't you want to see what happened to him! He died because he was trying to *help* you. Won't you return the favor, Veronica?"

"I don't know what you are talking about!"

"We've been trapped so long. You remember Trinna? She's been here the longest. She was the first. Her grave became the oubliette, which in turn became all our graves."

Veronica's dreams suddenly came bubbling up to her conscious memory. It was as though they were there all along, just under the surface, and now they assaulted her sense of reason like impetuous imps. She remembered Trinna's story — the Pagan ceremonies, the fire, her young lover Bevin and his horrific act of necrophilia. The dream swam in her head along with the legend of the Templar Head Ralph told her. She realized he was right. All legend is based on

447

some truth, and she had seen that truth played out in her dreams.

Marie-Claire tilted her head like a mother explaining something complex to a child. "Trinna and Bevin started it all. They unleashed something into this world that wasn't meant to be here. An ancient, elemental beast that roams these grounds, trapped in a limbo between the lands of the living and the dead. And it doesn't like to be alone. It traps us here, so it can feed off our fear and misery. It sucks us like a parasite, keeping us lethargic and subservient. All victims of the oubliette become *its* victims. It holds us here, so we can't move on. We can only exist in an eternity of darkness and uncertainty. We just want to pass to the other side, Veronica, but it won't let us."

Veronica spoke carefully. "That sounds awful, but what does this have to do with me?"

"All our stories were fed to you in your dreams because we wanted you to know us and understand who we were. That way — we hope — you'll say yes when we ask for your help."

"Help how? I don't understand."

"You can defeat it and drive it back. You can help all of us move on. We're depending on you. Remember young Isabelle, the brave little girl who saved her brother? And Father Michel? There is also Dorothée and her lover André-Benoit. Josette-Camille and her baby, and so many others who summoned you to save them…"

Sandbourne was right. Marie-Claire contacted her from the other side and lured her here. They all lured her here. Her temples throbbed as the memories of the ghosts of the oubliette accosted her consciousness. The line between reality and her dreams blurred, and fleetingly, Veronica wondered if even now she was awake or asleep. In a desperate attempt to rid herself of the vile specters, she pulled her head back and cried out, blaring as loud as she could.

"No! Just go away! Leave me the *fuck* alone!"

In response, Marie-Claire recoiled like a beaten dog. Her eyes flared with betrayal, and for a moment, a look of hate and anger overpowered her delicate features with such intensity that Veronica stepped backward.

Marie-Claire fumed. "Ungrateful fool!" she spat.

From inside the oubliette, Clark cried, "Veronica, help me!"

Other voices chimed in and called out for Veronica.

Oui, Veronica help all of us.

Only you can sing the song, Veronica!

We've waited so long.

Help us!

Free us!

Do the deed your destiny commands.

Quit crying and help us, bitch!

Veronica collapsed into herself and coiled up tightly. Her face pressed into her knees, and her arms wrapped around her legs.

"No!" she blubbered. "No! No! No!"

In the throes of terror, she imagined herself to be a rock, closed up hard and safe. Nothing could get in. She was solid, impenetrable, like a steely jeux de boule.

All became quiet.

Something gently nudged her.

Veronica opened her eyes and charily lifted her head. Marie-Claire crouched beside her and stroked cold fingers through her hair.

"Please, Veronica, help us?"

Veronica's gut twanged with a bubbling mixture of mortal terror and pity. She stiffly nodded her head and whispered, "Okay, yes, anything, just stop tormenting me, all right?"

The matronly woman rose and pranced back to the dead center of the tower room. She stood there smiling sweetly. Veronica considered dashing out the door, but hesitated as Marie-Claire benignly appeared to implode. Like a piece of origami paper, folding into a tiny fragment, she grew smaller and smaller until nothing more than a glowing speck remained. It hovered in the room's center several moments.

Veronica was about to make a move for the door when all the air in the room began to roil like a sudden autumn breeze bursting through fallen leaves. It was gentle at first, but quickly gained speed and spun debris around the circular chamber. The entire room suddenly turned into a churning vortex. Veronica gasped for air, but it was like breathing in a vacuum.

What remained of Marie-Claire floated in the center. Like an ember suddenly fed with oxygen, the essence of Marie-Claire glowed with white-hot intensity. Around it, the air spun in a whirlwind. Veronica struggled to inhale. She cowered in the grotto to escape the churning current, teetered on the edge of the oubliette.

The lamp tipped over and spiraled across the floor, shattering the colorful glass shade into a mosaic of projectiles. They bombarded Veronica's left side and sliced through her jeans and sweatshirt, drawing bloody welts. Pillows flew off the bed. One pelted Veronica's cheek and almost sent her hurling backward. Her fingers clutched the edge of the wall, and she hung on for her life. The sound became deafening, like a train it roared. The forceful airstream became too much, and Veronica's fingertips began to slip. Her nails dug into the stone, tearing and bleeding. As her index fingernail ripped off halfway to the cuticle, the wind abruptly stopped.

All was suddenly and completely still.

Veronica continued to clutch the wall stubbornly. She was afraid to let go. In the center, the speck that was once Marie-Claire glowed like a beacon and illuminated the room in a fiery red haze. Finally, Veronica accepted the calm and slowly released her life-grip. As her fingers relaxed, Marie-Claire exploded like a silent bomb. The force sent a rushing wave of heat into the room like backdraft from a furnace. Veronica's precarious perch was knocked off balance. She swayed at the lip of the oubliette, cried out once, and fell in.

Inside the Oubliette

Veronica inhaled deeply and coughed back a noxious flavor which coated her tongue like a blanket. It was the air. She could *taste* the air. A sickly sweet flavor, like rotten flowers; it hung in her nostrils, on her palate, and in her throat.

"You okay?" a hoarse voice asked.

Her reply was simply, "Yes," even though she had no idea if she was okay or not. Searing pain shot through the right side of her ribcage. She twisted her torso, and another pain accosted her head. Throbbing, like she had been hit in the head with a baseball bat, her tender temples felt like they would burst.

"Did you call for help?"

She recognized the voice. It was Clark. Call for help...yes, she was going to get help for Clark...

"I need to call for help," Veronica mimicked.

The odor wafted into her sinuses and mouth again. She smacked her lips and spat. It was stronger than before. The dead flower tang now mingled with the stench of rotting meat. She coughed as she realized she wasn't just *smelling* — she was *tasting* — the aroma of death.

"*Did* you call someone? Does anyone know we're down here?"

The image of Marie-Claire stabbed her mind's eye. She shook her head to drive the vision away. "What happened?" she asked and looked up with bleary eyes. She saw only a furry darkness.

Clark whispered, "You fell in. I'm not sure how. One minute you say to me that you are getting help then you scream then thud! And you almost land on my legs. I thought you were dead at first. You've been lying there many hours."

"I'm *in* the oubliette!"

"Is help coming?"

"*We're* in the oubliette?"

"Oui. Before you fall, did you tell anyone?"

Veronica paused a moment to clear her head before answering. "No. No one knows we're here...at least no one who can help us."

Clark was silent. The pit was silent.

She sat with her back against the wall. While caressing her temples, she felt a swollen welt where she must have hit her head. She combed her hair with fidgety fingers, and crumbled a dry clump of blood.

"How do we get out?" she asked.

No answer.

Veronica blinked several times and wondered fleetingly if she was dreaming. A thin stream of hazy light filtered down and dimly illuminated the center of the floor. The perimeter remained hidden in the shadow, like a donut of darkness. Veronica squinted, and as her sight returned, saw the ground was littered with human skeletons. Sharp, decaying, grinning skulls were piled up all around her like a macabre nest. She felt her ribcage and grabbed the jagged, broken bone that had sliced her side while shrieking, "Oh God, oh God, oh God..." She whipped the bone across the small chamber. It hit the wall and shattered. With all her might, Veronica prayed she was dreaming and shouted, "Get me out of here! Get me the fuck out of here!"

Clark didn't respond to her outburst. He was only about six feet away and directly across from her, but was sitting against the wall, so his upper body was veiled in darkness. She could only see his legs jutting out into the center, illuminated area. As her tantrum deflated, and she finally sat quietly, she heard him softly sobbing.

"You okay?" Veronica asked.

He snickered. "I *thought* I was okay. I *thought* help was coming. Instead of helping, you fall in here with me like an imbécile!"

"I'm sorry. I was gonna get help but..." she trailed off, uncertain how to explain the apparition of Marie-Claire. "Then I guess I must 'a slipped and fell."

Clark inhaled deeply and coughed. "I'm crying, but I'm so dry, so...déshydraté...no tears come out!"

Veronica leaned against the cool wall and kicked away the bones while muttering, "Gross-oh-so-fucking-gross." As she cleared a small circular area, her tennis shoe tapped something that "tinked". She hesitated and saw a silver cylinder glint among the bone shards. The flashlight had fallen in with her!

She snatched it, turned it on, and aimed at the opening. She could only see the roof of the grotto, nothing more. The Tiffany lamp was the likely source of the faint illumination, but it was not in sight. She scanned the sides of the oubliette, searching for any means of escape, but the stone was totally smooth, with no climbable crevices or ledges. It appeared to be slick, covered in mold and milky-white spider webs. She cast the beam down to just above Clark's head, stopping before completely bathing him in light.

Clark looked like he was dead.

Veronica cringed at his visage. He had always been a thin man, but now the skin stretched tight over his skull and was a sickly grey. It looked like he was wearing a mask — a death mask. A festering gash on his forehead oozed puss through dried blood. His lips were swollen, purple, cracked, and covered with open sores. He winced at the unexpected brightness. A feeble hand rose as if to protect his face from an assault. Veronica gasped and clicked off the light, but not before noticing her messenger bag. It had fallen with her.

She sat back in uncomfortable silence until Clark finally asked, "That bad, humph?"

"No," Veronica lied. "You...ah...dah...listen, I think I have something for you..."

She turned the light back on, but kept it pointed away from Clark. She rummaged through her bag and proudly pulled out a bottle of water like a magician pulling a rabbit out of a hat. She forced a broad smile onto her face and turned the cap.

Clark's dead eyes brightened. "De l'eau! You have *water*?"

She handed him the bottle without shining the light near him. With surprising strength, he snatched it from her hand. He poured the lifesaving liquid into his mouth. In his eagerness, he over indulged and precious drops spilled down his chin.

"Easy, not so fast," Veronica cautioned.

Clark didn't slow down, though. He chugged the water while snorting and coughing.

Veronica reached out a gentle hand to push the bottle down, so it wouldn't spill out so fast. Clark squealed in retaliation. Veronica jumped, gathered her wits, and explained, "Be careful, Clark, you shouldn't drink so much at once. You're gonna choke."

Clark ignored her. He slurped the water, paused, wheezed a moist breath, coughed, sputtered and then quaffed some more.

"Slow down," she warned, but he chugged until he gagged and threw the water back up in a foamy spray that covered the dusty, dry bones by his feet.

"See, told you. Your body can't handle too much at once. Let that settle in your stomach and then drink some more." She plucked the liter-sized bottle of Evian from his trembling hands and gently tucked it in the bag by her hip.

Clark groaned in despair. He hunkered over while thin strands of drool spilled from the sides of his mouth. "I am dying of thirst. You have to give me more water."

"Just wait a little bit. Let your tummy calm down."

"I *can't* wait!" Clark wailed.

"Yes, you can, Clark. Just give it some time, and I'll give you more."

He waited mere seconds then asked, "Can I have some more *now?*"

Veronica turned away like a stern parent. "No. Not now. Wait, or you'll just throw it up again."

Clark grunted angrily and after a few quiet seconds made a soft lapping sound.

"What are you doing?" Veronica asked.

He ignored her.

She slowly cast the flashlight in his direction. He was holding two femurs, moist with vomit, one in each hand, and licking them like a child with dual lollipops.

Veronica closed her eyes and turned away. "Please, let this be a night terror. Oh God, please, please let this be a night terror..." she whispered over and over again until her head became cloudy with throbbing dull pain. Before she knew it, merciful sleep took over.

"Don't go to sleep," Clark objected meekly. "You probably have a concussion. Miss Veronica, sleeping is not a good idea."

But he was neither compelling, nor sincere, and she slept rock-tight in the depths of the oubliette.

Chapter 128

Inside the Oubliette

Veronica woke hours later. Pain bit into her head through the temples, and she fleetingly thought she had a hangover. She turned on the flashlight hoping Clark wasn't there, and she was actually safe in her hotel bed sleeping off a bottle of cheap wine.

But he was there.

When he groaned, she immediately turned the light off. She didn't want to see his creamy, bulging eyes and big yellow teeth again.

"You are awake finally," he said and dryly continued. "Good, now we can die down here *together.*"

"Don't worry, Clark, we're gonna get out. There's gotta be a way."

He answered with a defeated sigh, and she stood erect for the first time. Dizzy and wobbling, she steadied herself by reaching out to the slanted walls. The shape of her environment reminded her of the old television show, *I Dream of Jeannie.* Barbra Eden would sit in the bottom of her bottle on a nest of luxurious pillows. The interior of the oubliette was shaped like that magic bottle, but there was no nest of pillows. Instead, there were broken bones, vacant skulls, and a few fragments of ancient clothes and miscellaneous buttons, jewelry, and gold teeth.

Veronica groped the wall, searching for cracks and crevices like a rock climber, but there were none deep enough to dig into. She wished she could "blink" her head and get out of this mess. She peered over her shoulder at the decrepit soul. Clark certainly wasn't Major Nelson.

"Can I have some more water now?" he asked groggily.

"Sure, just take it easy so ya' don't throw up again."

"I am *dying* of thirst."

"Here," Veronica offered. "Take one drink."

Clark snatched the bottle and took a long draught.

That's mine, Veronica thought fleetingly.

Clark smacked his lips and savored every drop. He handed the bottle back. "Thank you. I think you saved my life." He rested his head against the wall and this time did not throw up.

Veronica returned the bottle to her messenger bag. Almost half was gone. She noticed the treasure box nestled among her belongings and thought how all the money in the world was worthless to her now. What she really needed was a *cell phone!*

Veronica thumped herself in the head as if to say "I could 'a hadda V-8!" Her cell phone was tucked away in the side pocket of her messenger bag. She immediately retrieved it and punched 9-1-1.

Clark lifted his head. "What are...you have a *phone?*"

"I have a phone!" Veronica declared as she pressed the receiver to her ear.

"You have a *phone!*" exclaimed the plumber. He grinned with big, yellow, bleeding teeth.

The phone breeped the warning signal for low battery.

"Oh shit," Veronica whispered and squeezed it tightly as if doing so would hold all the juice inside.

She willed the phone to ring. Instead, she heard three quick off-key tones and a fuzzy monotone voice declare, "The number you have dialed is not in service. Please check the number and try again. This is a recording..."

"Shit!" she cried and clicked it off. She had precious little power and knew it would die completely in only a few more minutes.

"Is it working?" Clark asked.

"Yes and no. I got a recording when I called 9-1-1. Plus, the battery is low. I probably only got enough juice to make one more call."

"What is 9-1-1?" Clark asked, his French accent lilting on the last "one".

"Emergency, you know..."

Clark coughed. "That is *not* emergency!" he scolded.

Veronica sheepishly realized her mistake. "Well, in the States, that's the number to call for help."

"Stupide! You must call the *police* for help!"

"Yes, I realize that..." she started, but Clark interrupted.

"You must dial seven, two..."

Veronica ignored the plumber's instructions and contemplated the situation. Obviously, her relationship with the local police wasn't all "peaches and cream". They had it in for her. Detective Hertel thought she was emotionally unstable and was certainly bitter about Christophe influencing the mayor.

If I call the police now, will they even believe me? She wondered. Will they care? And what if the operator doesn't speak English? Will I be able to explain why we need help in broken French before the battery runs out?

Clark hacked and sputtered; bits of blood and bile oozed down his chin. She could ask him to talk, but he was weak and prone to fits of uncontrollable coughing.

"I'm gonna call my sister," Veronica declared.

"Qui?" Clark asked.

"Nikki can call the police for us."

Clark gagged before imploring. "No! Call the police. Your sister cannot..." his voice trailed off as he continued to cough.

"She's our best hope. I can't speak good French, and you can barely speak at all. My battery will only last a minute or two. We can't take the chance the cops won't understand us."

"Then call my brother..." Clark gasped for air with raspy lungs. "He's a contractor. He has ladders and ropes..." his sentence went unfinished as the plumber lapsed into an uncontrollable hacking fit.

Quietly, Veronica sneered. "Yeah, I saw the great job he did on the bridge. I think I'll just call my sister."

She clicked the phone and watched it slowly whirl to life. The display screen was dim, a warning flashed: "Low battery — charge now." With horror, Veronica saw something else on the display screen — only one signal bar.

Veronica hit the speed dial for her sister's cell phone.

The line was filled with static and rang just once, then nothing. No connection. The call had dropped.

"C'mon, damn it," Veronica cursed and tried again.

Faintly, it rang and breeped another "low battery alert." It rang a second time, then a third.

"Pick up, Nik!" Veronica pleaded.

"My brother lives a few kilometers from here. He can be here in minutes..." Clark insisted.

"Shh!" she asserted as the phone rang and breeped again.

Then Nikki's voice, distant and distorted with static, answered. "Hey, how...you?"

"Nikki! Listen, you gotta help us..." Veronica began.

"I think we have a bad connection."

"I know, just listen carefully..."

"Can you hear me?" Nikki inquired.

"Yes, I can hear you! Can you hear *me*?"

"Okay, go ahead!" Nikki answered cheerfully.

"I'm trapped in the oubliette inside the castle. You have to call the police. Did you hear that? We're trapped in this pit. It's called an *oubliette*, and it's in the tower room of the castle." Veronica kept her voice steady and clear. "This is an *emergency*. Clark is down here, too, and I think he's..."

Nikki interrupted again with an enthusiastic, "Ha-ha! I got you! *This* is a *recording*! Please leave a message at the beep, and I'll call you back...sucker!"

"What? Nikki, for Christ's sake what the hell!" Veronica roared. The connection crackled, and she hurriedly started her story again. "Nik, we're trapped. You have to get help for us. We're in the oubliette. Clark and I..."

The line stopped hissing. The phone was dead.

☙✿❧

Eighty miles away, Nikki trotted through the mirthful crowd at the wine festival. She ducked as a fire-eater blazed his torch to the delight of spectators. Christophe was just ahead. He glimpsed back, and she shouted, "Wait up. I'm coming!"

"So, what do you think of the Châteauneuf-du-Pape?" Christophe asked as she bustled up beside him.

Nikki giggled. "It's a freaking blast, man. When we gonna drink some wine?"

Christophe pointed to the center of the square where a crowd gathered. Nikki wiggled through the bodies and in the center found a fountain gurgling wine. Several people stood around it and filled their glasses while singing:

> I want to sing to you
> Of this old Châteauneu
> Of that've bottled just for you
> It will work miracles.

For when this wine makes us tipsy;
Venus will crown our mirth!

"That's the Pope's drinking song," Christophe explained over her shoulder. "John the twenty-second once owned this château. This festival goes back many years. The farms in the region are renowned because the wine requires thirteen different types of grapes. It is some of the finest in the world. Would you like a glass?"

Nikki nodded. "Heck yeah. Let's have one on the Pope!"

Christophe held a cup under the cascading fountain. Beside him, a merrymaker wavered and almost fell into the vat. His friends whooped and pulled him back just in time.

"Makes ya' wonder what might 'a fallen in there already," Nikki observed with a chortle.

"Such things you probably shouldn't think about. Here, drink up, you look thirsty."

"Totally parched. Thank you!"

Nikki and Christophe toasted as the evening flickered on. Shop owners lit candles on verandas and street lamps flamed to life. Somewhere a string jazz band played. Nikki gazed at Christophe, and she let her lips part slightly as the twilight cast romantic shadows over the festival street.

Christophe looked down at her.

Nikki lifted her chin.

He opened his mouth.

Nikki's phone chirped. She moaned. "Sounds like I missed a call."

"Check your message. I'll be right back." Christophe dashed off toward a cluster of booths with merchants selling their wares.

Nikki tapped the buttons on her phone. She could see from the caller ID it was Veronica. *About time she quit pouting.* Nikki tittered as she heard her sister's initial reaction to her outgoing prank message: "What! Nikki, Christ!" The message was choppy and unclear. "Nik, we're...you have...we're in the oubliette. Clark and I..."

Nikki looked at the phone quizzically and then quickly dialed her sister back. The call went straight to voicemail. She left a message. "Hey, Vern, my outgoing message *got* you! That was pretty funny, huh? I didn't catch what you said, though. Where are you? *The Oubliette?* Is that a restaurant or something? Did you say you were with *Clark?* Well, wherever you are, I hope you're having fun. Christophe and I are having a blast at the wine festival. You should really consider coming down here. Give me a call if you change your mind."

Christophe stood in front of her, holding a floppy patch-quilt doll that was shaped like a mermaid. "Was that Veronica?"

"Yeah, what's in your hand? A doll?"

"How is she? Is she coming to the festival?"

"I dunno. I called her back but got her voicemail. Is it for me?"

Christophe looked at the doll guiltily. "Actually, I got it for Veronica. It's a mermaid, and she likes mermaids. I saw this and thought of her."

"Oh," Nikki answered. "Well, she just called from some restaurant called *The Oubliette*. It must have been crowded 'cause she was yelling. She's there with Clark."

"Clark?" Christophe asked.

"Yeah, he's one of the workers she hired." Nikki saw a moment of disappointment flutter in Christophe's eyes and she embellished. "He's kinda the big, rugged type with lots of muscles. Owns his own plumbing business. Not a bad looking guy. Sounded like they were having fun. And good for her, she deserves it!"

"Yes, she sure does. Maybe you should take this after all." He handed her the black-beaded eyed mermaid.

Nikki held it up for a split second. "It is the cutest thing I've ever seen!" she proclaimed and stuffed it into her purse.

Fireworks suddenly burst in the sky, and she snuggled against his side as they watched the display.

Chapter 129

Inside the Oubliette

Veronica waited in the quiet dark for help to come. The dull pain throbbing in her head seemed to stupefy her, and she dimly wondered if she had a concussion. A wave of nausea came and went. She pondered if Marie-Claire and the other shadows were still up there, waiting for her, watching her.

Is *this* what they wanted? For her to come all the way to France just so she could sit and rot in the bottom of this God-forsaken pit? Marie-Claire asked Veronica to help them, but how? What did that even mean? What was she supposed to do? What the hell *could* she even do, trapped down here like a fly in a jar?

Veronica realized her bladder was full. The tiny radius of the oubliette didn't leave much room for bodily functions, and she sheepishly whispered, "Clark? Are you awake?"

There was no answer, so she clumsily scuttled over a few feet, unzipped her jeans, and peed on a pile of bones. Clark stirred. She forced herself to finish just as he came to.

"What was that?" he asked.

"What was what?" Veronica asked in return.

"That sound, like running water..."

"Oh, that. I had to go to the bathroom."

Clark was clearly distraught. "You urinated? Just now? And you didn't tell *me*?"

Veronica scrunched up her nose. "You were sleeping."

"We could've saved it and put it in a container for later."

"Save it for what?" Veronica asked without thinking.

"To drink, fool! When the water runs out, we will need to stay hydrated."

"That's ridiculous. We don't need to save urine. My sister's gonna be here soon. Here, have some more water."

Clark eagerly drank again and then asked, "The next time you urinate, please tell me, okay?"

"Fine." Veronica said unconvincingly. "It won't be much longer," she added. "Someone will miss us soon and come looking for us."

Clark twisted the bottle cap in the hazy light. "Apparently, no one missed me."

Veronica didn't have a kind answer, so she lied. "That's not true. I missed you."

"Then why didn't you look for me?" Clark implored. "Why didn't you have the workers search the castle? Did you even call anyone? Tell the police? Tell my brother or my family?"

Veronica wasn't used to him speaking so boldly. Seven days in this pit had transformed the amiable employee into an angry, bitter jerk.

"Well, I didn't know you were trapped..." Veronica began to explain gently.

"But you knew I was *missing*," he persisted. "For days you didn't see me, even though I was supposed to be working for you. Why didn't you set up a search party?"

"I knew you were gone, but I kinda thought, you know, I guess I kinda figured you just quit your job or something."

With a snigger he challenged, "You thought I would just leave and not come back? I work hard for you Mademoiselle Veronica! I stay late to make sure your water runs and I set up an outdoor toilet for you to use. I dig up your septic tank to find your problem. I call my brother to fix your bridge. I even find a pretty dress and give it to you. And you think I would just quit and not tell you?"

His words stabbed Veronica like cruel daggers. She wanted to change the topic. "Speaking of the dress, you know, I wore it to the masquerade party!" she quipped.

"Humph, well that makes me feel much better," Clark retorted.

"Christ, Clark. Look, I'm sorry. I should 'a sent someone to look for you. I was just so busy finishing the castle. I didn't stop to think..." She fought to find the right words, and when none came, simply finished with, "...about what happened to you. Man, I was so self-absorbed. Clark, I'm sorry."

Clark didn't answer. He turned over and went back to sleep while she sat in cold, dark silence.

Chapter 130

Inside the Oubliette

On the morning of her second day in the oubliette everything went completely black. Veronica blinked as she woke, but saw nothing but darkness. The hazy light that illuminated the center of the oubliette was gone. The Tiffany lamp was off. Did the bulb finally burn out? Or did someone turn it off? Was someone here to rescue them?

Veronica jumped up, snapping brittle bones beneath her feet. Nikki must have heard her message. Was she up there, or maybe she sent the police?

"Hello! Help! Au secours! We're down here!"

Clark groaned as she jarred him from sleep. "Is someone here?"

"I think so!" Veronica answered. "The light went out. That means someone must 'a turned it off. Hello up there! Can you hear me? Help us!"

"Or maybe the light bulb burned out," Clark said wryly.

"*Or*...maybe someone is up there, and they saw that it was on, so they turned it off! Hello! Can you hear us! Help! Help!"

"So, you think someone just strolled into the tower room, turned off the lamp that was lying on the floor, and is sitting there now in the darkness? Unlikely."

Veronica huffed before answering. "Well, maybe they thought it fell, and they're searching in the other rooms 'cause they know we're here *somewhere*."

"I doubt they can hear you even if they *are* up there," Clark replied.

"Oh, they can hear me alright. This whole castle echoes..."

"Not down here it doesn't. The sound is trapped. Just like us. I think they must have made it that way so that the kings and queens wouldn't have to listen to the damned down here crying out in agony."

"I heard *you* yell for help when I was up there," Veronica began and then stopped as the stabbing memory of Marie-Claire pierced her reality. Knowing how manipulative the specter was, she wondered if Marie-Claire *allowed* her to hear Clark. Perhaps it was a trap all along, and Clark lured her in.

"I think that was different," Clark began. "I don't know how you heard me. I was barely whispering. But on the night of the party, I was still strong and yelled as loud as I could, and no one ever heard me. Even with all those people, no one heard me scream."

Veronica fell silent. The complete darkness enveloped her like a chilly blanket and then she asked, "You were down here while the party was going on and you could hear us?"

"Yes, of course, I could hear the music and the laughter. I could hear people talking as if they were right next to me! Some were even in the tower room, just above me. There was an angry woman named Gigi and two men, and they talked about you. One of the men called you the 'quasi ex-girlfriend' of someone named Robert. Said his new girlfriend was a 'super-hottie' and that you were lucky to have ever dated him. Said he gave you your big break in the interior design business. I tried to call out to them, but they kept gossiping and didn't even hear me. They were just a few feet away, yet they heard nothing!"

"Those were the Traveler's Channel people scouting for the filming...which never happened."

Clark continued. "I heard the countdown to the unmasking. I heard people scream shortly after, and I even heard the police sirens. I was so *overjoyed* when I heard the sirens because I thought help was coming for *me*! But it wasn't."

"Yeah, they came for Dr. Sandbourne. He had 'a heart attack."

"I know. I could hear what everyone was saying. I even heard when they interrogated all the guests. Being at the bottom of this pit is like sitting at the bottom of a megaphone, Veronica. Every sound is amplified. That is why I know there is no one up there now. You can't hear them, can you? If there was someone in the castle right now, you could hear them *breathing*!"

Veronica coiled up with her flashlight and let the beam shoot straight up. Clark was visible once again. His cheeks were sunken; his eyes bulged. He looked like a refugee from a concentration camp.

He looked like he was two minutes away from death.

He looked like a George Romero flesh-eating *Dawn of the Dead* zombie.

Veronica closed her eyes, so she wouldn't have to look. She wondered how long it took to die of thirst and starvation. She recalled reading that most people can last several weeks without food, but can seldom go more than a week without water. How many days had Clark been down here? About six or seven, maybe more, she surmised. He was lucky to still be alive.

Veronica's stomach rumbled even though she'd been trapped less than twenty-four hours. She opened her mouth to ask him what day he fell, but then held her thought. She had given him some water. That would help him last a little longer. Maybe.

Chapter 131

Inside the Oubliette

Smack! Smack! Smack! Veronica opened her eyes and momentarily forgot where she was. It was completely black. Smack! She blinked, but there was no difference between open and shut eyes. Smack! And what the hell was *that sound*? She rubbed her temples, slowly regained her bearings, and remembered she was in the oubliette. She grabbed the flashlight. Smack!

Clark was illuminated. He cringed in the brightness like a caught thief. "Rien! That is bright!" he cursed. "But it helps. Shine the light here, on the wall."

"Why? What are you doing?" she asked while obliging.

He smacked the wall again and flipped open his palm in the light. A greedy grin spanned his dry, craggy lips like a Cheshire cat's, and he licked his hand. "Spiders," he answered. "Just tiny ones, but they taste okay. I ate most of the big ones already. They hide in the crevices. See, there is one!" He pointed to a crease in the bricks with his skeletal finger and then gave it a hearty *smack!* He popped the wiggly arachnid in his mouth happily.

Clark was getting stronger. Veronica recalled how he was barely able to move yesterday when she first discovered him. The water she had given him had helped. He had some strength back.

And she felt weaker. How long had she gone without food? The last meal she had was dinner at the hotel more than two days ago. She was thirsty, too. She wanted a drink, but didn't imbibe. Clark needed the water more than she. Veronica would save it for him. That was the right thing to do. Save it for the one who needed it most.

"There, on the wall behind you. It's a big one. Get it!"

"Eew! I'll pass." Veronica was hungry, but not *that* hungry.

"Can you get it for *me*?"

Veronica hesitantly complied, shined the light behind her, and crushed it with her meaty palm. Clark quickly scrapped it from her hand and popped it in his mouth.

"In some places these are delicacy," Clark declared. "Insects covered in chocolate. They are rich in protein. You should eat. Keep up your strength."

"Maybe later," she mumbled.

"I'm feeling much better today. My stomach is not aching so much. The water helped." He paused as if waiting for her to respond. When she didn't, he kept talking. "I could really go for some more. I am thirstier now than before. How odd is that?"

Veronica knew why he was thirstier now. It wasn't odd at all. It was a phenomenon that she had read about. After becoming overly dehydrated, the body stops craving water, but if given just a little, it naturally wants more.

Clark nodded his head politely as she handed him the bottle. Veronica watched him quaff a large amount, and was about to speak up when he tilted the bottle back down.

"Merci," he said while sweetly nodding.

Veronica brightly commented, "They'll come for us yet today. My sister must've heard the message by now and surely called the police. They should be here any time."

"And if they don't?"

"Then they'll come Monday at the latest," Veronica logically surmised. "I'm supposed to meet Nikki at the airport because our plane leaves Monday morning. When I'm not there, she'll come back here looking for me. So the *most* we have to wait is, what, five days?"

"You can make it five more days, but I don't think I can. I've had no food, other than spiders, and just a little water. My body can't take much more."

She forced a cheery smile. "You'll be fine, Clark. You're lookin' better already! Just remember we just gotta play it safe and conserve the water. Take small sips in case we need it to last 'til Monday, okay?"

Clark cocked his skeleton head. "You really trust Nikki to come looking for you?"

"Yeah, of course, she's my *sister*," Veronica retorted defensively.

"She won't let you down?" he asked suspiciously.

"I know Nik can be flaky sometimes, but she always comes through in a pinch," Veronica confessed.

"My brother would have been here by now," Clark said matter-of-factly.

"She'll be here. Believe me," Veronica snapped.

"D'accord, je vous crois. I believe you," he acquiesced while shrugging his shoulders. He adjusted his tone and inquired, "You are close to your sister, or no?"

"Yeah, very." Veronica sighed. "I mean, she drives me batshit-freaking crazy sometimes, but that's what sisters do, right? It was just the two of us growing up. Mom worked all the time and left us to fend for ourselves, so we became pretty tight."

"What about your papa?"

Veronica chuckled at the way he said "papa" and sighed. "He left us. Just took off one day and didn't come back." She paused and explained. "It's a long story."

"We have plenty of time. Five days 'til Monday," Clark joshed.

Veronica sniggered, not only at his wit, but at the absurd notion of telling her family story to someone who looked like an extra from *Schindler's List* while sitting at the bottom of a dungeon in a castle in France.

She clicked off the flashlight and sat back for a few moments in complete blackness before conceding. "My mother was a Las Vegas showgirl. For real, you know, Las Vegas, Sin City, and all that. She danced in a chorus line and waited tables. That's where she met dad. My mom told me it was 'love at first tip'. He shoved a twenty into her bra, and that was a lot of money back then! She thought she had found her 'whale'. He would come and visit her every couple weeks, started buying her presents, wined her, dined her, stuff like that. Then one day she said, 'So when are we getting married?' and he said, 'Right now,' and they went to a drive-through wedding chapel!"

Clark smacked another spider and said, "Excuse me. Please continue."

Veronica laid her head against the slimy stone wall. "Mom told me she thought he was her knight in shining armor. The way he spent money, she figured he was rich. He told her he lived in California and was an 'oil man'. What he *didn't* tell her was that he lived on the crappy side of Bakersfield in an area called Oildale. His only connection to the oil industry was a job sweeping floors at one of the refineries. The little bit of money he had was a small inheritance he got after his parents died. He would travel to Vegas every few weeks and had managed to gamble most of it away by the time he and mom got married.

"Well, mom tried to make the best of it. She convinced him to use the money he had left to buy a trailer on the outside of town. She got a job as a waitress, and a year later I came along. My sister followed a few years after me. Nik is too young to remember them fighting all the time, but I do. And then one day, dad left us. Right around the time..."

Veronica's hazy childhood memory suddenly came back to her. It felt like a thousand hot pinpricks stabbing the back of her neck. With a hoarse voice, as if choking on her own memory, she continued. "I remember dad leaving right around the time I started having these real bad night terrors. I was real, real hard to handle. I'd wake up screaming every night because the 'monsters' would come. I told mom and dad about them, and I remember dad said I was crazy. Said I had 'mental problems'. Said I needed to go the state hospital."

Silent tears seeped down Veronica's face, and she absently licked them as they rolled past her lips. "I remember mom wanted to take me to see Dr. Sandbourne 'cause she heard he was the best. Yeah...now I do remember. Dad said he couldn't afford 'no fancy doctors and that the state mental hospital could take care of me for free'. He and mom fought. Mom finally took me to see Sandbourne, and dad got pissed and left. Just like that he left us."

"I'm sorry," Clark commented sincerely.

Veronica sensed the tension and perked up. "Mom took good care of us, though. She got me decent medical care and did everything she could to raise Nik and me. So what about you? What was it like growing up in beautiful France?"

Clark proudly told his story. "You had a hard life. Mine was not easy either. Our family was not rich, and we had to work hard on the farm..."

Veronica hugged her legs and rested her head on her knees while listening to Clark's life story. He told her about herding goats into a big red barn, summers in Provence, and becoming a plumber's apprentice at the early age of fifteen. They went back and forth, story after story, to pass the time as the hours trudged by.

Inside the Oubliette

Somewhere in the middle of a story about L.A. traffic, Veronica realized Clark was asleep. She sat quietly and mused over how absolutely dark the oubliette was without the glow of the Tiffany lamp. The flashlight was right inside her messenger bag, but she wanted to save the battery, so she kept if off, choosing instead to wait patiently for sleep to come for her.

Slowly, the blackness began morphing into a deep shade of crimson. Veronica observed the redness creep in from the perimeter of her vision. Four dark-red blotches soaked the corners of her mind's eye. They started small, but grew larger and larger until they finally consumed most of the blackness. They throbbed, like strobe lights, bursting and pulsating. She tried to lock her gaze on the red blotches, but they refused to remain still, and constantly bobbed just out of focus, making it impossible for Veronica to look directly at them.

The game of *follow the dancing red blotches* unnerved her, and Veronica twitched with irritation. She distantly recalled a poem, or a quote of sorts, she once read on the menu of a quirky restaurant that served dinner in complete darkness:

Once I feared the dark
Its black filled me so with dread
But I learned the dark is never black
Just a deep, deep shade of red

She dined at that restaurant with Robert and a client. The memory of that long-ago random evening preoccupied her, and the red blotches momentarily stopped dancing. She recalled the events of that meeting. Even though Clark was sleeping, she spoke it out loud, finding it more comforting to listen to her own scratchy voice than the impudent red silence.

"The client was blind and insisted we meet him at some kitschy place in Santa Monica. Think it was called *Opacity,* or something like that. It's one of those trendy places that serve an entire meal in the dark. No light at all. The experience is supposed to sharpen your senses. You know, you taste better, you smell better, sounds are amplified, and you rely *a lot* more on touch while moving your hands across the dinner table.

"Our client, Christ I can't remember his name, think we called him T-Bones or something like that. He was a Jazz musician; born completely blind. He had a beachfront condo with a million dollar view that he couldn't even see. Told us he could *taste* the scenery, though. Yeah, said 'the salty air and the mellow flavor of the rising, warm sun played like a melody across his palate every day when he woke up'.

"He was one our first clients — one of *Robert's* first clients — when he opened the Beverly Hill's studio. That's why he made us eat there. Said he wanted his interior decorators to *see* things from *his* point of view.

"Ya' know...he inspired me. That day in that dark, quirky restaurant I planned an interior that wasn't based on form and color, but rather on tactility, aroma, and taste. The mosaic on his bathroom floor was accented with cool jade 'cause I wanted him to *feel* the morning when he first woke. The living room carpets were this luxurious, fluffy shag that ya' couldn't resist digging your toes into. I covered the wall of his home recording studio in an alligator patterned quartz surface, and in the den, I put these funky lamps made out of rock salt, so he could *taste* the light if he wanted to. The design won an award and was even featured in *Dwelling Magazine*. Ha, one of the first of many that *Robert* would win."

Veronica paused as if to give Clark a chance to speak and ask an obligatory question, but he was still asleep, so Veronica pretended to answer him with, "The meal, of course I can tell you about the meal! It was delicious. I had a filet mignon, and it smelled incredible. I knew it was coming before the waitress set it down because the aroma suddenly filled the entire room. And the water, how I took that cool, icy glass of water for granted! I remember reaching for it, tapping across the table with my fingers until they brushed along its side. Moist with condensation. Tinkling little ice cubes. It tasted so good..." She smacked her dry lips and imagined a long, savored swallow.

"I ate mushrooms for the first time that day, ya' know. Never liked 'em before that. Thought they tasted like dirt. But they put mushrooms on my steak, and I didn't even know 'til I took a bite. Didn't even recognize them at first. They tasted amazing! It was like a whole new flavor for me! That's the weird thing about the dark; it washes away all preconceptions. You can do things in the dark that you can't get away with in the light. I yawned during dinner and didn't bother to cover my mouth. I could 'a made funny faces at Robert if I wanted, he wouldn't have known. Hell, could 'a picked my nose if I wanted to. No one could see. No one would know. The dark keeps its secrets well. Ya' know that, Clark?"

Clark didn't answer; though she could hear him inhale deeply and snore just a little.

She continued. "The crazy thing is that complete darkness is actually red just like the menu says. T-Bones said people see red 'cause their retinas are still firing. With no light, they just kinda don't know what else to do. I don't know if that's true, but right now, Clark, I can see that red. I don't see blackness, or grey. I see *red*. A throbbing red that kinda matches my heartbeat I think. Do you see it, too, Clark?"

He snorted in his sleep, and Veronica watched the red blotches dance around her line of sight. They finally joined together, making one large, oblong oval that panned across her view evasively. Like it was teasing her, tempting her to follow it, it bobbed and pulsated just out of focus as Veronica slowly drifted off.

Chapter 133

Inside the Oubliette

Veronica figured it must be morning and thought about waking Clark, but then realized she had to pee. She unzipped her jeans and relieved herself silently, carefully, so she didn't disturb him. He wanted her to save *it*, but Veronica wasn't about to do something so gross. *Besides,* she thought, *what could she possibly* put *it in*? Surely, not the water bottle! That would be disgusting, especially since she'd need to drink out of it at some point, too. She licked her cracked lips and wondered how much longer she could hold out.

Dehydration was taking its toll and hardly any urine came out. She zipped her jeans and stared into the abyss in Clark's direction. She couldn't see him, of course, but knew he was just a few feet away. He exhaled deeply to confirm he was still there.

She figured it must be around seven or eight in the morning. Groggily, she tapped her cell phone's power button to see what time it was. Of course, Veronica knew the battery was dead, but she was still half-asleep and wasn't really thinking. Surprisingly, it made the familiar chime to let her know it was springing to life. Any sleep that lingered in her brain was zapped with a surge of adrenaline when the phone turned on. Veronica clutched it expectantly as the LED screen whirred to life and a photo of her and Nikki beamed happily. She frantically opened her contacts, but just as quickly as it turned on, the *low battery* warning flashed. The phone shut back down just before displaying the time. 1:09am.

Veronica pressed her cheek into the smooth, cool stone wall and groaned in frustration. Her heart beat chaotically from the momentary excitement. She tried the phone again, but it was completely dead now, without even a glimmer of life.

And it was only one o'clock in the morning; much earlier than Veronica had thought. Time dragged mercilessly. She counted the hours, whispering numbers while grasping her fingers one at a time, and finally decided it had been about forty hours since she fell in. She did more finger calculations. If she had to wait until Monday to be rescued that meant she still had— her tired brain struggled to do the math — over *one hundred* hours to go.

She squeezed her eyes tight, as if to force sleep to return, but instead, they slowly opened back up. Without light, it didn't seem to matter if her eyes were open or shut. She would close them only to have them gradually open wide again and again.

The red blotches came back. Her staring eyes perceived them moving peripherally around the oubliette. They seemed to throb, in and out, making the walls *breathe* with them in unison.

In and out, in and out, she sensed the oubliette wheezing all around her like a skinny, broken lung. With each exhalation, it collapsed a little more, like it was shrinking. She froze; suddenly afraid to move because she didn't want to *feel* the mildewy, silky, spider-webbed walls encapsulate her like a cocoon. A few desperate tears squeezed free and escaped down her quivering face.

Clark snorted. The unexpected noise reverberated against the encroaching walls. Veronica jumped, and he coughed. It sounded like he was right next to her rather than several feet away. The crimson blotches flashed in front of her and loosely formed the shape of his face. She was sure that he was poised just in front of her, close enough to kiss her — close enough to stick out his pasty white tongue and lick the salty tear trails from her cheek.

Her heart beat faster as the crimson blotch-face moved in. Closer, closer until he was close enough to chew into her flesh and tear off a meaty chunk of skin. *I don't want more of your water, Mademoiselle. No, your blood will do just fine instead...*

Veronica snapped her head back and thwacked the stone wall behind her. She whimpered in pain and fear. The sound of her own sniveling gave her a shiver that rattled the core of her intestines. Though there was no food in her stomach, she felt nauseous and thought she would throw up.

Fumbling with wicked adrenaline, she dug into the messenger bag to retrieve the flashlight. Her shaking fingers grazed the smooth, plastic water bottle. They lingered there, caressing the grooves of the cap before tentatively digging deeper into the bag. Then her pinky brushed against another bottle. It was the tranquilizers from Dr. Sandbourne. She pushed past the pill bottle until she found the flashlight and pulled it out. The pills rattled as the flashlight bumped against it.

Her thumb rested on the switch, but she was afraid to turn it on — afraid of what she might see before her. What if Clark really was only inches away from her? Sitting there with a big, yellow, bloody-toothed smile like a demented Cheshire cat waiting to take a bite out of the quivering canary.

She sat stock-still — afraid to make a move — with her index finger poised to turn on the light. Her heart beat in frenzied rhythm, and she imagined it was trying to escape. Her heart wanted to break out of her chest. Yes, she was suddenly sure it was attempting to *pound* its way through the ribs that held it in place like prison bars. It would use its severed arteries and veins like sinewy appendages and tear apart her sternum, bursting free like a red and white shrieking alien.

She gasped as the grotesque imagery assaulted her sense of reason. Deep inside, Veronica knew her thoughts were irrational, but she couldn't calm them, nor control them. She momentarily focused on one lucid thought. She *needed* to chill the fuck out before going completely batshit crazy!

The tranquilizers. They would relax her; force her to sleep, soundly and deeply, with no dreams. But they would also knock her out, so she wouldn't be able to hear if help came. Plus, they would dehydrate her even more. They were, after all, supposed to be taken with water...

The childproof cap resisted her weak grip initially, but then happily snapped open. The alien in her chest tried to slice through her breastplate and snatch the pills, but she was too fast and quickly rolled one onto her palm. She cradled the pill tenderly for a moment. The alien squealed with delight at her hesitation. Veronica opened wide, and they whined as she popped the pill in her mouth.

She gagged a little. She *needed* a drink to wash it down.

The water, though, she rationalized, was for Clark. The man was on the verge of death. He needed it so much more than she, and it had to potentially last several more days. She had to resist for his sake.

The pill was chalky and stuck to the roof of her mouth. It caused her intestines to roil, and they began seizing again. Surely, she would throw up, and that meant she would be depleted of precious fluids.

Veronica sat gagging as the redness breathed in and out all around her. Clark snored peacefully just a few feet away. She quietly, shakily, unscrewed the cover to the water bottle. Hurriedly, she took a drink and washed down her bitter pill. Clark whimpered in his sleep, but she didn't feel guilty. After all, it was *her* water.

Chapter 134

Inside the Oubliette

A sharp whiff of sulfur accosted Veronica. She snapped awake just in time to see the flickering match burn out. Clark lit another. He held it out in the middle of the room casting dainty shadows across the oubliette walls.

"What are you doing?" she asked with a whispery, hoarse grumble.

"Lighting matches I found on the ground," Clark answered matter-of-factly.

He lit another, and she saw the name on the matchbook. *The Paris Underground.*

"Hey those are mine!" she whined. "They must 'a fell out my bag."

"The light is nice, no? Is like a candle flame until it burns out." The match illuminated the pit with a glimmering radiance. Clark's facial features were bathed in deep shadows that reminded Veronica of a Jack-o-Lantern.

Clear-sighted reason resonated in her waking mind. The alien in her chest and the dancing red blotches were swept away into distant shadowy corners.

"You're wasting my matches, Clark," Veronica said levelly.

He huffed and sighed dramatically. "Here! There are only a few left anyway," he proclaimed as he handed them to her.

She snatched them and instantly was unsure why she felt she needed them so badly. After a thoughtful moment, she handed them back. "Go ahead, light 'em if you want. I guess we don't gotta save 'em. Besides, I'm happy to *share*."

She dug inside her bag and retrieved the water as the skeletal man gleefully lit another match. "And here, have a drink," she offered with a contrived smile.

"Oh the water! Thank you so much for the water Mademoiselle Veronica!" He took a slurp and stopped drinking just as she began to gently scold him for taking too much. She took it back, smiled politely, wiped the opening with her shirt and gingerly took a sip. Through the bottom of the bottle, she could see him eyeing her incredulously in the flickering match light.

"What are you doing?" he rumbled with surprise.

She forced herself to slowly swallow one small sip and waited a moment, so it could refresh her dry pallet. She answered sweetly and slowly. "I need water, too, Clark."

"But I have gone without any for over a week! I need it so much more!"

She didn't want to start a fight. She knew that peacefully sharing the water was their best option for survival. "I only took a few drops, Clark. Just enough to wet my whistle." She pursed her lips and blew out a few cheerful chords before explaining. "We can share and make it last 'til Monday. We just gotta take small sips." She twisted the cap back on the bottle and noticed about a third was left.

He appeared to pout in the dying flame and grunted, "You could survive until Monday without water. You are stronger and haven't been here as long as me. I need every little drop, or I could die."

The water she just drank gurgled in her stomach, and she felt a slight head rush, as if she had just slammed a shot of tequila. "Don't be so dramatic. You aren't gonna die. And I'm only taking a little. Don't worry, you'll still get most of the water."

"But I need it *all*!"

She grew impatient. "It's my water, Clark," she snapped. "I can have few drops if I want."

Under his heavy breath, he murmured, "Greedy American bitch," and turned away from her. They sat in silence as the hours crept by.

❧❦❖❦❧

Thursday morning Christophe led Nikki through the doors of his villa and threw their bags on the foyer floor while proclaiming, "We're back! My home sweet home."

Nikki trotted across the terra cotta tiled entry that spilled into the massive living room. Directly across were double doors to a veranda overlooking the city of Amboise. "You know, this place rocks, Chris. It's like my dream house. Definitely don't mind spending time here."

He tapped out a text on his phone while absently saying, "You can stay in the spare bedroom again, the one that overlooks the pool."

Nikki grinned without smiling and turned her back to him. "Of course he wants me to stay in the *spare* bedroom," she muttered. "Always the gentleman, aren't you, Christophe..." her voice wasn't loud enough for him to hear, and she let it trail off as she sprinted to the veranda.

To the left was a spectacular view of the city, to the right the deck hugged the corner of the villa and led out to a swimming pool and tennis court. Now these were *her* kind of accommodations, much more modern and luxurious than that cruddy, old castle. Christophe came up behind her. She pretended to jump, as if he startled her, and spun to coyly face him.

"Do you want to take a ride with me to pick up Babette? My brother's been watching my dog. He doesn't live far from Château du Feu Ardent. Maybe we could pick her up, and then stop by and see how your sister is doing?"

Nikki pecked casually at her phone. "Naw, she hasn't returned my call yet. She's still steaming. Trust me, I know my sister. Best to just leave her alone 'till she cools off. Hey, but I know what we can do! Let's go swimming...just tear off our clothes and jump in!"

Christophe shook his head. "I wish I could, but I need to get Babette. I should probably take her for a run and scare up some birds in the fields. She hasn't seen me for days, poor girl, a hunt will be good for her. Please, go ahead, though. Make yourself at home."

He stepped back inside and left Nikki alone to pout on the patio. She shimmied out of her jeans and tank top while strolling to the edge of the pool, tossing them on the deck as she went. Sitting there in just her bra and panties she updated her status: "Hanging poolside at Christophe's. His villa is amazing. How lucky am I to be with a guy who's both hot and rich! Oh, gotta run, going skinny dipping!"

471

Chapter 135

Inside the Oubliette

The back of her ankle throbbed. Veronica didn't really notice it before. Her head ached so much from the mild concussion she surely had as a result of the fall, and her stomach was so knotted from thirst and hunger, that she scarcely noticed the dull pain along her Achilles tendon. She felt with her hands — gooey, sticky, wetness. Something wasn't right.

Clark and she hadn't spoken in hours. Now she needed him. "Clark, I think something's wrong with my ankle." She held out the flashlight. "Can you hold this while I take a look?"

Clark sniffed and reluctantly agreed. "As long as I get a sip of water."

"Fine, okay," she said as she guided his hand to the flashlight. His fingers were thin and brittle; as if she could give a little squeeze and his bones would break like wooden matchsticks.

He flipped on the light. She reached around, grabbed her foot then twisted her torso to see the back of her ankle. The scratch from the bat — or whatever it was that swooped down on her that night in the library — was a swollen, bright red, and covered with yellow pustules.

Clark gasped at the nastiness. A man who could pass as an extra in a zombie movie found her wound disgusting.

"Does it hurt?" he asked.

"Yeah a little," she said as she craned her neck for a better look.

"It is infected," he stated. "You need to take antibiotics before it spreads to your blood."

Though Veronica felt woozy, she replied. "It's just a little scratch; ain't *that* bad."

"Even a little scratch can feed a big infection. If it goes untreated and spreads…"

"My ankle is the least of our worries right now…" she interrupted.

"You'll get gangrene and die!" he snapped back.

"I'll be fine…"

"Or if the flesh begins to rot, they'll have to amputate your foot."

This resonated with Veronica. She had heard of people with gangrene infections needing a limb removed. Like a cowboy in a western biting the bullet while the ol' doc poured whiskey down his throat and sawed off his leg. That *could* happen if they didn't get out soon.

As she contemplated the new urgency of their rescue, Clark asked, "The water?"

"Oh, yeah." She handed it to him. A quiet moment passed then he gave it back. She sat frozen, holding the bottle thoughtfully. "I could *clean* the infection with water…" she began.

Clark snapped before she could finish her sentence. "No! We have to *drink* the water!'"

"But you just said I could lose my foot or even die if it turns gangrene!"

Clark shined the light on her ankle quickly and quipped, "Ah, it is not so bad after all."

She took the tiniest drink possible before nodding sarcastically. "Yeah, gee, okay, I believe you!"

Clark clicked off the flashlight and waited a moment before playfully challenging, "I spy something...ah...something...black!"

Veronica laughed, the water roiled in her tummy, and though she felt like vomiting, she snarked back with, "Is it *this freaking pit!*"

"Yes, of course it is *this freaking pit!*" he answered.

They both guffawed. The ridiculous game of I Spy continued several rounds until sleep finally came for them both.

*I*t's my water! That's what Veronica told herself as she snuck a quick sip. Clark snored hoarsely across from her. She let the liquid slide slowly to the back of her throat and down her esophagus. As she tucked the bottle back into the bag, Marie-Claire sat down next to her.

The American girl couldn't really *see* her, but she *knew* the matronly French lady was there. In the deep, dark redness, Veronica was capable of knowing things without seeing them. Like a thick, murky, conduit, the redness intensified her senses, and she no longer needed to see something to know it was there.

"Mademoiselle Veronica!" Marie-Claire said cheerfully.

Veronica wondered briefly if her eyes were open or shut, then decided it didn't matter as she tentatively answered, "What?"

"Are you ready?"

Trembling, Veronica answered, "For what..."

Marie-Claire smiled warmly. "We brought you here all the way from the city of angels because you are *our* angel. From the beginning, I knew you were special. Everything Dr. Sandbourne said was true. You have the gift to connect with the other side. Now you just need to use it to help us."

For a second, the friendly, motherly voice calmed Veronica. "I still don't think I get it," she groaned like an incorrigible child.

"Use the Head to command it, and drive it back. Invoke the ancient name, and order it to back down, so we can pass onto the other side. That's all you have to do to free us!"

Veronica pulled the crystal skull out of her messenger bag. Though there was no light in the oubliette, it glinted. "Okay, how?" she asked while holding up the Head like a trophy. It grew warm in her clammy hands.

"Call it by name!"

"What name?" Veronica asked.

"*Its* name! Address it then command it to stay back. While you keep it occupied, we can all pass to the other side. It's that easy!"

"But I don't know its name."

"Sure you do. Just say it!"

Irritation stung Veronica. "No, I don't *know* its freaking name!" she snapped. The Head grew hotter in her hands. Her burst of anger seemed to charge it.

"The name was written inside the front cover of the Bible you found in the catacombs," Marie-Claire explained calmly.

"That book is a *Bible*? I didn't realize...hey, is that why Sandbourne told me to read the Bible just before he died? Did he want me to know this name you're talking about?"

Marie-Claire's demeanor seemed forced as she carefully explained. "Yes, dear, *that* book is a Bible, and yes, that's what Dr. Sandbourne was trying to tell you.

He gave you that clue. You *did* read it, didn't you? You carried out his *dying wish*, right? The name is plain to see when you open the book. Plus, Dr. Sandbourne left notes on the yellow paper. He made it so *easy* for you to figure out!"

"Oh," Veronica began sheepishly. "I didn't realize what he was telling me. I thought he wanted me to, like, find religion or something. And then I gave the book to Ralph to study; didn't even realize it was a Bible. I remember he glanced at the paper, but I didn't pay attention to what was written on it. Sorry, I guess I can't help you after all..."

"No, Veronica, you *have* to figure it out."

"How 'm I s'posed to do that?"

"Think real hard, and you'll remember the name," Marie-Claire encouraged.

Veronica was annoyed. "Why don't you just *tell* me what it is?"

"Because the dead can't speak it!" Marie-Claire hissed.

Veronica's fingers tingled as if the Head was electrified. It continued to radiate, and Veronica felt the sudden urge to throw the skull like a hot potato. She forced herself to calmly say, "I don't know *how* to help you."

The specter coaxed her with nervous urgency. "You already know the name. Just think about it. Put the clues together and..."

"I haven't eaten in four days! Hardly had any water. I'm injured with an infection, and I'm tired. I don't even know if I'm awake or asleep! I can't possibly figure out your silly clues."

"It took all our strength to lure you here. You have to do this for us."

"That's the problem," Veronica wailed. "I don't want to be here! I never asked for this. I just want to go home!"

"Once you help us, you'll be free to go," Marie-Claire soothed.

Veronica didn't hear her, though. "I want to go *now!*" she cried. "I want to be back in my cruddy studio apartment in West Hollywood, and work in my crappy office where I don't make any fucking money, and lousy clients criticize my work and refuse to pay, so I can't afford my God damn bills! I want to buy groceries at the gas station because all I have is my Mobil credit card and then have my dumb sister take me out for dinner with one of her rich, stupid dates just so I can eat a decent meal, and I want to watch the insipid reality decorating show that my ex-boyfriend is producing, and it's making him rich, and I won't even care if he dumped me because I wasn't pretty enough to be on it! I want my life back! I don't want you! I don't wanna do this!"

"You're the only one who can. You're our only hope, Veronica."

Veronica felt dizzy, as if the oubliette was churning. The skull burned in her hands. "Well, I guess that means you're all fucked then, huh? 'Cause I can't help you," she snapped angrily.

Marie-Claire didn't miss a beat. "Then you're *fucked* along with us, Veronica. Trapped down here to die a slow, painful death and then join us as its captive." Marie-Claire hovered over her with hands on hips. "I was wrong about you. You can't help. You're too weak, too stupid, worthless to us," she scolded. "Couldn't even decorate this castle decently. English toile accents in the upstairs bedrooms? Really?"

"You're mad about the *toile?*" Veronica asked incredulously.

"The Fontaines and their bourgeois friends were right about you, just a vacuous, incompetent, self-absorbed American who has no business restoring a majestic piece of French architecture. You're better suited to styling dog's houses and homes for blind people."

"My work is more than that! It's won awards, been recognized in *Dwelling Magazine,* and..."

"Humph! Work that doesn't even have your name on it. That is Robert's claim to fame, and you have nothing to show for it. You let him steal from you. You're weak, easy to manipulate, easy to use..."

"Robert didn't *use* me..."

"Then you meet a man here, and let your own sister steal off with him. Can't even fight for someone who loves you! Ha! Surely, you're too weak to fight and save us!"

Veronica burst into tears. "You mean Christophe *loves* me?"

Marie-Claire grinned warmly, but said nothing.

"Christophe?" Veronica asked. "You tricked me into saying his name just now..."

The phantom gently nodded as she slowly imploded like a folding piece of origami. Veronica braced herself, but there was no explosion left in Marie-Claire's wake. Instead, she just shrunk peacefully into a benign speck that faded silently into the redness.

Veronica's body wilted onto the floor of the oubliette. She cradled the skull by her belly, curled into a fetal position, and asked herself, "*Christophe's name?* Is that *it?* It's that easy?"

Shaking, suddenly, Veronica felt her body heave violently. As she thrust out a hand to steady herself, her index finger dug into an eye socket while her thumb plunged between two rows of teeth. She squealed as a tongue caressed her cuticle. It felt like a thick emery board filing her fingernail. She shrieked and jumped.

Clark spit her thumb out of his mouth. "Are you okay?"

Veronica forced the disgust out of her tone before answering, "No, I'm not. Clark, what the hell are you doing? Stay away from me!"

"You were talking in your sleep, and I just wanted to help," he answered sheepishly and skulked back over to his side of the oubliette.

"Well, don't do that!" she cried.

"Sorry, are you okay?"

Veronica caught her breath and excitedly rambled, "Yes, I'm fine. More than fine actually! I think I understand what I need to do now. I *get* what they want. It all makes sense."

"They want you to do something...?" Clark began.

"Do they talk to you, too, Clark? Do you know? What do they say to you?"

Clark waited several moments before he answered. "Just relax, dear. Your dream is over now."

"I can't relax, Clark," Veronica spewed. "I just figured it out!" She swiped sweat from her brow and rapidly explained. "I have the Head, and I think I know the name, too. That means I can free the souls who trapped us here and then they'll let me go — let *us* go, Clark!"

She lowered her voice and explained. "Everyone who died down here came to me and told me their stories in my dreams. For weeks — months even — I've been dreaming about them. I feel like I know them, like they *really* are my friends, Clark. That's why I can't let them down. I'm their only hope to save them from the demonic elemental thing that keeps them trapped in some kind of horrible limbo. Know what I mean?"

Clark didn't answer her right away, and when he did, he simply said, "Can I have some more water, please, Veronica?"

⋗⋗❖⋖⋖

As swallows swooped across the crisp Paris sky, Ralph studied the ancient tome while lounging on his veranda. A floppy hat shielded his eyes from the setting sun, and shielded his line of sight as a young maid set a bottle of Perrier on the table beside him. Startled, he jumped and fumbled his magnifying glass. He grunted as he shooed the servant away.

"This is amazing," Ralph effused before she got too far.

The girl paused and asked, "The water is good?"

"Come back here!" Ralph ordered. She shyly complied, and he continued. "I'm not talking about the silly water. Do you know how valuable this book is?"

The girl cringed as Ralph flamboyantly waved his hat in the air. "No, sir."

"I *told* Veronica it was priceless!" he boasted as he pulled out a chair and ordered her to, "Sit down. What is your name? It doesn't matter; just sit down and listen to me. I have to tell someone, anyone, even you. What is your name?" He didn't give her a chance to answer as he pushed her into the patio chair, forcing her to sit, and continued, "My first impression was right. This book was kept by the Knights Templar. They guarded it, protected it. But do you know why?"

The maid crossed herself and nodded at the eccentric man. She had worked for him three years, knew he was prone to outbursts, temper tantrums, and eccentric behavior, yet she had never seen him like *this* before. She smiled thinly and wished he would let her go.

"You are Catholic! Ha! Oh, I am sorry whatever-your-name-is, but you are in for a rude awakening. This book, this ancient tome, is an early edition of the Bible — a *Nicaean* Bible!" Ralph paced back and forth. His eyes flitted rapidly over the brittle beige pages. He stood silent for several seconds.

"Will that be all, sir?" the young maid finally asked.

Ralph chuckled. "Of course that is not all! Veronica swears that Dr. Sandbourne told her to 'read the Bible' right before he died. A cryptic thing to say, don't you agree? He obviously cared about Veronica, so maybe he wanted her to find solace in the Bible after his passing. Maybe he was concerned about her personal lack of faith. Or *maybe* he was telling her something more literal. A message..." Ralph stared intently at the maid, yet his eyes were distant, not focused.

"The Head!" Ralph yowled. "The Templar Head protected them, made them invincible in battle, and controlled a force more primitive than mankind. They knew its name. You see there is great power obtained over an entity when you know its name. Even God protects His true name, does He not? He has been called Yahweh, Allah, and Jehovah, but no one knows His *true* name because that would make Him vulnerable. And that is the beauty of what we have here! For written on the inside cover, as if by the hand of a child, is the name of the entity the Templars controlled."

She squirmed in her chair and bravely asked, "So what does 'dis all mean?"

"It means this name controls some kind of being, a demon, and it is unbelievably powerful and dangerous." He paused and then contemplated. "Veronica had asked me about an elemental...a djinn. Said Sandbourne thought one inhabited the Château. Such an odd reference to make unless..."

Ralph grabbed the phone and dialed Veronica's number. Voice mail *again*. He left a message. "Veronica, this is Ralph. You *must* call me. I know what Sandbourne was trying to tell you!"

He swiped a handkerchief across his brow and took a long swig of his fancy water. The maid cautiously rose, nodded meekly, and turned to leave. Ralph leaned over and patted her rump as she scampered off.

Chapter 137

Inside the Oubliette

Once Veronica heard the familiar wheezing-snore, she knew Clark was asleep. That meant it was time. She held the Head close to her chest and whispered into the spot where its ear would have been. "Christophe, Christophe, Christophe!"

She waited for something to happen — and waited — but all remained quiet in the depths of the oubliette.

She repeated the name several more times to no avail. Finally, she tried a new approach. "I command you to...to...leave Marie-Claire and the others alone," she ordered. For a moment, Veronica felt silly. Then she felt angry, and soon after that confused.

A wave of exhaustion swept over her, and her temples radiated with fever. She fought the urge to sleep, though. Raw determination kept her whispering into the imaginary ear of the curious crystalline skull until Clark stirred.

"What *are* you doing?" he asked.

Veronica twitched irritably at the sound of his voice and answered, "Summoning an evil genii, so I can drive it off — until you interrupted me. Go back to sleep, so I can finish."

"No. I can't. Not tired."

"Then please be quiet while I conjure the demonic force."

Clark ignored her. "You imagine things, Veronica. No food, little water, the fever from the infection, it all makes you see and hear things that are not there. I feel it, too. I am so weak I sometimes forget where I am, and dream I am at the pub with my brother, or holding my wife's hand as we both feel our baby kick in her round belly."

"Your wife is expecting a baby?" Veronica asked.

"No, we divorce two years ago...right after the miscarriage. That is how I know these are just illusions. Fantasies because of lack of food and water. You must ignore them, or they will drive you crazy, Veronica."

"I'm not crazy," she snapped. "At least I'm trying to do something to save us."

She shoved the Head back into her bag and pulled out the flashlight and water. The light flickered when she turned it on, not long until the battery died completely.

She carefully twisted the cap off the water bottle. Drinking had become a sacred ritual. Once open, she held it out like an offering, and they both inspected the water level. She tapped the side with her pointer finger. "To there," she proclaimed.

Clark nodded, accepted the bottle as if it were a chalice of communion wine, and as always, gulped down slightly more than the agreed upon amount before gingerly handing it back.

Veronica forced herself to take just one small sip. To keep her mind off the savory liquid, she absently asked, "What time do you think it is?"

"I don't even know what day it is, do you?"

"No," Veronica lied, even though she knew it was probably Thursday night — maybe early Friday morning, but that was wishful thinking. She didn't want to listen to Clark complain about how long he'd been trapped, so she shrugged and changed the subject. "I spy something...red, Clark."

"Rouge? Humph, so the darkness looks red to you, too?" he asked.

"Yeah," she said glibly.

They sat in silence and observed the redness together.

⋟⋞ ❖ ⋟⋞

Christophe came home at ten-thirty Thursday evening. Babette slogged by his side. She ran hard that day. The panting golden retriever plopped down by her water bowl and closed her eyes as Christophe tossed two headless, featherless pheasants in the freezer.

Next he crept into his own foyer, unsure if his houseguest was asleep or still awake. He peeked into Nikki's room as he walked down the hall. She was sprawled on the bed, atop the covers, wearing something sheer, flowing, pink, and lacey.

He turned quickly, but she snapped awake as if she had been waiting and asked, "Christophe? You finally home?"

Sheepishly, he ducked into the doorway. "Yes, didn't mean to wake you."

She stretched, rolled over, and arched her back as she scooted upright against the pillowy headboard. "You didn't."

"How was your day, not too boring here alone?"

"Bored? Are you kidding? I swam a few laps in the pool and got a tan this morning, then rented a bike and rode around town this afternoon. I like it here, Christophe. *This* is the life."

"I wonder if your sister is enjoying herself as much as you during her final days in France."

"I'm sure she is. Hooking up with Clark like that was probably the best thing for her. I'm sure he's keeping her busy. If ya' know what I mean." Nikki winked and snickered.

Christophe nodded knowingly. "Goodnight then. Help yourself to anything if you want a midnight snack."

"Hmm, anything huh, then a snack sounds great," she teased.

"Do you want me to get you something?" he asked awkwardly.

"Naw, why don't you just come on over here," she drawled, patting the pillows beside her.

He blushed like a boy and answered, "It's been a long day. We covered six acres and dressed two birds. I'm exhausted. I need to get some sleep."

As he stepped back into the hall and turned out the light, Nikki flapped her arms against the mattress in frustration. She knew he was hung up on her sister.

She just needed to figure out what to do about it....

Chapter 138

Inside the Oubliette

While Clark slept, Veronica cradled the Head in her arms. She whispered softly to it, hoping something would happen. Hours passed with no result. She was about to give up when everything subtly shifted. The room wobbled slightly, the redness lifted, and a familiar voice spoke. "They're tricking you. Gonna use you like a peasant whore." It was a man's voice. She had heard it before but couldn't place it.

Veronica rocked shut into a ball of denial like a crab retreating into its shell. She didn't want to acknowledge the presence, and thus, encourage him to speak more. But her silence didn't dissuade him. "They want to sacrifice you like a gamey slab of mutton on a Pagan altar. Seduce you like a Protestant prisoner. Bait you like an indignant priest preparing to fall from grace. And discard you like a colicky baby hurled down a hole."

"Leave me alone," she seethed.

Hands on shoulders spun her swiftly. Veronica squealed as she twirled in a complete circle. Vertigo made her stagger, and she realized she was on her feet, and no longer slumped over in a lump on the oubliette floor. Though afraid of seeing his visage, she opened her eyes. To her surprise, no one was there. And the redness was gone; replaced by a dark greyness that, though formless, was absolutely vast.

She flung out her arms. They touched nothing. She was in the center of an immense space. Grimy and grey though it was, the fact it was wide open made her titter, spin, and flap her arms like a girl whirling in a meadow on a summer's day.

"Feels good to stretch, doesn't it," he asked, but his voice didn't lilt, so it sounded like a statement. "I rotted in that blasted hole for nine days before I died."

Veronica staggered to a halt and stood face-to-face with Sebastian. She recognized his swarthy figure even though a dark hood covered his head and only the vague outline of a crooked nose was distinguishable.

He continued. "Dying is worse than death. People who say they are more afraid of dying than death have absolutely every right to be afraid."

Everything behind him seemed veiled in a gauzy haze. It was like she was peering through loosely threaded cheesecloth. She slowly recognized the intricate ionic columns of the ballroom. They were still adorned with drooping floral swags from the party, and just at the edge of her range of sight was the long banquet table, still covered in dishes of decaying food.

"We're in the ballroom," she stated.

"Shh, keep your voice to a whisper. We don't want anyone — or anything — to find us now, do we?" Sebastian stepped toward her. His scraggy beard and biting eyes came into focus. Grinning, he continued. "Yes, in a matter of speaking.

This is the ballroom as it exists in that limbo world where the demon dwells. Where we all dwell. I like to call it 'home sweet home'. None of the others do, though. They are altogether fixated on leaving. Well, *most* of the others are. A few of the insane ones don't have the capacity to really care one way or the other."

"Am *I* dead…too?" Veronica stammered.

He laughed and didn't answer. Methodically, he strolled in a circle around her. She followed him, spinning ever so slowly in the center of the dance floor. Finally, he said, "No, you aren't dead. Not yet. But don't worry, it won't be long now."

"Then what is this?" she asked as trepidation fluttered her vocal chords.

Sebastian leapt forward fluidly, and before Veronica could recoil, he had an arm draped around her waist and the other clasped her hand. He glided. She followed, and together they waltzed. "Just a little visit," he whispered in her ear. "You'll return to your body soon, at least for a while."

Veronica squirmed in his arms. "I gotta help them get out of here. Gonna try and save everyone, even you."

Over Sebastian's shoulder, she caught sight of the spot where Dr. Sandbourne collapsed. Police tape sectioned it off, and the hardwood was still stained with blood. Despite the fact that the entire scene was bathed in melancholy hues of grey, the splotch on the floor gleamed with bright red intensity.

"Here's the rub," Sebastian stated as he grinded his groin into hers. "They are tricking you. You won't ever get out of here, and the only thing you need to worry about is whether you want to rest in relative peace for eternity, or face something much, much worse."

"Marie-Claire told me what to do. I just have to figure out how to control the damn Head-thingy, and we'll all be free," she explained hopefully.

Sebastian hummed into her ear and softly sang, "Fight the monster only you can see, and dream the dream you only dream for me…"

"Right, I gotta fight the monster. That's the answer, it was there all along. I just need to figure out the name. I know it has something to do with Christophe…"

Sebastian stepped back, lifted her hand high, and gave her a dramatic spin before pulling her back into him. "Foolish girl, you succeed, and you'll find something worse than death. Don't do it. I'm warning you."

"Of course *you* don't want me to do it. I'm not stupid. I know why you don't want this to work. This limbo place is better for you, but everyone else deserves to escape."

He dipped her deeply, almost all the way to the floor then dramatically pulled her back up. As she returned to his arms, he pressed his lips against hers. It happened so quickly she didn't have a chance to shut her mouth. As he kissed, he spoke, "Sweet dreams, Veronica, you'll see me again quite soon."

She violently squirmed out of his arms. Her cheek smacked something smooth and hard as she flung her head. It was the slick, moss-covered oubliette wall.

She was back. The Cloaked Man was gone, and she was left with just the emaciated plumber to keep her company.

Inside the Oubliette

eronica thought Clark was asleep and jumped when he asked, "Give me the flashlight and your phone, s'il vous plaît."

"The cellphone battery is completely dead," she answered vacantly.

Fever made her head fuzzy, and she was enjoying the red sea of obliviousness she had been floating on for the last several hours. Distantly, she recalled dancing in the ballroom with Sebastian, and she wondered if it was real or just her imagination.

"Turn on the flashlight; let me look at it; I have an idea!"

Clark's voice annoyed her as she contemplated the Cloaked Man's warning. "It's hopeless, and the battery in the flashlight is *almost* dead," she answered flatly. "We shouldn't waste it because when help comes we need to flash, so they know we're down here."

"The battery is *almost* dead?" Clark persisted.

"Yes, that's what I said!" Veronica snapped.

"Then I need to try it now. This can't wait."

Veronica sighed to illustrate the annoyance he obviously couldn't see in her steely stare. "Try what?"

"Use the flashlight battery to charge the cellphone."

"But they're totally different," she grunted.

"I think maybe I can wire them together, using the wires in the flashlight to connect to the cellphone's rechargeable battery."

"That's impossible..." she began.

"And you are an engineer who knows of these things?" he retorted. "It doesn't hurt to try. Give me the flashlight and the phone."

Veronica huddled around her precious items. "No, you'll break them messing around in the dark."

"We have nothing to lose, and if it works, I can call my brother like we should have done in the first place."

"So, that's what this is about. You're blaming me for calling my sister instead of your stupid brother?"

"You had *one* call to make, and you chose *her*? That was stupid! Now do something smart for a change, and give them to me."

"You know, I wouldn't be down here in the first place if I hadn't come to help *you*!" Veronica huffed back. "You should be grateful! You'd be dead by now if it weren't for me and my water. You'd be a dried up bag of bones just like the rest of 'em down here!"

Clark didn't respond.

Veronica sat in the quiet blackness a brief moment. "I shouldn't have said that. I'm sorry."

Clark didn't answer right away. When he did, it was with a calm, assertive, authority Veronica had not heard him use before. "If you give me the phone and the flashlight, I may be able to get help for both of us. Getting out of here is what we *both* want."

Veronica sheepishly handed over the items and listened as Clark unscrewed, tinkered, and tapped.

"Do you have anything else in that bag; a knife or a scissors?"

"No, this is my carry-on, stuff like that won't get through security," she began and then interrupted herself with a shout. "Wait!" She dug into the messenger bag's side pocket. "I left this in there. What a stroke of luck, huh?"

Clark's cold fingers brushed against hers. "Yes, we're the luckiest people in the world. What is it?"

"A metal fingernail file. Will it help?"

"We'll see!"

Clark tinkered with the objects. At one point, he flicked the flashlight, so he could see the inside the cellphone. Veronica saw it was totally torn apart. She had little hope his plan would work, but at least she had a little hope, and eagerly waited for him to produce results.

And waited.

And waited.

Until Clark shrieked.

"What!" Veronica cried.

"It burns! Acid, from the battery is on my hand! It burns."

"Wipe it off, quick," she offered.

"How?" he cried.

Automatically, Veronica offered him the water. "Wash it." Clark grabbed for the water, and Veronica immediately changed her mind and pulled it back. "Wait. You'll waste it."

"Give me the water," he insisted.

"No, I'll do it. You'll spill it."

They each had a hand on the water bottle. Veronica pulled back, but Clark wouldn't let go.

"Let me have it, Clark!"

He released his grip, and cried out like a beaten dog. Veronica took the bottle and carefully poured a few precious drops onto the corner of her raggedy T-shirt. She grabbed hold of his icy, brittle-boned hand. It was like grabbing a dead man. She used the moistened part of her shirt and swabbed at the wound.

"It's making it worse!" he cried out.

"Hold still," she scolded as she fumbled, found the flashlight, and clicked it on. It worked even though entrails of wires spewed out one end like it was disemboweled. Clark hunched over in pain. The acid from the battery was red on his white hand. She did her best to wrap it with a bandage made from a torn shirt. "You'll be okay."

"It hurts."

"I know. Here, take one of these." She offered him a pill.

"What is it?"

"A pill. It'll numb the pain, and help knock you out, so you don't feel anything.

You'll feel better when you wake up."

"If I wake up at all. My body is so weak. That thing could kill me."

"It won't *kill* you! It'll help you calm the fuck down."

"Fine," he snapped and then bargained. "I'll take it. Just give me the water so I can swallow."

"You just had some water a couple hours ago."

"I haven't had any water all day!"

"You don't *need* water," Veronica reasoned. "Just chew the pill and eat it up."

"Give me the water. You are keeping it all for yourself and drinking it when you think I'm asleep. I can hear you, slurping away like an American pig. Give me the water, so I can take the pill."

"It's *my* water! And if it wasn't for me and my water, you wouldn't be alive...and this is how you repay me? You insult me and call me names?"

Clark's face flushed an irate crimson. His voice was shrill as he yelled, "Just because you have the water it does not give you the right to be greedy. I *need* it more than you, but you don't care, do you? You only care about yourself. Selfish, entitled American! What if I swallow this pill and choke? You wouldn't care, would you?"

"I've done everything I can to help you, and you just want more and more. You don't need water now. You can have some when you wake up. Just take the pill, and you'll fall asleep, and you won't be thirsty."

"I need water!" he roared.

"There are only a few sips left!" she spat.

Clark sprung to his feet in a sudden display of agility that Veronica wouldn't have imagined possible. He lunged for the water, but she swiftly passed it from her left to right hand. He spun and grabbed for it again. Both the bottle and the flashlight were balanced in her right hand, and the flashlight flew from her grip. Its beam swept across wall as it sailed through the air. It landed across from her and shined straight up, illuminating Clark's head like a halo. He was a silhouette towering over her. She couldn't see his facial features. He was completely lit from behind, but somehow his wide beady-toothed, Cheshire-cat smile beamed at her.

She shielded her head as he drew back and lashed out with the fingernail file, which thinly sliced her forearm. *He's attacking me*, Veronica thought distantly as the redness closed in to help its champion. Everything became bathed in a scarlet haze. Veronica rose like a boxer and poised herself to fight back.

He swung again while madly anguishing, "Selfish, stinking, American bitch!"

Veronica blocked him like Holyfield, and he gnashed her wrist — though he aimed for her face. She bellowed in pain and jabbed with a clumsy uppercut to his gut. He wobbled backward, but determination didn't abandon him. While sliding down the slimy wall, he stubbornly kicked, sending boney debris and dust swirling into the air.

The American Bitch retreated as far from his reach as possible in the narrow chamber, but still caught a swift kick to the shin. She crumbled to the floor. He crawled on hands and knees to her and snatched the water bottle as she cradled her wounded leg. He scrambled to retreat, to his side of the oubliette, while frantically unscrewing the cap.

The redness drove her forward in a blind rush of rage. She snagged the water bottle back from him. "Mine!" she snarled.

Clark tried to stand, but she shoved him hard back down. His head thwacked the wall. He slumped over into a peaceful heap. She waited for him to rise and attack again, but he didn't.

Veronica leaned back and indulged in a savory sip of precious water — and then another. Her arm throbbed, and she dabbed it with the end of her moistened T-shirt. She shoved the wires back into the end of the flashlight and screwed it together. She didn't turn it on. Instead, she placed it by her side, ready to grab it and click the button when Clark awoke. She reclined on the dusty bones and waited for Clark to get back up.

But he didn't.

Ralph steadied a hand protectively over the ancient Bible as he wove in and out of the Friday traffic. Everyone was escaping Paris early for weekend romps in the country. He spoke loudly into his cell phone. "Veronica, it's Ralph. You getting my messages? It doesn't matter. I'm on my way to the Château to see you right now. Should be there in a little while, and boy do I have a surprise for you!"

He punched another number on his phone, listened as it rang several times, and then left a message. "Christophe! What are you doing right now with that beautiful Nikole that you cannot answer your phone! Listen, I just wanted to see if you heard from Veronica? I'm on my way to the Château right now to find her. If you see her, tell her to call me. It's important!"

Chapter 140

Inside the Oubliette

C lark? Are you okay? I'm sorry. I didn't mean to push you so hard."
Veronica waited for a reply. He had been silent for hours. At first, she
thought he was faking it and would pounce on her at any moment. She
had sat stiffly for an eternity braced for an attack, but none came.

After a while, she decided he had fallen sleep, and she dozed off, too. Upon
awakening, she still heard no sound from the plumber and figured he was pouting.
The long, silent minutes drifted by, and in an effort to waken him, she offered,
"Clark, want some water?" She held the flashlight, poised to turn it on, but was
afraid of what she might see if she did. "Clark?"

Something hummed, buzzed, and zipped through the redness and landed on
her arm. She shrugged it away, but it kept darting around her head. Every so often
she could feel the slightest wisp of air as insects whirled past her face.

She pulled her shirt up over her head to keep the annoying bugs off her flesh.
Thump, thump, thump — rhythmic beating — she could hear it, feel it, and for
a brief moment, she even thought she could *see* it as the redness pulsated around
her. Must be her heart struggling to keep up with the demands her dehydrated
body was putting on it. Without water, her kidneys were failing and that made her
heart work overtime. She read somewhere that without water the body slowly
poisons itself.

Besides severe dehydration, infection also ravished her. With a compromised
immune system, her poor, little heart was working as hard as it could to keep
blood flowing to fight the infection. She imagined it finally giving up, saying,
"Fuck this job! I'm outta here," breaking through her chest, and scrambling up
the oubliette walls to freedom. A boulder of depression rolled onto her soul at
the thought of her own heart betraying her.

"Don't lose heart," she dimly whispered to herself.

The beating echoed softly against the cone-shaped oubliette walls. The more
she thought about it, the more she surmised it couldn't be her heart. The sound
was not coming from *inside* her. That meant it must be Clark's? Yes, that had to
be the answer.

She pulled her head out of her shirt like a turtle emerging from under its shell
and implored, "Clark? Talk to me. I'll tell you more about California," she
bargained. "Do you want to hear about Disneyland? About Mickey Mouse and
the rides and the food? Oh, they have cotton candy and churros and frozen
bananas covered in chocolate..."

Clark didn't respond.

Another insect landed on her face, on her cheekbone just below her eye. She
shooed it off and briefly thought about the nourishment it contained. Clark was
right — insects are a great source of protein. Swallowing a few might help her get
her strength back. Maybe the next time one buzzes her head she'd try to snag it

rather than just brush it away...

One zipped past her ear while another landed briefly on her hand. They sounded like flies. She tried to smack one dead, but it was too swift and easily escaped. It zipped around her head several times as if to taunt her before swooping off.

The buzzing flies momentarily grew silent. Distantly, she heard inhalations, like someone breathing. Veronica was not completely convinced the redness wasn't playing tricks with her sense of perception. She held her breath to make sure she wasn't actually listening to her own breath.

In and out, in and out. She was sure she heard it. Clark — it had to be — and this notion made her smile. He was okay. She hadn't hurt him too badly when she pushed him after all! He was just sleeping it off. She thumbed the flashlight — she could turn it on and see if his chest was moving....

Afraid of what she might see, she waited and listened to the rhythmic inhalations instead.

"Clark?" she asked, but got no answer.

She pinched her eyes shut and turned the flashlight on. She waited for Clark to protest. He usually groaned in the unexpected light, but not this time. She could still hear steady breathing, though, so Veronica opened her eyes.

Clark's eyes were also open. They were wide and staring directly at her. They didn't blink. His mouth gaped and flies whizzed in and out like bats in a cave.

"Clark!"

One landed on his unblinking right eye. She clicked off the light and pushed herself as far back as possible. Clark was at least six feet away from her, but it felt like he was right next to her, inches away, glaring at her with frozen bug-infested eyes. She covered her head with her arms. A fly landed on her pinky finger, and she squealed.

Even though she was hunched with her arms covering her head, Veronica could still hear breathing. It came from above...then came footfalls. Someone was walking around in the castle!

Her mortal terror turned to instant, insane glee. Veronica bellowed. Her dry throat cracked. "Is someone up there?"

She listened and waited. More footfalls, steady, regular. They were not of someone running to her aid, but of someone leisurely strolling. The sound was slightly hollow with a mild echo, and she quickly deducted it was coming from the parquet floor in the dining room. He or she walked slowly into the library. Veronica was amazed at how accurately she could pinpoint the sound. The breathing matched the pace of the footfalls. It was heavy, like that of a big man. He stopped just for a moment in the library by the entry to the ballroom.

Surely it was the police! Her sister had called them after all. "Help! Follow my voice. I'm in the oubliette!" she called.

The footfalls remained steady, consistent. This person wasn't bolting to her rescue. *He can't hear me*, Veronica thought. *Clark was right. No one in the castle can hear you from down here.* She clicked the flashlight on and aimed it straight up. If he even so much as glanced in the tower room, he'd see the signal.

The footfalls became louder, thunderous, like he was coming closer.

Excitement bubbled in her belly, and she imagined the taste of food and water. In just a few moments, she would be able to drink all she wanted. Her immediate thirst overcame her, and she pulled out the bottle. Only a few drinks were left. She slammed it. The last of the water was gone in a matter of three gulps.

She jumped up, holding the flashlight high, turning it on and off, and aiming at the ceiling.

She called, "Down here! Down here!"

"Veronica?" someone asked.

"Yes! I'm down here! In the oubliette!" Veronica stood on tip-toes and cried out to her rescuer. "Hurry!"

"Veronica?" The voice sounded like it was coming from the keep.

"Yes! It's me."

She heard her name called again. "Veronica?"

The voice sounded familiar.

"Down here!"

There was no answer. She waited a few moments and tried to dig her fingers into the slippery wall. She managed to get a slight hold and inched herself up slightly.

"Can you hear me?" she shouted.

The castle sat silent.

"Hello! Are you still there?" she asked.

There was no sound for several moments. Then the oubliette walls reverberated with a deafening shriek. Shrill and horrifying, Veronica could not be sure if she was listening to the sound of a human, or something else.

"Are you okay?" she yelled.

There was a quick answer. "Oh my God!"

She finally recognized the nasally voice. "Ralph?"

There was another cry, and this time Veronica also heard scuffling. Frantically, she implored, "What's happening?"

"It's blocking me from getting any closer to you!" was his answer.

"What is? Marie-Claire?" Veronica asked, assuming the manipulative specter was preventing her rescue.

"Does Marie-Claire have gnarled black hair, razor sharp claws, and oddly-human eyes that slice into your very soul?" he asked.

Veronica's gut stung. "No," she answered meekly.

"Then this ain't her," Ralph replied.

⇜❖⇝

Nikki lounged beside the pool with a floppy hat, enormous black sunglasses, and a fruity cocktail that was the same blue color as the chlorine water. She sucked in her tummy and adjusted her electric-pink bathing suit top as Christophe approached.

"Hi, honey, you're home early! How was work today?" she beamed like a fifties housewife and giggled as he sat on the patio chair across from her.

He smiled thinly and said, "Ralph left a message earlier. Said he was going to

489

the Château and is wondering if we've talked to Veronica lately. Has she called you yet?"

Nikki casually picked up her phone and scanned at the display. "Nope, nothing since her date with Clark. But that's not unusual. She gets like that sometimes."

"Gets like what?"

"She's very stubborn and goes dark for days, even weeks."

"Goes dark?" he questioned her terminology.

Nikki shrugged. "Yeah, she turns off her phone, ignores emails, ya' know, goes *dark*."

Christophe cradled his cellphone thoughtfully and tapped numbers with a stylus. "I'll try, even just to hear her voice, so we know she's okay."

Nikki breathed an almost imperceptible sigh of relief when he dictated a message.

"Veronica, we've all been trying to reach you, Ralph, your sister, and me. Just want to make sure everything's okay. Call me...call one of us, okay?" Christophe said and slowly clicked the hang-up button.

Nikki licked at the straw in her drink and asked, "So whaddaya wanna do this weekend? It's my last in town..." she trailed off.

Christophe gazed over her lean, tan body and lingered on her thighs before answering. "You are so beautiful. And a funny girl, with a lot of spunk." He smiled broadly and then furrowed his brow seriously. "But you're not *my* girl, Nikki. I should have said something sooner. I guess I thought maybe...but the truth is I made a mistake that night when I kissed you at the party. I intended to kiss Veronica. I know she isn't interested in me. I understand her heart belongs to her ex-boyfriend, Robert, and now she's dating this plumber-guy. I should've said all this sooner, but I thought maybe you and I would eventually hit it off. And we have become very close, but I still pine for your sister. I'm sorry. You are my friend, a dear sweet person who I've had so much fun with. You've had fun, too, no?"

Nikki sulked and nodded. "Yeah, we've had good times."

"And we can have more. Let's spend the weekend wine tasting. Take a drive through the valley; maybe stop at the Château and check on your sister and see if she and the plumber want to come with us."

She rolled her eyes to the left and guiltily looked up at him over the top of her thick sunglasses. "I gotta tell you something about *the plumber* and Vern," she started.

Christophe cocked his head and a tuft of hair flipped onto his forehead. "Yes?"

"You just told me the truth, so you also deserve to *hear* the truth," she explained with a sigh of resignation.

Christophe paused and considered the earnest tone of her voice before conceding. "Yes, okay, continue."

She carefully stated, "Well, Vern and Clark," she carefully began. "They're just hanging out in that old castle as happy as two rabbits in a rabbit hole. And they're fucking like rabbits, too. That's just the way Vern is. She's having a good time and really doesn't want me around bugging her. If we go over there, well, it'll just piss her off. I'm her sister. I gotta respect her space, ya' know?"

"I didn't realize," Christophe began, but Nikki didn't let him finish.

"I should have told you before. I knew you still had a *thing* for her, and I just didn't want to see you hurt. I mean, finding out someone you like is still in love with their ex is hard, but it's another thing to learn that person is fucking some scuzzy plumber. And to think, she picked him to fuck over you — man, that's gotta be a blow to the ego! I mean, it's one thing if she ain't interested in you, but to shack up with some dude with shit under his fingernails instead...eew! I just didn't wanna see you hurt, big guy."

"Thanks," he answered.

He vacantly allowed her to pluck his phone out of his open palm. She casually flung it onto a fluffy beach towel and dropped a tube of sunscreen into his hands instead.

Nikki flashed a beaming smile and said, "Let's just hang here and drink some wine because c'est la vie! You and I can enjoy the next two days with no worries about anyone else." She flipped onto her stomach and unsnapped her bikini top. "Let's just not think of Vern and her sleazy sex-capades, okay? We can be buds and just hang out and have fun without her. Wanna rub me down a bit, Chris?"

Like a zombie, he slowly squeezed the tube of sunscreen onto her bare shoulders. She squirmed and arched her back as he robotically massaged it in.

Inside the Oubliette

Veronica feared she knew what blocked Ralph from the oubliette, but she asked nonetheless. "Who's up there with you, Ralph?"

"The Templar Demon," he answered gravely.

"You mean the djinn?" she asked dimly.

"I don't think this is really the time to argue about what we should call it…" His cocky voice fluttered.

"Yeah, right." She felt detached from the surreal world around her.

"Do you have The Head down there, dear?"

"Yes!" She snapped from her stupor and dug it from her messenger bag.

"You gotta hurry," he shouted as a cacophony erupted.

She heard screeching as sharp claws scraped across stone, mixed with the sound of scuffling footfalls.

"What's happening up there?" she asked.

"It's getting pissy! Do you know the *name?*"

"Yeah, it's the same as Christophe's!" she proudly answered and lifted the crystal skull high, aiming it at the struggle taking place several feet above.

"Then use it quick…" he was cut short with a hollow thud. He wheezed heavily, as if the wind had been knocked out of him.

Veronica recalled from her dreams how Baldebert whispered the name to activate the skull. She did the same. "Christophe, I order you to back down."

From above, Ralph cried out in agony.

"Christophe, leave him alone!" she commanded again.

"Veronica, use the Head to stop it!" Ralph wailed.

"I am!" she called and then to it, tersely instructed, "Back off, Christophe."

"Quick! Call it by name!" he pleaded.

Frantically, she bellowed, "Christophe, I order you to back down!"

She dropped the flashlight. With a clunk, it landed on a filthy pile of bones and illuminated Clark. The plumber grinned maniacally at her. From above, the jarring sound of breaking bones echoed down the oubliette.

Ralph howled.

"Stop, leave him alone!" Veronica shouted. "Christophe, I order…"

Ralph interrupted her. "Not *that* name; the other one…"

Veronica's skin prickled as she sickly realized the name was *not* "Christophe". She sobbed. "What *other* one?"

Ralph coughed and blubbered like he was choking, and the only audible syllables were, "Terr-ah-ga…"

"Ralph!" she bawled over and over again. "Ralph! Ralph!"

But Ralph never answered her again.

❧❧ ❖ ❧❧

The crimson wine clung to the inside of the glass as Christophe swirled it. "See how thick? That's good; shows the wine has a nice body."

Nikki raised her glass and swiveled it next to his. They lounged in the poolside cabana with a plate of fromage, jam and crackers, and two bottles of smoky cabernet on the table between them. She held up her glass and ogled through it as if studying Christophe with a magnifying glass.

"The wine isn't the only thing around here with a nice body," she answered.

Christophe shyly smiled and retorted, "Yes, of course, *you* have a nice body, *too*."

"I meant *you*, silly!" she exclaimed.

"Let's toast to this beautiful sunny afternoon." He cordially tipped his glass toward hers.

Nikki scowled playfully. "Let me show you how to toast LA-style. First, lift your glass high, and then we clink, sink and drink!" She clanked his glass hard, tapped hers on the table, and slammed half a glass of red.

"You *sip*, you don't *clink, sink and drink* cabernet!" He shook his head disapprovingly, but grinned none-the-less. "It's going to be an interesting night, isn't it?"

"Damn right it is, Chris!"

Chapter 142

Inside the Oubliette

eep within the aperture, the American girl beseeched, "Ralph, please tell me you're okay. Please, just say it. Say anything."

Ringing silence was the response.

"I'm sorry I didn't know the name. I thought it was "Christophe", but I was wrong. I've been wrong about so many things. Forgive me?"

After an eternity with no answer, she reclined upon a bed of bones, her predecessors, and prepared to join their ranks.

"I'm done. I give up, okay? I'm ready to just die already."

Veronica shut her eyes and waited for something to happen.

A sinister form hovered at the cusp of the oubliette. It studied her for several minutes before slinking through the opening. Lanky arachnid-like legs scaled the fissure until it stopped just a couple feet overhead. A drop of silky-white foam dripped from its maw and landed gently on her shoulder.

She twitched. "Just do it fast," she whispered.

It flinched and swiftly scooted back up the oubliette and skulked away. It would leave her be for now, but it would be back.

Chapter 143

Inside the Oubliette

eronica was still alive. She had fully expected death to grip her one way or another, but several hours passed and nothing happened. Mortal terror lifted after the first hour and was replaced with nervous agitation. Veronica waited expectantly.

And waited…and waited…but nothing came to do her in.

Ralph almost saved her. She had been so close to rescue! And now he was — Veronica didn't want to accept the truth — he was lying up there hurt. Yes, he was still alive, just knocked unconscious. Or maybe he had escaped. Perhaps he ran away and was now bringing help to come back and save her!

The redness of the oubliette pulsated like a beating heart around her. It matched the rhythm of the throbbing pain in Veronica's ankle and forearm. It resonated a single phrase: *Ralph is dead. Ralph is dead. Ralph is dead.*

"Another one *dead* because of you, Veronica!" a chorus of voices cried in the megaphone-shaped oubliette.

Marie-Claire and all the specters chanted the single truth that Veronica didn't want to face. They hovered nearby, ever-present, wafting in and out of her reality as she drifted in and out of sleep. Veronica jolted, and the taunting voices grew quiet.

"I didn't mean to kill anybody. No one was supposed to die," she whispered to those who judged her. "I came here to decorate a castle. I came here for you, Marie-Claire. I wanted to finally do a big design by myself, without Robert's name attached to it. I wanted to show him, and the rest of the world, I could do it. Wanted to make some money and get out of debt. And then I met Christophe, and I thought maybe I could fall in love, too. But I didn't want anyone to *die*! I didn't want to fall into this miserable hole and get trapped with a dead plumber." Veronica heaved with anguish. "I didn't ask for any of this. And now I just want out. Why can't I get out?" She blubbered.

As she cried herself to sleep, the shadow people answered her. "You can get out, as long as you help all of us out, too."

Veronica demanded, "How, how, how…" as she submerged into oblivion.

Chapter 144

Inside the Oubliette
Day Four
Friday, 9:25 PM

It was Friday night, but Veronica didn't know that. Time had stopped for her long ago.

"Ralph?" she asked every so often. There was never a response.

Emptiness consumed her insides with a thick blackness matched only by the outside darkness of the oubliette. Like she was being submerged in oil, it swathed her completely.

Veronica didn't dare turn on the flashlight. She didn't want to see Clark; didn't want to face the man she killed.

"For water," the specters added. "You killed a man over a couple measly drops of water."

His corpse lay a few feet away, and Veronica was afraid to look. Even though the darkness was absolute, she sat with her eyes tightly shut.

"I didn't mean to kill you, Clark. It was an accident," she pleaded. But in the darkness of the oubliette, Clark didn't accept her apology.

❧❧❖❧❧

Nikki twirled in the shallow end of the pool. Her bare breasts glistened under the hanging patio lanterns as she called out, "Come on, Chris, come swimming with meee!" She splashed at him as he dodged from the safety of the cabana to the French doors.

"You are the craziest girl I know!" he shouted back. "Let me get my swim suit."

Nikki swiveled her hips and pulled off her bathing suit bottom while proclaiming, "Who needs a swimsuit? We don't need no *stinking* swimsuits. Just get your ass in the pool." She held her bottoms high above her head and waved them like a flag before tossing them at the man ducking inside.

Christophe shut the door behind the giggling girl just in time to avoid a wet bathing suit to the head. He mouthed the words, "Missed me," from behind the safety of the glass door. She shrugged a casual shoulder and reclined in the water, floating on her back and exposing her full, naked form.

He went to his bedroom and steadied himself by clutching the bedpost as the wine filled his temples with warm temptation. Babette popped her head up lazily. She was curled on a dog bed in the corner. She watched her master with a cocked neck and expectant brown eyes.

As Christophe pulled his bathing suit out of the dresser, a helpless vision of Veronica resonated in his mind's eye. He paused as he pulled down his trousers and wondered what she was doing at that precise moment. He imagined she was with Clark, probably enjoying an evening together. Despite what Nikki told him, he couldn't imagine her having sex with him. No. Instead, Christophe chose to think of a lonely girl merely seeking comfort and companionship.

"Oh Babette, how I wish it had worked out different between her and I."

Babette sniffed the air as if that would help her find an answer for her master.

"I know I blew it. I can only wish her the best, and hope she's happy...whatever Veronica is doing, I just want her to be happy."

Babette huffed the way that tired dogs do, and laid her chin on her paws. Christophe whispered, "Stay," grabbed a towel, and jogged back out to the pool to let Nikki distract him for the rest of the night.

Chapter 145

Inside the Oubliette
Day Five
Saturday, 12:05 AM

Veronica bawled dry tears. Her body heaved from anguish. The slices on her arms where Clark gnashed the nail file throbbed. Her ankle seared with pain like it was on fire. It was swollen to twice the normal size, and the wound was sticky and festering. With no fluids to keep toxins filtered, the infection spread unchecked. She imagined it surging through her body like a warm swarm of insects.

Desperately, she pressed the empty water bottle to her mouth. No wetness. She pushed harder until her parched lips split open. Thick blood soaked onto her tongue, and she imagined it was cool, refreshing water. She drank it down.

When finished "drinking" she ceremoniously screwed the cap back on and returned the bloody water bottle to her messenger bag like normal. It bumped against the prescription pills as she tucked it inside.

"Pills," Veronica said.

If she had full use of her faculties and her regular strength, the word would have resounded against the thick stone walls with ecstatic enthusiasm. She proudly realized that she still had the pills! But her delirium was so intense and her body so weak that the word was just a scratchy whisper.

There were ten, maybe twelve, pills left. In her fragile state, just a few pills would probably do the trick. Ten, though, that would be enough to kill her twice!

She shook the bottle. The pills pleasantly rattled. She grinned and cooed like an infant playing with a toy. The pills could end it all — no more suffering, no more guilt, no more thirst and hunger.

Hoarsely, she asked, "What would these pills do? Would they make me big or small? Should I go ask Alice when she's ten feet tall? Huh, Cheshire Cat? Chesh, what do you think?"

In the redness, she imagined Clark's disembodied grin form into a Cheshire Cat beside her. The phantasm answered, "You don't need to take those pills, Veronica. Just rest some more, no need to be dramatic. Sleep now, just sleep."

❧❦ ✤ ❧❦

Christophe bent down and kissed Nikki on top of the head. She leaned forward and together they both fell against his bedroom door. "Oh!" she exclaimed as he cried, "Whoa!"

Laughing, they regained their balance, and he firmly clutched her shoulders. "I'm going to bed now, and you should, too."

"Alright, let's go," she said and pushed him against the door again.

"No! You be a good girl," he teased. "And go to *your* room."

"Are you seriously still st-stuck on my st-stupid sister?" Nikki sputtered.

"It doesn't matter. What matters is we drank three, count them..." He held up four fingers and smirked. "*Three* bottles of my finest reds. I have a rule, no sex after drinking three bottles of wine. It only leads to very bad things in the morning."

"Sounds like the voice of experience!"

"Yes, I have experience, my dear. Once they called me the most eligible bachelor in all of the Loire. Trust me, I had *many* experiences."

She pushed at him again, but he held his ground, and she merely bounced off his bare, broad chest.

"Then why not add one more to the list?"

"I don't add women to my list. I'm not that guy anymore, Nikki. All those girls, those relationships, if that's what you want to call them, they were all so shallow. So...so *blah!*" He stuck out his purple tongue and grimaced. "I'm going to sleep now. See you in the morning." He bent and gave her another tender kiss on the brow, turned, and slipped into his bedroom.

Nikki stood there several moments in the dim hallway and stared dopily at the slightly ajar door. She shrugged her shoulder and followed him inside.

Chapter 146

Inside the Oubliette

eronica heard something. *Was it a voice?* She lifted her tired, throbbing head and asked, "Who's there?"

No one answered, but Veronica sensed a presence. She cradled the flashlight. Her voice cracked as she persisted. "Is someone there?"

This time there was a reply. "Oui, I'm right here; where I've always been."

It was Clark.

Overwhelming relief surged into her sluggish soul. Guilt and depression melted away. *Clark was okay after all!*

"You're all right?" Veronica answered excitedly. "Oh my God, Clark, you were asleep for...I don't know how long...hours. Christ, are you okay? I thought you were..."

"Dead?" he finished her sentence.

"Yeah, but I wasn't sure. I kept trying to wake you, but you just slept. And then Ralph came to help us, but something happened. I heard him scream then there was a struggle. I don't even know if it was real or a dream. I don't know anything anymore. I don't know what day it is or why my sister isn't here. I don't even know if I'm going to live or die."

"You're going to die, Veronica."

Veronica haltingly asked, "What-did-you-say?"

"You are going to die, Veronica. That is your answer. And you should be grateful. Dying is the best thing that could happen to you. Just accept it. It will make everything much easier."

"Clark, what they hell are you talking about?"

"I'm talking about the inevitable. You're going to die, so why not get it over with? It's easy enough to do. You've been thinking about it, no? Eating those pills. Pop, pop, pop! Pop those pills, Veronica. It is only death that awaits you. And trust me, there are some things that are worse."

Veronica aimed the flashlight at him. She hadn't turned it on since Ralph had been there. A weak thumb pressed the switch slowly. She hoped the batteries were dead, so she wouldn't have to look. The light flickered with full intensity, however, and illuminated Clark's bloated carcass. His thin, rice paper-like skin was now puffy and blue. The eyes were yellow and crusted with puss. His jaw hung wide open, more open than nature should allow, and Veronica imagined that the tendons which secured it had lost their elasticity as the body decomposed. Flies twirled in and out as their offspring squirmed in the mouth like naked baby birds in a nest.

Even though it was infested, the jaw moved up and down, and the bloated tongue wiggled to form words.

"You can't defeat it. You know you can't. You are too weak, and there is no one who can save you now. You're better off dead, Veronica. Better off if you swallowed every last one of those yellow pills right now. You have enough to do the deed. Your body is weak, dehydrated. It won't take much to destroy it. Accept your fate like I did. Because you won't be able to handle the alternative, Veronica."

"No!" she cried and threw the flashlight at the animated corpse. It hit squarely on the forehead, causing the flies to swirl up in a spiraling, buzzing vortex. The flashlight landed with a thud in the center of the pit and flashed like a strobe.

The insects blindly batted against her flesh. She shielded her face as they dive-bombed her and became tangled in her matted hair. Her fingers manically ran through her greasy tendrils. The flies were everywhere. Some landed on her, while others flew straight into her like mini kamikazes.

She rubbed her hands up and down her entire body trying to evacuate the insects. Several clung to her festering ankle. She shrieked with revulsion. They had landed on her *open* wound — *did they lay eggs there?*

She cried out again, and one flew in her mouth. She tried to spit it out, but instinctively, her throat swallowed. The fat, juicy insect slithered effortlessly down her esophagus and into her gut. Disgusted, she coughed, but nothing came up. Her body happily accepted any kind of nutrition at that point, and it wasn't about to forfeit a nutritious morsel of protein, no matter how revolting it was.

Veronica curled up and became as small as possible as the insects twirled around her. Her frantic feet kicked at the bones and debris as she tried to force herself into the cool stones of the oubliette wall. Veronica pretended she melded into them, disappearing into the bricks and mortar and away from the corpse and the flies. The redness engulfed her, and she imagined it wrapping around her like a mummy...or like a spider binding its prey. Veronica enjoyed being swaddled. It felt comforting and protective. It buffered her from the horrors in the pit.

In the safety of her imaginary nest, Veronica's stomach gurgled happily and digested the bug. It had been a big one — a large fatty, about the size of a blackberry.

As she drifted in and out of consciousness, she imagined being cocooned in her Snuggie blanket, sitting in front of her TV in her West Hollywood studio apartment, dining on a big bowl of succulent, buzzing blackberries.

Chapter 147

Inside the Oubliette

Flies tasted good. Veronica was repulsed by the fact she knew this. It was true, though. They tasted nutty, most similar to almonds, with slight "minty" undertones. Though mushy, they had a subtle crunch to them. It was almost a "pop", which was most likely their huge, multi-lensed eyes bursting on the impact of her molars.

Another one landed on her arm. She smacked it quickly, mushing it into a gooey glob of protein, and licked it from her palm.

"They don't taste as good as spiders, though, I bet," she said to Clark.

Clark didn't answer. She was grateful for that.

Veronica wasn't sure if Clark really had talked to her earlier. Her dreams, her imagination, the wicked way the oubliette seemed to twist reality, all left her questioning everything. She pondered whimsically if anything was real. Maybe the whole thing was a dream. The thought momentarily comforted her, and she wished with all her might it were true.

She sat upright, strength returned to her atrophied muscles because of the infusion of protein. She reached her arm up high, another fly landed on it, and she smacked it.

"Fly fishing!" She giggled at her clever play on words. The laugh turned into a hoarse cough. "Missing the water, though..."

Veronica knew if she didn't get water into her body soon, no amount of flies would save her. The best she could hope for was that since Ralph had come looking for her, then others would, too. Perhaps Nikki would be here soon. She wondered if she dared to hope that help was still on the way.

After filling up on a meal of flies that would have fed a hundred hungry spiders, Veronica glumly decided that Clark wouldn't allow her to have hope. As her tummy made rumbling, gurgling, digesting sounds, she whispered, "What happened here will haunt me forever, won't it?"

Thankfully, Clark still didn't answer. But he didn't need to. He would always be with her. His specter would follow her for the rest of her life — however long or short that might be.

❦❧ ❖ ❦❧

Sunlight seeped through the translucent curtains in the master bedroom as morning gnawed its way into Christophe's fuzzy head. A crusty eye slowly opened. He saw Nikki lying next to him. He quickly pushed himself up on his elbows and saw she was naked — and so was he.

Babette, still in her dog bed, watched him kick the twisted sheets off his ankles and take the slow walk of shame across the room to the master bath.

Inside, Christophe washed his face and swirled mouthwash across his dry palate. While drying his hands, he noticed an empty condom wrapper on the marble vanity.

He stared at it as Babette strolled in, sat next to the bidet, and observed him curiously.

"Oh, Babette, what did I do?"

Babette answered by hunching over and licking her crotch.

"You don't say."

She stopped and gazed back at her master. Christophe held her non-judgmental stare while scanning his fragmented memories from the night-before.

Distinctly, he recalled going to bed *alone*. He had practically fallen asleep the moment his head hit the pillow. Did he black out? Was he really *that* drunk?

From within the bedroom, Nikki cooed, "Christophe, come back to bed! It's too early to get up. Come lay with me for a while longer."

For reasons Christophe could not control, his penis responded to her voice with a twitch. Not knowing what else to do, Christophe sulked back to his bed and the eager blonde beneath its covers.

Chapter 148

Inside the Oubliette

Someone wiped her brow. A soothing, cool hand caressed her feverish forehead, and it felt *so* good. Veronica hadn't even realized how hot she was until she felt the icy touch. It made her shiver in a brief spasm, and she grinned dopily for a moment.

The hand cupped her cheek. *Who was touching her?* Her groggy mind attempted to focus and finally remembered. *I'm in the oubliette with Clark's corpse!*

Veronica was instantly alert. Urgently, her eyes searched the dark for the culprit, but sight was the most useless of her five senses in the dark pit.

The hand touched her again. This time it brushed the greasy hair out of her eyes.

"Who's there?" she managed to whisper, even though she didn't want to know the answer.

The specter of the thin Holy Man in the old, tattered cassock vaguely appeared before her, as if his figure was suddenly illuminated with a hazy, grey light. He knelt beside her and answered calmly, "I am here, with you, always."

Delirious, yet hopeful, Veronica asked, "Are you God?"

"No," came the gentle answer. "But I can lead you to Him."

She took a moment to assess the situation as her brain found clarity and focus. His touch made the fever subside, and she lucidly asked, "Am I dead?"

"No, you're still alive."

"Damn it!" she cried. "Why can't I just be dead already? Oh, sorry, didn't mean to swear, Father."

"It is perfectly alright. You've been through a lot. You earned the right to swear." He grinned with curling, crooked lips.

"I think I recognize you. You were at the party...and in my dreams. You're Father Michel, right?"

He nodded. "Yes. I'm glad you remember. I wasn't sure how effective we were at penetrating your dreams."

"It's a little fuzzy, and I don't recall all the details of your story. I know you lost your parish, your lover, your best friend, and your faith."

"I've been blessed, though, with renewed faith. I know He waits for me now, along with Gaston-Elise and Claudeen. He's waiting for you, too, Veronica. It isn't too late to have faith and trust in Him."

"I've never believed in God," she said. "Seems pretty hypocritical to start now."

"That's the amazing thing about His grace, Veronica. You can turn yourself over to Him at any time. You just have to show faith. He'll forgive you as long as you believe in the Father and the Son and the Holy Spirit."

"Seems too easy. You're saying I just have to have faith, and that's it. I'm in, even though I never believed in God my entire life?"

"Faith is easy, Veronica, you simply release all your doubts, and there it is!"

"But I *killed* Clark! I'm a murderer. That's a pretty big sin, right? I'm sure God isn't gonna let that one slide."

"Even a sin as immense as murder is a tiny infraction in the eyes of the Lord. It can be absolved. All sin can be cleansed."

"And Ralph is dead because of me, too," she avowed. "If I had known the name like I thought I did, I could 'a saved him. Not to mention Dr. Sandbourne. He came all the way here to rescue me and look what happened to him. I got a lot of sins to account for, Father. I don't think a little blind faith will do much for my eternal soul. I'm damned no matter what. There's no way I can be forgiven."

The priest whispered a silent prayer, waited a moment, and then answered. "But there is a way. You can make a penance and all will be forgiven."

"A penance?"

"Sure, many have earned their way into Heaven with penance," Father Michel assured her.

"What's that mean?"

"If you release all the trapped souls here, your sins will be absolved. God is giving you the opportunity to remit what you've done. You just have to take advantage before it's too late."

"So, I do something good, and it erases my mistakes?"

"One can never erase the past, but you can set things right for the future. By helping us, you free yourself. It's that easy, Veronica."

Veronica became frustrated. "But *how* do I free you?" she whined.

Father Michel leveled his kind eyes into hers and carefully stated, "You have to distract the beast long enough for all of us to move on to the other side. Fight it. Challenge it! You don't need the Head. Your determination and willpower alone are enough to engage it and drive it back."

"No, Father, I can't. I'm too weak, and I don't even know *how* to fight."

"Veronica, I can't force you. No one can. We can only ask for your help. The choice is yours alone to make. Time is running out, though, so if you do this, you have to act fast."

"Do what exactly? I tried to drive it back with the Head when it attacked Ralph, and it didn't work. I don't know what to do!"

He explained, "You have to face it in its domain. Confront it where it lives," he explained. "Remember, you are a conduit between worlds."

"But I'm only a conduit when I'm asleep. It just happens. I don't control it," she whined.

"You're more in control than you think. The power you wield is immense. Only fear is keeping you from fulfilling your destiny. Go forward with confidence, child. All obstacles will prove to be imaginary."

"If it really were that easy..." she began.

"Just close your eyes, fall asleep, and imagine yourself entering our world. You'll do just fine. You'll see. Don't worry. I will pray for you."

Before Veronica could answer, he was gone. In his wake, as if the priest had shielded her, all the pain and misery returned to her body. The fever seared into her brain, her ankle throbbed, hunger gnashed in her gut, and thirst scorched her throat. The oubliette became dark, and she was once again trapped inside her miserable skin.

ঌৡ❖ঌৡ

Nikki's left arm and leg were draped over Christophe. He couldn't fall back to sleep and lay there for hours trying to figure out how he could have caved in to her advances. He rose, and she groaned in protest. He sat on the corner of the bed, cleared his throat, and began.

"Last night..."

"Was a lot of fun, wasn't it?" Nikki interjected. Though she was groggy, she hadn't lost her snap-quick wit.

"No, that's not what I was going to say. Nikki, you're always fun to be with. You make me laugh. But I need to know if..."

She poked at his ribcage playfully and interrupted. "If you're ticklish?"

He squirmed. "No. I *know* I'm ticklish." He gently cinched her hand and continued. "I need to know if we..."

She sliced into his questions again. "If we got shit-faced drunk last night? Why yes, we did, Mr. Man." She pouted and slithered up behind him as he gazed past the gauzy, veranda curtains at the rolling hills of the Loire Valley.

He rested his face in his hands and hunched over. "Nikki, I need to know if we slept together last night. You're right. We did drink a lot of wine, and I guess I don't remember everything too clearly."

She stopped playing, became stoic and still, and paused dramatically before answering. "Of course we slept together, silly!" She wrapped her arms around his neck and giggled gleefully.

Christophe pulled her hands off his chest. "I see," he stammered and rose.

He looked down at her in the sea of white downy pillows and comforters that was his bed. Though she held the blanket up to her chest, one perfect, round breast peeked out. Nikki didn't try to cover herself.

"Christophe!" she cooed alluringly, but Christophe turned and left his bedroom, with Babette at his heel, before Nikki could say more.

506

Chapter 149

Inside the Oubliette

Veronica didn't know she was sleeping the day away. The fever made her confused and stupid, and she often forgot where she was.

They came to visit her. One at a time, the specters surrounded the girl. They wanted her. They needed her. They prayed for her. Once every so often, the fever would release its grip, and she'd become aware they were there. But she didn't care.

Because she had spiders in her hair.

"La-la-la Veronica doesn't care 'cause she's got spiders in her hair," Veronica sang and giggled at her goofy rhyme.

The redness of the oubliette throbbed as she made up more poems. "I don't care 'cause I got spiders in my hair. Don't you dare mess with me 'cause I got no juice left to pee!"

She rolled in the bones with ecstatic laughter. Endorphins released by extreme dehydration made her euphoric — and oblivious to her environment. "I got my hair done, Robert. It was done up real pur-tee like! You would 'a liked it. Christophe would 'a liked it, too, if my ho-bag sister hadn't gotten in the way! What a little bitch, huh?"

Ethereally, she saw Cheshire Cat's smile in the dancing globules of the red oubliette. "Hey, Chesh, how's it hanging? You seen my ho-bag sister around lately? If you do, scratch her eyes out for me, okay?"

The Cheshire Cat's smile nodded, and she drifted back into a deeper sleep while murmuring, "I don't care 'cause I got a ho-bag sister..."

❦❧❖❧❦

Nikki pranced around the kitchen in Christophe's thick, terry cloth bathrobe. Though it was the middle of the day, she refused to get dressed. She prepared a meal of vermicelli and sundried tomatoes in a butter-garlic sauce. A plate of cheese and wine accompanied the meal set out on the kitchen counter.

"Sweetie, come on, let's eat. I'm starving!"

Christophe emerged from the hallway that led to his study. He had spent all day there with the door closed. He wore a suit jacket and carried a binder with papers. "You cooked. I didn't know...I'm on my way into the office right now..."

"You're *working*? On a Saturday? I thought we could have a nice meal and maybe talk."

He grabbed a baguette and tore it in half. "I'll take this with. Sorry, didn't know you were cooking."

"Just sit and eat and listen to what I have to say..." she began, but he firmly interjected.

"Frankly, I don't know what there is to say, Nikki. It was a mistake, and it shouldn't have happened. I don't want to hurt your feelings, but I can't do...," he waved the baguette at her, at the food, and in a wide circle above his head, "...*this*!"

"What do mean by *this*? You mean we can't eat lunch now because we slept together? Wow, that's pretty lame, Chris."

He shook his head and grabbed his car keys from the counter. "I gotta go," is all he said as he dashed for the door.

"Wait!" she called behind him.

He glanced back inside before shutting the door.

"I'm not saying *this* is anything, Chris." She mockingly waved both her hands around and smiled with twisted lips that showed she was taunting him.

"I'm leaving now," Christophe said.

As Nikki objected, he closed the door and left.

Chapter 150

Inside the Oubliette

The flies were gone. Veronica's stomach churned hungrily. She wasn't sure if she had eaten them all up or if the clever little critters realized she was a threat and were intentionally keeping at bay. Like insects avoiding the web of a predator spider, the flies now instinctively eluded her.

"Come back little flies. I need to eat you," she called. "I need nourishment. Come here and *get in my belly*!"

But the flies did not return. She hadn't eaten any in hours, and the little strength they had provided quickly diminished.

"Chesh, where the flies at?" she asked languidly.

Chesh didn't answer.

Veronica squinted, desperate to see the disembodied smile, but it wasn't there. "Chesh, where *you* at?" she inquired.

There was no answer.

"Even my imaginary cat abandoned me," she groaned.

The euphoria Veronica felt earlier was fading. She envisioned despair churning the oubliette like a washing machine. Rhythmically, she rolled along with it into the bowels of anguish. Veronica held onto the slimy wall to steady herself as she felt the oubliette spin. Her hand slid easily along the smooth film of mold that covered the stone.

She remembered seeing the mold in white, slick patches when she first shined the flashlight on the oubliette walls several days ago. It made any hope of climbing out absolutely impossible. It was like a thin layer of silky salamander skin.

A piercing thought rippled through her fragile body. That mold needs some kind of moisture to grow, condensation most likely. That means the mold is alive and probably has some nutritional value. At the least, it's slightly moist and must contain some water!

Veronica wondered what the mold tasted like.

Though her mind was fevered, she also knew that mold could be toxic. If it were found in a home during renovation, a special cleaning crew needed to be called to remove it. Certain varieties of mold spores were harmful if inhaled. It even could be deadly. Veronica had no way of knowing what kind of mold was on the walls of the oubliette.

She wiped off a thin layer and rubbed it between her thumb and middle finger. It felt velvety at first, and the more she rubbed it, the thicker it got, like the consistency of snot. She sniffed it. No odor. *Was that a good sign?*

Black mold. She vaguely recalled hearing that black mold was dangerous. This mold was white, though, almost translucent.

"What's the worst that could happen, huh?" she asked herself as she licked the tips of her digits.

It had no taste at first. As the miniscule amount slid down her throat, she felt a subtle tingling. The aftertaste was bitterly-sweet, like bakers dark chocolate. She caressed the wall for more mold. The palm of her hand was covered in a thin layer, and she licked it, slowly at first, then faster as the moistness entered her stomach. Her entire body shuddered with pleasure as it coated her gut. The mold was *good*!

Reinvigorated, she scrapped off more and more. She never seemed to get enough. After just a couple licks, she had to swipe again. She stopped using her hand. Instead, Veronica licked the wall directly. The stone was cool and gritty against her lapping tongue.

Then she discovered that the mold was particularly thick in the cracks between the stones. She slid the tip of her tongue into the slit and slid it along, sucking up as much as she could. The mortar was slightly salty, making the flavor even more interesting.

Veronica enjoyed it. Fleetingly, she thought this meal was even better than the one at that pitch-dark restaurant. The flavors did more than dance across her palate. They did backflips, twisty-twirls, and somersaults!

Every once in a while she came across a tiny spider. She joyfully lapped it up, too. She thought of Clark. He would have liked this. They both could have licked the wall together.

And they both would have fought over licking the wall together.

"All mine now, Clark. Too bad, huh?"

As if in response, the Cheshire Cat's disembodied grin returned.

"Chesh, you're back!" Veronica exclaimed.

It joined her along the wall, licking and lapping and laughing. Veronica imagined a full-bodied kitty cat next to her. She even reached out to pet it. It purred and rolled over on its back.

"I wonder what *you* taste like, Chesh!"

The cat meowed teasingly in response. Veronica felt euphoria returning, but this time it was even more intense than before. She convulsed hysterically at her friend the cat and playfully nibbled at its paw.

"You can eat me if you'd like," the cat said amiably.

Veronica giggled at the goofy kitty. As she did, the room throbbed in sudden bursts of red. Like fireworks, everything was filled with bright, vibrant colors. The hues swirled together, and Veronica lay back for a moment and stared straight up. It was like being at the bottom of a giant kaleidoscope. The room spun and danced. Veronica even thought she heard music. She lapped at the wall some more. *God it tasted good!*

As if in response, the colors took shape and began sashaying around the oubliette like prancing ponies. Veronica could *see* the flavors. The bittersweet mold looked like a pretty white pony, a perfect replica of My Little Pony to be exact. The salt flavor was a turquoise-colored sea horse—a mermaid-horse—with a bright yellow flowing mane. The spiders were miniature black stallions with hundreds of tiny prancing legs.

And Chesh — she leaned over and nibbled on Chesh's paws some more — Chesh looked better than all the other flavors. Chesh was a fiery red mustang. It had orange stripes, like a tiger, and a huge, toothy grin. She liked the way Chesh tasted the most.

"You're sure you don't mind me eating you, right?" she politely asked.

Chesh purred an affirmation. "Of course not. Be my guest. You're starving. You deserve to gobble up any sustenance you can!"

She gnawed blissfully at the friendly, furry paw until she passed out from sheer joy. She awoke several hours later to find Clark's mangled hand cradled against her bosom.

Chapter 151

Inside the Oubliette

aking happened in incremental stages. First, Veronica flashed momentarily into consciousness, but quickly dismissed the notion like a sleepy teenager not wanting to get up for school. A little while later, a stabbing pain in her tummy made her reach down and cradle her abdomen. As she did, she realized dimly that she let go of something that she'd been cuddling in her arms as she slept.

Another hour slipped by before Veronica woke a third time. She coughed her way to lucidity. The mold not only gave her a maddening stomach ache, but it left a film in her throat making it raspy. She gagged as her body worked the toxin out.

A half hour after that, a semi-clearheaded Veronica finally came to as the memories of eating the mold came rushing back to her. She recalled all the events with crystal clarity. Licking the wall, hanging out with her imaginary cat, the beautiful swirling colors — it was like an acid trip. With sudden, morbid intelligibility, she wondered if the mold may have produced a hallucinogenic response, like some fungus, mushrooms and such, are capable of doing.

Was I tripping balls?

She reached out to brace herself as she sat up. Something flopped off her chest and landed next to her hand. She thought of Chesh. *What is that...?*

Cold dread climbed up her throat. Veronica remembered nibbling on Chesh's paws. The cat told her to eat it. Absolutely absurd now, that crazy notion seemed perfectly plausible hours earlier during her delirium.

But Chesh ain't real.

Veronica inched her hand toward the thing that had flopped on the ground. She stopped before touching it, afraid of what she was going to find.

"No, please, don't let this be real. Please, make it all a bad dream. Please, no," Veronica begged to no one in particular.

She sat there frozen, half propped up on her left elbow, for more than an hour. Her arm holding her upright grew numb and was about to collapse. Before it did, she suddenly reached out and grabbed Clark's half-eaten hand. It was stiff, like hard rubber, and the exposed meaty parts were sticky like thick, maple syrup.

Veronica hurled the hand back. In her mind's eye, she could see it, grey and bloated with black, gooey blood dribbling between the tooth-torn pieces of skin.

Next, her trembling hands reached up to her mouth. She wiped it frantically, scrapping the dried blood and pus off her chin.

For the next several hours, Veronica lay catatonic. She reclined on a dried-up bed of bones and willed her body to shut down. Her heartbeat slowed. Her brain activity decreased to just the most primitive of functions. Breathing was almost imperceptible. Like a hibernating animal, Veronica fell into the deepest sleep she ever had. It was filled with nothing — no dreams, no thoughts, nothing but bleak, black peace.

Chapter 152

Inside the Oubliette

eath refused to take the American girl. Even though what she consumed was thoroughly disgusting, it did provide some nourishment, and her body stubbornly clung to life. She awoke wondering if anything could possibly be worse than the hell she was currently in. Was any torture, any pain, any imaginable situation worse than what she was going through?

Veronica decided no.

Her last resort seemed the most logical option. With the flavor of Clark's decomposing flesh hanging heavily on her tongue, Veronica reached inside her messenger bag for the sleeping pills.

A few maggots squirmed in the depths of her bag. She wondered dimly how the pests got there. One stuck to her forefinger, and she flicked it toward the opposite side of the oubliette. As she did, her hand brushed against something hard. Her nail caressed a button. It was Clark's chest. She withdrew quickly, realizing his corpse was only inches away. He was no longer on the other side of the pit. He was right there *next* to her!

She shrieked and instantly burst into wailing sobs. If she were hydrated, her face would have been covered in tears, but instead, it became scalding hot as she cried out again and again.

She knew that Clark's exaggerated Cheshire Cat-like grin was directly in front of her. Crazily, she imagined him reaching out to grab her throat with his half-eaten hand. She pressed meekly against his chest. She realized his gaping maw was in perfect position to spew the pearly maggots into her open bag, like a shiny, sticky waterfall. Her breast heaved with a surge of consternation. The alien inside was finally going to burst free.

Veronica covered her face with her forearm, preparing for the inevitable. She was completely sure Clark was about to stick out his maggot-infested tongue and lick her face. When he did, it would all be over. She didn't need the pills because she would die of a heart attack — of sheer fright — the second that bloated, grey tongue touched her.

But it didn't.

Clark remained there, leaning in her direction, but didn't move. There was no attack, no licking, nothing at all.

It took almost an hour before she calmed enough to realize she must have dragged him closer to her when she had gnawed on his hand. Then his corpse simply shifted and slouched over, probably because rigor mortis was wearing off. The body had lost rigidity and went limp because decomposition was setting in. That's what happened. Clark's core muscles were turning to mush, and gravity pulled him down — at least that reason sounded plausible to Veronica's fevered mind.

Bravely, she summoned the courage to firmly push him back. A few of the maggots landed on her forearms as she shoved. The body made a crunching noise, as if his brittle bones were breaking. This made her pause for a moment.

"Fuck it!" she exclaimed and with all her might buried her shoulder into his and pushed him across the narrow room. Clark landed with a thud back on his side.

Shakily, she grabbed the pills. The bottle was covered in writhing worms, and she flicked them off one at a time. She wanted to be certain they were all gone, because if one accidentally fell in when she opened the bottle, and got mixed in with the pills, she'd accidently swallow it — that would be disgusting.

But nutritious.

She flinched at the thought. No, she didn't need to eat any maggots while committing suicide. That wasn't part of the plan!

But why not? She had eaten a dead man's hand; nothing could be more repulsive than that. Those maggots were probably ten times more nourishing than anything else she'd eaten — the flies, the mold, the rotting flesh. She certainly couldn't be squeamish over a few measly worms at this point.

The thought struck her like a slap in the face. The maggots were rich in protein. There were plenty of them, too, a lot more maggots than flies. And they were juicier than flies — filled with fluids — much needed fluids.

If she wanted to live, that is, if she truly wanted to remain in hell, holding onto life by a sinewy tendril, she could simply eat the maggots.

The pill bottle was now clean of the infestation. She had removed all of them. She struggled with the childproof cap. It cut into her paper-thin skin and held fast. Taking out the fingernail file, she poked at the edges of the cap until it finally snapped off. She had grown tired from the exertion and sat the pills aside before falling asleep.

⋖⋗ ❖ ⋖⋗

Nikki stirred olive oil into the leftover vermicelli. It was an odd breakfast, but she didn't feel like preparing anything without Christophe there. He hadn't come home last night, and she surmised he slept at his office.

She thought about her sister. She knew Veronica was furious. This was the longest the two sisters had ever gone without talking to one another.

She called Christophe again, but he didn't answer.

"Hey, Christophe, don't avoid me now. There's something I gotta tell you — something important. Just give me a chance to explain, okay?" She left the message and hoped this time he would finally call her back.

The sticky vermicelli glistened in the pan. She lifted the spoon and sucked up a few of the little noodles. Vaguely, she recalled that vermicelli translated into "tiny worms" in Italian.

Chapter 153

Inside the Oubliette
Day Six
Sunday, 10:23 AM

With the bottle of sleeping pills in one hand, and a squirmy dollop of maggots in the other, Veronica literally weighed her options. She fondled the repulsive creatures for a full hour. Getting used to the way they slithered over her flesh helped desensitize her to their disgusting nature. They rather tickled, and Veronica smiled briefly as they caressed her.

The pills, on the other hand, were hard and sterile. Produced in a laboratory, they seemed artificial in the truest sense of the word. Like an easy way out, the pills literally felt like death in her hand.

Death, it was easy, wasn't it? Since Veronica didn't believe in God or a hereafter, she imagined it would be similar to the nothingness she felt earlier when she went catatonic. If she were gone, there would be nothing. Since she wasn't alive to sense or experience anything, there would be no pain, no fear, no thirst, no guilt, no shame, no hunger, no longing, no regrets, nothing. That was tempting.

That theory only held true if everything she'd gone through since arriving in France was sheer fantasy...if she was truly crazy. Because if the ghosts were real, that meant the soul was real. It survived mortal death and was subject to pain and misery in the hereafter. Plus, she had been warned. Her death in the oubliette would result in her being trapped with the others in some limbo-like world, kept for eternity like a slave by the elemental-djinn. That did *not* sound tempting.

Another option, thought Veronica, was to do what Father Michel said. If she could somehow enter that limbo-like world, then maybe she could fight the djinn. Perhaps that's what she needed to do all along — go to battle on its turf.

She had nothing to lose.

"Might as well go down fighting, right, Vern?" she asked herself. "One last throw down? A rumble down under? An old-fashioned brawl?"

The alien in her chest seemed to like the idea of going to battle, and it rattled against her ribcage.

Veronica grinned in the darkness with her own Cheshire Cat smile. In that instant, she decided to fight. As she sucked up a handful of maggots, primitive survival instincts kicked in. Like a meek animal — like a rabbit backed into a corner — she prepared to fight. Veronica surprised herself by emitting a low, guttural moan. She actually growled out loud in anticipation of the brawl. Her senses heightened in preparation, and her alien heart infused adrenaline through her body.

If she was to fight, she needed her strength. She sucked down every last worm and nestled down for a good, long rest. With a little luck, she would awake revitalized. She'd be ready to fight.

❧❧❖❧❧

Nikki was done fighting. She sat on the veranda with Babette at her feet.

"He really loves Vern, doesn't he, dog?" she asked. "And there's nothing I can do to change it."

Babette licked one of Nikki's toes.

"Damn it, too bad Christophe won't do that."

She plucked on her phone:

Status Update: I'm coming home tomorrow! Gonna leave the boy behind. Too much baggage with that one. But I kinda like his dog...

She snapped a picture of Christophe's lovable pet and posted it with the update.

After a long pull of wine from a fingerprint-smeared glass, she finally called her sister.

Voicemail again. While pinching the ridge of her nose between her eyes she sighed, "Vern, call me back already, okay? Listen, nothing is going on between me and Christophe. He has a thing for you. Hear that? He wants *you*. I'm just hanging out at his place with Babette. He's not even here. He slept at his office last night. Come over, okay? Share a bottle of wine with me. Let's talk. You can't stay mad at me *forever*. After all, I'm your sister!"

Chapter 154

Inside the Oubliette

eronica bent over Clark's corpse. It stunk. But she didn't mind. She actually began to enjoy the fragrance. It was sweet, thick, musky, and natural. Just the scent of bacteria emitting waste as they broke down the carcass, that's all it was. It happened to everyone when they died — to every living thing. The maggots, they were simply a part of the process. They helped dead things decompose faster. Baby flies, that's what they were. Little, wriggly, children, getting nourishment so they become juicy and fat when they grow up.

"They're sort 'a like caterpillars that are getting ready to metamorphose into beautiful butterflies. Caterpillars that happen to look like tiny, white worms. So small, about the size of the mother of pearl beads on that necklace mom gave me for my last birthday, and about the same color, too," Veronica told herself.

The flashlight was dim, the battery almost completely dead. Occasionally, she'd shake it, causing it to flare up, and she'd get a good look at the caterpillars crawling in and out of Clark.

If Veronica had a mirror, she would see that her own face was now gaunt and shallow like Clark's was six days ago when she first fell in the oubliette. She had ashen skin, bulging eyes, and a yellow, crooked smile. With a recollection that resembled fondness, she remembered how Clark had licked spiders from his hands. He had told her, "Some countries pour chocolate over spiders and consider it a delicacy."

"Why yes they do!" Veronica replied to Clark as if he just uttered the words. "They put chocolate on top of all sorts of creatures like ants and slugs and even caterpillars." The flashlight went dim and a fat, juicy caterpillar morphed out of the redness and danced in the air by Clark's Cheshire Cat-like grin. "Hey, Chesh, look, it's a hookah-smoking caterpillar..."

"And what about escargot?" the caterpillar asked. "Just a fancy name for snails. Creepy, dirt-digging snails that look a lot like worms when you pry them out of their shells. Sautéed in butter and garlic, and they cost forty euro at those fancy restaurants in Paris."

"Yep," Veronica said as she scooped maggots from Clark's gaping maw. "You're right."

"Nothing wrong with noshing over a healthy serving of creepy crawlers now and then," the hookah-smoking caterpillar declared.

"You know in America there's a television show, *Factory of Fear*, where contestants eat bugs and worms. They just suck them down like they're the sugarcoated gummy variety.

"And they do that for money!" the hookah-smoking caterpillar cracked. "You're doing this to survive — to live! And ultimately, to fight!"

As she plucked the writhing worms from Clark's decaying flesh, she had a realization. I will never be the same again. This will change me forever. How many people in the world have eaten maggots off a two-day-old corpse? Not too many I suppose…

She was primitive now, more animal than human. Doing whatever was needed to survive, Veronica had chosen primal instincts as her savior.

The maggots on her fingers shimmered as she lit one of the last matches. *Nope, most people have never done this,* she thought as she sucked them down one at a time. She imagined them flavored with salt and pepper and a savory butter-garlic sauce. Then after some consideration, decided she preferred them raw and bloody, like any animal would.

Chapter 155

Inside the Oubliette

It hovered above Veronica, and she knew it was there. She could hear its nails click against the stone. The crystal skull throbbed in her hands. It was warm. Veronica caressed the smooth surface lovingly while her stomach gurgled happily. She felt strength return as her body absorbed the nourishing maggots.

Its lanky shadow drifted near the mouth of the oubliette. *Like a spider*, she thought. The spiders that infested the desert town where she grew up had webs that funneled into tiny black holes. The creatures would sit stoically just inside of their dens waiting for an unsuspecting caterpillar to crawl too close. Then they'd jump out, snatch their prey, and pull it into their lair.

"But you aren't a spider, are you?" Veronica whispered to her captor. "You're the ancient thing that the Druids worshiped. They called you a fire elemental. Dr. Sandbourne called you a djinn. Ralph called you the Templar Demon. They said that you're an entity as old as the Earth, made out of smokeless fire. You're just waiting for me to die, aren't you? You're guarding me right now, making sure no one comes along. You won't allow me to be saved because, as long as I'm alive, I'm a threat to you. But once I'm dead, I'll be just like all the rest. I'll join Marie-Claire, the priest, and all the others. You'll keep me trapped just like them."

She felt primitive rage quell in her mind. Like a trapped animal, she instinctively growled — low and threatening. It grunted back at her.

"I'm not gonna lay here and die for you," she whispered.

The elemental hissed at her defiance. Veronica felt all the rage of the past week come to a super-sharp head. Anger at her sleazy sister for seducing Christophe, anger for not being able to save Dr. Sandbourne, anger at the police for suspecting her of murder and sealing off the castle, anger at Gigi Jones for being a bitch and not coming back to film, anger at Clark for luring her into the keep, anger at Marie-Claire for trapping her down here, anger at the Priest and Sebastian and all the other shadow people for entering her dreams and manipulating her, anger at herself for not knowing the name and not being able to save Ralph, anger at the Cheshire Cat and the alien in her chest. Veronica was filled with nothing but anger, and at the heart of all her rage was that thing at the cusp of the oubliette.

"None of this would have happened if it wasn't for you." She held up the skull and rose to her feet. She wobbled. Though her body had some nourishment, it was still weak. Her knees trembled, and she almost lost her balance. "I command you to go back to hell, or wherever it is you're from. Leave this place! Leave these souls alone. Leave *me* alone!"

It snarled shrilly in retaliation.

Veronica braced herself with one hand on the wall, while the other held up the skull. She wasn't sure what to do next, but it didn't matter. A gust of heat, like a backdraft, shot down the pit and knocked Veronica off her feet. She fell but didn't hit the bottom. Instead, she kept falling — down, down, spinning round.

Veronica left the reality she knew and entered the world of the dead — a limbo-like wonderland where things were similar but far from normal. Veronica entered its domain.

ॐ✧ॐ

Nikki and Christophe scanned the crowd at the gate. She still wore her pajamas — yoga pants with "Juicy" scripted across the back, and a baby-doll Powerpuff Girls T-shirt — and squinted the sleep out of her eyes as she searched for Veronica. Christophe had picked Nikki up at 3:00 AM to take her to the airport. She never completely woke up despite the double espresso from the airport café.

"If she doesn't get here soon, she'll miss her flight," Nikki murmured. She glanced at the clock on the wall, which flashed 5:10 AM.

"Maybe I should see if she checked in yet," Christophe said.

"She's always late for stuff like this. We almost missed our flight to France because of her."

A loudspeaker voice announced, "Les passagers du vol numéro 24 à destination de Los Angeles sont invités à se présenter à l'embarquement porte B2."

"They're calling me." Nikki looked into Christophe's chocolate eyes.

"Your sister should be here now." He searched the faces as they filed in line.

"Ya' know, she prolly took an earlier flight. Hell, she's prolly already home! That would explain why she never came over yesterday after I called her. She got bored, switched her flight, and has been in LA for days."

"Yes, perhaps. Maybe I should have her paged?"

"Wait, there's something I gotta tell you..." Nikki had a peculiar look in her eyes, and it took a moment for Christophe to realize it was "seriousness".

Not wanting a mushy scene, he quickly interjected. "The airline can check to see if she checked in." He hurried off.

Nikki waited several minutes until he came back.

Shrugging and shaking his head, he said, "No, they don't have any record of her checking in yet. I wonder if she slept late."

"Then she'll catch the next plane. I'm sure she's doing this on purpose. Always the drama queen, that one. But there's something you need to know..."

"Nikki, don't. I told you already, we are good friends, buddies. I wish it could have been more..."

"Fuck! Listen, Mr. Most-Eligible-Dude, get over yourself for five minutes, and let me talk!"

Christophe gasped, but he held his tongue.

"When we slept together..." she began.

"Oh, no, I don't want to get into this..."

"Listen!" she snapped and stomped her foot. Several people turned to look as she loudly declared, "I didn't fuck you!"

Christophe stared at her dumbly for a moment.

In a more demure tone, she explained. "Yeah, we slept together, in the same bed, but we didn't have sex. We didn't have anything. You were already passed out when I crawled in. I snuggled beside you, but you were the perfect gentleman."

He narrowed his lips suspiciously. "But I found a condom wrapper in the bathroom," he challenged.

Nikki looked sideways coyly and rasped, "Well, big boy, it wasn't like I didn't *try*! You weren't into it though. After a couple minutes, I gave up and fell asleep."

Growing angry, he asked, "Then why did you *tell me* we slept together?"

"I was yanking your chain. I tried to explain, but you took off to work and wouldn't return my calls."

"Damn, Nikki, why'd you do all this?"

"I dunno." She shrugged like a child caught red-handed in the cookie jar. "I'm just used to getting my way, I guess. You were like a challenge, like a freaking white whale or something. I thought for sure I'd crack ya', but I guess you really do have a thing for Vern."

"Yes, but I know it'll never work out between her and I anyway. She's with the plumber now..."

"Oh. About Clark," she began and flushed as she confessed her white lie. "There really isn't anything going on there. Least I don't think so. I kinda embellished that so you'd get your mind off of her."

"So, she's not in love with him?"

She continued. "I'm sorry. I didn't think you had it for her that bad. I shouldn't have done this. Forgive me, please?"

Christophe didn't accept her apology. Instead, he pried. "And Robert? What about him? Is she still in love with Robert like you said?"

She winced, hung her head, and let floppy bangs hide her eyes as she confessed. "No. She took their split hard, but it's been nearly a year. She's pretty much over him now."

The fluid voice on the intercom piped in. "Les passagers de première classe sont priés de se présenter à la porte B2 pour embarquement immédiat."

"You better get going," Christophe said.

"Yeah, and you should, too. She's prolly pouting inside her fairytale castle, waiting for tomorrow's flight. Go to her. She wants you. Hell, she *needs* you — needs you a lot more than I do." She playfully pushed him away.

The loudspeaker voice made one last call for passengers. Christophe leaned over and planted a tender kiss on Nikki's cheek.

"Au revoir, Nikki."

"Au revoir," she echoed as she slung her bag over her shoulder and strolled to the gate, swinging her hips so that Christophe could enjoy the view as she walked away.

However, he wasn't watching.

Veronica was no longer spinning down. She was standing in the library. Swathed in dismal hues of grey, it was not the sharply decorated designer room she had created. The vibrant blue, red and gold silk pillows were dingy and colorless. Magnificent multicolor tapestries that once graced the walls, were now dull and dark. The entire room was slightly blurry, like a picture just a tad out of focus. It was also heavy, as if the humidity was incredibly high, but Veronica didn't feel warm. The atmosphere was just *sticky*. It clung to her like air in a sauna, seeped into every crevice of her body, and squeezed her like a sweaty, smothering down blanket on a hot August night.

Her flesh prickled. It was extremely sensitive. Dimly, Veronica was aware that she could actually *taste* the syrupy air through her skin. It was sweet, like dried flowers decaying in the sun. It made her want to vomit.

The crystal skull, or some mental manifestation of it, remained in her grasp. She studied it intently, hoping it would give a clue as to what she was supposed to do. Faintly, it flared with a smoky yellow glow. But that was all. If it knew any secrets, it wasn't revealing them — at least not yet. She shoved the skull into her messenger bag, which was conveniently draped over her shoulder, and hoped the esoteric relic would eventually become useful.

She was surprised at how incredibly *real* everything felt; yet, it was the most unnatural environment she had ever encountered. She pinched her arm, felt a nip of pain, and watched a small welt form on her skin. She was real, not ethereal, and that meant she was vulnerable here.

Moving took considerable effort. It felt like she was wading in jelly. Veronica slowly made her way through the forlorn facsimile of the château she loved so much.

The ballroom doors were cracked open just a hair, and Veronica eyed them suspiciously. Sebastian and she had danced in there during one of her "dreams". She wondered if he dwelt there now. The thought of his clammy touch sent a chilly bolt through her gut, causing her to purposefully walk closer to the opposite wall.

She lumbered past the fireplace, all the while keeping a suspicious eye on the ballroom's doors. The fireplace was murky and cold, and she felt it *breathe* a slow and subtle exhalation onto her super-sensitive skin.

Startled, she turned to look at it. No longer warm and inviting, its masonry façade was craggy and the stones jutted like jagged teeth. The fireplace was a giant face, and the hole its hungry mouth. It throbbed, as if taking deep, labored breaths.

Just as Veronica took a tentative step back, it twitched suddenly, and nipped at her — snapping like a turtle — as if she were a passing fish in a stream.

Veronica squealed. When she did, the whole château shuddered and rumbled. As if in response to the sudden commotion, voices cried out in the distance. They sounded raw and oddly harmonized, as if a hundred tormented souls wailed in pain at the cue of a sadistic choral conductor.

The fireplace opened its maw to chomp again.

Veronica didn't have time to contemplate the odd voices. She sidestepped in anticipation of the fireplace striking again. However, she found herself moving slower and slower. The jelly-effect became thicker, as though the air around her was coagulating.

The ravenous masonry lurched and grazed her buttocks. Veronica barely escaped its assault as she painstakingly fled toward the foyer.

She sluggishly careened around the corner. The faster she tried to run, the slower she went. Out of the corner of her eye, she saw the three Roman statues turn their heads in unison, following her path with stony stares as she passed.

They moved!

This made her want to freeze in fright. To her amazement, instead of doing so, she zipped faster than before. The murky, sticky jelly effect was quickly replaced with the sensation that she was moving one hundred miles per hour!

Through the foyer, past the stairs, she flew at what seemed like lightning speed. She came to the front doors within a split second. Overjoyed at evading the library, she let out a grateful sob of relief. As she did, her body twitched, the château shuddered, and voices howled out. Again, as if in direct response to her audible cry, her surroundings seemed to shift. She no longer moved like Superman on speed. Now she twitched in painful, quick spasms.

Veronica raised her hands to push the front doors open. As she did, one of her fists punched herself instead. Like it was spring-loaded, her wrist snapped, and her knuckles caught her jaw.

The other hand felt as though it was tethered to a bungee cord that had stretched to its limit. It took great effort to move it at all. She summoned all her might to make it barely reach the doorknob, only to have her hand suddenly slam against it as the "bungee" released at the last moment.

The force *did* push open the doors, though. As they swung, she leaned forward, using them to help break her fall. Vertigo consumed Veronica, and she tumbled outside.

She rolled onto the front steps until she came to a stop before the fountain. Oddly, she felt incredibly comfortable sprawled on the hard cobblestones, and she remained there, frozen, waiting to regain her sense of balance.

The fountain beside her gurgled with slurps and pops that sounded like excruciating stomach gas. She turned her head and watched it "fart" black, bubbly tar-like water out of its spout. It stank like a combination of rotting shit and hot asphalt. The stone cherubs swimming in the sludge looked like sewer-rats as the muck poured over them. All had their heads turned toward Veronica, and they all smiled devilishly at her.

Not sure what to do, she waited for something to happen. Nothing did.

Above the sky was grey; not the sleepy grey caused by rain clouds, but an opaque grey that hung in the air like liquid cement. She gazed past the festering fountain and across the tree-lined path behind it. The once lush, protective trees flanking either side were now towering, gnarly, black sentries. Their branches clutched at each other above the road like outstretched arms playing the children's game *London Bridge is Falling Down*.

She imagined that traversing the path would cause the trees to clamp down their branches, trapping her in their clutches like wicked bridesmaids and groomsmen during a twisted version of the wedding march.

Veronica surely didn't want to walk under that foreboding canopy. Going back inside was out of the question, and lying there wasn't a luxury she could take advantage of for long. She wasn't sure what to do next, but she needed to figure it out soon.

Christophe cursed the traffic leaving Charles De Gaulle airport that blocked his path. Several emotions surged through him — overwhelming joy knowing that Veronica wasn't in love with any other man, searing anger at Nikki for tricking and manipulating him, gratitude that Nikki finally *did* confess, and intense shame for allowing himself to be tricked in the first place.

As a bus cut in front of him, Christophe also felt overwhelmingly stupid — stupid for not being able to tell the sisters apart at the costume party.

"What a complete idiot am I?" Christophe rhetorically asked aloud.

He plugged his phone into his car and commanded loudly, "Call Ralph." The phone rang several times before Ralph's voicemail picked up. "Damn," he cursed before leaving a message. "Have you seen Veronica? Did you go to Château du Feu Ardent like you said you were? She didn't make her flight, and I need to find her right away. Call me back as soon as you can, my friend."

Misty rain made the traffic more congested than usual. Frustrated, he dialed Veronica's phone number over and over, hoping that she would suddenly pick up, but Veronica was not "available at the moment".

Something dashed behind one of the sentry-like trees. It was quick, and Veronica only caught a brief glimpse of a small, dark form.

She rose and was surprised to find that her movements were relatively normal. Standing made her dizzy, but she managed to remain upright with little effort. She scanned the distant trees, hoping whatever it was had gone away.

It hadn't.

It popped up like a gopher coming out of a hole. It was small and crawled fluidly on the ground toward her before slipping down and disappearing under the surface.

A fallen tree branch on the cobblestone pathway served as the only handy weapon. She took several tentative steps down the stairs and toward the fountain, knelt, grabbed the stick, and turned back to the approaching threat.

It bobbed up again. It was about twenty feet away, close enough to see that it wasn't a gopher after all. Hairless and covered in filth, down and up it went again and again. As it closed in, Veronica saw it wasn't even an animal. No, the creature approaching her was in fact *human*. It was a naked infant — it was a *baby*!

It fluttered across the murky ground and then dipped back down. Oddly, it appeared to be *swimming*. Up it would come, do a couple quick strokes, and then down it would dive again. Veronica realized the ground was not solid, but liquid. Soupy and black — it was the consistency of the liquefied sewage that had sucked her into the castle's catacombs.

She inched herself backward, up the steps of the castle, and quickly surveyed the grounds. The stairs, the asphalt driveway, the fountain, and the cobblestone pathway leading to the gatehouse all seemed solid and stable. Every inch of the ground covered in soil, however, was soupy. She now saw the earth roil like delicate waves in a thick, black sea. Veronica noted she needed to be careful so as not to step into the sludge accidentally. She had no clue if she would sink, float, or be able to walk on it, but she wasn't interested in finding out.

The baby grew closer. It was disturbingly dull in color, greyish-black like a rat, and wrinkled like an old man. Not sure if it presented a threat or not, she posed with the stick over her right shoulder like a batter...and waited.

Up and down it swam, drawing closer with each stroke. Veronica now saw the leathery skin was covered in welts and scars. A tiny tuft of dark hair remained on the top of its head. Otherwise, the thing that was once a child was completely naked. Tiny hands and feet, once surely adorable and cute, were now gnarly claw-like appendages that sliced through the sloppy earth like oars on a rowboat.

Veronica whispered a faint curse as the infant's face came into sight. As she spoke the words: "Jesus Christ what the fuck..." the entire world rocked around her. In the distance, voices cried out and moaned. The infant stopped short for a moment and stared directly at her, as if seeing her for the first time. Its wide, blue baby eyes were the only human trait remaining. The mouth was drawn up into a menacing pucker, and the nose had flaring nostrils several times larger than what seemed normal. The ears were raggedy like tattered bat's ears. Veronica felt she was looking at a demonic cherub rather than anything that may have once been a human infant.

After assessing Veronica for several impossibly long seconds, the demon-baby continued its swim. Veronica saw for the first time that it was *not* on a direct course in her direction, but instead was heading slightly to the left and behind her. There, only several yards away, near the apple orchard, was Josette-Camille. The specter with the bloodstained apron waited with outstretched arms for her child. Surrounding her were glistening silver balls undulating slowly on top of the liquid soil.

Veronica brought the stick down as she watched the baby join its mother. Together the two tossed the sparkling balls to one another. Mother and child seemed to navigate the mucky terrain quite successfully, but Veronica still wasn't sure how she'd fare if she stepped on it.

After several uneventful moments, she felt completely free of any threat from the baby, so Veronica turned her attention to the goopy ground. She poked it tentatively with her stick. Only a few inches deep, the stick hit solid bottom. Perhaps she could walk through it after all!

As Veronica weighed the pros and cons of making her way through the shallow sludge, a gangly figure crept behind her. It was the same sickly grey color as the infant, but was the size of a small adult. Virtually hairless, it had a round, bald head and twitched violently as it reached a shaking hand out to touch her. Veronica was too engrossed with her stick in the mud to realize it had snuck up on her. With a violent jerk, it clasped her shoulder and squeezed tight.

Veronica squealed with an earth-shattering wail that made castle bricks rattle and branches shake off the quivering trees. Voices cried out in the distance as if accosted by the sound. Josette-Camille and the baby whimpered and covered their ears. The entire world came to a standstill as Veronica cried out at the top of her lungs, "Nooo…!"

Veronica was like a magical being. Christophe had never encountered anyone like her. She captivated him completely and was tantalizingly different from the women he usually chased. She didn't pretend to be anything she wasn't. Demure, brilliant, passionate, and unafraid to express her opinion, Veronica was the opposite of all the vacant, pretentious women he used to date. She excited Christophe to the point of trepidation.

He reflected on the night of the masquerade ball as he sped down the freeway. He had intended to confess his feelings to Veronica that night. It had taken him weeks to muster the courage, and he was shaking a bit as he walked into the ballroom. He was so focused on making the moment special. He wanted to give Veronica the fairytale romance that he knew, deep down inside, she craved.

The sister wearing the black gown greeted him warmly when he entered. Veronica and Nikki looked so much alike, and Veronica had specifically told him earlier that day that her party dress was *black*! He assumed it was her. There was no doubt in his mind. Though he understood *how* he made such a grievous mistake, he couldn't wrap his mind around *why* it took him so long to figure it out. He had an entire conversation with Nikki, shared a passionate kiss, and stood beside her as she unmasked. There was so much confusion when Sandbourne collapsed, Christophe didn't even realize he was standing next to the wrong sister until he looked down at poor, desperate Veronica as she tried to resuscitate the doctor.

Christophe should have said something right there and then, but he blew it. Absolutely blew it. The confusion, the chaos, the police and all the questions — it all made Christophe freeze like a scared, little rabbit.

Then they were swept off in different police cars and taken in for more questioning. He was grilled thoroughly and made numb from the experience. He barely believed the tragedy of the night was real when he met Nikki outside on the courthouse steps.

He had every intention of explaining to her that he made a mistake, but before he could utter a word, Nikki planted a thick kiss on his lips and gushed, "I'm so glad to see you! They questioned me about everything! Oh, I hope Vern is okay. She doesn't speak French too well, and I think they think *she* had something to do with Dr. Sandbourne's death."

"They know she had nothing to do with it," Christophe had answered. "They're just pretending they live in an episode of *Law and Order*. Don't worry. I know the mayor. I can make some calls on her behalf. I really hope she isn't frightened. The police here have a big bark but a little bite. Let's go back inside and wait for her…"

Before he could finish, she piped in with, "Vern will be fine! I'm sure she's on the phone with good ol' Robert right now. Even though they broke up, she still goes running to him every time she's in a pinch. She just can't get over him, ya' know. And he *always* comes to the rescue. She says the make-up sex with him is great! Gawd she can be such a little sleaze sometimes!"

That was the beginning of Nikki's game. Christophe naively fell right into her trap, and now he could only blame himself for not questioning her motives. As he reached the outskirts of Paris, traffic diminished significantly. He stepped on the gas and sped across the rolling hills of France toward Le Château du Feu Ardent.

❧❧ ❖ ❧❧

A voice sternly cautioned, "Stop making so much noise."

Veronica spun and faced a sallow-eyed corpse. Her jaw dropped, but before she could utter a sound, its claw-like hand cupped her mouth.

"Not a sound!" It seethed angrily. "Your thoughts serve as your voice here. Even whispering aloud sounds like deafening thunder."

She noticed that its lips did not part as it spoke. She heard everything in her head.

Veronica hastily took a step back and out of its grip. Naked, gangly, and forlorn, the thing that must have once been human gazed at her vacantly. Streaks of red crisscrossed its emaciated, hairless chest as if something vicious had mauled it. Chunks of torn flesh dangled from its exposed ribcage. It reached a desperate, jerking hand toward Veronica. She stood petrified, unsure if she should stay or flee. The figure took a gingered step forward and dipped its round head, as if showing it meant no harm. Completely bald, it reminded Veronica of a light bulb.

Veronica then recognized Dr. Sandbourne bowing before her. She softly uttered his name. "Doctor Sandbourne...?"

In her mind, she heard the thing that was once Dr. Sandbourne rage.

"I told you not to speak!"

Before she realized what hit her, he barreled forward and knocked her to the ground. Jumping on top of her, he scratched and clawed into her face. She brought her forearm up to defend herself, and he bit into her flesh like a ravenous dog.

At the top of her lungs, Veronica roared. "Get off me!"

She pushed at the creature, but suddenly moved in slow motion. He, on the other hand, was fast and frantic and pissed off. Sandbourne reeled a gangly arm back and swiped at her. His claw-hand grazed across her cheek and lips. She felt warm blood ooze down her face.

"I'm sorry, Dr. Sandbourne, I tried to save you! I know I should have listened to you. I'm so sorry!"

She heard another voice, this one fainter than Sandbourne's, gently tell her, "You *must* stay quiet, Veronica."

Obediently, Veronica shut her mouth. She tasted the metallic flavor of blood, and her tongue felt the meaty swelling of her sliced bottom lip.

Looking up, she noticed several other figures hovering above Sandbourne. They surrounded her and her attacker, slowly closing in, and as they did, Veronica recognized familiar faces. All from her dreams, all the victims of the oubliette, all smothered around her as Dr. Sandbourne gnawed into her flesh.

The figures reached out with groping hands, grabbing, pulling, and scratching at her. Veronica stopped struggling. She was no match for all of them, and her tired body went limp. A resolved peace crept over her. Time stopped, and Sandbourne also moved robotically slow. Though she dreaded existing in purgatory with the other trapped souls, she decided she couldn't fight any longer.

Acquiescing, she looked into Sandbourne's crazed face. The kind man she once knew was replaced with a wild-eyed beast. Though he moved lethargically, he opened his maw to clamp down on her throat. She eagerly anticipated the moment, but instead, Sandbourne was swiftly pulled off of her. Veronica felt suddenly light and free.

"You're going to be fine," a soothing voice spoke. "You're not going to die."

She opened her mouth, and in an instant, several voices erupted in her head.

"Do not speak, Veronica!"

Okay, I won't, she thought.

A woman's voice explained. "The sound of your voice is deafening here. It is like driving spears into our ears."

Before she could help it, Veronica thought, *what just happened?*

"Sandbourne, being downright mad, wasn't able to control himself," was the answer.

Another question popped into Veronica's head. *How can you hear me?*

"All of your thoughts are audible. Don't try to quiet them. Doing so will only drive you mad like Dr. Sandbourne," the voice replied.

Veronica finally recognized it as Marie-Claire.

So, that's what happened to him, she thought. I feel so guilty.

Marie-Claire answered. "Don't. Such miserable feelings can consume you here. Instead, focus on how you can save him. How you can save all of us, and absolve your sins."

Something like an insect buzzed next to her ear. It took a moment for Veronica to realize that it was her own voice, reciting every thought, feeling, impulse that ran through her mind. She felt naked and exposed, without even her inner dialogue private.

The specters surrounded her. They closed in tightly and gazed at her in awe — like she was a valuable, arcane object — like she was their savior.

Numerous questions raced through Veronica's mind, and their voices piped in, answering her before she even knew she was asking a question.

"This is the realm between two worlds. It's like purgatory. This is where we're trapped."

"The elemental isn't here right now. But if you keep screaming, it'll come. It despises the sound of a human voice, especially a scream, even more than we do."

"Beyond the gatehouse is our freedom. That's where we want to go. We all just want to escape."

"No one goes beyond the gate; to even approach it could summon the elemental."

"It punished Dr. Sandbourne for trying to warn you. He fought so hard to keep his thoughts private in order to protect you. He didn't want it to hurt you. That's what drove Sandbourne mad. He tried to hide from his own mind, and that's not possible here."

"It feeds on our souls, drawing our energy, and keeps us weak. That's why it traps us. We nourish it."

"This domain was created by the Hag to imprison it. It can't go far beyond the castle walls. This is its prison. It is *our* prison."

"Veronica, you can free us, though!"

Veronica felt like she was spinning. Encircling her were Father Michel, Marie-Claire, Isabelle, Julien-Luc, Cicero, Josette-Camille, and Trinna.

They continued to invade her head, all talking — or thinking — at once.

"We have faith in you. We know you can do this. We entered your dreams and brought you here for this exact moment. It is time for you to free us."

Veronica pulled the crystal skull from her pocket. "I'm still not sure what I have to do, but damn it, I'm gonna try," she thought.

They silently cheered her.

"Let's start by figuring out why it doesn't want anyone to go near the gatehouse!" she proudly announced in her head as she turned to march down the tree-lined path. Toward the entrance she went, with a trail of specters following behind.

❧❦❖❦❧

Christophe couldn't deny Nikki was attractive. Her tight, slender body and party-girl attitude was similar to many of the models he dated. Plus, he genuinely liked her. She was fun. So when she convinced him there was no chance between Veronica and him, of course he thought giving it "a go" with Nikki was worth a shot. Having a fling with *her* wouldn't be difficult at all.

Plus, from Nikki's point of view, he had been pursuing her all this time and was madly in love with her. Admitting the truth would have been cruel and heartless. He wasn't *that* kind of guy.

So on the day he and Nikki went to the wine festival, Christophe decided to try Nikki on for size. He reasoned that his feelings for Veronica didn't matter if they weren't reciprocated.

"That was my second mistake," he whispered to himself. "I never should have considered an affair with her for a moment. She picked up on that and fed off it. I led her on, even if just for a little bit. It was enough to fuel her fire. If I had just leveled with her from the beginning, she wouldn't have played so many games with me. Damn, why did I let myself be tempted at all?" The composed man banged an angry fist on the steering wheel.

He had tried to make it work with Nikki, but every time he came close to giving in, Veronica flashed in his mind. He knew that if he were with Nikki, even just once, it would forever ruin his chances with Veronica. No matter what Nikki said, Christophe knew Veronica wasn't the type of girl who would tolerate a lover who had been with her sister. He knew deep down inside Nikki was a temptation he must resist.

He careened on a roundabout and exited onto the twisty road that took him to Rue Crevier and Le Château du Feu Ardent. *Almost there*, he thought. *Time to make this whole thing right!*

✑❧ ❖ ❦❧

Veronica faced the tree-lined pathway. Through it, she saw the gatehouse. It was foreboding and mordant and impenetrable. Chains and metal spikes decorated it. She took several tentative steps forward while the specters followed at a distance. She also noticed other figures hovering in the background. She caught glimpses of them darting behind trees and peeking out from inside buildings.

Before she could fully formulate the question in her mind, someone answered her.

"There are *many* souls trapped here, Veronica. All victims of the oubliette. Only a select few of us communicated to you in your dreams; otherwise, it would have been overwhelming. So, it isn't just a handful of souls you're saving. There are over a hundred of us. We all have a unique story. I was the first, and I saw each one of them join me." It was Trinna speaking.

Veronica cast the girl a sideways glance. Trinna came up alongside her. She wore tattered rags, and her hair was still singed from a fire that blazed nearly seventeen-hundred years ago. Veronica wondered where Bevin was.

Trinna answered. "He crossed over. He's waiting for me on the other side. I'll finally see him again!"

For the briefest moment, Veronica felt happiness emulate from Trinna. It was like a small burst zapping the shadowy bleakness. Trinna glowed in faint, warm colors before being scolded by the others.

"Stop it, Trinna!"

"You'll only aggravate it. No matter the joy you feel, you *must* remain melancholy."

Marie-Claire explained. "You see, Veronica, it's *connected* to us. It feeds off our sorrow and pain. If we dare allow ourselves to have pleasant thoughts, it gets very angry and very violent."

Veronica thought, "No wonder you guys are all so miserable. But you know, that gives me an idea…"

She paused midway on the path. Above, the canopy of trees rustled as if sensing her below them.

"I wonder…" Veronica began.

But before she could finish, Marie-Claire warned, "Don't stop. Keep moving."

Veronica paused for a confused moment. "Why?"

"Don't linger on this path. Just go!" was the answer.

Veronica obliged and took a step forward. The walking-through-jelly sensation was back. She moved at almost half her normal speed.

"Keep going, Veronica," Father Michel urged.

Looking down, Veronica saw the ground was roiling around up her ankles. It crept up her legs like creeping vines.

"What's happening?" she thought.

"Forces here are trying to stop you. Now go, Veronica, before it's too late!" the priest said.

She forced her feet forward, but progress was miniscule. The ground seeped up her calves, her hips, and her pelvis. It felt cold, moist, and muscular. It was constricting her as it crawled across her flesh.

"Help me," she implored and reached desperate arms out to the souls around her.

Father Michel moved forward and held her hand tenderly. His touch was icy and ethereal. "We can't. You have to do this yourself."

"Fuck! Do I have to do everything?" she thought rhetorically, but got an answer nonetheless.

"Yes, you alone must fight it."

The earth crept up her belly. As she took another laborious step, she felt something hard scraping across her ankles. Looking down, she saw roots from the trees wriggling like eager worms. They wove around her feet, anchoring her to the spot.

"This isn't working..." she thought.

"Go! With all your might, fight it and keep going!" the specters encouraged.

Veronica willed her other foot to take a step forward. The squirming roots worked their way up her legs until they completely covered her thighs, causing excruciating pain as they squeezed and burrowed into her soft tissue. She wanted to cry out, but knew she couldn't.

From above, a branch lurched down and blocked her path. She automatically shielded her face with her arm. The limb jerked like an arthritic hand. It was fast and clamped her wrist. Tangling around her forearm, it quickly restrained her. Veronica feebly fought against its incredible strength.

Before she knew it, another branch reached down and snatched her other hand. Pulling from opposite directions, Veronica was positioned spread eagle, with all four appendages pulled outward. The earth continued to work its way around her body like a hundred tiny snakes constricting her.

She tried with all her might to pull free, but the earth, the branches, and the roots moved at lightning speed while she floundered at a snail's pace. She was no match.

"Fight harder! You can beat them. They are just *trees*!" Marie-Claire urged.

Hanging there like a defeated crucified Christ, Veronica found that last statement amusing. To come all this way to be done in by *trees* seemed ridiculous. Despite the extreme pain, Veronica managed the tiniest laugh.

At that moment, the branches and the roots hesitated and relaxed their grip ever so slightly.

"You don't like that, do you?" she thought and laughed again.

The earth started to drip off her body like wax from a candle.

She laughed some more, this time with more sincerity.

The roots acquiesced, and her feet were freed.

Veronica kicked and giggled while dangling in the air. Only her arms were bound now, and she twisted to break free. One let go.

Hanging from just her left hand, she guffawed. "Looks like your bark is worse than your bite, huh, Mr. Tree?"

The branch released her, and she fell on her rump into the wet earth. Giggling insanely, she splattered the mud like a naughty kid on a playground.

"Ha! Don't like happy thoughts, do ya'?" she mocked.

The specters loomed back as her madness escalated. She splashed some muck at them as they danced backward.

"Where you going? Don't you see, I know how to fight this place now!"

Veronica pulled herself up, wiped mud off her palms by rubbing them down the length of her jeans, and then sprinted down the tree-lined path.

"I know how we can beat this," Veronica thought as she skipped easily to the gatehouse.

The excited spirits kept their emotions in check as they eagerly followed from a safe distance.

❧❀❧

The bridge was adorned with bulky, orange equipment. A backhoe, a small crane, and a truck were parked at the front. Christophe got out of his car and studied the scene. He wasn't sure if the construction on the bridge was finished or not and didn't want to risk driving over it if it was unstable.

The logical part of his mind decided it was doubtful Veronica was at the Château if the bridge was still under construction. After all, she'd be trapped. Christophe surmised she must be staying in town. He decided to go look for her there. He figured he could call around to all the inns and hotels. She liked the quaint bed and breakfast style châteaux. He would start by calling them first. He got back in his car and contemplated backing up, but something intuitive pulled at his sense of reason, and he hesitated.

❧❀❧

A green, moldy growth painted the gatehouse like a rancid infection. Barbed wire, chains, metal spikes, and boiling hot oil squirted from the top in a never-ending cascade, down the massive doors. A small drop splashed on Veronica's hand and burned like a sting from a wasp.

The American interior decorator stood before the obstacle and wondered what to do next. Her brilliant plan shriveled as she faced the impenetrable gatehouse. She glanced sideways and saw that her cheerleading specters were all skulking in the distance. They, too, seemed suddenly daunted by her task.

A dark figure emerged from their ranks. He swooped gallantly to her side.

"So, what are you going to do?" Sebastian asked.

Veronica spun and faced the Cloaked Man. She hadn't noticed him until then, and his sudden presence made her shudder. "I'm gonna open that gate and free everyone," she stated flatly.

532

He leaned in as if studying the massive, fortified doors. "How are you going to do that?" he asked coquettishly.

"Well, I thought if the trees released me when I laughed, that I could also get the gatehouse door open by..."

"By laughing at it." He finished her sentence, grunted, and asked, "Are you going to stand here and laugh at the wall? Is that the plan?"

"Well, it sounds stupid when you say it like *that*." Veronica scowled and wished Sebastian would go away.

"I'll leave you alone if that's what you really want. I don't mean to upset you," he responded to thoughts she could not keep private. "Please, go ahead with your plan. I'll just stand back and observe from a distance."

He glided out of her line of sight. Oddly, she felt alone without him there. No one was near her, and she suddenly realized this was a battle she'd be fighting by herself.

Taking a deep breath, Veronica exhaled with a hearty chortle. The walls shuddered, the trees quivered, and the air grew denser, but that was all.

From far away, one of the specters whined. "It hurts when you do that!"

With more determination, she cracked up again, this time louder and longer than before. The world around her gyrated as if in protest. Marie-Claire and the others feebly whimpered. The gatehouse rattled, but the scalding oil continued to pour down its façade, the gnarled ivy remained in place, and the doors stayed shut tight.

Sebastian came up behind her again, and she jumped slightly.

"Keep it up, and you'll summon the djinn," he cautioned. "Remember, it doesn't like the sound of a human voice, especially one that's happy."

Veronica clamped her mouth. Without meaning to, she thought, *then what the hell should I do?*

Sebastian smiled as he answered. "It's not too late. Go back to your body, quick, and just die a quiet, peaceful death at the bottom of the oubliette."

"That would mean no one would be saved. If I am gonna die anyway, I may as well save the others. I'll figure out what to do. I wasn't brought all the way here to fail now."

"No, you were brought all this way to serve as *bait*." He leaned in and winked as he said, "Don't worry, you're doing a good job."

Veronica couldn't help herself and thought, *what do you mean by bait?*

One of the specters warned, "Beware of his artifice, Veronica." It was Cicero peeking out from behind the others. The once brave warrior was gaunt and frail. Though he still carried his sword and wore his uniform, there was nothing fierce about him. His agitated eyes jittered around as if fearing retaliation for speaking up.

Sebastian hissed at the centurion, and Cicero furtively shuffled back among the other specters. The Cloaked Man steadied his gaze at their savior and advanced. In an instant, he stood directly in front of her, mere inches from her face, as if he moved at the speed of light.

"They made a bargain with the djinn. In exchange for their freedom, they would lure you here and offer you up like a sacrifice. You and that skull and the knowledge of its true name. The total package — that's everything it needs to be free and invincible."

"Ha," thought Veronica, pleased that she found a flaw in his story. "I don't know the name!"

"That doesn't matter. What matters is what's going to happen to the person who *has* that name."

Veronica looked at him cross-eyed. She pulled the skull out of her bag and peered into it as if looking for an answer. "You tell lies, manipulate situations to suit your own needs, and can't be trusted. I know who you are, Sebastian, and I won't allow you to trick me." She stepped past him and glared intently at the gatehouse.

"This is no trick, my darling. This is your destiny. You're going to be trapped here for eternity. The difference is that you'll endure this place all *alone*. While everyone else goes free, you're going to be stuck here. That's the price you pay for being the big hero."

"You're trying to distract me. Just leave me alone. *You're* just afraid of what awaits a wicked soul like yours on the other side of that gate. That's why —"

"You think this is about *me*, Veronica?" the Cloaked Man snapped. "I have no part in this game. I'm just a bystander. I even sat by and watched them weave my story into your sleeping mind. They took liberties with it, you know. Made me out to be the bad guy because they didn't want you to trust me once you got here. You must believe me. I'm trying to *save* your life."

"I don't care if I die while saving the others. Death is better than withering away in the oubliette. If that's the sacrifice I gotta make, then so be it."

Tenderly, he said, "How tragic! You've finally taken a leap of faith only to belly flop right into a vat of shit! Okay then, I acquiesce. I've done all I can do to dissuade you. Do what you will, Veronica, but just remember, there *is* something worse than death."

She pushed Sebastian out of her way, and he dissipated like mist. The gatehouse was now her only obstacle. She just had to figure out how to open it. Thin slivers of white light shined through it, like promises of something good on the other side. She let the beams of light fall on her hands, and she playfully grabbed at them, as if she could catch them.

After several minutes, she stepped back from the gatehouse and turned to face the Château. Fearlessly, Veronica opened her mouth wide and shrieked. The specters looked around expectantly, then ran and hid. The sky turned dark, almost black, as Veronica screamed and screamed and screamed, "Come and get me motherfucker!"

☙ ❧ ❖ ☙ ❧

Christophe sat in his car grappling with what to do next. He searched for local bed and breakfasts on his phone and dialed the nearest one. A grumpy, old man flatly said he had "No American guests" and hung up. Christophe called another and another, all with the same response with varying levels of rudeness.

Maybe she *did* catch a flight home already. Perhaps Nikki was right about that.

After all, there was no reason for her to stay in France after her work was done. It would cost only a small fee to change her flight. The notion hit Christophe like a bullet, a small fee that would have been charged to her *bankcard*. It would show up on her account activity!

He dialed the bank and spoke with Miss Desandé. "Bonjour, it's Christophe. I need a quick favor. Can you look up the activity of those American girls who opened that account with the Swiss funds a couple of months ago?"

Miss Desandé answered with an exasperated sigh. "Oui, but you know the bank's protocol. When calling in for customer information, you have to state your name and employee identifica —"

He cut her off. "It's me, for God's sake!"

"And *you* should know you have to follow procedure."

Begrudgingly, he started. "I'm Christophe Sinclair..."

"Your *full* name..." Miss Desandé cautioned.

Without hiding the annoyance in his voice, he stated, "Tervagan Christophe Sinclair. Employee identification number seven, four, zero, zero, four. Now please access the account."

"You mean the account of the stupid women who tried to cash in old francs?" she asked coyly.

"Oui," he answered sharply.

Miss Desandé complied. After a few moments of listening to her tap on her computer, she replied, "Under recent activity I see one of them, Nikki Dixon, bought two bottles of cabernet at the same wine festival you were at last week..."

"Not that girl, the other one. See what Veronica purchased over the past week."

She plucked some more at the machine. Christophe tapped his fingers on his dash in time with her. Finally, she came back on the line and said, "No activity since last Monday. She checked out of the Château de Vallagon a little after two o'clock. That is all."

That was odd. Surely she would have *some* activity over an entire week. Christophe knew she didn't like to carry a lot of cash. Plus, if she did leave France, she would have used the card for the plane ticket and rental car. This meant she surely must still be in the country!

"Anything else, Tervagan?" she chirped.

"No," Christophe answered absently.

After they hung up, Christophe sat there contemplating. The only place she could possibly be was in the Château. He pulled the keys from the ignition and stuffed them down his pants pocket. With absolute purpose, he ran across the bridge toward Le Château du Feu Ardent.

⁂

Veronica screamed as loud as she could while the specters cowered at a distance. The blare caused many of them to cover their ears and writhe in agony. Her throat began to hurt, and she closed her mouth with a dramatic smack, allowing silence to return.

Nothing happened.

Hopelessness consumed them all with a giant, suffocating hand.

Slowly, the specters crept toward her again, like beaten dogs unsure of an unstable master. They circled her while their hopeful eyes fluttered nervously. One of them wore a faded red dress. Though muted by the greyness of their surroundings, Veronica still recognized Dorothée's velvet crimson gown. With a painful stab, Veronica recalled watching her accost Dr. Sandbourne at the masquerade ball.

Curious, Veronica asked, "What did you do to Sandbourne?"

Dorothée shook her head bashfully and faded behind the others.

"Wait!" Veronica pleaded. She followed the evasive spirit. "I saw you attack him. At the party, as he was walking toward me, you wrapped yourself around him and *hugged* him to death."

Dorothée couched her reply, "It wasn't like that."

"I saw it. I could hardly believe it at the time, but now I am entirely certain you *killed* him. I just don't understand why?"

"We all wanted to protect you that night. Sandbourne was getting in the way."

"What do you mean *getting in the way*? He was looking out for me."

"He was about to tell you something you shouldn't hear. That's all, but it doesn't matter now. All that matters is *this*." She pointed, smiled, and nodded at the gatehouse.

Veronica rumbled, "He told me to read the Bible right before he died. Was that it, or was there more? What was he going to tell me?"

Dorothée held her charm and grace as she diffidently answered, "It would have only confused you and it wasn't important, dear Veronica."

"I'll decide if it was important or not. Tell me!" Veronica spoke out loud, causing everything to rattle and quake.

Dorothée quivered but didn't answer.

A musky, rotting odor permeated the scene. Veronica gasped, suddenly overwhelmed by the noxious, yet familiar pong.

Dorothée artfully flitted out of the way as all the specters made a wide pathway. From out of the opaque backdrop, the djinn appeared.

Veronica fought an overwhelming urge to flee. This was her moment, though. She knew that there was no running away and no place to hide. She would make a stand for herself and all the victims of the oubliette. And if it didn't work, she would at least die trying.

The elemental demon born out of smokeless fire was about ten feet away from the interior designer from Oildale, California. Though Veronica was a small, broken woman, the elemental was also surprisingly unformidable. It was diminutive, about the size of a rabbit, with a long, horse-like face and a scrawny, emaciated body. Its eyes locked on Veronica. They were surprisingly human, with large whites and pale-green irises. Veronica waved her hands at it as if she could shoo it away.

Instead of running, it stood up on its gangly hind legs, like a miniature horse rearing up. As it did, it grew larger. Its haunches arched over its barrel-chested torso like legs on a spider. The sickle-shaped claws on its front paws grew to nearly a foot in length. The head was almost as long as Veronica was tall. It towered several feet over her.

Veronica took two tentative steps back. It leaned in, and the nostrils on its upturned, piggish nose flared. She saw worms and insects crawling on its flesh as it thrust its face into hers, sniffed deeply, and then it reeled back.

She ducked just as its massive jaws clamped shut in the air. It quickly recovered, and an infested claw swiped at her. It grazed her back and knocked her to the ground. Red-hot pain rippled between her shoulder blades.

As she cried out, it cringed at the sound of her voice. The other paw snatched her arm and pulled her to her feet. She squirmed in its grip, but could not break away. Her free hand pulled the skull from her bag and held it up for the demon to see.

It shrieked and released her. She dropped to the ground and rolled several yards away from it. Jumping up to her feet, Veronica stood poised with the skull in front of her, like she remembered Baldebert doing in her dream.

The djinn skulked back and eyed Veronica fearfully. It suddenly seemed so harmless that Veronica nearly felt sorry for it.

"Stay back; just stay the hell back," she whispered as it shrunk down again.

While it was scared and small, Veronica turned her attention back to Dorothée and commanded, "Dorothée! Tell me what Sandbourne wanted to say!"

The specters had formed a semi-circle around her and the djinn like kids on a playground watching a fight. Dorothée hung her head and avoided eye contact with Veronica. Sebastian gladly stepped forward and offered an answer.

"Sandbourne was about to tell you the name of the demon. He figured it out while reading the Bible you found in the catacombs."

Veronica waved the skull at the djinn as she cried out, "You kept Sandbourne from telling me the *name*? But that's what I need to know to fight *this* fucking thing!"

Veronica continued to hold the skull in front of her. Though it gleamed fiery red, it was obviously useless without the name to trigger it.

The djinn snarled. It took a casual step toward Veronica.

"Don't listen to Sebastian!" Marie-Claire warned. "Fight the beast and free us. That's all that matters now."

"I could if I knew the name!" Veronica answered.

The creature born of smokeless fire glowed with red-hot intensity. Lips parted to reveal saber-like teeth with the most evil Cheshire Cat-smile imaginable.

Veronica swiped the skull at the djinn, and it leapt back — but not out of fear. It had a bounce in its movement. It was playful, like a kitten. It pounced around her in a complete circle, swiping occasionally with its petite paw as though she were a trapped mouse.

Desperate, she rambled off random names, hoping one was correct. "Bob, Tom, Jerry, John, Jim, Carl...ah, Fred, Frank, ah, ah..."

"You *know* the name Veronica!" Sebastian offered.

Veronica didn't have time to debate in her head if she should trust his advice or not, and she sputtered, "Robert, Ralph, Clark, Christophe, Andrew, Jacob...ah..."

The djinn suddenly moved at lightning speed and whirled around her so fast she could barely see it. It barreled into her gut at full force. Though it was small, its immense power sent her flying several feet in the air before landing hard against the gatehouse doors.

She tried to cry out, but there was no air left in her lungs. Hot oil poured from the funnels overhead and seared Veronica's body. It felt like she was on fire. Blisters festered on her skin, and she smelled her own flesh cooking.

Veronica pushed herself away from the gatehouse and landed face-down in the mud at the feet of the full-sized djinn. It glared at her with its fierce human-like eyes. Not just a stupid animal, it was obviously contemplating something. Veronica hoped it was mercy.

She coiled into a ball as the pain roiled through her defeated body in thunderous waves.

The elemental leaned back on its spider-like legs. There was no mercy in its eyes as it prepared to pounce. Veronica bit her bottom lip and braced herself for impact.

☙❧ ❖ ☙❧

The gatehouse door opened. Veronica heard the familiar creaking hinges. The chains simply fell free, and the barbed wire dissipated. Everyone paused a moment and watched as something from the other side pushed its way through.

The djinn snarled at Veronica. As she cringed, it turned and lunged between the gatehouse and the specters. It growled defensively, preventing them from going through the open doors.

Veronica realized it couldn't attack her and guard the doorway at the same time. With its attention diverted, she seized the moment and mustered up all her courage to attack. She whispered urgently to the Head, asking it to please give her strength, and bounded forward. She jumped onto the djinn's back like a cowboy tackling a bronco. Veronica held onto the nape of its neck with one hand and with the other brought the skull down hard on its head.

Crack!

It seemed momentarily stunned, and went down on one knee. She prepared to strike again, but before she could, the djinn twisted its neck from side-to-side and violently arched its back. It threw her off. She rolled end-over-end away from the entrance.

As she tumbled to a stop, it pounced onto her, crushing her beneath its massive body. It pinned her down with its sheer size — bigger than a horse at this point — she was like an insect trapped beneath.

She pelted the Head against its buttocks, but to no avail. It just sat there and effortlessly crushed her. All the air escaped her lungs. She could not draw in another breath. As she struggled, something snapped in her chest. A shooting pain under her heart could only mean one thing — her ribs were breaking.

Veronica twisted, but it didn't matter. She was completely immobilized. She gasped for air, and another rib snapped in her chest. Her face was pushed into the goopy ground, and only one eye peeked out. She finally stopped struggling.

A few feet away, someone walked through the gatehouse doors. The form was vague, almost invisible. She could tell it was a man, but he faded in and out of focus. It was as if she were looking through a camera lens as it rapidly zoomed in and out. She squinted as he passed by, trying to see who was breaking in from the other side. For a brief instant, the figure stopped, looked around, and appeared crystal clear.

It was Christophe.

He disappeared back out of focus as the djinn shifted its weight and drove her face deeper into the ground.

Everything went black.

With the last bit of air in her lungs, she whispered, "Christophe..."

The djinn responded to her voice by turning over so it faced her. Another rib snapped. The pain forced her one eye to open just in time to see Christophe jog up the pathway to the Château.

The djinn opened its festering maw. It was inches from her face. Its rancid breath filled her mouth and coated her tongue. It tasted like death. Despite the noxious, sickly-sweet flavor, she was grateful to have air once again in her lungs. She breathed several times deeply.

Its human-like eyes scrutinized her as if debating. Its gaze relaxed a moment before it reeled back and opened its jaw. A solitary drop of drool dripped onto her forehead. It seared like acid. She begged for mercy, "No, don't..." as it chomped down on her face. Its incisor punctured her cheek and sliced into her mouth. Blood poured down her throat.

Her airway was once again cut off, this time by her own blood. The only thing she could do was squirm futilely as she drowned in it.

Amazingly, her willpower made her suddenly move at lightning speed. Squirming under the djinn like a wiggly worm, she was able to twist her hands free. It opened its jaws to bite into her again, but this time she quickly clamped her hands around its throat and viciously dug in with her fingernails. Slimy things that lived in its fur slithered across her knuckles, but Veronica did not let go. Feeling more beast-like than human, she ignored the crawling creatures, which nipped at her hands like crazed fleas. She burrowed her fingers mercilessly into its flesh. It pulled back, offering an unobstructed view of its scaly neck, and without hesitation, *she* bit into *its* exposed flesh.

It shrieked — more from surprise than pain — and rolled off her. She sat up like a shot. Worms, insects, hair, and an array of slug-like creatures remained in her mouth. She spit them out in a spray mixed with saliva and vomit. While catching her breath, air flooded her lungs, causing excruciating pain. She hunched over and coughed out blood. Bright red, it contrasted strikingly against the monochrome ground.

She stumbled to her feet. As she stood, drool streamed from her busted mouth. Torn flesh hung from her jaw. Her bottom lip was half torn off, causing her to look like a stroke victim with an exaggerated droopy frown. A spot on the center of her forehead smoldered where the djinn's drool singed her. Blood and bile seeped out of her swollen eyes and mangled nose.

The djinn stood poised to pounce on her again. Feebly, Veronica bent and grabbed the crystal skull off the ground in front of her. She held it up like a decrepit old man waving an angry fist.

The djinn hissed, but did not advance. Veronica had no fight left in her. She shook the Head as menacingly as she could and waited for it to barrel into her one last time. Instead, it once again shrunk down to the size of a harmless bunny. Its human-like eyes glinted happily. For the briefest, insane moment, Veronica saw it smile at her. It appeared to be amused. It snarled slightly, and then blissfully bounced away.

She watched incredulously as it pranced up the tree-lined path, toward the Château, like a rabbit who was late for a very important date.

Stunned, she remained frozen and poised for battle.

"Relax, it's gone," Sebastian finally assured her.

"You did it, Veronica. You drove it away," Marie-Claire confirmed.

Veronica gazed at the familiar specters. More came into sight. They slinked out from behind trees and emerged from the ground like corpses rising from graves. She smiled a goofy, crooked grin and answered, "I did it?"

The open doors to the gatehouse creaked and slowly began to drift shut. Veronica leapt forward, and grabbed one of the edges with ravaged fingertips before it could completely close. Warm light from the other side touched her raw skin. Its caress made the pain go away. The door was heavy, though, and it took all her might to keep it propped open.

"Hurry!" she instructed. "Now's your chance. Go! Every one of you, leave while I hold it."

Veronica pulled the door wide. As she did, the light engulfed her and slowly eased her pain and healed her wounds.

The specters filed by and gave themselves over to the fate that awaited them beyond the gate. Veronica watched with awe as crisp sunshine cascaded over each figure as it crossed over. They were completely enveloped by it, transforming into beings of light as it washed over each one. They were sublimely beautiful as they metamorphosed.

Joyful tears escaped her bruised and busted eyes as she watched. Once totally transmuted into light, each figure slowly rose and floated up toward the white-hot sun. More brilliant than any sun Veronica knew in the real world, this one drew them in until they were just tiny flecks of light dancing across the most brilliant, blue sky she had ever seen.

Marie-Claire passed by.

Veronica called out to her. "Marie-Claire, you were right! I did it!"

The matronly specter smiled, nodded, and turned her head quickly as she crossed the threshold.

The door began to slip from her hold. Veronica twisted to gain a firmer grasp. As she did, another set of hands helped her. She turned to see Sebastian beside her. He now bore the majority of the door's weight.

"Thanks," Veronica said.

Together they kept the entrance open as one by one the specters shuffled by. Isabelle, Dorothée, Julien-Luc, Cicero, Josette-Camille, Trinna, Father Michel — all went swiftly through.

She called, "You were right Father Michel! Penance *is* possible. I do have faith, now, I do!"

Next came Clark. The plumber was no longer a gaunt shell of a man with a maggot-infested maw, but instead he looked like he did the first time they met. Lean, yet healthy, with bright, cheerful eyes and a wide, toothy smile.

Veronica said his name as if it were an apology. "Clark…"

"Farewell, dear Veronica. You did a fine job setting this up!"

She began, "I'm so sorry Clar…" however Sebastian interrupted and leaned in to ask, "Are you sure this is what you want, Veronica?"

"It's what *everyone* wants," she answered as the plumber slipped past her. "Except you. Sebastian, I'm truly sorry you're gonna face hell on the other side. Maybe someone over there will see the good things you did, too, and have mercy on you."

"Don't worry about *me*, Veronica. Right now it's your lover you should be concerned about."

"My *lover*? You mean Christophe?"

"He's in there…" Sebastian nodded to the Château, "…with the djinn. Everything worked out as planned."

"Why would anything happen to Christophe? He's done nothing…"

"He was the key all along. Him, his name, his *real* name, is what the djinn needs, as well as you and the skull and the Bible."

The truth fell into place like puzzle pieces suddenly coming together.

"His real name, they kept it from me all along, didn't they? That's why Dorothée killed Sandbourne at the party, isn't it? He was going to tell me."

"Yes, he was. And he even tried to give you a clue, when he broke through and told to read the Bible. He was *trying* to tell you the name he discovered within it. It was written there on the inside cover. And Sandbourne even made note of it on that yellow notepaper, you just needed to look! Trust me though, the others were quite pleased you never actually figured it out."

"But why, if I needed it to save them, why prevent me from knowing?"

"Because you aren't *really* saving them! They traded their freedom for Christophe, his name, for the Head and the Bible, *and* for you. You aren't a hero, you're a transaction."

"You mean they made a *deal* with it?"

Sebastian beamed. "Now you're getting it! Marie-Claire masterminded the whole plan. She realized the djinn could use you as a portal to travel from this world to the other. She offered to lure you here, get you to find the Head, the Bible, and even deliver the namesake, Christophe, in exchange for hers and the others' freedom. She came to you in your dreams and played you from the beginning right up to this moment."

"She wanted my help. They all wanted my help…"

"No, they wanted *you*."

"But why *me*?"

"You, my darling, are a gateway. Remember what Sandbourne told you? You are unique because you can straddle both sides at once. You are just what the djinn needed to break the spell cast by the Hag. Through you, it is free; unleashed

541

on the *entire* world."

"Unleashed, through me? How?"

"Oh Veronica, you don't really want to know."

"It's in there right now, with Christophe..." she began.

"Yes, it is. I doubt it will be much longer though. Soon it will be free, just like it wanted. And you, Veronica, will be trapped here, it's solitary captive. Don't worry, I've decided to stay behind, keep you company." He winked at her, then gave a friendly smile to a passing spirit, and nodded. "Farewell, enjoy the afterlife!"

Veronica let go of the door and began running toward the Château. She fled in slow motion, though, barely faster than a minute hand on a clock. Sebastian stood holding the gatehouse doors like an usher as the last few souls shuffled by.

"Don't worry, dear Veronica!" he called. "You don't have to face eternity alone. It will be you and me, and the djinn makes three!"

Inside the Oubliette

Christophe pushed through the gatehouse doors. Beyond the tree-lined path, he saw two cars parked by the fountain. One was the orange, boxy Twingo that Veronica drove, and the other was a crème colored Jaguar — Ralph's.

So Ralph is here, Christophe thought, relieved that Veronica was not alone.

As he began jogging up the path, he heard someone softly say his name. "Christophe..."

He stopped short. It sounded like Veronica, but she was nowhere around. He swallowed an icy lump and shivered even though it was a warm, August morning. A bolt of urgency surged down his spine, and he rushed toward the Château.

He knocked on the door. The only reply was silence.

"Hello?" he called out. "Veronica? Ralph?" He didn't wait for an answer as he pushed through the doors into Le Château du Feu Ardent.

Quiet. There were no voices — not a sound. The castle was dead silent.

He walked through the foyer, glanced into the deserted kitchen, and then strode into the library. Half-filled champagne glasses, feathered masks, and crumpled cocktail napkins were scattered around the room. No one had cleaned yet. Everything was exactly as it was on the night of the masquerade ball.

Fallen police tape lay in tatters across the threshold of the ballroom. The doors were ajar, and he pushed them open, releasing a dank, sour odor. Tables were still covered with plates of rotting food.

Veronica certainly would have had this cleaned up immediately upon returning, he thought.

He stepped inside. A pair of rats feasting on festering crème-filled crêpes eyed him greedily as he entered. They scurried down the once-white table linen and across the bloodstain in the middle of the floor. Once at a safe distance, they stopped, turned around, and glared at the unwelcome intruder. He made a sudden movement with his fist and the rats bolted.

Standing there, Christophe recalled the night of the party. In his mind's eye, the room was illuminated and filled with masked revelers. He envisioned Veronica and Nikki in their beautiful gowns. They truly looked so much alike! Self-loathing tore into his gut as he once again felt stabbing regret for mistaking Nikki for Veronica. There was nothing he could do now except find her and make it up to her, beg forgiveness, and convince her that it was *she* he wanted to be with all along.

He gave the rats their privacy and left the ballroom. Back in the library, Christophe contemplated where to look next. The sickly-sweet odor of rotting food and stale alcohol hung in the air. And there was something else. A penetrating scent that bore deep into his nostrils and dimly reminded him of the local butcher shop. Christophe smelled raw meat.

Next, he decided to check the girls' bedrooms. Nikki's was untouched. He remembered it looked that way when they had returned with the police. Veronica's room, however, was now empty. It was disheveled as if she had packed and left in a hurry. Dresser drawers were half opened, hangers were strewn across the floor outside the armoire, and a single shoe sat abandoned in the closet.

The entire Château felt *wrong*.

He fingered his cellphone and considered calling the police. Before he could dial, he heard a faint cry from deep down the hallway of the keep. A cold rock rolled over in his gut.

"Vern?" Christophe shouted.

Softly, she answered. "But you know my name is Veronica..."

Excitement and fear gripped his throat simultaneously and played tug-o-war with his larynx as he shakily responded. "Veronica, is that you?"

Distant singing answered. "Dance with me, we'll start slow. Clasp my hand, now lose control..."

He bolted toward the voice.

Around the twisted passageways he went, careened around a corner, and stopped suddenly. In the center of the hallway sat a solitary suitcase.

"Veronica?"

He saw the door to the keep was open. As he entered, he could clearly hear Veronica's voice singing off-key.

"Bite the monster only you can see. And dream the dream you only dream for me."

Her voice came from within the tower room.

"Veronica, are you okay?" he asked.

"Spirits in the maze, burning brighter. Like a dream within the haze, dancing fire. Deep inside malaise, hungry spider. Force your screams to blaze, spinning spiral...."

He entered the tower room. It was dark, and he groped to find a light switch, but there wasn't one.

"Veronica, are you in *here*?" he asked, peering into the pitch-dark room.

"Let the whispers guide you down the hole. Cheshire Cat, whispers near, smiling wide, have no fear!"

He shuddered, spun, and looked madly for a lantern, a flashlight — any kind of light source. Seeing none, he cursed and tore back down the passageway and into the library. He grabbed an oil lamp, turned it on, and trotted back to the keep.

"I'm coming, Veronica, just hang on!"

Into the tower room he sped, stopped short at the doorway, gasped, leaned over, and vomited.

The room was covered in blood. Ralph's mangled remains lay in the center. What was left of him was prone on his back with arms raised over his head defensively. The skin from his forearms was shredded down to the bone, as if he had unsuccessfully fought off an attack from a meat-grinder. His intestines were hanging out of his stomach. His right foot was twisted back unnaturally, and the white tip of a broken ankle poked out through a brown argyle sock. His signature white jacket looked tie-dyed pink; having apparently soaked up a massive amount of blood.

Ralph's face was still perfect. Untouched, it had little blood on it, and was cocked slightly toward the doorway. The eyes were open and locked in a death stare with Christophe. For a wild second, Christophe imagined his friend's face in motion, talking, laughing, making crude jokes, and rolling his jovial brown eyes.

Christophe turned away from the dead man's gaze. He noticed a crimson stream meandering through the grout of the cobblestone floor. Bits of flesh were speckled in the ruby rivers like tiny islands along tributaries.

Christophe wiped vomit from his chin and hung his head. Unable to behold the visage for another moment, he stepped backward, swayed drunkenly, and spun around the doorway so he stood with his back to the wall.

He fought the urge to bolt down the hallway in front of him. The bile in his stomach churned, and he spat on the floor several times. The smooth, cool, moist bricks behind him felt hard and real. He dug his fingers into them, scratching desperately for reassurance. Like a small boy kneading a blanket for comfort, he felt safe with the thick, stone wall between him and the carnage on the other side.

He remained there several moments. As he calmed down, reason took hold, and he decided to call the authorities. Without moving his strong, muscular body from the comforting wall, he pulled his cell phone from his pocket. As he did, it surprisingly rang. He shrieked and dropped it.

"Damn," he cursed, knelt, and retrieved it.

The display read: VERONICA. He rubbed a thumb over the screen, but couldn't bring himself to press down and answer the call. It rang again and again. He shook his head as if doing so would restore reason to his frenzied mind. He pressed the answer button on the fifth ring.

He heard her sing to him.

"Calling you to play, I'm your master. Don't you want to stay, falling faster. Looking for the way, hidden answers..."

Bile burst out of his throat so fast it also squirted out of his nose.

"Now you must obey, stupid bastard!" she continued.

He coughed and gagged. He reached into his pocket and retrieved a tissue with a shaking hand. A solitary tear dripped down his square jawline, and he meekly asked, "Veronica, is that you?"

She answered with a new, excited tone. "Christophe! I'm calling you to play!"

The urge to flee was even more intense than before. He quickly reasoned that he could go back to his car, phone the police, and wait there. She beseeched him one last time, "Don't you want to stay?" And then the phone went dead.

Despite having rushed all the way there to find her, Christophe now wanted nothing more than to be far, far away. He fought the illogical urge to run, and sheepishly called out, "Veronica, where are you?"

"I'm right here, love. I've been here all along." He heard her voice coming from inside the tower room.

Where could she be? he thought. Ralph's ravaged corpse was the only thing he saw in that room.

He dialed the police. The phone rang just three times, but it felt like an eternity.

"Bonjour?" a lazy voice answered.

Christophe rattled off awkward driving directions. "Take the D176 out of Montrichard and look for Rue Crevier about ten or twelve kilometers...turn right toward Le Château du Feu Ardent...there is a bridge, but it is under construction..."

The annoyed voice on the other end asked, "*What* is the situation, sir?"

He flinched as he soberly answered, "A body." In French, he explained, "Mon ami a été assassiné. Venez vite, c'est le bordel! Son corps est en morceaux partout."

The voice on the other end asked whom she was speaking with, but Christophe didn't answer. Instead, he urged, "I think someone else is hurt, too. I can hear her calling, but don't know where she is. I have to find her. Just hurry, s'il vous plaît!"

Christophe hung up. Mustering his courage, he stepped across the tower room's threshold and once again beheld the bloody carnage that befell his friend. Carefully, making sure not to step on any pieces of Ralph, he navigated his Italian leather shoes across the round room. He pulled a lacey ivory-colored duvet from the bed and spread it over the corpse.

Looking around, he asked, "Veronica?"

No answer. The room was still except for a few flies that flitted around Ralph's festering corpse. A sudden waft of decaying flesh invaded his sinuses, and Christophe coughed back the stench. He held his hand over his nose and mouth as he asked again, "Veronica, where are you? I can help; just tell me where to find you."

He noticed the princess bed was immaculate. Since he had pulled the duvet off to cover Ralph, the comforter underneath was free of blood. He decided to sit. Oddly, the room took on a different perspective as he rested on the luxurious bed. He saw it from the point of view of someone who just awoke from a good night's sleep while staying in a cozy château B and B.

He gazed at the pleasant wall art, which displayed scenes of pastoral French life. An elegant fireplace was graced with delicate topiaries and crystal vases on its mantle. Ralph's body was out of view, and except for a few random dollops of blood, from this vantage, the room appeared serene and perfectly normal.

To his right was a nightstand. The lamp that once graced it was broken in pieces on the floor. He wondered what happened here. Who did this to Ralph? Leaning over, Christophe could see shards of glass mixed in with the pools of blood. He leaned over a bit more, moving slowly, carefully, and then he quickly lurched down to see if Veronica was hiding under the bed.

No one was there. That was the only place she *could* be. Frustrated, he stood. Surveying the room confirmed there were no closets or doorways. There was no place to hide except for the fireplace.

He looked at it again. Surely, no one could climb *up* the fireplace...then he saw it wasn't a real fireplace. The mantle was brand new, pristine against the archaic architecture. It was faux, designed to disguise a hole in the wall.

Christophe approached it. That was when he saw the discarded hammer and tools, now covered in blood, near the mouth of the fireplace. In the floor was a hole — a pit to be exact. An *oubliette*, he realized. He recalled Nikki saying that Veronica and Clark were at a restaurant called The Oubliette. Of course not! They were in an *actual* oubliette!

He rushed to the edge and held the lantern at the cusp so he could look inside. Curled up on the bottom, about fifteen feet down, was a dirty, emaciated Veronica. He could see the top of her head resting on her bunched-up legs.

Across from her was another body. It had dark, thinning hair encircling a baldhead and wore workman's clothes. Christophe noticed the pallor grey color of his skin. It was surely a corpse, and it was rotting next to a near-dead Veronica.

"Vern," he whispered.

No response. Stock-still she sat. He wondered how many days she had been down there. *When had she fallen?* And *how?* How in the world did she and the plumber get down there together?

He called out again. "Can you hear me, Veronica?" He leaned in deeper, holding the lantern as far down as he could. Something was wrong with her ankle. It was swollen, bruised, and festering. She was hurt. "Are you okay?"

He teetered on the lip.

She didn't make a sound. He stretched farther and swooped down the lantern to illuminate the pit as much as possible. "Vern?" he asked with a thin, shaky voice.

Her head moved just a bit. It turned slightly to the left as if hearing him for the first time.

Joy welled inside him. She *was* alive! Just as fast, a sickening wave of dread also consumed him. She was alive, but just barely. "Talk to me. Say something," he implored.

Her head flopped back down and she said nothing.

"Please, talk to me, ma chérie..." his voice cracked and trailed off. Christophe reached his free hand out to her even though she was several feet down and impossible to touch. "S'il vous plait!"

Veronica whimpered in response.

"Veronica! That's my girl. Talk to me if you can. Tell me if you're okay." The edge of the oubliette rubbed against his belly as he slipped suddenly into its depths. He caught himself just in time and inched back to a point of safety.

"I'm fine, Christophe," she said calmly.

He imagined she was in a state of shock. That explained the bizarre singing. She had probably not eaten or drank anything in days. "I'm going to get you out of there," he told her.

He hoisted himself and the lantern back up. The edge of the oubliette where he had lain crumbled. Tiny shards sprinkled below and Veronica groaned.

Christophe dusted his hands off and forced his mind to find a solution. He needed rope or a ladder — something to get her out of there — and it had to be sturdy. Nothing like that was in this room, though, and he didn't want to leave her to go searching.

Staring vacantly at the bed, he had an epiphany. The sheets had to be at least seven hundred thread count, meaning they were strong. He quickly tore them off and tied them together. He pulled the knot as tight as he could to make sure it wouldn't come loose. At the end, he looped it around so all she had to do was slip her legs through and sit in it like a swing as he lifted her up.

Veronica grunted from the bowels of the oubliette.

Christophe flung the end of the sheet-rope over the edge and slowly lowered it. "Grab this, Veronica. Slide your legs through and hold on tight. I'll pull you up." He glanced over the lip and was relieved to see her climbing into the makeshift harness. She moved slowly and methodically. He was grateful, though, that she was lucid and strong enough to get in.

He anchored his end of the sheet around the bedpost to use it as leverage. "Are you ready? I'm going to pull you up," he called out.

She grunted in response.

Christophe smiled. Under his breath, he reassured, "You *are* going to be okay."

He yanked the bed sheets, and they scraped across the jagged lip of the oubliette. He leaned backward, using his body weight to hoist her. Slowly, she inched higher.

She said his name, and the unexpected sound of her voice made him shiver. "Christophe?"

"I'm here," he answered.

"You came back for me!" she gushed.

"Of course I did, dear."

"I thought you'd stay with Nikki."

"I made a mistake. I wanted to be with *you* all along."

A coiled hand cusped the edge of the oubliette. Veronica reached out blindly.

"Easy, take it slow," he cautioned.

Her other hand appeared, and both dug furiously into the cobblestone floor. Her nails splintered as she burrowed into the stone and pulled her torso up.

"Careful!" he warned. "Not so fast..." Before he could finish, her head and shoulders appeared.

In the flickering lantern light, Veronica's gaunt face distorted like a caricature of herself. She jerked spastically and pulled the top half of her body over the ledge.

Christophe wanted to go to her and help, but he held onto the sheet, fearful that she might slip back down — and fearful of what she had become.

Another quick jerk and she pulled her lower body over the edge. She slithered on her elbows a few feet. Once completely clear of the pit, she hunched over as if exhausted and laid her head in a puddle of Ralph's blood.

Now was Christophe's opportunity to rush to her side, but still he hesitated.

She spoke. "I can't believe you left Nikki and came back for *me*. You must like me after all?"

Nervously, he spluttered. "I always liked you. I wish things happened differently. But I will make it up to you. I promise."

Her arthritic-looking hand reached out and grabbed the edge of the duvet covering Ralph. "What's this?" she asked.

"Don't touch that!" he admonished.

"Why?" she cooed as she tugged the duvet and exposed Ralph's gutted entrails.

"Ralph is under there," he said while jumping up. He grabbed the duvet out of her hand and laid it back over his friend. "He's dead. Something awful happened."

Christophe skirted back toward the bed quickly, keeping a wide breadth between him and Veronica.

She pulled herself up on her elbows. Thick blood clung to her shirt in coagulated clumps. "Now how could that have happened?" she asked.

Christophe thought he detected rhetoric in her tone but quickly dismissed it as he answered. "I don't know. That's how I found him. I thought maybe you'd know."

"I'm so hungry," she said.

"The police are on their way. In the meantime, I can run and get you something to eat or drink…" He excitedly jumped up, suddenly eager to be out of the room.

She interrupted him. "No, don't leave me. Stay with me, Christophe!"

Begrudgingly, he stopped and retraced his steps. This time he sat on the bed, near the headboard, and farther away from her. "Okay, don't worry. I won't go anywhere."

"You'll stay with me forever, right, Christophe?"

"Of course. Right now we have to focus on getting you better."

As she lifted her head, the light caught her facial features. Christophe could see her more clearly than before. Her eyes were covered in a yellow film and puss oozed out of the corners. Her cheekbones were severe and her lips white and cracked. She had obviously been down there several days without food and water. She wriggled in the gelatinous blood and got up on all fours. He saw her ankle again. It was swollen and crawling with chubby white maggots.

"What happened to you?" he asked. As he spoke, he realized his tone wasn't sympathetic, and he added, "How did you get down there, dear? And the plumber?"

"We fell." She pulled her knees up and crouched unnaturally on her haunches. For a brief moment, she reminded Christophe of a rabbit standing on its back legs.

When she didn't elaborate, he chided, "How did you *both* fall in there?"

The question seemed to annoy her, and she evaded it by whining, "I'm so hungry!"

"I can get you food…" he offered again.

Before he could finish, she leaned over and appeared to sniff the air above Ralph's corpse. She quickly pulled back the duvet again and dug her nose into his open belly. Christophe watched, stunned, as she bared her yellow teeth and bit into his rancid flesh. She pulled back on a string of entrails. They dripped down her chin like thick pasta noodles.

Veronica was eating Ralph.

Christophe jumped up and demanded, "Stop! Veronica, you don't know what you're doing!" He leapt to her side and pushed her face away from his best friend's intestines. She grunted defiantly. "You're not well. Just relax and wait for help to arrive. You'll be fed real food and water soon."

Veronica gurgled and gagged. Her eyes rolled back in her head. He covered his friend back up as she slumped onto her side and started to shake. Her body was in spasm.

"I'm so hungry, Christophe." She sighed as foam bubbled out of her mouth.

The bed sheets twisted around her feet. He untangled them and wrapped the pristine Egyptians around his beloved like a swaddled baby. Veronica seemed to go momentarily limp. On bended knee, he coddled her, holding her tight to protect her from herself. He used one end of the sheet to wipe her face clean of vomit and blood. Her skin was so dehydrated it felt like parchment. Christophe dabbed gently.

"I know you're hungry. Just sit tight. The police will be here any minute. We'll get you to a hospital and on an IV in no time."

Christophe thought about carrying her to the bed. She was so frail, though. He decided it wouldn't be wise to move her. He noticed the complimentary water bottle on the fireplace mantle. A small sign offered it free to guests. Rising momentarily to his feet, he snatched it and held it up for her to see. "Want some water?"

Her eyes flared at the sight of the bottle. Veronica lunged for it with lightning-speed. Her skeletal hand grabbed it fiendishly, and an excited squeal escaped her desiccated lips. Her breath smelled like sour milk. Her tongue danced a moment across her yellow teeth. It was white and cracked and covered in cankers.

"Look, Clark, we got more water!" she exclaimed.

Christophe held her tighter to comfort her as he said, "Clark is dead, dear."

"No shit, stupid. But he can still talk to *me*. Can't you, Clark?" She leaned her head toward the oubliette as if waiting for a response. None came.

Christophe twisted the cap off. "Just drink it. Here, be careful. Not too much or you could throw it up..."

"I know that!" she cried and threw the bottle into the pit. "There, Clark! Drink the water. You can have it all because I got Christophe! Don't I?"

Christophe rocked her like a child. "Yes, you do. I'll take care of you. Make sure you get better. I promise."

"And you promise you'll always be with me?"

"Yes, dear, I promise."

"You won't go running off with my sister..."

Christophe cringed as he explained. "No. That was a mistake, and I'll never make it again. I'll be with you forever."

"That's a long time...forever. You sure you can hang with me that long?" she asked flirtatiously. For a brief moment, the Veronica he remembered was back. Her eyes glinted, and she smirked coyly.

"I'm sure," he affirmed and caressed her cheek.

She bit him.

At first, Christophe didn't comprehend what happened. He even laughed for a split second as she playfully nipped his index finger, but the spurting blood gave him a reality check.

He jumped up while holding his gushing digit tightly with his right hand. She had bit the tip completely off.

Veronica flopped on the floor by his feet.

She wormed her way out of the sheets as he cried out, "Fuck! Why'd you do that?"

Veronica was on all fours. She advanced toward him.

"Stay away," he warned and took several strides backward toward the doorway. "You're not in your right mind. Just stay there."

She cocked her head like she was assessing his fear, and crouched on her haunches as if preparing to pounce.

Christophe shot to the door.

Veronica moved unnaturally fast. Within a second, she was on top of him. Her coiled claw-like hands scratched and dug into his neck.

"Veronica! Stop!"

She clung to his back like a lioness bringing down prey. He spun blindly in a circle while trying to swat her. Her teeth sunk into his shoulder. The strapping man thrust himself backward into the wall, smacking her body into the hard bricks. Her bite released, but her nails still dug into his face. He reeled back again and slapped her into the stone. This time she let go and fell to floor like a rag doll.

He stepped back and glared at the woman he loved incredulously. Blood ran down his face from gashes around his eyes and lip. It also poured from the tip of his finger like a spigot.

With her back to the wall, she looked up at him adoringly. "You said we'd be together forever."

"You're sick, Veronica. Just stay right there until help arrives." He grabbed the broken Tiffany lamp from the floor and held the jagged end toward her threateningly. With his bleeding left hand, he fumbled for his phone. He was too injured to dial, though. "Damn," he cursed. "They better get here soon."

"Then we don't have much time," she observed and hurtled toward him.

Christophe swung the lamp and struck the charging interior designer squarely in the jaw. Her neck spun, causing her body to turn in a semi-circle. She landed on the floor with a thud and blood splattered everywhere.

He had hit her hard. It should have been enough to keep her down, but still she got up and charged again.

"Stay the hell back!" he threatened as he belted her with the lamp a second time. Shards of broken glass lodged in her face. Thick, black blood oozed out of her wounds like motor oil, but still she advanced a third time.

"I don't want to hurt you, Vern. Stop, please, Vern, Vern! Don't make me hurt you!"

She did. For a brief moment, she stood in the center of the room and stared at Christophe as if seeing him for the first time. She seemed to grow in size. No longer frail and injured, Veronica looked formidable and threatening.

"Don't worry. You can't."

She pounced on top of him again. This time the fractured lamp was no match for the thing Veronica had become. It crumbled as it struck.

"But you know my name is Veronica," she whispered as she embraced him.

She nuzzled her face against his lovingly.

Christophe kicked and hollered. "Let me go. I promise I'll get help for you.

Doctors, psychiatrists, whatever you need."

"Why, you think I'm crazy? You think this is all in my pretty little head?" She squeezed him tight in a bear hug and dragged him toward the oubliette.

"You've been in that hole for days. You're malnourished, dehydrated, hallucinating. That's all. You're not crazy, but you aren't well either."

She tugged him along the blood-soaked floor. He writhed in her grip but could not break free. She was amazingly strong and with little effort moved the big man across the room to the rim of the oubliette.

"What are you doing?" he asked.

"You promised we'd be together forever. Welcome to forever, Christophe!"

She pushed him over the edge.

He desperately grabbed at the air while spiraling backward. His injured left hand caught the lip of the mantle. He held on for dear life. While teetering on the threshold, he implored, "Please, Veronica, don't do this. I love you."

"Relax, dear Christophe. It's only death that awaits you. Trust me, there are some things much worse."

She pushed him in.

❧ Fin ❧

Epilogue

Nikki lazily poked at the orange in her glass of iced tea, forcing it to the bottom. The man across the table snapped his fingers at a passing waiter. Nikki cast her lawyer a disapproving frown and then smiled politely at the harried server.

"So, Ms. Dixon, I am afraid you're stuck with the Château. There's nothing we can do but sell for a fraction of the value."

It was a brisk November afternoon in Burbank. Nikki scooted her chair closer to the outdoor heater and sulked. "It just doesn't make sense. I don't *want* the stupid castle. After everything that happened there..." her voice trailed.

The stoic attorney's eyes fluttered slightly as he said, "The place was abandoned for over twenty years, and during that time no taxes were paid on it. Plus, the city of Montrichard had to invest a significant amount of money into restoring the bridge, not to mention cleaning up the crime scene. And, of course, losing the lawsuit for the accidental death of the plumber pretty much tapped you out. All the money in the Swiss bank account has been confiscated by the French government to pay those debts."

"Great. So then let's call it even and be done with it!" Nikki groused.

The lawyer feigned compassion as he explained, "Like I said before, in accordance with French law, the castle was considered abandoned. By living there with your sister for three months you laid claim to it, and all liens associated with it. You took possession, and therefore, it is yours. And all its debts are your responsibility."

"But why don't they just take it and put it up for auction?"

"Frankly, they would if they thought for one minute it was worth it. But the history of that place is so sinister that no one would buy it, what with all the crimes that took place there. You are liable in their eyes, and that's all they care about."

Nikki erupted. "My sister committed no crime. She's innocent!"

He cocked his head. "They found her blood, her fingerprints, her hair, her *teeth* marks on Christophe's...face it, Ms. Dixon, she killed him, and Ralph, and Dr. Sandbourne, too. She's lucky the plumber's death was deemed accidental; otherwise, she'd be charged with a fourth. Instead, they opted for unintentional manslaughter."

"They can't blame her for all those crimes. There wasn't even a trial. Whatever happened to 'innocent until proven guilty'?"

"There was never a trial because your sister was never found. If she does ever turn up, you can bet there will be a trial."

Nikki's hard façade cracked as tears streamed down her lightly blushed cheeks. "Don't they realize I've lost my sister? What else could they possibly want from me?"

"Look, there's one interesting offer on the table. A priest called last week to inquire about the book — the Bible — that your sister found. He wants to take a look at it and if it is in good condition, he says his church might offer between thirty and forty thousand US dollars for it. I suggest accepting what they give. It will help you pay the balance of your debt...and your legal fees."

"Of course, my legal fees." Nikki stuck the orange in her iced tea with her straw and waved it at her attorney as if scolding one of her students. "Fine. Tell them yes. They can buy the stupid Bible."

"Okay. I'll have my assistant make the travel arrangements. When do you want to meet with them?"

"Meet with them? Travel arrangements? What the hell? I'm not going back there!"

"Ms. Dixon, you really must cooperate here. The investigation into the murders is ongoing, and the authorities requested to talk to you again. You don't want Interpol to get involved, do you? And if you want to sell the castle, we need to meet with a realtor. There is a lot of business that needs your attention, and that business is all located at Le Château du Feu Ardent."

Nikki plucked carrots from her chicken soup defiantly and shouted, "Fine, let's go! Winter break is coming up; plan the trip then." She flipped the orange into her soup with a splash and asked, "While there can we try one more time to find my sister?"

"Sure," the lawyer said. "We can try."

Nikki drawled, "Then let's go. Le Château du Feu Ardent, castle of blazing fire, I'm coming back...."

CPSIA information can be obtained
at www.ICGtesting.com
Printed in the USA
FSOW02n1827270317
32230FS